ARNULF WOLFBLOOD

S. C. Pedersen

ARNULF
WOLFBLOOD

Book One of
Arnulf – A Viking Saga

Translated from the original Danish
by Sinéad Quirke Køngerskov

Forlaget Zara

Arnulf Wolfblood
by S. C. Pedersen

www.scpedersen.dk
Facebook: Arnulf – A Viking Saga

Copyright © 2020 Danish original *Arnulf* S. C. Pedersen
Copyright © 2020 English translation Sinéad Quirke Køngerskov

Forlaget Zara ApS, 2020

Translation: Sinéad Quirke Køngerskov
Cover design and layout: Lars Bech-Jessen, www.bogmager.dk

First Edition 2020
ISBN 978-87-7116-363-6

Forlaget Zara ApS
Svendborgvej 7
DK-4000 Roskilde
Denmark
www.forlagetzara.dk
e: kontakt@forlagetzara.dk

Thank You

Dedicated to my beloved children, Ragnhild, Asbjørn, Sigrid and Hjørdis.

A deep and heartfelt thank you to historian Kåre Johannesen for his enthusiasm and his impressively vast and detailed knowledge of all things Viking. It is an enormous help and support and thank you, too, for his never-failing encouragement

With the utmost respect, my thanks to the Viking Age combat group *Ulfhednir* for inspiration for the battle and fight scenes and to Peter Marius Stampe and Christoffer Cold-Ravnkilde, in particular, who generously shared their insight and great knowledge of warriors, battles and strategy, which made recreating Jomsborg effortless.

Thanks also to master skald Rune Knude, who lifted the veil on the secrets of skaldic verses and let me taste Suttungr's mead.

And a huge thank you to Jomsviking Bjarne Dahl and Jomsviking Qanun Bhatti.

A warm thank you to illustrator, Louis Harrison, for designing Arnulf's wolf shield.
A huge and happy thank you to my wonderful translator, Sinéad Quirke Køngerskov, who fearlessly took on the challenge of translating my Viking-saga-like-language into English. Glory to the brave!

And last, but not least, a loving thank-you to my husband who with great faith gave my pen free rein.

Cattle die, kin die,
Every man is mortal:
But the good name never dies
Of one who has done well.

Cattle die, kin die,
Every man is mortal:
but I know one thing that never dies,
The glory of the great dead.

The Hávamál

Gallery

Arngrim Rune, Jomsviking

Arnulf, son of Stridbjørn

Aslak, shipbuilder from Egilssund

Astrid Burislavsdaughter, earl Sigvalde's wife

Bjørn the Bretlander, Jomsviking and Vagn's foster father

Bue the Stout, Jomsviking and son of earl Vesete from Bornholm

Erik Hakonsøn, son of earl Hakon

Frejdis, Arnulf's intended

Gyrith Stentorsdaughter, Toke's wife

Hakon, earl of Norway

Halfred, Helge's helmsman

Haug, Jomsviking from Bornholm

Hedin, Frejdis' father

Helge, Arnulf's brother

Hildegun, Toke and Jofrid's mother

Hød-Ulf, Norwegian farmer

Ingeborg, Torkel Lere's daughter

Jofrid, Toke's sister

Ketil, Little Ketil, Jomsviking

Kjartan, Jomsviking

Leif Cleftnose, Viking from Haraldsfjord

Palnatoke, founder of Jomsborg

Ranvig, Toke and Gyrith's daughter

Rolf, Arnulf's brother

Sigrun, Frejdis' mother

Sigurd, Jomsviking, earl Vesete's son and Sigvalde's brother-in-law

Sigurdur, tradesman from Iceland

Sigvalde Strut-Haraldson, earl of Jomsborg

Skarde, king Sweyn's hirdman

Skargeir Torfinnson, Jomsviking

Skofte, earl Hakon's thrall

Stefanus, an English monk

Stentor, Gyrith's father and gothi from Haraldsfjord

Stridbjørn, Arnulf's father

Sweyn Haraldson, king of Denmark

Svend Silkenhair, Jomsviking, Vagn's cousin, son of Bue the Stout and grandson of earl Vesete

Toke Øysteinsøn, son of the chieftain of Haraldsfjord

Torkel the Tall, Jomsviking and Sigvalde's brother

Torkel Lere, earl Hakon's vassal

Toste Skjaldely, Viking from Haraldsfjord

Tove Strut-Haraldsdaughter, Sigurd's wife

Trud, Arnulf's mother

Vagn Ågeson, Jomsviking, Svend Silkenhair's cousin and grandson of Palnatoke

Æthelred, king of England

Øgmund White, vassal of Tønsberg

Øystein Ravnslayer, deceased chieftain of Haraldsfjord

Åse, Øgmund White's wife

Arnulf stood on the top of the hill and gazed out across the sound. The sun had gone down, but the sky was still rose-coloured where it had left the horizon, and the water was lapping gently. A shoal of fish twinkled at the water's surface as Arnulf searched every ripple intensely, but not even the smallest of boats was out to upset the calmness of the sound. He snorted with disappointment. A light evening breeze whispered through the fresh spring grass, and darkness began to creep out from the forest behind the village. A dog barked, and Aslak Shipbuilder called to his journeymen on the strand where the sound of the axes was dampened by the newly-clefted oak keel. The evening's stews were simmering over the many fireplaces in the houses, and the day's chores were amicably divided and completed between the households. Weaving and baskets were lifted in, the last of the firewood was chopped and the fish-catch of the day was hung to dry, as the blacksmith finished up hammering an axe head in the forge. A group of boys threw their wooden swords on the ground and began to tease some girls who were carrying meat from the storage hut and Finn Bow slapped his wife on the behind as he strode past with three freshly caught hares over his shoulder. Trud stood, her arms akimbo, scolding her youngest thrall, but Old Olav gently intervened, and Trud's anger waned, as the thrall hurried away, stooping. No one seemed to be in a hurry to go indoors and eat, for the air was intoxicatingly mild, and the newly sprouted greenness a soothing sight after the grey-white winter.

Arnulf pulled a lock of his long hair from his face and squinted. It was too late now for Helge to come gliding home on the black water. He would wait; let the sunlight shimmer on the men's chainmail and weapons and shed light over his newly acquired wealth. On arriving home from plundering and looting, Helge would always stand at the bow of his dragon ship, his cape thrown dashingly over his shoulders, his outspread arms loaded with silver, as he proudly called his father's name. Stridbjørn would greet him with his great bronze-plated drinking horn full of mead, and they would drink to each other as soon as Helge had set foot on land. Helge would then catch Rolf in a manly embrace and lift up his mother, as

9

if she weighed nothing, while the eyes of the village women would glow, and their cheeks turn rosy. Children would flock to the returning warriors and admire their conquests and new scars, and the thralls would busy themselves, frying and boiling. Stridbjørn's longhouse would resound with song and laughter, and Helge would sit in pride of place and give his full, detailed report of this year's voyage, so the youngest, shuddering, would have to seek out their mothers for comfort. And long into the night, when everyone was finally sated and drunk, with stomachs distended from bacon and beer, Helge would turn to Arnulf, offer him his sword arm and they would wrestle. Last year, Helge said that he believed Arnulf's grip would be skilled enough by spring, and he had promised to bring him home a real fighting sword.

He sighed. It was not to be today! Overwintering at the royalseat was dragging out, but never before had a man of Stridbjørn's lineage been invited to the feast of the king himself, and Helge had to protect his reputation and increase his honour. The snow was long gone, lambs and calves were once again suckling in the field. No other cold spell had seemed so long and gloomy to Arnulf as this year's!

A last gull-cry was heard over the waves. He followed the sea bird's low flight with his eyes and noticed how its call caused his blood to flow faster in his veins. It was the sea that drew him, the sea which filled his limbs with burning salt-water, and it was his restless longing for the sea that frayed his composure. His heart was already out on the waves. Best to follow his heart and throw himself out with the tide, and best to go with the storm away from the coast and the long-winged seabirds. The gulls had screamed loudly this spring. They egged on the daring journeys of fire-minded men; they called on will and bravery, and they shouted to each other that now it was Arnulf's turn to plough the waves. He clenched his fists hard. Together with Helge he would rally out and turn his back on Egilssund, together with Helge!

Arnulf closed his eyes and flared his nostrils. The salt-air was crisp and there was a force in the herbs and earth. His heart was pounding. He was about to turn and go, when he caught sight of Frejdis down at the cows, on the meadow, on the other side of the hill. She sat with her back to him, milking the one-horned cow with an experienced rhythm. Her blonde hair flowed down her back like gold, and she had pulled her shift up over her knees so as not to stain it with the squirting milk and rolled up her sleeves to her elbows. Arnulf smiled and felt light on his feet. Frejdis' cheek was pressed up against the side of the spotted cow, and her winter-pale skin glowed against the earth's fresh green grass. Her hips were

10

round beneath her shift, and Arnulf felt himself swelling with pleasure. He could never look at Frejdis without his manhood stirring and standing like Odin's spear. Freya had given her those hips just so men would aspire to grasp them!

Arnulf stepped back quickly and ran with agility down the mound to get to her. Frejdis had not seen him; the wind rustling and the cows munching and rummaging in the grass made it easy for him to sneak up on her. She hummed. He knew the tune for he himself had composed it. Her shift dress had almost completely slipped off one shoulder and the sight of it made Arnulf's genitals throb fiercely. The gentle spring sun had not yet touched her vulnerable, pale skin, and softer skin than Frejdis' was not to be found! It even made a swan's down seem rough. He hunkered down. The one-horned cow turned its head and looked at him questioningly, and Arnulf jumped like a lynx, before it could reveal him.

Frejdis let out a whine when Arnulf grabbed her by the shoulders and pulled her down onto the grass, causing milk to splash on her legs. He pushed her to the ground and caught her flailing arms effortlessly. Frejdis' eyes flashed, and she angrily shook the hair from her face and tried to free herself, 'Let me go, you horny colt!'

Arnulf laughed and sat astride her hot, wriggling body: 'I wanted some milk!'

'You are stark raving mad! Now the milk is wasted! Free me this instant!'

She tried to bite him but could not reach and had to settle for lying there, furious and fuming. Arnulf let go of her hands and looked at the neckline of her shift, which revealed her well-endowed, shapely womanliness. He reached for her breasts, but Frejdis smacked his hand away, 'You're heavy, I can't breathe, move!'

'I feel wild every time I see you!'

'You were born wild, Arnulf Stridbjørnson!'

Frejdis pushed him with all her might.

'Feel here how wild I am!'

Arnulf slid off her and onto the grass and pressed his groin into her. Frejdis sat up and pushed him away, annoyed, 'Stallion blood runs in your veins, but I'm not your mare!'

He grabbed her wet feet with a firm hand and licked the milk off her ankle, 'Young stallions mount those mares that stray from the pack!'

Frejdis tried to pull her foot away, but Arnulf held it tightly and let his tongue run up to her knee.

11

'I didn't stray from the pack! I was milking, and now you've poured half the milk out of the bucket! My mother is going to be angry! And you can stop all that! What if someone sees us – your brother, for example?'

Arnulf greedily sucked the milk from her skin and nibbled her calf, 'My brother? His ship hasn't been seen in the sound yet.'

Frejdis grabbed his hair and pulled his head away from his leg, 'Not Helge, you sulking-calf. Your other brother, Rolf.'

Arnulf freed himself and let his finger follow the curve of her knee, 'You mean my boring, responsible, reputable farmer brother? To Helheim with him!'

'Arnulf!'

Frejdis' eyes were reproachful, but her hand was gentle as it stroked his hair, 'You're not the only one who has an eye for me, you know.'

Arnulf sighed and rolled over onto his back. He frowned and softly he composed a ballad:

Stridbjørn's sons
Proud of two
One of sword
One of field
The grey bear
Grimly buzzes
The last son
Makes woe of worth

Kinsman of the wild
Path freely chosen
Wandering limbs
Wayward words
Honour stealer
Walks alone
Of wolf's kin
Begat

'Sssh!' Frejdis lay on her stomach beside him, and Arnulf grabbed a lock of her long hair. He ran his fingers through it and rolled over to bury his face in the rest of her golden mane.

'Do you know that you offend the gods with your beauty?' he muttered lustfully. 'Even Freya doesn't have such long hair, such sea blue eyes and such round legs!'

12

She laughed and pulled her hair away from him, 'Now you are truly a bonehead! And your father has good reason to be proud of Helge and Rolf. Few men have such good sons to boast of as he. And if he's mad at you it's your own fault. Not two days have passed since you lamed his best stallion.'

Arnulf rose up onto his elbow and pulled a blade of grass from its roots, 'It needed to be exercised after the winter.'

'You broke the plough!'

'Only because my arms are too strong for thrall-work!'

'And you let the sheep run wild!'

'It's not manly to herd sheep. It's a boy's job. My sixteenth summer is starting now, and when Helge returns and takes charge of his new ship, he's taking me with him on the next voyage.'

Arnulf tiddled Frejdis on the neck with the blade of grass. She caught it between her teeth, 'Against your father's wishes!'

'Veulf, the Woe of the Wolf, Stridbjørn calls me and Veulf will I remain! Since when have I followed his will? He should just rejoice that his eldest son now gives his youngest an opportunity to be split in twain.'

Frejdis dropped the blade of grass, her eyes growing dark, 'Don't say that! Helge has gathered men to go a-viking over many springs. He's taking you with them because he considers you ready.'

Arnulf smiled and lay on his back again. The grass was wet with dew, and though the air was warm, the ground was cold. For a while, he stared up at the rose-coloured clouds that floated across the sky, like sea foam. Frejdis lay her chin intimately on his chest, 'You've missed him a lot this winter, haven't you? It's the first time he's been away so long.'

Arnulf turned his head towards her. Had he missed Helge? He had missed him so much his bones were frozen with longing! It was almost a year now. Helge had only been home for a short time during the harvest, when he had had to set sail again to trade his newly plundered wares and then had been summoned to the king's royalseat.

'Rolf has always done as my father says, and my mother loves him because he would rather plough and tend to animals than go sailing and fighting, but there is more to the world than seeds and bacon. I want out, Frejdis! Away from this village! To go out and seek, try my luck, win glory and silver!'

The words made his longing tear at him like a roaring spring current.

'Helge has brought your father enough silver,' she replied quietly. Arnulf looked at Frejdis' white forearms and felt his desire flare up again. His fingers glided over her arm, 'What has Rolf said to you recently?'

She laughed and pulled back her arm, 'Rolf? He talks. He shows me what he is doing and tells me about his plans with seeds and animals. Everything succeeds in his hands.'

'Now I'll show you something that will make you forget about Rolf and his seeds!'

Arnulf grabbed her hand and brought it down to his hardness.

'Agh, you only have one thing on your mind.'

Arnulf was hoarse, 'You just have to feel it. Then you'll never think of my brother again!'

Frejdis giggled and gave in. Arnulf closed his eyes with a sigh, as her hand slid under his kyrtle and into his trousers. Frejdis nodded with a teasing smile, 'Yes, it's handsome. But it doesn't get the corn to grow and it won't bring prosperity home from across the sea.'

He lowered his voice: 'Come closer, and I will whisper to you what it can get to grow! In its company you'll never be bored, and that could easily happen with a man who only cares about his ploughshares and heads of cattle!'

He grabbed her by the calf and found his way under her shift. His fingers bored deep into her soft buttock.

'Ow! You're pinching!'

Arnulf relaxed and fumbled with the buckle. Frejdis rolled onto her back, 'Keep your trousers on! Grim will soon be finished eating and then he'll be here to keep watch over the cattle. He'll see us!'

'A thrall who gossips risks getting his eyes gouged out. Grim won't betray us!'

Frejdis pulled her shift down to cover her ankles and Arnulf gave up, 'Fine, fine, but then promise me you'll come to the forest will me tomorrow! We'll find a clearing that even the animals don't know about.'

Frejdis' eyes laughed, but she shook her head, 'I'm freezing, it's still too cold to be rolling around in the grass now, and are you not supposed to be helping Aslak with the ship tomorrow?'

Arnulf shrugged, 'He can easily do without me. I worked for him for months on Helge's new ship, but there is no honour in building a knarr.'

'Honour? Wealth is wealth whether it be looted or traded!'

Frejdis got up and walked toward the one-horned cow that had moved further up the hill. Her hips swayed seductively. Arnulf jumped up and ran after her. He had to get those hips! They swayed so invitingly; he couldn't help it.

'Ship! Ship! A ship is coming! Frejdis! Arnulf! A ship is coming, a ship is coming!'

Little Ivar stood on the mound, winded, and waving his arms, as he pointed out on the sound with spiky fingers. Then he ran.

Arnulf's heart was pounding and the blood began to pump so fast that he was bewildered. Helge! Helge had returned! He looked into Frejdis' shining eyes and burst out laughing. He uttered a shrill yelp and jumped up into the air.

'Come, Arnulf!'

Frejdis grabbed his hand and seemed to forget all about the one-horned cow. Arnulf started running so fast that he dragged her behind him. He clasped her hand as if he was already wrestling with Helge, and she wailed. At the top of the hill, he could see that darkness really was about to envelop the sound, but the ochre-yellow woollen sail from Helge's longship shone through, like a star on the water. Down by the strand, people crowded together excitedly, and the air resounded with shouts and laughter. Those women who had had to do without their men for such a long time pushed forward, children cheered and waved to the ship and tried eagerly to distinguish fathers and kinsmen in the deepening dusk.

The tension was palpable, and more than one person seemed to be standing and mumbling a prayer to the gods, for not always did all the men return home or have their health and limbs intact.

Stridbjørn walked briskly along the plank-coated road that led down to the water dressed in his best embroidered kyrtle, his splendid crimson cape around his shoulders. His chest-long grey beard was carefully combed, and there was a wide silver chain around his neck, for Helge should be met in style. In his hands, he held his shiny bronze-plated drinking horns, the mead sloshing about in them; the other men laughed and patted his back. There was always a feast whenever Stridbjørn's Helge returned home. It was a certainty. For when Stridbjørn held a feast, it ensured no one had anything to complain about afterwards, for he was rich. Rich from all the treasures his son brought home with him and generously allowed the family to share. Trud had also quickly thrown off her woollen brown dress and put on her blue dress with silver buckles that she kept for special occasions. The large amber necklaces shone against her chest, and her solid, twisted bracelets jangled. No man's wife was prouder than Trud. Stridbjørn laughed at her and lifted his drinking horns in the air. Arnulf did not care in the least about how he looked. What did it matter if his kyrtle was white or grey as long Helge came home! It was just a pity that the ship was coming in so late! It would be night before the roast was tender. The thralls could have the evening stew.

Aslak Shipbuilder's journeymen lit torches, and Trud stood with her head held high at Stridbjørn's side and jingled the keys on her belt. Out on the longship, the torches were answered, and as it came closer, so too did the darkness, but the yellow sail shone like the full moon itself.

Rolf, laughing, joined Stridbjørn and Trud and stroked his blond beard expectantly. Stridbjørn handed him one of the mead horns and flung out his arm. Rolf has also changed out of his everyday clothes and had washed himself scantily because, although Arnulf doubted that he had longed for Helge half as much as he himself had, it always pleased Rolf to receive his highly admired brother. The torches on the strand flared, and their glow was reflected in the bronze jewellery and moist eyes. Arnulf felt Frejdis lean in towards him, he put his arm around her tightly and hugged her. It was nice that she was there and good that Helge would see them together as he was disembarking from the ship. Was there a better place to lay your arm than around a warm-blooded woman? Following the voyage with Helge he would go to her father's house with his newly acquired riches and put them on the table as proof that he could support Frejdis. She should be his, and Stridbjørn should plead his case, even if he would have to strangle his father with his grey beard! That Stridbjørn was named after both battle and bear did not scare Arnulf and he smiled. The people of the village often looked sideways at him because of his fiery mind and his thoughtless deeds, but once he had proved his real worth and been on the voyage, then they would think better of him. Frejdis should not want for anything. She should have as many amber and silver chains as she could wear around her neck and her pantry should burst with pork and game! And she should have so many thralls that she need not do anything all day but comb her golden hair and share her loveliness with him on a bearskin by the fireplace.

'Shouldn't you go down and welcome your brother?'

'I should ...'

Arnulf turned towards her and took her face in his hands. He wanted to tell her how happy he was that Helge had come home and how strongly he felt for her, tell her that his whole body trembled and that he wanted to scream and jump, but instead he kissed her with such passion and hunger that it made her teeter and giggle. He let her go and ran down the hill and out over the sand, wading out into the water to bypass those in front, to get to where the ship's bow would come aground.

'There you are!'

Rolf lashed out at him and slapped his fist into his with a clap. He did this when he was in a good mood and he liked when it stung and slapped Arnulf's hand back, but Arnulf could now stand up to Rolf and his brother noticed it.

'Well, you overgrown foal, do you have a skaldic verse ready for your brother? Sing, you are good at it.'

Stridbjørn ruffled Arnulf's hair, for today he was proud of all his sons. Arnulf did not answer but looked towards the ship, where the sail was being taken down. It was close now. So close that he could begin to distinguish the men aboard and hear the rhythmic splashing of the oars. The ship glided as proudly as an eagle on the water, but its golden dragon head at the bow had been taken down and the figure which stood in front of the Vikings was wider than Helge's. Arnulf stared, then his eyes began to water. It was Halfred, Helge's helmsman who was standing there! Arnulf bit his tongue and felt the blood drain from his cheeks. Was Helge not with him? Why was Halfred in his place instead of sitting at the helm? Was Helge still at the royalseat? He should have sailed with them; the king had had him long enough. Was he engaged with his housecarls? That was not inconceivable. The disappointment gripped Arnulf with an icy hand, and behind it, the fear.

Halfred raised his arm and shouted to Stridbjørn and Stridbjørn answered his greeting. An uneasy murmur ran through the crowd, but Helge's absence at the bow did not hamper the joy from all those who now recognised their men and kinsmen behind the ship's shields adorning the shield rim. Arnulf waded out into the water up to his knees and felt it sucking greedily at his feet. Halfred's eyes were dark, and the weather-beaten warriors behind him kept their smiles and happy reunion to themselves, as they glanced at Stridbjørn. Several of them had wounds and bloody bandages, like they had recently been in combat, and Halfred had a nasty gash across his forehead. They were not good signs. Arnulf's woollen kyrtle felt clammy.

Halfred jumped ashore and grabbed Stridbjørn's outstretched hand. Arnulf had difficulty breathing. His chest was so tight and hard that his vision became blurred. Stridbjørn's eyes burned like liquid iron, and his face was as white as snow. Trud stepped forward and grabbed Halfred's arm, as Stridbjørn's mead horns fell to the ground.

17

'Where is Helge? Is not he with you? Is he sick?' Trud's voice was shrill.

Halfred looked at her, and his rugged face twitched, 'Helge is dead, Trud! He died. Killed on the way home in Sælvig yesterday morning.'

The words cut Arnulf like a knife. Everything went black before his eyes and he thought he was going to faint. His vision swirled, but he heard Trud's painful screams slashing through the darkness and over the sound and he felt Frejdis' warm hand in his. Dead! Was Helge dead? Helge, his beloved brother. Helge, who would return home to take him on a-viking. Helge, who would give him a sword. It was not true; it could not be true! Frejdis hugged him as hard as she could, but Arnulf's hand was limp and he was gasping for air. The pulling of the sea and the rippling of the sand under his feet caused him to waver.

Halfred's words triggered a great lament for Helge, and many of the women by the ship burst into tears, but Stridbjørn stood like a rock and maintained eye-contact with Halfred, though his lips quivered, 'Killed, Halfred? By whom?'

Halfred pulled at his braided beard. Trud sank, groaning, and pulled the amber necklace from her neck, while the weeping women flocked around her.

'By a Norwegian chieftain, Øystein Ravenslayer from Haraldsfjord. Helge had lain with his daughter against her will after drinking at a marketplace, and Øystein resented him for it. He spent half the winter waiting for us near the royalseat and followed us to Sælvig.'

Halfred brought forward a sword that Arnulf recognised as Helge's. Serpenttooth it was called, after the interlaced serpent adorning it. It was a hefty blade and inlaid with silver. The sword was without scabbard, and Stridbjørn's hand shook as he accepted the precious weapon. Halfred sighed deeply, 'It fell on the deck when Helge's arm was hewn off by Øystein, but Helge himself ended in the sea and sank. That is why we could not bring him home.'

Arnulf's stomach turned, and he felt a fierce stinging in his throat. Frejdis put her arm around his chest, as she wanted to support him, and Arnulf could hear his own anguished groans. His eyes burned. His lips quivered. He freed himself from Frejdis, clenching his teeth and his fists so strongly that they trembled. By Tyr if he would stand here, blubbing before the eyes of thralls and women like he was a child! His brother was a warrior, and he had fallen in battle, and with that fate he could not be displeased. Stridbjørn spoke not a word. Halfred let go of his beard and continued, 'Helge fell in single combat and we avenged his death and killed Øystein and all his men and burned their ships. We took his son with us as a thrall. If you or Trud seek more revenge, you can take it out on him.'

Halfred waved, and two men from the ship threw a young man over the shield rim and flung him at Stridbjørn's feet. He was distinguishably dressed in a dark blue embroidered kyrtle and his hair and beard were brown and well-kept. A Thor's hammer hung around his neck on a thick silver chain and heavy silver bracelets wound up his arms. His hands were securely fastened, his gaze, defiant and furious as he looked up and tried to stand. Halfred grabbed the rope tied in a noose around his neck and pulled him down again, but the Northman fought hard to stand and only knelt when a knife was pressed into his neck.

Halfred spat contemptuously at him, 'You need not fear retaliation from the men in Haraldsfjord, Stridbjørn, for all tracks are erased and they will never find out where their chieftain ended his days. And never has a man fought so bravely as your Helge. When he lost his arm, he swung the axe in his left hand and shouted that there was no reason to hold back just because he had cut himself, and when Øystein's sword cut him off from life, he asked me to take his greetings home and apologised that the reunion would take a little longer. Then he himself sought the sea, and I struck Øystein down before he was given time to brag too much of his misdeed.'

Stridbjørn nodded. His knuckles were white against the pommel of Helge's sword. Trud sobbed, heartbroken, and threw sand in her hair. Rolf stood silent and livid, his thumbs in his belt, his breath hissed as he stared out at the black water that had swallowed his brother. Arnulf looked at the sword in his father's hand. Helge had promised him a sword like that! Now there would be no eventful voyage, no fighting and no looting; now Helge's new ship would never carry his brother to fair deeds at the front of the bow, and he would not win any valuables to lay in front of Frejdis' father. His body felt like a vessel, which had been shattered and everything inside seemed to flow out and disappear into the sand. Halfred threw the thrall's rope on the ground and put his hand firmly upon Stridbjørn's shoulder, 'Helge is among the Einherjar now and when the gods rally warriors for the last battle at Ragnarök, he will be at the front.'

'Thank you, Halfred.'

Stridbjørn's voice was maudlin but firm, 'And thank you for everything you have done for Helge. He never could reproach his men for anything, you have always served him faithfully and bravely.'

He looked around and raised his voice, 'My son is dead, but we will have a feast nonetheless! We will drink in his honour and rejoice that his place in Valhalla no longer stands empty!'

His words were greeted with loud cries and Halfred drew his sword and began to beat the flat side rhythmically against the bow of the ship while he shouted Helge's name. All those bearing arms around him drew them and struck them against something that gave sound while they intoned his cry. Even Rolf struck his hand against the ship. The sand seemed to shake from the thunder and cries and Arnulf straightened himself and took a deep breath. He wanted to scream and punch or run away and hide in the darkness. Every muscle quivered as the pain in his chest took hold; it felt like he was being hit by a splintered arrowhead of ice, but he went quietly over to Stridbjørn and Rolf.

Now that the grim message had been delivered, the joy began bubbling uninhibitedly around them. After some yelling, the returning warriors sheathed their swords and began laughing and swinging wives and children around in the air. Men greeted each other with manly, strong-armed clasps and gifts were found and shared, while a few had to be helped ashore as they were limping.

Trud, weeping, stumbled away supported by the women, and several began walking towards the village with their arms around each other's shoulders or carrying bags and chests from the ship. Stridbjørn walked over and put his hand on the ship as if it were a beloved horse, 'You carried him well,' he said softly, 'I owe thanks to you, too!'

Then he glanced at Arnulf, 'Tie the new thrall in the empty thrall-hut, Arnulf, and tell the others over there that I will beat to the death anyone who goes near him.'

If Helge had not died, Arnulf would immediately have refused, believing the task to be below him, but now he obeyed silently and grabbed the thrall's rope. The Northman sent him a fiery look; Arnulf tossed his head. The prisoner stood and seemed willing to follow without resistance and Arnulf noticed that he had difficultly standing on one of his feet. Stridbjørn turned and placed his hand of Rolf's arm and they began to follow Trud, as more village folk fell in behind them and called Helge's name again. Stridbjørn held Serpenttooth out in front of him, his arm straight. It was the least honour he could show his deceased son. Arnulf followed them with his eyes and Frejdis gathered up Trud's fallen amber beads and looked at him sadly before she took her leave. She knew that when something serious happened to Arnulf, he would rather be alone.

Arnulf did not rush the badly limping Northman but began to slowly walk away from the ship and along the water to the end of the village where the thrall's huts were squeezed in by the forest. It was good to get away from the others, good to get out of the torches' reach and into the concealing darkness where no one could see his face. His legs were heavy and suddenly every step felt unsure and new, as if Helge's death had, with one fell swoop, changed the world's pace. The water sloshed quietly against the shore and the moon was almost full over the sound and the forest's black crowns, and it shined with all its power, as if paying tribute to Helge. Its silveriness poured over the sea that now was his grave. Arnulf's trousers were wet up to his thighs, he shuddered and fought the urge to just sink down and give way to the tears. Helge was dead. His brother was dead. Everything was gone for him now. It was not only Helge; it was his whole life, his voyage, his burning urge to travel, his wanderlust and all his hopes of winning Frejdis.

The Northman's shoulders stooped as he limped through the sand, and Arnulf stopped and looked out over the water. A sail could no longer be seen out there no matter how bright it was. Now Helge would never get to launch his new ship. Arnulf knew exactly where he would have been sitting in the row of men. Aslak Shipbuilder had been so pleased with his help; he had given him permission to carve an eagle in the plank of the very oarlock. And Trud had worked on the sail with the thralls throughout the winter. At the very least, Stridbjørn should have been allowed to cremate his son's lifeless body on the ship. Helge should have had it with him in Valhalla, it should have been burned with him, filled to the brim with horses and weapons, but Helge himself had sought the sea with his mortal wound. Why?

A sudden jolt tore the rope out of Arnulf's hands. The Northman had taken flight and jumped like a hare towards the forest. His feet had not failed him in the least. Arnulf roared and took off in pursuit, anger sweeping through him and giving his leg wings. By his blood should the thrall trick him like that and hide in the woods in the dark! He would teach the miserable son of a stinking murderer to know his place!

The prisoner ran quickly for he had everything to gain, but Arnulf was familiar with every rock around the settlement and was mad enough to be the swifter of the two. The bright moon illuminated everything clearly. He found the Northman at edge of the forest and threw himself on him, so they tumbled to the ground in the withered leaves. The prisoner tried to bite him, but he could not defend himself with his hands tied behind his back and Arnulf took hold of the rope and stepped on it, forcing

21

the Northman's neck down to the ground. He jumped up, the anger making his eyes see red. Helge was dead, and the prisoner's father was to blame for the killing. He shook with uncontrollable rage and slammed his foot into the stomach of the Northman who uttered a stifled cry and writhed in pain. Arnulf would take his revenge, take revenge for the pain in his heart that bit like a serpent, revenge for Trud's crying and for Stridbjørn's hidden despair. Such terrible sorrow could not be contained in the body, it had to be let out, have air, revenge! The Northman wailed and Arnulf screamed, and felt the tears flowing down his cheeks like liquid iron. He kicked the man again, this time in the ribs, and so much that it hurt his foot. The prisoner tried to protect himself, but Arnulf kicked him again, this time in the side, unable to rein in the raging fury that tore at him. Everything around him disappeared and rage and grief coursed through his body like a spring tide. Revenge! He must have revenge! Halfred may have already killed Øystein and made him pay for his atrocity with his life, but Arnulf also had the right to avenge his brother, and Rolf had it, and this wretch at his feet had certainly earned every kick he could plant on his poor body.

The Northman gasped and tried desperately to roll away while he looked up at him, his face convulsed. Something in his gaze made Arnulf collect himself and, with an effort, he ceased his violent attack and his surroundings returned to him. His kyrtle was soaked in sweat. The Northman lay crumped on the forest floor, gasping as though he was about to give up life. Arnulf stepped back with a firm grip on the rope and, breathless, let his anger ebb a bit. The prisoner, groaning, rolled around onto his knees with his forehead on the ground, his breathing rattling. The moon shone so strongly between the bright green branches that Arnulf could see him clearly. He could not be more than twenty years. From Norway. Helge had talked enthusiastically about Norway. About fjelds. Fjords. Rivers. But Arnulf could only hate this Northman.

The prisoner began to get his breath back, now he groaned mostly from pain.

'Get up, you dog, and be glad that I don't cut your throat!'

Breathless, the Northman lifted his head, 'You have broken my ribs!'

'I won't cry myself to sleep over that tonight! Get up!'

The prisoner struggled to his feet, but he was weak, and he had to lean heavily against a tree, still bent over. Arnulf waited, for he would not carry him. The Northman recuperated slowly and looked at him. There was no harm in his bright eyes, rather deep despair and sadness, he coughed painfully and closed them for a moment.

'Let me go, Arnulf.' His voice was hoarse and Arnulf looked at him, astonished, 'Go? Are you mad? I lost my brother! Your father just killed him, and you ask me to let you go! As if you deserve anything other than to be beaten for the beast that you are!'

'And I have lost my father!'

The Northman opened his eyes and tried to stand up straight, 'I lost my father and several of my friends.'

He paused abruptly and groaned, but continued, 'My uncle was also aboard the ship. Your grief is not half as great as mine, and it was not me who killed your brother. Let me go!'

He leaned his head against the tree and looked quite worn. Arnulf spat bitterly, 'Should my father have lost his son and afterwards let his murderer's cursed offspring run free?'

'My father lost his life!'

The Northman had fire in his eyes again, 'And your damned brother ravished my sister, so now she is carrying a child she does not want!'

Arnulf felt his blood boil with renewed fury. How dare he!

'Stridbjørn will soon get answers out of you! And only if you beg on your knees, will I stay quiet about you trying to run away and demanding your freedom. Do you not know the penalty for a thrall that flees?'

The Norwegian's eyes flashed, and he straightened himself, 'I am no one's thrall! And I have a name just like you, Arnulf! Toke is my name. Toke, Son of Øystein Ravenslayer. That name is known far beyond Haraldsfjord, and more men than you know will be so full of grief upon learning of Øystein's death that they be willing to avenge him!'

Arnulf snorted disdainfully and was not impressed, 'A thrall is what you are and Trud will determine your name.'

Toke shook his head but did not give up, 'Loosen my rope and say I escaped from you. You will not regret your deed, and I will reward you richly the day you visit my fjord.'

Arnulf felt an amusing urge to kick the Northman again, but he stopped himself, 'Helge was coming home to fetch me. Are you too stupid to understand that? We were supposed to go a-viking together. He had a sword for me. I have helped Aslak to build his new ship and now he's dead!'

Toke bowed his head for a moment, 'You must really hate me!'

'Of course, I hate you!'

Arnulf shouted it. He was furious at the thrall's insolent speech and that he had lost his temper and let a stranger see his tears.

'If you want to go a-viking, then there is all the more reason for you to release me, for my ship is in Norway just waiting for me to pick men for my first voyage without Øystein,' exclaimed Toke. 'Come with me, Arnulf and let your grief remain here! I will go west this year. An Icelander told me about a good place with much silver.'

Arnulf shook his head and squinted with rage, 'Should I turn my back on my family and run away with a thrall? Who do you take me for? Toke Øysteinson you will go out and sail as much as I, and once Stridbjørn has time to grasp his thrall-whip, he will break your pride, so you crawl in the dust before him.'

He pulled the rope so Toke nearly lost his footing. The Northman was silent as he focused on following Arnulf, who was walking quickly as he was full of anger. No more words were voiced on the road to the thrall's huts and Arnulf shed no more tears, but he felt as if his heart would burst and he wanted to get rid of the mad Northman and all his talk as quickly as possible.

The thrall's end of the village was empty for they were all preparing the festive food for the returning Vikings, but Arnulf found an oil lamp on a door pillar that he used for light as he pulled Toke with him to the smallest of huts. It was used for barrels and pots. Arnulf shoved Toke brutally against the centre post that supported the leaky roof: 'Sit!'

The Northman looked sharply at Arnulf but obeyed. Arnulf loosened the rope from his neck and used it to bind his arms securely to the post. Toke looked up at him, 'Think about my proposal, Arnulf. Many would appreciate the offer to sail with my longship and they trust that I have inherited my father's luck.'

Arnulf put his fist on Toke's chin, 'Your father's luck? Any more of that talk and I'll knock your teeth out! Better you think of getting used to what I have told you about a thrall's life, for you decide how painful your life here will be!'

He blew out the lamp and deigned not to give Toke any further attention but went out of the hut, slamming the door on his way. Oh, that Helheim would fetch that Northman tonight! That man was utterly intolerable! Hassle, that was all you got out of keeping thralls, squabbles and hassles. Arnulf spat bitterly. That he should find himself quarrelling with an unfree man, when he had just learned of Helge's fate! He would go home to the longhouse now, go home and listen to what Halfred and the other warriors were recounting about their stay in the royalseat. He would drown his grief in mead, and he would, for a moment, try to forget that he had lost a brother.

Perspiration flowed down his back even though the air was cool, and his legs felt as soft as boiled cod. Arnulf bit his lip. His body shook. Shook so much that he could hardly use his hands. He spat again and clenched his fists so tightly that his knuckles cracked, but the tears would not stop. They wanted to overpower him and force him to the ground, writhing in pain. Damn! Men did not cry. They drank! Arnulf forced himself up on his feet and started to walk away from the thrall's huts, but they did not go towards Stridbjørn's longhouse, they were taking him back to the sea and they began to run. He gave in. Slowly at first, but soon he was running like a charging bull, running so hard that his heart throbbed, his lungs ached, and he could taste blood in his mouth. He wept with his mouth wide open as he ran along the strand, past the village, past the ships and Aslak's boatyard, along the meadow and all the way to where the trout-filled brook entered the sea. Here he fell to his knees and curled up into a ball, rocking back and forth, wailing frantically while the pain washed over him like a raging fire, each flame worse than the other. Helge was dead. Helge was dead.

*****

Only when the last tears had left him, and his eyes felt bone dry did he lift his head again. The moon was still out, reflecting in the water. Mirrored in Helge's grave! Arnulf sat up, humiliated and miserable, but the rage had not burned out of him yet. The blood hissed in his veins, like the water when the blacksmith plunged red-hot iron into it. His body reflected his state of mind; his heart was almost bursting through his ribs. By Thor, why had Halfred already avenged Helge? If only he had sailed home, then Stridbjørn could have picked men to take with him to Haraldsfjord for blood-revenge, and then Arnulf would have been sharpening an axe and buckling a sword to his belt instead of lying here, blubbering like a little girl!

He got up slowly. His trousers were wet from the dewy grass and he felt dizzy. The torches were still burning on the strand where Halfred and the Vikings had landed. Helge's new ship stood not so far away, mounted on struts, complete and ready for its first launch, its red-painted dragon head on its bow. It stood black against the moonlit sky with its

25

light, proud sweeping shape. No one had contradicted Aslak when he exclaimed that a better ship had he never before built in his entire life. In Helge's ship he had gathered all his skill and ingenuity, and not the slightest detail could be faulted. Now it would never carry Helge, nor sweep over the waves as it obeyed his hand on the tiller, nor raise its wings as the wind took hold of its tightly woven wool. Its fate was sealed, a dream was dead.

Arnulf staggered back along the water's edge towards the longship. His throat felt tight again and he found it difficult to breathe. Everything but the ship disappeared from his view; it was as if it grew bigger than the night sky behind him and blacker than death itself.

No one but Helge had the right to sail that ship! It was his; that anyone else should sully the smoothly planed planks by going aboard over the shield rim. It would be an affront to his brother to give the ship away, and Helge's body would lie there on the seabed, looking up at its keel, knowing that it was taken from him.

Arnulf started running again. No, no one should touch Helge's ship, he would make sure of that, and if he could not push it out onto the water and let the current carry it away, he would give it a fatal wound, a wound that not even Aslak could repair! Out of breath, he reached the ship's boatyard and ran over the thick layer of shavings and wood chips. The big felling-axe was leaning against the new keel Aslak and his journeymen had carved in the last few days. Arnulf gripped its handle with both hands. With a roar, he swung his weapon and planted the sharpened axe head deep in the ship's side planks with so violent a force that the iron cladding crumpled. He wrenched it free and struck again with all his weight, struck so splinters flew, and the hull gave. The thinly clefted planks could not resist his fury, and the wood groaned and burst, while the nails slipped out and fell to the ground. The gaping hole in the ship's waterline grew steadily larger and Arnulf's strength doubled with the glowing stream of despair that guided his arms. Again and again, he attacked the wood as if he were hacking all the way through to Asgard to bring Helge back. The pouring sweat soothed the pain in his chest as he hammered away on the ship's side, and he threw himself into it blindly, screaming his unbearable loss out. The axe completely gutted the carefully clinker-joined planks, mutilated the shield rim, tore the keel and tried to behead the red dragon from its life.

'By all the gods and jötnar! Are you completely mad, lad!'

A crippling blow to his upper arm stopped his axe's bite as Arnulf's elbow was seized with an iron hand. Aslak's bearded face appeared before his eyes, through the sweat, showering his forehead. The shipbuilder's complexion was dark with anger. With a roar and a wild look in his eyes, he tore the axe from Arnulf and cast it down to the strand and in the next moment he shook Arnulf so hard his teeth rattled.

'You accursed brat! What have you done? I should cut off your hands this instant! If it were not that Stridbjørn begat you, then ...'

Aslak was shaking so much from the anger that he could not form the words with his mouth. Arnulf tried to free himself from his painful grip, but Aslak was no small man, and his arms were hardened from a life of working with planks and axes.

'That ship belongs to Helge,' Arnulf said defensively, his teeth chattering. 'No one else should be allowed to sail it. I'm just giving Helge what is rightfully due to him!'

Aslak twisted his arm around to his back, so Arnulf screamed and thought it would break. The shipbuilder's fingers clasped his neck with a life-threatening force.

'Well, so that is what you are doing! Miserable whelp! You are a curse to us all! Hack a hole in the ship – what were you thinking? And what misdeeds were you going to commit afterwards? Burn down the whole village? Do you think Helge would thank you for destroying his ship like that? I wonder if Stridbjørn and Trud are sitting now and weeping bitter tears that the wrong son is dead! What have you ever done for them apart from bring them disappointment and unhappiness?'

The words struck Arnulf like a fist in the stomach and he forgot to resist. Aslak was quick to push him away from the wounded ship, Arnulf stumbled, groaning from Aslak's grip. The words rang in his head, and the pain in his arm was terrible. Was Aslak right? Was that what his parents thought of him? All the power that had been raging in him ceased and a deep misery weakened his limbs. Aslak was really mad, so he could well have shouted the truth. The despair was almost worse than the grief. If Arnulf's death could bring Helge back, he would trade places with him with the flick of a knife!

He let himself be led to the village without listening to Aslak's outbursts but before they reached the main longhouse defiance reared up in him again. Whatever the shipbuilder and Stridbjørn thought of him, the new ship was still Helge's and should follow his brother on his last voyage, his voyage to another world!

Nobody was between the houses; everyone was at home by their own hearth except Halfred and the Vikings who had farms further away from the sea. They would be Stridbjørn and Trud's guests for some days, resting after the last voyage, and Arnulf did not like the prospect of being humiliated in front of such brave men. He stiffened and dug his heels against the front door of his father's house, but Aslak wanted to go in and took a stronger hold of his arm. The pain was excruciating, and as Arnulf would not scream again, he saw no other option than to beat the door down.

Stridbjørn's house was so large that in addition to the sleeping places along the walls and the open fireplace in the middle, there was also room for a long oak table with benches. Usually it was shoved aside as much as possible, for it was comfortable enough to sit on the beds and eat or whittle with a knife close to the warming glow of the hearth, but now the table had been taken out and set for the feast, and the benches had been wiped down and covered with soft hides. Trud's large loom was next to the door so it could easily be carried out in good weather; shields and skins adorned the walls, for both decoration and protection against the draft. From the roof hung smoked venison bound up with dried herbs; axes, bows and swords hung on display at a suitable height so curious little knaves could not get their hands on them.

When Arnulf and Aslak entered, the men had seated themselves with horns of mead, while the women and thralls cooked and fried. Stridbjørn sat in the end seat with Halfred at his side, Serpenttooth lying in front of them, together with the large bronze horns. Trud was still crying but remained at the spit and did not seem to want to give up her hostess duties with so many guests at the table, and in the corners, or on the sleeping skins, children sat with open eyes, whispering.

Arnulf had slammed the door so hard that all eyes turned, astonished, directly towards him. Aslak forced him in, pushing him from behind as he released his grip. Arnulf fell but jumped up onto his feet immediately, and Aslak strode in, pointing vehemently at him, turning towards Stridbjørn in the high seat, 'I do not wish to add to the sorrow that Halfred has brought to this house, but as great as your oldest son was, your youngest one behaves carelessly. Arnulf scuttled Helge's new ship with a felling-axe and with such thoroughness that it is unlikely to be seaworthy again any time soon, if ever!'

Stridbjørn stared at him, dumbfounded, but then anger spread red across his face and several of the men shouted excitedly. Arnulf straightened himself and stared his father straight in the eye as Stridbjørn got up slowly and took a deep breath. He looked like a wounded beast about to attack, but just before he could roar, Arnulf cut him off, shouting furiously, 'Would you not even give Helge the ship in a funeral pyre? If

Halfred had not been so careless as to let Helge's body sink to the bottom of the sea, you would have been the first to put him to rest on the deck and throw in the torch!'

Stridbjørn opened his mouth to answer, but Halfred jumped up suddenly, pounding his fist on the oak table so Serpenttooth clinked against the bronze horns, 'How dare you! If you were my son, I would have removed the tongue out of your insolent flab on the spot! Do you think that there is time to fish for the dead when you are fighting as if it were the very end of the world? As Helge sank, I was fighting Øystein!'

Arnulf clenched his fists as he screamed, 'Had I been there, I would never have let my brother disappear like that and Thor knows it!'

'That is enough!'

Stridbjørn's voice thundered, causing the women and children to jump, 'Be quiet, Arnulf! Is there no end to the shame you would cast on your father's house? Only those who have never themselves felt a cut throw salt in the wounds of others, and those who have never defeated bigger opponents than foxes and deer have no right to invoke a war god's name!'

He moved threateningly towards Arnulf, who was not intimidated, but Trud stepped forward and stood between the two furious men. She raised her arms, her voice was firm but low, 'My youngest son is young and that his blood runs fiercely is known by everyone. He acts without thought and is just as consumed with sorrow as I and should, therefore, be excused.'

She looked around, seeking each of the Vikings with her eyes, 'Here we drink and when mead and grief are mixed with improper words, swords are unsheathed all too easily, but I have already lost my eldest son today! No matter how foolishly Arnulf has behaved, let him go and forgive him! The damaged ship should not cost you any loss Aslak, and if Arnulf insults you again tomorrow Halfred, you may take him into the woods and teach him all you want about honour and respect.'

Arnulf stared at the floor, deeply ashamed that his mother had to come to his defence. As if he were a child who could not look after himself. And as if there was reason to repent! Was he the only one here who wanted a respectable funeral for Helge? What would Heimdal think when the Valkyries brought his brother empty handed over Bifrost?

Halfred muttered something to himself and sat down with a nod. Rolf got up and pushed a horn of mead into his hand and pulled his father down into the chair again. He looked sharply at Arnulf and pointed towards the door, as Trud asked Aslak to sit at the table and wait for food in good company. Although most were in favour of Arnulf being made accountable for his actions towards the ship right on the spot, no one went against Trud as a housewife's word was law at her own hearth and her grief had to be respected. Arnulf looked around but met only pitiless eyes, and the floor began to go from underneath him. With a furious outburst, he spun around and headed for the door. If it should be like that, then they could be all be free of him! Apparently, a son of the house was not welcome at his own brother's funeral feast!

He slammed the door behind him with more force than he thought and staggered to the low wicker fence surrounding the house, stopping and swaying by the open gate and hid his face in his hands. His arm hurt, really hurt, and he could still feel Aslak's fingers biting into his neck. From inside the longhouse came the sounds of a toast being made and he could hear laughter and shouts from the other houses. Song. Everyone was at a feast except him, and he felt sick with self-pity. Even the dogs had snuck in and were begging for bones. Arnulf shuddered. His trousers were still wet and his kyrtle was clammy with sweat. The moon seemed to be staring at him with its large pale eye and the walls of the houses seemed to be turning their backs on him, as if they were trying to hold onto the warm rays of light seeping out of their cracks and half-open doors.

Bloody village! Bloody skrællinger who live in it! And bloody Helge, who betrayed him and let himself get killed over a moment of lust! Not one of the men here would ever offer him a place on a ship to go a-viking. He would be forever doomed to trudge on the heels of Rolf across the stony fields or haul herring out of the sea. Bloody life! Did they not understand anything? He had seen sixteen summers and was willing to travel and fight and just like that he was expelled because he had cut a little hole in a rowing boat! Chased out of his home without so much as his cape or hunting bow! He was almost ready to free Toke in the thrall hut and turn his back on Egilssund for good!

Fuming, Arnulf walked along the plank-covered road and out of the village with his head down between his shoulders. His legs knew the path into the woods; he could even find the way in his sleep. The path led to the trout-filled brook and honey trees and from there he had his own animal paths to follow.

Arnulf roamed. He had some places deep under the tangled branches of the densest trees that he went to, but he went to the woodland whenever the mood took him. The trees knew him, the animals knew him and, not least, the wolves at the large rocks. They lived there in crevices and caves. Arnulf had been visiting them since his tenth winter. He did not fear the wolves and they never attacked him. When he showed up at the rocks, they ran around him restlessly and snarled deeply and menacingly, but afterwards they let him be and kept to themselves at an arm's distance. Arnulf respected them but saw himself as one of the pack, and more than once he had howled along with them when the full moon rose just above the large rocks, causing his wolf blood to flow uneasily. Frejdis was the only one who knew what he did out there and that it was not only the wolves' howl that scared the children at night. Once, she had said that it was to be expected when a man with a bear in his name named his son after both the eagle and the wolf. It was the animals fighting in Arnulf that made him so wild. The mixed blood. Arnulf did not have an opinion on it but he certainly felt restless.

And on this spring's night more than ever. Restless, he jogged haphazardly through the trees while he mumbled rebukes at everyone and everything. Mostly at Helge, who had so cruelly disappointed him, but also at Stridbjørn, who always praised his other sons, boasting of their ability. Did he think that he could improve Arnulf by doing that? No, not in the least! Helge had thought about it completely differently. It was he who had given Arnulf his bow and wooden sword and it was he who had taught him how to use both weapons far from prying and judgmental glances. Helge never blamed him for anything, he just directed his movements and showed him how to hit and strike. He might well have believed that Arnulf was trained now, given that he had let himself be killed at a young age. It was an ugly business! Absolutely terrible!

Only long after midnight was Arnulf tired of his hard words and in a whisper, he asked Helge for forgiveness as he crouched by the mosquito-lake's bank. It was also here that he fell asleep, exhausted by his own fury and tears and without the slightest protection against the year's first stings of the buzzing insects. Things could be the same. Everything could be the same. And if the wild beast took him in the night, it would only be a liberation. Bloody life!

*****

The dawn did not bring him any relief. Arnulf was just as miserable and the dew had not dried on his clothes. His skin was dotted with mosquito bites, his arm still hurt, and his stomach reminded him that he had not had dinner. But for the time being, he was not totally helpless. He had his shelters in the woods and also snares and traps that he could set up.

Arnulf found a supply of dried meat under some rocks near an elderberry bush and after a reasonable meal he roamed around on the animal paths and tried to get a hold of his thoughts and feelings. As long as he walked, he was doing something, and it was easier to think about everything. Destroying Helge's new ship was not a particularly proud deed and it was unfortunate that he had also earned both Aslak's and Halfred's anger. It was hardly wise to return home before those two had had one more night to ease their minds. And he certainly did not want any of Frejdis' pity or to hear more of Trud's crying.

The forest shone a delicate green and the sky was clear and blue. Arnulf pushed the gloomy thoughts from his mind and went hunting. As he had neither bow nor spear, he could not chase down any prey but during the day he sneaked up on wild boar and red deer. He pretended he had shot them and had to take refuge in a birch tree as the wild boar played his part in the game a little too vigorously, grunting so that it could drive him from the sows and piglets.

When evening fell, he found the low shelter he had built out of branches and braided forest grass well-hidden amidst a pine wood. He had laid a sleeping skin in it and it was a good place to sleep, but he did not get much peace, as he tossed and turned as he thought of Helge. Was he already in Valhalla? Could the Valkyries find him at the bottom of Sælvig? And how would they get him up? Maybe they did not need to breathe while diving, but what about the horses?

Arnulf lay and said goodbye to Helge that night. He spoke long and intimately with him, remembering their winters. Year by year he remembered what he and Helge had done and experienced. In reality, they had not spent that much time together, for all men sought Helge's company, but Arnulf and he had shared a special bond despite the great age difference. Helge had never talked down to his youngest brother, rather he tried to be his equal in all ways. Perhaps it had been his way of alleviating the sorrow that the loss of three children between Rolf and Arnulf had inflicted on Stridbjørn and Trud. Torhild had been ill, a bear took Astrid and Ingvar had drowned on a fishing trip.

Arnulf tried to let Helge go and accept that he had to settle for Rolf in the future, and although he did not really succeed, he got a strange peace of mind from it.

*****

Arnulf started for home the next day but he paced himself so that it would be evening when he arrived and spent a long time fishing in one of the trout brook's many lakes. He had very little desire to look anyone in the eye, but he could not stay in the woods forever and he trusted that once he had heard people's accusations, they would be calm again. He was also starting to miss Frejdis and now that Helge was gone, his father would have more use for him, no matter what Stridbjørn thought of his behaviour. Aslak was rarely angry for long and Halfred probably would not want to fall out with his host. Perhaps they would interpret Arnulf's being away for two days as remorse. Besides the weather had started to turn. A sharp wind swept through the forest and Arnulf knew he could do without a night without proper shelter especially if it was going to rain.

Confidently, he fried his fish over a small fire and walked towards the village when the sun went down, but he went around by the salt meadow and hill and approached from the side where the thralls' huts were. He wondered if the Northman had yielded or if he was still just as stubborn and rude? Arnulf should have asked him about Helge's death, for Halfred was known to be a good skald and could well be suspected of having embellished some of Helge's last fight just to please Stridbjørn and Trud. Toke might have seen him fall, just as he had seen his father die. And it was not unimportant to know how a great Viking had taken leave of his life. Yes, Arnulf should ask Toke and preferably now before his father tormented any talk out of the thrall.

*****

He approached the village cautiously and stopped at the forest, but it was deserted between the thralls' huts, as they would cook for themselves later, so Arnulf was able to sneak unseen into the smallest hut, even so he took care not to be seen. There was no need to invoke further anger and attention for Stridbjørn had after all decreed a mandatory death penalty for any thrall who went near the Northman. When he opened the door to the thrall hut, the stench of urine hit him from the dimness. Toke sat bound to the centre post, hanging in the rope so that his hair hid his face, but he heard Arnulf come in and slowly raised his head. Arnulf went inside and silently watched Northman. Toke's eyes were red from lack of sleep, his lips were dry and cracked, and his breathing was laboured through his half-open mouth. His hands were so swollen by the post that his fingers bristled, and Arnulf assumed that no one had been in the hut since he had left it. He frowned. He did not like it, as it was surely supposed to crack the

33

Northman's pride, but to completely destroy a thrall was just as stupid as throwing silver into the sea.

'Leave me alone!'

Toke's voice was hoarse and his eyes glowed faintly, 'If you are not here to free me, then go, do not torment me anymore.'

He looked like a wounded wolf in a trap.

'Did you see Helge die?' Arnulf asked. Toke uttered a hissing sound that apparently was meant as bitter laughter, 'I saw my father die, now go.'

He had difficulty speaking, his mouth was so parched. Arnulf turned his back on him and walked out. He had to know. He had to know if Halfred had told the truth, and there was no reason for Toke to die from lack of water before he had told him. Arnulf went into the nearest thrall hut where Old Fulla was sitting, spinning her wool. She was blind but her yarn was strong and smooth, so she was permitted to live despite her advanced years. Arnulf found two big clay mugs on a skewed shelf which he filled from the water barrel and he took some wholemeal bread from the fireplace and put it under his arm. The water was not fresh but Toke probably did not care and once he had drunk it, his tongue would probably be looser.

Fulla seemed to sense that it was a free man who was in the room and bowed low over her work. Arnulf left the door and went back to the little hut where Toke had again let his head hang down to his chest, and this time he did not look up when he heard the door. Arnulf squatted in front of him and put the mugs on the ground. Toke's shoulders straightened when he saw the water, and he looked up quickly with doubt and desperation in his eyes, as if he feared that Arnulf would just leave the water there to increase his suffering.

'Here,   drink!'

Arnulf raised one of the mugs to his lips. Toke tried to drink but started to cough so the water ran down his chin and into his tight short beard. Arnulf let him catch his breath and gave him the mug again and the Northman drank, first in small sips but soon so forcefully that he was choking.

Arnulf was angry that Stridbjørn had let his thrall's thirst become so bad.

'Calm down, otherwise you'll just throw it up again. You'll get as much as you want.'

The mug was soon emptied, Toke took a deep breath and seemed to get a bit of strength. He looked at Arnulf with deep gratitude in his eyes and Arnulf put the mug down on the floor, 'I've been in the woods for a few days. You're probably hungry, too?'

'Yes. No one has been here since you left.'

His voice sounded better now. Arnulf shrugged, 'They probably thought it would do you good to sit and get used to being a thrall.'

Toke closed his eyes and laid his neck against the post, 'In that case, I'll be sitting here for the rest of my life!'

'Maybe.'

Arnulf looked at Toke's swollen hands. They had to be excruciatingly painful and there were cakes of solidified blood on the rope, he had struggled with it so much.

'I'll loosen your hands while you eat, but don't try anything! Do I have your word?'

Toke looked at him again, his bright eyes sparkling as the hint of a smile pulled at the corners of his mouth, 'Only a free man can give his word, a thrall's voice counts for less than an ox's.'

'That is true, but I will take your word for it. You are not thrall-born.'

Toke nodded and Arnulf loosened the bloodied knots at the post. It was not easy because they were securely tightened, and Toke's wrists began to bleed again when the rope loosened its bite on his skin. Toke groaned loudly and seemed to be about to faint. His arms were so stiff that he had difficulty moving them. He fell on his side and curled up his hands with his face convulsed, so unbearable was the pain when the blood began to run freely again from his wrists.

Arnulf let him be and Toke composed himself soon after, clenching his teeth hard as he tried to come up. Arnulf had to help him, and Toke stared at his battered wrists as he tried to bend his elbows.

'They are as dead as dried cod,' he muttered bitterly.

'They'll recover, I think you'd better start eating before anyone comes. I'd imagine my actions here could well make trouble for both of us.'

Toke took a deep breath, 'So Stridbjørn did not send you?'

'No, he thinks I'm still in the forest. Eat up.'

Toke had to hold the bread between his wrists, for his fingers would not obey him. He ate quickly, like a fox who had stolen a bear's prey. Arnulf sat down, watching. The Northman did not seem uncouth. Øystein Ravenslayer had no doubt been just as proud of him as Stridbjørn was of Helge. And Øystein had been extraordinarily rich; the bracelets that Toke wore were not underweight. He seemed strong and probably excelled enough with both sword and axe that he was good to have on a ship, so it was a shame to use him for bonded labour. It was a waste of a useful Viking.

Arnulf was curious. Rarely did strangers come to Egilssund and Toke must have travelled and seen many things with Øystein. Arnulf wanted to know where Haraldsfjord was in Norway, and what sort of Icelander had told Toke of a silver-rich looting place? He wondered how far it was from here.

The bread disappeared and the second mug was emptied. Toke rubbed his hands while he strove to move his fingers. Arnulf could see that it hurt and Toke was so weak that he swayed. He put his hand on his chest, feeling it, as he grimaced.

'Did I really break a rib?'

Toke shook his head and leaned against the post, 'They're painful, but not broken.'

'How did Helge die? Was Halfred right in what he told us?'

Arnulf leaned forward. Toke nodded as his eyes glazed over again, 'Yes, he told it as it happened. Helge got the best death he could wish for. He and Øystein fought long and hard and he wounded my father several times before he lost his arm. No one interfered in their fight until afterwards. Everyone stood around them, looking on.'

The Northman's face was gloomy, 'My sister was avenged, like your brother was. There is no blood between us, Arnulf. I will not take your life, though it is within my right to do so. Stridbjørn has already lost one son.'

'Your right!'

Arnulf snorted, 'You really are mad! You sit here, bound like a thrall, and I should be happy for my life because you will not commit blood-vengeance!'

Toke moaned softly and looked at him earnestly, 'I will not insult you and you should not bring shame on me, because we are equal in lineage and rank, and you know I speak the truth.'

'Am I supposed to have the same status as a thrall!' exclaimed Arnulf, angrily. Toke's exhaustion was replaced with a furious look, 'I am not a thrall, I am a free man being held captive, and the day will never come when I volunteer to do Stridbjørn's will!'

Arnulf's challenged Toke's gaze and the Northman seemed to want to put his life behind his words. Arnulf tried to get him to look away, but Øystein Ravenslayer's son was sure in his stare, and it seemed that a tough fight was waiting for Stridbjørn before the thrall's yoke could be placed on the Northman's shoulders. Arnulf enjoyed the jesting. Toke could not be cowed. He was alone and far from home, and maybe it was not just the lack of sleep that had made his bright eyes look red, but he had a firmness in his eyes like Helge had and he apparently respected Arnulf as a man, not a boy.

Arnulf suddenly broke out in a smile. Toke's spite was replaced by astonishment and Arnulf shook his head, 'I'm glad you are not my thrall. Not every horse can be ridden.'

Toke gently returned the smile, 'No, some can only be used for breeding and you understand that better than most!'

He bent and cautiously stretched his wrists.

'What do you mean?'

Toke ended the discussion by looking away for a moment and let Arnulf have the victory, 'What were you doing in the woods Stridbjørnson?'

Arnulf squinted narrowly, 'Looking to the wolves, Northman.'

Toke nodded slowly, gasping, 'The thralls talk of a mad man who scuttled Helge's new ship. Was that what you were going to talk to the wolves about?'

Arnulf spat on the compacted-clay floor, 'You don't talk to a wolf! You growl or howl with it!'

'Only if you're brave enough!'

Toke looked down at his hands and clenched them carefully, 'I want you on my ship, Arnulf. I like you. You obey only yourself and you know what you want.'

Arnulf rose abruptly, 'I promised to knock your teeth out if you spoke any more about taking a voyage together and it is rare that I do not keep my word!'

Toke looked up, 'My teeth would give you no joy and they are my only weapon right now.'

Arnulf did not answer but gathered up the rope as Toke stretched his fingers, 'You must be thanked for the water and the bread. I needed it.'

'You shouldn't thank me. I might come with the thrall whip in the morning. I have to tie you up again.'

Toke nodded and reluctantly tried to join his hands behind his back, but his arms shook so much he could not control them. The swelling had almost subsided and Arnulf had no great desire to tighten the rope around his injured wrists again. Toke could try to escape now. He could jump up. He would certainly be the stronger of the two with his hands-free, but he had given his word.

'Put your hands in your lap, I'll tie them in front this time, so you can use them when Stridbjørn frees you, but don't waste time trying to bite the rope. You won't get far before the night has passed, and my father will let the dogs flay you alive if he discovers it.'

Toke nodded. He looked weak enough not to be thinking about escaping. Arnulf wound the rope twice and did not bind the knots any tighter than was necessary. Toke tried unsuccessfully to suppress a groan. He leaned his head against the post and squinted as Arnulf tied the end of the rope firmly to the post, 'You can lie down now. Try to get some sleep.'

'Why are you doing this? Your father is livid enough with you as it is.'

The words were clipped and Toke did not seem so proud anymore but degraded and tortured.

'Not all horses can be tamed. I wanted to know if Halfred spoke the truth and you seemed so miserable. Rest now.'

The Northman nodded with a sigh, 'I will not betray you.'

Arnulf took the mugs and scattered breadcrumbs on the floor, 'That's for you to decide.'

He stopped at the door. Toke seemed very lonely by the post.

'Good night, Toke.'

Toke bowed his head, 'Just go now, Arnulf. Even if your father is angry, you should nevertheless be glad that you still have him. Not everyone has.'

He tumbled heavily to the ground. Arnulf did not answer but closed the door, thinking. The Northman was not wrong, but right now it would probably be easier to be an orphan. Stridbjørn could be quite hot-headed and hold grudges longer than was necessary. Arnulf walked quickly away from the thrall huts. There was more life in the village now after the men from the ship had come home. They were busy, there was plenty to do after the winter; the fields needed to be ploughed and sown before they could prepare for the summer voyage. Aslak had his hands full in the shipyard, for it was not without reason that Helge had asked him to build a new ship. The old one had been worn hard and the fight against Øystein's men had inflicted a lot of new damage. If the ship could not be repaired enough, the voyage might be abandoned, and although the women loved their men, it would be strenuous to have them tramping round at home for a whole summer without anything sensible to use their strength on. Strife, that was the only outcome of idleness, strife and far too much interference in the routines of everyday.

That spring when Stridbjørn had declared that he would henceforth let his sons sail, as he himself would be staying home because of his age, Trud had been very unhappy. She had shouted that a grey beard had not held other and better men than him from going a-viking, and Stridbjørn had had to roar at her before she fell quiet. That summer, Arnulf had stayed in the forest most of the time, practicing with his bow and Rolf had cleared the stone from a new field, but when Helge came home at harvest time, a calmness came over the family again, and Trud did not have to go without any plundered goods despite Stridbjørn's staying home.

Arnulf kicked a stone as he passed Finn Bow's house. A dog ran after it, almost knocking over Old Olav, who was not so steady on his legs after a blow from an axe in his time. He leaned on his stick, looking questioningly at Arnulf, who hurried on without greeting him. If Olav had something he wanted to ask about, it would have to wait until tomorrow, but the old man was not the only one whose gaze followed him. People watched him, sending stolen glances that Arnulf returned challengingly. Even the blacksmith lingered for a moment over a red-hot ploughshare at the sight of him. Did it really mean so much to them that he had hacked the ship? Did no one understand why he had had to do it? Did they begrudge Helge his own ship? Arnulf shivered and brushed the hair from his face as the wind was tore at it. Those women, who were not yet making dinner indoors, stopped their chores and were silent as he passed, and he heard them whispering behind his back. Was everyone gone mad? Had he done something that he didn't know of? Why did they not leave him alone and go in, it would soon be dark.

'You came back!'

Little Ivar, rosy-cheeked, came running up to him with a small axe in his hand, his big eyes sparkling, forcing Arnulf to smile.

'Yes, I have come back.'

Arnulf ruffled his hair in a friendly manner, and Ivar jumped eagerly beside him, 'Did you see any wolves? Aren't you ever afraid of sleeping in the woods at night?'

Arnulf shook his head. What had he to fear?

'Have you talked to Rolf?' Ivar punched him playfully. Like lightning Arnulf covered himself with an invisible shield, 'With Rolf? No, why?'

Little Ivar suddenly looked away and stood up, 'Oh, nothing.'

He fidgeted a moment, then scurried away and began to hunt for a puppy. Arnulf picked up his pace. What had he to talk to Rolf about?

39

Hopefully not too much! He lashed out at one of the willow fences that encircled most of the houses and turned towards Stridbjørn's longhouse. With any luck his father was in a sociable mood now. He had no desire to spend another night in the woods.

Dinner had just finished when Arnulf entered. The men sat around the long table, drinking, as the thralls put the pots and dishes away. Trud stood at the head of the table with two full drinking horns in her hands. There were dark circles under her eyes and her hair was falling out of its bun.

Arnulf did not close the door but remained grimly standing, his hand on the frame, ready to answer any reproach. Everyone in the room turned their faces towards him, and Stridbjørn looked up from his high seat. He seemed to be just as drunk as was his habit to be at the winter solstice feast, but his face was not cheerful. The mood was suppressed under the host's grief and the Vikings around him were subdued. Rolf sat by his father's side, but he looked away and did not greet Arnulf. A new silver buckle adorned his shoulder and Arnulf had not seen those bracelets before. Serpenttooth was still on the table but the big bronze-gilded drinking horns were in their place. Gloomily Stridbjørn lifted his mead horn and growled, frowning, 'Veulf has returned! Come in and close the door lad, sit with us if you are finished roaming and gnawing bones with the forest wolves.'

Arnulf shut the door behind him, and Trud walked towards him, 'Are you hungry?'

'What I need, I find myself in the woods,' Arnulf cut her off but Trud did not let that stop her, 'Bread does not grow on trees. Sit at the table and I'll find some food for you.'

Arnulf hesitated and looked at the broad-shouldered men on the benches. There was no seat for him unless some of them made room.

'Come here, Prowler, sit by me. Asbjørn, be nice and shove up a little,' said Halfred as he waved Arnulf closer. The fact that it was the helmsman who helped him to the table, softened the gaze of the others and Arnulf sat down, but with a grumpy expression. Rolf rose abruptly. He eyes flickered, 'I will see to the grey mare. Rane believes she will foal tonight.'

'Then Rane can keep an eye on it,' exclaimed Stridbjørn testily. 'Sit down and support your father. Surely you have something to say to your brother.'

Rolf walked away from the table, 'It's no rush, and the grey lost the foal last time so I will not leave Rane alone. Good night to you all and thank you for good company.'

The men said goodnight as they looked knowingly at each other. Rolf nodded curtly to Arnulf and left Stridbjørn. Arnulf looked at Trud, who was busying herself with the bread knife. What was wrong with Rolf? He would not ask, for it was best not to arouse more attention than was good, but there was no conversation after he sat down. Arnulf glanced at the scarred, weathered faces. Last time the Vikings sat here at harvest time, the sound of laughter had lifted the rafters, and Asbjørn's singing had caused the kids to put their fingers in their ears, but now he sat, fiddling with the silver axe that hung on a chain around his neck, and Stridbjørn drank deeply from the horn and wiped his beard on his sleeve. Halfred handed a full mead horn to Arnulf, 'Here, drink with me. I will count it as the closest I'll come to an apology from you.'

Arnulf looked down at the tabletop but accepted the horn. He drank and suddenly realised how much he needed it. He emptied the horn, letting its strong content flow through his body like a caress. Halfred laughed softly, and Trud placed bread and meat in front of him, 'Eat.'

Arnulf grabbed the bread and Halfred pulled at his braided beard, 'Listen, my young Hotspur, for I have something to tell you.'

Arnulf looked sharply at him but Halfred shook his head, 'We won't talk about the ship nor Helge's burial. But when I was at the royalseat, Helge sang one of your skaldic verses for the king, and he really liked it.'

Arnulf let his hand sink, his body weak, 'Which one?'

'The one about Regnar Hundingson's berserker-raids. The king asked if Helge himself had composed it and your brother proudly told him about you.'

Halfred paused a moment and took a swig of mead while he let Arnulf digest the words.

'The king asked Helge to take his unruly little brother with him on another visit, for a good ballad was always welcome at the royalseat as tribute. He gave Helge a gold ring in skald payment.'

Arnulf mashed the crust of bread. It was hard to hear. Halfred drew a twisted gold ring from his finger and put it in front of him. He laughed harshly, 'Helge was so foresighted that he wore it on the hand that fell on the deck. I thought it should belong to you after his death, because without you he would not have gotten it, so I allowed myself to take it home.'

41

Arnulf bowed his head. His mouth quivering, he pushed his feet into the floor. Halfred's rough hand lay heavy on his shoulder, and Arnulf sighed, trembling.

'Thank you, Halfred,' he whispered, staring at the ring. 'And thank you for not hanging onto your anger.'

Halfred gave his shoulder a squeeze, 'You are young and hot-headed. A little too young. When we sail out again, I won't be taking you with me, even though Helge would have done it. I cannot have unaccountable men aboard the ship, you understand that well enough.'

He let Arnulf go, 'But if you honour your brother and learn to act sensibly, then we can talk again next year.'

Arnulf nodded and put the gold ring on his middle finger. It was big but sat there secure enough and it felt as if it was still warm from sitting on Helge's finger. This ring had belonged to the Danish king himself! And Helge had performed one of his songs! Arnulf raised his head and met his father's gaze. Stridbjørn looked at him, his eyes swimming, but his face was gentler than before. Arnulf clenched his hand so that the ring's gold curves cut into his finger. By Bragi! He himself would go to the king, and with so mighty an epic that nothing like it was ever uttered before in his hall! Stridbjørn should also be able to pronounce the name of his youngest son with pride and Trud's eyes be overflowing with tears of joy. He would create ballads all summer long and, in the winter, ride the black stallion to the royalseat, for he was welcome even without Helge!

Arnulf bit into the bread and Trud filled up his drinking horn. He drank thirstily and let the mead loosen up his tense muscles. No one said anything while his ate but everyone seemed to be thinking as Arnulf sat, chewing his meat carefully. The fire flickered on the hearth and the women quietly finished their chores. Frejdis. He wanted Frejdis. He longed for her warm. Maybe he could visit her before she went to bed.

Asbjørn began to talk about a wrestling match that had been held at the king's winter games, and Hugleik the Lame recounted a duel he had once attended. Both swords had broken, he remembered, and the two warring men had broken all the rules and settled the rest with their fists. Stridbjørn shook his head and said that he would only bet his life in a duel with a Frankish sword in his hand, but Hugleik had heard of a blacksmith in Havn who could replicate the Frankish of blacksmithing. Asbjørn thought it was a lie, but Rune Crookedneck confirmed Hugleik's claim, despite believing that the only weapon you could really rely on was the axe.

Arnulf listened and picked at the bread. It was good to get his mind off Helge, listening to a story that Rune told that he had heard from a Gotlander about two families blood feud over a fair woman. The story was followed by several others, for many had been heard around the tables at the royalseat and they could easily be told again. Arnulf soon forgot everything else around him as he took a sip of mead, his eyes wide.

As a rule, new stories were something that were kept for harvest time when the men had come home from the voyage, and he impressed every word that was said upon himself carefully. Later, he would retell them for himself and perhaps make skaldic poems from some of them. It would not be disadvantageous to sing some of the ballads the king already knew if one day he received an audience with him.

'Listen, Stridbjørn, I have not seen to your new thrall since Arnulf tethered him in the hut. Have you forgotten him or is he supposed to die of hunger and thirst?' asked Halfred. Stridbjørn looked up from the edge of his mead horn, 'No, I have not forgotten him. Tomorrow I will set him loose and pull his kyrtle from him, and then he shall carry water for Trud no matter how many lashes of the whip it takes to put him in his place.'

'It won't be easy to break him,' said Arnulf as he waved down a thrall to replenish his horn.

'Not easy?'

Stridbjørn snorted, 'An easy opponent steals the sweetness of the fight, but that thrall has not been born who will not ultimately obey my commandments.'

Arnulf drank deeply from the foaming mead, 'That Northman is truly stubborn and Trud has enough thralls to carry water. Putting him to work like an animal is a waste of a good man. Tell me Halfred, did he not fight like a bear before you got the ropes on him?'

Halfred nodded with a wry smile, 'Yes, that is a battle you would have been delighted to see Stridbjørn! The Northman stood in the middle of Øystein's ship, lashing out, despite him being only one man and completely surrounded, as anyone here attest.'

The Vikings on the benches mumbled affirmatively and a few scattered remarks praising Toke's courage could be heard. Asbjørn leaned across the table and belched heavily.

'Since you are defending the thrall, Arnulf,' he said with a sly look, 'What do you think your father should do with him?'

Arnulf looked slowly around the circle of men. Hugleik the Lame twisted his moustache curiously, and Rune Crookedneck put his finger against his lips. Stridbjørn glared as if he had no great confidence in his son's opinion in such cases.

'I think that he should be allowed to follow Halfred on the summer voyage and afterwards buy his freedom with the treasures he has won,' answered Arnulf. Asbjørn broke out in a roaring laugh and beat his drinking horn on the table so it sloshed, and several of the other men laughed. Stridbjørn stared ominously at Arnulf, and Halfred's eyebrows were raised in astonishment.

'Ha, Stridbjørn!' cried Asbjørn. 'And you say that your youngest thinks less than a steer! The lad has the ability to trade! What a brazen proposal to ask his own father! But if you send the Northern thrall out with a sword, then you will get his weight in silver at harvest time, I will stand for that, I have seen him fight!'

Stridbjørn pounded his fist on the table, 'As if Helge's death can be atoned with silver! It can only be purged with blood and humiliation! Moreover, you know that the thrall will run away the moment he gets the chance, and even more so with arms in his hand! Your throat, Asbjørn, would be the first to be cut!'

Arnulf shook his head, 'If you give him your word that he may purchase his freedom at harvest time, he will give you his word that he will not escape.'

Halfred laughed loudly, but Stridbjørn flung out his arms, 'Should I put my faith in the words of a thrall! Or worse – give him my own! Did you lose your last bit of sense in the woods? Accursed is my house and my seed, and poor is the man who has only one son left!'

He leaned back panting on the high seat and fumbled for his mead horn. Arnulf emptied his. He was angry. His proposal was not bad, and he certainly wished Toke his freedom after what he had lost and suffered. The mead was spinning through his body, making him dizzy and restless.

'And how do you know that the Northman will keep his word?' snarled Stridbjørn. 'You speak as if you already know him.'

'That I do!' Arnulf retorted, as he threw the horn away. 'He is proud like every great man's son should be and he doesn't deserve his fate. What Helge and Øystein had against each other has nothing to do with Toke, and he has lost more than any of us, for he also had his friends and his uncle aboard the ship.'

'Toke?' screamed Stridbjørn and stood up, his fists on the table. 'Well, well, so he is called Toke! It almost seems like you have been talking with my thrall while you were tying him up in the hut. Have you perhaps even made friends? Friend! With your own brother's murderer!'

Arnulf jumped up, 'Toke is not Helge's killer! And yes, I have spoken with him and, in fact, just before I came in here, I gave him bread and water to safeguard your property from dropping in value. If it had been him who had slayed Helge, then I would have killed him instead!'

'You have done what?'

Stridbjørn's head was raging-red, 'Here I have issued the death penalty for any thrall who dared to give food or water to that boor, and then I am betrayed my own son!'

Halfred lifted his hands in a reconciliatory gesture, 'Calm down, both of you. An easy opponent steals the sweetness of the battle and if the Northman has eaten and rested, you will be pleased tomorrow, Stridbjørn.'

Stridbjørn silenced him with a gesture and pointed furiously at Arnulf, 'In the circumstances I find it most appropriate that it is you who will whip the thrall in the morning, and may the gods comfort you if you do not do it thoroughly!'

'Never!' exclaimed Arnulf, but Stridbjørn raised his voice, 'And if you do not do it, I swear I will use the thrall-whip on you in front of the women and the unfree until you toe the line and ask for forgiveness!'

Angry sweat ran down his spine and Arnulf squinted narrowly, 'Unfortunately, I can't beat the thrall for you, father, for I have a pain in my hand from hacking with the felling-axe!'

Stridbjørn let out a roar and reached for the sword's pommel and Halfred jumped up and grabbed Arnulf's shoulder, 'I think you have had enough mead now, Arnulf! Come out and take a piss with me instead of standing here, infuriating your father. Let's go!'

Without waiting for an answer, he pulled Arnulf with him over the bench, while Stridbjørn howled for Trud to get the thrall-whip immediately. Arnulf put his hand on his broad-bladed hunting knife in his belt, but Halfred's grip was not one to fight against and the fireplace and beds sailed past him until they reached outside, and the night air hit his face.

Halfred did not let him go until they stood beside the pig enclosure and Arnulf felt that his footing was not completely certain without the helmsman's hand. He grabbed a post and took a deep breath as the blood pounded in his ears and Halfred, grunting, pulled his trousers down.

Chased out of the house again! It was difficult that people got so worked up when they saw him and exhausting in the long run!

The wind had increased and helped to clear his senses and the air was cold. It streaked through the interwoven wicker and Halfred sighed deeply. Arnulf fumbled with his belt.

45

'You are a beast,' growled Halfred and considered his growing pool, 'One day you will get yourself into serious trouble. People know you here and know what to expect, but a stranger would never be mollified by your mother's talk. You are not a child anymore and you are well versed in the difference between courtly and rude behaviour and you should know to keep your anger in check when needed.'

Arnulf targeted a heap of pig shit but missed, 'Is what I do so wrong?'

Halfred chuckled and shook dry his manhood, 'It is one thing to be right and wrong, but it is something else entirely that your father is master of the house and should be treated respectfully, especially when there are guests present.'

He hauled up his trousers and closed his silver-buckled belt, 'If I were you, I would stay out here and cool off a bit. The rest of us will soon go to sleep, and then you can sneak in and find a seat.'

Arnulf looked down. Odin's spear swelled in his hands, and raised its head seeking Frejdis. She was probably asleep but could easily be awakened. Halfred nudged him with a laugh, 'No, well you're not a child anymore, Arnulf! But keep in mind that it was Helge's desire that ultimately cost him his life.'

Arnulf mumbled and bashfully stuffed his bulging lust into his trousers, 'Then I'll come later.'

Halfred whistled cheerfully, looking towards the thrall huts, which offended Arnulf. Did the helmsman really believe that he intended to go there now? As if his longing for Frejdis could be turned off with a simple thrall girl!

Halfred left him while he hummed a stanza of the ballad about Frey's lovemaking. Arnulf straightened his kyrtle and ran his fingers through his hair. Frejdis was his goddess, his jewel, yes, she was the moon itself! His tormented mind would find peace in her light and his broken heart would be healed in her lap. He watched Halfred go and slowly began to stroll along the barns and outbuildings. It was quiet in the village; only in Stridbjørn's longhouse was there still light, but soon they would go to sleep. As soon as Halfred went in, the men would find their sleeping skins, and after the mead and the food, it would be a deep slumber.

The moon still had power in the sky, so Arnulf could easily see in the dark. Rolf said he had the eyes of a wolf and that it was not natural for a man to be able to distinguish so clearly when the sun was gone, but Rolf himself never went out the door as soon as the day's work was over. Arnulf stumbled in the grass. His wolf sight did not help relax the grip of

46

the mead on his feet and he started to laugh himself silly. Stridbjørn was really mad this time, the old fool! He should be thanking Arnulf because he bothered to feed Toke, but no, no, the old bear always growled.

Arnulf had to stop and get his balance again before he crept towards Frejdis' low house. She was sleeping soundly now. Sleeping with her flowing hair radiating on her face, shimmering like the full moon. He smiled. Maybe he should just sneak over to her bed and kiss her without waking her. Just listen to her calm breathing; lie there beside her and feel her scent.

The dog would not betray him, he knew it well, and her parents, having drunk just as much as all the others, were snoring deeply. They were not wealthy, and the farm had seen better days, but none were scorned for not owning much and they were respected. They had no thralls, and of their children only Frejdis had survived the infant years, so her parents loved her and that they hung the scarce bronze they had on her neck was understood by all. Their animals were inside at night to keep the house warm, while Trud had enough thralls to collect and split logs.

Arnulf tiptoed around the crooked gable wall and crept to the loose board under the abandoned swallow nests. It was here that Frejdis lay on the other side of the wall, and they had often pulled the board slightly to the side to whisper to each other late into the night. When Arnulf roamed the woods, he would often find a way to pay her a nocturnal visit without the others knowing, and Frejdis would sneak a half a loaf out to him to take back to the wilderness. She did not laugh at his craving for solitude, but she cared nothing for his antics with the wolves. When she asked him to stay away from them, he laughed saying that every man had his own way to get used to danger, and that he who did not fear the forest's grey hunters could look his enemies in the eye better than others.

Arnulf squatted and scratched softly on the board. Another would probably think it was the mice at work but Frejdis knew the sound and if she was there, she would wake up and answer him. He put his ear to the wall and waited a little, but when Frejdis did not respond, he knocked lightly. There was still nothing, so Arnulf pulled the board slightly and put his mouth to the hole, 'Hello, Frejdis, are you asleep? It's me, wake up!'

Then came the sound from inside and he heard her sleepy voice, 'Shh! What do you want? I am sleeping now, Arnulf, go away.'

Arnulf laughed softly and knocked a little harder, 'Come out, Frejdis, I need to touch you! You didn't go into the woods with me and I am fierce hard with longing!'

47

He giggled wildly and sat in the dandelions, but Frejdis whispered offended, 'If you are so needy, you can find a willing girl somewhere else! You have drunk so much it stinks of mead even in here.'

She sounded awake now. Awake and a little too dismissive.

'Come on, you're not in the habit of being prudish! You won't regret it, I'll just stroke your hair a little, so very gently and delicately that you'll barely be able to feel it. Come out, the moon is shining as clear as day, and it's lonely here without you!'

'Go now, Arnulf, I can't.'

Frejdis' voice was anxious and urgent at the same time, and she had her mouth right up to the hole. Arnulf did not give up, 'Go? Well, I won't go! Come out or I'll shout and wake the whole house so even your half-deaf grandmother will be in no doubt about who's here!'

'I can't,' exclaimed Frejdis with a quivering voice. 'Don't you understand? Have you spoken with Rolf?'

Arnulf came onto his knees, 'With Rolf? No, he's out, foaling!'

He sputtered with laughter at the thought of Rolf with a wet foal between his legs and began to sing softly:

Ashen he abandoned
The table tersely
Arnulf's brother
With coarsened courage
Eyes wide
Wavering

'Shh!' gasped Frejdis horrified, 'That's spite! Wait, I'll come out, but, by Mjolnir, stay quiet!'

Arnulf bit his lip to keep from laughing and leaned back heavily against the wall. Why did everyone think he should talk with Rolf, the bleating beast! Rolf Lambbrave, Rolf Scythewing, Rolf Scaredyfarter, how should he go about talking to a man who ran as soon as he saw the shadow of his own little brother? No, bravery and a manly heart had been Helge's, whereas Rolf went around the smallest goat so as to be at peace, and he rarely gave words other than grievances and reproaches to Arnulf.

Frejdis came out quietly wrapped in her yellow-trimmed cape and Arnulf jumped up and went to her, smiling and with open arms, 'You look lovely, Daughter of Freya, come here, let me warm you, the grass is cold.'

Frejdis bowed her head and pulled her cape tightly around her. Golden hair fell down her face and her shoulders began to shake as if she were crying. Arnulf blinked the mead's mist from his eyes and embraced her tenderly while he stroked her hair. Frejdis leaned against him and gave in to a silent, quivering crying, and Arnulf hugged her tightly without asking for anything. The night was yet long and if Frejdis would cry, she should be allowed to sob against his chest as long as she wanted. He could feel the tears soaking his kyrtle at the shoulder and trickling in under the neckline, but instead of being comforted by his caresses, Frejdis sank down in front of him and hid her head in her hands. Arnulf hunkered down on his knees and squeezed her hands gently, 'Frejdis what happened? Did someone hurt you? What it is that I don't know?'

She shook her head, so her cape slipped off one shoulder, baring her neck, which was adorned by a double row necklace of large amber and silver beads. Arnulf stiffened and took hold of it, 'That's Trud's midsummer chain! Why are you wearing it? Frejdis, answer me!'

He heard his voice light with cruel fears. Frejdis had not stolen the chain and so precious a gift was not given without reason. She looked fearfully at him with swollen eyes. Her lips trembled, struggling for words, each one a deeper-stabbing knife that she did not wish to throw, 'They came when you were in the woods, Rolf and Stridbjørn, with Trud's jewellery ... Oh, Arnulf!'

She pulled away from him and bit her knuckles, while her eyes filled with tears. Arnulf stared at her aghast while she continued to sob, her shaking hand at her mouth, 'Rolf was playing the suitor and my parents ...'

She closed her eyes tightly, 'They shed tears of joy and plied them with everything that was in the house.'

Arnulf raised his hands and opened his mouth, but no sound came out. Was Frejdis really sitting there, telling him that she had given Rolf her yes? He shook his head violently, reefing at his fringe. It was impossible! It was a bad dream! He was drunk, lying in the pigs' enclosure and having nightmares! Rolf could not have usurped Frejdis in such an abrasive manner, he knew that Arnulf loved her! Even the young thralls knew that she was his, everyone had seen them together, and was it not Arnulf's marten skin that her new winter cape was lined with? To think that he could betray his brother like that! Rolf would pay for this, and as soon as he showed himself! And even just a few days after Helge's death! No one should act so distastefully! It mocked the mourning, it was inexcusable, it was heartless! Rolf had icily exploited his grief and acted while Arnulf was disgraced and exiled in the forest.

He moaned and drilled his nails deep into his scalp. Helge's scuttled ship seemed to come sliding out of the darkness to crush him

49

under its desecrated planks, and behind it stood all the other misdeeds like hideous trolls with eyes shining gleefully! A greater evil doer than Veulf Stridbjørnson did not exist in all of Egilssund, yes, not throughout its entire outlands! Of course, no parents in their right mind would want him as a son-in-law, and certainly not when Rolf had asked first. Rolf, with all his overfed animals and tightly sown fields! They could have at least fought for her! Let the weapons determine which one was the best for her.

'Frejdis how could you!'

Now Arnulf was crying. Distraught and unashamed in the least by it.

'I love you! I would have betrothed myself to you after the voyage, you know I would, and you would never have gone without anything! How could you say yes to Rolf?'

Arnulf grabbed her shoulders and leaned his head against her chest, 'I love you more than my miserable life, do you not understand that? Don't marry Rolf, do you hear? It will be the death of me, the death of me, here and now, tonight!'

Frejdis hid her face in her hair and hugged him to her as if she were drowning, 'What could I have done? It will never go well between us. Next year I will have a baby and what can you give it to eat? Leftovers from Trud's pots? Rolf doesn't trot around, waiting for his heritage. He is energetic and blessed by Freyr, and he can feed and protect his family. Your house is rich, but we feel winter's hunger and I want better for my children.'

Arnulf looked up. Was he worth so little? People believed he could not even find food for an infant. Was bread more important than the man? Had he not sincerely loved Frejdis, sung to her and brought her fur and game from the woods? His hands took her roughly, 'Now lessens the life in me, Frejdis!'

Her glance over Trud's precious amber and silver pearls mirrored his horror, and despair twitched at her mouth and took the power of the words.

'Tell me what I must do,' whispered Arnulf imploringly. 'Anything you want, I'll do it! I am no less strong than Rolf and I can learn to cultivate fields and breed animals as well as anyone else. I will not come home empty-handed from any voyage! I can't bear to see you with him, not for a single day!'

Frejdis looked down and pulled her hands away to wipe her nose on her sleeve, 'It's too late now. I can't go against my father's words and break his promise to Stridbjørn, not in spite of all your love and song. And no one believes in you, Arnulf. No one trusts a man who dishonours his reputable father and roams about like an animal in the forest.'

Arnulf did not answer but glided his fingertips light as a feather across her cheeks, and she took them and kissed his palm fervently. Her lips burned him, and his hand sucked the pain into himself so as never to forget it. Her gaze was fixed as she got up and slowly loosened her cape buckle at her shoulder, and Arnulf jumped up, the blood flowing through his limbs. Without words, he asked Frejdis' white shoulders with his hands, while he felt his skin thinner and more vulnerable than ever before, as every hair on his body begged for her presence. If Rolf had her for life, he would have her now! Tonight she would caress him like glowing coal and grate scars on every muscle, and from that moment he would drag his cursed life into the darkness and loss and eternal longing.

Silently Frejdis let her cape slip to the ground and slipped off her dress. Her skin glowed brighter than the moon itself, and Arnulf was humbled by the sight of the divine beauty and at first dared only to touch her hair. Frejdis' breasts swelled with the promise of endless joy and chubby, round-cheeked children and her hips were rounded prouder than the keel of any dragon ship. He grabbed them and pulled her to him, sucked hard on one nipple and squeezed the soft buttocks while Odin's spear obeyed. Frejdis grabbed his hair and pressed against his abdomen with a surprising violence and hunger like she wanted to throw everything else away and forever sink into his embrace. He kissed her neck, her eyes, tasted her chin, tickled her earlobes with his tongue and sought to become one with her warm softness. He would disappear into her lush body and leave his own in the dewy grass, never to return to it. Like the Franks forging iron and steel into each other when they beat their swords, he would twist and thrust his body into hers until no one would ever think of separating them again.

Desire burned in his manhood, and Frejdis fumbled, short of breath, with his belt. His trousers slid down, and he wasted no time taking them off, but took her as they stood up against the rough house wall and penetrated her, panting, as he discovered that the hunger for her grew with each thrust. Frejdis whimpered and closed her eyes. Her nails bit into his neck and shoulders and her hair tickled his sweaty face while he worked with an unquenchable force, and her half-open mouth found his with a painful sweetness.

Without warning, something large hammered violently into Arnulf from behind, and a hand grabbed his hair with so wild a strength that it tore him from Frejdis with a jerk. He struck out with his arms and tried to regain his footing as he heard Frejdis let out a startled yelp, but at that same moment something hard hit him in his face, so the world flickered before his eyes. Arnulf hit the ground on his back, knocking the air out of his lungs, while blood filled his mouth and ran from his nose. Before he could sense anything or defend himself, a foot kicked him in the crotch, making him double over in pain.

'May the gods curse you, Arnulf, and Helheim beat you with pestilence and death! Do you think I want your miserable seed planted in my woman? I will teach you to lie with my betrothed. Shame on you, you fiend!'

Gasping, Arnulf felt his groin and hunched his shoulders while he was swamped by pain. Rolf! The lurking son of Loki! His body twitched with shock and pain. Never had he hated Rolf more than at this moment. How callous of him not to allow his brother one last farewell embrace, now he had stolen Frejdis and, with her, the joy from his life.

Rolf's voice was thick with anger, but his snarling was subdued, for despite the indignation, there was no need to awaken and involve others and he stood looming over Arnulf like a leaning oak tree. Frejdis snatched her dress and cape and, stifling a scream, fled on her bare legs. Arnulf, breathing heavily, pushed his hands into the ground to get up and noticed his lower lip was burning, but the rage drowned out the pain and he shook his head and looked up. Rolf did not seem to have time to wait, because he pulled him up brutally by the hair, just to lash out at his face again, and Arnulf tumbled against the wall of the house, stumbling in his trousers that hung down around his knees. He spat blood and raised his arms to protect himself against his brother's rage, while sparks danced before one eye, 'Wait, stop!'

Rolf's solid fists waved in front of his head, 'If I ever see you with Frejdis again, I will kill you, do you understand that? She is mine and no one else's. No one will laugh at me behind my back, you horny buck.'

Arnulf dried the blood on his lips and, panting, came up on his legs, supporting himself with the house. His knees shook under him, and the pain throbbed sickeningly between his legs while his trousers kept his feet in a snare-like grip.

'You took her from me!' he hissed. 'You stole her like a thief, while I was away!' Arnulf straightened up and spat again, for the blood was running out of him, 'I love Frejdis more than you ever will! You just love yourself and your land, and had you had the courage to ask Frejdis in private and not turned up at her parents with Stridbjørn and all his promises of wealth then you would never have gotten her yes! It is not four days since Helge died and you have already played suitor! He meant so little to you that you mock his funeral feast by yanking the solstice jewellery from Trud and giving it away.'

Arnulf pressed the back of his hand against his split lip. Rolf squinted and seemed to find it difficult to restrain himself, 'Could it not be that this joy brought Trud relief from her sorrow? Helge would welcome my actions, and you talk about mockery! What man can afford to howl about respect, while his penis glistens of a stolen woman's juice? What do you know about what I feel for Frejdis? You love as the bull loves cows, but I want a family, to have children, and when I have built myself a new farm, Frejdis will bring blessing to it and to my life!'

Arnulf reached angrily for his trousers, for it was shameful to stand and argue with his balls shining in the moonlight, 'So let us decide it honestly with weapons in our hands. Don't think I'm afraid to fight you over Frejdis, your earth-pansy!'

Rolf did not let him buckle his belt before he kicked the legs out from under him, and Arnulf fell to the ground with a stifled outburst. He tried to escape before Rolf fell upon him, but in vain. He could not get up with his trousers around his ankles, and Rolf's foot hit his exposed end, so the humiliation spread like fire. Beside himself with rage, Arnulf got up, again and again, but each time Rolf landed him in the grass. Never had Arnulf felt as humiliated as he did now, rolling around, driven by Rolf's kicks and punches with his manhood dangling and shrunken with pain and disappointment. Rolf did not seem to have avenged his dishonour enough and with a fiery attack he forced Arnulf to crawl in the grass, but when he loosened his wide belt to beat him with it, Arnulf completely lost his temper.

The hilt of the hunting knife in his belt grazed his hand, and he grabbed it with the same speed as a lynx extending its claws in a spring. The weapon was moulded to his fist, and Arnulf jumped up, his legs together and threw himself against Rolf, blade first. Øystein had deprived him of his beloved brother, but Rolf had taken something that was worth ten times more! Frejdis was his life, his triumph, his breath! She was the blood that flowed in his veins, the dream that spun his songs and his only real longing! Arnulf could not bear to see her in the arms of Rolf for even just a single moment, and never had he believed that his own brother would betray him so terribly!

The knife hit Rolf in the chest, stabbing him and he opened his eyes wide as he fell backwards.

Arnulf kept his hold on the hilt and was hit by the warm, spurting blood. Rolf lay writhing and rattling on the ground, fumbling at the wound. It seemed like his whole body was cramping, then he lay still, and for a moment Arnulf thought his heart had stopped beating. He stared aghast at Rolf and heard a gurgling moan from his own throat, but then his heart beat again and its hammering pounded in his ears and the sweat poured down his skin. His body panted for air and felt strange to him.

Rolf had closed his eyes, the blood oozing out of him and his jaw twisted open, but he was not breathing and Arnulf staggered back, stumbling in his trousers. He had killed Rolf! He had killed his own brother! He was a murderer, and the most heinous one, a brother killer! And Rolf had not been armed! It was cowardly, it was a misdeed, it was villainous! Arnulf blinked and felt the burn in his throat. He had forfeited his life! No man escaped unpunished from manslaughter, and none were subject to greater hatred and contempt than a dishonourable killer.

Arnulf looked at the bloody knife. His hand would not let go and his fingers were cramped white on the hilt, like there was a curse upon them. He rose as if in a trance. The village folk would kill him or drive him away. He would be outlawed and exiled at the next Thing. Stridbjørn would drown himself with shame in a barrel of mead and Trud would grieve herself to death. All in Egilssund would pity them and condemn him and all his misdeeds. Every one of his actions would be remembered and everyone would count themselves fortunate for not having brought up such a degenerate son. Tears burned his wounded lip. And Frejdis! She would hate him as no woman had hated any man before! An overwhelming weakness brought down his arms, but then panic grabbed him and it squeezed so hard that everything went black. Frejdis would return in a moment. Perhaps she had fetched help, and maybe she thought she just had to wash her intended's scratches clean, but come she would, and she would find Rolf.

Arnulf pulled up his trousers resolutely and snorted a bloody snot from his nose. He would not wait here. He would not be overpowered and tied up like the offender he was, and all the death longing that Helge's death had aroused in him was abruptly swept aside, for he was young, too young to end his life now! He was the last of Trud's and Stridbjørn's sons, and whatever he had done, he deserved to live!

Arnulf could move his fingers again and he thrust the knife into its sheath and started to run. How could he have done it? Stabbed the knife in Rolf! Bloody hot temper! And damn Rolf! It was his own fault, by Tyr it was! You do not thrash your brother with a belt as if he were a dog, a thrall!

Arnulf stumbled over a tuft of grass and fell into a woven fence but he was on his feet again in an instant. Rolf was dead. Helge was dead and Rolf was dead. Rolf with his steady, strong hands and his mild, blue eyes. Rolf who had made shields and swords of wood and skins for him when he was little and had led the horse on his first ride. He taught him to catch fish. The summers Helge and Stridbjørn were out a-viking, it was Rolf who had supported Trud by taking care of the fields and animals while he reproachfully, but patiently, found himself party to Arnulf's whims. He could recite all the Kveldulf skaldic verses and all the stories about Starkad.

Short of breath Arnulf stopped in front of Stridbjørn's longhouse. He had to lean on a log pile, and it seemed to him that the house swayed, like it would break loose and run away from him. Arnulf spat blood and covered his eye with his hand. The house was silent and dark, but his thumping heart and gasping breath threatened to awaken those sleeping on the other side of the plank wall, and he listened intently, expecting to hear Frejdis' shrieks at any moment when she saw Rolf. She would wake up the whole village and people would jump up in the belief that there was a fire or an attack from the sea by unpeaceful men.

Arnulf held his breath as he ran towards the door. Any moment all the men would be against him and he had only his knife. He needed a weapon to defend himself with, otherwise he would be finished. With a weapon in his hand, he would bring the fight and better to be killed in a sword fight than be overpowered and sentenced.

Arnulf knew exactly how the door should be opened so as not to make a sound, and he slid in behind it like a shadow, his senses stretched to the limit. Everyone in the house was asleep. Halfred had been right that they would go to bed as soon as he went back in, and a soothing snoring was rising from the tightly packed sleeping places. The fire smouldered, and the dogs lifted their heads and wagged. Arnulf crept over the floor. Stridbjørn lay on his back with his mouth open, snoring loudest of all, and Trud had huddled herself together, her back against him. Even sleep did not smooth the furrows that had worn themselves deeply into her forehead over the last few days, and her hand clenched around the edge of the blanket. Arnulf was weak at the knees. If only he could throw himself on the ground and beg for forgiveness! Promise to behave better! Stridbjørn could beat him as much as he wanted to with the whip if that would stop them expelling him with horrified disgust and hatred. Arnulf clenched his shaking hands. He had not meant to murder Rolf; he did not understand his own actions. He had been ready for single combat and mad enough to win it too, but murder, never! He looked about searchingly. Serpenttooth was still on the long table, the flaming glow tinging its blade. The inlaid silver-threaded pommel seemed warm and alive, and the intertwined serpents along the edge called to Arnulf with glittering eyes. The mouth of one of the serpents was open so the tooth the sword was named after was clearly visible. Helge had given four thralls in exchange for it, because it was so rich in silver and masterfully executed. He had even had to raise his voice to the blacksmith, a broad axe resting on his shoulder, but they had gone drinking together afterwards, and Helge had dipped his new weapon in the sacrificial blood during next blot. He had loved that sword. Arnulf had often seen him pull it from its sheath at night and lay it beside him under his sleep skin. It was easily sharpened, with the weight placed closer to the hilt than was custom, so the wounding-serpent glide more easily in the hand and lifted its tooth effortlessly. Sleep had not come to Arnulf the night he had held the sword for the first time, his arm had wept with longing for the unattainable blade, skaldic verse was born and Helge had even had to promise to find his brother a similar weapon before the dawn had come.

Stridbjørn was old and Rolf was dead, so Arnulf went resolutely to the table and grabbed the hilt. He started when he lifted it. Helge's sword! Serpenttooth was famous for many a deed, and now it was his own hand that wielded it and it felt as if the sword's strength and danger was slipping through his arm like gold snakes running into his blood, giving him new courage. Helge would smile at the table in Valhalla, if he knew that Arnulf had taken his sword for he would be glad that Serpenttooth's saga was not yet over. It should be Arnulf's inheritance from him, and the only one he would get now.

Arnulf turned his back on Trud and Stridbjørn and hurried out. He grabbed a plain wool-lined wooden scabbard from a hook on the wall but did not wait to put Serpenttooth in it before he started running away from the house, leaving the door open behind him.

He clenched his teeth and hardened himself as he went towards the thrall huts. If he should get through this, it was important not to think about anything other than the way forward, and with the sword in his hand he had a reasonable chance of escaping. Arnulf swept through the darkness on swift feet. Wolf feet.

He turned in between the scant huts and swallowed the salty blood that continued to fill his mouth. His lip felt torn both against his teeth and where Rolf had hit it, and the pain from the other punches and kicks was beginning to encroach. Arnulf tore open the door to the smallest cabin, fumbling into the black darkness. Toke was sleeping deeply at the post. Arnulf tugged at his hair and searched for the rope, 'Wake up, Toke, you are going home now, back to Norway, to Haraldsfjord!'

Toke lifted his drowsy head but then sat up abruptly and let out a muffled cry when Arnulf cut him with the sword in his attempt to release his hands, 'Arnulf? What are you doing here? What has happened?'

He shook his head and had difficulty waking but appeared to be in a much better state than earlier in the evening. The rope broke, and Toke raised his hands with a sigh.

'We must leave immediately; the others will be here in a moment. I killed my brother! Can you stand?'

Arnulf grabbed Toke's arm and pulled him to his feet, and the Northman faltered and, groaning, bent his wrists.

'Your brother? What do you mean? I thought my father killed him!'

'Not him. My other brother, Rolf.'

In that moment Frejdis' screams resounded through the night, shrill and terrified, and each new howl was wilder than the other. Arnulf stuck the sword roughly into the sheath and hooked it to his belt, 'Will you come with me now and win your freedom, then come and run for your life, or stay here and be a thrall forever!'

Toke shook away the last of the sleep and his voice was curt, 'Good, Arnulf, I am with you!'

Arnulf slapped him on the shoulder and turned, 'Quickly now!'

If the Northman wanted to go, he had to fend for himself and prove his worth, he had, after all, slept and did not need to use his hands to run. Arnulf rushed out of the hut without any more words, Toke tumbled after.

Outside Arnulf set off, running, while frightened thralls opened the doors of the other huts and peered out, and he steered away from them as fast as he could while he hissed to Toke, 'The men will think that we have fled to the forest and that they can find us with the dogs, so we are better going on horseback. Many of them are grazing by the frog marsh, but the thrall down there will see and betray us, so if there is time, we will have to kill him.'

'No,' Toke shook his head and looked back. 'We cannot ride to Norway; we have to have a boat. The wind is strong and under the cover of darkness, we can get far.'

'Are you mad? They'll catch up with us in the longship as easy as anything as soon as it brightens!'

Toke looked at him earnestly, his hand pressed against his ribs. 'A boat, Arnulf! Maybe the wind will quieten at dawn and give us a head start and if necessary, we can sink it so it will not be found and recognised and get passage aboard a knarr.'

Arnulf turned towards the strand, while he thought quickly. There were lit torches in the village behind them, and the dogs were barking. Several women screamed, and angry cries and orders reached his ears. He still seemed to be able to distinguish Frejdis' voice and it burned him like fire and made his feet uncertain. Toke was right, despite it seeming far riskier to be on the open water than between the cover of the trees that he was so familiar with, and the wind was an unpredictable ally in which to place their lives. If it waned, Halfred could put forty oars in the water from the dragon ship.

Beneath him the grass was replaced by sand, and Arnulf doubled his efforts as he ran down to the water's edge. The wind tore at his hair and whipped foam on the sound. Toke was right behind him, his strained breathing revealing that he barely had the energy to keep up. The Northman did not have the strength to escape far on foot at their current speed, and Arnulf headed determined towards Aslak's boat yard while he fervently hoped that no one in the village would think to scout the sea. They would believe that he and Toke had run into the wood; they simply had to believe that! If no one discovered the missing boat before the sun came up, it would increase their chances of getting away considerably.

'Aslak has a boat we can take.'

Arnulf pointed forward. Several larger and smaller ships were pulled up onto the strand but under an awning was the shipbuilder's own. *The Sea Swallow* Aslak called it, and the boat was not so big that it could not be sailed by one man. When the men went a-viking during the summer, Aslak went out to make his agreements with people in the villages round about. Years earlier he had designated which trees to fell and then laid the keel for their new ships and led their construction. When the thwarts, the keelson and the mast fish were laid and only the deck was missing, he would sail on, his bag heavy with silver and let the villagers themselves make the vessel ready.

The Sea Swallow was quick and easy to sail, and Aslak had lavished it with much detail, carefully painting the cut-outs crimson, for a shipbuilder's own boat should impress and at first glance show its master's abilities. What would he think when he discovered his pride stolen? It was best not to think about it and Arnulf avoided looking too much at Helge's new, damaged ship as he passed it. He waved to Toke to follow him to the awning and tumbled against the front of the boat as he grabbed the rope, and although the Northman's face was convulsed, he took the rope with the strength of a jötunn, helping Arnulf to push *The Sea Swallow* across the sand with his shoulder against the planks. The boat lay a good bit from the sea, for Aslak did not like the winter storm's harsh ice to reach it, and he had journeymen enough to lug it over the sand. Out of the corner of his eye, Arnulf saw the torches dancing windblown towards the salt meadow and forest, while others disappeared towards the frog marsh; fireflies flew before his eyes and he felt as though *The Sea Swallow* was fighting stubbornly against its appropriators. His muscles quivered and his lip hurt and if the waves had not hit his feet with their coolness, he was sure he would have given in to the terrible guilt that roared in him like a wild animal and collapsed.

'Come on, Arnulf!'

Toke pulled him out with him into the hot-tempered water and jumped over the low shield rim. Arnulf followed and breathlessly began to grope for the sail's lashings. The boat rocked and lurched dangerously, and the waves crashed against the side, splashing water into the vessel. Toke took the helm with half-open hands, and Arnulf cut off the remaining bonds with his knife, for there was no time to waste and the water was rough and dangerous.

'Up with it. Come here, let me help.'

Toke steered with one hand and was able to use the other one well enough to pull the rope. He was accustomed to sailing, Arnulf could tell that immediately, and like a frolicsome colt *The Sea Swallow* turned one last time, then the Northman had dominion over it and caught the wind in the sail. Arnulf gripped the bailer, casting a nervous glance towards the shore. *The Sea Swallow* slid willingly out of the sound, and he saw no torches on the way to the strand, and his hand began to shake so the bailer beat against the shield rim. The men would head into the woods. They would believe that Arnulf was alone and had fled towards the wolf hills and only when the thralls said that Toke was with him, would they think of the ships. But thralls said nothing if they were not asked, and even though they did not know Toke, an unfree never betrayed anything of another man's escape unless he was forced. And while Stridbjørn and Halfred and Aslak would roar furiously as they searched for him, the women would carry Rolf into the house to wash his wounds and let Trud see him. Arnulf let his arms hang. Trud would fall on her son's bloody chest and moan worse than when the Æsir lost Balder, and Frejdis would be near madness from grief and hatred.

'Bail!'

Toke's voice was urgent and his look hard as if he knew what Arnulf was thinking. The excitement of going home to Norway seemed for a while to have completely won over his fatigue and pain. Arnulf clenched his teeth and threw water out with stiff hands. *The Sea Swallow* needed to be dry. It would not do to sit in water up to their ankles and the course would be more difficult to set if it splashed about onboard; every drop of water had to be bailed out, out, out. He clutched the shaft, like he had clutched the knife when he attacked Rolf and noticed that his hand was still sticky with blood. Arnulf dropped the bailer. Rolf was dead. He was a brother killer. He had killed Rolf. Murdered an unarmed man.

Toke reached out for him and forced his wounded hands together around his. The pressure was strong and Toke's smile was warm. His joy gave strength. Arnulf's wounded lip trembled as it began to bleed in his mouth again. The Northman did not condemn him, and instead of accusations and reproaches, his gaze promised friendship and help.

'Thank you, Arnulf!'

Toke let go and steered the boat towards the open sea, 'Do not think now. See if they set out for us and find out what is in the boat. We will need drinking water and food and a sleeping blanket would also be good.'

Arnulf squinted narrowly and stared back towards the village, but there were still no torches on the strand and the houses disappeared into the darkness, which mercifully hid their escape. One of his eyelids felt heavy and was throbbing. He tried to breathe deeply, but his body was tense, and his breathing was choppy. It tingled under his skin and his stomach had turned into a sharp stone.

Aslak's ship chest was stowed under the thwart, but apart from some blankets it was empty. The food sack and the little water barrel was not filled, for it had not been Aslak's plan to sail out before Helge went a-viking with his new ship.

'There are blankets.'

'Good.'

Arnulf began to feel the cold. The wind was stiff and the spring night chilly and his trousers were wet up to his thighs. No sensible person set sail without an extra wool kyrtle, leg warmers and water-repellent leather clothing. Egilssund's shore glided past him, and he could see the sea further out and shivered. His body trembled, unrestrained, just like in the worst winter cold. He had never sailed at night before but knew the waters well and as long as they had landmarks, their journey would be sure enough.

Toke's eyes glowed as if fevered and he resembled little the broken man Arnulf had seen sitting bound in the thrall hut, but if the Northman fainted, it would not surprise Arnulf in the least. Toke pulled the sail, 'Which way should we sail along the coast? We cannot make the trip to Haraldsfjord in this boat, we have to find the nearest trading market. Maybe we can sell it there and find ship's passage, if not to Norway, then away from here in any case.'

Arnulf dipped his sleeve into the water and held it against his lip, but instead of relieving it, the salt stung, 'The nearest trading market is located at Gormsø. It's not so far from here and trading will certainly be underway now before the summer voyages. Steer the ship to starboard at the mouth of the sound. If the wind holds, we will be there tomorrow afternoon, if not ...'

He was hoarse and looked back as if lost. Toke nodding contentedly and followed his gaze, 'We can do it! They will not notice that the boat is missing until tomorrow unless they search under the awning and we are sailing well. It is not any boat you chose for us!'

Arnulf brushed his hair from his face, 'Stridbjørn and Halfred will chase me all summer; that we have a head start now means nothing. They'll figure out that we'll head for Haraldsfjord.'

'Maybe, maybe not. You need not fear so much.'

'I killed Rolf!' exclaimed Arnulf testily. 'I will be an outlaw and exiled. What is it I should not fear? They won't rest until they have put a rope on me and pulled me to the Thing, if they don't kill me first.'

Toke shook his head, 'Do you have any other brothers?'

'Not alive.'

Arnulf moved restlessly on the thwart.

'Then Stridbjørn will not want his last son dead,' stated Toke. 'And certainly not your mother. They will mourn and rage and possibly curse you far away, but inside they will be relieved that you managed to escape. Halfred will never set foot in Haraldsfjord.'

Arnulf did not answer and huddled up. Maybe Toke was right. Why would anyone really want him dead? Who would it help? He hid his head in his hands, trying not to think. He could feel the boat bounding on the waves, so the water splashed against the bottom. Aslak had cut clutching beasts along the shield rim, clutching beasts with bird heads.

61

Toke steered the boat closer to the shore and turned it with a practiced hand along the coast, as the sound became the sea. The wind was stronger here. It reefed in the sail and *The Sea Swallow* floated swiftly in its power. The Vikings had often spoken of the wind on the Western Seas when they had talked about this year's trip. You could become wind-battered on the sea, especially if you did not have a low tent to seek shelter in now and then.

Arnulf tried again to sigh, but it felt as if his insides were rolling around in an earthquake. That their escape seemed to be succeeding gave him no peace; on the contrary, it was unbearable to sit with nothing to do, his blood grating in his veins like ice water.

He had lost Helge, lost Rolf, lost Frejdis and his parents and friendship with every inhabitant of Egilssund. Was there any longer a reason to live? His fate was sealed, the Æsir had turned from him. His thread of life was measured and was hardly much longer than the night. The rumour of his misdeeds would spread across the country, reported at trading centres for curious womenfolk, and they would sail after him over the sea carried by tale-lusty Vikings, and wherever he settled, it would reach him and drive him on, forever a curse to all. Contempt would follow him and with it a constant threat of revenge killings.

The murder-knife lay on the bottom of the boat where he had thrown it after having cut the sail free, and he lifted it up slowly, staring at the blade. Blood was not red at night. Blood was dark, it was blue; it was the colour of a shadow like a waft from Helheim's rotten breath. His fist tried to crush the hilt and never had it persisted so much at anything before. His arm was strong, strong enough to wrestle with Helge, strong enough to row an oar and go a-viking, it would be an easy stab. He turned the knife, so the blade was facing between his ribs.

'No!'

Toke cried out, releasing the helm as he lunged forward and grabbed his arm. Arnulf resisted, 'Let me go!'

'No! Arnulf, do not do it!'

Toke's grip drilled into his bone, but Arnulf fought with a desperate ferocity, and he tumbled about in the boat with Toke over him. He tried to stab himself with the knife but could not reach, and Toke struck out after his hand to weaken its hold on the weapon.

'Let go! You have no right to stop me doing it!' howled Arnulf as he tried to bite his opponent, but Toke put his knee against his shoulder with all his strength, 'I will not let you! Put the knife down!'

Arnulf writhed and moaned with pain, 'I killed Rolf, I am damned, let me do to myself what the others will do to me anyway when they catch me!'

'No one will kill you, you idiot! Do you prefer the friendship of Helheim over mine? You scorn the gods by wanting to throw away your life, give me that knife!'

Arnulf planted his fist in Toke's chest, where he knew that the Northman had the most pain, and Toke cried out but steadfastly kept his hold on Arnulf's arm. Furiously Arnulf tried to push Toke away with his knees while Serpenttooth's sheath drilled sharply into his thigh, but Toke twisted his legs around Arnulf's and caught his knife hand with both hands.

'You gave me my life, and now I give you yours, you steer Dane!' he shouted angrily and banged Arnulf's hand against the edge of the ship's chest. Arnulf screamed and dropped the knife, and Toke snatched it and stuck it in his belt, and then, panting and white in the face, he retreated to the helm with his hand on his ribs. Arnulf groaned and curled up in the water in the bottom of the boat, holding his hand and crying and weeping like a child. He just wanted to die and for Jörmungandr, the Midgard Serpent, to rise up from the sea to swallow the boat whole and put an end to the suffering. It was unbearable. His body was about to explode.

The water soaked his clothes and he froze and sobbed and spat.

'By Freyr, Arnulf, are you a boy or a man?'

Toke, struggling, heaved him up onto the thwart beside him.

'Veulf,' moaned Arnulf, holding his arm close to him, 'Never call me Arnulf again.'

'You should not have killed Rolf if you did not mean to do it! Mjolnir beat me if you are not worse to sail with than a whole shipload of jötnar, now breathe.'

Arnulf pressed his knuckles against his forehead, and Toke opened the lid of the ship's chest and pulled out one of the blankets, 'Look here, calm down, let the madness leave you! By Mimir's head! I will have to buy chainmail on Gormsø, otherwise my ribs will not keep you company all the way to Haraldsfjord.'

He threw the blanket around Arnulf. The fight seemed to have cost him his last strength, and he was breathing with an open mouth.

'I am cursed, and you stink of piss and what's worse?' muttered Arnulf darkly.

'It is your own fault, so you have to live with that, but one day you might find your tongue cut out!'

Toke rubbed his hands, his face convulsed and leaned heavily against the shield rim for support. Arnulf blew his nose into his fingers, his breathing rattling. His hand hurt terribly, and he held it before him, 'And you have broken my hand!'

Toke uttered a harsh laugh, 'A blow for a kick, now we are even in every way!'

He grabbed his hand and squeezed it while Arnulf writhed in protest.

'Well it is not broken, and you could have just let me go when I said.'

Arnulf pulled the blanket around him and did not answer. Toke looked towards land and straightened the boat's course and *The Sea Swallow* turned obediently despite the waves. Arnulf rubbed his hand and felt the moisture from his clothes penetrate the blanket. His heart pounded in his chest, like it was trying to get away from the murdering hand and out of the body that had tried to kill itself. Had Toke not intervened, he would have ended up on the road to Helheim now, going down to Niflheim's icy, dead world where Nidhogg lay gnawing on corpses. He had earned it! Helheim would have put him under a poisonous snake and even the dead would shun him.

Arnulf hurt everywhere and felt ice cold, and his hand was beginning to swell. He felt miserable, lonely and ashamed.

'Is that the first man you killed?'

Toke stared out over the stern's carved bird head.

'Yes.'

The answer was only a whisper. The Northman nodded slowly, 'So it was a bad choice to start with your brother. The first time is never easy.'

He looked like he would have to give in to the fatigue seriously now. His gaze was almost blank, and his shoulders were stooped. Arnulf put his hand in the water to swallow the pain, and it trickled black on his cuffs. He was alive. He had escaped the people of Egilssund but not life itself, and while the thumping pulse slowly eased, he tried to come to terms with his fate. A quick death was not punishment enough for his crime.

'You are not the only one who the Æsir have turned away from,' said Toke quietly. 'We are both equally cursed, Arnulf, cursed with life.'

He stroked his fingers through his hair with a painful sigh, 'I must look my kinsfolk in Haraldsfjord in the eye and tell many of the women and children that their men and fathers are not returning home. It would have been easier if I had died in the skirmish! We were twenty aboard my father's ship.'

Arnulf looked at him, 'Helge had forty men with him!'

'Yes. It was an unequal fight.'

His hand was tight on the helm, and Toke wrinkled his brows bitterly, 'I asked Øystein for permission to challenge Helge to a duel, so the revenge of his misdeeds should only stand between us, but my father said that he was angrier than I was, and that an old fox should be killed first. When Halfred killed him, my brothers-in-arms were furious and threw themselves into the battle.'

He clenched his free hand, 'If Halfred has boasted of the battle, he is a lesser man than most.'

Arnulf shook his head though it triggered stars in front of one of his eyes, 'He didn't boast, only told us how strongly you defended yourself.'

Toke snorted, 'Of course I defended myself! In any case, until Asbjørn succeeded in striking the axe handle on my forehead.'

He paused and sat a long time, brooding over the helm, while the boat glided past a headland. Arnulf licked his lips and felt his tense muscles loosen as he looked against the hurtling clouds and estimated that the wind would not quieten anytime soon. He thought of Helge's last fight. Saw him before him, Serpenttooth in his hand. Helge had always smiled as he fought, smiled and looked his enemy right in the eye. It must have been only after Øystein Ravenslayer had splintered both the shields that he had hewn off the arm; it must have been like that. Toke's father could not be called a coward since he had dared to attack a ship with twice the crew of his own, and Toke was clearly his descendant. Arnulf regretted his harsh words and actions. He had treated the Northman unfairly. Unfairly and rudely. He glanced at him. From now on Toke could count on him as his friend and no more blows should fall between them, by Helge's sword! Toke's face was worried and distressed, and his eyelids were heavy. He had to be completely exhausted, he had had little sleep, and his grief was great.

'Lie down and sleep, otherwise you'll fall overboard in a moment, and I know the course.'

Toke straightened up, 'Only if you give me your word that you will neither commit murder or suicide meanwhile.'

'You yourself have my knife, and I promise to keep the sword in its scabbard. Just lie down, Toke, and thank you!'

Arnulf reached out his shield hand and Toke grabbed it warmly. 'Before the moon is new, Arnulf, so we two will be a-viking together!'

He took the bailer and emptied the boat of water, then he pulled the second blanket out of the sea chest and with a relieved sigh curled up on the hard planks. In an instant his breathing was heavy, and Arnulf grasped the helm firmly.

Helge and Rolf were dead, but he would not cry or act like a child again, never ever! In the future, he would only do what was right, and others need not know anything of his pain and self-contempt. From this moment on, no man would blame him for acting indecently or petulantly, and Toke would not come to regret taking him on voyages. That the gods hated him and had abandoned him in disgust didn't need a skaldic verse but being completely unprotected was not good for anyone. Arnulf would choose a new god. A god for the excluded who was as lonely and had as a contrary a mind of his own, just as outlawed and derided. The wolf had lent him his name, and the wolves by the hills in the forest had accepted him into the pack, therefore Fenrir would now be the god he invoked and sacrificed to. Bound and condemned he stood on his island in the sea, but Arnulf knew that the jötunn wolf would lick his hands if he ever found it. Strong was Fenrir, stronger than all the Æsir together. He would not deny him his gloomy protection, and he feared not his evil force. Arnulf smiled deeply. He did not know how long the Norns had spun his life thread, but Fenrir would last until Ragnarök for that time to kill Odin himself, so he could probably spare a small piece of thread to lengthen Arnulf's slightly.

The Sea Swallow sailed past the high cliff at the flint hill and Arnulf was wary of the low-lying, serrated reef that was inhabited by birds in front of them, and which was difficult to see in the dark. Other men had been banished before him and had defiantly turned their misfortune into skald-worthy deeds. Praiseworthy men, whose history was known and admired. Life was not over; he was going into the unknown, on the way to his first voyage and he was not alone.

It was not Helge who would lead the longship, but Toke was just as burly a Viking, and the Northmen were no less brave than the Danes. Fenrir would watch over his conduct, and, like the black wolf he was, would maraud over the sea and fight and plunder as well as anyone! Without Toke he would have been running around in the woods, the dogs at his heels and would certainly have met a miserable death by now, he owed much to the Northman. Faithful he would be and highly he would esteem his new friend from Haraldsfjord. It was his first oath in the wolf Fenrir's name!

*****

The wind held all night, and *The Sea Swallow* followed her course steadily towards Gormsø. When the moon broke through the drifting clouds and shone on the coast, it lit the rocks and stones, making it easy for Arnulf to recognise the landmarks. At the first light of dawn, he kept a close eye on the sea behind him, but no sail was to be seen, and he felt convinced that he and Toke were not being followed.

Arnulf was sleepy and stiff from holding the helm; the more his fatigue increased, the more the cold plagued him. His thoughts had kept him awake but it had been good to make peace with them. Toke woke up only when Skinfaxi pulled the sun over the horizon and the sea birds flew out to sea. He sat up with a loud yawn and rubbed his sore hands together, sending Arnulf a grateful smile, 'You should have woken me earlier.'

Arnulf smiled a little and shook his head, 'You needed it. Besides, you were sleeping like a hibernating bear.'

Toke took stock of the shore and the wind and seemed satisfied, 'We got a good head start. How long until we reach Gormsø?'

'We should be there about noon; the boat is sailing faster than I had expected.'

Arnulf brushed his hair from his face. He was thirsty and his stomach was also beginning to make demands.

'Then you must sleep until then,' said Toke, wriggling out of the blanket. He laid it on the sea chest and looked appraisingly at Arnulf, 'You look terrible, you cannot show up anywhere looking like that. Wash yourself and your kyrtle too; it is better you be wet than look like a man who has just conducted a midsummer blót.'

He began to take the sail down in order to stop the boat for a short while. Arnulf looked down at himself. There was blood everywhere, even in his hair, and Rolf's blood had sprayed across his stomach. His lip was swollen and sore and his eye was hard to open completely.

'How is your hand?'

Arnulf spread his fingers, 'Alright. I can use it.'

'Your brother hit you good.'

Arnulf did not answer and Toke unfastened his belt and pulled his shoes and trousers off. He had soiled himself in them and the stench was reeking.

67

'Gods, what a mess!' he exclaimed, ashamed, and threw them in the bottom of the boat. 'Take off your clothes, I will wash them for you while you sleep, it is warmer now and my blanket is fairly dry.'

Toke pulled the silver bracelets from his arms and took off his kyrtle and allowed himself to slide over the shield rim into the water, and when the boat lurched dangerously for a moment, Arnulf had to act as ballast by leaning against the opposite side. Toke held on to the boat with one hand, 'Whew, it is as cold as Niflheim in here!'

He dived in and Arnulf regarded the Northman's muscular body. A Viking's body it was indeed. Several scars from cuts and stabs ran across his pale skin and the blue-black marks on his ribs clearly showed where Arnulf had kicked him.

Toke washed himself, snorting and laughing as he shook the water out of his hair, 'It is fresh down here, just wait, it will buck you up!'

Arnulf saw no need to leave the dry boat, but he lashed the helm and removed his sword belt and gently pulled the soiled kyrtle over his head while he felt and noted every place Rolf had hit him. The wind bit into his skin, and he dipped his kyrtle in the water and carefully washed his face with it. His eye was hot, and the icy sea water tingled on his lips, salty and undrinkable.

'Give me a hand!'

With his help Toke climbed, shuddering, into the boat again and huddled into himself, as Arnulf continued to wash blood from his upper body. The Northman grinned crookedly, 'It probably will not be today that you find a girlfriend in Gormsø. Your eye is completely black.'

Arnulf scowled gloomily and cleaned the blood from under his nails. The Northman's self-assuredness was almost intolerable after he had washed away the shame of the thrall's hut.

'Why did you kill Rolf?'

Arnulf let his hands sink and sucked air between his teeth. He stared at the finger that bore King Sweyn golden ring. Toke had no right to ask. It should be enough for him to know that there was a murder, which was Arnulf's concern, and the circumstances were too embarrassing to be talked about. Nevertheless, Arnulf wanted to confide in him; not carry his pain alone anymore.

'He betrothed himself to Frejdis while I was in the woods.'

His tongue could not really shape the words, it suddenly felt thick and clumsy, 'I didn't mean to kill him, it just happened.'

Toke frowned and nodded, 'Because he kept beating you?'

Arnulf tried to hide his scarred torso with his arms, 'Maybe.'

'And Frejdis? Was she worth it?'

Arnulf looked away. If she was worth it? He would swap Rolf for her a hundred times, nothing in all of Midgard was worth half as much as Frejdis!

'Yes!'

Toke crawled to the helm and handed him his blanket, 'I myself am married to the loveliest woman born under the Norwegian fjelds. Women get men to commit the most magnificent acts, but also the most fateful. Lie down and sleep, I will wake you when Gormsø comes into sight, I assume I cannot fail to see it?'

He hoisted the sail again, and Arnulf mumbled indistinctly and freezing, pulled the blanket around him. *The Sea Swallow's* planks were hard against his aching limbs, and he put his arm up over his head and hid under the harsh wool. The waves beat against the boat's sides and through the blanket he could see Toke adjust the helm a little and commence with the laundry. Arnulf had a headache and was dizzy with fatigue and he was thirstier than he cared to be. Yet he found no rest until Toke had finished his washing and had hung his clothes on the mast's shrouds.

*****

Arnulf felt not the slightest bit rested when Toke woke him in the early afternoon. He was soaked in sweat, and the echo of a death cry fluttered reluctantly away with a fleeting nightmare. The sail was not so tense anymore and the waves had subsided. Arnulf sat up painstakingly with a groan, putting his hands on his head. He was hungry and thirsty and sore, and his headache had worsened. His lip and eye were throbbing, and had it not been for the nightmare, he would just have crawled under the blanket again and continued to sleep until the hour of his death.

'Here.'

Toke handed him his kyrtle. It was clammy, but drier than Arnulf had expected, and he put it on reluctantly and looked around.

The weather had cleared, and the warm sun was blinking in the water. Not far away three small rocks stuck out above sea level, and just behind them he saw Gormsø with its flat sandy beaches and green fields. Several boats were pulled up on the sand, and further inland numerous tents and stalls with carved posts and patterned tablecloths were set up. Two wide piers were built along the large knarr that came from afar, burdened with boxes and jars and barrels.

Arnulf felt the excitement trickling through his body. The past several summers Rolf had taken him to Gormsø when the folk from Egilssund were getting the knarr ready. Loaded with wool and fur and amber, it was sailed out to trade for the items they themselves had not managed to produce, and Arnulf usually had a good pile of furs to sell. The trading days were summer's best experience and were always associated with joy and laughter and meetings with relatives and kinsmen from other villages. There were not many Arnulf's age in Egilssund, but Gormsø never lacked youths to drink and vie with, and Rolf had often had to be gruff in his voice when Arnulf was to go home again.

Everything was different now, and Arnulf was suddenly frightened at the thought of meeting people, especially someone who knew who he was. Usually the inhabitants from Egilssund sailed to Gormsø after the midsummer feast, so he allowed himself to hope that most of the traders in the square were unknown to him, but he could not be sure. He felt his eye gingerly and glanced at Toke, who sat tensely on the thwart with a hard grip on the helm. The Northman had tried to pull his sleeves down as far as possible, but they did not hide his injured wrists completely, and anyone who saw them would know immediately that he had been bound and had fought hard to escape. He did not look like an escaped thrall, but the rope marks were suspicious and combined with Arnulf's battered face and Aslak's famous boat, it did not make it easy for them.

Suddenly Arnulf had very little desire to dock *The Sea Swallow* at Gormsø. The plan in the night that had been so obvious, appeared risky and dangerous in the bright daylight.

'Should we wait until it gets dark?' he asked hoarsely. Toke shook his head firmly, 'Then we would lose too much time, and they have seen us. If we wait here for night fall, people will only be too inquisitive.'

He looked at Arnulf, 'But maybe it is best if we are not seen together. I am unknown here and can answer for myself, and if you stay by the boat you can probably avoid the worst of the unpleasantness. You can pretend you are sleeping, while I search for ship's passage. There are several larger ships here which are possibly on long-term trading expeditions.'

Arnulf nodded and fastened his belt around his waist. Serpenttooth lay safely and guarded against his thigh, and Toke sent him a stern look. 'No more murders, Arnulf, keep that sword in its scabbard no matter what is said to you today, promise me!'

'What do you take me for?' asked Arnulf again, and Toke shrugged, his gaze softer, 'More than you think Stridbjørnson, but I know how touchy a man can be the day after his first killing, and Frejdis seems to still have a deep hold of you.'

He pulled the sheet and turned the bow right towards Gormsø and Arnulf straightened his kyrtle and swore to himself that he would not talk to anyone unless it was absolutely necessary.

The marketplace at Gormsø was large and well attended from spring to harvest time. In addition to his countrymen, Arnulf had often seen Northern traders who sold whetstones, ropes and walrus teeth. People from Birka also came here with their iron and wax and sometimes treasures from the east. They had silk, brocade and spices. Frankish tradesmen occasionally came by to barter weapons and glass for amber, and last year a Westerner had sold tin.

Every year Arnulf had sought out coveted wares in every booth and admired jewellery and weapons, but as he approached with Toke, he was sombre and vigilant. He recognised none of the ships on the beach, nor any of the sleeping tents that were pitched behind the many rows of stalls and trade tents. Everywhere teemed with life, and the trading seemed to be going well. Several men were expensively or foreignly dressed, and the sound of a flute playing, and the smell of sizzling meat reached Arnulf as *The Sea Swallow's* keel met the sandy bottom, and he and Toke jumped out to push her up on land. There were few people at the ships, and his rumbling stomach and parched palate protested against Toke's proposal that he pretend to be sleeping in the boat. The Northman had to be starving too after the last day, and it did not help that the beer and food tents had been set up closest to the water's edge to tempt weary newcomers as much as possible.

Toke wrung the water out of his trouser legs and pulled down his sleeves, 'I will come back as fast as I can. Be careful.'

Arnulf nodded and leaned up against the boat with his hand on Serpenttooth's opulent pommel, 'I'll only stay here if you don't let me starve to death on the strand.'

Toke grimaced. 'You have not endured half of the hardships I have suffered since my meeting with Helge, think on that while you wait!'

'Was it not me who came with bread and water?' snorted Arnulf outraged, sending Toke a scowl. The Northman did not answer but smiled disarmingly, offering his hand, and Arnulf grabbed it firmly. If Toke could just get them the opportunity to get out of the country, then he would hold back his demands and endure his thirst a little longer.

Toke walked towards the stalls with a quick stride, as Arnulf sat with his back against *The Sea Swallow,* sighing heavily. The boat was wet but his kyrtle was so moist that they could have been one. He looked at the traders' eager gestures at the stalls and heard their cries and laughter. A blacksmith had brought his tools and had built a forge. His hammer sounded across the square, mingled with the neighing of horses and the clucking of hens. Some lads were preparing to test a new bow, and a young woman with a huge smile showed a roll of cloth to an Eastern-looking man, who gladly drew a bronze chain from his belt pouch. At a long table, two men were bidding on the same bearskin and were almost at arms. Arnulf bit his tongue to force a little spit in his mouth. Unfair it was that he should enjoy the fun from a distance, while Toke ate and drank and mixed with good people. He risked becoming both wrinkled and grey-haired here in the sun if the Northman were to set the pace, and the beer mugs were being clinked together in the tents so it could be heard all the way to Egilssund!

Arnulf sat for a long time, depressed, against *The Sea Swallow* and tried not to be overpowered by dark thoughts, while the thirst slowly became more difficult to endure, but when the torments seemed unreasonable, he got restless. It was too stupid to find yourself in such a state so close to a beer tent! No one knew him over there and no one needed to ask anything; it was not forbidden to have been in a fight! Just a single mug of beer and a hunk of meat. That would not take long and Toke would never know.

Arnulf combed his hair down over his swollen eye and walked lively towards the tent. He smiled wryly to a few girls carrying baskets on their hips and thrust his fingers into his belt satisfactorily, when they began to giggle behind his back. Did he not look just like any other lad womenfolk wanted to stare boldly at, and had Frejdis not even praised his bright hair for how it fell? As to the rows of stalls containing any dangers for those who had guts and a man's heart, how foolish to be as scared as a child!

Several men were sitting and talking in front of the beer tent, resting on the long benches, and large, tankards for beer hung on racks behind the Beer Seller's chunky barrels. Arnulf made sure that there were no familiar faces among the drinkers and then asked for a glass of beer from the best barrel. He threw himself down on the edge of a bench and immediately forgot everything around him, as the spicy beer poured down his throat like soothing rain after a relentless drought. Never had he been so thirsty before in his life! To think that tension and escaping could dry up one's body so much!

The beer flowed through his aching muscles, soothing them, and whispered calmly to his limps that they should relax, and the sad spectacle of the bottom of the mug reached Arnulf long before his thirst was just about bearable.

The Beer Seller lifted his bushy eyebrows cheerfully, as Arnulf demanded more beer, and he filled the mug again, while several of the men on the benches, laughing, lifted their mugs to Arnulf. He greeted them courteously and drank again, not caring what others thought of him. Today he could drink, just like Thor had done at Utgard Loki's, and when the second mug was empty, it was easier to shoo away the haunting thoughts of Rolf's death and the merciless judgment which the Thing cast on brother-murder. He belched sincerely happier than for days and carefully dried the foam from his lips.

Arnulf wanted the mug to be filled up again, and it annoyed him that he thereby became the object of the other drinking men's amusement. They laughed at him and toasted him while they nudged each other with their elbows, and Arnulf returned their toast and spat on the ground. He should probably make sure to eat something before he drank more beer so it would not go to his head, but it was so nice just to sit. A black-bearded tradesman, whose attire showed he was from Gotland, moved closer to Arnulf, 'It is hard to be as thirsty as you are, my friend!'

He grinned at the others, 'When a young knave drinks heavily and has obviously been in a fight, he has lost his girlfriend to another! Am I not right, Black-eye?'

Arnulf snorted and bit back a sharp reply, for he had promised himself that he would behave honourably toward strangers. He drank deeply and put his mug down on the bench, 'I drink because I'm thirsty. I do not ask why you are drinking.'

He spat again and didn't feel very hungry anymore. It was too bad the Beer Seller's mug was small on the inside, for he was most definitely reaching the bottom again, maybe the cooper had cheated them.

'Now we will talk nicely again,' said Blackbeard. 'A good story belongs to a good mug of beer.'

Arnulf emptied the mug, 'You would not want to hear my story anyway. More beer!'

His tongue felt strange in his mouth. Maybe Rolf had hit that too when he split his lip. The Beer Seller accepted the mug and filled it up from the barrel, but did not give it back, 'What do you have to pay with, youth? My beer is better than most and is not shared out for nothing, and you do not seem to have any purse on your belt, but maybe you are willing to break some of that ring you have on your finger?'

Arnulf was angry. The king's gold ring was Helge's skald pay and Arnulf's inheritance! Dared the lice-infected pelt of a beer seller make such a suggestion! Why could they not all just let him sit in peace and wait for Toke?

He frowned gloomily, 'You can have my knife, I have no intention of keeping it much longer, and for it, you can certainly fill up my mug a few more times.'

The Beer Seller nodded and handed him the mug, and Arnulf was well able to drink more.

'That seems to be a fine knife you have,' said Blackbeard with an eye on the sheath. 'You cannot drink it up its worth, would you not prefer to trade it. You can sell it to me and pay for the beer in silver.'

Arnulf stared at him angrily, 'Do you think I can't drink like a Viking? When I make an honest trade with the Beer Seller, I'd rather you didn't involve yourself. If you wish, you can buy the knife from him afterwards.'

Blackbeard frowned, but a plump red-haired man laughed, 'Ha, ha, do not drink up your sword as well, you drunken colt! She must be beautiful, that girl you mourn, but it would not surprise me if you have stolen both blades, that sword seems to me to be much too fine for a lout like you.'

Arnulf hammered the mug on the bench so the beer sloshed over the edge, and put his hand on Serpenttooth's pommel, 'The sword is my rightful inheritance, and it can easily separate your ugly goat face from your fat neck! I have killed a man before you, if you care to know it, and it did not take him long to die!'

The redhead lifted his hands disarmingly but continued to laugh. 'It was probably not him who hit you. No, no, you do not need to respond, just drink as much as you want, I do not care.'

Arnulf took a deep breath and closed his eyes for a moment. He should go back to *The Sea Swallow* now, he had already drunk more than was sensible, and so much beer could be perilous on an empty stomach. He let go of the sword and grabbed the mug, 'I killed my brother.'

Arnulf suddenly laughed. So it was said, it was not harder than that!

Blackbeard and Redhead glanced uncertainly at each other while Arnulf chugged the beer, so it tickled his toes.'

'Are you making that up?' asked the Beer Seller, but Arnulf shook his head so he got dizzy and had to grab the bench, 'Certainly not, I killed him yesterday, so you can surely grant me a little funeral feast.'

He laughed again, silly and frenzied. A wake! Of course, Rolf deserved a funeral wake and it should be one about which many words were spoken long after.

The Beer Seller came forward and took the mug determinedly from Arnulf and put his fist on his hip, 'Lying or not, it is time that you pay and find another place to agonise yourself for your age cannot tolerate any more beer!'

Arnulf laughed unaffected. It bubbled out of him. Rattling through the body, 'You'll get your payment, but stories are so sad! Would not you rather hear a song?'

He pulled out the knife and threw it against a tent pole, so the bloody blade quivered. All merriment became silent around him.

'The knife is covered in blood!' exclaimed the Beer Seller with disgust and pulled it out with a jerk.

'Of course, it is!' cried Arnulf exuberantly. 'My brother's blood, I told you!'

The bench swayed under him and the wind made the tent's canvas flutter, so it was dizzying to look at. His hands trembled as he fumbled with the belt, 'Do you want the sheath too? They belong together, for it is also has blood in it!'

Arnulf got up but had to sit down again, for the ground beneath his feet was suddenly unstable and he got to his feet stumbling.

'Is there anyone here who has seen Aslak Shipbuilder?' cried the Beer Seller looking around. 'This lad came here with his boat. The shipbuilder had better take care of him until he had cooled down.'

Arnulf spat and crawled along the bench towards the Gotland merchant, 'You know what, folks? I am afraid that I forgot to take Aslak with me when I borrowed the boat, but I'm sure he will pay well to get it back. Is it not something for you, Blackbeard, or you, you fat fox? An easier trade than to sail the boat to Egilssund has not made before, and now you shall have the song I promised you!'

The red-haired man stood up angrily with clenched fists, but, emboldened, Arnulf struck time with his hand on the bench and grabbed a hold of the black beard,

Stridbjørn's son
Pathless wander
Kinsman hunt

Blood man's penance
Hatred harvester
Brother's bane
Foul pay
For a killing deed

'Bjarke!'

A fist grabbed Arnulf's shoulder with a jötunn's grip. A fist with lacerations on the wrist.

'Bjarke, by Freyr! So this is where you are sitting, filling yourself!'

Toke forced Arnulf to his feet and held on, despite Arnulf's knees being as soft as butter.

Furiously, Blackbeard retrieved his beard from Arnulf's grip and Arnulf happily embraced the Norwegian, 'Toke, my only friend! Come here and drink with me! These bleating sheep do not believe what I say to them, now be good and tell them that I'm right!'

'Do you know him?' asked the Beer Seller brusquely, Arnulf's knife in his hand.

'Do I know him?'

Toke rolled his eyes, 'He is my brother-in-law, Æsir curse me, and he drowns in every barrel of beer he can lay his eyes upon!'

Toke looked around at the men's serious faces and saw the knives. He smiled winningly, 'You look like Ragnarök is upon us! What has he been filling your heads with? Last he said that he had strangled King Sweyn, and a time before that that he had lain with earl Hakon's mother! A bigger liar than Bjarke does not exist in the entire land, you should pity my poor sister, who is married to him!'

The men seemed to thaw slightly, and Arnulf had enough sense to keep quiet and let Toke speak. He clung to the Northman's shoulder, nausea burning his throat.

'But the knife,' objected the Beer Seller. 'It is covered in blood. He claims that he killed his own brother with it yesterday.'

Toke laughed so it was contagious, 'Bjarke has no brother! It was my dog he stabbed down, and as you can see, I was angry about it. And now you must excuse us, for it seems I have not beaten the folly out of my wretched brother-in-law skilfully enough, so we must leave you to talk things through once again. Peace follow you and enjoy the beer!'

'What about the boat?' cried the black-bearded one suspiciously. 'He came on Aslak Shipbuilder's boat, the Beer Seller himself saw it, your words are hollow, Northman!'

For a moment Toke's gaze flickered, but he kept his smile, 'Aslak arrived after sunset yesterday and gave us the chance to try his boat on a trip up the coast, the chieftain of my village would like to send for him if I find his skills worthy.'

He nodded respectfully and went off with Arnulf before the men could ask any more questions, and Arnulf saw them shaking their heads at the beer tent and toast each other behind him. Toke put Arnulf's arm around his shoulder and hurried them away from the tents and stalls back towards the strand. They did not reach far before Arnulf lost his footing altogether and landed on his knees while he threw up, so it splashed in the grass. Toke groaned and turned his back, and Arnulf coughed and gulped so he was almost choking. By Helheim's half-depraved face if this was how the first oath to Fenrir was to be! He had behaved inexcusably! He had revealed himself completely without knowing who he was talking to! Toke would surely hate him now! Arnulf was more ashamed than ever and tried to stammer an apology, but his tongue would not really obey, and everything went black before his eyes. He should just lie down and die now. Right here, where the grass seemed so soft. Had Toke not said that he should pretend to be sleeping?

Arnulf closed his eyes and pulled his knees up to his aching stomach. He had only to put his forehead against the grass for a moment, then a numbing darkness would spread around him as if the earth itself was forgiving him for his defilement and misdeeds.

'Arnulf, by Tyr! How much did you drink? Get up, man up!'

Arnulf struck out half-heartedly after Toke's rough hand, 'I have no use for an oath to Tyr. You should know that Fenrir is my god now. Swear by him and leave me, then I'll die here now without anyone noticing it ...'

Toke snorted indignantly, 'I will give you, Fenrir wolf, you beast! No sensible person puts his fate in so fickle a creature's power.'

He grabbed hold of Arnulf's hair and pulled him up to sitting and then urged on him, 'Listen, while you are still awake. There is an Icelander named Sigurdur who is willing to sail his knarr to Kaupang in Norway at dawn. I promised him I would pick you up immediately so he could see you, but I hope he pulls his hood well down over his eyes when he does it.'

Arnulf sighed deeply and tried to think clearly. Kaupang? It sounded like a bird, a Faroese bird! He stared at Toke, but the Northman's face floated before his eyes, and Arnulf had to blink rapidly. Toke was lacking one of his bracelets, but he had an axe on his belt.

The weapon was far from the worth of the silver, so the Icelander might have accrued the rest. Arnulf squinted his eyes but could not open them again. It felt like falling backwards into a bottomless pit. A deep, soft hole that took kindly to him. And it was not cold in Helheim, not in the least!

*****

The earth writhed under Arnulf in staggering sways, and his head lay on the blacksmith's forge, being hammered into a sword's blade with cruel blows. He rolled himself up, groaning, nauseated and stomach aching. The light was sharp, as if Skinfaxi was drawing the sun directly towards him, and Arnulf coughed dryly, tasting vomit. His body's cramped muscles testified to the new nightmares, which passed and were forgotten before his thoughts really came together. He blinked and heard the cries of gulls and the flaps of the sail.

'Good morning, Stridbjørnson! If you ever end up in Valhalla, do not assume that you will be allowed to sleep until late morning. Einherjar jump up battle ready when the rooster crows!'

Arnulf hid his face in his hands, 'Shut up, Toke!'

Toke laughed at him, 'Is this the thanks I get, after having dragged you aboard the ship and apologised for your condition most of the evening? Truthfully, you give your friends' faithfulness a hard test. If I was not so happy to be on my way home, I could easily tire of you!'

Arnulf opened his eyes, struggling to sit up, 'No offence meant. I know you must be furious with me! It was not my intention to drink so much ...'

He rubbed his forehead and looked up. Barrels and crates in lashed stacks stood around him, and the deck was littered with leather-bound bundles, which he guessed contained wool and linen cloth. The big worn anchor on the deck attested to its many years of raids, a small boat for landings lay beside the mast fish, its keel face-up. The knarr was wide and cut deep in the water. Some men sat around between goods and coiled ropes and talked or played board games, getting up now and then, when the ship had to be turned. It smelled of fish and sour milk, and Arnulf suddenly had to throw up again. He just managed to throw his torso over the shield rim before the corrosive gastric juices poured from his throat. Toke held on to his belt with a laugh, and the tradesmen chuckled and made derogatory comments about him. Arnulf slumped to the deck with his back against the boarding plank and, pale, nodded back. He felt sick to his bones and could hardly endure the rocking of the vessel.

'Well met, Bjarke Olaifson, I hope the beer was good!'

78

A tall brown-bearded Icelander with harsh traits sat at the helm, steering the ship with a practiced hand, and Arnulf presumed that it had to be Sigurdur. The helmsman was lavishly dressed with both a sword and an axe on his belt and appeared to be the man to defend his thriving trades. Several scars furrowed his face, testifying to more than one Viking voyage, and he stared appraisingly at Arnulf.

'Well met, Sigurdur. Well may I thank you that you bothered to take the trouble with me yesterday.'

Arnulf snorted and accepted the water bag, which Toke handed him.

'Other men before you have been carried on board over time, but it is rare that I sail with folk I have not first looked in the eye.'

Arnulf drank and felt a little better, 'You don't need to fear anything from me.'

Sigurdur gave a burly laugh, making his beard jump, 'With that face, you show up with? You look like someone who needs only a small excuse to pick a quarrel, but Toke has spoken well about you, and I hope he is right.'

'Bjarke is as peaceful as a calf,' said Toke quietly. 'And that he helped me escape my bondage to the earl Torsten, speaks only to his advantage. I do not think Bjarke surmised that the earl would be so furious about my marriage proposal to his daughter, and you cannot blame him for needing a mug or two of beer after the journeymen's heavy-handed treatment.'

Sigurdur shrugged, and Arnulf blinked at Toke's explanation, but did not ask anything. Bjarke Olaifson? Earl Torsten? There sat a wise head on Toke's shoulders, he had to give him that!

Sigurdur was silent, and Toke had both sausage and bread, and despite the nausea Arnulf forced them down and felt better. Now it was mostly his head that plagued him.

The sun was high, the wind was even, and fresh foam formed on the bow. Arnulf looked at the coast but did not recognise it; he had never seen the settlements that glided past before. Sigurdur watched the current and wind and gave orders to trim the sail. The tradesmen kept to themselves, no longer talkative, and Toke sat with his arms on his knees, brooding over his thoughts. Arnulf was tired. He did not particularly like the Icelander, who seemed to be familiar with the waters and carefully navigated around rocks and shallow waters in good time. The ship was heavy and turned arduously, reminding Arnulf of a worn ox that only grudgingly obeyed under the yoke, but a good ship it was, with enough space to have both cattle and sheep on board.

He slid further and further down, until he finally surrendered to the deck with his arm under his head. If no one asked him anything; surely, they would not begrudge him a nap and besides Toke was excellent at finding reliable answers. What else was there to take care of?

*****

Arnulf half dosed until early evening. When he sat up again, his headache was gone, and he pulled his sleeve up halfway and let his arm hang over the shield rim. The cool breeze on the water tickled his sore hand, and he liked its breath around his fingers. Toke was still closed and silent, but Arnulf was restless and wanted to talk. They were, after all, on the way to a foreign country and settlements, and he would like to know a little about it in advance. The Northman sat staring at the horizon, like he hoped to spot distant fjelds, and the late sun coloured his skin golden.

Arnulf slowly dried the sea foam from his hand and felt it swelling. He reckoned he could rely fully on its grip and clenched his fist hard a few times.

'What's her name, her you are married to?'

Arnulf kept his voice low so Sigurdur's men would not hear him. Toke roused and turned his head, 'Gyrith. Gyrith Stentorsdaughter.'

Arnulf nodded sympathetically. Gyrith, it was a good name!

'How long have you shared life?'

'Two years.'

Toke's face softened.

'Do you have children?'

The Northman smiled, his eyes shining like amber, 'A girl. Ranvig. She must be able to crawl now. Her hair is as bright as ripe wheat.'

Arnulf smiled back, 'Then she will be beautiful.'

'She is beautiful.'

Toke sighed deeply and stroked his short beard, 'I would rather not have been with my father on the journey of revenge, but my sister was crying, and my family was furious. There may be sense in going a-viking and increasing your wealth, but once you have a woman and a child, then it splits one's soul.'

Arnulf filed a frayed nail against the planks, 'Rolf would not go a-viking, only Helge.'

Toke nodded, 'Every man must do what seems best for him. I love to sail and take great pleasure in a good fight, but in reality, men's whereabouts and actions are not so important. We practice these great deeds or die randomly, while women go on with their lives and can tame even the wildest berserker.'

He looked wistfully beyond the waves, 'A son will grow up, perhaps to die by the sword, but a daughter will give joy and grandchildren and sing the coldest winter warm. For me, Freyr and Freyja are the most important of the Æsir, and when others pay tribute to Thor and Tyr before a voyage, I do so to Freyr, so he will take care of my loved ones, while I am away. I can take care of my own life.'

Arnulf bit his nail. Toke could not be many years older than himself, but he spoke like he had seen thirty summers. Arnulf understood him well, and yet not. The women guarded the children and it was probably important for a man to ask the Æsir for protection when he went out on a dangerous voyage. It mocked the gods of war not to do it, and it had indeed gone wrong for the Northman!

'It was neither Thor nor Freyr who sent me to loosen your ropes.'

'No, and Tyr did not help my kinsmen on Øystein's ship either.'

Toke eyes were dark, 'Do not expect a warm welcome in Haraldsfjord, Arnulf, but as long as I draw breath, no man will lay a hand on you. Your brother has desecrated the most courted woman in the fjord, and your father's helmsman killed a known and reputable chieftain. I will answer for your life, when we arrive, but later you yourself must win the respect and benevolence of the people.'

Arnulf bowed his head. He had not thought that far. Due to his lineage, the hatred and shame would hit him, and some would probably believe that there should be a revenge killing. Norway was a refuge, a shelter from Stridbjørn's anger and the Thing's exile, but he was not welcome. He looked up.

'If you want it, then I can say that you are Bjarke Olaifson and keep the truth to myself.' Toke's bright eyes were sincere, but Arnulf frowned with a grim shake of his head. He could be called many names, but he would not deny his family, and he was no less a chieftain's son than Toke and stood by his actions. Toke nodded appreciatively, while the shadow of a smile slid across his face, 'So that is what we will say, Arnulf Stridbjørnson and Freyr stand by us.'

'I'm Stridbjørn's son, until I die, and proud of it, but my name I will determine myself,' said Arnulf seriously.

'Veulf?'

81

'Veulf!'

'No, Arnulf, just as little as Fenrir is your god.'

'So, let's see which of the Æsir stands closest to whom and determine the name later.'

'That wish I can grant you, but do not think so ill of yourself!'

Arnulf looked away with a snort. What did Toke know about how you thought about yourself after murdering your brother? Arnulf felt his eyes burning a hole in the loose deck planks. If he looked at Toke now, the Northman would turn to stone, and Toke seemed to know it, because he got up and walked away.

Arnulf groaned softly. Perhaps the inhabitants of Haraldsfjord really would commit a revenge killing and grant him peace for life! Free him from his brooding self-hatred. Arnulf sighed, pained, and held his head in his hands.

Rolf had only done good towards him, and his loss burned like coal in his chest! If only he would rise from the grave and demand atonement! If only there were a punishment, which made it possible to pay for the misdeed he had committed!

An exile only served to remove people's fears of a mad man's madness, it did not alleviate the heavy, stone yoke of guilt and it did not give the heart peace. Did not give back joy. A choked life. A tree, whose roots were no longer able to suck, withered, but unable to die. Arnulf's breathing sweltered like dragon fire. Cursed!

*****

Sigurdur gave the order to tack the sail and the ship turned in a curve and glided directly towards the shore. It was time to take shelter for the night, a treacherous twilight could easily ground the ship prematurely.

Arnulf tousled his hair and rubbed his face, forcing his discouragement into his heart. Now he was Bjarke Olaifson and Bjarke had nothing to regret, he was an innocent lad.

The men on board found the food bags and tent cloths, and the anchor was dropped, while the small boat was put in the water. It was not long to the shore, for the seabed went down abruptly. The Icelander had chosen his landing with care and would be close to his ship. Two men were chosen to sleep on the deck and watch the current and Arnulf and Toke were on board when the boat rocked to the strand for the last time.

The packed food could be eaten cold, but Sigurdur asked some of the companions to gather wood for a bonfire near the ship for the spring night was frosty. The tradesmen still remained at a distance from Arnulf and Toke. There did not seem to be any additional sleeping skins or tents, but Arnulf did not care. He was on the run and willing to settle for what there was, and he had slept uncomfortably before on his foray into the woods at Egilssund.

The tents were erected and the fire lit, and a one-legged old man shared bread and dried meat and passed the buttermilk round. Arnulf helped himself to the food, and Sigurdur said he and Toke would have to find some blankets on the ship and settle for them as there was a lack of tents. Toke replied that the sand was soft, and the dunes gave shelter, and that he did not worry about the Danish weather since he knew the cold on the fjelds.

The tradesmen did not speak many words as they ate, and apparently barely tolerated Arnulf and Toke's presence. Sigurdur spoke with the grey-haired man about the sailing further towards Norway, and Arnulf munched the tough meat and muttered to Toke that their shipmates were not spreaders of cheerfulness, despite the fact that Toke had paid more than was reasonable for the journey to Norway. In Kaupang, Sigurdur and his people could trade their goods as well as in Gormsø, so much had he understood from their mutual talk. The Northman did not answer, but looked, depressed, into the fire, and Arnulf became silent so as not to seem rude with his whispering.

As soon as the meal was over, Sigurdur wanted to sleep, and Arnulf fetched blankets on the ship while Toke picked out a good high dune with a sand hollow behind it. He levelled the sand and lay the axe down, but Arnulf kept his sword belt, because he felt safest as long as he could feel Serpenttooth's sheath against his thigh. He carefully spread one of the blankets out on the sand, and Toke yawned, tired.

'You can think what you want, but we are on board this boat with bleak people,' exclaimed Arnulf, making himself a sand pillow under the blanket. Toke threw himself down with a heavy sigh and pulled the axe within reach, 'The ship is good, and we are moving steadily forward, so it is probably best not to interfere too much with whatever it is that is plaguing Sigurdur's men.'

He considered his wrists briefly and pulled the second blanket over himself. Arnulf sat down and straightened his sword, 'Sigurdur was a Viking before he became a tradesman. I don't like the look of him.'

'Well, he was a Viking and his eye is good enough to keep on course, now sleep! If you want to go plundering, you need to practise being able to sleep and gather your strength, no matter what thoughts you are grappling with and how hard the ship rolls. Good night!'

Arnulf lay close to Toke and took his share of the blanket, 'Helge would also have said that. So how old are you, Toke?'

'Twenty winters, and if you say more, I will hack this axe into your forehead!' muttered Toke moodily with the blanket over his head.

'I would have betrothed myself to Frejdis next summer.'

Toke groaned, 'You really only obey yourself, do you not? Trying to commit suicide, just as you salvage life, getting drunk at the worst possible moments and yammering on like womenfolk when honest men want to sleep. You should not be betrothed to anyone, you shall go a-viking with me, Garmr take you!'

Arnulf made a face, lying still but was wide awake. Night had not yet fallen, and the sky was light on the dunes. On a night like this last year Frejdis had danced naked on the strand meadow. With waving hair and luminous moon skin, she was as light-footed as a mist over the grass, and a stranger would probably have taken her for a woodland Vanir. Arnulf had sung and drummed for her dance, sung so the nightingales were silent.

He squinted. What was Frejdis doing now? Lying and lamenting Rolf? Who would she betroth now, after Rolf was dead? His half-cousin on Ørnholm? Surely. How he wished he would have an accident! He fathered sheep over there and they were fat with thick wool. Frejdis could sit and spin and weave with him for the rest of her life and sell her cloth on Gormsø while the children were playing with balls of yarn.

Arnulf clenched his fists. Did she think ill of him? Would she follow if one night he came to carry her off? They could travel to Iceland, Gotland, west, or wherever she wanted to, Frejdis was too good to spin her life away! She was still Arnulf's whether she wanted it or not.

He dragged his thoughts away from her. Thought instead of Helge, who was feasting under Valhalla's golden shields, and Rolf, who was in Gimle, the righteous men's last residence. Helge would die again in Ragnarök, but Gimle would be spared.

Toke breathed deeply. Arnulf was restless under the blanket, thoughts breaching his head like waves breaking against the shore. He drove them back one by one, but was attacked by new ones, and lay motionless like a spear shaft so as not to wake the Northman. Foolish to worry his night's rest away like that, but sleep would not come. The sky darkened, and the moon slid imperceptibly over it. So different were he and Rolf and Helge from each other that they could not even be united in death. For a brother killer only Helheim was open.

A little sand trickled down the dune, and Arnulf let his gaze slide up and stiffened abruptly.

Sigurdur stood on top of the dune like a dark shadow, the moonlight shimmering in the drawn sword in his hand. In a semi-circle around the dune Arnulf spotted the silent armed figures who approached noiselessly, and he suppressed an outcry and felt sweat dribbling down. He and Toke were about to fall in an ambush! The Icelander and his people had intended to commit murder under cover of darkness! Slit their throats, steal the wealth and weapons and then get rid of the toil of having to sail to Haraldsfjord!

Arnulf poked his finger hard into Toke's side and whispered breathlessly, 'Wake up, Toke! We are about to be attacked!'

Toke had not been deeply asleep and he was awake immediately, his entire body tense. His warrior blood had not betrayed him.

'How many?' He whispered back under the blanket.

'Sigurdur is just above us, and there are more.'

'So we take him when he jumps.'

Arnulf slipped his hand down the sword's hilt. Toke could easily reach the axe, and Sigurdur's men had apparently expected their prey to be fast asleep. The Northman's muscles were hard against Arnulf's shoulder, hard and alive like a cat about to pounce.

The tradesmen crept towards the bed in the sand, but even though they bore weapons, they seemed to want the experienced helmsman to carry out the murders.

Sigurdur began to run down the dune in a flash and Arnulf and Toke jumped up to greet him. The Icelander let out a cry of amazement but recovered himself immediately and met Toke's axe with his sword, letting sparks fly. With an excited roar Arnulf faced the surprised traders and swung Serpenttooth dangerously. A mighty force flowed through his arm from the sword, the hilt seemed to glow in his hand. All Helge's victorious battles were in the blade, and it was thirsty and eager to serve its new master and as light as a hazel branch to wield. Like a hissing, coiled snake, Serpenttooth waited for its strikes to be freed.

Dubious, Sigurdur's men moved back a little, and Arnulf spun around to help Toke, who caught yet another sword blow with his axe. It centred on overpowering the Icelander as soon as possible, before his companions wanted to get involved in the fight. Arnulf lunged violently for his throat while Toke swept the axe low. Sigurdur parried Serpenttooth's attack but was hit in the thigh with the axe and crashed onto the sand with a yell. Arnulf put his blade on his chest and Toke turned, winded, towards the perplexed men. If they attacked now, they would lose their helmsman, and the idea did not seem to appeal to them. After all, the helmsman's life was worth more than Toke's jewellery and Arnulf's sword, and it was his ship they were sailing.

Wailing, Sigurdur held his leg with both hands and Arnulf, grim, picked up the dropped sword. His heart was pounding as if a troll had taken him, and he bared his teeth and held Serpenttooth so hard against Sigurdur that drops of blood appeared and trickled down his chest. Toke went authoritatively towards the men's scowling glances, 'Miserable pack of jötnar! Here you could make yourself an honest trade, and to thank us, you try to stab us while we sleep! I am Toke Øysteinson and me you treat with respect or you will pay for your misdeeds with your life!'

He swung the axe in front of him, so blood dripped from it, 'From now on, I am the new helmsman on the ship, and those that do not want to sail with me to Norway, can go ashore here with their goods! Throw your weapons down now and tell me whether we are in agreement!'

Arnulf thought that the fight was easily won, and was almost disappointed, but then the youngest of the tradesman gave a furious cry and ran towards Toke, his sword raised. The others did not fail him, but followed after, roaring and waving their weapons in the air. Undaunted, Toke swung his axe with both hands and without hesitation he attacked the young man, cutting him to the ground and then like lightning he jumped back to Arnulf and Sigurdur and planting the axe in the forehead of the Icelander.

Blood and brains splattered onto the sand, and Arnulf stared dumbfounded at Sigurdur's clefted head. The onrushing men stopped the attack, horrified expressions on their faces. Toke had killed two men in a single breath, and Arnulf looked at him with an open mouth. A more energetic Viking could not be found! Obviously, nothing would stop him in his quest for home!

Toke's eyes were wild and he laughed triumphantly at his opponents, 'My new axe bites well and it can withstand more blows yet! Come and revenge your dead, for tonight Helheim is set for a feast!'

He ran up the dune quickly and Arnulf jumped after him, a sword in each hand. The Northman was mad; Arnulf had known it from the first moment he saw him, but what a brother-in-arms! The Æsir themselves would not be ashamed of his company!

Arnulf stood by Toke's side and counted ten men at the foot of the hill. They were all here, including the two who were to sleep on the ship. Despite Toke and he having the advantage of standing on high ground, they were shieldless, and despite Toke's killing shaking off the attackers, it sparked hatred and revenge in their eyes, too. If they knew how to use their weapons, they would be impossible to stand against. Arnulf snorted and did not want to lose either his exposed legs or his life.

The angry ship folk surrounded the dune, but not all had the courage to run up it and Toke yelled encouragement to Arnulf and charged the bold ones, his axe swinging deadly, 'See the cowardly chickens! When the cock is dead, they have no courage!'

Arnulf had two men against him and did not quite believe Toke's words. He caught an axe strike with Sigurdur's sword and stopped the other man's sword blows with Serpenttooth a finger's width from his hip and wrestled with him, hilt against hilt. The difference in their heights gave his body the most weight, and even though his feet slithered in the sand, he pushed his opponent back, but had to jump immediately afterwards to avoid being hit in the legs by a new axe swing.

Toke struck a man in the shoulder and another in the chest, and his luck gave Arnulf the strength to splinter an enemy's axe handle with Serpenttooth and thrust his sword into his throat.

The man tumbled back, lifeless, and Arnulf uttered a victory cry and charged the next attackers with a contempt for death. He had killed again, but this time he was not at fault, and should he die now, it would be during a fight, that was worthy of a skaldic verse. He felt the blood of the wolf and the eagle boiling beneath his skin. Every man's fate was to die, but not everyone's reputation to live!

Three men began to lash out at him, and Arnulf took a step back and kicked sand in their eyes. It had its effect, for the attack stopped amidst spitting and swearing and Toke, who stood and pulled the hook of his opponent's axe, got the idea and was free of him. Sigurdur's men also tried to throw sand but they were too low to hit and Arnulf kicked well from between his strikes. Every parry, Helge had taught him, he remembered, and Serpenttooth itself knew its way to the enemy blades and sought out flesh.

A deep-chested man had a shield with him and pressed Arnulf backwards, but Arnulf cut deep in the upper shield rim and hit the man in the knee when he raised his shield. He struggled to get back to Toke and tried to tear the shield from the wounded man while out of the corner of his eye, he saw as one of the other men threw an axe. Toke had temporarily made room in front of them but was hit by the axe in the upper arm and lost his weapon with a scream. The axe took hold in the bone, and Toke faltered, tearing it loose and throwing it away. He grabbed his own axe with his left hand and managed to narrowly avert a whistling sword blow, but his knees went from under him with the effort.

Arnulf let the shields be and in two leaps was back at Toke's side, who, bleeding torrentially, was on his feet, his sword side turned away from Sigurdur's men while he stared his opponent doggedly in the eye. Arnulf feared that his arm was broken, and with a furiously scream drove a large grey-bearded man back and tried to knock the sword out of the hand of Toke's attacker. It failed and the grey-bearded man fell upon him again, while the other man lashed out at Toke again. The Northman parried the blow, but fell down, and the attacker pulled out his knife and threw himself on him.

Arnulf lashed out frantically. His heart was in his throat, threatening to choke him, and he gasped for breath, sweat pouring down into his eyes. By Odin's wolves, would the beasts be allowed to take the life of Toke! Carrion for ravens is what they all should be and carrion they would be before the next cloud had drifted past the moon!

With effort, he stuck Serpenttooth in the hand of Greybeard and slung Sigurdur's sword into the back of Toke's opponent who flung out his arms and fell. The Northman struggled to get up but did not appear to be injured again, and Arnulf saw the remaining men run up the dune together as they howled to Greybeard to beat Toke to the ground again.

'Follow me! Down to the ship!'

He exchanged blows with his opponent and again got a grip of the Islander's sword.

'Are you crazy? They will beat us down like corn!'

Toke groaned and swayed as he blinked.

'Do as I say!' roared Arnulf and hammered both swords into the shoulders of the grey-bearded man, who sank on the spot. The tradesmen smelled blood and showed no fear in the faces anymore.

'For Fenrir!'

Shouting, Arnulf ran down between the men, defending himself, heart and soul, with his sword side and Toke followed after, dealing with those who stood to his shield side. He handled the axe well with his left hand and did not waste energy on unnecessary blows. Sigurdur's men seemed to be surprised at the head-on flight, and Arnulf pushed past them with fierce sword strikes.

The ship was not far off, and the fire was still burning in front of the tents. Arnulf jumped against it and made sure Toke was at his heels as he heard the hot-tempered tradesmen's cries from behind them as they took up the pursuit. It would not take them long to reach the shore, and although several were dead and wounded, they were still enough of them to win a quick victory on flat ground.

Arnulf stopped so abruptly in front of the tents that the sand spewed into the fire, and he threw Sigurdur's sword away and snatched a burning branch from the fire. Gasping, he held it over his head and turned against their pursuers, who slowed down with gleeful looks. The victory seemed within reach.

'Stop!'

Arnulf stood beside Toke, who, hunched, pressed his wrist against his wounded arm without letting go of the axe.

'One step further and I throw the branch out onto the ship and set it on fire!'

The men stopped. They glared evilly at Arnulf and muttered to each other as they doubted whether or not Arnulf would stand by his threat. All their belongings and the year's earnings were aboard the Icelander's ship, and if fire broke out on the vessel, they would be forced to sell the jewellery and weapons they were carrying to get passage on the next ship home.

Toke panted, 'Fenrir spoke to you, Arnulf! Only a true son of Loki takes on a ruse so vile!'

His eyes glittered under his sweat soaked hair.

'It wasn't Freyr in any case, Toke Fiendslayer,' Arnulf felt quite pleased with himself as he stared challenging at his foes, 'Lay down your weapons, even your smallest knives, and let us end with peace between us! Toke is helmsman on the ship from tomorrow, and at dawn it sets sail immediately for Haraldsfjord. The dead men's goods you can split between you and afterwards sail anywhere you want, but until Haraldsfjord you must swear by Odin not to attack us again.'

The one-legged old man, who only now came limping after the others, stepped forward and met Arnulf's gaze sharply, 'You can have my weapon for my silver is worth more than your blood, and it must ensure my old age, but the Æsir will not acknowledge a forced oath to Odin.'

Arnulf squinted narrowly and looked around, but then nodded, 'Well, so let it be by weapons, but I'll throw the branch as soon as my fingers burn, then let it do what it will willingly.'

Grumbling, the one-legged man lay his sword in the sand, and only after he had given up his, did the others follow reluctantly. Axes and knives and swords were laid in a heap, and Arnulf gave Toke the burning branch and fetched a sleeping skin from one of the tents, on which he laid the weapons and tied it together. He stuck Serpenttooth in his belt, threw the sleeping skin over his shoulder and looked ominously at the defeated, 'Toke and I will sleep on the ship for the rest of the night, and I will keep the fire burning for the whole trip to Norway. You can get on board at dawn, but at the slightest misstep I will burn the ship down. You should know that neither Toke nor I have anything to lose nor do we fear death by flame in the least!'

Sigurdur's men seemed to take his words seriously, and Arnulf lay his hand on Toke's shoulder and pushed him gently with him to the landing boat. Toke was deathly pale and still bleeding a lot as he stumbled away, his arm dangling. Arnulf threw the weapons aboard, pushed the boat out and helped the Northman up. A few hard oar strokes later they came to the knarr, and here Toke's strength failed, and he sank down onto the deck, his back against a crate.

Arnulf found a few oil lamps and lit them, so he had the fire at hand, 'How bad is it? Is the arm broken?'

He held one lamp close to Toke.

'No, but it is not a scratch.'

Arnulf bent over Toke's arm and made the tear in his sleeve bigger, so it was possible to get to the gaping wound. Bone splinters sat in it and Arnulf felt nauseated. He pulled Toke's knife from its sheath and wiggled them out, as gently as possible, as Toke writhed, wailing.

'It should be kept together.' Arnulf put his knife on the deck, 'Do you know if we have wound clips on board?'

'I know nothing, but that life is bleeding out to me. Give me some water!'

Arnulf began frantically searching for linen rolls between the goods and threw a water bag to Toke. He found what he sought, and tore strips of cloth, while Toke drank deeply, but when he went to bond the arm, the Northman waved him away and held the wound with his hand, 'That will not keep the arm from bleeding. Take oil from one of the lamps and heat it over the flame from the other. When it is boiling, pour it into the wound.'

Arnulf grimaced, and Toke snorted, leaning his head against the crate, 'Did Helge not tell you that? Glowing iron can also be used, but in open wounds oil is best.'

He smiled with a hard twitch of his lips, 'If you give wounds, you must also be prepared to receive them.'

Arnulf carefully held one lamp over the other and glanced at the strand, 'You slew two men with almost the same strike! I will make a skaldic verse about you, Toke Øysteinson!'

Toke spat on the deck, 'You fought well, too. You are a worthy brother for Helge, and you saved my life. Freyr reward you!'

'Just let Freyr keep his, I'm happy not to be sitting here alone!'

Arnulf smiled as pride surged through him with raised swan feathers, but Toke frowned, 'Do not smile too much yet, I will get sick from this. Fever does not need a large wound to lay a man out cold, I have seen it before.'

Arnulf disagreed, even though ice ran down his back, 'You just have to endure until Haraldsfjord, then the sight of Gyrith will make you hold on to life like never before, mark my words!'

Toke drank water from the bag again, 'Child's talk, Stridbjørnson!'

In on the strand, the wounded men were carried to the tents.

Toke tried to stretch his bleeding arm but had to use his healthy one to help. He put his sword hand on the shield rim and looked away, waiting with heavy breathing, 'Afterwards you can take the barrel with the strong beer out, for after this I will need something other than water.'

Arnulf nodded. The oil boiled.

'Are you ready?'

'Yes.'

Toke bowed his head. Arnulf did not like his task and clenched his teeth hard before he poured the oil over the wound. It startled Toke, and he screamed like an animal as his arm shook, as if a bear was shaking it but he did not release his grip. A malicious laugh carried over the strand from the tents, 'It is good to hear you scream, Toke Øysteinson! I hope it hurts, and that rot sets into the wound! You should know that I am proud of that throw!'

Toke groaned horribly and did not answer, and Arnulf stifled an angry response and bandaged the battered arm thoroughly. Sigurdur's skrællings could laugh, but they fought no better than dogs!

He gently loosened Toke's fingers that had tried to drill holes in the upper plank, and the Northman's right arm fell limply as he closed his eyes. His chest heaved. Arnulf gave his shoulder a squeeze and got up to get the mugs. The beer barrel stood near the helm, where the Icelander had watched over it, and even though Arnulf believed he himself could do with a drink of beer, he filled just one mug.

Toke drank thirstily while Arnulf took the water bag and looked at the flammable woollen sail. He was not quite sure whether he really would set fire to the ship, if it came to it, but the main thing was that the tradesmen believed he would and for the moment they seemed to. Arnulf gathered some wool sacks together, 'Come, lie here.'

He gave Toke a hand, and the Northman faltered over the ropes and bundles and sat down on the wool with a sigh. Arnulf emptied a couple of bags and put them over his legs, and Toke, weak, asked for more beer. He got it and drank deeply again and lay worn out while he mumbled apologetically, 'I will take guard tomorrow when I feel a little better, but it is tiring to bleed so much.'

Arnulf shook his head, 'We'll hardly be attacked again tonight, but what will we do in the next few days? Tie the men up?'

'No.'

Toke eyes were dark, 'There are still six days of sailing ahead of us, and no man should sit tied up for so long. I have never hated anyone as much as I hated Stridbjørn after those two days in the thrall hut and hate has before broken the toughest rope and led to murder. Right now, they fear us and are angry, but they understand our action and we need them to sail the ship.'

He ground his teeth and pulled one sack over his shoulder, 'A trader looks after his wares as a mother looks after her children, and as long as we have the fire in the lamp, they will not touch us. We will keep the sheep fenced in in the corner like sheep dogs do and set them free in Haraldsfjord.'

Arnulf stuffed sacks around him carefully and smiled encouragingly, 'I'll growl just as well as the lame bristly-haired one back home in Egilssund. Rest now!'

Toke nodded and closed his eyes, and Arnulf sat beside him on the thwart at the helm and looked towards the fire on the strand. He took the oil lamp in his hand.

The wounded were taken care of in front of the tents, and the dead were buried deep in the sand.

Arnulf brushed the hair from his sticky forehead. Killing was part of going a-viking, but Helge had never killed if it was not necessary, and Arnulf had not imagined that he would take so many lives so quickly. He shivered. You bound the dead man's strength to yourself when you killed. Boys became men, and men were insurmountable and, although Helge had been strict with Serpenttooth, he had had a hird of deceased warriors behind each blow he had struck. Arnulf felt no stronger than the day before, but he was still angry. The men he had chopped down had deserved their fate, and that it was Arnulf, who had been their slayer, the Norns had long since determined. He looked at Toke under the sacks. His fate was also sealed. Either his wounds would heal and his arm recover in a few months or it would bring poison in his blood and he would die, but Toke's purpose was to return home to Gyrith and Little Ranvig, and that will and longing were strong opponents to the poison.

Arnulf stroked his finger over his scabby lip. Trud knew all about wounds and had cared for many of Stridbjørn's and Helge's, but Arnulf had always been too self-absorbed to properly watch what she had done, and he bitterly regretted his indifference. He should have had that knowledge now!

*****

No new events disturbed the moon's journey across the sky, and Arnulf was overpowered by fatigue and gloomy thoughts about Helge and Rolf. He sat on the deck, struggling to stay awake while he regularly stared back towards the tents on the strand, where he could hear a man groan loudly now and then. Toke slept restlessly, and towards dawn Arnulf dozed for a moment and dropped the lamp but managed to avert fire in a rope coil at the last moment.

When it began to brighten, the tents on the strand were taken down, and Sigurdur's men got ready to go on board. They cooked a breakfast of porridge over the dying fire and rolled the blankets together, and Arnulf got up stiffly and shook life into his body. A comfortable night's rest it had not been, but under the loose planks he found bread and salted pork and at least satisfied his hunger. Toke should not be wakened, the Northman needed all the rest he could get.

One of the wounded tradesmen had died during the night, but the other injured were supported down to the water's edge and Arnulf pushed the small boat to them from the knarr. He forced the tiredness away and met the men with a harsh greeting as they fought to get over the shield rim, menacingly brandishing the oil lamp, which he then put right in front of him. They scowled and remarked how close the flame flickered against the flammable sail and nearby rope pulleys. Arnulf authoritatively ordered the anchor up. He started when he did it. Despite the severity and that it was only a knarr and not a dragon ship with forty oars, it struck him that Helge had been doing this every spring when he had sailed out to sea. With a commanding voice, he had shouted to his men and secured the angle of the sail with a chieftain-like pull on the helm. The tradesmen obeyed and gathered themselves farthest from him, more reticent than ever.

Arnulf agreed with himself that their course must be the same as the day before and shouted that the sail should be set. He grasped the helm, and a good breeze set the ship sailing, but it had not sailed far through the water before Arnulf had to admit that the vessel in no way let itself be controlled as easily as Aslak's nimble boat. The heavy hull was slow to turn and could not be readily tamed by an untrained hand. Arnulf had never led a large ship before and noticed several gleeful eyes resting on him from the group of men, as he tried to preserve his dignity and issue the right orders. The sail was set as he wanted it, but the trading vessel keeled and sailed askew away from the coast, and Arnulf saw no alternative other than to wake Toke and ask for help.

Toke was not sleeping heavily, but he was disturbingly hot to the touch, and when he opened his eyes, they were blurred with fever. The Northman did not seem to be worth much as a helmsman, and Arnulf was ashamed to have awakened him.

'How's the arm?'

Toke shook his head and frowned, 'Just give me some water!'

Arnulf had to help him sit up and help him hold the mug. Toke did not complain and asked in a whisper if they were sailing.

'Yes, but I can't steer the ship.'

Toke nodded and took a deep breath, glancing at the bloody bandage, 'The old one, the one who is missing a leg, he can steer.'

Tired, he closed his eyes and seemed to want to lie down again.

'How do you know that?'

Arnulf had not seen anyone other than Sigurdur at the helm.

'When the storm is the worst, set the oldest one on the helm. He knows the sea,' muttered Toke, 'Now let me be a little. It is disheartening that the strength bled out of me yesterday.'

Arnulf helped him to sit comfortably and called loudly for the old man. The one-legged man was so weak it was fair to trust him, and he was not the most headstrong of the flock.

He limped across the deck and waved his hand as he settled down on the thwart beside Arnulf. His hair was as grey as his woollen kyrtle.

'You want me to steer the ship, Bjarke, is that not right?'

His bright eyes were sharp to meet, but he just smiled and turned the bow with experience into the right course, 'You can fight and shout and move forward, but when the sail is to be set and the course kept, then youths should remain silent and let the experienced ones decide.'

Arnulf sat tensely on the deck in front of Toke with a firm grip on the oil lamp, 'Toke'll steer the ship as soon as he gets better. He has sailed many times before.'

The old one shrugged, 'Has he? We will see. I wonder if he would rather be put ashore and get some proper treatment for his wounds? He risks losing his arm like this.'

Arnulf shook his head violently, 'But he won't and the journey to Norway can't be postponed, so you just think of the ship and I'll think of Toke.'

He bit his cheek and stared out to sea. It was a long way to Haraldsfjord, too long. Little was the one-legged's strength and thin-skinned was his sinewy hand, but he had time to wait by the helm and if Toke was going to be sick for a while, Arnulf would end up succumbing to sleep deprivation.

The old man looked at him deeply, as if he sought to know Arnulf's thoughts, and he muttered something to himself as he pulled his cloak around him tightly, 'I do not know what it is you two are fleeing from and I am not asking about it, but you do not need to fear me. This is my last voyage. I want to get home safely with my goods – more than any of the others here – but I do not know the waters beyond Kaupang and the coast along Norway is full of rocks and streams that I do not know.'

Toke strained to lift his head from his bed and looked at the old man, 'Sail the ship along the coast and cross over to Norway half a day before you otherwise would to reach Kaupang. By then, I will hopefully have rested enough to take over, for the Norwegian Sea flows in my blood.'

The one-legged man agreed, 'That is a deal, Northman, but if you are not prepared to guide me when we see the fjelds, then I am heading for Kaupang and disembarking there with my goods.'

Toke's head sank back again onto the wool sack, 'That is reasonable, old man. And you can reassure the others that the same goes for them if I succumb to fever.'

He waved to Arnulf so as to whisper to him, 'Wake me when you cannot stay awake any longer, for the mongrels over there are no tamer than they were. They will bite again if we sleep and do not be stupid! You are tired. Promise me, by Fenrir!'

Arnulf nodded and took the outstretched burning hand, 'Sleep and stay healthy, Toke. Gyrith awaits you!'

Toke smiled and trembled, 'Gyrith!'

He grimaced and closed his eyes, and Arnulf let go of his hand and lay it on the woollen sack. By Geri and Freki! Toke had to recover quickly! Arnulf did not even know where in Norway Kaupang was. What would he do there, if Toke lost his life? He felt more alone than ever and seemed destined to hear the Norns laugh through the waves blowing against the ship. Arnulf clenched his hand so King Sweyn's twisted gold ring cut into his fingers. He looked down at it. Helge's skaldic verse payment. Arnulf should have been with him in the royal hall and sung. No worse than a man who had drunk Suttungr's mead! Like Odin himself!

Stridbjørn had sons three,
All died but one,
Hunted by Norns,
Æsir and men,
Despised by companion,
Kith and kin,
The tired man
Dwells in despair!

*****

Toke was sick for as long as the vessel followed the Danish coast, and Arnulf did what he could to help him through the fever and pain. The Northman tried to endure his trials with dignity, and Arnulf gave him water and beer and cooled his burning forehead as he whispered to him about Gyrith and Little Ranvig to get him to think of something good. When he himself had to sleep, Toke manned up and sat doggedly close to the sail, the burning lamp in his hand, keeping watch, wrapped in a woollen cloak.

At night, One Leg anchored the knarr up close to a suitable strand and sailed ashore with the rest of Sigurdur's men, while Arnulf and Toke stayed on the ship. Arnulf would have given silver for an able watchdog. He felt tired and dizzy, as if he was drunk, and he began to doubt whether he would be able to cope with travelling any further on so little sleep.

The tradesmen cared for their wounded and cast dubious glances at Arnulf and Toke. They were pale from fear of whether or not the oil lamp from sheer fever or fatigue would be knocked into the highly flammable sail by accident, but Toke snorted at them and kept his faith of reaching home despite his suffering. He had been wounded before and thought he could sense that the fever would soon leave, and when the grey-haired old man announced they were nearing the two sea currents that wrestled on the Danish north tip, he livened up, his eyes clear.

One Leg suggested that they should put ashore and await the next day's dawn before crossing over to Norway, but Toke got up from his resting place and ordered the sail be tightened and the stern turned to face the open sea. He sat down on a sea chest and held his wounded arm while he talked with the old man about how best the ship could sail through the capricious currents and Arnulf almost forgot to keep an eye on the tradesmen in his eagerness to scout out over the waves.

At a safe distance from where the two seas roughly bellowed to each other, he saw Denmark disappear behind him, as the waves got wilder against the keel. A deep sigh freed itself from his chest, and he let his outlawry stay in the cursed country that had sucked the blood from both of his brothers. Only now, as the last sight of strand and forest disappeared on the horizon, was he free from his judgement, and as long as Toke was silent, no one would know anything about the sinister secret Arnulf carried with him. He caught himself in a great smile, tears running down his cheeks and wiped them quickly away. At this moment, Veulf Fenrirfaithful was actually sailing and the world lay open.

One Leg believed it safest to sail towards Götaland and then follow the coast on to Norway, but Toke adamantly refused and asked him to give way at the helm for a while. Arnulf opened his eyes wide but gave him the lamp and took advantage of the moment's opportunity for sleep and threw himself, exhausted, onto the sacks of wool. The sail was taut like a pregnant cow's stomach over him, and the sea's rolling waves felt safe, like Trud's rocking arms had once done. Trud! Now she had no children to cradle anymore, only grey hair and wrinkled skin. Six times she had given birth but was rewarded with nothing but death and grief in her old age. Arnulf bored his face into the wool sacks. If Rolf had just arrived a moment later, then perhaps Frejdis would be with child and could have given his mother her only grandchild.

The distant sound of the Fenrir wolf's howl was heard over the sea and, through the wool and the ship's hull, Arnulf clearly sensed Jörmungandr wailing answers from the depths. They knew the prophecy, the sons of Loki, and it made them uneasy, because when brother slew brother, it was a sure sign that the Fimbulwinter and Ragnarök were at the door!

*****

97

Arnulf felt Toke shake his arm, but his sleep was deep, as if he had been sleeping for half a month, and he found it difficult to let it go.

'Wake up! Come and see!'

Reluctantly, Arnulf forced open his eyes and sat up, his limps as heavy as rocks. Toke stood, swaying over him, weak to look at, but with fire in his eyes and the dawn on his skin. He smiled broadly and seemed to be recovering as he pointed with a quivering hand.

Arnulf was alert and he pulled himself up onto his feet, astonished, with a hand on the shield rim, 'Have I slept all night? Why did you wake me?'

He looked out over the sea. The rosy sky whispered over the waves, and Arnulf opened his mouth, amazed, when he caught sight of the mighty mountains that rose from the sea beside the ship for as far as the eye could see. Like the grey jötunn of Jotunheim, the spear-sharp rocks shot up so high into the vaults of heaven that clouds foundered on them and Toke laughed softly, leaning heavily on Arnulf's shoulder, 'Norway! Just wait a little, then you will see! That is how I wanted you to see it!'

Excited and breathless, he stared expectantly toward the jötnar land and Arnulf got chills when the sun rose in front of him like a king's eye, bathing the fjelds in its red glow. The grey cliff's outline was set on fire and it returned the greeting by changing colour, and Toke sank down wearily on his knees and leaned against the ship's side, 'My country, Arnulf! The land of giants, trolls and free men! And under the greenest pastures in the most lustrous fjord lies my home.'

He looked like he was about to lose consciousness, and Arnulf laid a worried hand on his forehead, but it was cool like the morning wind.

'The fever is gone!'

Toke nodded weakly, still smiling, 'Yes, it is gone, but the night was long, even though the old man held the helm most of the time. He is sleeping, and I will have to rest now. Keep the ship out here, at a good distance from the coast and follow it. It is safe enough. Tonight, we will land in Mågefjord. Wake me in time and I will try to take the helm if I can.'

He cast a last glance towards the shore before he keeled over on his sleeping skin, and Arnulf tenderly laid the blanket over the happy, returning-home Northman, who immediately fell asleep. Then he sat at the helm, watching the marvellous landscape while the disgruntled traders murmured at the other end of the ship. Kaupang was not far away if you turned the ship, and it did not seem to please Sigurdur's men to be so close to such a large trading market and then sail in the wrong direction, but Arnulf was past caring. He caressed the worn helm, fond of the rugged, mountainous country from first glance A country whose bones stuck up through the hardy grass, sharp as polished iron and grey as countless hordes of wolves.

*****

For days Arnulf sat spellbound with the lamp in his hand, staring at the Norwegian coast, as the ship glided past with a steady wind in its sail. The sea was friendly, and the weather was good, but the mild spring air became steadily colder and the wind was biting, and Arnulf found some woollen cloaks that had belonged to the deceased tradesmen. Toke was beginning to recover from the blood loss and the fever and often took the helm, steering the vessel knowingly between the countless islands and reefs that lay like a defensive shield in front of the actual coastline.

Now and then the massive rock face opened and gave Arnulf a glimpse of wide fjords, shiny as polished silver buckles that seemed to wind deep inland, and each time it happened, he got a scintillating urge to follow their course to see what they hid. Some seemed to be lush with wide grassy hillsides and thundering waterfalls, while others swarmed with birds, so their screams echoed over the ship. Occasionally, he spotted distant settlements, which lay where it was best to lay anchor. Other ships also passed by, but each time Toke saw these vessels, he sailed far around them or went into hiding behind the nearest islands. The trading ship was too easy prey now that the men were few and unarmed, and Toke saw no need to tempt his country men's ability. He did not fear them but wanted to go home, and it could not go fast enough.

Arnulf was full of admiration that Toke never seemed to doubt the course among the sometimes-unpredictable occurrences of rocks and islets. He must have sailed here several times and nodded affirmatively when Arnulf asked him about it.

'Øystein took me on a voyage for the first time in my twelfth summer.'

The Northman laughed at the thought, 'My mother was very much against it, but when he allowed her to pick three of his bravest Vikings to take care of me wherever the journey led, she agreed. When I was fifteen, I believed her care to be humiliating and that it had to stop, but only when I could defend myself from my housecarls with a sword, did Øystein believe I could take care of myself.'

Arnulf smiled. It was good to hear Toke so happy, and the cool wind along the mountains seemed to do him good and kept him awake most of the day. His arm still caused him a lot of pain, especially when the sea was hard, and his strength was such that the one-legged man had the helm most of the time, but when the waters were fairly easy to navigate, Arnulf was allowed to steer the ship under the Northman's patient guidance.

Sigurdur's men seemed to have accepted their fate, and they got the best out of the time by expelling it with either small chores involving the various items or conversations and board games. One Leg wandered freely on the ship and was responsible for the preparation of the food, and it suited him well.

'There where the shore breaks and goes to the northeast, there lies Haraldsfjord,' explained Toke, while Arnulf sat at the helm. 'In the fjord, there are three settlements, and in the innermost lies my father's longhouse.'

His face was mild, 'There are also farms in the fjelds, and the cows are soon to be put out to pasture, so in the summer some people live up in the cottages. Behind Øystein's house is the meeting place and the blót stone, which my grandfather Sigtryg Ironside set up.'

He interrupted himself and shouted quickly about the sail and asked Arnulf to turn the helm a little.

'The people in the fjord have kept my father as their chieftain and his father before him. They both brought great prosperity to the settlement.'

Toke fell silent and his eyes were dark, and Arnulf decided not to ask anything more. Øystein Ravenslayer was dead now, and Toke was surely expected to take his place even though he was young, and it would be a heavy and dangerous legacy to bare. Arnulf bit his tongue and carefully held the helm as Toke instructed. Toke would surely be a good chieftain for Haraldsfjord. He lacked neither courage nor resolution and few would have been able to cut down the two attacking tradesmen faster than Toke had done. But the closer the ship came to Haraldsfjord, the more troubled the Northman seemed, and Arnulf did not envy him having to look his friends and family in the eye and share the news of twenty dead men.

*****

On the evening of the seventh day, Toke moored the ship at a large bird island that seemed to be used as overnight accommodation for fishermen and seafarers. He let Sigurdur's men disembark and sat in the bow with a

100

mug of beer, staring reservedly towards the north. Arnulf took a piece of dry bread and sat shivering beside him. He broke it in half, and Toke accepted his share but did not eat anything, and Arnulf let him be. He missed firm ground under his feet and thought of the village in Egilssund. Now Rolf's funeral feast had been drunk and his own misdeed brought before the Thing, and the judgement of outlawry and banishment handed out. Stridbjørn's pride was arguably broken, and his bad-tempered hum bitter and ominous, and Trud's body was aged and weighed down by grief.

Arnulf's eyes were hard and it felt like split flint in his stomach. He cast his guilt away, noting that it got better every time he did it and he forced thoughts of Egilssund away and turned his attention to some jellyfish floating below sea level.

In on a little island, birds were resting in their nests, nervous and offended at being disturbed, and Toke set down his mug roughly and held his arm with his head bowed. As long as the tradesmen were lurking for him, he kept his torment to himself but, in the evening, when they had left the ship, he had difficulty keeping in the pain anymore and drank so the beer barrel emptied.

'Is it very painful?'

'Odin knows!'

Toke looked up, 'I am going to have to hold my sword in my left hand on this year's summer voyage and should probably be happy if it not also the same next year.'

'So, you'll need your housecarls again.' Arnulf smiled, 'I would be proud, if I may be allowed to protect your right hand.'

Toke spat in the water and let go of his arm while running his fingers through his hair, 'Be quiet, Stridbjørnson! No one could wish to be bound to a particular man on his first voyage.'

'I'm serious.'

Toke nodded, pale, 'If you really are, then I thank you and accept your help. It is not certain that others will care much about my life after hearing the tidings I bring. I throw shame upon a proud lineage by daring to return home after having squandered both ships and men.'

'It was your father who threw his kinsmen into misfortune by leading them into an unequal battle, not you! People will be glad to see that his son is alive! Rather one man home than none, now eat. You are weak enough, despite having eaten.'

Toke looked absently at the bread, 'There is a man in the outer settlement – Leif Cleftnose – he wishes me no good.'

Arnulf stole a swig from his beer mug, 'What have you done to him?'

Toke frowned and took the mug from him, 'Nothing. But he has long believed it would be best for the people of the fjord to follow him instead of Øystein, and he has his followers. He considers me to be just a big whelp.'

Arnulf picked a bit of mouldy crust from the bread. How presumptuous of him, Leif, to think so, presumptuous and stupid! The older males in a pack of wolves tended to know when the younger ones were a threat and made sure to subdue them in time or drive them away.

Toke began eating without showing any desire for food.

'What is your sister's name?' Arnulf wanted to know.

'Jofrid.'

'And your mother?'

'Hildegun.'

'There are many women that await you!'

'Me and Øystein.'

Toke threw the bread away, his gaze wandering restlessly from fjeld to fjeld. Arnulf picked it up and gave it back to him insistently, 'Was it not you who said you can rest no matter what thoughts you were wrestling with and how hard the ship struck the seas? That is probably also true for food. Eat and gain strength for tomorrow.'

Toke sent him an angry glance but took the bread and turned his back on Arnulf so as to eat in peace. Arnulf left him and stumbled across the deck. Yawning, he promised himself that it was the last night he would share sleep with Toke and rubbed his forehead to ward off the onset of a headache.

Leif Cleftnose. He must look a sight! To get a cleft nose would probably enrage even the most docile person! Who had clefted it? Øystein Ravenslayer? And who, incidentally, was the raven that Øystein had killed?

Shivering, Arnulf stretched out on the sacks of wool and beat them into a bearable form. If he had not been so tired all the time, he would have long ago cursed this accidental bed away. Sour wool-stink, old bread, hard meat and an ice-cold night wind! The Norwegian spring was as frostbiting as the winter in Egilssund! But bedstraw and sleeping skins and shelter – there was much to look forward to in Haraldsfjord. He hoped.

*****

102

Haraldsfjord's mouth was wide and surrounded by towering snow-tipped mountains. The water was calm and the wind slow, so the wide knarr sailed slowly into the vast fjord, and Arnulf had time to consider the impressive waterway. The fjord must be as deep under him, as the cliffs that rose above him. He felt small and insignificant under the silent stone jötunn and straightened his back defiantly.

Toke let the one-legged old man have the helm and ordered Sigurdur's men to the aft, for in his ancestral fjord he would stand in the bow, as proud as any dragon's head. Composed and serious, he stared straight ahead, and all conversation between the tradesmen ceased. Arnulf looked up to the fjelds and felt a shudder at the thought that so must the Einherjar stand, wordless and waiting, in silent motionless tribute when the Valkyries brought newly dead warriors home with them to Valhalla.

There was no sound on the fjord, no birdcalls. The ship glided softly through the glinting water, following its twists, and with a masterful hand seemed to plough between the mountain's feet. Imperceptibly the mountains slowly penetrated closer to the water, narrowing the opening and, after yet another swing and some single rocks, suddenly it was revealed to be almost cliff-free, as if huge mountain trolls had cleared the stones away and evened the ground a bit. Friendly pastures wrapped themselves around the receding fjeld's feet, and eider ducks and geese found shelter in the sparse rush growth. Pines and shrubs were growing by the water, which had a gravel bottom, leading up to the fjord's first settlement.

The stone-clad houses and wicker fences seemed to cling to the uneven slope, and Toke asked the old man to steer the ship closer to the boat-covered shore and take the sail down.

The dogs started barking, and people came running from their houses and chores to see who was disturbing the peace. It struck Arnulf how much more exposed a Norwegian fjeld-settlement was to assault and looting than a Danish one, where residents often had a good view and could detect enemy ships in time. It was probably for the same reason that men did not let time pass but gathered themselves quickly on the shore with arms in their hands, as children looked out nervously, but curiously, from behind the safety of the women and the thralls.

A burly, broad man with a white wolf fur on his shoulders stepped out in front of the others. His unruly brown hair was bushy, and his beard was lush, but his face was marred by long scars, and of his nose, only two stumps remained. He stood, legs apart with his fists on his belt, and Toke raised his hand in salute as the ship rocked calmly, 'Well met again, Leif Cleftnose!'

His voice called loud over the water.

'Well met, Toke Øysteinson!'

Leif spat in the dirt and looked inquiringly at Toke and the ship, 'You sailed out on a snekke with good men on board but return home in an understaffed trading boat! Where is Øystein and the others? Where is my nephew?'

'You shall have your answer in a moment,' said Toke, 'For you must gather your people and sail after me to the meeting place immediately.'

Leif Cleftnose squinted one eye and slowly twisted a lock of his long beard, while the men muttered around him.

'And why should I obey that order? The animals are being gathered for the pasture journey, and there is enough to do here for the occasion. If Helge Stridbjørnson has captured your father, I can tell you immediately that I will not provide any ransom for the old fox.'

Toke waved to the one-legged old man to raise the sail again, and the ship began to move forward steadily.

'You will come soon enough,' he shouted as a farewell. 'For what I have to say affects all in the fjord and, not least, yourself.'

Without giving Leif any further attention, Toke commanded the ship be turned towards mid-fjord, and Arnulf saw the Cleftnose's furious gaze bore into his back. He followed the men's excited conversation in front of the village until the fjord swung. At the bow, Toke's shoulders shrank and Arnulf wondered what kind of man Øystein Ravenslayer must have been. Leif did not seem to want to succumb to one who was weaker than himself, and that Helge had lost his life to Øystein now seemed fair to Arnulf.

Toke ran his fingers through his hair, fixing his gaze towards the next bend, and when the ship rounded some vegetation, another village came into view. It was on less of an incline than the first and had more grass around it, and the man Toke spoke to there was much more welcoming and cordial than Leif Cleftnose. His eyes were bright and mild, and though he was still in his prime, his hair was already grey. He was called Toste Skaldshield and he urged Toke to anchor and come ashore for a mug of mead and a rest, but Toke gave him no more of an explanation than Leif and asked him to just gather his kinsfolk and follow him to the meeting place.

The last stretch of the fjord was straight and ended in a shallow lake and around its banks was the last of the three settlements. Arnulf went to the foreship, put the lamp down and looked out. The houses in the village were big, and several ships were pulled up on the shore, among them the biggest longship he had ever seen. Lush green fields of grain and animals spread out far behind the village, where a fair valley seemed to continue the fjord's beauty to finally lick up along the side of the fjeld and spawn a network of tortuous paths. A waterfall glittered like a silver ribbon where the valley ended. Both mountains and houses were mirrored in the lake, and Arnulf's mind was quiet. This was what Toke had yearned for. Even the gods of Asgard had to admit that it was beautiful here! Øystein Ravenslayer's village was worthy of Freya!

The people became aware of the ship in good time, but when the wind almost deserted the sail, it was slow to arrive. The closer the ship came, the clearer Arnulf could see how well-dressed and well-fed even the thralls and the oldest seemed to be, and how well the houses were built and decorated.

Toke stood motionless at the bow, while the people gathered on the banks, but when a light-footed woman with long, dark hair and a child in her arms came running from the main longhouse, he uttered a tortured sound and extended his arm forward. She screamed and waved and could not keep her feet at rest in the sand but danced around and lifted the child up, waving her hands.

The knarr had barely scraped against the short jetty before Toke jumped ashore and ran to the strand surrounded by greetings and shouts from the crowd. The questions rained down on him, and more than one wrinkled, worried forehead squinted at Sigurdur's ship, but Toke seemed to hold them off without answering anything. Only when a woman shouted, asking if Jofrid had been avenged, did Toke say yes, and his words triggered cheers and pats on his shoulder, but Toke only had eyes for Gyrith and Little Ranvig. He threw himself into her arms and hugged her, he took Ranvig on his hip and burst into tears. Ranvig howled and Gyrith wept as she laughed. Toke faltered and fell to his knees but was immediately helped to his feet.

Arnulf looked quickly around the ship. Sigurdur's men had dispersed themselves around the deck and made ready to sail away immediately. They cast anxious glances towards the many armed men on the shore, and Arnulf nodded to One Leg as he put his hand on the shield rim, 'Good wind to Kaupang, and good trading.'

'Thank you, Bjarne. And welcome home!'

Arnulf grimaced and lifted Serpenttooth's sheath as he jumped overboard and went ashore. The one-legged man clamoured for the sail, and the trading vessel was turned and set out while Arnulf stopped on the shore, waiting tensely. For what he did not know.

No one seemed to notice that the ship was sailing again, and Arnulf could not see Toke in the crowd any longer. He put his hand on sword hilt. He trusted the Northman, but Toke had no further use for him, and as soon as it became known who he was, who knew what would happen.

Some children flocked curiously around Arnulf and pointed, impressed, at Serpenttooth but Arnulf looked at them grimly and with a wave indicated that they should keep their distance. Cries and questions were stifled abruptly, for Toke climbed up onto an upturned rowboat and raised his hand. His wounded arm had begun to bleed through the bandage after the many hugs, but he did not seem to notice it.

'Even the greatest skald will not be able to put into words my joy at being home again!'

Toke was hoarse with emotion and let his gaze slide over the familiar faces, while despair pulled the corners of his mouth askew, 'But you see that I come alone.'

He looked all around the circle, 'I have asked Leif Cleftnose and Toste Skaldshield to gather their people and come to the meeting place, for there I will share what has happened to me and my ship companions and answer all questions.'

Toke searched out Arnulf and waved him forward. Arnulf swallowed and went quickly to the boat with a thumping heart. Everyone looked at him, and he felt like a horse being dragged around on a marketplace, so the buyers could judge its worth. He tried to answer the many glances with sincere kindness, but a smile would not come, and his knees felt loose and unreliable.

Arnulf stood in front of Toke, and the Northman lay his hand firmly on his shoulder, 'This is Arnulf. He is my friend and travelling companion, and I owe him my life, so welcome him.'

A flood of tears suddenly pressed Arnulf from behind his eyes, and he felt Toke's grip switch to an encouraging squeeze. The people of the settlement looked at him with kindness, and Gyrith came forward, smiling. Her brown eyes sparkled, and her teeth were white and flawless, 'Be welcome in Haraldsfjord, Arnulf! You have travelled far and, undoubtedly, have need for rest and a hearty meal before everyone gathers at the meeting place. Be my guest in Øystein's house as if it were your own home and know that no one here can thank you more for Toke's life than I!'

She blinked away a tear and gave way to an older voluptuous woman with a keen eye and a warm smile. Her brown hair was grizzled and gathered in a large silver pin and her face was softly furrowed, 'I am Hildegun, Toke's mother, and I also welcome you, as any of Toke's friends are welcome here. Toke is my only son, and you have saved his life. Today I have two sons!'

Arnulf breathed deeply and thought he ought to respond but remained silent, feeling his cheeks burn. Instead of talking, he bowed his head deeply, and Hildegun seemed to understand him.

A young woman with a bulging belly nodded towards him, and Arnulf noticed how similar her features were to Toke's and assumed that she had to be Jofrid, his sister.

Toke jumped off the boat and grabbed Gyrith passionately, and they walked to the plank-covered road leading up into the village. Jofrid took Ranvig on her hip and waved Arnulf to go with her, and the conversation ran again freely among the people, as they expectantly and uneasily followed Toke home. Arnulf could see from their fearful questioning of each other who Øystein's ship closest companions were, and he was breathless from it.

Øystein's longhouse was greater than Stridbjørn's. It was higher than the other houses and located further back, and all posts and gables were carved with serpents and clutching beasts painted in bright colours. Three snakes intertwined with each other around the door, and above them yellow runes were carved into the wood.

Toke spoke quietly with some men who seemed to stand very near him. He asked them to wait outside the house and apologised that he wanted to be alone with his family for a little while, and they nodded and looked at his bleeding arm and formed a guard at the door to protect the peace of the house.

Toke and Gyrith went inside and Arnulf bowed his head before the runic power and, full of respect, stepped over the high doorstep. The room he entered seemed almost bigger than the house looked from the outside, and the thralls had managed to get the flames to flare up on the long fireplace and lit candles in the hanging lamps. When Arnulf had become accustomed to the dimness, he saw that the inside was not much different than in the house in Egilssund, but that everything was bigger and more magnificent, and even the smallest and most insignificant details were richly decorated. The sleeping places were wide and the skins thick and colourful blankets shared space on the walls with silver-inlaid weapons and lavishly decorated shields. Arnulf felt like a poor peasant-forester when he compared Øystein's wealth with Stridbjørn's, and he now better understood Helge's reports of strange splendour and grandeur.

Three thrall women worked frantically at the pots and Gyrith fetched mead, while Toke, tired, let himself sink down on a bunk and leaned against the cloth-covered dividing boards with his eyes closed. Jofrid and Hildegun found clean linen and jars and Hildegun put dried herbs in a small pot and commanded the thralls cook them.

Arnulf sat on the edge of a bed, a little away from Toke, and Gyrith handed him a mead horn and asked him to drink deeply. Then she sat down beside Toke and, whispering, stroked his hair, and Toke nodded with a sigh and drank the mead, leaning his head against her shoulder.

Arnulf tasted the drink. The mead was stronger and sweeter than that Trud used to brew, and he drank it in little sips as he looked at the sleeping places and guessed who slept where.

Jofrid sat down, panting, and laid her hands on her stomach, which now and then changed its form, and one of the thrall women gingerly lifted her legs up onto the sleeping skins. Ranvig crawled across the floor with a wooden sheep in her hand, and Toke saw her and, smiling, raised his head. The girl had light curls and bright eyes and looked just like Toke had described her, just a little rounder on the cheeks.

A thrall poured steaming lamb stew into a polished wooden bowl and brought it to Arnulf with some dark bread, and Hildegun found a splendidly embroidered red kyrtle and laid it beside Toke. While Arnulf ate, Gyrith and Hildegun helped Toke out of his torn kyrtle and took care of his wounds. Toke made a sound, when Hildegun removed his dressing, and his mother frowned at the sight of his arm and reached for the ointment and bandage, 'Can you lift your arm?'

'No.'

Toke found it hard to endure her touch, 'I can bend it. A little.'

Gyrith handed him the scalding herbal elixir that the thralls had brewed, but Toke grimaced at the sight of it and refused to drink it. Hildegun took the mug and pushed it certainly in his hand, as if he were a disobedient child, 'Drink!'

Toke, shaking his head, put the mug down on the floor, 'Why? It does not work anyway; I do not have a fever anymore.'

His mother looked up from his arm, her face deeply serious, 'Odin himself shielded you, since there is no rot in it. Thank him for it and maintain the wound with care, otherwise he may regret his favour and let you live with a withered arm for the rest of your life.'

Shamefully, Toke bent his head and combed his fingers through his hair. He reached for the mug, 'Forgive me!'

Hildegun smiled wistfully and stroked his bearded cheek, 'Toke!'

He slowly forced down the concoction and rinsed his mouth out with water after, and Hildegun looked at his scabbed wrist but did not ask anything. Gyrith helped him into the red kyrtle, after Hildegun had bandaged his arm, and she changed his silver chain around his neck with one that was noticeably heavier and brought food. Arnulf thought that Toke looked like an earl now and, pensive, scraped the bowl clean. Øystein's son would not talk to the village folk dressed as a simple man!

Hildegun placed his wounded arm in a sling of yellow linen and sat quietly at Toke's side and waited while he ate. At no time did the severity leave her face, and Arnulf wondered if she had suspicions about what had happened to Øystein.

A man stuck his head in the door and announced that the first of Toste Skaldshield's ships could be seen on the fjord, and Toke nodded and handed Gyrith the half-full bowl. He wanted to get up, but Hildegun took his hand and held him back. She just sat and looked at his hand but then very softly asked, 'Is Øystein dead?'

Arnulf held his breath and put the bowl on the floor and Gyrith lifted Ranvig up and gave her to one of the thrall girls and waved them away. Toke sighed deeply, his face convulsed in agony, while he also looked relieved that Hildegun herself had asked the question, and Jofrid straightened up with a hand on her lower back.

'Yes.'

Toke hugged Hildegun's hand.

Gyrith collapsed onto the floor, biting her knuckles silently, and Jofrid's shoulders began to shake. Her hair slid down her face, and Hildegun closed her eyes for a moment. When she looked up again, they were glossy, but she did not cry, 'And the other men?'

'Them, too.'

Gasping, Gyrith cramped in front of the fireplace with bleeding knuckles and Jofrid made a noise like a kitten with her head in her shawl. Hildegun lovingly caressed Toke's hand and pressed it hard against her chest, 'I knew it the moment I saw you. A black dís stood in your shadow. You have an unpleasant meeting in front of you.'

Pained, Toke looked into the flames, and Gyrith huddled up to Jofrid in the bed and threw her arms around her. Arnulf felt sorry for the women and winced. His grief for Helge and Rolf was beginning to rankle like an old wound. He wanted to comfort Jofrid and Gyrith who struggled to cry softly so it could not be heard outside, but he felt like a traitor, since it was his own people who had performed the misdeeds.

For a while no one said anything, but then Toke got up, swaying. For a moment he held his arm but released it with a resolute look. His face seemed ten years older than before, and his eyes glowed as if he was ready to meet his death. Arnulf also rose, and Hildegun went serenely to the end wall and took a sword with a black amber-inlaid scabbard from a hook.

'Sigtryg's sword?'

Toke had awe in his voice, and his mother nodded and hooked it to his belt, 'If your own and Øystein's is lost, may my father's blade guard you from now on. There are runes on the pommel. They never failed Sigtryg.'

She quickly wiped a tear from her cheek and tight-lipped, fixed the sheath, 'Leif Cleftnose will barely hold a funeral feast for Øystein. Thor strengthen you.'

The same man who had previously announced Toste Skaldshield's arrival announced that now Leif's vessels were also in sight, and others were waiting at the meeting place. Toke went to Gyrith and Jofrid and stroked their hair in turn.

'Come with me,' he said softly. 'I would like there to be at least four people in the square who are fond of me when I have said what I have to say.'

He looked careworn at Arnulf, who waved his hand, deprecatingly, 'Don't think of me, you have enough of your own to deal with and you did what you could. Tell them everything.'

Arnulf's voice was gruffer than intended, but when Toke dared to face the people with his cruel message, Arnulf also dared to reveal who he was. Toke nodded grateful, 'By Freyr, Arnulf!'

'By Fenrir!'

Hildegun helped the sobbing women onto their legs and asked them for Toke's sake to stop their tears for a little while, and Gyrith, bravely, took Jofrid's arm, and muttered, trembling, that excitement was detrimental for the pregnant. Jofrid bitterly cursed the child who was to blame for twenty men's death and her own dishonour, and Arnulf looked at her swollen belly. It was Helge's child who kicked in there! Helge's flesh and blood, who even before its birth had decided the fate of three fjord settlements. He wanted to shout to Jofrid that she should take care of the life of the child as she did her own! He was the uncle of Helge's heir, and he had not broken the law. He or Rolf should have fostered the child! A stream of violent emotions spread like fire across his chest, but now Toke went towards the door with Hildegun after him, and Arnulf had to put a lid on his troubled thoughts and follow. At least he himself could take care of Jofrid now if the large meeting developed in an unpleasant direction.

People swarmed outside as Toste Skaldshield and his village companions arrived, and they headed for Øystein's house, chatting. When Toke came out, it silenced all conversation abruptly, and the sight of his haggard face and the weeping women behind him, got people to stiffen, as if a cold blast from the mountains had frozen everything without noticing. Everyone seemed to presume that Øystein was dead, and they shrank back from Toke and his family with pity and fear in their eyes as he wordlessly walked towards the meeting place. Arnulf put his hand on his sword hilt and felt his eyes burn. He followed after Jofrid and Gyrith without looking at anyone and felt every stone he stepped on through his leather soles. It was so quiet in the village that the oar strokes from Leif's ships could be heard over the fjord, and Arnulf saw them find a place and moor among the other vessels in the narrow sandy strand.

A tall black-haired man with a curly beard came up beside Gyrith and put his arm around her protectively. He was missing a hand and had the same look as her, so Arnulf concluded that he must be Stentor, her father. Gyrith clutched hard on his hand stump but said nothing, and Stentor looked briefly at Arnulf, as he threw his cloak over his shoulder. Arnulf was uncomfortable, because the man had one brown and one yellow eye, and there was a force around him, which had its roots in something other than muscle.

The meeting place was spacious and even and seemed to be used for grazing. In the centre was a little mound, so the speakers could be seen and heard by all. Beside it stood a large flat stone with carved image motifs on the sides. Arnulf recognised Mjolnir, Sleipner and the sign of the sun, and the dried blood on the stone revealed that a blót had been held recently to ensure the missing men a safe home voyage.

Toke walked slowly up the hill, and although his posture was erect, he seemed to be weighed down, the heavens resting on his shoulders. Hildegun and Gyrith stood at the foot of the mound, and Jofrid sank down on one of the stones that was laid in a circle around it. The men Toke had spoken with most when he arrived remained closest to him as the other village folk thronged around the mound except for the side facing towards

111

the valley, which seemed to be reserved for Leif Cleftnose and his companions.

The silence was palpable and even the younger children were silent, seeking their mothers with big eyes. Arnulf waited with a forced calm and Toke, gazing far out over the fjord, did not seem to want to say a word before the last person had arrived.

Leif's voice echoed between the ships and just like Toke he had dressed so well that his silver flashed up to the meeting place. Proudly, he left the breath of the fjord and stomped, shouting loudly, up through the village with a group of armed men while he gestured and make an aggrieved face at being summoned. There were no women or children with him, and Arnulf took it as a bad sign that Øystein's rival came combat-ready to the gathering. He held Serpenttooth a little firmer. The Thing's square was sacrosanct in Egilssund. It was only allowed to carry knives to meetings, but that law did not seem to apply here.

Toke hardly noticed that Leif Cleftnose did not look favourably on the place reserved for him, and Leif stopping his talk, took stock of the situation. Burly housecarls accompanied him, and several of Toste Skaldshield's companions scooted over so as not to stand too close to them. Gyrith dried her cheeks and sent Leif a sharp look, and slight as she was, she straightened up and went and stood like a shield between him and Toke. Dark as a dís of destiny, she guarded her child's father, and the shadow of a smile slid across Stentor's face.

Toke looked around. All eyes were fixed upon him. He seemed terribly alone on the mound, and if Arnulf had not been a stranger in the fjord, he would have joined Toke up there.

'As you can see, I returned alone and Freyr alone knows how I suffer at having to stand here today.'

Toke's voice trembled slightly and a woman burst into tears and leaned against her husband's shoulder.

'Øystein Ravenslayer is dead, and those that were with him ...'

He swallowed and searched for Gyrith for courage, 'His ship companions did not fail him, and now they have found their places beside him and the Einherjar in Valhalla.'

Toke closed his eyes, and Arnulf's hand began to shake on the sword hilt. He looked down and heard gasping and weeping ripple through the crowd, and several people sank down in the grass, groaning, though most seemed to have sensed and prepared for Toke's terrible message. There were no screams and curses around the mound. The crying was quiet in Haraldsfjord; the bitter tears lingered like dew on the valley's grass.

Jofrid complained again with her hands on her stomach, and Stentor's hand was clenched white on the Thor's hammer that hung around his neck. Toke said no more but gave way to grief, and Arnulf recalled the evening on the banks of Egilssund where Halfred had shared the news of Helge's death. The bystanders' sobs and sighs tore at him, but Leif did not let the mourners have peace and shouted angrily, 'His companions did not fail him, but you are here anyway! Explain yourself, Toke! Which man was my brother's son's killer? Who was stronger than twenty of our best men, and where was your blade as they fell? From such a fight only traitors and cowards remain!'

Toke's eyes shot lightning, 'I fought so those who faced me will remember it to their last breath, Leif! We waited for Helge Stridbjørnson for half the winter outside King Sweyn's royalseat and met him in Sælvig. He had forty men with him, and Øystein refused me to spare our own and face Helge alone in single combat to avenge Jofrid, as is a brother's duty. He wanted to do it himself, and it was the death of Helge. The fight was fierce and wounded Øystein, and Helge's helmsman, Halfred, avenged Stridbjørn's son by killing my father, and after that everyone fought.'

Leif listened, his eyes narrowed, as he stroked the edge of his axe with his thumb. His men stood silently behind him with harsh faces like they intended to appear threatening to Toke, and Jofrid twitched her lips grimly when she heard about Helge's death and seemed satisfied.

'We defended ourselves bravely, and the battle was long before everyone, but I had departed from life. I was overpowered and taken to Egilssund where Stridbjørn let me sit, tied under heavy torment, in a thrall hut without water, for two days.'

Toke stretched out his rope-bitten hand. Hildegun suffered at his words, and Gyrith's lips trembled, but Leif Cleftnose seemed only to regret that Toke had not remained a thrall in Denmark.

'Finally, I was so weak, I feared I would not be able to stand against Stridbjørn as I intended to, but then Arnulf came, as if sent by Odin, and he freed me and gave me bread and water against his father's orders.'

'Against whose orders?' exclaimed Leif, sending Arnulf a crushing glance. Arnulf stared challengingly back at him and went a little up the mound when Toke hesitated. The earth burned beneath him, and the inquiring eyes stabbed him in the back, but his chest was hotter than Fafnir's breath.

113

'Against Stridbjørn's orders. Helge was my brother.'

There was a gasp through the crowd, and Leif Cleftnose sneered hatefully, 'His brother! So are you a relative of a woman defiler! What did you get out of betraying your father and associating with a thrall?'

Arnulf's whole body was tense and his skin trembled like the skin on a lightning-scared horse. Sweat broke out, but he could not fall back or wait for his answer, could not give Leif the opportunity to bite his throat.

'Nothing other than knowledge of how Helge died.'

'And why do you stand here now and not in Egilssund? When a man loses his son, should the dead man's brother not stay home and be his parents' comfort and support?'

Toke considered Leif intensely, and the bystanders followed the exchange of words with bated crying.

'Because I killed my other brother, Rolf, later that evening.'

The blood pounded through his rigid sword hand grip on the hilt, and Leif let out a roar and spat contemptuously, 'A brother murderer! A murderer who betrays his own and escapes the country with a thrall! Toke! Your company was better when you set sail!'

'Arnulf is my friend, and if you mock him, you mock me!'

Toke's voice was thick with anger.

'Is he?'

Leif's spiky nose stumps quivered, 'A man who can kill his own brother while his family is in mourning is probably also devious enough to abuse the confidence of a chieftain's son! He has tricked you in gratitude to save his own skin, and only a dishonourable son does not avenge his father's death! Helge's blood and lineage flows in Arnulf's veins. Kill him!'

'It was Halfred that killed Øystein, neither Helge nor Arnulf!' returned Toke furiously, but Leif parried back lightning fast, 'And who did Halfred serve? He carried out Stridbjørn's wishes, but you have sold your honour for a drink of water! Avenge your father and show yourself worthy of wearing Sigtryg's sword or surrender your position! He who prevails in Haraldsfjord must be stronger in will and deeds than everyone else! There are too many women in your house, Toke. You think and act like them!'

Toke's face was white and he looked like he could attack Leif Cleftnose at any moment, had he not been so weakened, and Leif knew he ran no risk with his humiliations. Stentor was uneasy and exchanged glances with Toste Skaldshield who motioned for him to keep quiet. Many supported Toke and would stand behind him against Leif, but if he himself was not the man to stand his case, then he was not a worthy son for his father. Arnulf knew that if Toke were to win over the people, he had to put Leif in his place now.

'Only those who have never languished mock thirst.'

Toke kept his answer quiet to save strength, 'Arnulf had his reasons for that killing, and as far as I know, you have never regretted some of your own! I am ready to meet you and prove my strength, just as soon as my wound has healed sufficiently, and those who shout loudest about others' honour, usually lack it themselves! When I give a man my friendship, I stand by my word, and Arnulf and I owe each other our lives several times over.'

The silence was oppressive. Arnulf held his breath. People glanced at each other, and Arnulf saw worry and sorrow mingle with anger and determination in their eyes.

Leif laughed briefly, 'Then that is what we will say, Toke Øysteinson. When you have enough strength for the fight, my sword and I will continue our talk about honour, and I believe that the appointment of a new chieftain should happen at the same time.'

Toke acquiesced and wiped his hand across his forehead, 'That agreement I would like to conclude with you, Leif. But until then, I will accept my heritage and decide for the fjord and settlements as my father, and his father, did before me. If anyone wants to oppose this, let him come forward and say what he has against me, I will listen. No free man should obey a chieftain he does not respect!'

He looked searchingly, and Arnulf saw only good will and nodding heads around him, but Leif had more to say, 'I believe that just a single day with you in the chieftain's seat is one day too many! Regardless of the good men we have lost, it will soon be time to organise this summer's voyage and who should steer the ship's course? I will not submit to a cripple who has lost his luck, and I believe I speak for everyone in my village. You cannot hold your sword with that arm, Toke, and Øystein could not keep a hold of his! You are so sick that you are shaking, stay home and let yourself be cared for by your women, I promise that *Twin Raven* will come home richer than ever before!'

Leif Cleftnose stared challengingly at the people, and Toke straightened himself, even though everyone could see the sweat pouring off him. Arnulf sucked air between his teeth. If Toke did not lead the voyage, it could very well cost him the opportunity to remain chieftain. Leif Cleftnose seemed to be the man to steal silver so it would satisfy most, and if luck was with him, it would be difficult for the people to see why Toke would make a better chieftain than him.

Arnulf drew Serpenttooth and held the blade proudly, 'I have promised to be Toke's right arm during the voyage, and this sword's exploits can undoubtedly compare with yours, Leif! Toke was able to steer the helm on the way up along the Norwegian coast, and we wouldn't have arrived any sooner if someone else had been helmsman.'

Leif drew his axe with a roar, stamping his feet in front of Arnulf. The scars in his torn face seemed to almost glow, 'How dare you speak in this matter, you miserable Danish skræling? If Toke will not kill you, I will do it myself, by Thor, and avenge my nephew!'

He raised his axe, and Arnulf was ready to react, but Stentor quickly jumped in between them with raised arms, 'Stop!'

His amber eye shone so it ran cold down Arnulf's back, and Leif seemed to respect him enough to listen.

'Only consecrated blood may be shed near the sacrificial stone, and whether or not vengeance shall be taken is for Toke alone to determine!'

Leif grumbled and, screeching, tore the air with his axe head, 'So cast the runes for Arnulf and let Odin determine his fate!'

Stentor shook his curly head, 'Man does not encumber the gods with questions he himself can answer. And *Twin Raven* is Toke's ship after Øystein, and he can deny you a place on it, so compose yourself, and do not seek to determine its journey, Leif. You have good people behind you and are right in saying that only the best man must lead Haraldsfjord, but give Toke the breathing space you yourself would have liked, because as you rightly say, he is sick and his wound needs treatment.'

The Cleftnose exchanged glances with Stentor, but put his axe in his belt again, and Arnulf lowered Serpenttooth. Toste Skaldshield came forward quietly. His calm face helped Arnulf breathe again and people dared to move again.

'Whoever will sit in the chieftain's seat is for people to decide not the sword. I think that Odin himself held his hand over Toke and brought him back to the fjord as a gift, and it takes great courage to return home and talk honestly about so cruel a defeat as Øystein Ravenslayer and his men suffered. Give Toke time to rest and let him lead the voyage with a fjord chieftain's authority, then we will see how it goes with his luck. And if you have now said all that you wanted, Leif Cleftnose, I would like to hear the rest of his account, because I do not like to have a story interrupted, whether it is good or bad.'

Leif tugged at his beard, muttering, and Toste turned towards Toke and raised his hand encouragingly. Toke blinked, as if he were dizzy, and Arnulf doubted if he could hold out against Leif much longer.

'There is not much more to tell, Toste. Arnulf and I escaped to the trading market on Gormsø where we got passage on the knarr we arrived with. The men on board attacked us on the first night, and it was a severe struggle, during which several of them fell, and I got an axe in the arm, but Arnulf threatened to burn the ship if they did not sail us to Haraldsfjord and, believing him, they laid down their arms.'

Toste nodded, his eyes glowing warmly, 'It seems that your young friend has demonstrated both wisdom and courage, and with me he will continue to be welcome regardless of his origins and dubious actions.'

Arnulf was strangely affected by Toste's support, but Leif was not yet tongue-tied, 'So we let Toke lead *Twin Raven* as he wants, but while we are talking, I understand that there are unguarded goods and silver floating around the fjord. My men are well armed, and it will be easier to take the knarr than to catch a cod! Lend me the *Raven*, and I will show you how a little willpower can bring home our deceased men's honour-prices to their widow and orphans.'

Toke was about to give in to fatigue and seemed to be feeling really unwell. His shoulders stooped and he kept a hold of his arm, but his eyes were wilful and his voice firm, 'I gave the tradesmen my word that they could sail in peace as soon as I arrived safely in Haraldsfjord, and my first act as chieftain of the fjord is not to break an oath! *Twin Raven* is not yet ready. It is lacking a sail. It shall remain where it is.'

Leif Cleftnose snorted and turned his back on him, 'But I have not given my oath to anyone, and my ship is ready enough to obtain precious wares if I were the one to row! Those who are thirsty for silver can follow me now, and when *Twin Raven* is voyage ready send your messenger, Øysteinson.'

He strode off towards the ships with his men following, and several youths from the other settlements joined him with eager cries. Arnulf watched them go with disgust. So easy it was to enlist support when there were treasures to be had in reach! Leif Cleftnose must have guessed what Toke had to say when he saw him in his own village, otherwise he would not have behaved like an earl with a hird.

Gyrith sat with Jofrid and began to cry again, and the wailing rose higher at the meeting place. More left or fell into gloomy talk, and Toke staggered down the mound to Stentor and Toste. There was no more to be said, everyone had their own to attend to and Toke was deathly pale and trembling.

Toste Skaldshield put his hand carefully on his shoulder, 'Well said, Toke! If Leif thought he could topple you off your mound by swaying folk with fine words, he made a mistake and now he knows that Øystein's power has not left your village despite his death. Leif Cleftnose is a good man and a strong Viking, but he worries most about himself. His regime in the fjord could well turn out to be harder than most would care for. I have to be with my companions and kinsmen, even though I would prefer to be a guest in your house, but you should know that I am wholeheartedly behind you, even if it should cost me grief with Leif.'

Toke nodded slowly, 'Thank you, Toste! I was hoping you would say so, and I know that Øystein wanted me to take up his duty if he fell.'

Toste released him with a glance at his people, 'Be wise now, and do not get yourself into more bother with the Cleftnose. Promise me that you will not fight him before you are strong enough and do not rush to make *Twin Raven* ready. Leif's disrespectful behaviour will reflect more on him if you continue to act with dignity.'

Toke nodded again and looked out over the fjord. Leif stood, gesturing by the water's edge and placing men in two ships, and Arnulf thought of the tradesmen and the one-legged man and clenched his teeth. The old man would not reach home with his goods now, and before he died, he would condemn Toke for broken promises and believe that it was he who had sent his Vikings after the ship. Toke seemed to think the same, and it hurt Arnulf that Leif, laughing, would make fun of his and Toke's oath and for allowing such an easy prey to escape the hands of the fjord's men.

Toste raised his hand and left them, and Toke's friends gathered around him while Hildegun quietly asked Stentor to cast runes, so Toke's arm could be healed. Stentor promised to do so immediately, while the sun's light still had the power to banish evil, and having embraced Gyrith, he departed the square with long strides.

Toke had many questions to ask and answer and sat feebly on a stone, and many settled in the grass around him. Arnulf remained standing, for he did not feel completely at ease, and Jofrid sent him a bloodshot glance, her lips pressed together. Never had Arnulf seen such icy contempt in a woman's eyes, and he looked away shamefully. That Helge had wronged Jofrid he could not undo, and it was fair of her to hate any member of the family who was to blame for her grief and humiliation.

118

Toke's sister stood up, strained, and walked proudly over to Arnulf. Her bosom swelled under her dress and her cheeks were round with the advanced pregnancy, 'If I were a man, Arnulf Stridbjørnson, I would challenge you to single combat here today!'

She stared him straight in the eye, breathing in short bursts, 'Now I must wait for Leif Cleftnose to stand by his threats to kill you and have to suffer the further indignity of having to entertain you as a guest in my house, but welcome you are not!'

Arnulf bowed his head, 'You judge me too rapidly, Jofrid Øysteinsdaughter! Although I am Helge's brother, I can't take responsibility for his actions, and I myself am the first one to lament them, because I lost the person I was most fond of when Øystein took his revenge. I want no enmity with you, and you won't have to give me as much as a spoon. Save your hatred! Your humiliation has already been adequately avenged.'

He looked up, and Jofrid's fiery eyes overflowed with tears. Arnulf's voice was gentle, 'Your brother is my friend, and if anyone should be tended to, it is you, for you carry a heavy and precious burden.'

Jofrid snorted furiously and gathered her shawl around her shoulders, 'A child born of a rape is never precious, and as soon as it is born, I will leave it out for the wolves! It is my right, whatever Toke thinks and if it pains you, it will please me even more! Woe to thee, Arnulf, for Helge's misdeed led to my father's death! Once you and Toke have set sail on the voyage, my sorcery will overthrow your quest with bad luck and Freya will stand by me, just until your troll of a brother can welcome you amongst the dead!'

She turned on her heel and left Arnulf standing dumbfounded. He groaned and shook his head in disbelief. Leave Helge's child out! Over his dead body! The frightful jötunn-shrew! How could Jofrid be so heartless that she intended to do what poor people-in-need did and even get pleasure out of it! She was Helheim's sister, not Toke's! And the threat of sorcery and curses when Toke would never have made the trip home without Arnulf's help, the ingratitude! That child more than any other should live and by Fenrir!

Arnulf stared after Jofrid's swaying buttocks and tried to assess how long it would be until the birth, but he had never thought deeply about such matters before, and women could be big for several changes of the moon without anything happening other than that they found it even more difficult to breathe. If he and Toke were on the voyage when the infant was born, they could not prevent Jofrid killing Trud and Stridbjørn's

119

first grandchild, and having to bear responsibility for that killing, too, was more than Arnulf could take. The child was to carry the family on, and if it were a boy, the chieftain's seat awaited him in Egilssund, Jofrid should – and had to – listen to him. Make a promise!

Hildegun went by Arnulf with heavy steps. Her eyes were dull and her posture stooping as she headed for the sacrificial stone, where she pulled out her slender knife. For a moment, Arnulf was afraid that she was going to take her own life from sorrow and went after her, but then she slowly unfastened the large silver pin that held her hair and with an expressionless face began to cut it off and lay it over the stone. Arnulf stopped uneasily. The talking around Hildegun hushed and even Toke was silent while his mother carefully laid handful after handful of long, shiny hair on the stone until, finally, the silver pin adorned the stone's blood dark surface. She lay down her amber beads and silver rings too and went towards the fjeld without looking at anyone, and Toke beckoned a man to him and asked him to follow Hildegun at a safe distance. Everyone had the right to grieve in peace, but Haraldsfjord's first woman should not be completely without company.

Arnulf joined Toke and let Jofrid be for it would not do for her to give birth now. The men in the grass began to speak again, and Gyrith sat beside Toke on the stone.

It was quickly known which families had lost most with Øystein's defeat and they agreed who should temporarily come to their aid. Toke looked ready to roll off the stone at any moment but remained stubbornly sitting. He would not hold a wake until after the voyage and said it was important to work out the space for newly caught thralls after *Twin Raven* was manned, for it was imperative to rally more hands before the summer ended. A tall freckled man with spiky red hair felt it would be better to have as many men as possible on the voyage and instead send a boat later with the plundered goods and buy thralls in Tranevig, for there prisoners from the east were sold regularly, and they were easiest to subdue.

Arnulf was tired of standing and sat down with Serpenttooth resting over his knees and began to suck on a blade of grass. He thought of Toke in the thrall hut and did not believe that free men were easy to subdue, wherever they came from. In Egilssund, Stridbjørn had not had anything other than home-born unfree. Toke gave the redhead some credit, 'The Eastern thralls are little cut out for winters on the fjeld, but it makes sense to be as many as possible heading out. Styrbjørn Broadblade and Tord Vifilson must meet here with their snekke ships within fourteen days, for with them the voyage should be guaranteed a good return.'

The redhead shook his head, 'They sent word ten days ago, but since we had nothing new to say about your and Øystein's absence, they set out on their voyage together.'

Toke frowned, 'I had an agreement with those men! It is not like them to break their word. It is much safer to plunder from three ships than from one.'

'They had waited long enough, Toke, and it was only reluctantly they left. Even you would have made the same decision.'

Toke nodded, tired, and supported his forehead in his hand, 'So we sail alone. Maybe we can collect Eskild from Laksholt on the way.'

The freckled man laughed bitterly, 'Leif Cleftnose will not go for that! No, we are just ourselves this year and will have to live with that.'

Toke looked up, 'It is getting harder and harder to loot westward if you are not numerous enough. The skrælings are beginning to fortify the largest settlements, but Thorgrimur the Black told me about a cove where the worshippers of White Christ have settled. He has already attacked them twice, but they keep coming back with new riches, because they believe that the spring that runs through their homestead stems from the blood of one of their fallen. A miracle they call it. Stupidity it is rather.'

The redhead wrinkled his nose, 'Never trust an Icelander! Most of them are the children of murderers and outlaws.'

'You are only saying that, because it was an Icelander who turned the head of your betrothed!'

Toke grinned feebly at Arnulf, 'Did you hear that, Stridbjørnson? It was therefore it nearly went wrong for us during the escape from Egilssund. We trusted an Icelander!'

An elderly white-haired man with only one eye looked seriously at Toke, 'Do you know that Hildegun sacrificed a thrall-young to Odin, so that he would lead you home safely?'

'Did she really? That was clever of her! When did it happen?'

Toke straightened himself a bit and looked up into the fjeld, where his mother had gone.

'At midnight, a week ago. A raven screamed immediately after the blood ran out of him.'

Arnulf glanced quickly at Toke, 'Eight days ago? That was the night the tradesmen attacked us!'

Toke clenched his hand, 'And I slew two men in almost one strike, yes, indeed, it was Odin himself that wielded my sword in the dune! Never was my arm as strong as that night! Whose young thrall was it?'

'Skule and Ram's second oldest.'

'Then send them to the pasture with the cattle so they do not become too hot-headed to handle in the village.'

'Jofrid has already done it.'

Toke struggled to his feet and grimaced, 'Jofrid. She is getting big with child.'

Arnulf jumped up and offered him his arm, 'She doesn't want the child. She says it must be exposed.'

His outbreak revealed all too clearly a plea for help, and Toke sent him a long look.

'There are so many dead, Toke, should we not cherish the life of the unborn? We are both kin of the child. Family.'

Toke looked at his outstretched hand, his eyes empty. Arnulf managed to seize him as he fainted and Gyrith gave a startled squeak. Toke's weight caused Arnulf to falter, and the Northman's head dangled from his arm. A man, whose coarse black hands revealed his knowledge of fired iron, lifted Toke from Arnulf without exerting himself and carried him toward Øystein's longhouse, closely followed by Gyrith. Jofrid came hurrying, and several others went excitedly after the blacksmith, leaving Arnulf standing alone. Toke did not wake, and Arnulf looked puzzled at the people without knowing what he should do with himself. The village's people gave him no further attention. Those that did not follow Toke continued to talk, and Arnulf snorted and kicked a tuft of grass, while an overwhelming urge to run away pulled at his body. Thoughts and feelings swarmed about each other like a herd of horses put out to pasture after winter, and Arnulf headed away from the meeting place and trotted down to the fjord to be by himself. Toke would probably recover after he got some rest and there were plenty of kinsmen to care for him.

Arnulf spat at a pile of sheep shit and hunched his shoulders. Care. He crossed off the path and in between some semi-underground storehouses. If only Frejdis had been here! The loss tugged at his stomach and hurt his lungs. Arnulf stuck his thumbs into his belt. Frejdis no longer loved him. Her disgust was certainly not much less than Jofrid's, but he loved her still, hot and wild, worse than ever, like a forest fire shattering spring ice, like a howling wolf! Toke would wake up and look into Gyrith's dark eyes, meet her smile and be strengthened by her caresses, and Jofrid and Hildegun would fuss over him and watch over his sleep like mother-bears, while Arnulf could plunge down from a fjeld, drown or be attacked by wolves without anyone caring the least bit about it.

He stopped by the water's edge and wiped a tear from his cheek. Toke had come home. Chieftain or not, he was held and esteemed, not ostracised and exiled. Not a brother murderer. And Jofrid was right! Arnulf was not welcome in Haraldsfjord! An unbearable misery swept through his entire body with a crippling fatigue. His sixteenth summer, the summer Helge should have brought him a-viking, the summer he really would have proved his worth as a man and won Frejdis forever, that summer had been his misfortune and despair! Now he stood at the bottom of some Norwegian fjord without knowing in which direction his next step should be while the Norns' guffaws denied his grief peace.

The mountains around the fjord were darker, casting long shadows, and the air was cold. Seabirds volleyed against the polished silver mirror and snatched their evening meal from the icy water without dipping their beaks in too deep. Øystein's mighty longship was jacked up farthest in the line of ships, and beside the village's small boats it seemed strange and alone among its kinsfolk, just like Arnulf felt among the Northmen. The bow of the sea stallion was higher than on any other ship he had ever seen, and it ended in two carved black raven heads that peered obliquely to each side with wide open yellow beaks and staring red eyes.

Arnulf walked slowly towards it. *Twin Raven's* planks were painted the same black, red and yellow colours as the raven heads, and a hammered silver serpent with an open mouth wound around every oarlock. All along the shield rim, carved ravens with long claws screamed and fought against meandering snakes, the writhing of their bodies masterly, in and out, between each other, painted red and black on a yellow plank. The bow was iron-clad and sharply cut, and Arnulf counted thirty thwarts on each side of the deck. With a real wind or sixty rowing men, the bow could cause considerable damage to the hull of any enemy ship, and he saw for himself how the Vikings had to grab their shield's rim so as not to tumble during a ramming.

Full of admiration Arnulf let his hand run over the smooth wood. Aslak Shipbuilder should see this ship! He would die at its sight, declaring his life wasted if his vessels were ever to be measured against *Twin Raven*. A king could not sit at the helm of a prouder vessel! With a pounding heart he grabbed hold of the shield rim and climbed laboriously aboard. It was that big! The empty thwarts greeted him silently while a yearning for deep water sighed through the hull. Arnulf grabbed the polished rudder and, for a moment, the salt spray of the North Sea splashed in his face while sixty hardened Vikings with flaming eyes and windblown hair and beards pulled on the oars. The mast rose, creaking, and a mighty dragon-adorned sail strained while a war horn resounded like an echo from out at sea.

Serpenttooth burned against his thigh, and the raven heads stared ahead through fog and storm, secure in their course like Huginn and Muninn, while the men released the oars and freed their shields for battle.

Arnulf sank down on the thwart, breathless, and hid his head in his hands. His fingers cramped around his long hair. He would sit here until he rotted, sit on the ship, his biggest dream so painfully close, and not open his eyes when exhaustion finally overpowered him but die of anguish and cold in the biting, Norwegian spring night. Soon darkness would cover him, and Toke would not sense anything of Arnulf's fate before it was too late. His fingertips furrowed into his scalp. Tonight *Twin Raven* would sail him to the realm of the dead, no one would miss him, and he would no longer be a burden on the hard-pressed people of the fjord.

Arnulf huddled where he sat, huddling into himself like a squirrel in hibernation, brooding over his pain, oblivious to everything around him. For the first time since his misdeed he was alone and felt neither the driving mist nor the falling of night. He missed Helge, he missed Rolf and he could not bear to think of Trud and Stridbjørn and just wanted to be a child again, a child whose greatest misdeed was to overthrow the loom and tease the young thralls. Rolf had even given him the knife he died by. It was purchased on Gormsø five summers ago, and Arnulf had wrestled his brother in the grass from enthusiasm and rejoiced over the knife for several days.

'Arnulf!'

Arnulf was startled and he looked up, his neck stiff. It was almost dark, Stentor stood on the shore with a torch in his hand. He had a fur lined cloak around his shoulders, and the fire flickered in his eerie yellow-amber eye. Arnulf looked away shamefully as if Gyrith's father had caught him doing something he should not, and Stentor went down to *Twin Raven* and thrust the torch in the sand, 'It is cold. Hildegun has come back, she saw you down here.'

Arnulf nodded and only now felt how much he froze. He stared out at the murky water without making a move to get up, and Stentor leaned against the ship. He had a braided leather cord in his hand, on which a small piece of polished wood was attached. Runes were in the wood, and he turned it slowly between his fingers, 'There will be times in every person's life where he clearly believes he can see signs that Ragnarök is drawing near.'

Stentor had a strange power in his voice, and his words forced a sigh from Arnulf.

'Hate flares up, dissension splits kinsmen and despair spreads; all signs from the gods that the final battle is near.'

Stentor smiled and caressed the ship with his hand stump, 'The only true evidence of Ragnarök is, however, Fimbulwinter, and no man has yet felt the slightest breath of that.'

His strange eyes held Arnulf firmly, 'You are incredibly young, Arnulf, barely a man, but I feel a great power in you. An immense force and a violent grief.'

Arnulf bowed his head, his breath wheezy, and Stentor placed a firm hand on his arm, 'Balder was killed by one of his own. How do you think Hod lived on after his death? That story no one has told!'

Arnulf looked up hard, 'Loki controlled Hod's hand and aimed for him!'

'But did Hod blame himself less because of that? Thoughtlessness and rage – the malevolent forces of Loki that often plunge men into misfortune, but you helped my son-in-law make it home and deserve a lot of forgiveness and respect for that.'

Arnulf shook his head, 'You are in good standing with the Æsir, and they seem to listen when you call on them. Tell me why they have turned away from me, for only Fenrir will walk a path with me now!'

Stentor let go of his arm, 'If Fenrir follows you, then you have a mighty guardian! But from Loki's seed springs every misdeed, so beware of its steps and do not let it walk in your tracks forever! Odin loves the wise, and Tyr the brave and those that prove their strength win Thor's favour! Come with me, before you are too weakened from the cold. I promised Hildegun I would give Toke wooden runes as soon as they were finished, and the evening meal has long been warm.'

He held the amulet in the air, and Arnulf looked in awe at the mysterious characters. Only a few were vouchsafed to master runic power and to bind words to stone and wood and compel them to act. Incomprehensible that it was possible to capture and subjugate so much power, incomprehensible and awe inspiring. He shivered with cold. Runes aroused his curiosity and talk of hot food seemed tantalising; death could well be postponed a bit.

'What do they mean?'

Arnulf's voice broke. He counted four black runes in the polished wood, and Stentor put the amulet in his palm and explained willingly, 'The first draws fever and rot from the body, the second heals wounds, the third takes away the pain and the fourth is a strengthening rune. I have chosen the strongest that exists for Toke has suffered much and will need great strength in the future.'

Arnulf reached for the wooden runes but nevertheless dared not to touch them. Odin's own wisdom lay in runes, and it was not without reason that the Æsir king had hung, for days, pierced in Yggdrasil, before enduring his suffering and sacrificing an eye to gain mastery of the mysterious runic characters. With the amulet around his neck, Toke would be sure to recover quickly and perhaps regain the use of his sword arm.

Stentor lifted the torch from the sand and struck out with his handless arm towards the village, and Arnulf, exhausted, let himself drop down from the ship and went with him. There was something safe about Gyrith's father, despite his scary eye and commanding presence, and Arnulf let his troubles remain on *Twin Raven* and imagined that Stentor were his uncle and Gyrith his cousin and that Øystein's house in Haraldsfjord was filled with family and friends. A vulnerable urge for peace grabbed him.

'How did you lose your hand?'

Stentor looked, without bitterness, at his hand stump, 'I took a blow for Toke during a voyage. He was very young then and Hildegun had asked me to guard his life.'

'You were one of his housecarls?'

Stentor nodded with a smile, 'Yes, I was. Toste Skaldshield was too, and several others who are now dead. That hand made my daughter happy, for Toke would have lost his neck if I had not made my sacrifice, and their love is as beautiful as Bragi's song.'

He put his hand stump warmly on Arnulf's neck, and his torch lit a shielding circle of light around them. Arnulf was close to tears and stumbled up the plank road while exhaustion took his breath away and emptied his mind of thoughts. He felt the heat of the fire and suddenly wanted to walk with Stentor in the dark for eternity, never reaching the house. Never again to have to look anyone he did not know in the eye and be wary of strangers' opinions or prove something and defend himself, just follow the torch into the black with nothing but Stentor's mangled arm for support, by Fenrir! The wolf that walked his tracks.

*****

Toke felt relief as soon as the wooden runes were hung on his neck, and although Hildegun preferred to see him lying on the bed, he got up the next morning and sat up against the sun-warm house wall on a sheep skin.

126

He sat there for most of the days that followed, and when Hildegun had other things to attend to, he sneaked into the fjelds, Gyrith in hand. His mother scolded them when they came back and said that unnecessary exertion was foolhardy when the body had a wound to heal, but Toke said that the quiet hike had given him his strength back, and he smiled as bright as Gyrith after their walk on the fjeld.

Arnulf left them alone and helped Stentor and Hildegun get the spring tasks done, so *Twin Raven* could be put in the water. He helped as much as he could so as not to be perceived as an unhelpful and unwanted guest, and as Stentor was missing a hand, Toke incapacitated and Øystein dead, his help was desperately needed. The sheep needed to be sheared and put out on the summer pasture and the winter damage to the roofs and fences needed to be repaired. Arnulf and Stentor sailed out to gather eggs and eiderdown from the nests on the many islands, and he went fishing with the Northmen when the spring salmon thronged into the nearby waterfall. Stridbjørn and Trud would hardly recognise their son again. Arnulf wiped the sweat from his brow, thinking of Rolf and all his hard work with the land and livestock. He was sore and stiff but did not complain, and when the evening stew was cooked and people were going inside, he sat by the fire and carved wooden animals for Little Ranvig and Gyrith, humming, wound wool around them.

There was no more talk of Helge or brother-killing and Toke's village folk were friendly towards him, but Arnulf often had to content himself with working alone when one of the Northmen suddenly left him or sat idly by, unable to do anything. The village was in mourning, and the vitality of spring, which caused the birds to chirp in the scrubs and the bulls to roar in the fjelds, was replaced by muffled talk and glazed eyes.

Jofrid was suffering from pain in her lower back and did not speak to Arnulf, and he avoided her as much as possible and did not ask more about the baby, but he confided in Hildegun. She sighed and replied that she put her own daughter's happiness first, and that a detested child would not live happily, 'Jofrid is strong of mind, and if she has said that the child must be put out, you can hardly talk her out of it. Helge was not thinking of children when he forced himself upon her, and you have nothing to offer his offspring.'

Arnulf objected that if the child were simply sailed to Egilssund, no one need worry further about it, but Hildegun shook her head wearily, 'And who would bring it to Stridbjørn? No one from here will take on that task and you yourself would pay for it with your life. Even if a man from outside the fjord made the trip, your father would probably reject the child in the belief that Toke had sent him a fake thrall young as a noose around his neck. Forget the baby!'

'So let me buy it as a thrall!' begged Arnulf. 'I will give all the goods I win on *Twin Raven's* voyage in exchange!'

Hildegun looked at him earnestly, 'Arnulf! Jofrid wants revenge on Helge and wants to address it her own way, do you not understand that? Do not stand in her way lest she uses her sorcery against you, for she is stronger than most women are and has the Vanir in her ear.'

Arnulf shuddered at the threat, 'She hates me!'

'No! She hates Helge and grieves greatly for Øystein, and you should hate your brother's heinous deed!'

Arnulf was silent and Hildegun, depressed, left him, and neither of them uttered more words about Jofrid's child.

Everyday Leif Cleftnose sent a man to Toke to ask after the readiness of *Twin Raven* and each day Toke had to bite back his anger and explain what was delaying work.

His arm was beginning to heal, but he found resting difficult and he often quarrelled with his mother as he wanted to do everything that had been neglected because of Øystein's revenge voyage. Hildegun insisted that her son did not do anything other than rest, but Toke believed he could use his left hand, as long as he was careful. To his dismay Stentor said Hildegun was right, and Gyrith tended to his wound with great care and plied her husband incessantly with food in order for him to put on some weight before the gruelling summer voyage.

Arnulf thought they fussed over him too much but refrained from smiling when Toke was pushed into a corner by his women.

*****

Toste Skaldshield sailed in one morning with one of Leif Cleftnose's men to agree upon who should sail with *Twin Raven* from each of the settlements. The number was roughly determined from the year before, but there were many other considerations, and several of the young lads saw their opportunity to go a-viking after Øystein Ravenslayer's previous crew had perished. At the same time, some of the most experienced men refused to admit that their strength was not what it once was and Toke wanted as strong ship companions as possible, as now they must go a-viking with only one ship and, with a heavy heart, he had to disappoint the inexperienced and weak, but Arnulf was the first he wanted with him. Those who owned the least goods but were able were preferred, so their families could enter the winter months richer, but no family could be completely bypassed, so Gyrith had to fetch beer and meat several times before the three Northmen got up from the meeting stones.

That afternoon five men started to put the rigging and sail on *Twin Raven* and Stentor announced there was to be a blót the night before the Vikings set out. Toke took his arm out of the sling and tried in vain to keep a hold of Sigtryg's old sword, and finally Leif Cleftnose's envoy could return home with news of the upcoming departure.

Stentor and Toste were both to go on the journey and Arnulf was surprised that Stentor, despite his missing hand, was in no way defenceless, when they practised sword fighting in the meeting place. Stentor tied his shield to his maimed arm and could strike as well as any man, and Toke laughed heartily when Arnulf bit the dust four times from the blows of his wife's father.

'Do you understand now why Hildegun asked him to guard my life back then?' he asked cheerfully, when Arnulf, breathless and supported by his shield, poured beer into himself afterwards.

'I will never again underestimate a limbless man,' conceded Arnulf, displeased. He threw the shield in the grass and slumped down on it.

'Courage! Look here what I have for you!'

Toke had a piece of cloth wrapped around something in his hand, and he took it with his right hand and tried resolutely to give it to Arnulf. He could lift his arm as far as his hip, sweat forming on his forehead, but he had to give up bitterly, grimacing, 'Accursed arm! I am not worth more than an old, lame and battered horse! Take it yourself!'

Smiling, Arnulf took the cloth from him and unwrapped it curiously. Inside there was a knife in a sheath, and Arnulf pulled it out, dumbstruck. The handle was gilded with silver and shaped like a leaping wolf, and it was made so cleverly that the grip fit perfectly in his hand. The wolf's eyes were sparkling red stones and the blade was strong and as sharp as a cat's claw. Three flat amber beads adorned the sheath, and it touched Arnulf. It was a precious gift.

'Do you like it? The smith worked on it for six days!'

Arnulf nodded, blinking, 'Thank you, Toke.'

'You needed a knife. Do not swap this one for beer!'

Arnulf got up, turning the knife in his hand, 'Not even if it was Suttungr's mead! Serpenttooth will not be ashamed in its company, it is a worthy of a chieftain!'

'A chieftain?'

Toke looked out over the fjord, 'Stridbjørn's son should not carry inferior weapons, Arnulf. Perhaps the knife can help an exiled heir find himself a new kingdom, Freyr stand by you.'

Arnulf frowned and loosened his belt to attach the sheath to it, 'A fugitive wolf for a fleeing man!'

'No! An attacking wolf who will stop at nothing! The blade is in front of the wolf, not at its hocks!'

Arnulf spat at a thistle and pulled the sheath into place, 'Only the Norns know where my path is headed and they're not friendly towards me, but now I won't go knifeless to my grave like a thrall and with Helge's sword and your knife, perhaps I will win my luck. I shall cherish your life with both blades on the voyage if need be, so Stentor need not fear for his other hand.'

Toke smiled wryly, 'Stentor has never feared anything, and luck is every man's possession. Whatever your destiny, I am happy to sail with a Danish wolf, especially one that has Fenrir's power in his bites!'

*****

The evening the blót was to be held, a sharp wind swept down over the fjeld and forced the grass to bend in the village square. Dark, heavy clouds reflected ash-grey in the fjord, and Arnulf, freezing, pulled his cloak tightly around him and thought of the mild spring in Egilssund. Toste Skaldshield and Leif Cleftnose had sailed in with their people in the late afternoon, and Stentor, together with Toke and one of the elders, had selected the animals to be sacrificed. As this year's voyage was of greater importance than usual, they had captured three fine young animals: a white kid goat, a white colt and a white calf.

The women had prepared the feast, over a large cooking fire, on the edge of the square, and the children, full of anticipation, had excitedly followed all the preparations, eager to lend a hand.

Arnulf was alert for any snide remarks Leif Cleftnose would make at Toke's expense, but the Viking had behaved courteously upon his arrival and had shown Øystein's son nothing but the respect he deserved. Man's disputes must be laid to rest in the presence of the gods. Stentor's golden eye glowed strongly out from under his black curly hair. Today, Gyrith's father was radiating the godly force of the Æsir, and no one dared come near him or charge him unnecessarily.

Arnulf swept a ticklish hair from his face. If the wind held, *Twin Raven* would fly over the water at dawn. He gave up trying to control his

130

flowing tresses and shivered. The fjord folk were gathered in a large circle around the sacrificial stone, and the white sacrificial animals tripped uneasily over themselves, as they were bound to sturdy pegs, driven into the earth. Three splendid gilded weapons lay over the stone. Arnulf recognised Odin's spear, Tyr's sword and Thor's hammer. No one uttered a word, and Toke stood, waiting, his cape flowing, beside Toste Skaldshield and Leif Cleftnose.

A horn sounded with a strange trembling shake, and Stentor solemnly entered the sacred ground and slowly began to walk around the circle with a gold-gilded cup in his hand. He was dressed in a knee-length snow-white kyrtle and on his chest glistened a silver Thor's hammer the size of his hand. A short cloak of polar bear skins rested on his shoulders, and an unsheathed sacrificial knife hung from his belt. With his amber eye and dignified manner Stentor seemed like Odin himself, and the gothi's radiance was so strong that Arnulf shrank into himself as he walked by.

Toke bowed his head reverently when Stentor reached the sacrificial stone and turned his face to the north. He raised the cup above his head and in his deep voice, thundered, 'Hail Odin!'

His greeting was answered by the whole congregation, and Arnulf cried, his blood pulsing threw his veins, penetrating his cold limbs.

'Hail Thor!'

'Hail Thor!'

'Hail Tyr!'

'Hail Tyr!'

Stentor drank from the cup, which he then handed to Toke, and Arnulf saw Toke's hand trembling slightly as he took it. Øystein Ravenslayer had been the first to receive after Stentor at the last ritual sacrifice, and for Toke to claim his chiefly right in the face of the gods themselves required a strong heart. Gyrith clutched the edge of her mantle, her eyes bright as she watched her husband, and Toke drank and passed the cup to Leif, who handed it to Toste, the last. When it came back to Stentor, he poured the remainder of the contents over the weapons on the sacrificial stone, and Arnulf clasped his knife-handle like a pouncing wolf. The Æsir had disowned him, and it felt wrong to be so near the power of the sacrificial stone. Tonight the gods of war were hailed, and Fenrir was denied access to both the circle and the congregation, for Toke had drunk only on behalf of his village folk, not for Arnulf.

Stentor raised his arms, invoking the attention of the Æsir and praising their greatness and power. He remembered the dead, now in Odin's company, and after naming Øystein, he recalled the names of the other deceased. Many of those gathered in the square spoke softly to themselves; a member of each family stepped forward and placed a lit torch by the sacrificial stone. Hildegun lit the torch for Øystein and Toke carried it forward. The fire flickered in the wind, grasping for the people. Stentor placed the gilded weapons carefully on a red cloth, spread over the grass. Toke's face was deeply serious. Jofrid wept silently, though her eyes burned with defiance. Gyrith did not seem happy either.

Toste put a large vessel down at the sacrificial stone, and Stentor, laying the sacrificial knife out flat on his hand, held it up to the storm-threatening sky. In the distance, thunder rolled down from the fjeld and triggered an excited murmur. Thor himself was present, and with him, no doubt, Odin and Tyr! The blót was blessed and the young chieftain was acknowledged. It was a good omen!

Leif Cleftnose and Toste Skaldshield grabbed the white colt and laid it on the sacrificial stone, because despite Thor's thunderous greeting, it was Odin who had to have his sacrifice first. The colt fought back, in a manner unbecoming of the promising steed, and Arnulf felt sure that the Æsir's king would appreciate his gift. Toke forced the animal's head back with his good hand and kept its throat over the sacrificial vessel. Stentor cut, the blood splashed and the life drained slowly out of the colt, proving its power and Toke's lucky choice.

It pleased Arnulf that Toke helped perform the blót to the gods of war, even though on the knarr he said that he had only ever made offerings to Freyr before a voyage. Now the power of Thor would help him, and maybe he would even need Odin's ingenuity before the blót was over. After the foal, it was the turn of Thor's kid goat and Tyr's calf. They bleated and bellowed, and the great sacrificial vessel was filled to the brim with consecrated blood, and as they finished, Stentor broke out in song while he again raised his knife to the sky.

Arnulf shuddered and looked up at the dark clouds. The wind rose, tearing foam from the restless fjord. The gods had their offerings and seemed pleased with them. He took a deep breath. Only recently, at the spring blót in Egilssund, had Frejdis carried the blessed seeds around the fields. Dressed in green and bronze and with her long hair flowing, she had gone barefoot across the freshly ploughed soil and, humming, thrown a handful of grain on each family's field. No man's virility was left unaffected at the sight of her swaying hips, but it was Arnulf she had smiled to, and he had bowed deeply to Freya's gothi. The sun was shining, the birds were singing, and Rolf was laughing, drinking extract of elderflower instead of beer to pay homage to the goddess of love and encourage fertility.

Stentor proclaimed that anyone who intended to go a-viking next morning was now free to bring their weapons to the sacrificial stone and have them consecrated in the warm sacrificial blood, and many men in the circle drew their weapons and stepped forward. Arnulf looked down. As if Thor would bless Serpenttooth as long as it hung on the hip of a brother-killer! If the blood hit the blade, it would probably rust on the spot or turn as soft as a willow twig; no, if the sword should be blessed, Arnulf would have to do it himself!

He withdrew from the group and went to one of the great cooking fires on the edge of the square. Kneeling, he took out his knife and cleared a spot of grass. Then he scratched a standing wolf with bared teeth in the ground. Its back hair was raised, and its eyes were wide open, and although Gleipnir kept Fenrir bound in its powerful hold, the huge wolf stretched its muzzle to the sky and held its tail high in the air.

Arnulf looked contentedly at his work; the flickering fire cast its glow over the image. Fenrir should have an offering, and Serpenttooth be no less consecrated in deeds than the other Viking weapons. Arnulf stood up and slowly pulled the blade from its scabbard. Resolutely he rolled up the arm of his kyrtle and drew the blade over his white forearm. The blood poured down the sword and over the earthen wolf. The blade's painful kiss was ice cold and Arnulf clenched his hand firmly and watched as the ground hungrily soaked up his blood sacrifice. No cheers or great words were necessary for out on his storm-battered island, Fenrir raised his head with a jerk and felt his gift soaking the stones beneath him. A horrifying howl pierced the air and, twitching his tail, the wolf began to lick the rocky ground.

'What are you doing?'

Arnulf was startled as Leif Cleftnose struck his fist on his shoulder, and Serpenttooth cut him deeper in the arm than he intended. Arnulf broke loose angrily and faced the Viking, 'What am I doing? Surely you can see that, and you have no right to stop a free man in his deeds, like he was a presumptuous young thrall!'

He raised Serpenttooth threateningly and shook his sleeve over his bleeding arm. Leif stared at the bloody wolf, squinting narrowly in disgust, 'Are you standing here making a blood sacrifice to Fenrir? Have you lost your mind? Are you trying to invoke the god's anger on *Twin Raven's* journey and have us all end in misfortune?' his voice roared over the wind and over the square.

'I'll sacrifice to whom I will, Leif Cleftnose, and as I see it, you didn't pray well enough to the god's for their protection, since you lost the prettiest part of your nose and got your face torn to shreds! Mind your sacrifice, as I mind mine, and beware of stepping on my sacrifice, lest Fenrir lets you lose a foot in the next sword fight!'

The words seemed to hit Leif hard, for his eyes caught fire, 'You miserable swine-louse!'

He was red with rage and saliva sputtered from his mouth, 'Gungnir pierce me if we do not see what Odin thinks of my next offering! If he accepts thralls, he will probably also accept brazen Danes, even if they are as poor as skrælings!'

He lifted his broad-bladed axe, still dripping with sacrificial blood, and Arnulf jumped back a step and rocked, ready.

'What is going on here?'

Stentor's voice froze Arnulf in his attack, and Leif, unwillingly, forced his arms down, 'Helge Womanshamer's brother, that killer-rat, is annulling the entire sacrifice and bringing misfortune on the voyage and fjord!'

He pointed furiously at the red wolf image, scratched in the earth, and Stentor frowned at Fenrir and gazed unfathomably at Arnulf. Arnulf was panting, mouth open and did not lower the sword. The nearest Northmen broke away from the circle and, worried, gathered around the conflict.

'I have said before what the gods think of bloodshed on sacred, peaceful ground,' said Stentor slowly. 'And I do not think anyone should interfere in Toke's guest's doings. Everyone has the right to offer what he thinks will be of most benefit, and those who do not agree must look the other way.'

'But he mocks Odin himself,' cried Leif incensed. 'He brings jötnar and malicious curses near the consecrated stone of the Æsir!'

Stentor shook his head, 'Arnulf stepped out of the circle and the congregation to sacrifice alone, and Tyr, who you just now sacrificed to, fears not Fenrir. As long as they both watch over Twin Raven's voyage, Tyr will be the strongest and will not let the wolf so much as scratch the seafarers. Put your trust only in him, but Arnulf, you must give me your word that you will not invoke Fenrir again in our presence, and next time make your sacrifices out of sight, lest the fjord folk turn against you!'

Arnulf bowed his head, and Leif snorted, 'Turn? They have turned! And if you hold your life dear Stridbjørnson, then disappear into the fjeld tonight and never return!'

He swung the axe over his head and planted the blade deep into the bloody wolf image, 'Now Fiendslayer has tasted your blood, Dane, and will not rest until it has beaten the life out of your body!'

Leif Cleftnose tugged the axe head loose, 'Seldom have I had to give a warning twice to make myself understood, but you are as thick-skulled as an Icelandic horned-sheep! Beware!'

He turned his back to Arnulf and made his way between the people. Arnulf slowly lowered Serpenttooth. Leif's outburst had not shaken him, but the indignation smarted. The gashed earth wolf was no longer alive, and the colour was draining from it.

'I'm sorry, Stentor.'

Arnulf did not wish to awaken the gothi's anger, and Stentor nodded curtly, 'You must like treading on sharp stones, Arnulf, but as long as you leave the Midgard Serpent, Jörmungandr, in peace in his watery calm, the *Twin Raven*'s crew will not come to harm, but from that which they bring upon themselves. But it is a poor housecarl who wounds himself the day before he has pledged his sword to another man's protection.'

'It's just a scratch!'

Arnulf's cheeks were hot. His sleeve was getting soaked. Stentor raised one eyebrow and quickly left him to continue performing the sacrifice in front of the waiting people. The surrounding people withdrew and followed him. Now was the time for making personal sacrifices at the sacrificial stone if anyone wanted to ask a chosen god for a special favour. Toke would undoubtedly bring a gift to Freyr, and afterwards Stentor would pass the speaker's stick around, giving those that wanted to the right to share what was in their hearts or pay tribute to the Æsir with proud, strong words.

Arnulf sheathed Serpenttooth. He no longer wanted to participate in the ritual, not even if the widdershins walk in the square and a last touch of the sacrificial stone blessed those in attendance. It was hard to share a feast with the village folk as the only foreigner in the fjord, disowned by his gods and countrymen.

Arnulf walked towards the strand in the deepening dusk, while he pressed his arm to his side to stop the cut from bleeding. Here, far from the bonfire and people, the bitterly cold wind stiffened his fingers and blew under his cloak and kyrtle, making him shiver and hunch his shoulders. To Helheim with Leif Cleftnose! To Helheim with all those who thought themselves the better judge of what he undertook! As if he were an unclean suckling-baby to be rebuked by others! At dawn he would embark a Viking! At dawn he would finally prove his courage and his perseverance and be taken seriously as a man! Years of yearning would finally be realised. Toke had even, with cheerful expectations, given him three good shields, iron-rimmed and with shiny shield bosses. Arnulf had painted them black, and to intimidate the enemy had decorated them with menacing wolf heads and entwined bodies in crimson. The most beautiful was sitting firmly on *Twin Raven's* shield rim, waiting in the windy darkness for the dawning of the day, the great day!

Arnulf arrived down to the mighty longship and leaned against the bow as he patted the colourful planks. Its soaring raven heads gazed out over the choppy fjord, and he could feel their silent, longing cry for the voyage and feats in the hull. Soon, soon the iron-clad bow would plough the cold water and wrestle against the wind and the high seas. Arnulf leaned his head intimately against the proud sea stallion. At dawn!

*****

The wind held overnight but the morning revealed clear skies. The fjord rippled like the skin on a harrowed horse, and the air was fresh and salty. *Twin Raven* lay, rocking against the jetty, packed with weapons and supplies, its strong colours shining in the sun under the two-headed bird, which was red from the sacrificial blood Stentor had poured over it.

Arnulf tossed the hair from his forehead. He stood close to the longship with a hand on Serpenttooth's pommel, his heart pounding so the sand vibrated under the soles of his feet. At dawn, some snekkes had sailed in with men and goods from the rest of the fjord, and the whole village had come out and were gathered on the narrow, sandy strand, their many faces expressing both joy and sadness at the parting. Stentor, having placed his gothi clothes, trotted back and forth ordering the thralls around, and ensuring the remaining water and beer barrels were rolled aboard and lashed with ropes. *Twin Raven* was expertly trimmed so ballast and Vikings were evenly weighted, and Leif Cleftnose was satisfied with his allotted place under the twin raven-heads, for he thought it entirely reasonable that the strongest man should sit closer to danger.

Toke and Gyrith's embrace was drawing out, and Hildegun bravely held back her tears as she clenched the splendid red cloak in her hands. The wind played with her short hair, and Jofrid, sitting on an upturned boat, wept openly over her brother's departure.

Arnulf took a deep breath and enjoyed the breeze. He had had trouble falling asleep the night before, but Helge came riding to him about midnight on a pitch-black horse wearing his helmet and chainmail. He had his arm again and a new sword adorned his hip, and never had he seemed stronger and more authoritative. He did not say anything, only smiled broadly and regarded Arnulf while the horse stomped, but when he reached out to grasp his arm, seawater come flooding in like a river in between them, and Helge had disappeared. The vision brought Arnulf deep peace, and he had slept heavily till dawn. Helge was with him, and his brother had not denounced him but had rather seemed proud of his quest. The dream was the good omen that neither Stridbjørn nor the gods had given before his first voyage a-viking.

Arnulf was so light and free that if he had jumped, the wind would have carried him to the highest fjeld. His blood bubbled and his fingers tingled as Fenrir's hot tongue licked the sore on his arm. Helge's proud smile flickered into his mind, and the eagle flapped in his stomach. Today he would stretch his wings, today the wolf in his name was silent and lay flat on the ground, for today was the sea eagle's day!

Though he was a stranger, Arnulf looked at the fjord folk with great affection. His gaze stopped at Jofrid, huddled careworn on the boat with one hand on her lower back, and he grinned. To think he had feared her sorcery! How foolish! Jofrid was just one of the many assembled sisters, and she was suffering with Helge's growing child, who was drawing on her life force.

The redheaded blacksmith nodded to Arnulf as he passed, and Toke wrenched himself free from Gyrith's embrace. Hildegun walked over and put the cloak around his shoulders. It fluttered so the silver threads glittered and Toke took Ranvig on his hip and hugged his little girl tenderly. He passed her to Gyrith and Hildegun threw her arms around her son. She had chosen skilfully from Øystein Ravenslayer's plundered silver from last year and had sent a man to the armoursmith on Bjørnenæs to commission chainmail for Toke. Now it lay, wrapped in leather, under the thwarts at the helm. Hildegun seemed to put more trust in that than in the god's favour. She would not lose her son.

A handful of elated young men approached Arnulf and stomped impatiently around in the sand. They stood before their first Viking raid voyage and could hardly wait for Toke to allow them to go aboard and set sail on *Twin Raven*. Leif and Toste, being experienced, distributed the thwarts among the men. Arnulf turned to face the wind and closed his eyes. Behind the joy and the roars, a thorn stung nastily in his side, and he secretly imagined that it was his own village folk of Egilssund he could hear laughing and shouting. Stridbjørn had just put his hands on his shoulders, and Trud wished him a happy journey, while Helge stood aside, allowing the ship to be manned, with a shiny spear in his hand. Frejdis' tears soaked his kyrtle; he could still taste her. Frejdis! Frejdis with her warm skin, her soft hair and her round arousing hips. Frejdis whose embrace put Freya to shame and whose shine cast a shadow over Valhalla's.

'Are you ready, Arnulf Stridbjørnson?'

Stentor stroked his curly black beard, his golden eye shining brightly at Gyrith, who was by Toke's side. Arnulf nodded, solemnly, 'Yes!'

'Good! He who has few goodbyes is fortunate, for his companions are travelling with him.'

He sent Arnulf a knowing glance but said nothing more for Toke started walking towards *Twin Raven* with long strides as he threw out his arm, and everyone's attention was directed to him, 'Let each man take his place, and set the ship free! The wind is good, and Njord at ease, so we should not hesitate any longer!'

The young men greeted his words with enthusiastic shouts, and Arnulf went with Stentor to begin loosening the tight mooring ropes. Toke threw his cloak behind his shoulders and was the first to go aboard, the Vikings followed by position and reputation. Thwarts from the mast fish's head to the bow were assigned to Leif Cleftnose's men, while Toke's men took those in the aft and Toste's companions, those amidships.

Arnulf waited to the last and solemnly let his feet take leave of the jetty's wooden planks. He jumped down on the full deck and climbed over the thwarts and chests to reach the furthest port thwart that Toke had intended for him. Stentor was sitting right in front of Arnulf, and Toste Skaldshield, having left his village folk around the mast, sat on a thwart facing them in *Twin Raven's* starboard side. Toke wanted his most reliable companions close to him at the helm. Arnulf moved his sword's scabbard aside and sat down. In the chest under his thwart, the clothes Hildegun had given him were carefully packed, and better clothes, he had never owned. Stentor secured his shield to the shield rim and fixed his cloak, while Toke stood with one hand on the mast and ensured everyone was where they should be. Gyrith ran into the water with Ranvig on her hip to be near Toke for as long as possible. She smiled as her tears ran, and Hildegun, standing with her arm around Jofrid, was tight-lipped and only had eyes for her son.

The last rope was released from the pilings, and Toke raised his arm, 'Set sail and set out!'

The large woollen sail was freed, and the wind immediately grabbed the yellow square and gave the black sewn-on raven air under its outstretched wings. *Twin Raven* broke away with a start, sliding away from its berth, as the youngest Vikings waved a boisterous goodbye to their kinsmen in the village. Arnulf took a deep breath as a wild trembling took hold of his body. Here and now he was setting out! Now he would be a Viking and leave boyhood behind! Now Arnulf Stridbjørnson would wield Serpenttooth on this bold voyage, everything lay in wait, everything could be won! He would scream his youth and manhood out, shaking the mountains as though he were an invincible stallion, and throw himself out over the stormy waters on flaming wings, for now he was setting out and everyone should know it!

The village folk waved back to the young warriors, and overwhelming joy invoked a hearty war cry from Toke's crew. Toke ought to quieten them, ought to shout a farewell to his people of words that would be remembered, and take manly control of the voyage and the battle fortune, but he stood silently at the mast, his splendid red cloak billowing around his legs. Instead the air rang with cries and wishes for great deeds back and forth over the water until the wind intervened and swept the voices away, and the village and valley waned into the distance.

Stentor had taken the helm from his chieftain, as Toke did not seem to be able to move, as long as Gyrith stood with Ranvig waving, in the shallow water. Arnulf clenched his hand around King Sweyn's gold ring and caught himself smiling. He would do Helge proud on this voyage! If ever they should meet and grasp forearms in Valhalla, Helge would laugh and punch him on the shoulder, acknowledging his little brother as his equal. He would show him to the Einherjar and proudly tell of Arnulf's deeds, and if he did well, Arnulf would return the gold skald's ring to him.

Twin Raven flew towards the fjord's first bend, and all on board looked back one last time except Arnulf, who looked at Toke. The Northman's gaze burned so fiercely at Gyrith that it was only now that Arnulf realised, just how unwilling Toke was to go. His face was contorted, his hand white on the mast, and when *Twin Raven* turned cruelly on the water, making Gyrith disappeared and Toke's eyes found Arnulf. In that moment, his despair was exposed, but he gathered himself together, and Arnulf swore with a wordless nod not to reveal his pain. A great man could not appear weak, and Toke safeguarded not only himself but his family and heirs by keeping the chiefdom.

The sail was set and Toke, tossing his head defiantly, took his place at the helm. Stentor gave his shoulder a squeeze, as he stood up: 'You will see her again soon. Time is rarely slow on a plundering voyage and summer is short.'

Toke sat down and grabbed the helm with an appraising glance at the sail's angle, 'She is with child again, Stentor.'

Stentor froze with his leg half over his thwart, and Arnulf laughed and turned to jab his friend in the chest. Toke had probably sacrificed more to Freyr on the fjeld than animals and blood, and with such a beautiful wife as Gyrith, the Northman had apparently not allowed himself to be hindered by an injured arm. Toke's lips trembled, but then a proud smile broke through that relieved his despondency, while Stentor slumped heavily into his seat. Those sitting in front turned to hear more, and the rumour reached the mast before Stentor could answer, 'With child again? Are you sure? And here I thought you were lying on your sickbed!'

He broke into a loud laugh and slapped his hand on his thigh, as many congratulations were shouted across the thwarts.

'Never begat a man with his arm, and Gyrith could feel it as soon as it happened. She did it with Ranvig, too.'

Toke beamed with joy and let the ship follow the vertical rock faces around another bend. Arnulf shook his head cheerfully, 'I told you, you would feel better as soon as you saw Gyrith, and I was more than right! You can store your runes safely for another time, Stentor, your daughter's power overshadows Odin!'

'As the puppy barks! Respect is more often forgotten by young blood than old but remember that over-confidence is punished by the gods!' bit Stentor again, but he did not look angry.

A youth at the bow shouted as Toste Skaldshield's village came into view, the banks swarming with people. The Midfjord Vikings were hailed by those remaining on the strand, but the last farewell was brief, for *Twin Raven* rocked eagerly forward. Leif Cleftnose's village folk also stood at the water, their cries not meagre.

The sea stallion danced on the outer fjord and threw its chest into the good-sized waves, and Arnulf sniffed the smell of wild water, glaring fiercely at the waves. Intoxicated, he was intoxicated and erect as an earl at the sight of the sixty resolute Northmen in front of him, who were ready to brave the wind and venture out without blinking. Better Vikings could no helmsman have, and he sat closest to Toke! Housecarl, he was a housecarl to the death, and he could not perform that deed soon enough.

Toste, at his side, seemed to also be affected by intoxication, for he stretched his arms over the vast sea, and shouted hoarsely, 'Words! Words! Who will give words to so proud a moment? Miserable it is if Haraldsfjord must see its sons off silently!'

'I will!' Arnulf rose, his mind ignited, 'I'll give verses for those who want to listen, poor heir of the fjord that I am!'

He set a foot on the thwart in front of him, clasping Serpenttooth's pommel, his other hand grabbed the spring wind by its strands. Shining eyes looked at him expectantly. Suttungr's mead flowed in his veins, but the strongest sound was the echo of Frejdis' laughter from the south. Arnulf's voice tamed the sea:

Rider of the fjeld
Fairest fjord son
On green grass path
The gelding grazes
Believe in your companion
Trust your kinsman
But most in yourself
Bear betrayal, corpses abound!

Good fortunes you win
Favour the fair
For victory and valour
Venture your quest
To pilfer and plunder
Prizes attest
Boldly you fight
Bent on your feats

The Norns' spools
Spin shimmering
With unbreakable bonds
The fates constrain
Wise One-Eye chooses
Housecarls from clashes
But the warrior himself
Swings his sword in hand!

Rider of the sea
White horse rider
Sharp-bowed skeid
Sets his sail
Mighty wings

Fierce venture glory
Fears neither voyage
Nor dark-minded curse!

Kings know you
Women desire you
Deeds skalds recall
Revered in halls
Runes encircle
Enchantment enfolds
To the stones' cry
Heroes reply

Odin the Great
Your Einherjar greet
Mead flows once more
Behind glorious doors
Kith and kin honour you
Remember the elders
Proudly your sons
Recall your repute!

'Well performed,' cried Toste excited. 'Now I need a beer, for such good verses deserve a toast! Woe to you, Arnulf Skaldtongue, for I will not give you a moment's peace, for as long as *Twin Raven* sails your verses must shorten my journey!'

Laughing, Toke released the helm and grabbed out after Arnulf's hand, as appreciative shouts thronged the deck. Only Leif shouted that Northmen knew how to sing for themselves and did not need the words of a Dane on their departure, but no one seemed to listen, and Arnulf did not pay him any heed.

'So bold a son I would not push away from me regardless of his guilt!' stated Stentor, as Arnulf sat down, and Toke thought Arnulf should abandon Fenrir and stick rather to Bragi, as they had to be close to each other in family.

Arnulf pressed the tip of his thumb against King Sweyn's gold ring, pleased with himself, and the Outerfjord Vikings in the foreship broke into a rambling song about Gunbjørn Stonefoot's ice-sea's voyage while Leif challengingly beat time with his wooden scabbard.

All morning *Twin Raven* stroked along the Norwegian coast like a low-flying sea gull, but towards noon the wind blew stronger and more unpredictably, and strong gusts of wind drove water between the suspended shields and over the deck. The longship was spirited between the sharp islands and reefs, and Toke sailed the ship further offshore and had a tough job holding course.

Leif passed more than one comment about the navigation and believed himself to have better advice for the steering, and the beautiful coastline that Arnulf had admired during his voyage to Haraldsfjord now bared its teeth, seeking the afterlife for the thin hull. The wind turned so it was now in front of the sea stallion and Toke had to constantly veer the vessel to cross against the weather. It cost him a lot of strength to hold the helm with one hand, and the sail was tough for the men to turn. Arnulf was sitting too far from the ropes to help, but he could see Toke sweating.

'If you have thought of veering for the rest of the day, we might as well put in now, for we have yet to get anywhere!' cried Leif Cleftnose from the bow. 'Øystein Ravenslayer was never afraid to tack in fresh winds. You let far too much wind out of the sail by slackening the ropes as you do.'

'What Øystein did earned him credit,' returned Toke with a forced calm. 'I prefer safe sailing rather than daring, and we risk capsizing from gusts of wind with too tense a wing. If you are unsatisfied, I can put you off anywhere you want, then you might find your next ship's passage on a bolder vessel!'

Leif threw out his arms, resignedly, and spat into the water, but he was silent, and Toste asked Toke for permission to take over the helm for a little while, as he was so stiff from sitting still for long.

*****

The day did not bring *Twin Raven* far from Haraldsfjord, but the next day was better, although the wind pushed the ship towards the coast as soon as Toke was not watching like a hawk.

Arnulf performed several of his own songs for Toste, whose ability to memorise words was amazing, and Stentor and Toke talked much about what name would bring Gyrith's next child most luck. If it were a son, Toke thought he should be named after Øystein or Sigtryg, but Stentor said that the Æsir should be consulted by throwing the runes and that good fortune is not always passed down with a name.

In the afternoon, the wind quietened, and a heavy rain swaddled the sea and coastal fjelds in a damp cape. Arnulf got his tallow-treated leather clothes out of his chest, and the atmosphere on board eased considerably. Rainwater had to be regularly bailed out the ship, the bread was soft before it was to be eaten and the men's well-cared for warrior beards seemed thin and sloppy.

Toke let the little mead barrel go around, and Toste spoke loudly of foreign women's lust after the embrace of Freyr's sons and about wealthy earldoms and the gold of White Christ's worshippers, but the mood was not cheerful anyway.

When evening came, the rain did not let up in the least, and Arnulf was clammy and had had enough of the grey-waves and rain-driven fjelds that he was relieved when the longship headed for land. The tents were erected in the shelter of a thicket, and the food was eaten cold, but shortly before dawn the clouds drifted away, and the wind dropped. The day proved to be surprisingly warm and *Twin Raven* splashed gently away, barely faster than it could be rowed by the men. The wet clothes were hung out to dry, and Toke stopped a fishing boat and bought fresh fish for dinner, while Toste found a gaming board and pieces and challenged Stentor to play Hares and Hounds.

Arnulf pulled his outer kyrtle off and watched; Stentor was an ingenious hare for Toste, which was one not easily defined by the hounds. Arnulf believed that Toste guarded his back line jealously and should make bolder moves but Toste knew Stentor's hare play too well to be fooled and ended in pushing him into a corner. The pieces were exchanged, and Toste vowed to run behind Stentor's dogs, but Toke laughed that he had only succeeded three times during the whole of the last summer, for Stentor kept his pack together like the leading wolf.

Arnulf leaned on the shield rim. The sun poked through his eyelids and he needed the warmth after the cold and wind of the last day and it could be felt clearly that the journey had turned south.

He had played Hares and Hounds, too. With Frejdis. They had been lying in the tall grass on the strand meadow, and he had let her win one time after the other while he had enjoyed her face and shining eyes. She was barefoot and kicked with naked legs, and Arnulf's spear had swelled, hot and throbbing, against the flattened grass under him. They had agreed that the next winner could make a claim against the loser, and afterwards Frejdis, laughing, had to remove her shift and let her whole body be tiddled with poppies, until the petals fell off them.

Arnulf pressed his knuckles against his forehead and felt it grow under his belt. He had twisted buttercups into her hair. First, he had tried to make a wreath but had then attached them into her yellow locks, one by one. Many of them. Many, indeed. Yet they had all fallen out, to Freya's honour, so vehemently had they embraced in her name.

*****

The evening before the big sail over the open sea, Toke put *Twin Raven* into a shallow fjord, and the Northmen camped on the bare sandy strand. Arnulf was restless after sitting quietly in the ship all day, and the thought of the vast water that had to be crossed made him change position more than once by the fire. Out there, far from the coast, great storms were whipping waves up to tree height and, even though, considering the season, they should have subsided, it was always risky to cross the domain of Jörmungandr. He remembered, with painful clarity, reports of ships that had not returned, and of seafaring men's vain attempts to save their unfortunate fellows who had been washed overboard.

Toke did not seem to worry but sat on his sleeping skin, picking his teeth, while staring distantly into the fire, and Stentor painstakingly combed his wind-tangled beard with a carved bone comb. Toste Skaldshield threw himself into the story of Tore Shieldbiter's single combat in Iceland, but Arnulf was too caught up in his own journey to listen. Questions persisted, and he missed Helge, who had known so much about the world outside of Egilssund and foreign people's customs and traditions, 'Tell me, Stentor, is it true that there are no Christians in Norway?'

Arnulf needed to talk. Toke broke away from his reverie and Stentor, growling, slowly pulled beard hair out of his comb, 'True and true, there are probably some, but thanks to earl Hakon no Northman has been forced from his ancestral faith, as has happened in many places in Denmark.'

'Not with us in Egilssund.'

Arnulf smiled proudly, 'Stridbjørn has never let a Christian be a guest of the village but Helge knew many and did not view them as lesser men. Once he even let himself be falsely baptised and then swapped his christening robe for beer for his ship companions. We got a lot of amusement from it.'

145

Toke laughed, and Stentor carefully shared his hair, 'I consider them to be curious men, curious and cruel. Not those traders, who for peace and earnings, wear crosses around their necks, no, the worst are those who settle together in monasteries and truly commit to the life of White Christ.'

Arnulf flung himself in the sand on his elbow, 'Why cruel? The Christians I have met on Gormsø don't behave very differently to others.'

The gothi spat into the fire, 'King Harald gave them the choice between baptism and the sword, so I wonder how deep their new faith sticks? His death pleased me immensely, and King Sweyn looks more kindly upon Odin. Some say outright that he might wear a cross outside his kyrtle, but he wears a hammer against his skin.'

Arnulf shook his head, 'Sweyn professes his belief in White Christ but otherwise doesn't interfere much in the village's faith, so Stridbjørn can have as many blóts as he wants, and our king is not cruel!'

'Probably not.'

Stentor blew a lock aside, 'But the staunch Christians and monastic monks hold the most abhorrent rituals during which they eat their god and drink his blood.'

Arnulf sat up, grimacing in disgust, 'I have never understood why!'

Toke shook his head in amazement, 'Christian worshippers say the White Christ himself ordered them to do it. Man-flesh eaters that is what they are. Even starving thralls do not exhibit such shameful behaviour in the winter.'

'Yuk!' Arnulf dug his fingers into the sand. 'They are equal to scavengers! Do you think the bloody deed strengthens their solidarity? Helge said that Christians living in monasteries live without women like the warriors in Jomsborg. But Jomsvikings live without women to safeguard their brotherhood and warrior strength.'

Toke smiled, 'Comparing monks with Jomsvikings is like comparing rats with bulls! More magnificent warriors than those from Jomsborg do not exist, and woe to them who meets them! The monks are pitiful scraps and ugly, too. They cut their hair short on the top of their heads, so they look like decrepit old men, kneeling time and again for their wooden cross, like the unfree do for great men.'

'Imagine worshipping a god you cannot meet standing with raised eyes!' Arnulf snorted, and Stentor nodded, black curls in his eyes. 'Cowardice is their virtue and pride they consider to be a sin. Weak are those without manhood, and very greedy their God, for he demands maximum wealth in his presence and lets his worshippers adorn themselves in thrall's shifts. Killing is against White Christ's will, therefore they do not defend their treasures with weapons. When the Vikings plunder, they throw incantations, but not once has it helped them against Tyr's warriors.'

Arnulf crushed a mussel shell, 'Men that only have one god and mock a woman's embrace will become extinct.'

Toke threw a log on the fire so sparks flew and flicked one of them off his arm, 'Without a doubt. Therefore, it is important to plunder monasteries as long as they are there.'

'Now you're talking!'

Stentor snorted, displeased, 'A good deed is to cut the heads off monks as often as you can for the strife and the divisions the Christians have brought with them, forcing good men to betray the gods of their heritage or flee from where they settle. White Christ talks about peace and many a proud Northerner has gotten peace from his followers and that with a sword throughout life! Has one man ever been killed because he did not honour Odin? Not one! No, Arnulf, Christians are cruel, not even women and children do they leave free!'

Thoughtful, Arnulf threw a stone in the water, 'I still don't understand the meaning of men living alone if it is not to train courage, skill and the use of arms like in Jomsborg. And what do the Christians do when their god doesn't hear their cries, and they can't sacrifice to another? Only a fool lets a single god decide his fate!'

Stentor stuck his comb into his belt pouch, 'White Christ is the weapon of hostile kings against Odin's chosen folk and therefore his worshippers need to be shunned like disease and crushed like lice, in my opinion. Do not worry so much, Arnulf. Use them to train your strikes and lighten them for as much silver as you can so they have a single justification for putting their dirty feet on Midgard, but do not try to understand why they do what they do, and now let us rest. Tyr loves the brave but renounces the reckless and it is foolish to shorten an important night's sleep with talk.'

He sent Arnulf and Toke a gothi look, reaching for his sleeping skins, and Arnulf crept obediently into his, but the conversation had not brought him peace. He had ants of excitement under his kyrtle and he stared up at the darkening sky. Strange men, the Christian worshippers, but despite his disgust he had to admit that he, like they, had only one god to stick to. Although Fenrir was unbeatable, Tyr had not feared it. Perhaps White Christ was the strongest of the gods to the south and, in that case, it was probably not wrong of his worshippers to hold him in such high honour. Odin was king of the Æsir, but he was changeable, and the favour he bestowed upon a warrior one night, he took from him the next.

'If you do not close your eyes, you will never fall asleep!'

Toke lay down next to Arnulf and gently pulled his bad arm to his side.

'I've never crossed such a big ocean before.'

'*Twin Raven* has many times and I with it.'

Toke yawned, 'If the wind is good, there will be nothing to make verses about.'

'And if not?'

Toke snorted, resting his head on the skin, 'Then there will certainly be nothing to sing about, as there will not be anyone to perform it afterwards, but there is no reason to worry. Odin calms the waters for those who seek his enemies for life, and Stentor has sworn by the oath ring to cut down every Christian worshipper he can, and so, my faithful housecarl, good night and think no more!'

*****

Arnulf woke up in the earliest dawn and thought he was definitely the first to be rid of sleep, but Toke was already up. He stood, a little away, at the water's edge, staring out to sea while he touched his arm. Arnulf wriggled free of his sleeping skin and went to him and Toke nodded without breaking his stare and carefully lifted his arm. He seemed uneasy and Arnulf shook sand out of his hair and blew his nose. The fires had burned down, and the morning wind gusted uncomfortably about his sleep-warm skin. *Twin Raven* looked dark and colourless and the sea, bottomless.

'I am afraid, Arnulf.'

Toke sighed and Arnulf glanced at him as he pushed a stranded jellyfish, 'You weren't yesterday.'

The Northman let his arm hang, 'No, nor all the times Øystein was responsible for steering the ship.'

Arnulf shuddered and sucked air between his teeth, 'What do you think about the wind?'

Toke shook his head, 'It is strong. There are waves when the land shelters us no more, but *Twin Raven* can clear them. We endured a storm there three years ago.'

Arnulf let Odin's spear taste dawn and aimed for the jellyfish, and some men began to stir the embers. He was not afraid himself. His body tingled and gripped, but it was not fear.

Leif Cleftnose tumbled out from his sleeping skin and came stomping over to them. He stretched, yawned and fastened his belt without paying Arnulf any notice, 'A fresh breeze, Øysteinson. Maybe we can make the crossing in less than two days.'

He squinted narrowly and watched the grey sky, while his nails scratched his kyrtle, 'It will barely be hard, see the birds. They are daring to fly out today.'

'Leif!'

Toke looked firmly at him, 'Would you trade places with Hafr from Hornsdale? I would like you to sit with me. If the sea is high, I will need the best men I have, and it is not safe to change seats once it is rocking.'

Arnulf looked surprised from Toke to the Cleftnose. Leif's face did not reveal what he was thinking, but he gave Toke a long look. To put their own disputes aside in order to take responsibility for a perilous voyage was praiseworthy, and Toke did not let his pride overshadow his reason. Leif had to be, undeniably, one of the best sailors in Haraldsfjord, and his help could prove necessary. He nodded appreciatively, and Toke nodded again, 'Thank you. Let us awaken the others.'

He turned around in the sand, and Leif Cleftnose silently smoothed his lush beard. However little Arnulf cared for him, he had to credit the Viking that he knew when a truce had to go before his own desire for gain.

Arnulf wanted to go after Toke, but Leif stopped him with a sharp glance, 'I can sit with Toke Øysteinson, for he will possibly become my equal if his beard manages to grow, but you are not worth more than a heap of pig dung and that is a stench that is hard to endure!'

Arnulf was flaming from indignation and bit his jaws together so it trembled by his ears. He stared into the sand to control himself and then looked up with a suppressed snarl, 'My blood is not inferior to Toke's, and for his sake I'd beware of my killing desire, Leif! But there is nothing wrong with my arm! Remember that as soon as we set foot on land again.'

Leif snorted contemptuously, 'Your blood is goat piss, and your arm is not so thick than that I cannot break it with my thumb! Shut up and live and be a good dog for your master or come on and find your death on the other side of the sea, but it will not be pretty!'

Serpenttooth flew out its sheath, but Leif turned his back and went, whistling, towards the awakening men while he stroked his fingers over the edge of his axe. Arnulf threw his sword from him with a roar and cast stones in the water, hard and long, while his wheezing caused his eyes to glisten. That boastful, louse-infested fjord-tick! He should squeeze the tallow out of him and strangle him in his own filth! How dare Leif yap at him like another rotten sea gull, the son of a thrall bitch!

The stones cracked down in the waves, beating upon the sea jötunn's scales, but nothing could worry Arnulf less! The Cleftnose could just wait, so he could! When Arnulf was finished with him, his nose would be the most beautiful part of him, by Fenrir!

*****

Breakfast was eaten quickly, and when the sun momentarily shot its glowing back in between the woolly fjeld clouds, Toke ordered the ship be pushed into the sea. Arnulf walked heavily on the sand as he followed Stentor up the gangway plank, for it would be some time before his feet tasted solid ground again. Leif Cleftnose sat down in front of Toste in Hafr's place, and the sail was set and grabbed the wind immediately.

Toke steered right out onto open sea, and Arnulf took leave of the fjeld country and followed the receding coast with his eyes. Surprisingly quickly, the steep fjeld sides became insignificant hills, and the vaults of heaven seemed to expand, pushing land and islands away. It breathed in the depths below *Twin Raven*, and the mood among the men was serious. No one broke the silence, as if they had made a wordless pact to sneak over the waterway as unobtrusively as possible, and Toke sat erect and grim on his thwart, ready to face whatever might come.

Arnulf sniffed the sea air and looked at Leif's broad back in front of Toste. The Viking's hanging hand was stringy, and sword bitten, testifying to a life spent as a warrior. Arnulf's gaze bore into his neck, but since it did not seem to do Leif any harm, he began to look for the narrow strip of land on the horizon behind them. Helge had told him about the great sea crossings, about how he found the way by following the path of the sun and stellar patterns, but also by keeping an eye on the flight of birds and the forms of the clouds, the drifting seaweed and the movement of the waves. The cold could be a bad opponent, so it was important to keep dry and eat plenty. When the body first becomes cold, the limbs weaken and actions become slow and that which otherwise seems easy, can seem insurmountable, the will would seem to seep into the water. Once Helge had made a winter sailing that had nearly cost him his toes.

Arnulf was not cold, but he did not find any of the signs Helge had talked about. The sailing was smooth and since no powers of the sea let themselves be distracted by *Twin Raven's* cleaved keel, the Northmen thawed, and their tongues loosened. The clouds held over the fjeld and,

150

like the waves, were huge; the sky cleared up, and the wind's pull on the sail was good. Sun and wind made the hunger sharp, and Arnulf helped himself when the food bag was passed around. The wind's rush in his hair elated him, and with Toke's experience and Stentor's godly favour, worrying was unnecessary. The skaldic verse about Holger Bullstrength's bear hunting clang in his inner ear, and Arnulf wanted to stand fully erect in the bow, riding the waves with his feet. Toke smiled and remarked that he had never before seen a man use so much effort to sit still, but Stentor remembered a long-limbed lad who had once been bound by the legs to a thwart because of his turmoil, 'I remember it, for I myself tied the rope. At that time, I had two hands.'

Twin Raven seemed to know the way over the wave ridges, and Toke regularly let his companions take the helm, and towards evening gave it to Leif, even though he immediately turned their course more southerly. Toke was against it, because he believed that that crossing was longer and that the direct route towards land was preferable.

'So, we just hit the Orkney Islands, and there is not much to be gained on those stones,' growled Leif, grudgingly, and held the helm firmly as he had set it.

'Possibly, but landfall is better than a wild-water voyage, and mutton from Orkney provides good looting strength.'

Leif spat into the water and held his own, 'A stone's throw too northerly and a little morning mist, then we go straight through Orkney and Shetland. Ask the men here if any of them have errands on the Faroe Islands! Øystein would never ...'

He met Toke's gaze, and none of them said more to each other, but Leif drew a finger width at the helm, and Toke muttered to Toste that he would sleep early and should be awakened by midnight.

Arnulf had difficulty finding peace between the thwarts when darkness fell, and the deck was so hard that soft sleeping skins made no difference to his comfort. The waves struck teasingly sideways on the ship, and Arnulf felt sure that his head was more downward than upward and was not used to it.

The crew slept in shifts, and Arnulf wondered how Toke could snore, as he lay on spring-thick sheep furs. The Northman had wrapped a leg-swathe about his bad arm to alleviate the ship's rolling, but a low wail escaped from him now and then, as the longship quarrelled with the sea. Arnulf pulled the sleep skin up to his ears and realised that there probably would not be much rest on the first night at sea. Leif Cleftnose seemed to feel suited to the helm and sat humming various stanzas in his beard, but

Stentor kept an eye on him, despite apparently sitting half asleep up against the boards. The amber eye glittered narrowly behind the black curls and secured Toke one dangerless sleep, and Arnulf lay under the gothi's protection and closed his eyes for shame's sake. If nothing else, he would lie and make a poem for Frejdis. A skaldic verse about the wind's song and the waves' glistening and Fenrir's howl over the sea, Bragi alone knew whether or not she would ever hear it.

*****

The night battered his body almost as sore and stiff as Rolf's fists had done that fateful night in Egilssund. The sea was high in the morning twilight, and it was uncomfortable to be thrown around when sleep was still sitting in his limbs. Arnulf's stomach felt weirdly nauseated, and water leaked in between the suspended shields. He sat up queasily and let the cold morning wind attack his hair.

Stentor held the helm and held council with Toste and Leif about the course, and Toke sat between the thwarts with his back to the shield rim, holding his arm. The uncomfortable night's sleep seemed to have been hard for him, but he sent Arnulf a pale nod and praised his sleep. Arnulf gathered his hair with his hands and looked for a bit of yarn, 'How is your arm?'

Toke grimaced, 'It hurts a little. I must have hit it a couple of times as I slept.'

Arnulf could not find any yarn and tried to braid his hair, but it would not hold, 'Where are we?'

Toke's eyes sparkled, 'One day from Norway, Dane. If you are hungry, then Stentor has the food bag.'

Arnulf waved his hand dismissively.

'Here.'

Toste handed him a braid band, and Arnulf gained control over his unruly hair.

'The wind is blowing north, so we have to head more to the south,' said Leif and pointed to the red sky, but Toste shook his head, 'It did not last night. We have already postponed making landfall half a day with all your coursing to the south. Just keep the sun in the back, then we will have coast again by midnight.'

'You slept when the wind was strongest,' returned Leif. 'And you can put away all the rune pieces again, Stentor! You said yourself that you do not consult with the Æsir about anything man himself knows well!'

Stentor snorted, but before he could answer, Toke sat up, releasing his arm, 'To Jotunheim with whether we hit land north or south, as long as arrive as soon as possible! The sun sets in the east, and we need to go due west, right the course as Toste says and keep peace in my ship! We are companions, not squabbling old women!'

He sank gloomily and Arnulf exchanged glances with the others. Leif shrugged, and Toke moodily rejected the mead jar that Toste handed him while Stentor with the best of his ability turned the bow due west.

Arnulf let Toke sulk and picked at the cut he had made for Fenrir which scratched under his kyrtle. He did not feel as cocky as the day before and was light-headed from the wind and water's flickering, and as the day progressed, his stomach did not improve. Some of the youngest Vikings threw up, and Arnulf hid his head in his cloak, but the wind slipped his hair loose of the band and annoyed him greatly. So as not to be completely windswept, he forced hid thoughts to Egilssund and tried to imagine what Stridbjørn and Trud were doing, but after everything that had happened, the settlement seemed like the distant chorus of an old song to him, and it only resulted in the agonising pain of thinking about Frejdis. His hunger weakened, but the nausea was worse, and Stentor loaned him an amber bead and said it would help to suck on it.

Twin Raven's ploughing from wave crest to wave crest was endless, and Arnulf watched impatiently for land in the afternoon. Helge had once made the trip in one and a half days, and the wind was so unbearable, the sea stallion advanced considerably. Toste made Toke a soft bed and forced him to nap, and Stentor did not think they had had such an easy sea journey before and toasted Njord with Cleftnose.

Arnulf, suffering from stiffness and boredom, straightened his legs without relief. Imagine having yearned so strongly for this! And they were neither storm hit nor frostbitten.

*****

The second night at sea was much better than the first, for Arnulf was tired enough to sleep despite the sea and did not let himself be disturbed by the splashing waves.

In the earliest light, he was awakened by hard-handed shaking and started drowsily. Stentor sat over him, a finger on his lips, and Arnulf heard excited whispers around him as he tumbled out of his sleeping skin. *Twin Raven's* large sail had been packed, and the tall mast laid down, and the Vikings sat low behind their shields, lifting the oars into place as quietly as possible. Toste helped Toke into his chainmail, and Arnulf wiped away the sleep and stared out to sea. He noticed a coastline, which was not so far away that he could make out the grey houses and boats on the strand through the mist and he grabbed the shield rim. Land! They had reached land! Land and villages!

A rooster crowed through the fog, but the people in the houses did not seem to have woken up yet, and Arnulf gripped Serpenttooth's pommel, short of breath from his thumping heart. Toke's burning gaze met him, and the Northman extended his hand, as Toste closed the buckle on his right shoulder. Arnulf grasped it firmly and wordlessly vowed his fidelity to Toke and Stentor handed him an oar, making a sign to put it gently in the water.

Silently the men got themselves ready on the ship, and Leif crawled forward to his companions at the bow, holding his axe off the deck. Arnulf took the oar, his hands trembling and began to row with the others in long strokes. He was so strong that he could put his feet through the hull if he pulled the oar like Thor and glowing shivers ran down his back, while Serpenttooth writhed from blood lust in its sheath. His first plunder! Soon he would run inland and increase his riches like Helge had done so many times before! In just a few oar strokes, his reputation would be forged, and his life's verse would begin! A fierce gratitude flowed through his limbs. Toke had kept his word! Just as he had promised in Egilssund, he had stood by his word and, by Fenrir, Arnulf would keep his word, too, and be a good housecarl!

The oar's wood felt alive against his sweaty palms, and the longship's strokes over the water resembled a snake after its prey. Softly and lying low, Toke sneaked his countrymen towards a hiding brink, and neither cry nor barking dogs revealed the Northern warriors. Arnulf cast his eyes over his shoulder at every other row, and the wolf's blood raged and turned his mouth dry and sharpened his spirit. Fast he would bite, hard and like lightening, for every stranger should know that Stridbjørn's son had gone a-viking and they should tremble at his name!

The settlement was larger than his own in Egilssund, but the houses were not unlike the Danish ones and wicker fences surrounded both the stables and workshops. Toke motioned to the Midfjord Vikings to lay their oars down and make ready their bows, because if the attack was discovered before they made it inland, the people of the village would have time to run into the woods with their goods and cattle. Arnulf was breathing in short bursts, and *Twin Raven* caught the shadow of the land and scraped its keel against the shore, as another rooster crowed. The men loosened their shields and began to jump ashore to push the sea stallion up onto the sand, and Arnulf grabbed his wolf shield and wanted to give Toke a hand, but the Northman disembarked his ship light-footedly, drawing out his sword.

At once a dog barked from the field, and although it was killed by an arrow through its neck, it had alerted the village. Toke jumped like a stallion up the slope, and Arnulf threw his cloak over his shoulders and followed him closely. The Vikings were greeted by horrified howls and cries as they made their way up to the village and people rushed out of the houses, half-dressed and carrying their young and old. Women screamed for their children, while men and lads took up arms, although they did not seem to want to use them for anything other than to ensure the weak could get away. A horn sounded, and a bell began to chime.

Toke ordered the archers to shoot at the people who were trying to move chests and strongboxes to safety but otherwise to let them escape, and Leif Cleftnose charged forward, roaring and swinging his mighty axe over his head. Arnulf believed he had never seen rabbits bolt as fast as the terrified skrælings that were flying over the fields towards the forest, their shifts flapping around their legs, and Stentor shouted that Tyr was not with them, since they now had to settle for cleaving the empty air with swords.

When Arnulf and Toke reached the enclosure, the village was not yet completely depopulated, but those who were fleeing last were not worth a fight, and Toke stopped where the plank road began. Arnulf confronted him with his shield lifted, for even children and the lame could handle a bow in the shelter of a doorway, and no chainmail would keep its wearer free from injury against a strong arrowhead. He drew Serpenttooth from its sheath and searched every corner for hostile shadows.

A house caught fire, probably because some furniture was overturned, and mad dogs and cackling chickens ran around, bewildered, between fallen fences and broken clay jars.

Stentor and Toste stopped, winded, by their chieftain, and Toke did not hesitate long before roaring triumphantly and with an arm movement motioned the plundering to begin. The youngest Vikings were quickest, for now it was every man for himself, and Arnulf felt a hand on his shoulder.

'Give Stentor your shield and run with them! He and I will stay here and keep an eye on the forest.'

Toke smiled warmly, but Arnulf still felt bound by his housecarl oath, 'There may be hidden warriors behind every door, and Serpenttooth is not known for failing.'

Toke shook his head, 'The people here will not bite again, believe me! And as chieftain, I have the right to that part of the plundered goods which most appeals to me, hurry now!'

He gave his shoulder a nudge, and Arnulf sent him a wry grin and handed the wolf shield to Stentor. With his sword raised, he ran between the abandoned houses and headed towards the far end of the village where the other Vikings had yet to begin plundering. He let the biggest longhouse be, regardless the greatness of their wealth, but the last thing he wanted right now was to argue with the Cleftnose about the skræling chieftain's silver.

Some of the Midfjord Vikings ransacked the adjoining buildings, and Arnulf ran past them and opened the door to a high-gabled house whose roof was thatched with countless small wooden boards. It was dark inside, and he had to stand for a moment before he could see anything, for the fire had burned out on the hearth. The room was large, and Arnulf noticed that instead of connected sleeping places along the walls, there were single beds and a table with narrow benches in the middle of the floor. Some chests stood beside a loom at one end wall, and Arnulf went towards them but stiffened abruptly, a small girl had stepped out on the floor in front of him. Although she was hardly more than eight summers, she grasped a wide slaughter knife, and she looked so furious that Arnulf stopped. Behind her in a bed lay a woman with fever-bright eyes, and Arnulf was indignant. Never would he have left children and sick behind, and the girl had to be admired for her courage.

The woman looked at him fearfully and pulled the blanket up to her nose, but Arnulf meant them no harm and grabbed her daughter to push her away. Wild as a polecat, she twisted out of his grip and stabbed at him, and the knife struck him in the wrist and tore the skin up to his fingers.

Arnulf pulled his hand away with an exclamation, angry at the unexpected pain, and the woman in the bed cried and pulled the girl to her, her eyes round. Arnulf looked at his hand. It was bleeding profusely, and the woman threw the blanket from her resolutely and fumbled with the keys on her belt, while she pointed to a shrine that stood under a low bed. Her leg was swollen and bandaged, and the girl dropped the bloody knife and pressed against her, as if she were only now aware of the danger, she had brought upon them.

Arnulf wound a piece of cloak tightly around his hand, irate from the humiliation that had greeted him, and the woman handed him a key, trembling. He took it with lowered eyes and went and retrieved the chest from its hiding place. It was heavy, but the lock was easy, and its content made Arnulf forget both his hand and his indignation, for twisted silver chains and bangles lay mixed with amber and glass beads, a treasure worthy of a great Viking! They were hardly looted goods rather bartered over a long time, and Arnulf looked kindlier on the woman and her daughter who, with mortal fear in their eyes, followed each of his movements. He could take them as thralls, get the leg healed on the mother, and sell them for at least a neck ring of silver, but the memory of Toke in the thrall hut caused him to hinder. So proud a girl should be allowed to grow up freely, she was so obviously braver than her companions.

Arnulf fished a single amber bead free of the others and motioned for the girl to lie up in bed. She obeyed immediately, and he handed her the bead, a smile tugging at his mouth, and threw some sleeping skins over both of them. What Leif and his warriors would do if they found them was not easy to think of, so Arnulf toppled both the table and the loom and emptied the pots and baskets that were in the house, so it looked ransacked and stripped. He caught a tearful glance from a half-raised fur and then, putting the chest under his arm, he left.

*****

Outside, the Northmen ran, jeering and laughing, around with bundles and chests, and Leif stepped out of the large longhouse and raised his arms with a victory roar. Silver and bronze he had taken, for both his neck and his fingers, and his companions struck him on the shoulder and showed off their swag.

Toste had found silk, and Arnulf, amazed, ceased his looting to feel it. He had once before seen silk in a booth on Gormsø, but he had never touched the precious material that seemed thinner than a butterfly wing and sleeker than any fish scales. Frejdis should have such a dress! So soft a skin deserved so soft a robe! If only Rolf had left them alone ...

Arnulf bit his tongue, before he suggested a trade to Toste. He confined himself to congratulating him on his find and showed his chest, but the shine was gone by the joy. Toste appeared to be satisfied with his loot and did not seem to want to further participate in the plundering, other settlements existed along the coast, and the youngest Vikings were

157

clearly dangerous in their plundering madness, 'Have you ever been in a church, Arnulf?'

'A church? No.'

'Then we can just reach it before Toke calls us on board again. These cowardly wretches should not be allowed time to think too much about a counter-attack, for even if they have fled, they can quickly enough get strange ideas.'

Arnulf let himself be dragged along to a tall wooden house with a wide door. Outside hung a solid bell in a tower the height of a man, and Toste pulled jokingly on the rope. Arnulf jumped back and dropped his chest at the deadening clang of the anvil, 'By Fenrir! What in all of Midgard is that good for? Stop it!'

Toste laughed and let go, 'The Christian worshippers do not think that their god can hear them if they do not make a noise that can awaken the Midgard serpent! This White Christ is certainly no Heimdallr!'

Arnulf shook his head and gathered the silver up into the chest, 'So much iron just to call up to a god? There's at least five swords in that bell!'

Toste handed him some glass beads and waved him through the wide door, and Arnulf followed, curious. The room inside was filled with benches in rows, and behind a table at the end wall were two planks joined to form a cross but otherwise it was empty and Arnulf, disappointed, looked around and tightened the cape flap around his injured hand. There was neither oath-ring, blót vessel, ceremonial weapons nor sacrificial knife, and not so much as a wood carving hung on the walls. Toste shrugged, 'Well, the others must have taken what was here. Candlesticks and goblets and such, sometimes of silver, usually stand here, and I have heard they are made of gold in the large churches. This is just an ordinary village, but they have a sense of trade.'

He threw his silk over his shoulder, and Arnulf followed him back along the plank road to Toke and Stentor, who still stood holding the wolf shield. Around them, the elated Haraldsfjord Vikings carried their loot towards the longship, and Stentor kept a count of the men, that none should be forgotten to the enemy. Leif Cleftnose came stomping with a rattling bundle on his back, and Toke smiled when he spotted Arnulf's shrine, 'Did you find anything good, Stridbjørnson? Oh, what have you done with your hand?'

Arnulf's cheeks grew hot, and he tried to avoid the answer, 'Nothing. I cut myself on the chest's lock.'

Leif guffawed and threw his bundle on the ground with a bang, 'The chest's lock? That is no cut from a lock! You forgot to check the girl for knives before you dropped your trousers, am I not right, you beginner-Viking?'

Arnulf's astonished face cheered him and several men laughed.

'You should, by Thor, wring the arms of womenfolk, so that occupies them more than what else is happening, remember that! But take comfort! You are, after all, the only one of us who came near that kind of fun this morning!'

Arnulf, furious, clenched his hands and fell silent. Better that Leif believe he had committed a rape than know the truth, for both the girl and the woman's life was in danger as long as the Vikings were in the village.

'Let us get going, how many are missing?'

Toste was trying to get an overview of the men, and Toke sent Arnulf a serious look. He did not ask anything, but Arnulf knew he was thinking of Helge's misdeed and glared again. Did Toke really know him so badly that he would simply believe Leif's accusations?

The Cleftnose gathered up his plunder and slapped Arnulf on the back as he walked, and Toke turned on his heel faster than was necessary. Arnulf wanted to explain himself, but just then one of Toste's men arrived and shouted that there had been a shot from the edge of the woods. Toke ordered the immediate withdrawal, and as nobody wanted to defend a successful looting with weapons, the remaining Vikings quickened their pace and started running towards *Twin Raven*.

Arnulf followed, fuming, while silver and amber rattled in the chest under his arm, and from behind the settlement a handful of archers came into sight but they were outside of firing range. The longship was pushed hastily out and Arnulf took his place and unwrapped his hand to take the oar. Stentor threw the wolf shield on the deck, and Toke ordered the mast be raised and the sail set, while the oars rowed *Twin Raven* away from the land and left the reckless skrælings on the strand. Leif sat in the foreship, and not long after the ship was at a safe distance from the shore, and the men let the oars rest.

Arnulf leaned breathlessly against the ship's side and saw the village folk throw stones at the Northmen. His hand was bleeding heavily and was more painful than he cared for it to be, but no one around him seemed to want to help him with it, and Toke deigned to give him a glance. Leif Cleftnose stood with one hand on the raven heads, waving towards land, while he laughed heartily, and Arnulf put his hand out over the shield rim and let it bleed in the water, 'Fenrir take you! I have not raped anyone, what do you take me for? Only fools judge a man by the accusations of others without having heard of him first!'

He stared challengingly at the silent Northmen, and Stentor answered quietly, 'We take you to be Helge's brother, Arnulf. What have you done with your hand that cannot be said aloud?'

Arnulf looked at his bloody fingers and exhaled deeply. The sight caused pain to bite all the way up his forearm.

'There was a girl inside the house. She was not very old, but she defended her sick mother bravely. I would not hurt them, but she struck me anyway.'

Arnulf's cheeks burned from the disgrace but Toke exchanged a brightened glance with Toste and Stentor, 'And what did you do?'

Arnulf could hardly take it, but had to deal with it, 'The woman was terrified and gave me the key to the chest. I hid them under some sleeping skins, so Leif and his companions would not find them, for they would hardly be so lenient.'

Toke burst into laughter, and several of the men seated in front of him turned and wanted to take part in the merriment, but he waved his hand dismissively, 'Arnulf! Thor flay me if you do not run around and rescue women and children instead of plundering and taking thralls, and then you cannot even defend yourself against them! Give him a drink of beer, Toste, he needs it, and then stick your hand in water! It is making more of a mess than Stentor during the winter blót!'

Arnulf believed he had received his share of the spoils but did as Toke said, although the cold salt water smarted just as much as it alleviated. He closed his eyes and felt his heartbeat slow to a walking pace, while his morning hunger volunteered a snarl. The chest stood between his feet and the sun reddened the sky to the east, his first plunder was over, and he was already rich. There was so much silver that it could not possibly fit in his belt pouch. An axe with a shield could be bought with it, or if he was lucky a fair horse.

'Here, drink!'

Toste handed him a mug, and Arnulf drank deeply.

'Let me see your hand.'

The Midfjord Vikings found linen and ointment and Arnulf did not make a sound as his hand was bandaged. Stentor let the food bag go around, and Toke threw three silver rings into the sea as thanks to the gods of war for their protection and a successful start to the summer voyage.

Twin Raven cleaved sea from land while the spoils were taken out and admired on the deck and barters concluded. Everyone gave Toke part of their loot, and Arnulf put his shield in place and began to look for more settlements. The next attack was going to take place in broad daylight and would hardly be as surprising as the first, but he tasted blood between his teeth and Serpenttooth was tired of its sleep.

Stentor drew Toke's attention to the sky and did not like its sallow colour, and Toste felt that they had only just reached the shore in time, 'We will have a storm at midday. If we had hesitated just a half a day in Norway, we would be badly off.'

Toke was not worried and was prepared to sail until the weather was too hard. No rocks disfigured the flat strand, and *Twin Raven* could be put ashore at any time. Arnulf gave him credit and trusted their luck, and when, not long after, he spotted cattle, he straightened up and grabbed Toke's arm eagerly, 'Look! There must be houses behind those hills, take the sail down!'

Toke peered towards land but shook his head, 'No, we will let them be, there will be more.'

Arnulf let him go astonished, 'Why? One village is probably as good as the next.'

Toke stroked his short beard, holding the course, 'Øystein taught me to plunder that way. With a fast horse and little headwind, the first settlement can reach and warn the next, and so we waste time searching in vain for buried silver and forest-driven animals while we risk a planned counterattack. No, by sailing past every other settlement, the rumours never reach the next village, and they feel confident when they see our sails disappear, but afterwards!'

Toke's eyes glowed like a lynx's, 'Afterwards we sail back and take all the ones we missed in the first place! That is how Haraldsfjord is so rich, my father and grandfather never returned home empty-handed, and they were both respected throughout the Northland because of it.'

Arnulf smiled, full of admiration. Helge had never gone a-viking like that and so much fighting had come out of it, that it heavily affected the women and children at home.

Although the earth around the looted village had been fruitful, *Twin Raven* had to pass a large woodland before Arnulf caught sight of cultivated land again. This time it was a larger collection of buildings, but the inhabitants had evidently been attacked several times before, for they had raised a defensive palisade of tapered logs which enclosed the whole village, and as soon as the longship approached, the sound of a church bell could be heard.

Toke let the sail turn so the wind went around it and held council on the deck. Although he leaned towards sailing past and feared it would cost too many lives to take the village, Leif Cleftnose shouted from the bow that the wealth behind the palisade was obvious and he was not inclined to be stopped by a row of boards. His village companions supported him, but the Midfjord Vikings spoke of the farms in Norway and believed that Haraldsfjord had enough widows and fatherless. The youngest on board had fever in their blood and joined Leif, and Arnulf shielded his eyes with his hand and tried to assess the village's resistance. Toke had many men with him and wood could burn.

Stentor suggested that they let the fortified settlement be and recommended attacking when they sailed past it on the way back and knew more about the success of this year's voyage, and Leif could see the sense in his words and gave in for the moment. Arnulf kept his disappointment to himself, but when the ship, a little later, approached a high-gabled farm that was so ostentatious that it had to belong to an earl, there was no talk about avoiding an attack.

While the first hard gusts predicted rapid weather changes, *Twin Raven* kept close to the coast, and Toke did not try to hide his arrival. Arnulf loosened his shield again and ensured that both his sword and his knife sat right on the belt. His luck felt strong, and a brisk game of sword play would not be out of the question, Serpenttooth was not there just to rust.

The earl's farm lay back from the seafront and had many pit houses and stables around it, and the main house was painted red and surrounded by buildings that formed a huge courtyard. Arnulf heard shouts and saw people running around up there, while cattle and horses were led to a woodland along with women and children. There did not seem to be many men, but those there were gathered around, armed, on the grass field in front of the strand, and although the Northmen were many, the earl's housecarls did not look like surrendering without a fight.

The sea stallion went aground and Arnulf jumped out after Toke, drawing Serpenttooth from its sheath. His injured hand murmured horridly over the hard shield grip, but Toke should not be without his guard, and the pain served only to increase his alertness. An injured man struck out skilfully; the din of battle was ahead!

The earl himself did not seem to stand among his people, and as Arnulf got closer to them, they did not seem to be in awe and cringed behind their shields. Again, the Æsir had smiled gently on Toke's crew, this time by letting the enemy's main force be of farmers, and Arnulf squinted like a wolf, letting Fenrir's courage sizzle in his body. He assured himself that no bows were pointing out from between their enemies and Toke looked back to rally his flock. Leif Cleftnose did not wait for anyone but unhooked the cloak from his shoulders and ran, howling, his axe bared, his beard flapping, and his companions let out a roar and did not give the grass time to stand in his tracks.

Toste led his brothers-in-arms, and Stentor and Arnulf flanked Toke and joined in the cry, while the earl's men advanced against them and formed a shield wall. Arnulf picked out a tall fair-haired man whose long legs would be easy to get at. A good blow should cause him to raise his shield, so Serpenttooth would be able to access free flesh. The sword tugged at his hand, as if he was holding a frisky horse by the tail, and the enemy gathered themselves together, but just before the clash, the ground around them seemed to be too hot, for suddenly the shields were lowered, and the men turned and fled.

Leif stopped, and war cries changed to jeers and scornful laughter, while the false warriors disappeared in panic over the fields and into the woods. Toste sneered at them, imitating their terrified sprint, and Arnulf spat into the grass disappointed. You would have to search long to find such an unmanly thrall-fledgling! How cowardly to play such a fool's game! He would have given his life for Frejdis and the village without so much as blinking an eye, by Fenrir!

Toke let the men go with a noble expression and, happy, thrust Sigtryg's sword in the air. Toste stuck his axe in his belt and jumped off on flexible hamstrings to get to the treasures before Leif, though the Cleftnose seemed to want to let him have the best loot this time, for he did not rush his men. Arnulf laughed and thought that the Skald-man probably lacked silver for his silk, and Toste's settlement companions let their first man have the honour, but Toke's eyes were hard like flint. He called several times in vain for his countryman and rocked irresolutely on his feet, and when Toste reached the settlements, he hastened after him across the field with a raised sword. The Northman's anger seemed intense given that whoever took the earl's riches, he would get his share of it, but Arnulf ran anyway.

Toste stopped ahead in the yard and clapped his hands triumphantly together, but in the next moment the door to one longhouse opened, and armed men swarmed out with a strong cry. Toke gave a yell and picked up his pace, and Arnulf clenched his teeth. Toste was surrounded and drew his sword, the earl's men's escape had been a ploy and Arnulf started to sweat.

A tall nobly dressed man with copper hair and a golden sword walked towards Toste, and Toke shouted shrilly to his men and ran, despite his chainmail, so Arnulf could hardly keep up with him. Behind them, Leif roared wildly, as if he were trying to divert and entice the earl's entire hird against him, and Arnulf heard the Haraldsfjord Vikings set off after their chieftain. A bull's fury pounded in his heart, and in front of him Toste was wounded in both hip and arm.

The earl's intention was clearly to not let anyone help rescue the distressed Vikings, for he let most of the housecarls fight the Northmen, while he exchanged blows with Toste.

Arnulf enacted his housecarl oath like a tick after blood, with his shoulder plastered against Toke's, his wolf shield close in front of both of them during the final leap into the courtyard, so he crashed into their enemies' line, as Toste screamed wildly behind the men. The clash of shields paralysed his arm and, with as much strength as he could muster, Arnulf drove the enemy blades back with a mighty sword blow. A red-bearded man roared right in front of him, his face convulsed with hatred, and an unmanageable number of arms and weapons were within reach and ready to kill.

Toke struck the leg of a man and shouted to Freyr in triumph, and his left-handed stroke fell accurate and heavy. Arnulf barely escaped an axe swung high and let indignation lead his sword arm, while it grated down Toke's chainmail. If they could just make their way to Toste, then there would be three to stand the few moments necessary, but the earl's men guarded their home and seemed hot-tempered enough. The sword hilt was sweaty to hold, and it was a difficult task to guard Toke's weak side in a brawl, for figures and attacks flickered like the mane of a runaway horse. Damn that so many weapons swished; Helge should have prepared him better for such fights!

A sword hit Serpenttooth just above the pommel, and Arnulf had to break the weight of his enemy. He managed to bump the earl's man away but was then beaten back by more crushing blows, the last of which split the wolf shield through the middle. The jammed sword tip pulled threads from his kyrtle but was worked free immediately, and Arnulf's opponent jumped around him to attack from behind. Toke stumbled and fell, and Toste screamed for help, but now Leif and his companions came charging.

It crashed and shattered so shield splinters flew as point and blade met axe and long knife, and Arnulf was pushed too far forward between the earl's men but was again thrown backwards from an iron grip on his shoulder. For a moment he staggered dangerously and lost his sparse overview but regained his footing and leapt over and got Toke up onto his legs, while a spear thrust against his shield boss.

Roars and cries resounded from all sides, and a thrown knife struck sparks against Serpenttooth, while the blood of a wounded man's head streak across Arnulf's face. Toke stood under his own power, nodding palely, and from the corner of his eye Arnulf saw Leif Cleftnose cut two men to the ground with both hands on his axe handle. Fearless seemed the Viking and he was strong, strong as if he cast a jötunn's shadow.

Arnulf struck out, life or death, he would not be accused of cowardice and Toste's last skaldic verse had not sounded yet! A shield edge rammed between his ribs and took his breath away, but his feet held, and he managed to knock the nearest man off his feet. The pain grappled with his breath, and a sudden powdery snow fell through the air. Arnulf, quick as a hawk, took a blow with the flat blade and pulled his shoulder away from a knife attack, while his trousers were torn up under his wolf shield and his thigh was scratched by a spearhead. He looked at the spear carrier and bared his teeth and, for a moment they locked eyes, as the housecarl tumbled aside at his brothers-in-arms' pressure.

An axe stuck itself fast in the edge of the wolf shield and tore it aside, but Stentor came to the rescue and made space ahead of him. The gothi seemed to be possessed by the strength of the bear, and a stab in the shoulder caused him neither to groan nor fall back. For a moment, all three stood free of the fight, and Arnulf, panting, pressed his elbow against his ribs.

More men came running out of the longhouse, and Arnulf recognised the tall man, who had fled from the field earlier. They must have gathered themselves and gone through the houses to assist their companions, and their help was desperately needed. The housecarls tried to stay close to their earl, but the Northmen came together in small groups and blasted their attempts. Despite the new arrivals, they were still in the majority, and the enemy's flock was scattered between the buildings during the fierce fighting.

Arnulf yanked up his shield and spotted Toste again. The fjord man lay coughing on his knees in a pool of blood at the earl's feet with a broken axe, his hand cramped and pressed against his side. His back was so badly slashed that his gasping lung was visible, and Toke let out a terrible scream. He wanted to charge the earl, despite three housecarls standing between them, but Stentor threw himself against him, so they both tumbled to the ground. Leif called to the earl, while Toke beat Stentor to free himself, 'Let me go! Have you gone mad, Toste is dying!'

Arnulf had to screen the combatants against a fleeing man's wild blows.

'You can't win this battle with an injured arm. Let Leif take it!'

Stentor loosened his grip, and the earl glared ominously at Toke and put his sword tip against Toste's neck. The chainmail and Stentor's intervention had revealed who Toke was, and the earl's face quivered with rage under his copper-red hair. His housecarls fell in around him like grain before a hailstorm. Toste's death would be little revenge for their defeat.

Toke got up tensely, and Leif raised his mighty axe over his head to throw it, but at the same moment, a man who had been lying as if he were dead jumped up behind Toke with a long knife in his hand. Arnulf tried in vain to reach him, but the man grabbed Toke by the hair and forced his head back, putting the blade to his throat. The Northman fought back so blood trickled down the blade, and Stentor flew to his feet with his arms raised, 'Halt!'

His voice echoed over the courtyard. The Vikings from Haraldsfjord knew the gothi's voice and stopped hesitantly, and even the earl's men let their arms stiffen, and for a moment the only sounds were the men's heaving and Toste's rattling gasps. Toke gave up his opposition with open eyes, while the earl's gaze was steadfast, icy and gloating. His man could, with a single swipe, rob the Vikings of their chieftain, and Toste's life ebbed away under his sword tip.

Arnulf let go of his shield and slipped his hand down around the knife hilt. A quick movement in the direction of Toke would cost the Northman his life and the man from the hird nudged the knife into the wound, so the chieftain would order the weapons be lowered but Toke fell silent. Toste spat blood and sank down on his side, and Leif roared, throwing his weapon, like Thor would have thrown Mjolnir. The axe met the earl in his chest and the great man writhed with a yell, while Arnulf slipped the blade from his belt. Oh, how it would suit the Cleftnose if Toke had his throat cut by the enemy! With his throw he had just abandoned the ruler of Haraldsfjord and Arnulf felt his arm tense rock hard.

Despite the blood gushing from his chest and mouth, the earl still held his gaze on Toke and contorted his face in a grin as he stuck his sword into Toste's neck. His surviving housecarl was free of paralysis in an

166

instant, and Arnulf jumped on Toke's opponent like a bull elk and beat the knife hand away from his throat before he had time to consider his next move. By Tyr's blood if that miscreant should be allowed to murder his friend! He should die and a shame it was that it had to happen so fast! The wolf-knife packed a mortal wound, and the man sank down without a sound, while Toke fell to his knees, feeling his throat. Arnulf grabbed him by the shoulders, but Toke seemed defensively alive, and Stentor did not let anyone come near them.

The earl's men who were still standing, looked at each other bewildered and several of them surrendered, throwing down their weapons, but Toke stood up, panting, without giving any sign to save lives. The Midfjord Vikings did not believe that their leader deserved to die alone, and Arnulf was hit by a dismembered hand as the rest of the hird was killed with yells and curses. Blood and guts flowed like at a pig slaughtering and Arnulf, weak in the knees, tried to swallow a few times. He pulled his knife out of the killed man and fumbled to get it into the sheath. By Helheim's disease! All for a queasy looting! His body burned and his eyes sought relief by the windswept sea. What riches could pay for Toste's life? And several of the Northmen were wounded.

Leif Cleftnose spat as he pulled his axe free of the dead earl's chest and wiped it on his cape, while Stentor, his face rigid, knelt by Toste and put his hand on the fallen's shoulder. Toke let his throat go and staggered over to the longhouse to support himself. The sword slipped out of his hand, and Arnulf smudged the sweat off with his sleeve, 'Are you badly hurt?'

Toke leaned his forehead against the planks, 'Yes. But not from weapons.'

Trembling, he held his arm but righted himself and kicked his sword with clenched fists.

Leif stomped around restlessly, his axe over his shoulder as he voiced his indignation while the men who were worst wounded were scantily bandaged, 'Why was he running here all alone, the scrawny Midfjord louse! He could have waited! Even milk-sucklings know that you must never attack like that, Tyr himself punished his folly!'

Arnulf went to Stentor and Toste. He felt every stone in the yard through his shoes, and a violent thirst tore at his throat. His limbs felt like stems that had been chewed several times over. The dead Viking did not look good and Stentor sighed and straightened the half-severed head, 'Of all the deaths that have hit Haraldsfjord, this is for me the worst. He was my cousin. Few better men are born.'

He stood up with an embittered look, his shoulder bleeding badly. Arnulf grabbed a dead man's cape and tore into it with his knife, 'Sit down again, Stentor, you have been hit hard.'

Stentor looked at Toke, shaking his head, 'It is not deep, just let me bleed a little.'

'Sit!'

Leif Cleftnose had stopped and stared commandingly at the gothi, 'Enough foolishness has been committed here, do not also let your power leave you!'

The hair blew wildly around the harsh face, and Stentor seemed to hold back an objection before he obeyed. Arnulf helped him get his arm out of his sleeve to get to the wound.

'Foolishness?'

Toke was hoarse and his eyes sparkled, 'If you had held your axe in peace, Leif, Toste would be alive now! You killed him with your cast of the axe and disregarded my life! If Arnulf had not been so resolute ...'

'Haraldsfjord would have a new chieftain now! Toste was choking on blood from his mortal wound, I did not betray him by letting him see his own death avenged!'

Leif tensed his muscles.

'It was the earl's last thrust that killed him! I risked both my own and Arnulf's life to come to his aid, and you saw him as a dead man already! Your cast was not to avenge anything, you meant to cut my throat and ensure your right to the ship and the fjord but Arnulf was too fast!'

Toke spoke loudly now. Arnulf stood on awakened legs and pressed a rolled-up piece of the cape against Stentor's shoulder to prevent more bleeding, and the gothi stirred uneasily. The Northmen listened silently and the Outerfjord Vikings moved closer to Leif, who had his hand on his hip, 'Should we have surrendered then without a fight to a handful of weaklings? Your life is not worth that price! And it is hard as you complain that you have faced death and rude to discredit my words! Is your arm really so weak or are you just afraid to meet me in single combat? There is no need to talk more here!'

Toke's gaze was fierce, 'My courage I have proven many times and my arm is injured because I held out against a superior enemy before today, but you have broken the peace of the voyage and betrayed your chieftain!'

Arnulf felt Stentor quiver, as if he had to fight hard not to involve himself. Leif Cleftnose spat at a dead man's helmet, 'What will you do about it, Øysteinson? Put my men and me off *Twin Raven* here? It will trigger a blood feud in the fjord! And before you talk more about deceit remember who just beat the enemy to pieces and saved your skin from danger! You risked your own life when you lost your head and attacked the entire hird with only one man at your side! The fjord people will not be served by so foolish a leader, and I deeply regret that your suicide failed.'

'You are only sorry that I am still alive and that you were not the first to come to Toste's rescue! Do you think he would have appreciated your deed? A chieftain needs to see if his men are in danger and act upon it and that I did!'

Arnulf's pulse throbbed intensely. If only the earl had stabbed the neck of Leif instead of Toste!

Stentor could not keep quiet any longer, 'Halt both of you! It is unworthy to argue like women over Toste's lifeless body. Brave hearts acted here, and disputes are always seen in a clearer light when they have passed. Make sure that the wounded are brought down to the ship Leif, and Toke you should thank Arnulf for you owe him your life more than once.'

He clenched his teeth and bowed his head, while Arnulf wound strips of cape around his shoulder. Leif ignored the gothi, his posture threatening, and Toke breathed heavily, the blood rippling from his neck. The Vikings waited tensely and Arnulf remained ready for sudden action. Toke picked up his sword and put one foot in front of the other. His voice was low, but his words made of fire, 'If you want to meet me now, Leif Cleftnose, then do it shieldless and left-handed. No man can then speak of a dishonourable fight, and your reputation will not suffer.'

Leif's eyes seemed to be filled with liquid iron but before he could answer, the group was unexpectedly broken up by two Outerfjord Vikings, who with loud cries dragged a kicking woman. She bit out after the Northmen, wriggling like an eel, but when she saw the dead earl, she uttered a despairing cry and burst into tears. The Vikings threw her on the ground, and the woman huddled, groaning, and hid her face in her hair.

Toke and Leif sent each other a long look, then Toke shoved his sword roughly into its sheath and Leif beckoned to his men for an explanation.

'She tried to burn the ship!'

Eigil Black pointed to the woman and looked at Leif incensed, 'She came from the forest with a torch, we just managed to stop her.'

Leif grabbed the woman by the hair and forced her face up, and Toke looked away, wiping his neck with the back of the hand. Øystein Ravenslayer had hardly ever left his ship unattended during a plunder and, without the sea as an escape route, a hated boatload of Vikings could quickly be badly off on foreign soil.

Arnulf finished bandaging the wound and gave Stentor a hand to get up. It was a relief that the woman had averted the duel with her attempted arson attack, and he took a deep breath. Toke was fast but Leif was fearsomely strong, so the outcome of the fight was disturbing to imagine.

The woman whimpered under Leif Cleftnose's grip and her courage seemed to have evaporated. She was richly dressed. Heavy jewellery graced both her clothes and her arms so she must have been a member of the earl's family, but judging from her age, his daughter rather than his wife.

'I have good men!'

Leif pulled the prisoner onto her legs, 'And they do not run blindly from their duties. You can take all the goods you want, Toke, but this thrall-wench here and the wealth she wears is mine. And by Thor, I will duel you as soon as my feet stand on northern fjelds again and until then my words are just as valid as yours!'

He pulled the woman off without waiting for an answer, and the crowd hastily made space. Arnulf scowled. Over his dead body would the Cleftnose's words be half as valid as Toke's, that man was indeed a sore oozing-boil! And what Leif would do behind the nearest pit house was shameful, Helge had forfeited his life due to such a deed!

The driving storm clouds were not darker than Toke's glance. Leif's lust was salt in his mockery, and Toke seemed to find it difficult to restrain his anger and looked stiffly at his gooey hand, 'Search the houses and take what there is and lay Toste in the earl's bed. He shall not have a poor funeral pyre.'

'It will be seen far away.'

Stentor fought to get his arm back into his kyrtle.

'Yes! It will guide Odin's daughters to a great warrior who surely deserves a place in his hird!'

Toke's irritability caused Stentor to be silent, and the gothi went to young Ingmar Thorirson, who lay with his head in his brother's lap and appeared to be gravely injured.

Arnulf tore another strip from the cape and handed it to Toke, 'Come. Take care of your neck, so it doesn't end up looking like Toste's.'

The Northman's kyrtle was bloody down along his chest. Toke took the cloth and grabbed his hand firmly. Behind the anger he seemed deeply saddened, 'Thank you, Arnulf!'

He would say more, but the words were gone, and Arnulf nodded, 'By Fenrir, Toke!'

He clutched the Northman's hand, so his knuckles were white.

Two men lifted Toste up and carried him into the house, while the others proceeded to ransack the buildings and Toke gently covered his gash. Stentor left Ingmar, writhing and boring his fingers into his brother's knee, and a woman's cry caused Arnulf to start. Leif, the wretched miscreant, the depraved mongrel mite! The earl's daughter had lost both her kinsfolk and her freedom, her bravery should not be punished with humiliation! Each scream was replaced by a new one, and Toke's fingers stiffened at the sound. He turned his back to Arnulf and went into the longhouse, while a pair of Outerfjord Vikings grinned and elbowed each other.

A beer barrel was rolled up from a pit house, and Arnulf's thirst got worse, so he drank deeply when the mugs were passed around, but the drink could not flush the revulsion away. Weapons and chests were piled up in the middle of the courtyard, and Toke reappeared with a lighted torch. He had a silver cup in the other hand and asked Stentor how injured the men were. The gothi looked tired, and his answer was quiet, 'Four have wounds that are more than scratches, Hafr from Horn Dale has broken a foot and young Ingmar will die.'

'And yourself?'

His amber eye glistened, 'A bee sting, Øysteinson, let us get away before the weather gets its teeth into *Twin Raven* for real.'

Arnulf looked at the dying Viking, who was struggling to speak. Five out of action and two killed; it went against Toke's voyage luck, and if Stentor's wound was a bee sting, then Toke's neck was tickled with a feather! He clenched his teeth and went to lend a hand; at least the spoils seemed to be good. He chose the best weapon and rolled it into a lost cape and Toke walked slowly along the proud house, setting fire to the eaves. Fat smoke waved in the wind down over the Vikings, and Arnulf threw the bundle of weapons over his shoulder and put a box under his arm; he let the mutilated wolf shield lie.

Hafr needed two men to support his limping, but the heavy silver chain Eigil Black had hung on his neck seemed to numb the pain, for he did not seem sad. Ingmar Thorirsson was carried by his brother into the burning house to accompany Toste, and as the smoke stung his eyes, Arnulf thought of Helge and Rolf. He spat at the dead earl and stepped over the fallen housecarls. The ground was slimy with blood, with more than one puddle composed from Serpenttooth's song, and Arnulf

171

straightened. He and Toke had fought heavily, and everyone had seen it, he had kept his word, Helge would have smiled! Had they been together now, Helge would drink to him and make verses about his deed, by Fenrir he would! Verses that would oust the stench and murmur of death and glorify the desperate, verses that would let heroes rise from cut iron and force the cries back into their throats, verses that would give Toste and the earl life again!

The fire and the wind did not go well together, and the Northmen's departure from the earl's yard was subdued. Leif Cleftnose came stomping with his new thrall, whom he again held by the hair, and Toke joined Arnulf. The earl's daughter looked bruised, but the look she sent the Northmen around her led Eigil Black to believe she probably had too much to avenge now to walk with her hands free, and Leif, laughing, let him bind her arms behind her, while he pulled up her dress and showed off his conquest. Toke stepped forward, but Arnulf felt his manhood stir at the sight. She was beautiful, though Frejdis was more beautiful. More beautiful and whiter. Rounder and kitten soft. With hair like milk amber.

Leif's companions were horny and believed the loot could be shared, and Leif threw out his arm, shouting that there was enough woman for all, as soon as the fires burned for the night, for he was always generous. Odin's spear stood like a candle for Frejdis, as his desire for the bondswoman subsided. Lovemaking should happen with laughter and hunger, not with screams and degradation. Arnulf looked out towards the sea. The earl's household would bring the testimony of his daughter's fate, and Leif deserved some pursuers chasing him down.

The waves beat furiously on *Twin Raven's* tail, and the wind had become dangerously powerful. It blew away from land and Toke did not allow the ship to be pushed out before the cargo and the wounded men were well on board. On land, wild flames ate the farm and buildings as tribute to Toste and Ingmar and Arnulf found his place and picked his cloak up from the deck. He slung it over his shoulders and sat down as an overwhelming weariness came over him, causing his hands to shake. Ashamed, he kept to the thwart while the sail was set, and the sea stallion danced free of the strand. Toke let the course remain steady and Arnulf took a deep breath, his pulse going up rather than down. Anxiety it was, anxiety! He had fought as if he was tired of life, and countless blades could have laid him cold easier than a hot knife through butter. That Toste and Ingmar burned alone was Fenrir's fault! Who else would have prevented the blow from hitting him in the back, two man against the hird, a madman's actions!

> The son of Stridbjørn
> Sword scarred and marred
> Frightened by battle
> Fearful from frays
> With wayless wavering
> Blood pale blade

'Are you injured, Arnulf?'

'Injured?'

Arnulf raised his head. Stentor ran his eyes over him, he had to speak loudly in the storm.

'No, I ... Maybe a bruised rib.'

Arnulf looked at his scratched thigh. Stentor nodded, 'It weakens the living to stand close to death, and you and Toke have sat on its claws. Your blót was not in vain.'

'Toste's was, and he gave more than I!'

The gothi had to be able to vouch for the gods' choice.

'Odin wanted him while he was strongest. Who wants to die of winter disease and decrepitude? Give Toste a skaldic verse, Skald-tongue, a verse that is worth dying for, then his kinsmen will not grieve too heavily.'

Twin Raven heeled hard and took in water, and Arnulf had to hold the shield rim. Although the ship straightened itself, the waves beat between the shields, puddling around their feet and Toke's mouth was tight. The sea was angry and the gusts erratic, and Arnulf acknowledged the danger and got a hold of his discouragement; only hardened men went a-viking! The sail was taut and hopefully would hold, and the daylight gave way to ashen clouds. Daunting how abruptly the weather changed! Arnulf, shivering, looked out at the horizon the long ship had recently sailed, and several of the Northmen thought that *Twin Raven* should put in again, the wounded's journey was difficult enough without the battering of the sea. Toke wanted to sail further and Stentor was silent and pale, but Leif shouted from the foreship that he had not risked life and limb in the earl's yard to drown immediately after. He had the thrall woman beside him on the thwart and probably had more desire for a campfire than rowing an oar. Toke replied that the ship could withstand higher waves and that the looted mead would replace the salt water in time.

Arnulf turned to face the wind. The sea stallion was like a wooden bowl on the sea, a bark basket, but the fear had lost its bite, and he lifted his feet away from the sloshing water. The men agreed to put into the coast at the next cove and Toke allowed the ship to sail closer along the strand. The foam boiled on the watery-field, and the storm began to howl, but *Twin Raven* took strength from the wind's song and glided through the water like snow drifting over ice. Arnulf pulled his cloak tightly around him, huddling. He had sweated so much that the heat had left his body, and the pain in his hand vied with the pain in his ribs. A warm fire. A soft bed. Sizzling bacon. And Frejdis! He closed his eyes. If Rolf were not dead, she would have embraced him, pulled him inside and seated him at the fireplace with a mug of beer while she, smiling with eyes glimmering, got dry clothes out of a chest. She would have leaned down over it so that her breasts would fall forward, and her buttocks would invite his manhood. Arnulf groaned. She was now another man's wife; why had he jumped to avoid the swords of the earl's men? The golden hair, the soft skin, his life's blood. Brother murderer. Why cower? He had killed himself with the shock!

*****

Toke put *Twin Raven* up on a wide rocky strand that kept back a forest. After the vandalism and the looting none of the Vikings needed to seek too far under the trees, but the shelter was still welcome, so the tents were posted at a reasonable proximity and guards put on watch. The fire was flat and fickle, and the tent canvases unruly, but soon the Northmen were no longer defenceless against the storm and Arnulf sat near a fire. Leif Cleftnose tethered his thrall-woman to a thorny bush a little away from the heat, letting her freeze, while he himself carried beer in land and Toke followed Stentor into a tent so he could look at his shoulder.

The earl's bread and meat were shared around, and the good food made it possible to endure the weather, but Arnulf was restless and ate little. The Outerfjord Vikings put up sheltering branches around the tents and drank to the first day of the voyage and Leif noticed with a raised mug that there were neither slain nor wounded among his village folk, Odin rewarded the strong!

Arnulf unwound the soaked bandage from his hand. It did not look good, a wound clamp would certainly help, and he got up stiffly. Hildegun had put both clamps and ointment in the sack, which Toke had brought into the tent. Arnulf shivered and gathered his cape around him. The

174

woman had to be freezing, but when he looked at her, she sat, staring right out at the storm, her gaze distant and without showing any sign of being cold. Her dress was torn so one breast hung exposed and Arnulf walked slowly towards her. When the thirst was sated and the fight retold enough, and the day did not offer anything more than to wait for clarification or evening, the Outerfjord Vikings would take her into the tent and do with her what they would.

Arnulf loosened the clasp on his cape. The woman looked at him without batting an eye and he offered his cape to her. Leif had taken her jewellery, her throat was scratched, and her tense breast leaked pearl drops of milk. Arnulf clutched the wool fabric hard. Somewhere in the woods a motherless child screamed from hunger, she had risked everything to burn the ship and stop the fight, no cape could shield her from her fate.

The woman looked at him as if he had voiced his thoughts and let her gaze slide to the forest. Arnulf lowered his arm. Another prisoner had once asked him for his freedom, but then he had thought of no one but himself, now his hand found its own way to the knife. She tensed when he drew it out, curling up like a cat, her face convulsed, and Arnulf moved slowly as he cut her arms free, so that she would not cut herself in panic. She made a noise when the rope fell to the ground, her tears flowing, then she was on her legs, bristling as she took a few tremulous breaths. She searched under her dress and tore something loose, which she quickly pressed into his hand, then she ran towards the forest, so even a wolf could not catch up with her.

Arnulf looked down. In his palm a gold cross on a chain shined, and he was taken aback. It was solid, rimmed with red glittering stones and decorated with the finest filigree work he had ever seen, an unimaginable treasure. A great man's cross. Or his daughter's.

A cry tore him away from his reverie, and he stuck his knife into its sheath. The woman disappeared into the swaying wood's edge, but Leif came running from the tents, raging like a wounded wild boar. The beer sloshed in the mug as he threw it away and the axe flew out of his belt, the Cleftnose was ready to kill.

Arnulf pulled the chain over his head and gripped his sword. Leif was going to kill him! No living power could intervene between them now, the woman's escape was just the last thing to be avenged! He drew Serpenttooth and stepped away from the bush, while the sight of the Viking's anger struck like lightning before thunder. Strange that life could suddenly be happy, even without Frejdis; Leif's axe could shatter the neck of a bull! Arnulf loosened his knees and lightly held his weapon. His heart beat so hard that his lungs could hardly bellow air, but then the sword's power flowed through his arm and Helge gripped the hilt with him.

He avoided the first blow and the next caught the blade. Leif's arm was stronger, and his axe sparked along the sword's edge, as if the sword were a trunk to be stripped of bark. Arnulf had to jump again, amazed at how quickly Leif could swing his axe around, and the fjord man wasted no energy, speaking or shouting, but stood assured, despite his drinking. Arnulf kept his distance and ran around his opponent, but Leif did not let himself be taken by surprise. With teeth bared and coldness in his eyes, he attacked again with a series of quick blows that forced Arnulf to defend himself and give way, foot by foot. It was obvious that Leif was not driving his blows through yet and was only giving a display of his abilities, and Arnulf had to strain not to stumble or completely lose control of the situation. He ducked and ran out of range, sweat running down his back. It was not enough for Leif to kill, he would humiliate, kick him around like a calf on a rope, force him to his knees and beat cries from him and there were plenty of spectators!

Arnulf growled deeply and did not let the Viking swipe first again. Serpenttooth aimed for his head, but Leif parried the strike, sweeping the sword aside so the following low blow missed. He did not look impressive and Arnulf went for him once again. The Northman received the attack with a humiliating calm and had no trouble staying alive, while Arnulf, out of breath, ran back and lay in wait for him while rage and fear wrestled in his chest. Leif was strongest, so Arnulf had to be the fastest, but his arm was strained after the fight in the earl's yard and the Cleftnose's confident attitude dented his courage.

Out of the corner of his eye, he caught glimpses of Toke and Stentor, who came hurrying out of the tent, but despite their irate looks, they respected fighting fair and custom and did not get involved. For Helge's sake! Serpenttooth was used to being victorious! Again, Arnulf jumped at Leif. By Geri and Freki if he would be subdued by that self-sufficient maggot! Leif Cleftnose fastened his grip, controlling the direction of the blows and Arnulf toiled in vain, while the strikes sent painful shocks through his forearm. Helheim swallow him raw, why were the shields aboard *Twin Raven*?

Leif struck the sword into the ground, kicking Arnulf in the back, causing him to fall with a yell. He rolled to the side and heard laughter, while the axe ripped up earth at his hip, came up onto his knees, holding Serpenttooth in front of him with both hands, and now Leif came at him with full strength. The axe hit rock heavily, the blade hooked and twisted the sword around, so he strained his wrists, and Arnulf had to give in so as not to lose his grip. He fought to come up onto his legs but could not resist the axe's next wrenching bite, his hands let go involuntarily and Serpenttooth flew from him.

Leif flashed a grin, and Arnulf jumped like a hare in an attempt to reach his sword, but the Cleftnose got there first. With one foot planted on the serpent-graced blade he stepped, threateningly, forward and Arnulf tripped doubtfully, pulling out his wolf-knife. The Outerfjord Vikings found this funny and shouted that with so sharp a blade, there would be no difficulty cutting an axe handle, as long as he just remembered to shake Leif's beard at the same time. Toke took a few steps forward but was stopped by Stentor, who had to grip him to hold him back.

Arnulf ran to the woods and broke off a spear-long branch, and Leif yelled for beer, for so long was it between the tiny nips, that he was suffering badly from thirst. Although the branch did not inflict any greater damage, his mouth was shut when Arnulf, with hard knocks, struggled to force the sword from his opponent and the Viking became incensed and had to turn quickly to ward off the stabbings. Arnulf pushed against his neck, and when Leif raised his arm, he drove his spear-branch between his thighs and ran around. The Cleftnose fell and the merriment around them died. Arnulf let go of the branch and snatched Serpenttooth in flight; his luck was back!

Leif got up and two shields were thrown to them, so the single combat could unfold in a more dignified manner. Arnulf put the knife in his belt and took one, but Leif let his lie and, with a two-handed hold, slashed against the shield's edge with a roar. The axe split the wood in pieces and left Arnulf with only half a shield, but the handle was damaged and fell off the boss, so that help had to be abandoned.

The sight of Leif, who now carried both a weapon and a shield froze the blood from his cheeks, and Arnulf retreated while he struggled not to be overcome by his own fears. The Northman lashed out violently, and Arnulf just managed to drive the blow away, the flat axe struck him on the shin, so his body crumbled, screaming. The pain was excruciating, and he wanted to grab his leg, but Leif struck again, and Arnulf had to put all his will behind his answering blow. He limped back and Leif did not begrudge him a moment's peace. His legs carried him, even though tears of disgrace blurred his vision and his weakened wrist had difficulty holding the sword.

Arnulf wanted to run away from the fight, but Leif followed him, forcing him to stumble towards the woods with relentless blows. The man might well have stolen Thor's belt the way he hit! And his gauntlets, too! The shield caught every lunge, and the axe's blows fell heavy as if a jötunn were throwing stone blocks. Sweat and power seeped, and Arnulf gasped for breath with an open mouth and tried to man up against his despair, if only Serpenttooth could at least hit Leif's hand, incapacitate him, even if it were only for a moment! For Fenrir! For Frejdis! Helge!

Leif came at him with the shield and hit his injured shins again, and Arnulf fell, wailing, to his knees. His body was shaking so badly that he no longer had dominion over it and a kick in the side sent him to the ground. Twisting, he stabbed the shield in fear of death, and Serpenttooth's tip cut deep but was restrained by the tough wood. Arnulf did not manage to wrestle his sword free, and Leif Cleftnose, snorting, pushed the shield aside. It went black before his eyes as the fjord man stood on Arnulf, his weight on his shoulder, and Arnulf fumbled to free his knife and strike his leg. The Silverwolf hit, but Leif raised his axe anyway in grim triumph, and Arnulf found unexpected strength. Garmr savage him, as if he would lie here begging for mercy! His shoulder creaked he fought so hard, and Leif uttered a sudden scream and dropped the axe. An arrow had pierced his arm, and Arnulf met his stunned gaze. Toke? Toke could not draw a bow nor Stentor.

Another arrow hissed, and the sound of cries from the camp made Leif step back.

'Leif! Arnulf! Quickly, we are being attacked!'

Eigil Black swung his arms, and Leif picked up his axe with his left hand while Arnulf, groaning, got to his feet. More arrows were shot out of the dim forest, and three Outerfjord Vikings came running with shields. One of the tents burst into flames, and the Norwegians left the bonfires, heads over heels, seeking the ship. A large group of men armed with longbows came out from the woods, and Arnulf started running as fire arrows began to squeal over his head. Damned that all sought to kill him! The man who had just saved him from Leif, could easily cause him a mortal wound!

Toke stood on the strand, shouting, and assuring himself that the wounded Vikings were carried aboard, but everything else had to be left, the attack was too violent and unexpected to allow a useful counterattack, the arrows hailed like heavy rain. Breathless, Arnulf reached *Twin Raven* and looked back. Leif came limping, supported by his companions as the fiery arrows hit the longship, threatening to set fire to it. More and more men came out of the woods, but they kept their distance, satisfied with using their bows, and Arnulf stuck his sword into its sheath. They wanted the Vikings out in the storm and the churning sea, to chase them off the strand in revenge for the killing and robbery, the earl's longhouse had lit up the land like a warning beacon! He fought to get on board and fell onto his thwart, unable to move again.

Twin Raven encountered the water, and Leif was the last to make it on board, hauled up over the aftship's shield rim, then the crew grabbed the oars and fled the coast with advanced strokes. Hræsvelgr was unfavourable towards the sea stallion, and the oars had to be pulled hard. The sea foam soaked Arnulf, and he hunched, droning, and finally got a hold of his throbbing legs. The ship would sink; death-by-drowning awaited them all, but exhaustion stifled both anxiety and sense like a woollen pelt. Leif sat next to him, suffering from his wounds, and Toke squeezed the helm, shouting that everyone had to take care against being washed overboard, Jörmungandr was awake!

The current was strong, and soon the arrows attack ceased. Twin Raven drifted, not letting itself be easily controlled and the Northmen raised their oars and took stock of the circumstances. Some thought the sail should be set, but Stentor wanted to ride out the storm, and the warriors on land mounted horses, apparently getting ready to follow their flight from the strand. Toke would, at all costs, keep land in sight and adamantly refused Hafr Hornsdale's proposal to sail out of sight now and put ashore later, but Leif was mad from both pain and the unfinished single combat and he wanted to go to the coast immediately and beat the enemy down.

Arnulf sat up on his thwart, holding on fast to it. Leif could neither walk nor strike, but no one dared to comment on it, and the Outerfjord Vikings were silent and held on when a huge wave crashed down on the deck and washed several shields overboard. Toke struggled to keep the ship along the coast despite the roaring wind, and Twin Raven groaned as it meandered over the crests of waves, while Stentor invoked Njord for protection. Arnulf peered towards land. A counterattack would have cost lives, but probably not all of them. If the longship sprang a leak from the storm, their escape would be in vain, and the coast seemed too far away to be reached by swimming. He looked at Toke. The bright eyes shone warmly, the Northman must have feared for his life, and Arnulf gazed warmly back. If they could make it this far, then no bad weather would get the better of them, and those who could put a friend in a brother's place had not lost anything!

Water was in the ship again and the bailer had to be used. Stentor threw a silver ring to the gods, and Leif listened abruptly, leaning over the shield rim where the shields were missing, while he clung to the planks, 'Arnulf! Come, help here! I cannot!'

He stretched out his arrow-shot arm and Arnulf sat up on his knees, 'Where? What's wrong?'

'Here! At the waterline, hurry!'

Arnulf looked over the edge into the raging sea. *Twin Raven's* side did not appear to be damaged, neither under the shield rim nor further down.

'Where? I can't see it.'

Leif did not answer, but suddenly Arnulf felt a tug at his neck and the next moment an indomitable force slung him over the shield rim. He wanted to scream, but black water closed over him, the cold beating the air out of the lungs as if Niflheim was enclosing his body. Wild with terror, Arnulf swallowed saltwater, beating his arms and legs to get afloat, despite Serpenttooth's weight. He coughed and sank again but gained control of his limbs and began to swim. Leif! That dishonourable tapeworm! It was impossible, no one could act so mean, throwing his opponent out of the ship instead of continuing their fight later, honourably and honestly! Never would he have believed him capable of such a callous ambush!

Twin Raven was already several boat lengths away, and Arnulf could see Toke standing half upright, throwing a rope out, but it was too short. The men toiled at the oars to turn the ship and Arnulf swam after them like he had never swum before. Fear overcame both cold and fatigue. He would die in the sea, no end could be more frightful than being left behind, strangling in your own horror!

Toke shouted, waving his arm, but a wave came between them, and Arnulf was pulled down again. The water was dark; nothing could be seen in the depths, but the sound of the storm's rumbling sounded like weapon noise from dead armies. He broke the surface, gasping for air. Toke's cries were distant, *Twin Raven* was impossible to row back, and Arnulf treaded the water. Only a fish could catch the ship now, and his body would not withstand the waves for long, weakened as it was.

Each time he was lifted up, the coast was visible, and Arnulf made a quick decision to swim landward. The current drove him sideways, his sword rubbing against his leg. People could be seen on the shore, armed men, and Arnulf gasped for breath, forcing his limbs to obey. Maybe they had not seen him, maybe they would ride on in their hunt to expel the

Northmen and would be gone when he reached the shore. Perhaps they would take him as a thrall, so he would have to flee. Maybe they would kill him.

He swallowed more water and had to throw up. His clothes were as heavy as chainmail and his sword pulled his hip down. Arnulf screamed to himself not to give up, just to swim, he could not let go of his inheritance, could not let Serpenttooth sink, no proud Viking threw his sword away voluntarily! The cold took hold of his hands and feet, sending tremors through his body. His eyes burned. The strand was too far away, and the sea too wild! He would never make it! Arnulf fought with all the might, all the anger, all the horror he could muster. Desperately slow he swam landward, time and again uncertain of the direction. The sword was heavy, ill-fatedly heavy! Serpenttooth would have to be sacrificed, Fenrir curse him! He searched for the belt, but his fingers were numb, and the buckle did not open. When he grabbed the hilt, he sank and had to let go to come up, he was going to die, die! His arms began to fail and the pain increase. They would find his body at daybreak, broken and torn.

'You are fighting too hard, let your body float!'

Arnulf stared around him, ice getting into his bones.

'Let only your head go under, you just need to come up and get air at every other stroke.'

Helge! Helge had taught him to swim. Arnulf obeyed and was able to do a few more strokes. When the sun went down over the sound, and the water was smooth as a bronze mirror, they had swum. Helge's strong scarred body and Arnulf's long limbs, he had been nine summers back then. His brother would take him in, Helge would not fail! From his deathbed on the seabed, he had seen Arnulf's distress, now he was here, darkness would not get hold of its prey! Helheim be damned!

Arnulf swam through ice, through his own blood, through pure pain. His fingers tore loose, the sea devoured his legs to the knees, thoughts fell like injured birds, only his heart and breathing were left. Through a shimmering red fog, the coastline slowly floated into his vision until shells and stones skinned his hands. A wave swept him up onto the rocky shore and Arnulf bore his forehead in the gravel, gulping water. A mountain lay on his back, his arms were forever anchored to the earth. He heard voices, and an echo of panic gave him the strength to look up.

Pattern-sewed leather shoes. Trousers of woven wool. An axe. In motion. Arnulf threw his head to the side, but the axe hit, and Sköll swallowed the sun.

*****

Skinfaxi's eye burned, without light, yet stark white; remotely through the fog at first, then growing closer, a dazzling, round throbbing, which grew more gruesome as he woke. The thirst smarted, his skin began to crack, Nidhogg's teeth gnawed at him.

Arnulf woke in his body and was hit by searing pain. It flowed over his forehead like molten iron, over his eye, down his cheek. He tried to see but was met only by a cobwebbed haze. Heard his own anguished groans, blinked and regained sight but only in one eye; slowly his surroundings came into view: an undulating ceiling, floating walls, flickering light. He wanted to defend himself, but his arms were rusty and heavy and hit out blankly into the air.

A figure bent over him and lifted his head cautiously, and the edge of a mug was pressed against his lips. The water was cold, and Arnulf drank deeply, becoming more lucid. The room he was in looked almost like a storage hut or a cleared workshop, and apart from the bed, the flickering candles revealed only a small table with a stool. A tall, skinny man was holding his head, speaking kindly in a foreign tongue, and Arnulf stared at him bewildered and stiffened abruptly. The man's hair was cut short, the crown of his head was bald and cowled and under his beardless chin, a silver cross hung around his neck. He asked questions, smiling, but Arnulf winced, horrified, wanting to be free of his grip. A monk! The thoughts tumbled over each other. Of all the enemies that had been on the strand, he had been taken as a thrall by White Christ's worst men! Stentor's talk about the monks' cruelty resounded hollowly in his mind and, by Tyr's death, if there weren't dried screams in the shadows along the wall! They would sacrifice him, eat him alive in their God's honour, drink his blood.

Arnulf shoved the hand away from his neck and sat up, but lightning struck his wound from the movement, and an overwhelming nausea upset his stomach. He managed to lean out over the floor before the vomit flew from his throat, then he curled himself up, wailing, his hands over his face, his senses dulled by the pain, it hurt so much that death would be mild. Pain!

The Christian put a steady hand on his shoulder, continuing his friendly talk, but Arnulf was only as calm, as a hare, facing a fox. He was dizzy, his arms trembling from exhaustion, he had not the least power of resistance to call upon, the bald crown had him quite in his hold!

The monk's grasp was warm on his swollen wrists and as he pulled them from the bound wound, his voice had an admonishing tone. Arnulf

182

tried to gather himself and, retching, sank back blank-eyed, and the man handed him the mug again without the slightest hostility. Why this care? Who was he, this cowled man? It was hardly him who had wielded the axe. And who had brought Arnulf to the hut? The monk? Why? The axe's swing had tried to kill, but someone may have averted his next blow.

The pain won over the will, and Arnulf clenched his hands and drank again. Tried to endure. His torn hand stiffened and he discovered a small neat skin nodule, which was sewn like wool cloth in a kyrtle. Were there no wound clips? And why do anything with the hand if White Christ was about to have his life anyway? The folds of a cowl could easily hide a sacrificial knife.

The Christian was silent for a while but then pointed at himself and shaped a word clearly: 'Stefanus.'

He repeated the name, and Arnulf blinked slowly, his own name he kept for himself. Stefanus pointed at the prestigious gold cross that had remained on his neck despite the fierce battle with the sea, and he spoke with joy in his voice, but Arnulf pulled the chain to himself, angrily. It was possible he was wounded and defenceless, but he would not be robbed! The monk raised his hand disarmingly and clasped his own silver cross, and Arnulf recognised White Christ's name in his tirade and tried to think clearly. Did Stefanus think that he too was in favour of White Christ? Was that why he had not already taken the cross, it was that valuable? In that case, he had to be mad! The monastery monks understood well the idea of gathering riches for themselves.

Arnulf had difficulty focusing his eyes and let things flow, and at the door he saw Serpenttooth leaning against the wall. Quickly he looked up at Stefanus; his sword was here! And under the blanket he found his knife still in its place, Stefanus must indeed be mad!

The Christian worshipper pretended not to notice anything, and Arnulf, tired, closed his eyes. What use would Serpenttooth be when he vomited, just from trying to sit up, there were no ropes necessary here, the pain kept him in the bed like *Gleipnir* itself. Misfortune and unhappiness, Jofrid must have carried out her threat and performed sorcery against him!

Stefanus pulled the covers up around his shoulders, and Arnulf could not bear to look again. Never had he been so weak, not even that autumn he lay with fever. The stillness of the night tamed his troubled breathing and hinted at the distance to the storm and fight, but the waves still rocked in his body, although they were gentle, even agony could be overcome by fatigue.

The cross slipped from his fingers, and Stefanus began to clean up the floor. Was it the earl's daughter, he had freed, was it she, who had saved his life? How could he ask a man who did not speak with an understandable tongue? Fenrir guard him, Veulf Whelpskin, for now there was none other than the giant wolf left!

*****

A strange song sounded at dawn, maybe it was just the glow of a dream. It reminded him of women's humming but was too deep in sound; in the distance the tones lingered, rose and fell without haste, quietly, without action and power. The song seemed to sway back and forth between the singers as if they were blowing feathers to each other, and Arnulf looked up. He was alone in the hut, the grey morning light seeping in through the half-open door. Outside he glimpsed an open space and a house wall, and the challenging crows of the rooster over-shadowed the deedless voices. He lay the back of his hand on his forehead and forced sleep from the body. They would come for him now! The monks had only kept him alive overnight to wait for day and when the sun rose, Stefanus would get ready for the sacrifice and get him! Had Stentor himself not told him about the cruel and bloody rituals?

Arnulf stroked his hand over his face and drew his knife under the blanket. The nausea was still gripping his stomach and the pain lurked threateningly. His limbs did not seem stronger than before. The stitched hand murmured, and his calf was hot and swollen, Baldur's death, how miserable! His muscles were stiff and useless.

They sang to the White Christ out there, Stefanus and his companions, their voices lissom, but Arnulf knew better! Gentleness and cowardice were their mantle, but they had blood between their fingers, and so much that they drank it! He moved uneasily. Stentor should be here now and fulfil his oath of Christian murder, his blade would find rich harvest, and Arnulf could use support, denounce this weakness! He would pretend to sleep when they came in, so he would have to be defensive, as best he could, he would die in full deed!

The song went on, undisturbed like the rising sun, and Arnulf listened. It crept into his body, got stuck in his breath, but the ballad was not entertaining. Did Toke think he had drowned? Had he seen Leif's heinous deed, or had the waves been blamed for the accident? And his eye! Arnulf muttered. The axe had hit over his eye; it felt as if it were knocked out! Was he now to live half-blind like Fjølner at home in the

184

village? His eye had been cut during a duel and rotted away over the summer, and since then Fjølner had found it difficult to judge his blows. Æsir's curse, Jofrid's sorcery; his life was to be sacrificed – why mourn a mutilation?

It burned beneath the bandage, although wound-fever was long in coming, Hlidskjalf break, he was so tired! Just holding the knife demanded exertion; it was Leif's fault, the traitor! Revenge, he should have revenge, he would chase the Cleftnose to the end of the sea!

The song ceased.

Stefanus had neither rope nor sacrificial knife with him when he walked in the door, just a steaming bowl, and there was nothing bloodthirsty in his step. Arnulf did not return his greeting but let go of the knife, it would probably not have struck hard anyway. Stefanus pulled a stool over to the bed and put his hand on his forehead. That there was no fever, seemed to delight the monk, and he pointed to the gold cross and nodded. Then he lifted his eyes and mouthed something with a different wording than usual and drew a cross in the air above the bowl. It smelled of soup, and his stomach was suddenly very busy making demands behind the persistent nausea, but Arnulf looked away when Stefanus lifted the spoon. It was bad enough being fed like an infant by a stranger, quite another to consume food that clearly had incantations said over it! Fighting Jofrid's sorcery was enough, White Christ could keep his malicious sorcery to himself!

Stefanus spoke enticingly and even slurped the soup, and the hunger was almost insatiable with the pain. If White Christ wanted murder, poison was not necessary, and no matter what was in the food, it could badly weaken his limbs even more. Stefanus sounded reproachful now, and Arnulf looked at him again. Would Fenrir not slurp what was given to him? There was strength to be had in the contents of that bowl, strength to heal the wound, and had it maybe cost Helge to associate with a foreign god and be falsely baptised? He kept his humiliation to himself and let Stefanus offer him the spoon, but he did not manage many mouthfuls, before he had to lean out of the bed and throw up again, so the straw rattled. His courage fled; how could he recuperate when food ran out of him faster than it could be forced in?

Stefanus did not seem surprised and put the bowl on the floor. He gave Arnulf water and began to loosen the dressing and Arnulf had to summon all his will to endure being touched. It felt as if his face was being ploughed through the middle, and he had to push his feet against the bed's footboard as the cut skin was exposed. He wanted to feel the injury with his fingers, but Stefanus took his wrists and shook his head. Instead Arnulf tried to open the eye, afraid for the fate of his vision, and though it was dizzying, he managed to lift his eyelid so much that a little hazy light penetrated through the crack. He looked quickly at Stefanus, and the Christian worshipper pointed at both of his eyes and nodded as he explained in his foreign tongue. Arnulf was breathing heavily. He could see! He was not blind, only his eyelid had been torn! It felt swollen, but the wound did not bleed, maybe Stefanus had sewn it like his hand.

The monk rubbed salve on it, and Arnulf complained, the suffering eclipsed the joy of the light, if only the cowled one would go! Go and let him be alone, so he could again seek refuge in sleep and get away from the anxiety and misery, away from mutilation, from misfortune and curses! Arnulf held a shock of screams back, hard hands spun his life's thread, the calloused grip of fate smart and urged defiance!

He looked earnestly at Stefanus, who was putting clean linen over the wound, 'How did I get here?'

He spoke clearly and pointed at himself and at the hut, his voice hoarse from screaming and saltwater. Stefanus wrapped the cloth around his head and replied, just as clearly in his strange tongue, pointing to himself and made a motion as he lifted something from the floor up to the bed.

'That was you? Why?'

The monk smiled and pointed to the gold cross and named White Christ. He must really believe that they shared the same faith. Arnulf nodded gently and tried to draw a ship in the air, 'And the ship? Did it sail away? Have you seen a ship? Toke? Toke Øysteinson?'

Stefanus shook his head, gesturing with his hand, as if he did not understand, and Arnulf breathed deeply. He was alone, the Northmen must have been convinced that he had been drowned or killed.

'Am I free or a captive? What will happen to me now?'

The gestures were lacking, and Stefanus seemed not to understand but gently pressed his hand against his shoulder, as a sign to remain where he was. Arnulf shook his head and immediately regretted the movement, 'You're wrong, I do not worship the White Christ, Fenrir is my god.'

The monk nodded eagerly at the word he recognised, and Arnulf closed his eyes. The axe had beaten the will out of him, but he had to get a grip on how he could escape the monks, but the thoughts writhed around each other with blinding pain. If he should not die, he would sleep, at least he had not lost his nose like Leif! That scar was disfiguring; a cheek-blow testified, after all, to courage. Helge had worn his scars, like he had worn his silver. Arnulf had to be patient, as patient as the giant wolf himself!

*****

Arnulf slept restlessly for most of the day. Now and then he was awakened by his own wailing, but the tiredness was heavy enough to pull him back into sleep, offering him relief. Stefanus gave him water when he was awake, and put a new bandage on the wound, but otherwise he sat at the small table, working carefully with something using long white goose feathers. What it was, Arnulf could not see, and he did not care, but in the evening, he was able to eat a little without throwing up, and the rest had loosened his strained muscles. It made Stefanus happy, who pointed to the gold cross and held out his hands, and though Arnulf did not like the proximity of the strange god to his sickbed, he was relieved by his improvement and that the fever was still holding off.

He could also sleep at night, but song and pain woke him at dawn, and when the worst fatigue appeared to be over, he did not find peace from his wound again.

Stefanus was out, and Arnulf moved tentatively and wondered if he dared to sit up. He could lift his arms without shaking and was no longer dazed, and under the blanket a neglected longing for Frejdis remained and grew, no, he should not die! Smiling, he decided to postpone his flight for a short while, but he did not get much pleasure from his decision until the monk came into the hut again with a greeting. Arnulf swallowed his disappointment and returned his greeting, and Stefanus sat, chatting at the bedside, and removed the bandage and seemed very pleased with what he saw. The salve jar was taken out with a barrage of incomprehensible questioning, but suddenly his fingers stiffened on the jar's edge and the cowled one listened intently.

Through the closed door an excited cry could be heard, followed immediately by the voices of others, and a wailing cry induced barking dogs and cackling chickens. A bell began to chime, and the sound of running feet and slamming doors made Stefanus get up, pale. Arnulf looked at Serpenttooth by the door, and gripped the knife's handle, while his pulse throbbed, splitting his forehead. Toke was coming! The Northmen had returned, who else would well get the half-bald ones out there to squeal in fear like scalded pigs? Hail Fenrir, he was not completely deserted!

187

The bell's chimes were silenced, and he pulled the gold cross chain over his head and fumbled with the jewellery in the straw so as not to be taken for a friend of the monks, while Stefanus dropped the ointment jar on the floor and looked like he did not know if he was going to run or stay. Other cries could be heard now; strong, commanding voices and Arnulf struggled to sit up firmly, holding on to the edge of the bed. To the monk's dismay, the door was flung open and a man entered, bursting the hope of Toke's help.

The intruder was young, and his axe bloody, his yellow hair long and fine, his bare arms scarred like an old boar skin. The short leather vest was marked with blows and both a long knife and a sax hung from his belt, and two blood-speckled silver crosses also dangled from it. He stopped, astonished, with the foot on the doorstep at the sight of Arnulf, who stared challengingly back and pulled out the wolf's blade, so it was visible. The man had killed, and more than once, and if, at first, he took Arnulf to be in fellowship with the monks, Helge and Rolf could easily get a visitor in Valhalla soon!

The Viking's eyes sparkled, and Stefanus took refuge behind the table and began, shrilly, to chant incantations with his cross held high in his hand. Terrified screams could be heard outside, and Stefanus knelt, tears running down his cheeks from fear of death. Without tearing his eyes from Arnulf, the blond youngster moved over to the monk, and with the same indifference as if he were kicking a dog out of the way, he put his axe in the monk's neck.

The Christian worshipper sank, his limbs rattling and jerking, and Arnulf did not make a move towards the sparkling metal, for the axe drank weak blood. His heart beat like a drum against the knife's handle, and his kyrtle was clammy in that same moment. The Viking took a slow step towards the bed, like he was trying Arnulf's cold-bloodedness. Despite the threatening attitude, his face radiated no dislike, and Arnulf found it hard to believe that he would share the fate of Stefanus. The stranger rested his weapon on his shoulder but then jumped forward, without notice, with a well-aimed blow. Despite his muscles throbbing, Arnulf kept himself motionless, tensed to the limit. The axe stopped within a whisker of his skin, and Arnulf felt the chilling edge in his uncovered wound.

The Viking's gaze was narrow but made room for response, though Arnulf still did not move. A swarm of bees was buzzing in his veins, and he had to control himself hard not to act rashly, 'Take that axe from my skin, Man of Thor, I will not mix blood with a monk!'

The stranger frowned, but then gaiety broke through, and he burst into a short laugh, lowered his weapon and wiped a drop of sweat from Arnulf's temple with his fingertip. Arnulf loosened his grip on the knife, and the Viking returned his axe to his belt, taking a step back, 'I am Svend Silkenhair, warrior from Jomsborg, son of Bue the Stout and grandson of Vesete, earl of Bornholm. Who are you?'

By Odin! A Jomsviking! Arnulf hid his self-consciousness and thought it advisable to keep his knife ready anyway. Winter Evening's proud, heroic skaldic verse heroes welled up in him, reports of the finest and strongest of all warriors, and with them Toke's respect and awe.

'Veulf.'

'Veulf? Nothing more?'

'Does a man's worth depend on the length of his name?'

Arnulf did not have much desire to lay out his reputation as an outlaw and brother-murderer against Svend's genealogy. The Bueson's grey-blue eyes sparkled, 'No. My name is shorter than yours!'

He looked curiously around the hut and saw Serpenttooth. Brazenly he took the sword and drew it from its scabbard and wielded it, 'Your sword?'

He looked appraisingly at the blade and felt its weight.

'Yes!'

Serpenttooth did not suit strange hands.

'It is good. I could take it.'

'Then you'll have to fight me first, that sword is my inheritance from my brother!'

Svend seemed to find this remark amusing and hissed the sword into its sheath, 'You? If I want to, I will make you my thrall!'

'Only if you win!'

Arnulf was ready for anything. Outside, the tumult and the screams stopped, and laughter was unleashed. The Jomsviking smiled, 'You will be badly in debt if you must owe me both the sword and the value of a thrall. Why are you here? Who wounded you?'

Arnulf did not back down, an unarmed man was a wingless bird, and as long as the warrior had his sword his mood was foul, Svend had killed easily. Stefanus' goodness had certainly not been reciprocated!

'I'm not wounded! I'm just lying here, resting while I think about how I should move on.'

Svend raised his eyebrow as he handed him Serpenttooth, and nodded towards Stefanus, who had faithfully followed his God, 'And the monk there?'

Arnulf grasped the sheath, appeased, 'I don't know him. I was on a voyage with a ship from Norway but fell out with one of the Northmen. We met in single combat but were interrupted by archers from the woods and forced out at sea in the storm with our companions, and my opponent was then mean enough to throw me overboard and leave my fate to the enemy on the strand.'

He spat on the floor, 'They beat me down when I reached the shore, and I woke up here.'

Svend stroked his finger over his lip, nodding thoughtfully, 'You have something to avenge, Veulf, was it a big ship? In which direction did it sail?'

'*Twin Raven* is worthy of an earl. We sailed south.'

'I have not seen any remarkable ship in the last couple of days, but a number of rivers run inland, your companions could be anywhere. Did they see you swim ashore?'

Arnulf stared gloomily at the open door. Toke could easily have sailed up rivers, but *Twin Raven* might as well have gone down.

'If Toke had believed I was alive, he would have come after me and I don't know why I wasn't murdered on the strand, for the monk there spoke only a foreign tongue. As for me, I am alone.'

Svend Bueson went over to the dead man and tore the silver cross from his neck, and Arnulf threw the blanket aside and stuck the wolf-knife in its sheath. It was good to hold Serpenttooth again, there was no reason to fear anymore. If only he had his full strength, he would have the courage to cross the country on foot and meet what there was.

Svend attached the silver chain to his belt, stepping over Stefanus, 'I believe I will think better of you as a friend than as a thrall. Can you stand?'

He held out his hand, and Arnulf looked up. Friend, friend with a Jomsviking! Had Valhalla itself dropped into Midgard? Several new and old scars furrowed Svend's face, and his eyes shone with self-won life as if he had snapped at death so many times that he no longer believed it to be dangerous.

'Friendship is worth far more than bondage, Bueson! And why should I not be able to stand? My feet are not broken.'

Arnulf grabbed his hand and swung his legs over the edge of the bed, but when he got up, a tree knocked down on him so violently did pain and dizziness jump from his wound. He lost his footing, exclaiming, and fell to his knees, and Serpenttooth clanged on the floor.

190

'Calm down, show your enemy's blow some respect! Is this your first wound?'

Svend pulled him up to sit on the bed, and Arnulf pressed his hand against his forehead, while the hut spun around him, 'Why do you think that?'

'Your skin is as smooth as a young maiden's, and no sensible man jumps like a wanton foal from his sickbed. Here, drink!'

The Jomsviking found the mug under the bed. The water cleared his vision, and Arnulf was extremely annoyed. Anyone could be inexperienced, but it was shameful to reveal it so clearly.

'Svend, you wooden-cock, where are you, there are no women here! Come out, you can get a pig to entertain you instead.'

The cry resounded fiercely and Svend flashed a grin, 'My father! He allows me peace in a woman's bosom no more than a moment! Come on, lean on me.'

He put Arnulf's arm around his shoulder and helped him up, and Arnulf had to lean heavily, so his quivering legs would not fail him again. The gold cross! He glanced towards the bed straw. So valuable a treasure should not be forgotten unless ... unless it was wiser to leave the Christian symbol instead of waving it under of the nose of unknown raiders. They would hardly let him keep it, and what if they took him to be a friend of the monk's anyway? Fickleness and Mimir's offering, had Odin given an eye in pay for wisdom, was a gold cross a fair price for life and freedom! Arnulf was sweating from the strain, stumbling as if he were drunk, and Svend took Serpenttooth and helped him put it on his belt. Condemned to be dragged out like an old hag, Thor punish the monks for making the doorstep so high!

The increasing daylight was still not sharp but was dazzling after the half-darkness of the hut and the unfamiliar surroundings and many men outside flowed together like flickering flames. His head felt twisted and wrong on his neck, and Arnulf stopped after a few steps, blinking. Svend Silkenhair's ship companions were busy looting, and all around bleeding monks lay motionless on the ground. The Jomsvikings seemed proud to look as they did: heavily armed and violently sword-bitten where the skin was visible. Some wore chainmail and scratched helmets, others had thrown off their kyrtles in the heat, and axes and spearheads were marked from fighting but newly sharpened.

The hut, Arnulf had lain in, lay beside some other small buildings in the corner of an open space surrounded by four unusually long houses, some of which seemed to serve as living quarters. The buildings were not joined and small plots for vegetables and herbs seemed to lay here and there, and sheep and cows trotted around, grunting, uneasy from the smell of blood. Gilded crosses, caskets, chests and colourful cloth rolls were piled up on the hard-stamped earth with precious glassworks and plump barrels, and in the middle of the courtyard stood a strong, rotund man, his legs apart and one hand on his hip. His features were coarse, and his chainmail distended over his weapon-endowed belt, two fingers on his shield hand were halved and his right ear was missing.

'Well, there you are! Loki screw me if I did not think you were in bed with a woman! And who is the weedy one you are carrying around? Is he not man enough for his legs?'

Bue the Stout looked at his son brusquely, but Svend, unfazed, pulled Arnulf towards the growing heap of stolen booty and let him sit on a chest. Weedy one! Although the body staggered, at least the anger had enough blazing force to stand on its own! The pulse throbbed in the wound like a cleaving axe through wood and Arnulf bowed his head, clenching his teeth. If the Vikings should consider him something, there should be no grumbling at least!

Some of the warriors came curiously closer, and Svend leaned confidently in over the Arnulf with a low voice, 'Are you in pain, Veulf? Know then that I myself am not able to feel pain, and that the men here are neither known in defeat or fatigue. They laugh when they are tickled by swords.'

Arnulf snorted defiantly, looking up, 'I have no pain, I was dizzy, and dizziness has never taken honour from anyone!'

Svend laughed softly, turning towards his father with his hand on the axe, 'The weed here is Veulf, my kinsman, who I have just caught lazing in a monk's bed. Welcome him, though he is temporarily slightly subdued, for he came from his ship companions in the storm and was not greeted hospitably when he swam ashore.'

Bue the Stout lowered his eyebrows and spat peevishly. 'If he is your kinsman, then King Sweyn is my little brother! By all the gods and jötnar, what will you do with him? You will have to make a good trade, if you want to get a decent thrall-price; he does not have his full strength!'

Arnulf had to bite his tongue, but Svend would not be cowed, 'I will take him to Jomsborg and see what he is useful for. He has the look of a wolf, so if it suits me, I will show him how a great warrior bites.'

Arnulf's breathing was quick. Go with them to Jomsborg? Even Helge had ever reached so high!

Bue blushed threateningly and several men came forward with expectant looks.

'You know Jomsborg's laws as well as I do, you cannot take him. He is too young and will never be able to pass the tests.'

Svend's grin sparkled, as he raised his hand, 'Surely I know the laws, but I also know that Sigvalde does not keep them as zealously as he should! Not least, I myself would have been denied because of my age, and everyone knows that Vagn was only twelve, when he was admitted. Veulf looked Snap's blow in the eye just now and he did not flinch!'

'A lad with Palnatoke's blood in his veins may well be seen as a man at twelve, and he, who does not give way to your axe, can be petrified from fear as well as bravery! Where had you otherwise intended Veulf to be on the journey home? When these goods are loaded, the ship will lie with its shield rim below rather than above water, there is no room for even a roasted chicken!'

'Then I will tie him to the bow. That face can be used to frighten the enemy as well as any dragon's head.'

Bue stomped the ground and turned, panting, towards a strong, elderly man with a seagull white beard, 'Then say something to him, Bjørn, he usually listens to you! Vagn! Where is Vagn? Vagn! Vagn Ågeson! Come here and talk sense to your kinsman, or else, Gungnir impale me, I will soon become a son-murderer!'

A large man with hands full of silver goblets broke the row of men. He looked young, and his dark hair was unruly on his shoulders, courageously he wore his strength, so fearlessly that it bordered on cruelty. Bue pointed, and a black spear hit Arnulf when he met Vagn's eyes. They were so filled with violence that they could cause a man's blow to hesitate. Vagn knew and, apparently, rejected his opponent, faster than any weapon could reach him, and though Arnulf stared sharply back, his defines was too late.

Vagn Ågeson threw the goblets on the ground and looked around the circle. Everyone seemed about to accept his judgement except Svend, who kept to his demands. The silence gave Arnulf the urge to scream. Vagn walked slowly around the heap of goods, sniffing like a stallion, 'I do not leave a companion in the lurch, young or old, who needs help. Would any of you refuse an outstretched hand in need?'

He turned to Arnulf, less threatening than before, 'You will not weigh down the ship any more than half of Bue's belly. Will you come with us to Denmark, Veulf? We shall sail the length of the kingdom, so you can be put off, where it suits you.'

Bue the Stout rolled his eyes but did not object, and Arnulf straightened, enduring the dark gaze. To an outlaw, Vagn's offer was, well-intentioned, though of little help.

'It would be a great honour to sail with you to Denmark, Vagn Ågeson, but I still think that Svend Silkenhair's proposal is best.'

Vagn startled, but Svend laughed to his father, 'You see, I was telling the truth about being kin to Veulf, proud blood does not let itself be either persuaded or scared! Is it not true that you yourself, Vagn, refused to accept half of Bretland in exchange for refraining from going to Jomsborg? My share of today's looting is Veulf.'

Vagn shrugged with a hint of a smile, 'I won both and will not stand in the way of a wholehearted endeavour, but you should know, Veulf, that many warriors have come to Jomsborg, but only the best were found worthy to stay. Neither Sigvalde nor we tolerate the sight of weaklings.'

Arnulf put his hand on Serpenttooth. The scratch no longer itched.

'Weaklings are not part of my lineage, and cowardice is not our habit, so no shame shall be cast over Svend for opening Jomsborg to me.'

'With us actions come before words, in turn, a promise is kept to death, so be quiet and listen, Maidenskin, so no one gets tired of you too soon!'

Vagn's return was dry and the words smarted, but Bjørn went past him and stood right in front of Arnulf. Although the white beard and the bald head revealed his age, he appeared no weaker than the others, and he stooped and looked inquiringly at Arnulf's wounds, then nodded his approval, 'The cut is healing exceptionally well, it is well-sewn. Who took care of you? We could use that man.'

Arnulf wanted to respond, but Svend beat him to it, 'You should have said something before, Bjørn the Bretlander, the monk is dead, I killed him.'

He cast a careless glance at the gash and, without warning, drew his sax and jumped against Vagn with a crushing strike. Vagn's sword flew out of its sheath just as fast, and he met the attack effortlessly, and with a look of indifference swept the sax aside and struck Svend harshly on the upper arm with the flat blade. The skin flushed, but Svend did not seem to notice, and none of the bystanders found the outcome surprising. Arnulf hid his amazement, and Bjørn's face was pitiful, 'If the ship were not so full, we should capture some wound-knowledgeable Christians and take them home. They have a reputation for being able to pull a sick man out of fever.'

'What do you think Odin thinks of his hird being weakened like that? Those, who have earned it, die, we others had better think of carrying the muck here on board.'

Bue looked impatient, and the men let Arnulf be, and returned, chattering, to the loot. Svend sneaked behind Vagn and tried his luck again, this time with the axe to help, but Vagn was still too fast for him and paid for the jest with a knock in the back. So, he began to collect his silver goblets and Svend put his weapons away and gave his hand to Arnulf, 'The ship is lying down in the creek behind the hill. The snekke is not so big, but we were not so many who set out.'

He tossed his head, and Arnulf took his hand and got up but let go of the hand again and started walking. His knees were very loose, and the ground beneath him unreliable, but even if he had to crawl, he would reach the ship by himself. Svend flung the chest on his shoulder and followed, and Bue's disapproval had completely disappeared as he slapped his son in passing, 'Take Vagn with a broken arrow next time, he will not see it, if you hold it in your sleeve.'

'Vagn sees like Heimdal himself, I would rather take an anvil, he would not think of ever getting that in his skull.'

Svend adjusted the chest, grinning at Arnulf, 'I have not yet managed to get at him, even at night, but just wait! That night I hid under his sleeping skins, I got the blade in his hair at least.'

Arnulf smiled. Although he knew no one would be able to avoid Svend's snake-swift attack, 'And Vagn? Does he attack you, too?'

He stepped past the last building; the wind smelled of the sea.

'Only when he finds my skin too colourless, we are kinsmen and blood companions, Vagn and I, and it is a commitment.'

'Blood companions?'

Svend jumped over a dead monk and walked along an upward sloping field, 'Yes. When a man is accepted into Jomsborg, his blood is merged with those who wish to do so, and that merging binds us stronger than brotherhood on a journey or in combat.'

Arnulf was unsteady on his feet and Svend stretched out his arm, but Arnulf refused help, 'How is Vagn your kinsman? Bue said he has Palnatoke's blood, but he bears Åge as his father's name.'

Svend nodded, 'Palnatoke is the greatest Viking who ever brought joy to Odin, and it was he who gathered the strongest warriors from among the Danes, built Jomsborg and issued its laws. King Borislav gave him land in his kingdom, in the southeast of Denmark in exchange for his protection in wartime. He was terrified of looting and killing, when

Palnatoke put his ships on his strand, but they reached an understanding, and Borislav gave him the county of Jom to build his fort. Palnatoke's son, Åge, was betrothed to my father's sister and became the father of Vagn and that Vagn is his grandfather's descendent is clear to everyone. It was a great sorrow for Palnatoke to have to die from him.'

'When did he die?'

The hill took Arnulf's breath away.

'He fell ill a few years ago and entrusted Jomsborg to Sigvalde, Strut-Harold earl's son, for Vagn was still too young and much too hot-headed. Since then the laws have been obeyed moderately, but Sigvalde is a great warrior, as clever as a fox and wiser than most men and married to King Borislav's daughter. Jomsborg's reputation has not been harmed.'

'I didn't think there were women in Jomsborg!'

'There are not many, but with a little kindness and silver you can always seek out a peasants' daughters or enjoy their thrall-girls and that way a healthy man finds out for himself, what he needs on voyages.'

Svend stopped on the hill, pointing, and Arnulf resisted the temptation to sit down. Accursed suffering! Down in a low-lying cove was a yellow painted ship, its bow pulled up on the strand. It was not flashy, but it seemed seaworthy and stable and from the hill Arnulf could see how the bags and bundles were placed between barrels and thwarts. Behind him lay the deserted cloister at the mercy of the Vikings, and Vagn was beginning to set fire to the buildings. Svend pushed the chest onto the other shoulder, and Arnulf followed breathlessly after him through the tall grass and tried to feel whether his wound was bleeding, 'How long have you been in Jomsborg?'

'Many years as Bue's son, but I passed the tests last year and was fully accepted among the men.'

Arnulf looked at his hand. The wound wasn't oozing, 'What tests?'

Svend laughed, 'All the questions you ask! It seems like they are tumbling out of that hole you have in your head, but be careful what expectations run the other way, the tests are worthy of the Æsir themselves.'

'What are they based on?'

'Courage, Veulf! Strength, endurance, weapons proficiency, pain denial and cunning in battle, and if, after that, you can compose a good skaldic verse and empty a beer horn in one go, it will serve your honour.'

Arnulf was silent. Maybe he should go ashore anyway in Denmark? He could find a ship going north, try to get back to Haraldsfjord and wait for Toke. Odin's death! As if Jofrid wanted him back there and what was he to do in Norway? After the summer's voyage Toke was probably not going to include him in the family.

The pain washed over the wound again, worse than ever, and the water's shimmer blinded him. He felt a grip on his kyrtle as his knees hit the sand of the strand and Svend's voice was distant, 'Up again, Maidenskin, we are almost there. I will find a drink of beer as soon as we are on board. The heat from the sun tends to follow open scratches.'

Arnulf struggled angrily to get on his feet, unhappy with his new nickname. He would have to have a hand on Svend's free shoulder on their way to the ship, and the Bueson dumped the chest in the sand and looked back, 'Sit down before you fall, I will find the beer.'

The first handful of laden Vikings appeared on the hilltop, and Arnulf sank down on the lid of the chest, while Svend jumped over the shield rim and began to look between the barrels. Smoke surged up over the hill, and the wind carried laughter and eager cries. Arnulf recognised Bue's booming voice. He counted the men as they walked, and reached five hands, before Svend cut him off with a full mug and some linen strips. The drink was strong and the sun warmed and Arnulf rediscovered courage and let Svend bind his wound as the Jomsvikings gathered at the ship and loaded their loot. Bjørn the Bretlander was thirsty at the sight of the beer, so a barrel was retrieved and opened, and mugs passed around. Arnulf could easily take one more sip. The beer trickled under his skin, shielding the pain from him, and his sight was better; now the sun was not sharp in his torn eyelid. He raised his mug to Svend, who had found a yellow glass among the treasure and stood watching the sea through its amber hue.

Bue commanded the cargo be carried on board, but Vagn jumped amidships and stated that they had to be select about the plunder, for as it was now, only gold rings could fit among the huddled prey. It irritated the Stout, 'So re-pack and discard the least valuable things overboard. It was not just for the sake of play that we attacked the monks.'

'We did that twice already, yesterday, uncle, and Veulf takes up place.'

Vagn sent Svend Silkenhair an amused glance and Bue snorted, 'Do what you will, Vagn, it will not help to sell the Maidenskin when we do not even have space for the silver, it would yield.'

Bjørn settled by Arnulf with the sack he had dragged and was of the opinion that there could be place for all, if Bue were to swim after them, 'But we can do something about the food, then it will not take up so much space but the weight will be the same.'

He began to share round, and the men who were not wrestling with bundles and caskets, took a food break. Arnulf made good of the chicken thigh he was handed and watched the Jomsvikings without shame. Vagn Ågeson was exceptionally beautiful to look at, but even when he ate, he seemed dangerous, so vigilantly he bit into the cold meat. Svend had put down the glass and was combing his hair with a bone comb, and Bue drank, so it trickled down his stubbly beard. So mighty a man must be strong, jötunn strong, and heavier weapons than his, Arnulf had not even seen at Gormsø's market.

Vagn gnawed the bone clean and threw it at Svend, who grabbed it and sent it into the sea, 'I think we should stop with plundering along the coast and turn the bow towards Jomsborg.'

Vagn reached down into the sack and pulled out some bread, 'We can take a ship and sail further north, but Sigvalde has waited long enough, and I need to hear some news.'

Bue growled, acknowledgingly, 'We have enough ships at home, and I have not seen my brother since the autumn, I am with Vagn.'

He looked around and was greeted by consenting nods from most.

'Odin follow us! And if you see a nice ship, Vagn, then take it, so your long legs do not challenge my belly during the homeward journey.'

A man shouted from the deck that everything was ready and that the last man on board had to settle for hanging from the yard, and the seated Jomsvikings sprang up to push the snekke out. Svend helped Arnulf on board and threw the chest over the shield rim, as the men set to pushing the vessel out into the water. Arnulf walked gently on bags and bundles, while the gangway plank was drawn in. The deck was only visible between thwarts and many had just enough place to fit their feet, so there was a moment's difficulty as everyone got seated.

On the deck long spears were laid along the mast fish and stacks of shields lay, prepared for use, and helmets and chainmail were also within reach, testifying to both will and force.

Svend led Arnulf to the foreship and asked him to sit between two thwarts with his back against the ship's side, he pushed himself onto the next thwart beside Vagn. Bjørn and Bue settled down beside them, as a crooked-nose man grabbed the helm, and the sail was hoisted and took wind, and the snekke curved its bow and the keel cut deep. On the strand, the remains of the goods lay among emptied chests and barrels as compensation for the damage the land had suffered, and Vagn began to clean his weapon, unhappy with having to rub shoulders with his kinsman. Svend was not bothered by the congestion and eased the situation, 'Now, we can better hold the heat if the weather turns and you are still better off than if you were to have me on your lap.'

Arnulf supported his elbow on the thwart and did not like the sea's rocking. Although the wind was even, he was surrounded by more swaying and flickering than on *Twin Raven* during the storm, and both his head and stomach were against him.

'Of all shed blood, monk blood is the worst!'

Surly, Vagn rubbed the soiled sword hilt, 'It is as fatty and sticky as resin, Nidhogg soak them! Next time I would rather squash the creeps with a stone.'

'It comes from the fact that they relate more to life than other men. They are as afraid as rabbits to meet the god they worship so vehemently, am I not right, Veulf?'

Thoughtfully, Svend ran a finger along a scar at his elbow, but Arnulf was reluctant to respond as he had so little experience. Maybe blood was thicker amongst people from the south, what did he care? The beer and the sea made his body sleepy, and the trip over the hill had cost him several days' strength.

'Where are you from, Veulf?'

Bjørn made himself comfortable on the narrow thwart and let out his desire to talk. Fenrir's flaps, why could the old man not suffice with chatting with Bue instead of plaguing him with questions?

'Denmark.'

The Bretlander laughed, 'Yes, that I can hear, but where in Denmark? Who sailed with you, and how did you end up away from them?'

Arnulf was the subject of prying eyes, and Vagn looked up from his sword.

'I left my village and sailed with the son of a northern chieftain who offered me a place on his summer voyage. And I was thrown overboard during the storm. From behind, by a man who had tried to defeat me in single combat.'

The words were met by indignant outbursts, and Bue shook his head, 'You let him live too long! Pity should only be given to those who are worthy.'

Svend knew more but fell silent, and Vagn's gaze cut its teeth into Arnulf, 'You left your village to sail with strangers, and you will not mention your home or your father's name and, moreover, will not be set off in Denmark. Veulf you are called. By whom?'

Arnulf fought. Curse his unclear thoughts! The men here were killers, and to deprive an outlaw of life would hardly count as murder.

'By myself, Vagn Ågeson!'

Svend rose abruptly, jumping up on the thin shield rim. Despite the waves his foothold was true, and he beat playfully with his arms, 'Now you know enough, my sharp-minded blood comrade, you would do better to tell something of yourself! Many men journey in Jomsborg, and not everyone has a story. Never has a good skaldic verse forced been from a tongue.'

'Then get down, and now! If you fall into the sea, the ship will not be turned!'

Bue flared, but Svend just took some dancing steps, drawing his axe, 'Why? When we put bow against bow in a fight, the man who knows his ship best wins.'

Vagn gripped the axe handle as the Bueson swung, pulling him to him, 'You are right, Svend.'

He pushed his comrade to the deck and turned to Arnulf again, this time more forthcoming, 'I am Vagn, son of Åge and grandson of Palnatoke from Funen. My mother is Bue's sister, and therefore I must side with Svend here, even if he is as mad as he is unpredictable and fears neither Helheim nor Odin. Bjørn Whitebeard is earl of Bretland, and he was foster brother to Palnatoke's wife and he is now my foster-father. He gave Palnatoke half of Bretland to council over, a heritage, which fell to me after his death, so now we control the country together and have just stayed there all winter.'

'Wait, dear kinsmen!'

Svend found a seat next to Vagn again, 'You forgot to tell him how unruly and violent you yourself are now that you are listing my virtues! You should know Veulf that Åge endured his son so badly that Vagn had to take turns living with him and his grandfather, Vesete, earl of Bornholm, when he was a child. When he was nine, he had already killed three, and no one could tolerate his cruelty and brazenness, he would only listen to Bue. In pure anguish they gave him a well-staffed ship when he was twelve and sent him to Palnatoke, but none in Jomsborg would receive him, least of all my father.'

Vagn grinned, punching his fist into Svend's side, and Bue and Bjørn shrugged, smiling. Arnulf was even more reluctant than before to reveal who he was but hid his concern. A cat catches a mouse once the mouse flees, 'But you sail together now?'

'Yes, yes,' Svend let his zeal lead the words, 'Vagn could not be cowed! Palnatoke offered him half of Bretland if he would sail back to Funen, but Vagn challenged my father's brother, Sigurd, to single combat, to let the weapons decide whether he and his men deserved admission or not.'

Now Bue the Stout laughed aloud, 'Do you remember that Vagn? Even though my brother is the son of an earl, you called him a bitch with no more courage and heart than a mare, if he would not accept your challenge. It was spite, so Sigurd had to consent and rally his people.'

Everyone around Arnulf joined in the laughter, and Bjorn the Bretlander slapped his knee, 'And what were they met by when they sailed out of the fort? Stone! Afterwards, Vagn and his young companions struck down thirty of Sigurd's men and injured many, but then Palnatoke opened the gate and welcomed them to the brotherhood. Since then Vagn has been as mild as a lamb, so fear not, Veulf! Tyr could easily put his hand into his yawn.'

The last one Arnulf found hard to believe, but he managed a smile and a nod. Perhaps he had been better off with the monks, regardless of their intentions. A few more days, and he would have had the strength to escape them. How Odin would not win Ragnarök once the Jomsvikings fought among the Einherjar was hard to comprehend.

'Of Bue there is not much to tell,' said Bjørn, teasingly, 'Other than that he and Sigurd are the sons of Vesete, earl of Bornholm, and that they both lead many men in Jomsborg. Palnatoke had four highly trusted men, and the other two are Thorkel the Tall and Sigvalde, who now councils in the fort.'

'I guess that several of the men in Helheim have a lot to say about Bue, since they are there prematurely at his behest, but now you have scared Svend's new friend enough. He is as pale as seagull's dung.'

Vagn smiled wryly and resumed polishing his sword, but Arnulf denied him, straightened himself with a hand on the thwart, 'No one here has scared me! If I feel something, it is only pride that I sit among such deed-rich men, and if I look pale, it's because I'm dizzy from looking at so many strong faces with only one eye.'

Bjørn the Bretlander shrugged and spat into the water, 'So lie down and rest yourself while you can, Veulf Maidenskin. With the cargo, we carry, we will tempt every ship that meets us from here to Vindland, and we would like to see our guests lend a hand when needed. Even if they have only half their vision.'

Arnulf nodded and, silently, took the sleeping skin, which Svend handed him. As if he were able to so much as lift Serpenttooth. If it came to a fight, a kitten could sneeze him to the ground, however much Bjørn would slap his thigh and spit! He crawled on his side and wound the skin around him. Fatigue softened the planks, and even the waves could not reach behind his eyelid. Over the silver misty marsh came Frejdis, barefoot in her dark green dress, with snake embroidery, then she ran away, while the voices around him vanished, and only Fenrir's deep growls under the keelson remained.

*****

'Did he not let you sleep, this monk? You snore, as though you have been kept awake for days!'

Arnulf looked up, bewildered, as if a whip had tugged the merest at his face. Svend's yellow hair was within reach, he was bowing so much, and the grey-blue eyes slipped, 'We others have already eaten, but Bjørn saved a chunk for you so you could recover some strength. Are you coming, Maidenskin? My father can always gnaw another bone clean.'

Arnulf sat up, accepting the extended hand. Maidenskin. That name was hard to get used to! Svend waited a moment before pulling Arnulf up onto his legs. They murmured horribly, and Arnulf had to hold on for a moment before he could follow Svend over the deserted deck, his body heavy and clumsy.

On the strand, the tents were put up, and a large fire crackled. Fine smoke wound up into the air, drifting out over the water, and the bung was removed from a beer barrel. The Jomsvikings sat around the fire, with mugs in their laps, while a man sang, and the smell of roasted meat made Arnulf realise how long it was since he had last eaten. Light-headed, he went with Svend and sat down behind the circle around the fire. The evening was warm and the water calm under the golden sky. Svend found both meat and a mug for him, and Arnulf adjusted Serpenttooth and greeted the Silken-haired over the beer. The sea was so peaceful. Treacherously midsummer mild, Freya's time would soon come.

The song finished and drew applause and Vagn stood up and began to recite a story. Black fire glowed in the dark eyes and the light cast a bronze glow over his skin.

'Was he a good brother, the one who gave you the sword?'

Svend spoke quietly to avoid disturbing Vagn's recount. The juices ran from the roast.

202

'He was the best.'

Arnulf swallowed the half-chewed mouthful hard, losing his peace, 'He did not give me the sword, I took it myself after he was dead, because my other brother ...'

Svend nodded, encouragingly, but Arnulf looked away, lowering the meat. The hunger was not so bad anymore.

'I have always wanted to be have brothers. You are wealthy. One is better than none.'

The beer alleviated the thirst but not the heat of the flames flaring up.

'I have no brothers. Both were killed.'

'You really have something to avenge, Veulf!'

Svend grimaced, but Arnulf shook his head, so his eyes sparkled. Gentle Idun, how long would he have to endure this pain?

'Not everything can be avenged, son of Bue.'

'Why not? Was it King Sweyn Haraldson himself who killed them?'

'The king? No!'

Arnulf raised his hand with the gold ring, 'He gave Helge this ring in payment for a skaldic verse.'

'Helge? Him with the sword?'

'Yes, him with Serpenttooth. He was a great Viking.'

A fleeting smile slid across Svend's face, as if he was holding back a biting remark, but he kept it to himself.

'It is a good name, Serpenttooth. I call my axe Snap.'

He patted the sharpened axe head. It was exquisitely decorated with silver, as grand as it was deadly.

'He who has no brothers, does not lose them. You have Vagn.'

Svend laughed softly, 'Yes, and I will not lose him, for I will die first!'

He took his bone comb out of a belt purse and began combing his hair. How he took care of it! Arnulf bit, without any desire for food, into the flesh, hunger weakened even the strongest. Vagn erupted into a skaldic verse, a powerful verse that he performed with great intensity, and his hearers listened engrossed.

'In my eyes, you are hard to kill, Svend Silkenhair!'

Svend shrugged, 'We all die, Veulf, it is a choice, a condition for Jomsborg's sons, and because we know that, we fight without fear.'

'Is that why you live without families?'

'Yes.'

Svend's hair shone like gold.

'Too many women would be left man-less and find it difficult to find food for their children. And, furthermore, the worries of women have killed more warriors than I care to think about.'

'What do you mean?'

The mug was empty. Svend smiled mockingly, 'They whisper to their men about omens and bad dreams and ask them to take care during the next fight, but you know what, Veulf? No man is worse off than if he should look after his own skin behind the spear. That is the day he gets hit, just as surely as Mjolnir always returns. A woman's love disturbs more than the bee that stung Brokkr.'

Arnulf coaxed a piece of meat from between his teeth. Had Svend known Frejdis, he would have thought otherwise! Just the thought of her instilled renewed courage, gave him something to fight for.

'Bue must surely have had a woman, you were birthed.'

Svend worked the comb through a tangle, 'She died shortly after I was born. I lived with my grandfather, Vesete, on Bornholm, after my father had gone to Jomsborg. When I was eight summers, he fetched me. No man in the fort can be under eighteen or over fifty, but I was no man, and Palnatoke liked me.'

His gaze was distant, and the comb stopped in its deed.

'He let you stay?'

'Yes, I grew up there. I have known many great men, and I have seen many new take their place. They were all fond of me. I got the beer. Took care of horses. Polished the weapons. No boy had more fathers than I!'

Bue's son smiled sternly, 'When I was fifteen, I tried to pass the tests, and again when I was sixteen. Last year I managed it. Sigvalde demanded that for the last one, I should stand against Vagn.'

He removed the hair from the comb and put it back in the purse, and Arnulf raised an eyebrow, 'But you have never managed to hit him!'

'No. He hurt me four times before Sigvalde interrupted the fight.'

'Your own kinsman!'

A doubtful snort escaped from Arnulf and Svend shook his head, 'That day he was the guardian of the laws, he did not do it to hurt me.'

Arnulf looked out at sea. Jomsborg's guardian. He himself had killed Rolf for wanting to beat him with a belt! What kind of men considered wounds and death to be nothing, and whose reputation made even kings tremble?

The horizon dimmed, and the first stars braved their light. Vagn sang no longer but walked slowly around the campfire with raised hands.

'Tell me about the laws.'

'The laws?'

Svend threw his arms around his knees, 'They were determined to strengthen the courage and unity and make the brotherhood unbreakable; Palnatoke was as clever as he was strong. No force has since been more feared than ours.'

His voice was thick with pride, 'Friendship or kinship may not influence who is accepted into Jomsborg. When a man belongs here, he must avenge any of his companions, as if they were his brothers. All must live in peace together and not sow discord, and if there is still mutual animosity, Sigvalde alone determines the dispute. No man shall flee from an equal opponent or show anxiety and concern, no matter how hopeless the circumstances may be, and news must first be brought to Sigvalde, also all loot. And no man may be absent for more than three days without his consent and he, who does not comply with any of these rules, is immediately expelled.'

Arnulf whistled, impressed. It was far from Toke and *Twin Raven* to the Jomsborg legion, and it was indeed doubtful whether King Sweyn had such similar men in his hird. Helge had felt invincible when he had let more than three ships with crews of summer Vikings go a-viking, but they were farmers and fishermen, capable of ploughing and finding cunning from mead.

Svend blew a golden lock from his brow, 'At least it was like that before. Now there are occasional single combats, and some believe they should have the right to a woman because Sigvalde has one.'

'And what about the old, those over fifty? Are they expelled?'

Svend smiled, 'Bjørn is an exception, for Vagn will not do without him. No. Those who want to, go home to family, and the rest prepare for the final battle.'

He supported his chin on one knee, looking thoughtfully at a low-flying seagull.

'The final battle?'

Arnulf sucked the bone clean.

'They perform blóts, put on their best clothes and then enter the battle where the fighting is hardest. Mighty deeds are done under such last fights, and people notice them. The outcome is always the same: joy for Odin.'

The grey-bearded old men brandished weapons with a bear's mind, while hoarse battle cries caused age to flee and made the watery eyes young.

'You yourself are not yet eighteen.'

Svend bared his teeth with a dangerous gaze, 'Sloppiness, right? But it will not be because of me that Jomsborg falls.'

He spat at a crab shell, and Arnulf threw the bone into the sea, 'Will Vagn be earl after Sigvalde? Would Palnatoke not have preferred that?'

Svend straightened abruptly, 'Veulf! Vagn is a killer! You can see it in his eyes. To stand against him is to stand against Tyr himself! He sees you as a dead man even before the sword is drawn, he has a look, a fatal glance that freezes even the boldest to ice. He is fully aware of his opponent, but has also seen the next and the next, yes, all around him and behind them all the others. As dead, mind you. Myself, I feel no pain, but Vagn does not even know when and how many times he has been hit. So, no. He must not command Jomsborg. Many others can do that.'

Arnulf was silent. The hairs on his arms bristled. Cold and merciless, even the wildest berserker seemed to come up short next to Vagn.

Bue the Stout proclaimed a toast to Palnatoke's grandson who sat under the appreciative cries, and Svend, whistling cheerfully, got up to sit with his kinsman. Arnulf supported his hand in the sand. The Jomsvikings' beer was strong, as strong and hard-hitting as themselves. He stared at the fire behind the men, at Bue, and Bjørn. Sigvalde's hird. Blood companions who died as brothers. He was not one of them and had never been one of the Northmen. Had he ever really been Stridbjørn's son? The eagle screamed in his blood. Helge's brother, but Helge was dead, and Frejdis taken from him. Fenrir howled out there, and an answer vibrated mutely in his throat. Veulf, Veulf the Wildminded, Veulf the Wayward, Veulf the Wrong-lived, Veulf the Fight Father's Shame!

*****

The weather stayed clear, but the wind was weak, so for days the snekke splashed lazily along the coast without putting much behind it. The Jomsvikings were unhappy and would not venture out into deeper waters, but Arnulf got peace to sleep as much as he wanted, and began to recuperate, while the wound closed. No one asked questions, and thoughts were hazy on his bed between the thwarts, flowing from Toke and Stentor to Stridbjørn and Trud, and not least to Frejdis.

Several times strange ships sailed near the ship, and not all with friendly crews, but as soon as Bue and Vagn spoke their names with

206

weapons in hands, the silver-hungry Vikings lost courage and rowed hurriedly in the opposite direction.

In the evenings, the ship was put ashore, and the tents were raised, and when the wind finally blew favourably, the snekke crossed towards Denmark with a foaming bow. The sea was raging but passable, and along the way Svend goaded Vagn into more than one hunt over goods and men. Arnulf started to get used to their reciprocal violence and sat up deathly-pale with the rolled up sleeping skin at his back to better follow the talk. He could open his eye again and pitied Odin, who for the sake of his wisdom had to settle for only half-seeing Asgard.

Bue approved of his son's game, for he believed that bear cubs only kept their teeth sharp with regular squats and how Svend never got hold of his kinsman was a riddle to Arnulf, for he was as quick and as cunning as a lynx.

Denmark came into view one sunny-sharp afternoon. As beautiful as Frejdis herself lay his homeland, floating on the sea, just as painful and unattainable, a lost kingdom, a deprived life. Arnulf turned from his ship companions and looked gloomily at the coast. He did not want to set foot on the grass a moment longer than necessary, but he kept his movement to himself and tried to figure out how many days he would have to endure the sight before the snekke would again put the Danish fields behind it.

Bue roared that the sight of Jutland already made him feel at home, and several of the men were suddenly tired of the sea and got the urge for freshly baked bread and shelter. Svend could indulge himself in a woman's warmth before the gate to Jomsborg was bolted and did not believe that a short detour would harm anyone, 'Tord Halfhand will hardly deny us a feast, and his daughters are as affectionate as kittens. What do you think, Vagn?'

Vagn Ågeson narrowed his lips, as Bjørn scratched his beard and cackled, 'Do not talk to Vagn about women, Silkenman, he has only Torkel Leres' daughter from Vigen in the head, and that fever has burned for almost a year.'

Vagn frowned but preserved his dignity in front of his foster-father, 'Sigvalde should not wait any longer for us than he has already done, and the day I wish it, Torkel will come to give me his daughter, whether he wants it or not. We are not changing course.'

Svend whistled disappointedly, but Arnulf was relieved by the Ågeson's haste. Denmark was a sleeping bear, light as a sparrow he would tread its fur. He ran his fingers along the upper strake and saw a red-painted longship gliding around the nearest headland and pointed. Svend rose abruptly, a hand shading his eyes, 'It is *the Blood Fox*! Ha! See! Little Ketil is coming.'

His words sparked jubilation, and the snekke heeled from the weight of the men in the foreship. Bue blew into a silver-plated buck's horn, and soon a similar greeting resounded from the light-footed fox ship. Men waved behind the installed shields, and Arnulf squinted narrowly, despite the pain, to better see over the flashing water, 'Who is Ketil?'

'Little Ketil? He is one of the most skilled axe swingers we have, so do not underestimate his short stature! He has cut off more feet than you have sucked fish bones, but his enemies always realise it too late.'

Svend laughed, waving his hand, and Arnulf saw a man standing on *the Blood Fox's* deck. He could not be called tall or very young, but his movements were sprightly, and when the ships approached each other, Arnulf could see how vibrantly the gaze burned in the weather-beaten face.

The shield rims met, and ropes were thrown and lashed, and Ketil jumped over the jarring shield rims and was lifted into the air like a child in Bue's bear paws.

'Ketil, you wolverine, you get even smaller every time I come back, are the barrels emptied of pork in Jomsborg?'

Little Ketil landed again and slapped his palm against the Stout's stomach, 'Not so, and the same can hardly be said of you, Bue, but it would be shameful if you did not have to get a new hide from the chainmail blacksmith also this year.'

Bue guffawed, and Arnulf watched the newcoming men from *the Blood Fox* curiously. They were not hugely different from the Vikings he had already sailed with; all strong fellows with hard stares and scarred skin, as blank as a young raven he flew among eagles.

The mugs were taken out and the beer barrel opened and Bjørn made room for Ketil, while laughter and shouts mingled over the ship's sides. Ketil toasted to the snekke's successful journey on the open sea voyage, and Vagn, stroking his chin with the back of his hand, wanted to know how things stood in the fort. At once, Little Ketil was serious and lowered the half-empty mug while the gaiety of those sitting nearest quietened.

'Sigvalde himself sent me Vagn Ågeson, and I was prepared to go all the way to Bretland after you. Earl Strut-Harald is dead.'

Vagn darkened, and the men who had heard Ketil expressed their regrets. Svend looked at Bue, and Arnulf nudged him, 'Who is earl Strut-Harald?'

'The father of King Sweyn, earl of Zealand and Sigvalde.'

He replied softly, and Bue put his hand on the axe in his belt, 'What does Sigvalde say?'

Little Ketil grimaced, shaking his head, 'Strut-Harald had many days, so his sons were not caught unawares. But King Sweyn sees it as his duty to hold the funeral feast of his earl and has invited both Sigvalde and Torkel the Tall and the men they wish to bring.'

Vagn emptied his mug in one gulp, and Bjørn tugged at his beard, 'None of them should go. Ravens will feed from that royal meeting, and Sigvalde and Torkel can do their own drinking for their father as much as they want to.'

'Of course, they have to go!'

Vagn threw the mug from him with a captivating gaze, 'Just not alone! The man who fears the king is a miserable thrall, but Harald's sons must not stand alone. I am going.'

He stared so ominously over the sea to the south that steam seemed to hiss from the water. Arnulf dared only whisper when he nudged Svend again, 'Is Torkel the Tall Sigvalde's brother?'

'Yes, he is, and a chieftain, too, like my father.'

Svend killed the next question with his hand and Bue the Stout nodded to Vagn, 'Sigvalde certainly must not do without me at the royalseat, we all need to sail. If peace should hold, the wolves need to eat equally.'

Arnulf moved uneasily. The questions stuck in his throat, and nobody found it necessary to explain anything to him in the least. Lille Ketil smiled harshly and lifted his mug.

'I did not expect to get a lesser answer, so *the Blood Fox* did not make haste in vain. And greetings to you, Bue, from your brother Sigurd and to the rest of you, too. They are waiting for you. Jomsborg resembles only a weaving house when Vagn and Svend are not leading the songs.'

Svend grinned and reached out for Vagn but the Ågeson was still annoyed and struck back unreasonably hard. Ketil let his gaze run over the ship's rich prey with an appreciative look, 'You are not hungry anymore, I see. How are things in Bretland?'

'We took what we found best, and let the rest remain, and there is peace and food for all in Bretland. The winter was mild, and the lambs are fat.'

Bjørn looked pleased, and Ketil nodded with a finger towards Arnulf, 'And the calf there? Was he also bred on your land?'

Arnulf straightened himself and Bue laughed briefly, 'Veulf? He is Svend's find, we others are not getting involved in it. My son believes there is wolf blood in him.'

Little Ketil looked at Arnulf appraisingly, from the feet up, as if he was estimating how violent a blow it would take to remove his feet from his ankles. A shiver crept up under the hairs on his neck and Arnulf found himself in their talk with a forced calm. Stridbjørn had tolerated him in the same way, but Svend's faith made him warm and softened his defiance. Wolfblood? That praise must have been voiced while he slept.

Vagn stood resolutely and untied the rope, and with such a practiced hand that Little Ketil did not manage to finish his drink before *the Blood Fox* began to drift away from him.

'Well if my ship is not pulling off without its master. That is going to cost you more beer, Vagn Ågeson!'

Vagn threw a rope over to the red longship and waved to the men by the sail, 'Last ship in Jomsborg pays for the feast. We are heavy, but we have it in mind to win, so enjoy the beer, Legslicer! The next drink is from your barrels.'

'No, wait a moment!'

Ketil jumped up and yelled at the folk on *the Blood Fox* to encounter the ship again, 'If we are to have a race, it is fair that you bale your snekke here of men, so we will lie evenly in the water.'

Vagn pondered for a moment and then loudly ordered half of the Vikings to change ship and Little Ketil drank deeply and climbed over to *the Blood Fox* with jeering cries. Bue became good humoured again, and Svend pulled the sail, no one seemed to miss the earth under their feet any longer. Arnulf was infected by the fever, and the displaced men found places on *the Fox* and made ready for flight. Sigvalde could boast proudly of his people, they were so willing to support and eager to return home! To count Vagn among his flock had to be as huge as it undoubtedly was fatal to have him go against them.

Soon *the Fox* and the snekke were foaming side by side and that the Jomsvikings knew both ships and each other fully, was easy to see, they passed each other so closely. Arnulf took his place on a vacant thwart. Vagn had taken the helm with the look of great man, and Bjørn and Bue held council over the beer barrel, which the Stout thought was best opened. Svend stood for a time in the bow and exchanged news with the people from *the Blood Fox*, but when the snekke distanced itself from the longship, he sat by Arnulf with a cheese under his arm and began to cut it. He seemed unworried, the cheerful scarred face seldomly got stuck in a weak-willed expression. 'You might think about warm bread, Wolfblood, but the cheese is good. We found a whole stack at a river farm.'

'Wolfblood.'

Smiling, Arnulf accepted the slice, 'Sounds better than Maidenskin.'

Svend laughed and stuffed cheese in his mouth, 'You have blood between the teeth, Veulf, and you stink of murder.'

Arnulf's lips shivered and abruptly lost their joy, Thrymr take Svend's penchant for backstabbing!

'What do you mean?'

'Mimir kick you! You can tell when a man has taken life, it shines from his eyes! You are just not used to it yet, but therefore you have wolf blood anyway. It burns.'

Arnulf stared at the cheese and bit hard. Fenrir's blood. How did Svend know that? He was rude, and that just as much as he was fearless! And did he suspect? No, impossible, who would have betrayed something? Arnulf brushed the hair from his forehead, 'Why is there animosity between Sigvalde and the king?'

Svend's gaze glittered, and Arnulf saw the movement's first draw and managed to defend himself, as the cheese-sticky knife came towards him. The sinews of Svend's wrist were tense to grip and the Jomsviking wriggled out of his grasp like a fly-trembling horse, and the next moment Arnulf felt the knife tip against his ribs, but Svend was satisfied, 'Look!'

He poked a hole in Arnulf's skin and quickly glanced at his knife before he stuck it in the cheese again, 'Wolfblood! Who says there is enmity between Sigvalde and the king of the Danes?'

Arnulf was sweating. The pulse beat in his gash like a dull mallet. He understood now, had seen enough of Svend and Vagn to understand the predators in them, warriors who never slept, never let themselves be surprised, the peace from being wounded was over.

'Vagn will probably not go for the beer's sake?'

Danger played on the Silkenhaired's mouth, 'No. The two great men are not friends, but it is a long way to enmity. Without Palnatoke and his men, King Sweyn would never have forced his father from power, so he is in debt. But after Sigvalde abducted him in the craftiest manner and forced him into the marriage bed with King Borislav's second daughter, many believe that the debt has been amply paid. King Sweyn did not like that it was Palnatoke himself who slew old King Harald, so where Sigvalde now has him only the One-eyed knows. Was it your brother you killed, him who cannot be avenged?'

Arnulf stiffened. The cheese crumbled between his fingers. The Bueson deserved to be smothered by his own golden hair! Serpenttooth seethed against his thigh, but a wild pain paralysed his body from the inside, a wild pitch-black pain. Rolf lay twisted in the grass, Arnulf's blood burned like boiling oil, and the wounded eyelids began to quiver. Svend averted his eyes and lowered his voice, 'I do not take without giving anything back, Veulf, and you need to be able to defend yourself. A beard only grows on a man who can keep his chin free from blows, I need to sharpen your claws in Jomsborg.'

He got up quickly and went to Vagn, and Arnulf dropped the rest of the cheese and slumped down from the thwart. The urge to cry made his lungs small, and he tumbled onto his side and curled up, while the wound pounded. Jofrid's sorcery! Fenrir's journey! Would he ever find peace again? He had the mark of a murderer, the mark of a murderer and was ostracised by the life of the living!

*****

The Blood Fox and the snekke stroked along Denmark's flank with flickering shadows and only fleetingly touched the sand of the strand when the darkness was thick. Vagn and Lille Ketil exhibited the greatest knowledge of winds and currents, and the ships took the lead in turn and did not let each other triumph for long in front.

Although the dangling hair ripped at Arnulf's wounds like pig bristles, the pain was withering and endurable, and the feeling of limp eels in his limbs was replaced by budding courage. The tear healed well, and it was becoming easier to blink his eye, and the familiar restlessness pushed the dizziness out.

Svend cut the stitches and pulled out the threads, and Arnulf felt his face, trying to feel his appearance. The scar was almost a hand's breadth long, and now and then the eyelid hung as though tired, but it did not affect his sight. Svend liked the scar and spent a whole afternoon talking about his own. He knew each of his wounds carefully but did not attribute them any more importance, familiar as he was with death in his shadow, 'The lame one rides well, and the one-armed can still swing a sword, so do not despise what daring deeds have to give, only corpses lie useless.'

Bue the Stout yearned for his brother, Sigurd, and Bjørn stretched his aging hamstrings, longing for land. Vagn controlled the helm grouchily, but Svend gave him company often enough while Arnulf let his thoughts go with the wind. The ships were reflected in both Egilssund and Haraldsfjord, but the rush to see Jomsborg overshadowed the pining, and with Svend he had not fared unluckily. The Bueson did not ask about the murder of his brother and kept the secret to himself, and the men on board seemed to get used to Arnulf and looked milder upon his presence.

King Sweyn's kingdom stretched far and wide, but it did not continually devour the sea, and the course was set eastward. Tents were erected for one night on Vindland's strand, and the next day the Jomsvikings, on both ships, began to retrieve clothes from chests and bags, comb their hair and polish their weapons. Arnulf had only the clothes on his back, but a swim in the waves and a loan of Svend's comb made him reasonably ready for the feast.

Ketil and Vagn settled their game, and let the ships follow each other for the last part of the journey, and Arnulf was no less elated than his ship companions. Lush green, brightly lit forests and fields greeted him from King Borislav's kingdom, with coves and sounds dotted unevenly along the coast.

Svend could certainly smell smoke and warrior sweat and had to stand up on the shield rim to scout and Bue, grunting, stabbed a spear in his hand for support, for if his son fell in the water now, he would certainly have to swim the rest of the way home. The Silkenhaired yelped when the snekke rounded one high-backed point, and Arnulf gripped the thwart, tears in his eyes. He could see it now, by all gods and Vanir, there, in the distance, he could see Jomsborg!

At the bottom of a long narrow cove was a mighty harbour, and behind it stood a huge palisaded rampart. It seemed to round away from the harbour, as if an enormous jötunn had thrown his neck ring at the water's edge, and mighty fortified arms ran out from the main rampart, embracing the harbour in a shielding grip right up to the entrance, which appeared to be blocked at the waterline.

Arnulf brushed the hair from his forehead and shadowed his eyes with his hand. Yes, a floating barrage lay lapping in the water; no, two! Behind them an incomprehensible number of ships lay moored at long jetties: snekkes, skeids and longships, and in the midst of the rampart a covered port yawned. It seemed to be iron bound, supported by massive stone foundations, and on top stood a wooden tower to the height of many men.

Arnulf gaped. As the snekke and *the Blood Fox* approached, the overwhelming fortifications and the ramparts clearly rose higher and higher, as if the tower sought the source of rain in the clouds. The harbour curved in towards the port, which was not far from the nearest jetty, and on each side, there was room for pit houses and workshops. One bank seemed to be used exclusively for shipbuilding and maintenance, for pulled-up and semi-finished vessels lay in rows on glowing wood shavings between plank stacks and heaps of newly made rope. On the other bank were raised forges, stables and storage huts and the ring of a hammer mingled with horses neighing and cattle bellowing.

Bue the Stout blew his horn, and soon after the call was answered, as men thronged the banks, pointing and gesturing. Vagn let his ship overtake Little Ketil's, flouting his outraged cries, and Bue laughed and waved his arm. The news of the arrival seemed to spread inside the fort, for many men came out of the gate, and Svend threw the spear and danced sure-footed from foreship to stern.

So many people! So steep a rampart! Arnulf licked his lips. It was grey-brown, coated with almost vertical wood, and at the top of the palisade a walkway ensured protection for the archers. Only birds could come up over the manmade steep, smooth slope with its thousands of tapered logs! Who but pure madmen could think to attack Jomsborg? Behind that rampart, there had to live more warriors than flying starlings in October. Arnulf clutched the shield rim. Sigvalde apparently had men, like a great king had a hird!

Vagn yelled and the snekke slowed in speed, for just ahead approached the first floating barrage, and it did not bid the ship welcome. Large trunks with iron spikes nailed into them cradled the narrow cove, chained to poles which were driven down into the seabed, and even a light brush from such a trunk would tear a hole in the thinly carved planks and founder the vessel. Only in one spot was a trunk placed aside to make room for an entrance, but a heavy lock hung in the related pole, so the opening could be locked at night or in times of unrest.

The snekke did not make many boat lengths before it had sailed past another barrage, and after that Vagn took complete control of the ship and began to steer with the greatest care. The cove was shallow enough that Arnulf could see rocks and seaweed on the bottom, and, to his surprise, he discovered that all around him were hammered piles of cut spearheads just below the surface of the sea. A narrow sailing channel wound unpredictably between them and only those who knew the way, would be able to get his ship to land unharmed. Even if enemy ships

214

cleared the obstacles, they would still be forced to arrive one by one, and those men who escaped the rain of arrows from the palisade, would ship-by-ship have to fight the Jomsvikings. Arnulf was speechless from the ingenuity of it. From the sea Jomsborg was utterly impregnable.

Three men came out together from the port, just as the snekke slid toward the middle jetty, and Vagn threw a rope so that the ship could be moored. One of the men was immensely tall, never had Arnulf seen a man so tall! His eyes were clever, and his well-trimmed hair was dark, surely he must be Thorkel the Tall, Sigvalde's brother. Arnulf would have to ask Svend, but now a companion of the tall one was running along the bridge and Bue the Stout jumped overboard with a roar and clasped him around the neck. They slapped each other on the back and bumped foreheads with hollow thumps, and Arnulf had to laugh, for Sigurd had to stretch far to reach around his brother's well-endowed belly. He was handsome, but not as impressive as Bue, and all the features of the Stout, which were clumsy and ungainly, were refined and tasteful with Sigurd.

Svend landed on the bridge and cheerfully greeted his uncle, and Vagn raised a dignified hand and called to the third man. Sigvalde, it could not possibly be anyone else, walked towards the ship with a broad smile, and Arnulf considered, in detail, the acclaimed Jomsviking. Broad-shouldered and thick-haired in appearance, red curls and deathly pale, with eyes wise and handsome and a nose that was unusually lopsided and ugly. Over one ear a blade had robbed both locks and skin; but he was no less scratched by the sword than his men. It was a wonder to Arnulf.

'Welcome back, Vagn Ågeson, and welcome also to you Bjørn and the rest of you.'

Bjørn the Bretlander flung his arm out and got up from the thwart, 'Greetings yourself, Sigvalde!'

He crawled over the shield rim and onto the bridge and Bue and Sigurd released each other. Vagn followed his foster-father and greeted Sigvalde with a hard grip of his arms, and Arnulf was the last to leave the snekke after the remaining men. He was tense, quivering with proud reverence. Helge should have seen him now! At Jomsborg's gate! It was important to stand firm without humility; Torkel was tall, but Stridbjørn's son stood straighter!

Little Ketil's ship docked at a second bridge and Bue sent Sigvalde a serious look, 'It is hard to hear about Earl Strut-Harold's death. We let the wind take the sail as soon as Ketil met us.'

A shadow drifted over Sigvalde's white face, and he nodded curtly, 'We sail for the funeral feast at the royalseat in ten days at the latest. Only

215

Ketil could have collected you in that time; he has a pact with the sea and weather. Is everything well in Bretland?'

He let his eyes slide over the fully laden ship and end at Bjørn. The white-bearded confirmed, 'Bretland thrives like Asgard itself. Vagn gives council such that an old man can die without regret. How did the message from the king sound?'

'It is proper enough. Sweyn Haraldson sent a messenger with peace, and I asked him, in the best way, to prepare for the feast and take the cost from my inheritance, but more about that at the table.'

Sigvalde pulled at his lush beard and looked like he was about to turn but then spotted Arnulf and stiffened, 'Who are you?'

Arnulf lifted his chin, sure in his gaze. If his voice trembled now, he had cut his own throat!

'I'm Veulf. I am Svend Silkenhair's housecarl.'

At that moment, he was not on the same footing as the Jomsvikings. Sigvalde smiled, but both Sigurd and Torkel laughed shamelessly, and gaiety spread through the bystanding warriors. Arnulf became short of breath, as furious indignation washed through his blood, and Serpenttooth hissed out of its sheath hungry to wound. His anger just increased the laughter and drew even more awareness to him and Svend slid as sleekly as a cat over to his side. Thorkel the Tall stepped forward and put his finger at the tip of the sword, 'Svend's housecarl? Bue's son has never before dared a risk so bold! No one here needs weapons to subdue such as a yapping whelp, it can be done with a mug of beer in the hand and without spilling so much as a drop.'

Arnulf could have boiled water with his eyes, and if Vagn had not step forward, he would have cut the hand off Sigvalde's brother, by Tyr's blood, he would have!

'Let Veulf live, Torkel, you will win greater honour from that. I do not want a skirmish between you and Svend just now, for Sigvalde needs both of you.'

He spoke quietly, but the road to Helheim stood wide open behind his words. Bright-eyed, Svend followed the exchange of words without getting involved, and Torkel blew at Arnulf and, grinning, pulled his shoulders, 'Truly so! He is still standing! You are right, Vagn, such a strong lad deserves to live.'

He let go of Serpenttooth as if he had touched something awful, and before Arnulf could react, Vagn's eyes met him with a night-coloured, thundering glance. It commanded the sword be sheathed immediately and his arm obeyed, as if the Ågeson had cast runes over it. Vagn nodded to

Sigvalde and walked towards the gate. The leader of the Jomsvikings was strict with Arnulf, 'A man who has not been tried and accepted among the men may not be in Jomsborg overnight, Veulf, and you are obviously too young and inexperienced to catch up with the Boy's Play practiced here. For Svend's sake, you can remain until tonight and eat with us, and you will be welcome again when you have grown a beard.'

Svend raised his hand, but Arnulf struck it down viciously, holding Sigvalde fixed with his eyes. The words were true, and surprisingly they did not come, but he had heard too much of the warriors' talk to let himself be beaten off the horse so easily, 'So test me now! Perhaps I'll be fit to walk in Svend's shadow without shame!'

Was he Helge's brother or not? Only he who grips the sword can win!

Sigvalde raised an eyebrow and looked questioningly at his chieftains. Thorkel the Tall frowned, but Bue and Sigurd nodded in agreement, and Sigvalde stroked his beard. Arnulf maintained his stare without blinking; he would not be turned away without a fight!

'Shed Vagn Ågeson's blood before midnight, then you can stay and learn, but you cannot call yourself a Jomsviking!'

A grey, glassy storm wave sucked the air out of his lungs. Make Vagn bleed! Sigvalde might as well have asked him to swim to Denmark with his head under water! Had Svend not tried to hit his kinsman for years without success? The wound was thumping, but Arnulf refused to show it, 'That is reasonable time to make a cut, I accept the challenge.'

A tinge of recognition was traceable in Sigvalde, then he beckoned to Bue and Bjørn and took his leave, and the jetty emptied of men. Arnulf was standing on stiff legs, and so fierce was his glare that the ships seemed to burst into the harbour one after the other. Svend chuckled, 'You really know how to make people take notice of you, Wolfblood, before cooking time everyone here will have heard of Svend Bueson's sharp-minded housecarl. Welcome to Jomsborg!'

Arnulf ran his fingers through his hair and spat in the water, 'Vagn will kill me!'

Svend tossed his head and started walking, 'It is no shame to be killed by Vagn, and the sun has only just topped the sky. Come, I will show you my realm, you yourself asked for a test.'

No shame! If only the golden hair of Bue's son would flame on the spot! Arnulf followed him, fuming, but his worry was soon soothed by the awesomeness of the mighty ramparts.

217

To reach the entrance, he had to go over a wide fosse, in the base of which high pilings were raised, and the gate to the port was heavy and iron bound so that it could stand unscathed, even if the entire wooden stockade burned down. A plank-covered road led over a bridge and in under the soaring tower, and Arnulf stepped onto it with awe, as if Odin himself were waiting behind the rampart.

He did not manage many steps into the fort before his feet stopped, but Svend was immediately hailed by a handful of young men and fell willingly into conversation. Arnulf did not hear what they were talking about, his eyes grew so big; not since Helge had shown him Gormsø for the first time, had they been bigger! The plank road seemed to go straight through the whole of Jomsborg, and along both sides were great vaulted longhouses. Along the inside of the rampart, under the wharf, was a second earthen rampart with pointed stakes at the bottom and a narrower road followed the curve of the rampart and seemed to follow the entire ring around.

Armed men were everywhere, no less imposing than Bue's and Vagn's followers, and although they seemed peaceful, the air resounded with cries and sword fights as though somewhere behind the slash-marked houses things were being fought to the death.

Svend's snapping fingers and his companions' laughter tore Arnulf from his frozen state but the Jomsviking did not fuss over the inattention and pulled his sleeve eagerly, 'Due to all you can see, your ears deafen, you should almost be allowed to start from the top; there will be enough time for acquaintances later and there are plenty of men.'

He beckoned to the others and led Arnulf to a wooden staircase beside the gate that led up to the wooden stockade. Each step was wide enough so many warriors could quickly run up it, and in the large gate tower a door stood open for further ascent. Solid ladders led up on each side to the archers' walkway on the palisade, but Svend did not think they needed to climb so high, and when Arnulf put his feet on the gravel rampart top and turned, all Jomsborg lay stretched out under him, incomprehensibly great, round like a tail-biting snake. He swayed and, open-mouthed, grabbed the pilings. The large plank road did indeed run through the fort, while another equally large road seemed to cross to the opposite side and divide Jomsborg in four. Three tower gates guarded the roads, and in each section of the fortress longhouses were erected like four-winged farms whose gables almost collided. The many square longhouse groups were, with a blacksmith's sense of beauty, laid in strict patterns, and they made Jomsborg look like a shoulder buckle.

Arnulf breathed deeply. He could see where the clangour of arms was coming from now, for in almost all courtyards there was combat training, so the grass was worn away. He saw piles for striking and targets for spears and arrows, and a single torn up track seemed to be used for riding exercises. In the middle of the fort was a huge open space, large enough for all the men to gather there and in front of the largest longhouse in the section to the south, which resembled a royal hall, a high pole was erected. At the top billowed a red banner with a gold dragon sewn on, and Svend pointed, explaining, 'The house with the pole is Sigvalde's. He rules over all men but is not least responsible for the south wing. The western wing is Thorkel's, the north my father's, and to the east Sigurd leads. Vagn lives in Sigvalde's house, as does Bjørn, and I live where I please, and everyone has become accustomed to that.'

Satisfied, he bared his teeth, and Arnulf shadowed his eyes with his hand.

'Between the houses, we train the use of weapons with each other, but on the banner ground we rally to battle every afternoon, you will get to see it soon. When everyone is there, and it is going to be a great battle, we go outside; we also use the woods behind Jomsborg, for it is something else to squabble between trunks than in open fields.'

He nodded towards a small peephole in the palisade, and Arnulf looked through it and could see a rolling plain beyond that surrounded the fort and stretched to a tightly grown forest belt.

'Vagn and I exchange blows up here, it adds to the excitement.'

The excitement? Arnulf would be quite wary of a push from Vagn with a tumble down the rampart as punishment for not paying attention.

'And how often does Vagn fall?'

Svend sprayed some gravel down the slope with his foot, 'Sometimes, Wolfblood, but, of course, it is all about knowing how to fall, we have to defend the rampart in wartime without giving life in exchange. Have you seen enough? Let us walk back.'

Arnulf would like to have sat the rest of the day, beholding Jomsborg, with his back against the palisade, but Svend pranced down the steps as if he had the hooves of a fjeld goat. The rampart barely moved in the shelter of the night, so Arnulf followed Svend, whose chattering took him around the rampart, and along the curved plank road. That was how Valhalla must lock Asgard out of its own greatness, the realm behind the rampart was worlds from all known, and Svend's voice was drowned in his heart-pounding pulse. Again and again, the Bueson was welcomed with pats and fist bumps, and Arnulf grasped arms with more men than he had ever before in his life met, but the Jomsvikings' reserved glances felt like embers under his skin. He was far from esteemed for his appearance, but no one said anything against Svend Silkenhair when he presented his wolfly housecarl.

When the seaport again came into view, Svend crossed in between the houses and began to tell him about the men who lived there, and Arnulf quickly gave up on the many names. All the longhouses except Sigvalde's seemed the same to him, but on each side of the doors hung the warriors' shields who laid their head under that roof. Strong images in brilliant colours impacted him, terrifying swirling animals, bloodshot weapons, mythical patterns that each man had chosen for himself, only the crimson rim edge did they have in common. A wolf shield could easily find room here, a black shield with red wolves!

*****

The large depopulated banner ground was covered with sand, and in many places, there were piles of weapons and unpainted shields. Neither swords nor axes were sharpened, and spears had blunt tips, for quick as the Jomsvikings were to draw blood, they seemed to want to spare their own. Svend confirmed and picked up a scratched sword from the ground that he weighed in his hand, 'We would kill each other faster than Ketil can take a woman, if we trained in formation with our own weapons. No man here is scared of being wounded but we are certainly not stupid! Blood must not be shed in Jomsborg.'

He looked down at the blunt edge with a grim laugh, 'Outside the rampart is, of course, another matter, and man to man, every now and then we use sharp blades. But enough talk and stories, Wolfblood. Let me see what you have got!'

He threw the sword to Arnulf and with great care selected one for himself, and Arnulf, surprised, grasped the hilt and took the shield that was handed to him. A mug of beer and a bite of meat would have been better now, and he would have liked to have seen inside one of the longhouses. Many men had begun to go indoors, and food could be smelled, but Svend was eager to trade blows, 'We ought to maybe find a few helmets, but it should do. Give me your best! If you want to pierce Vagn before midnight, we must warm up your sword arm thoroughly.'

Arnulf did not like being reminded of Sigvalde's test, but the words were encouraging, and what did he care about food in the middle of Palnatoke's famous fort? He had not practiced fighting in the winter with

Helge for nothing, and had his worth not been amply proven in his fight with the Northmen? Svend grasped a shield, and Arnulf took a broad stance at a sure length from him and leaned forward to try to lure him, sharp-eyed, the Silkenhaired would not get him to shrink as much as half a foot! Svend was agile enough, but Stridbjørn's son counted for something, by Fenrir, now he felt the wolf's blood!

Svend's face lost life, and he threw both the blade and protection from himself with a groan, 'Thor's death, Veulf! I am well aware that you are no hirdman, but are you so bad? Torkel is right!'

Arnulf clutched the hilt, expecting anything from Svend, so often had he seen him jump at Vagn, 'Do you not dare? Come on! You won't be disappointed.'

'Disappointed?'

Svend laughed hard and spat at his shield, 'You cannot do anything! Who taught you that? A mad dog?'

Anger flushed to right out under his nails, and Arnulf anchored his eyes angrily in Svend's, 'What do you mean? You have not seen me make a strike, but you already know what I can do! Take your sword and come on, you don't usually hesitate!'

No one in Midgard should escape from speaking ill of Helge!

'Good!'

Svend ran his fingers through his hair, snorting, 'But if you want to learn how to snap, you have to bite the pretension in you and listen! Where do you have that from?'

Cursed snout of a chieftain's son! A growl wriggled loose from his throat and Arnulf narrowed his eyes, breathing heavily. Jomsborg. The finest warriors. Svend was Bue the Stout's son, raised by heroes. The fluttering dragon banner beat with laughter over the square. Morose reluctance was bad pay for an outstretched hand.

'What am I doing wrong?'

'Ah!'

Svend's fire returned, 'Well asked, Veulf, the answer is everything!'

'What I can, I learned from Helge, my brother, and few men could stand against him. He didn't lose life, before meeting a chieftain from Norway.'

'Helge?'

Svend walked slowly around Arnulf, 'Helge? How many men could he hold at once? How many single combats did he win? How many fights did he survive? How many seasons did he serve in the king's hird?'

'He won a great reputation and wealth a-viking!'

Arnulf lowered the sword, keeping his rage on a tense tether.

'Did he? To rob terrified peasants does not a warrior make, forget your brother! The only thing you can use from him is the sword you carry; the rest is beer boasting and child's play.'

His sword hand shook, and fire-midges swarmed through the air. Either he beat Svend down as he stood and left Jomsborg forever, or he endured the mockery and accepted it. Helge's proud figure in the bow. His strong arm. His contagious laughter.

'By Fenrir, Svend Bueson, what is it you see that is so wrong?'

Svend snorted and jumped after his thrown sword and held it out, 'You hold the sword as if you would blow the hilt asunder. A sword should be held like a bird! If you pinch too hard you squash it and if you hold it too loosely, it will fly from you. And then you wring your legs like a needy bitch; get those feet in a position that you can use them, and stand like a man, not a servile thrall! If you attack with the sword in your right hand, then your right foot should point forwards and the left be turned aside while keeping your weight just above the middle, and if you are defending yourself, then your left leg should be in the front. And furthermore, your distance is totally useless; you stand too far away.'

He strode in front of Arnulf and stretched his sword arm towards him, so that the tip threatened his chest without reaching, 'Here! Here you can dodge and engage at the same time. The man who wins is the one who knows best that distance is based on his opponent's size.'

He pushed his shoulder forward and put the sword tip against Arnulf's neck, 'But the worst is almost that you are staring me in the face like a besotted girl! What do you find there? The well of wisdom?'

The ground disappeared from under his feet on the banner ground and Arnulf clung to the splinters, 'Helge always held his enemies in the eye. A fixed gaze is scary, and your opponent's own wandering will reveal where the next blow will fall.'

'A proven warrior does not reveal himself; you should look here!'

Svend let the sword tip slide down Arnulf's neck and stop just below the clavicle, 'Your sight is widest when you keep your eyes down, here you can better sense what is happening both around you and behind you, and then your opponent's grimacing does not disrupt your tranquillity. Sight is more important than everything else. If you can get out of your enemy's line of sight, you have him! The man, you see, is not dangerous, it is him, you do not see that will kill you! Never lose your overview!'

Arnulf stared at Svend's chest, nodding. It was, therefore, that Vagn always noticed Svend's assault in time! He was trained to see like a horse! Bue's son lowered his sword, 'The next thing Helge taught you was to kill, right? Get the weapon behind the shield and ensure the man's death?'

Arnulf nodded again, while a growing respect repressed his anger. How did Svend know that?

'Why would you kill, Veulf? The dead do not join your hird.'

Arnulf startled. That those words should come from a Jomsviking! Had Svend himself not chopped Stefanus down without offering him so much as a thought?

'To live, of course, to win the fight!'

'Yes, but because of that you do not absolutely need to kill him, a killing-blow can easily be frustrated in the mayhem.'

Svend struck out his hand, 'Arms and legs are easy to hit, and without grip and balance weapons are useless. A helmet shock paralyses sometimes more than it injures, but it is enough to clear an opponent out of the way temporarily. Of course, killing is necessary, but take his hand, and most will be defeated.'

Stentor lay, blood gushing, on his knees in front of Toke with his hand stump pressed against his stomach and the wind over the banner ground was suddenly cold.

'The last thing your brother taught you was to hit harder than your opponent, am I right? The heaviest blow is the safest victory?'

Arnulf shook his head in disbelief. In a moment Svend would probably tell him also how Helge drank, shat and screwed! Leif Cleftnose's bull-crushing axe hammered into the ground with a dull thud. New as a new-born calf.

'Do not say that the strongest do not have an advantage!'

'Of course, it is an advantage to be strong, but Little Ketil does not fight any poorer than my father, despite his age. Strike me!'

Arnulf raised his arm. Svend would block a blow to his cheek and thereby leave himself open, shieldless as he was, and Arnulf lashed out. Svend's sword slid as gentle as a maiden, effortless around his blade, his footing failed, and Arnulf received a sword tip to the throat. The Bueson, grinning, blew a lock from his forehead, 'Enjoy life while you have it, Clumsy-wolf, for it will hardly be long! What would you have done if I had let you live?'

'Hit you in the side.'

His teeth ground.

'And then?'

'Then? Then you were dead!'

'You think like a ram.'

Svend removed the sword from his neck, and Arnulf tilted the shield.

'A swipe, a bite, a jump, that is what animals do, men use their heads. Your attack must slide around, cutting, floating, covering, learning from the wind, the current. Do not just think from blow to blow, everything you do is one continuous movement, and the more effortless you look, the more enraged your opponent becomes and then they expose themselves in anger. See now! I hit you in your shield shoulder, you lift your protection, I slip over your thighs and slip into the opposite armpit before you can even grasp what is going on.'

The dull edge split air along Arnulf's skin with a swallow's certainty, and Arnulf's eyes grew wide. The blade tip did not rest softly under his arm.

'Between clashes you must lure your enemy's weaknesses out, and your feet should rest on smouldering coal, use them, move!'

Svend wove around Arnulf, while the sword swept shadow patterns in a disturbing series of cuts and thrusts, and Arnulf defended himself in vain. The known parries and follow-ups were broken, and the Silkenhaired's encounters hurt. Disease strike him, if that dung-heap did not flounce around and emptied the chest of all honour and self-belief? The sun began to warm.

'Try your movements slowly, make them large, see what happens.'

Svend slowed down considerably, making the blows clearer, and now Arnulf could follow and do something about them.

'That is it, indeed, the wood out of the limbs, breathe, find peace.'

Svend was silent for a moment and let Arnulf clear the blows, but then increased his speed again, 'The quicker, the less movement, a warrior's moves can be better sensed than seen, the feet should be with you; you obstruct yourself if they cross! When you are sure of what you want, boil your movements down to the bare necessities. Never let go of your overview. The small twists and cuts give way to the greater killing-blow, remember, your opponent can easily discern the bigger strikes.'

The impacts were painful, and Arnulf thrust fiercely after him, but Svend's sword must have been rubbed with eel fat, not a single block could halt its escape, and the sweat trickled under his kyrtle. Thrymr roast his legs if he would find himself being driven around defenceless for much longer! Svend laughed, 'Are you angry? If you cannot handle a little whacking without getting enraged, you should not stay until tomorrow. No matter what happens, you must find calm, wild fighting is not a courageous act, it is panic!'

His sword tip sucked Arnulf's hilt out of his hand, hit his stomach and knocked the air out of him. Arnulf snapped together with a yell and Svend stopped at last. 'Now I think you understand me. Get your breath, while I pick up a few helmets, and then we will start all over again.'

*****

As groups of Jomsvikings began to rally to battle on the banner ground, Arnulf felt no less scratched and worn out than the hard-used sword. Svend was not rough handed, just insensitive, and he did not possess Helge's understanding of only marking your strikes.

His scalp cooked under the helmet, so sweat dripped from his hair, but the Bueson had not the slightest sweat stain on his kyrtle as he let Arnulf sit while he went for food and drink. His arm did not look good when the sleeve was rolled up, and Svend's talk about making it sword ready had to be jokingly meant. Blue-splotched and rigid it was, hardly faster than a lame nag.

Arnulf pulled the helmet off and rubbed his palms against his sweaty trousers. How many times would Svend have killed him with a sharp blade only Odin knew, but despite the many bruises, any attempt to anger drowned in admiration. Svend could sing with that sword, could dance, could wriggle around his enemy and be everywhere at once, see all the possibilities, Arnulf's skills were only thrall worthy next to the earl's son's.

He tousled his hair and wiped his face in the sleeve. The incoming warriors chose their weapons without ceasing their chattering as more strolled in, and Arnulf recognised Bue and Sigurd. There was not enough space for all the men from the same section to face each other in battle at once, so Bue had divided them and let half go outside the rampart. Svend had explained how they trained alternately on the banner ground and on the plain. The Stout was apparently not finished greeting each of his companions, for new warriors still trotted past him with shouts and laughter.

Little Ketil and Vagn appeared, and Arnulf remembered the test again and looked up at the sun. It no longer stood at the top of the sky, so Svend must have played with him for quite a while, but now he at least did not have to search for Vagn in all the longhouses. In return the Ågeson

225

seemed to be well armed; he wore both an eye-protecting helmet and short-sleeved chainmail behind the heavy shield, and the long broad axe over his shoulder   did not invite close combat.

Arnulf drew the wolf-knife and tried the edge with his thumb. Stab Vagn. How? Should he just go over to him under a ruse? With the knife in his hand? If it first had to come out of the sheath, it would be too late!

'You can see all the way from the rampart that you are plotting something, so you will never get to him.'

Svend dropped onto the sand and laid sausage and bread on the shield, and Arnulf reached for the water bag, 'Why is Vagn also wearing chainmail? Many of the others make do with a battle-kyrtle.'

Svend sent him a twinkling grin, breaking the bread, 'He always wears chainmail in the time before we go on a quest. He enjoys its weight, and when the time for battle comes, he no longer feels it.'

'How clever!'

Svend laughed and bit into the bread but grimaced almost immediately, 'Agh! The bread is bitter! You must have touched it!'

He spluttered with laughter, shoulder slapping him, and Arnulf forced a sour smile. Only he, who did not fear to die, could strut! It was hard to laugh on the last day of his life, and he grabbed the sausage to cut it. So easy were fat and meat divided by the sharp blade!

On the opposite side of the square Vagn and Ketil now saw Svend and crossed boisterously over to him. Little Ketil was laughing vigorously and the Ågeson's chest jumped, causing the mail to slap him on the thighs. Arnulf rose abruptly with the sausage and knife in his hands. It felt like three wild stallions were about to kick him in the heart, and Svend flung out his arm and commanded his companions to sit down and have a bite with him. Vagn refused, and Ketil could hardly stand still, 'Have you heard what has happened to Ottar?'

'Ottar?'

Svend shook his head, 'No, what has happened to him?'

The two warriors burst into resounding laughter, and Ketil had to dry his eyes, 'Yes, what has happened to him?'

Vagn stuck his axe shaft in the ground, 'Well, you see, he bored himself a little too much in the abundance of winter, so he rode eastward with a few kinsmen to settle his old dispute with Haldor Skægge.'

The broad axe seemed to drip with poison under Vagn's gloved hand, and the wolf-knife pricked its ears, wanting orders, but Arnulf hesitated. The Jomsviking was well protected by a battle-kyrtle and chainmail, and his forearms were laced in leather, leaving only the lower part of his face and legs to be harmed by a blade.

'It went as it had to, but you know Ottar, the revenge was too miserable for him, so he cut off Haldor's head and rode around with it dangling from his saddle for the rest of the day.'

Ketil was flushed with delight, and Svend nudged Ketil, impatient, 'And what happened next? So much amusement he could not have had from the head?'

Should he scratch on the cheek? The broad axe would never let him get that far! Over the knee then? But if Vagn was lame now that Sigvalde needed him, Arnulf would end up with half of Jomsborg against him!

'No, but Haldor Skægge had crooked teeth in his mouth, especially the one front tooth. Believe me if Ottar did not get it right in the thigh as he rode around there, gloating, and the very next day the leg was both blue and black, to Ottar's considerable annoyance.'

Arnulf went a step further. The banner ground breathed, as if alive, under his rocking sole. It was now! Afterwards, it would be about getting out of the axe's reach, but where should the scratch be, where?

'He did not lie there for long and had only just breathed his last breath, when the earth began to shake, so heartily did they laugh in Valhalla.'

Svend flipped his hair, and the laughter shook the air around Arnulf. By Loki, did Vagn have sharp canines! The hand on the axe head juddered so a little skin revealed itself where the chainmail ended above the elbow. The tears rolled down Silkenhair's cheeks, and he got up and knocked his hand into Vagn's chest, 'Ottar, the miserable boasting flab! How like him. Wait till my father hears this, he will split through the middle!'

Vagn would not notice a graze on the upper arm, but the axe might have murmured to his master, the dark warrior turned in the same moment towards Arnulf, 'You look pale-nosed, Maidenskin, has Svend completely knocked the drive out of you? When he gets too eager, he cannot be stopped again.'

He looked reproachfully at his kinsman, and the corners of Arnulf's mouth pulled, while Svend assured them that he always started to work gingerly with a new man.

'Good.'

Vagn supported the axe against the shield and let the gloved fist stroke Arnulf's hair from his forehead harshly, 'Some scratches tend to be deeper inside than on the outside, so avoid using a helmet that presses, at least.'

A roar from Bue interrupted him; the Stout have combat now and until the sand was dark from sweat! Vagn swung the axe on his shoulder, and Little Ketil wanted to pull Svend up, but the Bueson declined with a half-eaten sausage stump in his hand, 'You will certainly get the hiding you want, but right now, I want to ensure that my housecarl here knows what use I expect to make of him. We will watch.'

He sat down again and with a cheeky expression bit into the sausage, and Ketil sent Arnulf a grin and trotted behind Vagn Ågeson. Arnulf let the knife drop into the sand and stared after them. The moment was gone, the game ran free. Never before had he been so indecisive on a hunt, never hesitated at the wolves, he had failed, lost his fire. A rock sank through his body and ground his feet into the earth.

'You hesitated to save your life. In combat those who hesitate always die first, but when other fighters give up, you still have your wolf blood. Come and sit. Eat and rest. Vagn will give his utmost today, and it is worth looking at.'

Arnulf sat down heavily with his arms around his knees. In the earl's courtyard Serpenttooth had had a bite of itself, nor had he doubted before Leif Cleftnose.

'You have killed me, Svend!'

'No, I have only loosened some milk teeth and you are not the first to be struck dumb in front of Palnatoke's grandson. Be a man for now the games of boys begin, worthy of a king, only women carry discouragement.'

Svend flung himself onto his elbows and nodded towards his father, who, with broad gestures, shouted and divided up the men and Arnulf pulled the shield to him and put down the sausage. Vagn and Little Ketil went along with one group, and Bue and Sigurd went to hold talks with the other. Then the warriors spread out in two long rows opposite each other. Most appeared to have agreed how they would stand, but behind each of the large groups stood a few handfuls who apparently had not found their place in time. Many were gripping long spears and excited cries flew around the sanded area. Ketil spat in his fists and tested the weight of his axe, 'Bue, you fat abscess, when I am done with you, you will regret your winter somnolence, even Sigurd will not recognise his creeping brother!'

He swung expectantly with the axe, but Bue laughed, shaking his shield over his head, 'You will be stepped on like a snotty snail, and the same applies to him, that ugly dog, beside you. His cock seems to be flopping as uninvitingly as his dirty hair!'

Vagn laughed at the accusation and shouted his men forward, 'Now we will come over and slaughter you all as one, then Sigvalde can sweep up the remains. Are you with me?'

A roar drowned out Bue's answer and the rows advanced towards each other. Arnulf forgot all about the sausage and absently replaced the wolf-knife in its sheath. Madness and death-defiance beamed from the faces of the Jomsvikings, and that the weapons were not sharp, seemed totally irrelevant. The spears were lowered, and the men crashed into each other in a tangle of bodies and shields. A noise like thunder came from between the longhouses: spear points hammering against shield bosses, and warriors pushing while the screams from the earl's yard echoed over Jomsborg. Arnulf's whole body shook so much it was difficult to remain seated, and the confusion seemed many times worse than in the battle with Toke, there were so many Jomsmen!

Sword blows crackled, and men fell on both sides, and the outer weapon-bearers ran so viciously at each other that they ran through the enemy's flank. Evidently, those Vikings, who were hit, should lie dead, and the more that lay, the more stumbled over them. Then Sigurd and Bue pressed their companions forward, and suddenly Vagn found himself surrounded and left alone on the battlefield. His struggle was as short as it was brave, and it was Sigurd who, with ill-concealed glee, stabbed him with his sax in the stomach.

Arnulf looked breathlessly at Svend. It lacked only blood, then the Jomsvikings would have wiped themselves out! Svend smiled wryly and, unfazed, butted teeth with the knife, 'What do you see Veulf?'
'What do I see? A lot of men who fought and are now pretending to have died.'
He stared at the fallen, who now stood up and gathered up the lost weapons.
'It is not untrue, but why did Bue's folk win?'
'Because they killed Vagn!'

Sigurd and Vagn Ågeson grasped arms and went their separate ways, and Svend shook his golden hair, 'You do not know anything about battle fights, do you?'

There was no mockery in his voice and Arnulf sucked his teeth. It was not worthwhile to contradict Svend, not when one had just been born again.
'No. What is it that I see?'

Svend straightened up, while Bue and Vagn gathered their fighters for the next battle. Emboldened gestures and muttered orders decided the new order.

'In a real fight the warriors often consist of three rows of men behind each other. The front bear shields and short one-hand spears, the next row stand in the small gaps, reaching over with the long-handled broad axes, and the men at the rear are armed with big, long spears. In addition, all have, of course, both sword or sax, long knives and ordinary battle axes.'

Svend patted the sand evenly in front of him and drew lines with the blade tip, 'Behind the men are archers, and every man has three javelins. The battle starts with slinging stones, shooting arrow and throwing javelins, and if the front men choose to carry two shields each, defensive coverage is possible in several layers and can be quite sound, but we practice all sorts of things. What you see right now is single row battle, later Bue and Vagn will form their companions into a more solid formation, and both must be practiced thoroughly, in order to be used in turn, depending on the battle's development and the slain.'

The slain. Arnulf nodded over the sand line. Broad axe warriors in the second row, and surely they had to be clad with hard chainmail.

'So here you have the middle and, on each side, the flanks. Those men you see placing themselves behind each row now, are wolves, runners, if you will, the skirmishing warriors who fight for themselves. In a triple formation, they are often placed as archers and afterwards they throw their bows over their shoulders and turn into wolves.'

Arnulf looked at the two new rows, they had again started to shout abuse at each other and beat swords against the shields' surfaces. Svend spoke quickly. 'Now notice the wolves. As soon as the men come forward, they will try to run in a wide arc around the flanks and bring down the enemy in the back, preferably from behind the last row of the opposite flank where their coming has not been seen. They kill, if they can, and otherwise create the utmost confusion from behind, but their task may also be to remain behind their own line and go into the hole that occurs when a man dies. See now Little Ketil, he is a wolf.'

The two battle groups went resolutely forward and Ketil stroked the sand behind the left flank with a watchful expression. Arnulf stared, so his eyes smarted. Now he himself was a wolf, now he went, senses tense, behind Bue's folk with melted butter in his ankles, ready to peel warrior holes like a shadow in the night! Just like Svend said, the free Vikings ran around the flanks, while the main forces thundered together, and no one was faster than Little Ketil with his axe. Two of Bue's wolves saw him and chased after, and Ketil retreated softly without abandoning his original direction. Svend laughed, 'Ketil would cut the hocks of the entire row, if he is not stalked from the start, so do not think that the wolves get peace to hunt their prey, they hunt each other with the same relish.'

The clash in the middle of the banner ground was no less fierce than the first fight, but Arnulf was completely occupied with Ketil's escape. Like a doe the Viking jumped from his pursuers, switching direction with surprise and hitting out, but he was too known by his companions. Another wolf came, and Ketil was killed, pushed up against the backs of the struggling men and Svend whistled in displeasure.

Not far away Sigurd was hit in the thigh, but Bue jumped near his brother and covered him with a shield. Vagn's one flank was pushed back, and again it seemed that it would bode unwell for the dark warrior, and Bue roared to his men.

'Look! Now Vagn will pull himself away from battle to get an overview. Bue takes his flank, but Vagn shouts for his best men to go to the opposite end to injure my father in the same way.'

Arnulf jumped up and tried to get a hold of how the warriors had been redeployed but it still looked most like confusion and bewildering weapon use. Sigurd was hit again and fell to his knees but was still not dead, and half of Vagn's group was pushed over the end.

'Why is Sigurd not dead? He was hit twice.'

'Only mortal wounds kill. Everyone knows how much he would be able to withstand if the weapons were sharp, but when you die, you have to lie down. On a real battlefield the dead can easily be crucial. If you can push the enemy back over their own fallen, many of them will inevitably stumble, for it is impossible to look back in full skirmish.'

He smiled grimly, 'Furthermore, it keeps the spirit alive when you have to bite the dirt. The more sand a man gets between his teeth, the more he tries in the next clash, but although it looks wild, we look after each other. The most critical blow is not fully carried out, and fractures are to be avoided wherever possible.'

Whenever possible, how thoughtful! Arnulf peered in vain to notice the critical blow, but maybe there was a difference between Jomsvikings and ordinary men's interpretation of the concept. Despite all Vagn's efforts the fortune of war was not for his people, for the men's ranks were broken in several places, and all of the receding flank fell. The other survivors gathered in small groups without seeming in the least bit defeated, and never had Arnulf seen so violent a zeal than in the eyes of

231

the surrounded men. With a bull-roaring, death-defiance they defended themselves, so splinters flew from the shields, and Svend nodded appreciatively, 'Look. Each and every one shall die, but if they had faced a force other than Bue's, they would still be able to seize victory. It is no coincidence who is teamed with whom, they know each other, and to know your neighbour's favourite fighting-pattern can be crucial. See how spears and broad axe warriors work together, they can affect both the long and short distances. If a shield-bearer pulls the sword, while his comrade leads with spears, they attack as one man with three arms.'

Vagn's spear broke, and he resorted to a long knife but was hit in the arm and let it drop. Svend's prophecy came steadily true, and the few remaining covered themselves behind the piles of corpses, but they gave intrepid resistance to Bue's Vikings down to the last man. Vagn used the sword with his left hand and attacked more than defended himself, and Svend smiled. 'One must never forget that intimidating behaviour is the last weapon that you lose. Remember, less experienced opponents can be kept at bay with roaring and the rolling of eyes. Vagn has only one arm now, but like everyone here he is fighting equally well with his left hand as with his right. You will be injured in battle, Veulf, everyone gets hit, so you must know how to fight on, depending on where and how deeply you are struck.'

Arnulf nodded, his mouth dry. He knew now that no king nor earl would have men enough to face against Sigvalde's Jomsvikings! Nothing that Helge had seen or heard could compare to this.

Vagn sank with a spear in the side, his trousers soaked with sweat, and Bue triumphed again and, laughing, helped his brother to his feet. The two forces went their separate ways, and Ketil had much to talk about with Vagn, while the helmets were pulled off for a moment.

'You are not eating anything.'

Arnulf shook his head, warm-bloodedly, 'Vagn needs to win now, does not he? If he loses again, he will have no peace from Bue for rest of the day.'

'He will win, do not worry, what else do you think he and Ketil are standing and speaking so vehemently about? My father knows it too, but he shows up anyway.'

The door to Sigvalde's house opened as he spoke, and Jomsborg's leader came out and leaned against the gable to watch. Thorkel the Tall also appeared dressed in scale armour, as if he himself were on his way into battle. Bue did not let his men breathe long and Ketil, sharp-voiced, spaced out his men in rows. Vagn went into that wing that had just been defeated, their expressions were dangerous; no heckling was necessary this time.

Arnulf licked his lips. Stallion fights were held in Egilssund, and he had seen Helge in single combat, but this far exceeded the domestic fights, and Svend did not spare explanation, 'Notice the distance between the men. There must be half an arm's length to the side-companion, so there is room to cut but still mutual protection; during a fight, a close arrangement will always become looser. Bue's men are preparing to meet Vagn's folk, they have an idea who is the strongest and who is the fastest, they seek out weaknesses and get ready to hit holes where they are most, but believe me if Ketil has not ordered the men to regroup just before the clash.'

He pointed, 'The spears are used to open the enemy's rows and create opportunities for breakthroughs, but they are never set out on the flank, for there, a spear-carrier is too exposed. With a spear the closest five enemies can be hit, and if you watch, you will see that two stings rarely go after the same man. A repeatable quick lurch will not always hurt an opponent but will press them and keep them occupied while others encounter to kill.'

Arnulf glanced at him and stared intently at the rows of long-handled spears that were now lowered by Bue's men. The rows moved quickly towards each other, and Svend shouted excitedly when Vagn's warriors ran quickly from each other just before impact and changed places in order to lunge forwards immediately after with lowered spears. Again the points rumbled against the shields, but now how the men worked together was more understood and Svend's word that the enemy, who was out of sight, was most dangerous, proved true, for too often those who were far from the offensive were killed.

The flanks spread out and tried to mutually surround and push each other backwards, and apparently it was the strongest and fiercest warriors who were set outermost, whereas the solid men hammered steadily from the middle and held the row together. Svend spat out sausage cartilage and confirmed pleasure when Arnulf asked.

'Now you can begin to see what really happens. Just as Ketil is most useful as a wolf, Vagn and Bue are always found on the flanks. Out there they are prepared to engage in hunting groups and ensure that the enemy does not destroy the wing. Sigurd, over there, is Bue's anchor man in this fight, he is the end of the middle and the first man in the flank, and from the anchor man the outer flank tries to curve against the enemy to be able to pre-empt the push. What happens in the middle?'

Several of the long spears were broken and the short ones were put to use alongside the striking weapons. Despite the confusion Arnulf managed to get more of an overview and tried to work out the meaning behind the fierce fighting. If a warrior came in front of his comrades, he was immediately pierced by spears from all sides, so it seemed most important of all to hold the row even. As soon as a man fell, the hostile group immediately tried to wedge a larger hole and divide the men from each other before they managed to move around or get a wolf to fill the empty space. Both Bue and Vagn seemed to have gathered particularly powerful men in small groups in different locations along the middle, for here the blows were most violent and opened wounds in the opponent's shield wall.

'Sigurd also stood beside the redhead, in the last battle, and Bue has not swapped his closest, is it just the smaller groups that are moved around in the row?'

Arnulf could not remember all the men from each other and tried to figure out how much switching Little Ketil had really caused among Vagn's men.

'Those, who work best together, often stand together. When all plans fail and the shield wall breaks into pieces, it is important to stay together with your nearest and make the best of the situation.'

Svend abruptly interrupted himself with a dumb grin, staring at Vagn, who had left his place in the flank and ran behind his men towards the centre. With a wordless command the wolves gathered behind him in the shelter of the warring Jomsvikings and suddenly his own line of men yielded a gap to the enemy. Vagn jumped through, shouting, closely flanked by a spearhead of men who, in an instant, let shields slide over one another like a snake's armour. So powerfully did they break through into Bue's flock with Vagn in front, that they split the row in two, continued through and spread out on both sides to attack the surprised men from behind.

Arnulf yelled at Vagn like at a wrestling match, and Bue saw his entire middle overwhelmed and surrounded. Exasperated, he made every effort to conquer one flank, but Vagn's folk rolled his formation together, and beat them to the ground, and Bue called all the remaining men together in front of him. Arnulf laughed out loud, now the Stout was beaten, Vagn's snake head had bitten the stout one in the heel!

Sigvalde and Torkel also seemed to be laughing by the large longhouse, and Svend rose elated, 'A boar snout. It cannot be more beautiful! That is how a boar reaps the fallen acorns from the soil, just do

234

not believe it will succeed every time. There you see how important the heroes are!'

Vagn let the slaughter begin while he trotted behind the men with a wry grin to Bue, his axe looming promisingly. Mighty were Sigvalde's warriors, and if they were led by men like Vagn Ågeson and Bue the Stout, then the ground itself would crack!

'Has Jomsborg ever suffered defeat?'

'Ah, Veulf. Defeat is a broad notion, and the enemy can be superior in number. Our victories are always paid, and the price cannot be haggled; keep in mind that with real weapons no man would remain. From here it looks easy enough, but once you stand there, once your own blood glows down your skin and your limbs set out, blow for blow, then you gain a warrior's insight and you can raise your voice at the table afterwards.'

Bue shouted scoldingly after the Ågeson, but it did not result in single combat for, at that same moment, the Stout was hit in the stomach by a spear. The skirmish ended in laughter, and the last men were spared, and Sigurd shouted that everyone should now be warm enough for a more solid line-up. Several threw themselves in the sand out of breath, and helmets and chainmail were removed, only Vagn still endured the heat of the battle in his leather-padded iron, even though he was so wet that everything seemed to slide on him.

Svend sat back down, pulling Arnulf with him, and Sigvalde disappeared behind his house, while Bue stomped around his brother with big gestures. The last sausage was sliced with Svend's knife, and Arnulf let himself partake again.

'Why did Bue die, Veulf?'

Arnulf looked over the resting men and held back the answer that had first fallen on his tongue. Long ago, when the sun was new in the sky, he would have thought it was because of the spear to the stomach, but then Svend would not have asked.

'He did not see the spear.'

'And why did he not see it?'

Arnulf stared at Bue, standing with the helmet under his arm, flushed from annoyance.

'Because ... because his helmet protects his eyes ... because there must be a blind spot in the helmet he uses!'

'Right! Ha!'

Svend banged his fists into the shield, so the sausage ends rolled into the sand.

'Such a helmet is safer than those that only protect the crown of the head, but sight is limited slightly. Veulf, tomorrow you will stand with me in the shield wall, you are not that bad after all.'

Arnulf smiled. Svend's confidence was honourable, although the bruised limbs began to recognise the eternal torment behind Jomsborg's rampart. He was aching enough already – how would his legs carry him after only a few afternoons on the banner ground? It all depended on a single small cut. A brief movement against the man who had just broken through Bue's shield wall, Fenrir have mercy! Soon nothing would ache anyway!

Like fiery stallions, Vagn Ågeson and Bue the Stout stamped the heavy sand from the sweat and the Jomsvikings donned chainmail again; they did not settle for helmets and battle-kyrtles, for the sun was rejoicing in its own power and the wind had blown itself out of the way. Arnulf followed how the shield walls now stood in dense triple rows, and the next conflict was, if possible, worse than the previous one. It was difficult to pierce in the new wall of warriors, and the men stood upright for longer, well-covered by each other. Svend asked and continued to explain, and Arnulf gave, with increasing clarity, the right answers.

Again and again, the Jomsmen came forward, clashing right in front of him, while the sand darkened, kyrtles were thrown down, and some fainted from the heat of their helmets. Water barrels were rolled up, the power and speed of the blows decreased, and Vagn's face was lobster red from exertion and nosebleeds.

The first men had to give up and sit down, and when Vagn, after a rather half-hearted fight, finally threw down his sword and tumbled onto his back, gasping, Arnulf jumped to a water barrel and filled the ladle for the Ågeson. The once-raging Vikings burned wearily over their weapons, and Jomsborg recovered in silent breathlessness. Even Bue hung drooping over his shield, and Little Ketil lay as if dead.

Cautiously Arnulf stepped between them. The exhausted Vagn was apparently not aware of him coming, and Arnulf could see the pulse pounding through the open hands. He stopped on one foot, the ladle dripping a few steps from the Viking and slipped his hand towards the knife's handle. Vagn could be hit now, in his own breathlessness, dazzled by sweat and worn out. The wolf-knife would slip quickly from its sheath, but there was not much honour to be gained from the cut, rather the disapproval of cowardice, Sigvalde had hardly envisioned his test would be performed so thievishly. Was it worthy of Helge's reputation? Was this how he would earn Svend's faith?

236

'Do not drip on the chainmail, Veulf, it rusts easily enough already.'

The dark spear-gaze lurked beneath quivering eyelids, and Vagn extended his hand towards the ladle. Arnulf was stiff. As if the Ågeson had not known he was there! Vagn's arm was so warm that the Jomsviking bit the ladle faster than a hawk snatching spoils from the grass! The ladle changed hands, and Vagn sat up and drank deeply.

'Will I help you out of your chainmail? It probably won't get wetter if I spill on it.'

Vagn shook his head, so sweat droplets streaked through his hair. With a sigh he handed the ladle back and rubbed his hand, 'No. I love my chainmail.'

He gave a short laugh and got up without so much as loosening the helmet, covered with sand that clung to his back.

'What do you think about the fight, Ulfhednar?'

Arnulf was silent. What did he think? How could that answer be spun into words?

'What is an Ulfhednar?'

Vagn looked at him like lava flowing over the rocks on Iceland. Then he smiled and left, Vagn Ågeson, Palnatoke's kinsman, Nidhogg skin him, the man would live when everyone else around him was dead! Live forever in burning skaldic verses! Arnulf let the ladle fall. Fall into the salt-bleached sand.

*****

Shortly after the training on the banner ground, Sigvalde called his closest men to meet in the longhouse hall and Svend resumed his tour of Jomsborg. Again, Arnulf had to place his concerns aside, although it got harder as the afternoon progressed. Faithfully he followed Svend, who let him visit several of the impressive longhouses. They were not much different from what Arnulf had expected, just overwhelmingly large and clearly inhabited by men of arms. He visited workshops and stables, the armour store and the injury houses where Sigvalde gathered with care the most wound-knowledgeable men who could be hired for silver; several of them came from remote areas to the east.

Svend showed Arnulf the sand barrels in which the chainmail was rolled free of rust, they greeted Sigvalde's white stallion that was grazing between the houses, and he let him try to strike against the pig carcasses, which were suspended with the aim of practicing sword bites in raw flesh.

Svend did not think they would get to see Vagn before the evening roast, for the feast with the king had to be carefully planned by the earl's sons, and Bjørn the Bretlander would certainly make a valiant but vain attempt to dissuade Sigvalde from going.

Without a care about the future Svend selected a glossy helmet from the smith that suited Arnulf well. It had no eye protection, but it covered his nose and allowed a clear view of both sides, and at the shieldmaker Arnulf had to explain how he wanted his wolf shields to look for the maker was also a master with paint and brush.

Arnulf had nothing to pay with but Svend ignored it with a shrug. Jomsborg armed its sons appropriately. Lack was not known at the fort.

'You should also have an axe, but all the joys do not need to befall you at once. We can get it tomorrow. Are you good with a bow?'

In that art Arnulf did not believe he needed to be outdone by anyone, and the arrows flew towards the targets until Jomsborg turned the colour of amber and the odour of food drifted towards them. The Bueson found it was then time to withdraw to Sigvalde's house for over his fire hung the fattest pork, and it was getting time to settle the promise to Jomsborg's leader.

*****

Sigvalde's longhouse did not seem less than a king's hall and it was so grandly decorated that Arnulf stopped as soon as he had entered through the door. Brightly coloured tapestries hung on all the walls, and several narrow oak tables with carved benches were lined up in rows around the burning mid-house hearth. The sleeping places were broad at the walls, with thick sleeping skins, and everywhere was bright, for countless small oil lamps supressed darkness from their hooks. From the rafters hung bloodstained shields and broken weapons, and Svend noticed Arnulf's gaze and nodded towards them, 'The conquered enemies' weapons. We have to get a little pleasure out of our efforts, but the sax above the seat of honour, over there, is Palnatoke's.'

Sigvalde's long table stood across the hall farthest from the door and from his seat, mid-table, the highest Jomsviking could survey his warriors who just now were gathering with hunger in their eyes. The seat of honour was painted red and silver snakes wove with great artistry around the edge of the backrest. On the wall behind it hung a gold-handled long sax of rare weight, so Palnatoke had not been a little man, and although the single-edged sword was his grandson's rightful inheritance, it did not appear to be used.

Bue and Sigurd were already seated by Sigvalde along with Thorkel the Tall and Vagn and a number of other masterful men and Little Ketil settled down, laughing, beside them. Not far from the seat of honour, a handful of women were leaning close to each other over the table and talking, their faces happy, and Svend pointed out Astrid Borislav's Daughter, Sigvalde's wife, and Tove Strut-Harald's daughter, who was married to Sigurd. Whether it was to honour the returning Vikings or simply to assert her husband's rank, Astrid sat dressed in blue with gold on her chest and wrists, and her chin was proudly lifted.

Svend pulled Arnulf along to one of the tables in front of the high table and threw his legs over the bench with familiarity, his back to Sigvalde. Steaming dishes were laid out between large round breads and mead horns were handed around, and those who came late, did not seem to be waited for.

Arnulf sat, tense, and took a full horn. As long as he had Vagn at his back, it was impossible to choke on the smallest bite, and the warmth in the hall was unpleasant. Sulking, Bjørn the Bretlander sat pulling at his beard at the end of the high table, and given the unrestrained mood around Sigvalde, Arnulf concluded that the Jomsvikings had agreed on the impending journey to Sweyn Haraldson.

Vagn had still not removed his chainmail but had pulled off his helmet and washed his face, and Arnulf restlessly rolled up his sleeves. He glanced back towards Sigvalde, but the redheaded Jomsman did not notice him, for Torkel was finishing a cheerful account and held the adjacent men's attention captive.

Svend handed a slice of bread to Arnulf and flung some pork on top it, but his throat was tight, pinched by pumping blood, and the mead seemed honey thick. Arnulf turned around on the bench and looked openly at Vagn who had swept the table clean before him and was eagerly slicing a sausage. It would not take many steps to get there, but Vagn sat on the opposite side of the table and could not be immediately reached. Svend seemed to have been infected by the fever, for he contented himself with sipping his drink and held a little too firm to his horn. Vagn lay the sausage slices in two straight rows and spoke loudly and Ketil leaned forward on his elbows to better keep up.

'Believe me, for we have long fought together, but one man seldom does that much harm when he breaks through a single line of men.'

Vagn's eyes sparkled, and he took a sausage from the row, while his table companions grew quiet. Arnulf handed Svend the horn, pulled out the wolf-knife and cut an end off the meat. The hand was calm but treacherously white. He skewered the meat and stood up, lightning hit him or not, Stridbjørn's sons were not afraid of perilous deeds!

'Here!'

Vagn pushed four sausages together, 'At selected sites within the formation, we form small groups; four men in each, supported from behind by a long spear, every other man is the leader and the rest, followers.'

Arnulf straddled the bench, sweating dribbling from under his rolled-up sleeves and he went towards the high table, as though he wanted to listen.

'So, the leaders break through, those following cover their backs, and the spears go with them, and here!'

The dark warrior collected four sausages further along the line, 'Here it is the same.'

Arnulf wedged himself unceremoniously between Ketil and a one-armed Viking on the bench and leaned over the table with the knife in his hand. He was so close to Vagn now that the sour stench from the battle-kyrtle could be smelled.

'When such groups are broken through, then those who succeeded gather together!'

Vagn rolled the sausages, but Little Ketil shook his head doubtfully, 'It is not going to work, Vagn, not at all.'

Arnulf stuck the pork in his mouth but kept the wolf-knife in front of him as if he were engulfed by Vagn's strategy and had completely forgotten that the point was jutting towards the others' noses.

'Yes, Odin's brew if it works! If we get just two groups through, that is at least eight men, and the wolves are naturally ready and prepared to join them.'

A sausage rolled away from Vagn, and he shot across the table to reach it. Arnulf threw himself at him, pork-spitting, and cut briskly at his face. The blade met resistance, but what it had hit, he did not see, for in that same moment a bear-like force flung him into the table, and everything went black before his eyes. Half-faint from the attack, Arnulf felt Vagn's iron fist in his hair, and even though his body screamed in defiance and escape; groaning, he forced it not to move. In front his cheek, which was over the group of four sausages, blood dripped onto the table.

240

There was a deathly silence along the benches as the men froze, and Arnulf heard only his own anguished panting. How much hair Vagn had pulled from the back of his head, he did not care to learn, but it was just possible to see the Ågeson's astonished face out of the corner of his eye. Vagn felt his chin, staring at his bloody fingers. Then his gaze slid along the table, searching, and ended at Sigvalde, and he burst into a resounding laughter, 'Sigvalde! Your sly jötunn fox! This is your work!'

Sigvalde answered his laughter, amused, and raised his mead horn, and the expressions of the men around the table came to life again. Vagn pulled Arnulf up and waved his hand free of the hair. The wolf-knife had lacerated his chin, under his lip, and Arnulf's legs began to shake. Die, he would die now for having scarred Jomsborg's proudest heir, the man who killed like others crushed lice, the man whose own father had banished him for cruelty!

Arnulf blinked away the mist from his eyes as the men's eyes weakened his courage. Vagn's face flamed, and his voice was clear, 'As you are so bold in deed, give me your hand and your knife.'

The jittering of his legs spread upwards and the knife's wolf writhed, glowing, in his palm. Arnulf was breathing slowly through his nose, Sigvalde's test was not hard compared to Vagn's! He who hesitated, died first! Vagn's expression revealed nothing, and Arnulf stretched his arm across the table with the knife in his open hand. This was just how it was for Tyr when he gave Fenrir his sword arm and felt the hot breath and saw the sharp teeth encircle the downy hair on his skin! The silence was even more poignant now, the calm before the thunder, before the worst possible pain, the silence that would seize his scream!

The hint of a smile lurked on the Ågeson's lips. He took the knife and grabbed Arnulf's hand and turned it over. His skin was rough and his fist hard, his muscles made of liquid stone. A fine cut drew blood above his wrist, and Vagn quickly pressed Arnulf's wounds against his own slashed chin. Arnulf gave an amazed cry as the blood mingled and ran down his arm. Of everything Vagn could have done, this was the last thing he expected!

Vagn Ågeson held his hand up and raised his voice solemnly, 'Now you are my blood-brother, Veulf, and if you ever pass Jomsborg's tests, then you will stand by it with an oath.'

He looked around, 'A whelp has torn me, a wolf whelp! Beat him now so a Jomsviking will be made of him, I only reluctantly spill my blood in vain.'

He let Arnulf go and grasped his hand in a firm grip, and Arnulf clasped it as though it were Helge he was wrestling with. The tears threatened to come, and he gasped for breath, Fenrir was fickle, Vagn was as fearsome as Odin himself. The promise in the dark eyes revealed the wildness of his fate, devoted to Ragnarök, he had mixed black blood with Arnulf, exchanged iron bands to death but Vagn's companions stood eye-to-eye with him, the Wolfblood would cow to no one!

Arnulf caught his smile and answered it with eyes of fire, and Vagn let go with a silent nod. Svend Silkenhair let out a triumphant yell, and Sigvalde's men shouted and banged horns and knife hilts against the table edges. Vagn laughed again, and Svend threw away the drinking horns and jumped up to shake Arnulf's shoulders and peel sausages from his cheek. Sigvalde rose with dignity. He waited a moment before demanding silence, and those beautiful eyes softened the appearance of the ugly nose, 'There are not many men with whom Vagn shares his blood, but those he has chosen, have never betrayed his confidence. You have won the right to stay, Veulf, and I must bid you welcome, just as long as you also know that you are free to go again at any time. Jomsborg's colts are heavily ridden, and some have their spine crushed too early.'

Arnulf nodded, unafraid of the words, his eagle flew so high that nothing could hit it! He took his mead horn, which Svend had filled again, and was with one up on the table where everyone in the hall could see him fully. The fears were killed, now dawned a new time! The words flocked, jumped like bucks with glistening backs, and mead sloshed over the horn's edge and it smarted in the bleeding wound. He looked at Bue, at Ketil and Bjørn, the rows of hearth-warmed men, at Sigurd and Torkel and the women, and last of all at Sigvalde:

'Far from farmhearth
A stranger I suffered
Misfortune and malice
Wrested my friends
From harm and hardship
With scoundrels I laid

Then included by heroes
The unproven rested
To learn by listening
To grow in greatness
To harden the whelp

To rise behind ramparts

Hail Sigvalde!
And hail Vagn and Svend!
Hail all you, highly praised!
Know Veulf greets you
No bolder warriors
Swung swords for kings!

My Fenrirblood flows
Steadfast and black
Destiny to force
On better path
Win favour of friends
And rally repute!'

'He dares to skald, the inflated midge-bladder, but just wait!'
Bue the Stout threw a rib at Arnulf, 'My respect you will have only if you can skald after standing in the shield wall tomorrow and Svend! You dare to protect your housecarl firmer than others, he would do well to believe that honour of Jomsborg is not earned by a single fortunate cut!'

Arnulf raised the horn to Bue and drank on his behalf, and the chatter broke out again between the men, as they hungrily reached for the barrels.

Arnulf sat with Svend and finished his drank, giddy with excited relief. His head throbbed where it had hit the table and his wrist continued to bleed soft and only now did he see how shamelessly he had shown his bruised forearms. Svend drove the meat between his teeth and yelled for more mead, and Arnulf, hungry from the taste of the salt, took a bite. Many along the table wanted to toast him, and the mead ran willingly down his throat, if he was to fight among the Jomsvikings, then he could also drink with them, and salt and fat would be rinsed off his palate.

At the high table Vagn toasted Torkel Lere's fair daughter in Vigen, her, he would have that day he had enough desire, and Bjørn abandoned his gloomy mood and sang along when Sigurd joined in. Arnulf drank manfully with his table companions and stabbed the wolf-knife into the table, so the blade quivered, and looked the mixed blood, which oddly enough seemed to flow around the blade itself.

'Now you must tell me exactly what these tests are about, Svend, since I'm the only one here who does not know it.'

The Bueson's golden hair was unfamiliarly dishevelled, 'To tell the truth, I do not know.'

A belch resounded from his throat, and Arnulf shook his head, 'What do you mean? You do not know? Who knows it so? Should they perhaps be performed whilst sleeping?'

He laughed and wiped the half-hardened blood off on his pants. Svend blew on his mead, 'You choose them yourself, Veulf.'

'Choose them yourself? And what is it that you choose yourself? Garmr bite you for that answer!'

Svend laughed himself silly but his brows wrinkled in an attempt to be serious, 'Now see my father and Little Ketil. My dad is strongest, but Ketil fastest, and one is not inferior to the other in battle. Should they prove one's strength at the tests? One's speed? It is a stupid earl who lets his men lift the same stone, no, Sigvalde decides merely that the first test is strength, and then the man himself chooses how he will prove his worth, you understand? Afterwards, in cunning, in pain, in endurance and whatever else follows, and the test in the tests is clever enough; that a wise man knows his own limitations and does not want to lose face in front of Sigvalde and the rest of us.'

He leaned into Arnulf and confessed, 'You must prove that you know yourself and choose correctly in a difficult moment, exactly as it happens in the middle of the battle. Only the last test does Sigvalde decide completely.'

Arnulf stared at Svend with a rigid grin. Choose correctly in a difficult moment? Loki himself was the father of such double-edged challenges! Was it the right choice to hack Helge's ship to pieces, to strike Rolf down, to flee the kingdom with his tail between his legs and not dare to stand by his own misdeeds? How strong was a man who was not threatened by death? And did man not endure double when it really counted?

'That is why so many do not pass the tests. Many of them are good men, but their arrogance and false grandeur hits them in the chest. Know yourself, Wolfblood, and you will be able to defeat most!'

'But Vagn! He did not pass any tests when he was accepted?'

'No. Not all fight in the tests, some stand out in other ways and thereby get elected to the brotherhood, but do not dwell on that now. In a little while, I will force you under a sleeping skin, otherwise you will not last tomorrow.'

244

He smiled wryly as mead dripped and jammed a finger in Arnulf's shoulder, 'You also need to know yourself with a horn, Maidenskin, and as long as you are a man in my hird, I decide!'

*****

The days of Jomsborg were warm and bright, but no place gathered more heat than the banner ground. Outside the rampart, the sea air cooled, and it could be felt on the wooden palisade, but between the shielding longhouses, the sand was fiery. As if to entice the wind to the feast, the gates of the fort stood open, and water was almost continuously drawn from the wells, and in the fortified harbour, birds and fish gave way to hot men craving relief.

When it was possible, Arnulf pulled off his kyrtle and rolled up his trouser legs, but most of the time Svend let him suffer under the helmet and battle-kyrtle, advancing blows until his arms and legs were almost useless. Despite their preference for practising in the shadow of the longhouses, their skin was cooked red and itchy under the leather-laces and Arnulf regularly threw water over himself to endure the suffering. The rigid battle-kyrtle bickered hard with the wet leather, gnawing at him, in turn, Svend's engagements were milder now, letting Arnulf catch his breath when it was needed.

In the formation fighting, Arnulf stood next to the Bueson, but despite all efforts, he was the first to fall in every collision, for encouraged by Vagn's call every Jomsviking vied to be the one who slew him. It was no penalty to lie dead in the sand, rather a relief as he was so woe-skinned and keeping track of things at foot height seemed a worthy challenge.

The chatter in the evening around the fire and the table was short; his exhausted body screamed for rest, and only in the darkness under the sleeping skin did Arnulf let himself be overwhelmed by pain and curl up like Ragnar Lodbrok in the snake pit. Svend thought he was sleeping like a baby, but Bjørn the Bretlander who, like himself took to bed early, defended him.

The wolves' shields were finished, and so furiously did the red wolves show their teeth on the black painted wood that Arnulf had to lift them with respect. The edges did not have a red rim, and none of them were hung up in the longhouse, he and Svend slept in, but Arnulf did not care. With the wolf-knife he scratched the strength rune on the back of them, like Stentor had done for Toke when he was sick, so no hostile blades would succeed in splitting the interlocking wood apart. Although

Arnulf was best with a sword, Svend Silkenhair found him both an axe and a spear, and he was also allowed to borrow chainmail to equip himself, even though Svend realised that he was not strong enough to train in it; he had so much to learn. The chainmail was a priceless treasure, worth as much as a farm with livestock and thralls, and his jaw dropped as Svend sought it out from among the combined battle-garb. Leather with metal plates attached, scale mail and chainmail, Arnulf could not swallow his amazement, Jomsborg's earl was as rich as a king, and he did his utmost to ensure protection for his brothers-in-arms.

During the day it was decided what men would sail with Sigvalde to the royalseat, and his dragon ship was painted again, and the preparations made. The Jomsborg leader wanted to have a great retinue, and his men had to perform well in front of Sweyn Haraldson's hird, so when the Vikings did not fight, clothing and weapons were inspected and cleaned, and the ships made ready. The white stallion would also travel as Sigvalde would not meet the king on foot, and as Svend was to follow his father room for Arnulf was also calculated on one of the vessels.

The wound above the wrist was closed and had lost its scab, and although Vagn did not talk more to Arnulf than before, Arnulf could sense his good will when they met. The Ågeson and Svend's axes sparred in the quiet cooking-time late in the afternoon, and it was a game that had been going on for the whole winter in Bretland, for Vagn was curious to test if a battle axe in each hand was superior to other weapon pairings. With axes spinning like a wheel, he attacked Svend from all angles and twisted both the shield and Snap out of his hand, and Arnulf sat with his back against the nearest longhouse, watching. He was as exhausted and sore as a whipped thrall, so while the kinsmen fought, his thoughts fled north over Jomsborg's ramparts, returning to Denmark.

The nights were also bright over Egilssund now, so Trud would let the door stand open in the moonlight with the dogs in front of the doorstep. Stridbjørn liked to sit on the bench outside, listening to the nightingales and Rolf would often sit with him, busying himself with a knife, while quietly talking about crops and chores.

Arnulf closed his eyes, supporting his head against the planks. The Midsummer blót. The flickering of the fire. The favour of the gods. Frejdis standing on bare legs by the blackberry brook. Last year, when the berries were ripe. She had scratched herself when she had pretended to run from him, scratched herself and whimpered, and stuck her foot in the water, but Arnulf had had a better cure for that kind of pain, sour must be driven away with sweet. He had pressed the blackest berries over the scratch and had tenderly sucked off the juice that dripped down from it. Frejdis had had other scratches when she first looked, but none of them was so deep that Arnulf could not heal it. Berry after berry was mashed and the blue-black sweet juice rolled over the downy skin.

He sighed. She would not have her dress stained, so he had pulled it off and caringly sought her white body. Blackberry juice could cure everything: mosquito bites, flea bites, bruises. With eyes closed, he had mistakenly taken the bulging nipples for blackberries, and the taste was no less sweet. Odin's spear had sought and found, and she had ridden him like Freya, every thrust had blessed the earth, hailed Freyr and brought the Æsir joy and so fiercely that afterwards Frejdis was the one who had to heal blackberry scratches on his back.

Arnulf stroked his fingers through his hair and felt his scarred face. Frejdis was worth losing his life for, worth enduring all Helheim's tribulations, worth waiting for until his hair turned grey. And life without Frejdis! It was exactly like that world to be found on the other side of the eyelids' guard, a Jomsborg filled with harsh fighters, tough swords and sharp eyes. Healthy men, who themselves found what they needed during voyages, men who put courage and skill above all else, men who could defeat berserkers and earls, but who did not know how invaluable a joy could be won! Men without blackberries. Men without meaning. By Fenrir, he was tired.

$$*****$$

Arnulf had been proud when *Twin Raven* had set sail out of Haraldsfjord, but that greatness was nothing compared to the Jomsvikings departure from Jomsborg. The sun was new when the first men started walking towards the ships with Sigvalde in the lead, and endless seemed the number of selected warriors who stomped out of the heavy gate, armed for Ragnarök itself.

The trimmed ships were already loaded with weapons and chainmail, and as the men took their thwarts, shield upon shield was attached to the rim. The colours were brilliant in the first light of the morning, the violent images strong in unity, and the red ring along each shield edge testified to the blood-bonded brotherhood, the Vikings stood ready to avenge all as one. Spearheads and cloak-clasps flashed, helmets and bronze-plated bow heads glistened, and although many of the vessels were not particularly large, their crews constituted a far greater danger than many a fully manned longship.

Arnulf followed Svend to Vagn Ågeson's skeid, moored at one of the outer bridges. The night before he had carried food and equipment on board and put clothes in his chest along with tightly wound rolls of narrow linen cloth for dressing wounds. The extra shields were secured, and a small anvil with hammers and a whetstone were arranged by the mast. The Jomsvikings knew how to prepare for tough battles and untethered rivets and chipped swords had to be repaired on site. Bundles of arrows with and without flammable tips, heaps of split flint for casting, wound clips and longbows; everything had found space on the deck or under the loose deckboards and sand barrels had rumbled chainmail half the night after which cloth soaked in linseed oil had ensured that ring-garments would shine like polished silver during the funeral feast.

The feast was being painstakingly prepared as if it were a great battle, but the thought of having to sit still in a ship for several days was encouraging and Arnulf could not get out to sea fast enough. His arms could hardly bear a shield and sword any longer, the overworked muscles ached from the grip, and which leg had the most right to limp was hard to decide. His shoulders were so sore after the burden of the previous days' chainmail that they could little tolerate a resting fly and his knees gave from the unaccustomed load. Although the belt placed some of the weight onto his hips, his shoulders bared the most, but the Bueson would not have a housecarl with him, who had never felt the weight of iron.

Arnulf stopped at the jetty, letting his gaze run over the dense rows of ships nudging each other like a pod of whales on the Faroe Islands. The Jomsvikings were lightly dressed in the heat, and although they hardly reached the royalseat the first day, their hair and beards were combed, not least Svend's golden, silken hair. Like Sif's golden locks they flowed around his shoulders and shed in vain lustre where no young maiden gloried in it. Vagn did not smell as he strode past on the bridge to take his ship in possession, and Arnulf followed so as not to be the last man on board.

Sigvalde let his dragon loose, standing at the mast while he watched the boarding. Tall and dignified he stood, strict and pure like his own snowskin. His longship was slowly rowed from bridge to bridge, and he examined his men thoroughly. Bue led the ship with his brother, and Torkel the Tall's white snekke slipped out as the first after Sigvalde. On *the Blood Fox* Ketil's crew was ready, and soon after Arnulf sat down, Vagn took the skeid's rudder. Sigvalde raised his hands with a shout, while his banner unfurled over the dragon, and a roar returned his greeting with resounding force. The Jomsmen on the strand and the wooden palisade wished their companions luck on the journey and, despite many setting out, Jomsborg was not left toothless.

His chest was overpowered by a deep sigh. This time it was not village looting and random plundering that awaited! King Sweyn's gold ring had been hot for days from longing for reunion with its former master, and the thoughts of the royalseat brought Helge to mind. Trud and Stridbjørn, if they only knew what their youngest son was engaged in, while they themselves were in mourning! Someday word would travel to Egilssund, tender tidings that would make even the eyes of the grey bear open in wonder!

Sigvalde's longship led the way out of the heavily fortified port, and ship after ship followed one after the other, a war eagle with young. Thorkel the Tall covered his brother Sigvalde's back, and Bue and Sigurd's ship cut the water sharply, followed by Vagn's skeid and Little Ketil's *Blood Fox*. Arnulf looked back over the meandering snake that was wriggling free from the entanglement of spears and nails. Jomsborg's rampart sank slowly into the gravel during the growing distance, like an echo of a powerful dream, a distant verse, an ancient story. Steadily the land engulfed the fort and towers, smoothing the sharp points, while the ships spread out challengingly, conquering the sea so even Jörmungandr shamefully abandoned any claim to the water.

The wind also brought honour to Sigvalde's setting out. Hræsvelgr flapped its wings, so the sails were tense and obedient, and Svend shouted to Ketil that the thralls could well start the fires for frying in the royalseat now, since given their speed, the sizzling pigs would be worthy of the Æsir on arrival. Little Ketil laughed and reminisced about Sweyn Haraldson's mead being the strongest he had ever tasted and believed he had never seen prettier women than at the King's hird. Vagn, displeased, set the course away from *the Blood Fox* and reminded the Silkenhaired that it was not for the beer's sake that he had sweated in chainmail for the past several days, and Arnulf let himself smile brightly for the kinsmen. So different were they, yet so close did they stand together, and since he had scratched Vagn's chin, the Ågeson had not had many moments of peace from Svend's sneak attacks.

Arnulf sat up and began to cut his nails. King Sweyn. What did he look like, the man who had rebelled against his father and taken his country in hand before time? He must be strong, since half the country had followed him into battle, and wise so quickly had he healed the wounds between the great men. Helge had spoken with Stridbjørn about him last winter, said that he had not been a bad son for his father, but that

249

King Harald had been a hard man. Many fears smouldered in hearts, even those of the hardy, fear of the Æsir's revenge: crop failure and misshapen livestock, storms and disease, for the king declared the Danes Christian and forbade blót and sacrifices and forced baptism on those unwilling by sword. Helge had whispered to Stridbjørn in confidence that the disgruntled chieftains and earls had barely given the young Sweyn a choice, either he led them in an uprising against Harald Gormson, or he would leave this life like his father.

It was therefore that Stentor could talk about the cross on King Sweyn's kyrtle and the hammer next to the skin of his chest; it was therefore that the people in Egilssund had never burned their shrine to the gods, and it was therefore no wonder that Sweyn had been so angry at his friend, Palnatoke, that it was he who had killed Harald. Helge did not believe that there really had been hatred between father and son.

Arnulf stuck the wolf-knife in its sheath. Outwardly there was a possible to say that White Christ stood close to the Danes, but the one who rode through the country, would learn how King Sweyn kept his people faithful and let every man decide over his farm and folk as he found best.

*****

Although Vagn had put some distance between himself and *the Blood Fox*, Svend continued to, now and then, shout with Little Ketil, and in the afternoon Bjørn the Bretlander had had enough on his thwart in front of the Ågeson and invited Ketil over for a beer. The agile warrior had no trouble jumping from ship to ship, and Vagn thawed when Bjørn thrust a mug into this hand and toasted to Torkel Lere's daughter in Vigen. Arnulf drank with him and wanted to know who he was, this Torkel, now his name was mentioned whenever the conversation turned to Vagn's chosen maiden.

'He is Hakon the Good's vassal and a hard, bloodthirsty fellow.'

Bjørn dried his beard on his sleeve, 'And just as well, Vagn likes the daughter, just as much as he dislikes her father.'

He sent the Ågeson a cheerful glance, and Vagn raised the mug and swore with vigour to kill the dog, before the year was out, 'He shall die, and as thoroughly as no man before has died!'

Little Ketil licked a runaway drop off the side of the mug and became serious, 'Therein you are undoubtedly right, but I would like to know what it is like when you die, thoroughly or not! Maybe the way you are killed reveals something about it, but whatever the cause of death, there must be a time, while the body is still bleeding and hot, where it is still possible to feel something, even if you cannot call or move.'

Arnulf's beer went down the wrong way and he started to cough, and Svend thumped him on the back, unconcerned and half-grinning, 'Possibly, Ketil, but how will you find out? Give us a signal when you die?'

Little Ketil smiled, and Arnulf breathed again, the thought was cruel! Had Rolf perhaps sensed what had happened to him that night? Had he, in some way, seen how his brother had fled the atrocity at his most miserable?

'The man I carried out of Sweyn Haraldson's hall sensed nothing – that I am sure of!'

Bjørn hummed, twisting a tuft of his white beard, 'He was killed emphatically, so no, Ketil. When you are dead, you are dead.'

'Yes, but how can you be sure?'

Ketil did not give in, 'The fallen on the battlefield clearly see the Valkyries come and would have to swing themselves on horseback, for although Odin's daughters are far stronger than most women, armed men are heavy and hard to move.'

'I think Ketil is right,' conceded Svend. 'Death always takes its time, otherwise the battlefield would be as silent as the night.'

'Death gives the valiant the opportunity to prove their worth, and no man in Jomsborg so much as blinks, even if the blade is about to hit him right in the face.'

Vagn emphasised his words, and Arnulf peered down into his mug. Certainly the Ågeson's eyes would not flicker, but even the most hardened warrior still ought to behave like a man.

'I do not know if it is possible to keep your eyes firm, if it is death itself that you see. Maybe they themselves would flicker a little, especially if the blow is coming straight at them?'

Ketil had completely forgotten to drink, 'When you pretend to strike, Vagn, we know well that we retain life, but who can vouch for a single flash, that moment that it really matters?'

Silence surrounded him on the thwarts, and Arnulf looked over the Jomsvikings' force. It was hardly a question of whether a man blinked or not, rather a question of how many times he did it before he died, as fast as the blow fell.

'Tell me, Bjørn, which man was it that you carried out of King Sweyn's hall?'

As blood-companion to Vagn he had the right to ask questions. The Bretlander looked up, frowning, the memory had to be a grim one, 'Which man, Veulf? Well, I will tell you.'

He snorted drops of beer into the seagull-beard, 'It happened the night Sweyn Haraldson held the funeral feast for his father. Palnatoke was there and I had men from Bretland in my company. The evening went well in every way, but then Fjølner, the king's companion, revealed an arrow wrapped with gold thread and let it pass around, so the owner could recognise it and come forward. It was easy enough for only Palnatoke had such costly arrows, the catch was just that it was precisely that arrow that had killed King Harald. Fjølner had saved it, and when Palnatoke acknowledged his master shot, Sweyn Kingson was so furious that he declared their friendship dead and commanded his hird strike each and every one of us down.'

Bjørn sighed, shaking his bald head, 'Palnatoke killed Fjølner on the spot and he had so many friends within the hird that we all escaped unharmed from the hall, or at least nearly all, for one was missing. Palnatoke considered the loss modest and wanted to continue the flight, but I was angry, because the man had been mine, and Palnatoke needed to see how one should honour a faithful companion.'

Although the others on the skeid may have heard Bjørn's story many times before, they listened with respect and did not seem to regard the Bretlander any less simply because he was old.

'I ran into the hall again, despite me not having any hird-friends in there, and I saw how shamelessly they threw my man around, almost tearing him apart. I got hold of him and threw him on my back, and then we ran to the ships with thunder and lightning in our heels!'

Bjørn laughed warmly, 'I have since had much pleasure from that story, and after that night Palnatoke never left anyone in the lurch, neither living nor dead.'

He smiled wistfully, and Arnulf nodded. The aging Viking could fill his place proudly on the ship. Great admiration he deserved. Such bravery! It was one thing to escape alive from an entire hird, but to volunteer to run back into it, that was ... that was not really much different than when he ran into the earl's courtyard with Toke! The mug froze on the way to his lips, and Svend saw it and raised his eyebrows questioningly, but Arnulf shook his head. He had had Leif Cleftnose and the Northmen at his back that day, although Bjørn must also have had Palnatoke and their companions. Wolfblood it was, wolf blood or pure stupidity!

Sigvalde moored at the coast late at night but in return allowed sleep to stretch out as the sun rose. There was no hurry to pack the tents again, and the morning meal was decent. The mood was oath sworn, and the light attire was substituted for leather and thick, warm jerkins, and chainmail was laid ready. Arnulf had to force the food down, as his stomach winced restlessly; it was bad to be uncertain about whether the evening would bring a feast or a fight. The gold ring was polished many times, but the sweat of his hand sullied it quickly again, and although Svend was cheerful as always, a dangerous glow shone from his eyes. Jomsvikings might laugh when tickled by swords, but they prepared for battle with great subtlety.

The wind could still not be blamed for their late arrival to the Danish king as the legion of Jomsborg threw sea-shadows along Denmark. In the late afternoon, those men who wanted to, put on their chainmail, while Arnulf, despite Svend's disapproval, settled for a helmet and luck, for his shoulders dishonourably refused to bear iron again so soon.

Sigvalde's scale mail armour was golden, and his cloak flowing and splendidly blue, and the lush red curls blazed down his back. Carefree, he spoke with the earl's sons, and Vagn did not seem in the least gloomy despite the uncertain future; on the contrary, he struck Svend twice with the utmost satisfaction.

Arnulf stared at the skald's ring. He should have made a drápa, there was no time now, but the thoughts flowed in strong words that gathered in flocks, craving a skaldic homage. King Sweyn, King Harald, kinsmen's deceit and kingdom's strife, Bragi's glance was fire blue!

*****

The light was golden as the entrance to the Kongsfjord welcomed the Jomsvikings and Sigvalde let the ships spread out in a loose formation that reached from shore to shore like a many-legged dragon tearing deep gashes in the fjord; the stripy backwash from the fleet furrowed the surface of the water for a good while. Sigvalde's longship led the way, and Vagn followed closely, in his skeid, with watchful eyes. Arnulf stretched his neck while Svend pulled the bone comb through his golden hair one last time. Obviously, the men in Jomsborg had been the finest warriors in Midgard until now, but the doubt came ice-cold and stealthily. The king's housecarls were hardly a bunch of weaklings, Palnatoke himself had once been among them.

On land, horsemen galloped in advance to announce the arrival and horns resounded along the coast. The fjord narrowed, pushing the ships closer together and Svend stuffed the comb in a belt purse and pointed, 'It was Strut-Harald earl, who kept the royalseat ready for Sweyn Haraldson when he was not there. It is one of the largest royalseats in the land.'

The coast became a sand bank further on, where a vast meadow pushed back a forest. In the middle of the meadow was a palisade wall, raised to the height of several men and round so it seemed to be like Jomsborg, although no rampart lifted it. This palisade was divided by high wooden towers, and from the closet waved King Sweyn's banner from a high pole. The longhouses arched their roofs behind the tapered trunks, as if Jörmungandr himself was winding his body in the Dane king's fortress, and the gate was open. Apparently, most people had been ordered inside when Sigvalde's ships were reported in sight, for apart from those just at the gate, the salt meadow was deserted.

Sweyn Haraldson's ships had been pulled up on the strand, so they took place up on both sides. Despite the large numbers, they did not lie very close together, rather it seemed as if they were placed to take up as much room as possible in order to force Sigvalde to put his vessels on land as far away as possible from the plank road leading up to the royalseat. Arnulf glanced at Vagn and Svend. Evidently, the king wanted to show his strength even at the gangway and, if necessary, provide his guests with a wide escape route in the heavy sand. He himself could not be seen, and not so much as a vassal came to the strand to bid Sigvalde welcome, but the lord of Jomsborg did not seem affected by it. He let his dragon run up the strand beside King Sweyn's own longship and the Jomsviking force followed immediately after him, boldly wedging snekkes and skeids in between the solid vessels. Although most of the Danes' ships were large longships, the Jomsfleet seemed yet more formidable, united as it was by the many red shield rims.

Arnulf jumped ashore and helped pull Vagn's skeid up onto the sand. His scalp became hot under the helmet, but just as much as a single facial scar created respect, just as little did he want it to have company. Sigvalde's white stallion was led down the gangway plank, and as soon as it felt solid ground, it began stamping and dancing around itself. The animal was fiery, tight-necked and suitably wild-eyed, but when Sigvalde swung himself up, it yielded, snorting and with its tail up.

Arnulf set foot on the plank road, blood-brother of the horse. Now he was about to see the man whose ring he wore, the man who had appreciated his brother and gathered a divided kingdom. Behind the palisade waited the hird that Helge had told him about and admired without end, the hird of Danes that the Jomsvikings found worthwhile to prepare so carefully against. Arnulf looked at Sigvalde's men who were gathering around their leader, and never before had they walked as straight and sharp-eyed as when the white stallion set its hooves on the planks and moved towards the royalseat. Despite the many Vikings, the horse's trampling could be clearly heard and Arnulf slid behind Svend, putting his hand on the hilt of the sword. Outlaw, exiled, and on the way to the kingdom's heart, Tyr's courage, Stridbjørn's sons were not to be brushed off!

Around the palisade a wide pit had been deepened, its bottom occupied with short needle-sharp iron spikes that bristled like pig hairs standing hammered-down with few fingers' space. It was impossible to tread the pit, and narrow slits in the palisade revealed a protected walkway on the inside. Small catapults were hoisted up in the towers, and the open gate had hammered gratings on the outside, so that it could stop any intrusion, even if it was on fire. The palisade was probably vulnerable to fire, but a strongly flowing brook wound its way under it to appear again at a bend ahead, so the royalseat did not lack water.

At the gate stood King Sweyn's iron-clad first guards, broad axes resting on their shoulders, and the silence was oppressive as Sigvalde rode through the gate, closely followed by Bue, Sigurd and Thorkel the Tall, who, with ill-concealed delight, looked down at the warriors of the royal guard. Vagn followed with Little Ketil and Arnulf held Serpenttooth firmly. Helheim's entrance. Sweyn Haraldson could bar the gate after those Jomsvikings in front, his housecarls waiting in a heap behind the palisade! That Sigvalde himself had once abducted him with similar fox cunning was hardly forgotten altogether.

Nothing happened, only the sound of feet and the clatter of weapons broke the silence of the royalseat, and Arnulf let his eyes stare, without gawking like a sheep or turning his head too much as the road led through the gate. The royalseat was full of warriors waiting silently and looking, watchfully, at the visitors. Uncertainty about the king's feelings for Sigvalde oozed from those assembled, and Arnulf stepped light-footed on the embers. King Sweyn's men stood close on either side, no less well-armed and harsh to see than Sigvalde's, and behind them longhouses lay like the teeth of a double comb, with one gable facing the biggest hall

Arnulf had ever seen. It was so long that it almost divided the royalseat into two and was painted in yellow and red. Every single support plank was masterfully carved and over the gable's front door hung a jötunn-sized ornamental axe as if it should scare the courage out of everyone who came before the king with deceit. Behind the longhouses were stables, cooking and brew houses, and Arnulf could even discern a paddock and some low buildings which probably gave shelter to the thralls. The king's hall seemed to have more doors on the long side, but Sigvalde let the horse go towards the gable door, where the broadest men of the hird had gathered, and it was now that Sweyn Haraldson came out!

King Sweyn was no taller than most men; on the contrary, and he did not possess Sigvalde's magnificent hair and dignified attitude, but a power shone from him that was so forceful that it was impossible to determine whether the man was beautiful or ugly. He was still young, with a great warrior's strength, the short-groomed beard was reddish-brown, the skin weather-beaten and the eyes sparkled like a harvest's blue sky. The hairy wrists were speckled with freckles like the neck and the nose curved up, his nostrils flaring like a sniffing stallion, the expression was victorious but the gaze benevolently open. A wild ruthless drag arched his mouth, but at the same time the face shone with trusting and confidentiality and Arnulf drew a deep breath.

This was the king who with well-known ease had won the fidelity of the bravest and whom Helge had spoken so highly about, and although Sigvalde was taller and sitting on a horse, he lost authority in front of the Danes' master.

Sweyn Haraldson broke out in a big smile, spreading his arms. He was beautifully but simply dressed, and apart from a few rings, without unnecessary gold. He did not need either jewellery or silk to highlight his power, only the sword hilt was uniquely and lavishly finished.

'Be welcome, Sigvalde earl son! Welcome as a dear friend, and welcome to every man following you. You have travelled far in a rough wind, but the bowls are full, the mead spilling out of the barrels and my women have longed to pleasure your hird! Come and drink to Strut-Harald earl's honour for your father was always a faithful companion and wise advisor to me.

King Sweyn's voice was exceptionally clear and penetrating, and his words triggered a subdued movement throughout the bystanders, as if everyone dared to breathe again and take hands off their weapons. Arnulf looked around and caught Bjørn the Bretlander's relieved nod. Every old

256

grudge had to give way to such a courtly welcome and the funeral feast's peace was now declared over the banquet in the royalseat.

Sigvalde answered Sweyn with a wide smile and jumped off the horse. They grasped each other's arms and let their hands slide down along the knifeless sleeves in order to gather in a hard grip, and after a brief embrace the Jomsleader's answer was no less audible than the king's, 'Greetings yourself, Sweyn Daneking, kingdom's gatherer and protector! With great joy, we are summoned to your seat, and cheerfully we will drink to your prosperity and my father's memory. Shame on the hird that leaves drops in the bottom of the barrel and meat on the bones! And if your women have longed, then I will give a silver ring to whosoever goes disappointed from the feast.'

King Sweyn laughed infectiously, slapping his palm on Sigvalde's shoulder, and like brothers the two men turned their back to the warriors and entered the long hall.

Loud talk immediately broke out around Arnulf, and many men among the Jomsvikings and Sweyn's followers seemed to know each other, for they came together, laughing and grasping arms, as brotherhood spread like ripples in water. Arnulf smiled. Jomsborg should be on the best terms with Denmark, Sweyn Haraldson knew that, and assembled those forces could accomplish much! It was odd how hunger abruptly displaced tension and how sailing really took its toll on the body! Only now did he sense the smell of the roasts, and suddenly the royalseat was not only inhabited by men but also by women, young and beautifully clothed in soft dresses. Thrall girls or not, they were alluring, and the trousers grew tight under his belt. Bue the Stout stopped with his hand on the door frame and called brusquely to his son, who already had his arm around a woman, and Svend Silkenhair let her go, laughing, and waved Arnulf into the house.

King Sweyn's hall was staggeringly long, and several fires burned like snakes on the floor. There were no sleeping places along the walls, rather narrow tables were lined up in long rows, bulging tables where pork and all kinds of sausages were fighting for space with cheese and bread, dried apples and honey, fish and shellfish and steaming pots. The mugs on the table planks were as accommodating as Hymir's vessels, and the benches were covered in pelts and had backrests, so the drinking could last most of the night, without anyone tiring of sitting. In the middle of the hall stood the high table with the seat of honour and the finest bench, and opposite was a less prestigious bench with a slightly lower high seat set up. King Sweyn and Sigvalde had already seated themselves, and now their closest men found their places on the two honour benches: Sweyn's on his side and Sigvalde's on his.

The walls of the hall were covered with precious tapestries, and where none hung, the planks were carved and painted in bright colours. In the hall's far end a serpent-entwined door led to a room that must be Sweyn Haraldson's own and lit torches were hung at short intervals. A group of flutes let luminous melodies escape, and eager drummers took up the pursuit, for the Dane king wanted a merry funeral feast for Strut-Harald earl's honour. Shields and weapons also found space on the walls, and wherever the ceiling opened in holes, smoke spiralled up, and Arnulf had to put his head back, it was so high! At each end of the table stood a lidless barrel, one with beer, the other with mead and smiling maidens dipped the thirst wakening mugs.

Although the hall could accommodate Sigvalde's longhouse several times over, the men were many, and Arnulf wanted to know how they would all be able to find space on the benches. Svend replied that only the best were allowed to follow the Dane king, the rest would be distributed in the other longhouses and the feasts there were often unrestrained and more violent than in the long hall, for other rules were sometimes followed as soon as the king was out of sight.

The Bueson did not think badly of himself, for although he did not aspire to the high table, that standing nearest to it he found suitable and with a glance he pulled his housecarls to him. Arnulf pulled the helmet off and sat down, while Jomsvikings and king's men continue to stream in through the gable door with thirsty eyes, and soon every bench was occupied, so shoulders rubbed each other. It trickled through the limbs, and everything that was done in the hall, fixed itself behind his eyelids. The king's hall! He sat at a table in the hall of the ruler of the land, counted among Jomsvikings, despite his life being forfeit! Suppose someone knew him or noticed his resemblance to Helge! Maybe he should have kept the helmet on, more as a protection against eyes than blades, but Loki's deceit, it was worth the risk!

The doors in the long wall were opened so the air could be kept clear, and Sweyn Haraldson rose with a raised mug. His eyes flashed, but he gave the first toast gravely, with good words about Strut-Harald. Most of the hall drank deeply to the earl's memory, and the next toast to Sigvalde's good health had also to be shown respect. Then Sigvalde stood up, praising King Sweyn greatly, and for the third time all those assembled drank manfully, the feast was initiated.

The mead was strong, so it was best to hold back – his actions on Gormsø were not to be repeated – and the sun still stood over the horizon. Arnulf looked at Sigvalde, who sat with his back to him, and at the king and the many men, who were eating, enthusiastically loosening their belts a few holes and arranging to have dry bread on hand so that the thirst could be maintained. Where had Helge sat? Where had he been when he performed the skaldic verse about Regner Hundingson? Behind Sigvalde's chair wrapped in the glow of the fire? Did it still echo in the rafters? And would King Sweyn recognise his skald-ring again, or had he given so many that he could not remember each and every one? Perhaps he had a whole chest filled with rings, forged to pull off his fingers and give away when he deemed it appropriate. His stomach was anxious.

'You are not drinking anything, Veulf.'

Svend lashed out hungrily for bacon and skewered a hefty piece with his knife.

'My shield is not red-rimmed, and you should know yourself with both weapons and mugs.'

Svend grinned, sinking his teeth into the flesh, 'You have learned much already Wolfblood. Now I can safely drink and trust that you support me when bird song begins again. Maybe you abstain because you fancy the girls?'

Arnulf smiled, breaking a piece from the rib roast and the Bueson tugged his shoulders, regretfully, 'The king has many women, but not more, than the most distinguished men get first, we others must hope for tomorrow night, and you are probably last in the queue, unless, of course, if you sneak out early.'

He laughed, clinking his mug on Arnulf's so it splashed on the table, and Arnulf sipped his drink, while Frejdis churned butter with rolled-up sleeves and swaying breasts. Would she begrudge him some company if the king himself commanded it? Fast-handed and fair-haired were the long hall's selected, but the sight of all the exuberance pricked bitterly in his throat; Frejdis begrudged him torment and misfortune, he was not as blind as a mole!

The bowls were soon filled again, meat-heavy spits were flung onto the middle of the tables, empty beer barrels were rolled aside for new ones and toast after toast was delivered at the tables and every occasion and deed was praised. The first of those needing to piss had to relieve themselves, and it must also have been enjoyable outdoors, judging by the elated faces of those who came in, fixing their trousers. The beer maidens spent more and more time on the laps of lustful warriors, and at the high table laughter roared in waves, for there was plenty to boast about. Svend Bueson had to share the story of Ottar's unfortunate venture for revenge, and several of the king's men could remember Bjørn the Bretlander salvaging his dead housecarl. Had Arnulf had peace in Denmark, nothing would have been able to stop him from drinking like the Jomsmen, but behind the laughter and the happy shouts Fenrir's distant howl could be heard over the sea. With bristled hair it warned about danger, the danger that hid just like Jörmungandr in calm waters, and at the high table the voices grew louder and the faces red.

Arnulf turned away a little from the Silkenhaired, straining to catch the words through the din at the table. The conversation was about horses for Sweyn Haraldson had sensed that Sigvalde's white was a magnificent animal, even though his own was naturally better. The Jomsleader was fervent and believed that his stallion had to be the more capable of the two, and now more at the high table shouted that the matter could be easily resolved with a breath of fresh air in the paddock.

Arnulf nudged the Bueson with his elbow and nodded toward the high seat. The warriors in the hall were sated and ready for a heavier distraction than courtly skaldic verses, and the Silkenhaired seemed to sense a change in the wind. King Sweyn stood up with fire and challenged Sigvalde and the Jomsviking shouted immediately to Little Ketil that his stallion should be found and lead to the paddock. Bjørn the Bretlander hurried over and took Sigvalde by the arm, but his subdued advice was brushed aside by a gesture, and the king left his seat of honour with a mug in one hand and half a duck in the other.

Arnulf jumped up and squinted to the helmet under the bench. A stallion fight was a good feast game, but what if the white won? Svend Silkenhair's mouth was tight, and table by table the men got to their feet, belching, all apparently happy at having to stretch for a moment and work up a new hunger in the paddock.

'Am I right, did Bjørn ask Sigvalde to give the king his stallion on site, or at least make sure it was lamed or half-blind, for the peace of the drinking should not burst because of a few hoofed beasts.'

The Bueson let his mug and food lie, his eyes not swimming in the least anymore, 'And if I know Sigvalde, he absolutely refused to bend in advance.'

Arnulf made his way after him towards the nearest side door, and Ketil was already out of sight. Among the men wagers were boldly agreed, although the stallions had not yet been seen together, and King Sweyn's clear voice, by the door, commanded the five mares in heat be led out of the stables.

Only once had a stallion fight occurred in Egilssund and Stridbjørn's black had won. The defeated horse had been gravely injured, but Stridbjørn had given another as compensation, and the mood had not been scarred because of it. How many stallions the king possessed was not easy to guess, but hopefully he did not prefer one in particular, so it could be lost in the game without resentment.

Outside the summer sky was still light, yet torches were carried through the royalseat. Bats were splitting the air over the empty paddock when Arnulf and Svend reached it, and shortly afterwards the mares were hurriedly herded out by the barn thralls. Troubled and bewildered they trudged around, and Arnulf leaned against the fence, while guests and warriors, flushed from beer, spread out around the paddock. When Svend Haraldson himself announced the commencement of the fight, he was no doubt not afraid of losing, but Sigvalde had not expelled Odin's wisdom by partaking of such things so soon after finding grace in the royalseat.

The men reverently gave way for the king and Sigvalde and the first stallion to be unleashed was the Dane Lord Sweyn's. Golden and white-maned, with a snow-white tail that swept the ground, high-shouldered and strong-legged. Without wasting time and attention on those gathered, it galloped on swiftly to the mares and selected a blazing black-brown; snorted and rubbed its muzzle against it.

Meanwhile, Little Ketil had the difficult task of holding back the white that he was leading in, and Bue had to take hold of the halter when it first caught the scent of the stallion and mares. Arnulf sensed its excitement just as he had sensed it at the gangway; something about the horse drew him. It was so mad!

The two animals were eagerly compared, and the white was slapped on the hind quarters, while the king's stallion greedily ascended the blazing mare to jeering shouts. Sigvalde's uttered a resounding whinny, and the golden one dropped down on stiff legs, sniffing and snorting. As soon as they saw each other, aggression shone in their eyes, incited by the mares' fragrance, and the halter broke when the golden-brown threw its chest against the fence. It creaked and the stallions reared and caught their legs in the cordon, but Bue grabbed the halter and the royal steed was driven back with pushes and jabs from a sword hilt.

The battle-will triggered both laughter and respect, and several bets were placed as Sigvalde declared that the weakest stallion would be credited to the victorious' owner. Sweyn Haraldson waged boldly, raising it with the saddle and bridle. Arnulf grinned crookedly at the Bueson, who also let himself get carried away by the excitement, and for a while the stallions were kept separate to increase their rage. The air resounded with neighing and stamping, beating tails and legs kicking the air sore. One of the mares was captured and dragged to the white horse, and now both stallions rolled their eyes as frothing foam spotted the ground. At last, the gate was opened and Sigvalde's steed was released as excited cries and pounding beat over the animals like a storm.

Arnulf stared, engrossed by the white. The quivering muscles, the thumping pulse under the hot skin, the ears twitched, the drive and destiny raged, everything flowed in Fenrir's blood from the animal, blocking out the surroundings. The wolves at the large rocks were his brothers, should he not know the animal before him like the One-eyed himself, know it with its own senses, foresee every move that would come? Would the grey hunters not otherwise have ripped him to death at their first meeting? The stray, Stridbjørn's useless son, who else had won himself an animal mind in the forest and goaded Egilssund's bulls into futile, wild roaming without ever being rammed with a horn?

It jolted from the heel to the neck as the stallion, impetuously and pointedly, set on the golden with its head lowered, its teeth bared at the same time, and the white bit, taking hold of its opponent's thighs, so the king's own squealed. Kicking, it escaped, turned on just one hind leg and drove his shoulder against the golden, biting behind the ear. Again, it had to yield, but it could rise itself highest, and its front hooves drew blood from the white's throat.

Arnulf stepped back with a gasp, and Svend turned towards him astonished. Geri and Freki, what use would it be to know the four-legged's battle better than the ones created by the Æsir? Arnulf waved deprecatingly, forcing a twisted smile. The fighters pounded each other so both tumbled to the ground amidst the warriors' cheers. The stallions fought, fought to the death for the right to beget a foal, but they did not own the mares after the victory. As housecarls, who under oath of allegiance, ventured life and limb for the earl alone, for glory and gold, or to live on as a name in a skaldic verse, rune-bound to stone, a scintillating account of new fighting men. Bragi's song and sounds of feasting, Sweyn Haraldson's mead was as strong as Heidrun's!

The Dane King had put down his mug and was looking at his horse, his arms crossed with an uneasy smile, and Sigvalde flanked him like a rock, only the jerk of his eyes revealed how tense he was. Torkel the Tall murmured to him, and beside them Bue's weight threatened to topple the fence so enthusiastically had he leaned against it, eagerly passing on his views of the events to Sigurd. Little Ketil sat like a squirrel on the gate with the rope in his hand, while the dark warrior let his lynx-gaze lurk more against men than animals.

The stallions clashed again and again, biting in between the hind legs, kicking and beating their weight and hooves against each other. Neighing and spluttering were interrupted by painful screeching, while the mares half-mad with horror trotted to and fro. The tension rose as the two nobles attacked and fled and then attacked again. The fence gave as bodies stumbled against it, and when one of the stallions momentarily pulled away from the fight, gasping for breath, men stood ready with long spears to poke courage into it again. The foam frothed, splattering their chests, and the blood flowed in sweat-soaked hair, but although the golden was largest, the white was heaviest and the Danish King's beast slowly began to find the mares less appealing.

Arnulf did not like the fight now. In the open, one would have long ago been driven out, but here, locked up behind the lath fence, in the proximity of the mares, their drives forced them to continue clashing, and the men's deafening cheers and excitement made them unnecessarily wild in the fight. Sweyn Haraldson shouted encouragement to his horse, and for a short while it kept straining, but when the white got a decisive hold of its pride, the golden freed itself, screaming and galloped to the gate where it stood with its head stooped, its flanks bellowing. Without shame the white gave itself to chasing it around the fence, biting its hocks, as the defeated one had to sit down. Limping, it came forward, and Svend Haraldson turned, frowning, from the horses. The folded arms loosened stiffly with clenched fists. The king was angry, he did not hide it but was honest, so without reproaches to anyone, he waved his thralls into the paddock to separate the stallions.

Arnulf let the horses take care of themselves, the contest had moved outside the paddock, and the game of looks replaced the biting and kicking. Sigvalde uttered not a word, but nodded deeply towards the royalseat's ruler without gloating, and Sweyn Haraldson announced briefly that he felt thirsty again and that it was warmer in the hall than in the cool evening breeze. The Bueson grimaced. The peace was worth many stallions, if only Sigvalde had just followed the Bjørn the Bretlander's advice! He could have bought a new stallion, as soon as the sun rose again, as many as he wanted, what had he lost by beating the white over the knee?

263

The good mood seemed to have suffered worse damage than the golden stallion, and silently the Jomsvikings and the hird followed the tight-mouthed king and Sigvalde back into the longhouse. At the door, Sigvalde lay his hand on Sweyn Haraldson's shoulder and quietly gave him back his horse, but the Dane Lord laughed coldly. He had more horses than any other man in the kingdom, so unless Sigvalde's ship was too small, he could safely take both horses to Jomsborg after the funeral feast.

Arnulf found his bench again, and the flute players tried to encourage the clouds to dance away, and when everyone was seated again, King Sweyn got up and raised a new mug, seemingly milder than just before outside, 'My stallion has failed me, but let us not weaken the beer with tears because of that! Possibly you surpass me in horses, Sigvalde Earlson, but better warriors than mine do not exist in the whole of Midgard, so drink with me in peace and make your father's funeral feast memorable!'

Arnulf drilled his nails into his palms. So cleverly did the king conceal his scorn! He would have had revenge, but the kingdom's gatherer did not draw the sword out of the sheath first. The king's men kept their laughter in check, while darkness brooded over Jomsborg. Sigvalde rose slowly. His luscious hair and beard coincided with the torches' flames and the mug was raised weightily, 'The toast for peace will I and mine wholeheartedly endorse, for it would be shameful to drink Strut-Harald's funeral feast in fickleness, but which of us two have the best men, it is difficult to foretell and cruel to learn.'

Arnulf let his gaze run over the high table's guests but the Jomsvikings sat with their backs to him, their postures betrayed nothing. The Bueson stirred uneasily and bit his lip to keep quiet. King Sweyn's face was hard, 'Perhaps then you have courage for another fight, Sigvalde? Your best man against mine? It would be too bad if all this food and drink were to go to waste, dead men do not consume much.'

Niflheim's cold breathed through the Danish King's hall, and while Bue and Sigurd glanced at each other quickly, Vagn Ågeson sat more immobile than a stone. Svend Silkenhair's breathing was wheezy, and Bjørn the Bretlander's escape with Palnatoke was suddenly sharp and alive, as if Arnulf himself had been present. Black sorcery, the side doors were far from the high table, and both fire and hird stood between them!

Sigvalde clinked his mug against the king's, and both men drank with great seriousness. Then Sweyn Haraldson wiped his mouth with his hand, seeking among those assembled, 'Skarde!'

264

A tall broad-shouldered man stood a few tables away. He appeared to be bull-strong; bare arms of knotted muscles and an expression that knew no defeat, even the blond hair and beard grew stronger than on other men.

'Skarde! Will you defend the hird's honour and avenge the loss I have suffered? If you later fester in Valhalla, I promise that your deed will not go unnamed and forgotten.'

Steely, Skarde looked the king right in the eye and nodded, 'Yes, I will, Sweyn Haraldson, fear not! I am man enough to report my own deed afterwards!'

Cheers and shouts thundered from the royalseat's hird, and all eyes were directed towards Sigvalde but Arnulf looked at Vagn, Jomsborg's best man. Many could, without doubt, take up the challenge, tried and experienced as they were, and not least Bue would be a formidable opponent for Skarde, yet the choice could only fall on the dark warrior. If Sigvalde was willing to risk losing Palnatoke's heir; Skarde did not resemble a random, farming Viking.

Gloomily, Vagn got up and turned to Skarde. Black flames shot from his eyes, and prouder than the Lord of Asgard he stood, 'I am Vagn Ågeson, Jomsborg's defender. It was my father's father, who killed King Harald, and a lesser man, I am not known to be, therefore it is I and not Sigvalde who will ask the sons of Jomsborg: will you let me remove the head of Skarde, or would another rather stand out in single combat?'

Now it was the Jomsvikings turn to roar, and Arnulf banged with them as the mugs left marks in the table's planks in time to Vagn Ågeson's name. Sigvalde smiled, and for a moment the walls of the hall had to bow to the pressure, so violently echoed the cries of the long tables, no one seemed any longer to fall into despondency.

King Sweyn let the commotion persist; his face distorted with rage. Vagn might have ripped open a badly healed wound by mentioning his kinsman's deed, but once again Sweyn Haraldson kept his self-restraint and did not let indignation control his action, he only seemed to wish the Ågeson an agonising death. Composed, he gave orders to push tables and benches away from in front of the high table, while the two warriors made ready for combat. Sigvalde and his closest companions were seated next to the seat of honour, and Svend Bueson jumped up to lend a hand, while Arnulf went to Vagn; they were blood companions, so assistance had to be offered.

The Viking seemed to have been expecting his fate and certainly did not look like one in need of help. He was already equipped with a battle-kyrtle and newly polished chainmail and his helmet lay under the bench, he lacked only a shield. Arnulf would not ask, and Vagn did not deign him a glance but stepped slightly away from the table and began carefully to inspect the leather laces and buckles with an expressionless face. The sword slid willingly from the sheath, an axe and a long knife hung within easy reach, the shoelaces were securely tied, and the belt appropriately tightened. A housecarl brought him three shields, which Vagn, after careful inspection, accepted and the helmet was slid down over the dark hair, shielding half of his face.

Although overlooked, Arnulf remained standing. If Skarde killed Vagn, he would lose the man in Jomsborg who had shown him the greatest confidence, and his mouth was dry at the thought of more losses. If Odin took Vagn, he would let Fenrir loose tonight! Skarde hardly allowed his opponent grace and, in any case, the Ågeson would refuse to accept it.

Vagn drew his sword and thrust the tip into the clay-stamped floor. He sank down on one knee and sat, for a while, gazing at the ground, the helmet's forehead against the hilt, while the square was cleared, and mead barrels rolled aside. He seemed to be lingering and sharing his call with the sword, while the Battle Father weighed their lives against each other. Bjørn the Bretlander went over quietly and put his hand on his arm, and Vagn looked up at his foster father reluctantly, as if he knew what was coming.

'I will not deny that you are right for this fight, but maybe it would be better to let Sigurd take it. He has his own way to settle disputes without wasting life.'

Vagn gave a quick shake of his head and stood by his sword.

'Then spare him at least, if you get the chance. It is better to humble the king's best man than to lay him out cold, enough beer has been drunk to easily trigger demands for blood revenge.'

Arnulf squinted to Sigurd. His own way? Skarde did not look like a man who engaged in negotiations, but maybe Bjørn would ensure the defeat; plenty of royal anger was already aroused! His stomach twisted; it was awful not to have any influence on what would happen!

'No, Bjørn!'

Relentlessly, Vagn looked the Bretlander in the eye, 'Combat like this must not be revenged, not even by my own blood-brothers, the peace of the feast has been declared! And a man like Skarde – do you really think he will live in shame?'

Bjørn sighed, fixing the chainmail on Vagn, and he pushed his hand under the battle-kyrtle, 'How is the shoulder?'

266

Vagn pulled himself free with a jerk and spat on the floor, 'I feel as though I have had it long and I fight just as well with it.'

Bjørn looked hurt, and Vagn stuck the sword in the sheath and took his hand in a firm but gentle grip, 'When did I lose your confidence, have I ever lost a fight? Wish Skarde luck, not me! And it is Sweyn Haraldson not Sigvalde that will have single combat.'

The Bretlander nodded and handed Vagn a shield and the dark warrior stepped out onto the cleared space, ready to meet King Sweyn's housecarl.

Bjørn suddenly seemed as old and tired as he ought to be, and Arnulf stood beside him with his eyes on Vagn. The old man should be sitting by Bretland's hearths, spared the noise of weapons and preparations for battle, even Thor had not won over Elli.

Skarde was not yet ready, and the men thronged close together on the floor and climbed up on benches and tables for a better view.

'What is wrong with Vagn's shoulder?'

The Ågeson had never seemed weakened during all that time Arnulf had spent in Jomsborg. Bjørn snorted darkly, 'Vagn's blows fall harder than most others, but he does not go through his fights unmarked, so even though he rarely lets himself feel anything, do not think he has peace from his injuries for very long. I know him, Veulf, as few men have ever done.'

Bjørn stroked his beard, 'Palnatoke gave him to me in heritage, and I have guarded Vagn like a shadow ever since.'

Arnulf nodded. The strong became weak when the old man was alone with him, Palnatoke had undoubtedly loved his unruly kinsman.

'Will he win now? Skarde is no weakling.'

'He will win until that battle comes, which he will not win, and that is how it has been for most Jomsvikings and their fathers before them.'

Bjørn remained silent, the housecarls made room and Skarde appeared amidst resoundingly sword hammering.

The bull-man was as well protected as Vagn and, apart from the weapons on his belt, he carried a mighty broad axe over his shoulder. The helmet was closed tightly, but the wild eyes glowed from the darkness, and although he might know Vagn's reputation, he seemed not to judge him to be a better man. His companions had put out shields, and the Jomsvikings began making noises of pride, so everyone in the royalseat would remember who had been at the feast.

Vagn looked his opponent up and down, mocking, and broke out in blaring scornful laughter, which his companions immediately took up and Skarde let out a roar that his hird answered, so it could be heard in Asgard. Then Skarde lay down his axe and selected a shield, and the two chosen drew their swords and stepped closer to each other. Arnulf's breath was shallow and hot in his chest, and Svend Bueson squeezed himself in between Bue the Stout and Sigurd in the front row. In front of the king and Sigvalde the table was clear, and Torkel stood behind his brother, his eyebrows deep.

Vagn and Skarde slowly began to circle each other, while their glances evaluated, searching for strengths and weaknesses. Swords and shields were elevated slightly and moved according to the opponent's movements like hoverflies. With dís-like effortlessness, Vagn danced more with his feet than during a fight of shield walls, ready to move out of reach as quick as lightning. A few times he attacked without engaging and Skarde defended himself with surprisingly agility, as big as he was. The cries around them ceased, and it was so quiet in the hall, that only the crackling of the fire and the breathing of the men could be heard.

Although the blackness radiated by Vagn would probably make most wary, the housecarl did not seem in the least bit afraid. Predator-eyes lurked under the helmet's edge with a dangerous obstinacy, and Skarde also tested his enemy without engaging his blows, only the changing of feet increased in speed. Closer and closer came the snakelike movements, and Vagn switched the shield and sword to the opposite hand. Skarde appeared to be able to follow him without difficulty, and now the Ågeson began to jog around him and past him, seemingly aimlessly, but the housecarl was not confused. The king himself had asked him to stand, and behind the loss of the stallion lay Palnatoke's humiliating killing of Harald to be avenged, so Skarde seemed to want to bite even if Vagn had been the One-Eyed himself.

Although expected, Arnulf started when Vagn Ågeson attacked in earnest, and although he looked and remembered what Svend had taught him, the fighters exchanged their blows so quickly that it was almost impossible to follow. Skarde pulled first, and again continued the lurking circuit, but now fierce and deadly, the teeth's sharpness was measured!

Arnulf let his thumb slide along Fenrir's scar on his forearm, he would willingly give blood again if the wolf would fight alongside Vagn! Skarde attacked, and with a single cracking blow split Vagn's shield through the middle, unleashing wild jubilation from his hird. The Ågeson was not near his other shields, and Skarde appeared to have perceived this, for he hastily threw his sword and shield away in favour of the broad axe, leaning against the table, and with a wild grin he threatened the life of Vagn with horrific blows. The dark warrior escaped without making any attempts to block and tried hard to get within range without losing an arm to the axe, but Skarde handled the heavy weapon with great skill and knew how to keep the Jomsviking at a distance. Light-footed, Vagn stepped around him, as if the chainmail and sword weighed nothing and Arnulf's aching shoulders shrank in shame. That the Ågeson had no shield was neither here nor there, for against so heavy a swung blade, protection was only a false companion.

Vagn was just quicker than the housecarl, but when he struck his sword against Skarde's mailed shoulder, the bull-man butted the end of the axe head in his chest with such inhuman force that the Ågeson was lifted on the tip and thrown backwards. He tumbled onto his back with a crash, ramming the high table, overturning mugs and pots, rolled over the planks past Sigvalde and landed on his feet, while Skarde flinched and lowered the axe. Despite blood penetrating the chainmail, the Ågeson rushed back against his opponent undaunted, and the next set of blows drove the bull-man backwards foot-by-foot without hitting anything other than helmet and shaft.

Breathing heavily, they again moved away from each other and Skarde let the axe stand before the king and took up sword and shield again while Vagn found his next protection. The housecarl's chainmail was also leaking blood, but neither of them seemed to be impaired. The attacks started in turn, and both wanted to determine the rhythm, while Arnulf kept his eyes rigid to capture the exchange of blows before the warriors withdrew again. Snake-like small cuts, sliding evasions, easy blockages that caused the enemy to stagger, chainmail-cleaving killing-strikes, stags of equal strength.

Vagn managed to catch the edge of Skarde's shield with his own and force it away, but the housecarl utilised the exposure and cut under the chainmail's edge above the elbow. Unfazed, the Ågeson sustained his pressure and Skarde stumbled backwards into the nearest Jomsvikings and with laughter was pushed out on the floor again. Arnulf heaved air in excitement.

The swords sang along the shield edges, tearing gashes in chainmail, hissing at one another like seals in a mating dance and beating dents in helmets, but both men were too quick to be hit decisively.

Unsightly, Skarde bled from behind his ear, and a stumble revealed how bad the tear had to be irritating him, but Vagn was hit again in the sword arm as he tried to seize the moment, and the Jomsviking had to exchange the sword for the lighter battle axe. The new weapon seemed to infuse him with new strength, for now wood chips and splinters flew from Skarde's shield until the handle broke, and a new one had to be used. It did not hold long for Vagn chopped it with so violent a jerk that Skarde let it go, tumbling to the side, and a new series of low blows caused the Valkyries to saddle their horses.

The housecarl beat the sword hilt into the Ågeson's elbow, and again the warriors stepped breathlessly away from each other and lowered their arms hesitantly, as the bull-man laid a hand on his last shield. If Vagn used the axe in his left hand now, he would probably be able to swing it better, but maybe the shield had become too heavy for the right.

Arnulf looked around at the contemplative men who were reviewing and taking note of every move from the clash on the floor. The king's housecarls in particular spoke eagerly, while the Jomsvikings settled for muffled conversations. King Sweyn sat erect with his hand on a sword's hilt and Sigvalde's face was deeply serious. Bue's brows were furrowed, and Torkel the Tall twisted his beard, disgruntled, apparently Vagn's single combats did not usually drag out, even Svend Silkenhair and Ketil had closed expressions.

They made ready for battle again, and Vagn stepped forward with a terrifying look. What had happened in him during the brief armistice, only he himself knew, but defeat was no longer possible! A wave of hatred flowed in front of the skewered-eyes, and although the height seemed to be clearly gone from his striking-arm, Skarde seemed to blink from something other than a headache. Arnulf glanced at Bjørn, who nodded to himself, and the old man seemed no longer tired, the open floor suddenly had the stench of death.

Without hesitation, Vagn charged the life of Sweyn's man and blocked the sword with the axe handle, hooked the blade and pulled the weapon from him with a roar, so a stir rushed through the long hall. Skarde defended himself, picking up his own axe, but the Ågeson got that one too, and that weight he placed in his tug slung the axe so high that it hammered the ceiling joists before it fell, and made those sitting nearest it jump like hares.

The cries broke out again around Arnulf, and Vagn's bleeding arm was trembling so much from the effort that he withdrew reluctantly and let it hang, while Skarde, amazed, shook life into his paralysed hand. Breathlessly, the dark warrior yanked up the shield, and in that same moment the bull-man stood with a spear in his hand. One of his companions must have handed it to him. The indignation formed spots before his eyes, and Arnulf clenched his teeth. It was rule violation, the work of wretches, but the hirdman slung his weapon anyway at close range, but like an osprey Vagn escaped, flung down the shield and snatched the spear's shaft and sent it on into the wall behind the king's seat of honour with a scream.

Arnulf stood on tiptoe and, ashen faced, the Ågeson took the axe in his left hand, while Skarde rushed forward and seized his lost sword. The spear quivered in the wall over Sweyn Haraldson's head, and the noise in the king's hall erupted as the furious men clashed in such a mad engagement that the housecarls shoved each other down for a better look. Icy cold Vagn defended himself with only one arm, and with such frightening ease and scorn in his movements that Arnulf's back jostled with the edge of the table behind him. How could he, the Jomsman was wounded, yet he jumped like a doe! Another opponent would undoubtedly have been overpowered by his own disbelief and anxiety, but the King had chosen his avenger with great insight and shrewdness.

The dark warrior accepted now, accepted and mitigated blow after blow, yielding, while he imperceptibly began to determine Skarde's strikes, and the hirdman continued to go even more irascibly for him; fiercely, the sweat pouring from his forehead. Bjørn the Bretlander began to laugh, and Vagn blocked harder, heading for the high table, while Skarde apparently felt victory within reach for he pushed forward beastly violent.

The housecarl hit the Ågeson above the wrist, and the axe fell from the fist, but at that moment, Skarde drove the sword against the Jomsviking's side with a triumphant roar, Vagn grasped the broad axe the bull-man had set by the table with two hands, and swung it full force. Even before it engaged, he turned his attention away from King Sweyn's selected warrior, and the bloody axe head crashed off the high table into two parts, while Skarde's head flew across the hirdmen and guests and with a dull splash landed in an open mead barrel.

The silence resounded worse than any death cry. Arnulf hardly dared breathe, and everyone in the hall stood as stiff as ice blocks, while the dark warrior, gasping, stared King Sweyn in the eye to the sound of dishes and sausages rolling off the broken table. Fenrir in flames, so disrespectful a cleft was pure madness, what should the axe find in the table? Skarde's headless body pulsed blood on and all around the feet of those closest. The Dane's leader had lost yet another battle!

Sweyn Haraldson rose, white in the face. He appeared to no longer find any sense in self-control, and his hand trembled as he pointed to Vagn, undoubtedly to issue an immediate death sentence in the next breath. The man who could declare the peace of the feast could also abolish it again and give his hird the freedom for revenge, but the first who would storm to his kinsman's aid was Svend Silkenhair, and then the battle would continue until the last man fell!

Arnulf jumped out onto the floor with a cry, to Sigvalde's consternation, now Vagn had to accept his help with or against his will, apparently no one else in the hall dared stop the kingdom's ruler from future misdeeds!

'Listen to me, King Sweyn, hear me, you gatherer and protector of the Danes!'

Arnulf looked the king directly in the eye and raised his hands, open, if he did not win now, either Jomsborg or the kingdom would be destroyed, and what if the king himself was to be killed?

'Mighty combats have been fought, courage and fidelity proven to the fullest, but still another contest should be held, for we are gathered for a funeral feast and not for conflict!'

King Sweyn lowered his hand slightly, hesitating and with a brief nod allowed Arnulf to continue, and Vagn straightened up with a surprised glance backwards.

'The peace of the feast is declared and the mugs full and stronger mead than that, which has been mixed with hird-blood, no one has ever before been able to offer their guests! I hereby challenge any of your skalds to dare stand in a contest, if you, my king, wish it to be so!'

The beating pulse made his knees shake, but boldly they remained, even if the roof fell down, his feet would not step aside. Sweyn Haraldson breathed deeply several times, as the colour returned to his skin. Then gesturing to Arnulf he sat down, while the warriors in the hall, astonished, found their seats. Vagn let go of the axe and staggered to the nearest bench and Sigvalde smiled subtly, while Torkel the Tall muttered appreciatively in his brother's ear. The Stout looked like he was seeing Arnulf for the first time, but Sigurd smiled broadly.

Bjørn rushed to Vagn to see to his wounds, and something similar must have happened before in the long hall, for despite their cold expressions, one of the hird men brought him linen for a wound dressing. The Bretlander wound the bloody arm tightly, but Vagn would not go out with him before the skaldic verses had been performed and Arnulf could hear the Bueson's eager voice mingling with Ketil's behind him. A forced calm descended, and he let his hands fall and bowed his head. Vagn's life, Jomsborg's fate, Helge's skaldic verse and Frejdis' downy-skin!

Arnulf looked up slowly, looked at King Haraldson himself:

272

'A wolf was grey
A wolf was red
The flock full mighty
United in rows
The grey led way
In wrestling and war

Soon mind would change
The kingdom to alter
Rejected the gods
Renewed the shrines
Growled at the bold
To crush the brave

Then bared the bite
Brisk was the pack
The wolf so red
With ruthless rape
Fiercely called for friends
In fairness to rule

The hardened Old Wolf
His hair raised high
Dared to tread
Boldly to battle
The red to brake
Resistance to breach

Filled with fury
Fellows now felled
Kinsmen and foes
In fearsome ferocity
Bloody the billows
Broke the prows

The red's companions
Proved their courage
Endured the wildness
With deed and will

Dishonoured the grey
A grim death won

Now Red Wolf commanded
For country and calm
To ease the hurt
To heal the harm
To gather and grant
Great gods' glory

Chainmail then burst
Brother became brother
Vigorously the wolf
Worthy and wise
Generous and good
Gave all gladness

Fear now foreigner
To challenge the red
In dispute and danger
Defeat is your destiny
Warriors' bane
The wolf king is

Hail, lord Sweyn
Honour to Haraldson
High Odin's hird man
And friend to White Christ
Merry and free
Men now meet

Mighty your strength
Manly your courage
No bolder Danes
Before departed
Never strifed prouder
Powerful men

Gods favour you
Fortune and future

Gold shall glitter
And wealth will grow
Risked but well-meant
Were Veulf's verses

Arnulf was no less drained of strength than Skarde was of blood, the words had burned the bones from his limbs, he stood in Helge's footsteps, holding the skald ring visible; now Sweyn Haraldson would have to decide which he found best! It was not a boatful of voyage-mooded Northmen who had listened, the men of the royalseat were well-accustomed to listening to good verses, but a lurking smile had slowly arisen on the king's face, and now he leaned forward in his seat, while applause broke out from the many gathered men. Whether their respect was due to the skaldic verse or the relief of the royal smile was hard to interpret, but the worst anger seemed to have been displaced and Sweyn Haraldson commanded silence with his hand, 'Well performed, Veulf! And cunningly done! No king may, after such homage, order swords to be drawn, I see Sigvalde has chosen his companions with care.'

His cheeks burned, and Arnulf bowed his head briefly.

'You have earned payment, both for the skaldic verse and for performing it promptly, but I see you are already wearing a ring of gold.'

The Dane king scrutinised the skald ring without revealing whether he recognised it or not.

'Yes, Sweyn Haraldson, a weighty ring I have, but only on one hand!'

Vagn Ågeson began to laugh, and the king laughed, too, and then most of the others. Sweyn's voice rang clearest among the laughter and he got up from the seat of honour, drew a ring from his finger and waved Arnulf to him. The floor was slippery with blood where Skarde had just bled to death, and the dampness could be felt through the shoes.

'Veulf is a short name, young Jomsviking.'

King Sweyn handed him the ring.

'Short, but easy to remember, and the honour of calling myself a Jomsviking I have not yet won.'

Arnulf took the ring, strangely moved by the moment. It was a patterned serpent, three times it wound around the finger.

'May luck follow your efforts. I see no reason to pit one of my skalds against you, and if they tire of your verses in Jomsborg, you can always come and perform them here.'

Arnulf's hands trembled as he put the ring on his finger, and Sweyn Haraldson looked around the hall, his voice louder, 'It is a paltry funeral feast when the guests of honour have to sit parched, without tables! Bring us a new one and prepare to start the feast anew, and if you have swung your arms tired, Vagn Ågeson, I think I dare to have you sit here again.'

His words were greeted with enthusiasm, and Arnulf completely lost his footing as Svend Bueson shook his shoulders from behind, 'Veulf! I am speechless! Now you owe Snap a fight for my axe gets quite sullen when it smells blood games in vain.'

Arnulf laughed, showing the ring, as Vagn called hoarsely from his bench. He sat leaning against the edge of the table with his hand on his chest, but his smile was as it usually was, 'Never before has a skaldic verse been the shield that saved my life!'

The warrior was short of breath, 'You think clearly, and that makes you dangerous, Veulf. By Tyr, I do not want to meet you with weapons in five years!'

The black spear became a torrential river, no less dark but streaming greatly and warm, and the answer disappeared into the water, Arnulf could only grasp the bloody hand.

'Enough you two.'

Bjørn, impatient, pulled his hands apart and helped Vagn up, 'You are not allowed to sit at any high tables before I have seen if your ribs are broken or not, but Veulf; had Palnatoke been here, you would be another ring richer.'

He brusquely nudged his foster son, and a silent victory cry dizzied Arnulf's body. Hail Bragi, who needed a drápa? There was so much gold in the king's ring that from now on his fingers would have to live separately. He had done it, he had stood in front of the Dane king and performed, performed so Helge would have roared with pride! A joyous storm dazzled his senses.

Vagn Ågeson was duly applauded on his way through the hall, and Svend thrust a mug into Arnulf's hand, pulling him over to Bue, where he triumphantly took a broad stand in front of his father, his fists at his belt, 'What do you think of my weed now, you bursting-bellied Jomsstud? Is he man enough for his legs now, or do you still have any objections?'

Bue snatched the nearest sausage and hurled it after his heir, and Svend grabbed it, laughing and stuck it in his mouth, while the Stout's chest stretched with an explosive laugh, 'As always, your mouth is a breeding ground for the most impertinent snot-cackle, but you do indeed get to keep that whelp a little longer. Veulf! Freyr's cock on a pig, soon I will start to grow fond of you!'

Not one of Bue's fingers failed to leave behind bruises on Arnulf's arms, but why feel pain from them, there were so many others already? Sigvalde was also satisfied, and while Skarde's headless body was carried away, and tables and benches were put back, talk about the single combat rose, and every blow that had fallen was weighed. Arnulf let himself take a seat by Svend and drank deeply, now others could stay sober if they wanted to, should he who had just won the king's gold not be entitled to drunkenness?

A new high table was brought out and Sigvalde took his seat as before, and boldly proposed toasts for both Skarde and Vagn, and someone even thought Veulf was worth drinking in honour to. As bad as the gaiety had been threatened, it fell just as intensely over the king's hall again, and when Vagn, a while later, appeared with Bjørn the Bretlander, joy knew no limits. His chainmail had been replaced with a new kyrtle, and somewhat subdued, the warrior took a seat next to Bue, but apparently Skarde's weapons had not disfigured him intolerably, Sigvalde still had his Jomsman intact.

The new skald ring had to take a turn around the table, and Sweyn assured that nothing could trigger hatred among the Vikings anymore, nothing could sweep aside the last remnants of vigilance. The strongest mead had to be tasted, too, and many competed to share the contents of the barrel, Skarde's head had fallen into. The thrall maidens poured willingly, again and again, and they grew more beautiful with every sip that trickled down inside and competition in drinking spread among the men. Laughter resounded again at the high table, the walls leaned from the waves outside, and the flute players' tones slipped now and then as the musicians also wished for a drink or two. Still looser tongues had something to boast of, and not one of the Jomsvikings appeared to be reluctant to brag. It was dark in the doorways, new barrels had to be rolled in and the Einherjar themselves would have found themselves at home with King Haraldson on this night, it was easy to agree with Svend about that.

The Dane lord rose once again, this time with a firm grip on the seat of honour, and he did not appear to have drunk much less than his men. The Bueson did not notice the king's attempts to speak before his head was turned with a jerk of the silky hair. The king still spoke as clearly as the Gjallarhorn, albeit a little slower than before, and Arnulf stuffed bread in the Bueson's mouth to shut him up.

277

'I believe that so mighty a feast as this should be remembered for something great!'

Excited shouts greeted Sweyn Haraldson, who politely belched behind his arm, 'I think we should hold a momentous contest, something that will commemorate more than just an ordinary game.'

Cheers roared again and Sigvalde struggled to get up, his mug splashing. He was able to stand without support, although the beer left his hand of its own accord, 'Well said, my King! But such a contest should be initiated by the greatest man to ensure that it is mighty enough.'

New howls lifted mugs, and Sweyn Haraldson and Sigvalde grinned at each other. Then they suddenly flew at each other because the royalseat lay askew, but somehow the Silkenhaired pulled it back on track.

'So I suggest we do that, which was done before at glorious celebrations where particularly outstanding men gathered together. And when you, Sigvalde, count so many notable warriors amongst your followers, I expect that you participate in the contest, as befits you and your warriors.'

Sweyn Haraldson threw out his arm, so the mug flew from him, 'We will make vows! Promises that even the Æsir can hear without being ashamed, and only the greatest heroes will be capable of fulfilling them!'

Arnulf roared too, it was difficult to remain silent for too long, and when there was no longer fighting or verses to perform, each and every bout had to be more fun.

'I promise that I, before the third winter's beginning, will have killed King Ethelred or displaced him and thus seized his kingdom for myself!'

Conquer King Ethelred's country! Had Harald's heir gone mad? Arnulf stared open-mouthed at Svend Bueson, Odin himself made no such promises! How could any mortal participate in that game? The Dane King was certainly not cowardly. And certainly not alone, for the whole hird jumped up, shouting, at least those who were able to, hammering sword hilts and axe handles in the tables, so that the floor shook. When thirst overpowered them again, Sweyn Haraldson looked encouragingly at Sigvalde, who had completely given up trying to keep the beer in his mug. The Jomsman nodded respectfully to the king, raising his hand, his expression forceful, 'And I promise that I, before the third winter's beginning, will have ravaged Norway with as large a force as I can rally, and will have driven earl Hakon from the country or killed him or lie dead myself up there!'

Arnulf stiffened, as if struck by evil sorcery. Impossible! Ineffective, the king's mead sank to his legs and his lungs had nearly given up all further acts from sheer horror. Invade Norway! Norway! The land of the wolf-grey fjelds and silvery fjords. The home of the man who had changed his fate and took him a-viking, the man he owed for sitting here alive! Rage Haraldsfjord with as large a force as possible! Burn settlements, mistreat and thrall-take Gyrith and Hildegun before the eyes of Little Ranvig while Toke and Stentor lay dead by the blot stone! Never! A groan slipped free of his chest, and heartless as stones the Jomsvikings sprang up in the great din of drunk men, which in no way was inferior to the hirds. His body was cold and warm at the same time, the mead and beer as toxic as snake venom and Arnulf had to twist himself around with his mouth as far away from the table as possible.

Svend Silkenhair laughed, grabbing him, but the beer, he offered was abominable, his innards cramped. Arnulf spat his mouth clean and, breathless, leaned his forehead on the table, they could believe what they wanted. The hair fell over his face like a cave wall. Norway. Never! But even Thor could not prevent Jomsborg's campaign, Fenrir's strength, how to stop such atrocity? Could Haraldsfjord be moved, bypassed, warned? Yes! Toke had to be warned in time! But then he would have to leave the Jomsmen! Again, a groan seized his body. Was Toke a-viking? Or was he at home now? Was he even alive? No, no, it was not until the beginning of the third winter, there was time yet, lots of time! Arnulf rose on his arms; ugh, to be like this!

It was so quiet again that the king could continue talking, 'It is a manly promise you have made Sigvalde, petty you are not, and I am happy to sit among such like-minded men! Now I will hear you, Tall Torkel, what you can add to your brother's words.'

Jomsborg's tallest did not hesitate, Strut-Harald earl's sons always stood ready, 'My promise is that I will follow Sigvalde in all that must come, and not flee until I see the back of his ship, and if we are fighting on land, I will not give way, as long as he stands with me in the shield wall.'

Torkel's words were also greeted and Arnulf grabbed a dried apple. The sour flesh alleviated his nausea slightly. When Torkel did not try to put ashore, the others would certainly not do it, Baldur's misfortune, where would it end? Did Jomsvikings strive only for killing and death?

'Well spoken, Torkel, no one can doubt your promise will be kept with courage! And now I would like to know what you, Bue the Stout, have to say in this contest, a lesser man than the other two, you are indeed not.'

279

King Sweyn no longer looked so wobbly, and Arnulf bit the apple in half. So firm a smile had only he who could control his face, the king was not at all drunk, at least not as much as his men and guests were.

Bue rested his paunch on the table edge, looking proud, 'I promise to follow Sigvalde on the journey and not only will I not flee before less stand upright than have fallen, I will hold out as long Sigvalde does, the Jomslaw in mind!'

The apple cut its way half-chewed down his throat, Sweyn Haraldson was luring Jomsborg to fall man-for-man! The warriors were many, but Norway was larger, the white stallion's victory was to be paid for dearly, earl Hakon was no flabby fart. Men like Leif Cleftnose would rally around him, men like Toke Øysteinson!

Sigurd also promised to follow Sigvalde and his brother with vigour to the campaign's end, and the king was clearly pleased. He mastered praising words and to beat King Ethelred with the Danish force was man's work, but still possible.

'And now I ask you, Vagn Ågeson! Give me an answer worthy of Skarde's death, for of all your companions, you were chosen as the best!'

Vagn rose slowly. He was not as thrilled as Bue and Sigurd, so maybe he had been caring for his wounds and holding back on drinking, black fire smouldered without joy. His eyes were hard against King Sweyn, 'I will not fail my comrades, I promise to follow Sigvalde and my kinsman Bue and hold out as long as the Stout wants it and is alive, and to this I will add that I, before I come home, will kill earl Hakon's vassal Torkel Lere and bed his daughter, Ingeborg, in Vigen with or without her kinsmen's consent.'

Vagn's word harvested violent outbursts, but no smiles could be drawn from him, and Arnulf pressed his knuckles against his forehead, as Bjørn the Bretlander promised to follow his foster son with all the courage he could muster. Sweyn Haraldson was full of appreciative praise and did not want to hear any more brave men make oaths, speech spawned thirst, it was not yet dawn, and Sigvalde himself had declared shame on the hird, who left slops in the barrels!

Arnulf struggled to get up, supported by the table. Someone had, with a painless knife, severed his knees, his feet stood, although the legs wanted to get over the bench, and a storm swept through the hall at head height. The Bueson had to know where a bed could be found, but Svend arm wrestled with his neighbour, as deaf as he was blind, the Silkenhair had to be soaked in beer before he maybe remembered that the northern longhouses were designated to Sigvalde's men. Stumbling, his feet followed, albeit not quite as legs should, but there were enough shoulders to lean on, for men sat seated so close together that it was hard to fall. The air was heavy and hot, so hot that the surroundings shimmered before his eyes.

The night air blew cool, and the royalseat's longhouses rocked restlessly on the ground. The noise was no less from most of them than in the royal hall, but the northern houses were in darkness and should be possible to reach. Arnulf had to sway from one support plank to the next along the great hall. Perhaps it would be Bue's son himself who killed Toke, perhaps Snap would swipe the last hand from Stentor, as he defended his daughter's honour!

Vagn would cut down Leif Cleftnose without the slightest difficulty, Øystein's beautiful longhouse would burn, and Jofrid! Jofrid would lose her child, when they tore the infant from her ... no, no, the infant she would have already left out for wolves by that time, he was as blind as Hod and the stretch to the nearest house was unreasonably far! Everything yielded in front of him, the dark wall arched in the air and the grass stood vertically, what ugly sorcery was at work here, he had almost managed to grip the gable! His body had to get up, Toke had to be warned, Toke, his best friend, Toke, who had left him wounded on a foreign strand, had betrayed him without searching, Jofrid's sorcery, the grass wove around his limbs like rope, he would never be free again, never, never ...

*****

'How long have you been sitting here? Did you sleep? Do you have a fever?'

'Since you ask! No, I do not have a fever, and I have certainly not slept, but sat down. I will survive this time, too.'

'Do you need anything? How is your elbow?'

'I have water. No! Now let the arm be a little longer, you tormented me sufficiently yesterday!'

The grass was cold and inhospitable, and someone must have torn his scar, for his head thumped. Another's cloak had been laid over his body, and annoyingly enough it hung so firm that he could not get out of it, by Fenrir! With a howl the dog who had slept beside him jumped up, and Arnulf placed his hand on a well-slobbered mutton bone, exclaiming. The king's mead was poisoned, now pain spread to his stomach, and the speaking voices broke into soft laughter, while the dog slunk away with its treasure.

'My word, you look alive, Skaldwolf. I can comfort you that you are not the only one who did not make it to their sleeping skin, others are lying here sleeping it off if you look around.'

Arnulf blinked back the darkness and heard his own groan as he sat up. The longhouse had landed again, and Vagn sat with his back against the planks beside Bjørn who stood, looking not so bright-eyed in the early morning. Arnulf froze, clammy. The taste in his mouth was disgusting, and he pulled the cloak tightly around him and picked up the water bag that Vagn threw at him. The Ågeson looked exhausted, blood was penetrating his kyrtle where Skarde had hit him, yet he seemed attentive and watchful. Was it him who had spread the cloak over him during the night?

Bjørn hid a yawn, brushing leftovers from his beard. The sun was beginning to reach over the wooden palisade, and men lay between the houses, sleeping drunk, where they had fallen.

'Good morning, Vagn. Good morning, Bjørn.'

Arnulf combed his fingers through his hair.

'Indeed, it is not a good morning, it is quite a horrific morning! Bjørn, try to find Svend somewhere, we have to hold a meeting before the king wakes up.'

Vagn looked contemptuously at those who had dropped and spat in the grass.

'Svend? What about Sigvalde? Or Bue at least?'

'You will not find any life in them yet, they were the last to bed and are lying with a whole bunch of womenfolk, find Svend and if he does not wake up immediately, I will come in and pull the golden hair from him, a strand at a time.'

Bjørn laughed and left with a nod, and Arnulf crawled to share back support with the Ågeson. Brokkr and Sindri hammered steadily deeper, as if he himself had, in his drunkenness, allowed them to erect a forge behind his forehead, and he laid the water bag at his knee, leaning his neck slightly back to keep his head completely still, 'He is cunning, King Haraldson, I do not at all believe he was drunk yesterday. How are you? Skarde did not take hold gently.'

'If I sit or stand, I feel as I ought to feel, but if I lie down, I am dying, so do not ask a second time! And King Sweyn is as wise as I feared, now it is important to drink cold water. Jomsborg cannot catch up with earl Hakon alone.'

282

Arnulf immediately regretted his nodding and dared not look at Vagn again, who was silent, drinking from the water bag, the night must have been tough for the fierce warrior. Instead, he followed, listlessly, the smoke that crept up over the roofs of the cooking houses. Women and thralls started their day; mildly, the porridge would alleviate many an overworked stomach, and a good rest was needed if the funeral feast was to continue in its due form so immensely was it laid out! The Jomsvikings had been excessively drunk; would Sigvalde remember what he had said? It could probably delight the king to see earl Hakon and the Jomschieftain tear the heads off each other. Afterwards, he could then remedy his father's loss and effortlessly win Norway back and insert a more obedient earl. Arnulf knew a Viking who was mean enough to want to betray his countrymen for the sake of his own fortune, and who could easily enough obtain the king's respect with only his appearance. Leif Cleftnose, earl of Norway! The thought doubled his nausea. Toke would immediately be out of favour and he would himself lose refuge in the fjeld kingdom. No, glass-clear nightmare, it was the beer that was still raging in the body. Before the Jomsvikings went north, Øystein Ravenslayer's son had already felled Leif in an honest combat for the chieftaincy. If only the arm was healed. Freyr's favourite, how he missed the Northman!

Bjørn and Svend appeared at the corner of the house, the Bretlander bearing bread and cheese, and the Bueson red-eyed and with the most tousled hair Arnulf had never seen on his head. He seemed surly to have been awakened, but at the sight of Vagn, he broke out into a wide smile, he had nearly lost his kinsman to Skarde. Excessively slowly, he pulled out his knife and brought it against the Ågeson's throat and Vagn threw an equally leisurely fist in his stomach, warmth in his eyes. Then the two newcomers sat on the grass, and Bjørn put food on the crossed legs and started cutting, while Svend, pained, rubbed his forehead, 'You went early, Veulf, where did you sleep?'

'Redder eyes than yours Thrymr did not see on his wedding day. I slept here.'

Arnulf gestured with his hand, and Svend laughed, rejecting the bread Bjørn offered, 'They may be red, but I can still see with them, and that is more than Skarde can with his. Can you feel the arm, Vagn? Is anything broken? Never before have I seen a man lift a fully armed warrior on an axe!'

The Ågeson sent him a dangerous look but then shook his head, 'I am a little sore, but it will be gone as soon as I have rested, and it is not for fun that Bjørn called you here, this is a council of war.'

Fatigue and disgust dwindled abruptly, and Arnulf straightened up, letting the cheese dispel the sour taste of vomit. He would not drink a single drop other than water as long as the Jomsvikings had to stay in the royalseat, not even if Sigvalde ordered a toast, by Fenrir! Svend was serious, and Vagn lowered his voice, 'I do not think Sigvalde will remember his promises once he sobers up, but they are binding anyway, and he will need help.'

Bjørn nodded bitterly, 'Great were the words yesterday, a little too great, and we Jomsvikings were served the strongest mead, I strolled around and tasted the contents of the barrels. Since Strut-Harald's death, the king has had ulterior motives, so we should be no less ingenious.'

Thoughtfully, Svend stroked the hair from his eyes. His kyrtle reeked of spilled beer, 'If earl Hakon gets wind of this, he will meet us with an insurmountably large force, yes, perhaps even sail to Jomsborg. I think we should put the voyage into action immediately and use the funeral feast to plan. We set sail as soon as it is over, and King Sweyn will help us, nobody else can quickly advance on Sigvalde with good warriors.'

Arnulf bore his fingers into the grass. After the funeral feast? That abruptly! But it was impossible! How would he be able to reach Haraldsfjord faster than Sigvalde's dragon ship? And what if the Northmen were not home from a-viking? No, Bjørn had to prevent it, he should say Svend's thoughts were far too hasty!

'I think you are right, kinsman, but it will demand cunning to lure help out of Sweyn Haraldson, he will not grant us so much as a dull axe, and we can hardly take Hakon of Norway alone, even if we come unexpectedly.'

Vagn put his hand on his chest and Svend nodded eagerly, 'Help will be quite difficult to get, but keep in mind that if King Haraldson should be angry at anyone, it is earl Hakon.'

The cheese made his stomach boil, and Arnulf put down the rest. Was that why he was worse for wear and suffered so diligently on the banner ground: to develop his skills enough to kill Norwegians? Bjørn did not seem to have problems with food, 'We certainly need to be quick off the mark if the promises are to be honoured as they were given! Sigvalde must appear happy tonight and get the king believe that his help is crucial. Any ruler can be flattered into going to great lengths, just look at how Veulf's verses won him over yesterday! As long as the king does not know how soon the voyage will be initiated, he will probably be more willing to make promises; three years is a long time and a lot can happen.'

Now all hope was shattered!

'And even more willing if he doubts whether the war voyage will ultimately happen.'

Svend leaned forward, 'If Sigvalde now admits to having bitten off more than he can chew and says that he would only consider leaving on the voyage dependent upon Sweyn Haraldson's assistance, then the king would certainly risk his men's lives without any further thought.'

Vagn nodded slowly, 'Hard pressure must be put on him. It is no use if we allow ourselves to set off with lame men and old ships, so you will have to talk to Torkel, Bjørn, for Sigvalde will probably not listen to you at the moment. If Svend can get Bue and Sigurd in on the plan, then Sigvalde could be persuaded to follow it, even though he may be rather headstrong.'

Svend and Bjørn nodded, and Arnulf stared down at his new gold ring. What if the Jomsmen would not even take him along on the voyage to Norway? How would he reach Toke? Maybe it was all just a bad dream, could he hear the laughter of the Norns or was it just thrall girls waking up under warriors' sleeping skins?

Bjørn put bread and cheese in the grass and got up with an open hand to Vagn. More talk was obviously not necessary, the Jomsmen seemed to be accustomed to putting words into action as soon as they were pronounced and accepted.

'Come here! If you are going to war in a few days, I demand to see your wounds again, then Veulf can watch over your sleep while I talk to Torkel. Tonight, the gaiety shall have no end, and what has been said here must remain secret from both our own and the king's men until Sigvalde himself reveals it.'

The older man pulled the Ågeson up onto his feet, Arnulf got up dizzily. Watch over Vagn? He could sleep by himself, if he could feel calm, a flaccid salted herring would be a better watchman right now. Ugh, how the nausea prod when his legs had to bear him! Bjørn seemed to read his thoughts, for he kept Arnulf back when Svend and the Ågeson started to walk.

'Why do you think Vagn did not sleep last night? Skarde has both kinsmen and companions in the hird, and I do not wonder if Sweyn Haraldson would look the other way if they were to wake up now and think they have something to revenge? Stay awake, Veulf, your blood companion himself chose you, and you would not want to betray his trust!'

285

Betray his trust! Not for anything in the world! But if Skarde's kinsmen were like him, then who in Jomsborg would then be able to take care of Vagn's life alone?

'Bjørn! I would die before I would leave Vagn's side, but I cannot stand against several housecarls alone!'

The Bretlander's harsh face softened, 'Do not do that. If you just sit there with your sword over your knees, no one will try to attack Palnatoke's kinsman. I do not fear open blood feud, only sneaky killing-knives and Svend will sit with you as soon as he has let Bue and Sigurd in on our plan. I myself will make sure that the mead today is not so strong that we can all think clearly.'

He smiled, shaking his head, 'In any case until nightfall. If the Einherjar think they can drink, they should try to compete with us in Jomsborg! If the training was not as hard for the warriors as it is, they would swell up like toads from all the mead. So moderation, young Veulf, moderation until that day you have just as much pain from battle injuries as everyone else.'

Arnulf shuddered, although the day started warm. Maybe it was in fact the Æsir's punishment that Svend had found in that monastery! What kind of a life was it to constantly have to fight, risking the loss of health and limb for loyalty and honour, drinking the pain away at night and sleeping with a cold sword at hand? Frejdis smiled with chubby grain-fed children at the legs, blond fine-skinned children. The sound of looms reached him, of giggles and wool being carded; keys rattling and dough-sticky hands patting flat bread, the blessings of Freya were not granted by Fenrir!

*****

Vagn was able to find some peace in himself. He had not laid down for many moments before a heavy slumber slid over him, freeing his breathe a little easier. There were plenty of issues to think about, and he must be in dreadful pain, Arnulf himself had seen the wounds when Bjørn bound them again, but the Ågeson could apparently decide to sleep like an animal in hibernation. The Bretlander had chosen an empty gable room in the outer house in the row where the bed was wide and well covered with sheepskins, and Arnulf pulled out Serpenttooth and sat at the closed door on a stool, Garmr had swallowed the flaccid herring!

Mighty snoring came from inside the long hall, it could be heard through the wall cracks, but the wolf's blood was outraged, he was not

286

infected by drowsiness! With serenity could Bjørn see to his errands, if evil-minded men tried to come through the door, Arnulf knew how to awaken the tumbled Jomswarriors into action, were they ever so faint! He smiled at the sword and spread-eagle wings out over Vagn's bed, but then dark considerations trickled in with a draught, peace did not aid the outlawed.

Norway! He was to go to Norway again, to Norway with the most feared men among heroes! Sigvalde would cross the sea with his force and sail north up the coast. The red-rimmed Jomsshields would merge together into a bloody chainmail, woe and tears would flow in the dragon ship's wake, and in his quest for earl Hakon, Strut-Harald's son would send hastily rowed small vessels to lookout on the larger fjords, and every village he saw would be burned to coax the Northman out. How many people Hakon would have time to rally was hard to guess, but if the Jomsvikings were fast, he would hardly be able to send an overly superior strength against them.

On the other hand, the Northman earl could hide in his fjeld country as long as he wanted, gathering men to land and sending messengers on horseback over the mountains; Sigvalde could hunt along the fjords for months without realising behind which island Hakon's fleet was hidden. With the wind he would stroke north, still further north, until the longships cast shadows at Haraldsfjord's mouth and hissed at the settlements there.

Arnulf stared at the ceiling joists. How did the last stretch before Toke's fjord look? There was a white rock, the Northman had shown him, and the flat island where he had gathered eider duck down was not far from the entrance. The next bay he had also seen with Stentor, a path winding across the pasture, and rocks and islets lay scattered in the water, yes, he would certainly recognise it! But before that? He squinted. Before that he remembered nothing but islands and cliffs and fjords, not the same, yet they flowed together, Fafnir's flames, had Helge not always told him to pay attention to the way and memorise any landmarks?

Vagn stirred uneasily, moaning in his sleep. He lifted his shield arm, as if to avert a blow, then he rolled himself together and found peace again with a loosely clenched fist against his forehead. Wildness was gone, vulnerable in rest lay the terrifying warrior, and Arnulf felt strangely tender towards him. He had a debt to the black-blooded, a weighty debt, would he ever come to win his blood-brother's confidence as Bjørn had done? Even Svend did not stand quite so near his kinsman.

287

Hard-hearted the Jomsvikings dashed forward, chainmail rooted to their skin, yet the mutual warmth appeared deeper than with other men, in the presence of death honesty and fidelity seemed to thrive with golden lustre, and he himself was just an uninitiated colt, who had to settle for pats and reprimands. Would their eyes water like Toke's when he thought of Gyrith and Ranvig, they probably had kinsmen somewhere in Denmark, mothers and sisters? Did they weep? The Øystein's son was also a trained warrior and not afraid of a single combat, but it was easy to mingle minds with him, was it in fact on *Twin Raven's* deck planks that Arnulf should have been fighting?

A moan had to be let out. Who was the enemy? Could Serpenttooth harm anyone if his will did not stand completely with it? In what shield wall did he betray the worst, was there a choice? If he failed to strike, would contempt then strike him afterwards from both sides? What did he owe the Northmen and did the Danes not strive after the life of the exiled? Arnulf. Veulf. Sentenced to a solitary stormy escape, mountain tops tearing at his chest, a tormenting stray over thorns! The hands fumbled over his face, slid along the scar and grabbed the hair and Serpenttooth fell clattering to the ground. Shamefully, he picked up the sword, but no one seemed to have heard anything, the flock of snoring rumbled undisturbed from the hall through the wall, and Vagn lay as if he were dead.

He shook his hair from his eyes and wiped the blade with trembling fingers. The air hissed in his lungs. What use would it be to embitter? The sword weighed on his thighs, and the intertwined serpents on the blade seemed to flash their eyes subtly. Sighs drove out the pain.

Helge's weapon. Serpenttooth. Horses died, women became old, but the swords were inherited, shared blood and destiny with the men who owned them, decided over life and happiness. The sword fenced everything that his side-companion did not notice, sweat and pulse, anxiety and defiance pressed through the hilt, a good blade was a third hand, was indispensable, irreplaceable, the weapon lived, lived fully and only for its wielder! Like Bjørn had promised Palnatoke to take care of Vagn, Serpenttooth reached from Helge to Arnulf, and after all that Svend had shown and taught him, his respect for the sword grew. It was a great inheritance, his brother had left, the best of all, and never would he part with his weapon, never!

Arnulf lifted Serpenttooth with a straight arm. Northmen and Jomsvikings, he was young, young and wild-minded, the bite was sharper day after day. Would Vagn not grieve if he knew that his blood companion sat here, worrying like a doddering old woman? It was the Æsir's favour and not punishment that he should sail in a great voyage with the strongest of all Midgard's warriors! The deed would resonate from kingdom to kingdom, and the feat that had to be done now, and would be retold for many winters, Norway was so large, it would be cursed if he encountered Toke. Øystein's son would probably forgive a couple of Northmen falling on the way, Haraldsfjord should have its warning in time, and he would be the settlement's defender, not attacker, by Fenrir's skin and bones! Both Svend and Toke could trust their friend!

*****

The funeral feast's second evening was no pale companion to the first. Rested after a good day's sleep, the guests and hosts gripped their mugs, the hunger was new and the food well prepared, and the king and Sigvalde did not seem to hold a grudge against each other, they sat so willingly and toasted.

Svend returned quickly to Arnulf and Vagn after his conversation with Bue, and that he soon fell asleep on the floor, Arnulf did not bear him any ill will for the Ågeson himself woke his kinsman in the afternoon. Some quiet talks between the earl's sons had taken place before the king's Hall was filled up again and Sigvalde must have listened and agreed to the battle plan for a more carefree man than he did not sit under King Sweyn's roof. Bue and Sigurd found themselves in one jest after another, and Torkel the Tall sat inside with several unrestrained stories that he was not content to keep to himself.

Vagn did not let the pain get the better of the festive joy, but Arnulf had difficulty following the Jomsvikings games. The feast was still on thin ice, thin ice over spearheads! After a single chunk of ham, he was sated, and so far, the water was preferable to the beer, whose warmth he still felt in his body. The nails pulled splinters from under the bench seat while the warriors in the longhouse were sharply observed one-by-one, but Skarde's closest companions did not reveal themselves in the crowd, and Arnulf was soon tired of looking for them. If they wanted something from Vagn Ågeson, he would know how to recognise them by that time. Instead hare ears pricked towards the high table, and the Bueson rolled his eyes resignedly as he was ignored for the second time.

The king would not wait for too long, for he wanted to learn if Sigvalde could remember the games of the last night, and the voices around the seat of honour ceased at the question, like corn before a

289

storm. A splinter found its way under his fingernail, and Arnulf abruptly let go of the bench. Sigvalde stood up, facing the hall, so everyone could see him, for everyone had to hear what was to be said.

With good-humour he admitted that his mouth had probably been a little too full, because as the beer had flowed in, the sense had flowed out, 'And if I should let myself be pulled out on such a journey before the third winter's beginning, then I must first know to what extent I can expect support from your side, Sweyn Haraldson, for without the help of the Dane lord will such a magnificent a mission be impossible. Sober I would probably never have made so mighty a promise.'

Arnulf pulled the splinter out with a shudder, and the king smiled contentedly, now the Jomschieftain sat, stuck in his own words, and no one before had so thoroughly forced the red-haired fox into a corner! Happy as he seemed to be for himself and his voice sounded gracious, 'Since I know how much you are a man who keeps his word, you will find enough courage to carry out the war voyage sooner or later, and alone you will not set sail. Twenty ships I will send you from here, the day you are ready.'

Arnulf pressed his finger against his trousers and glanced at the Bueson, whose face did not reveal what he was thinking, but Sigvalde stared at Sweyn Haraldson, amazed, and then looked round the hall, laughing unbelievably, 'Twenty ships?'

He shook his head reproachfully: 'Had you been an earl, those contributions would have been good, but they cannot be called kingly. Is that really all so mighty a lord as you can spare?'

King Sweyn frowned, leaning back, disgruntled and Arnulf straightened himself, the mood had changed quickly yesterday, it was not wise to push Haraldson! The answer was brusque, 'How much help would you need if you were free to ask it?'

Sigvalde flashed a winning smile, 'That is easy to ask and certainly affordable for a ruler whose generosity was recently put into verses in his own hall! I will have sixty ships and they all have to be great longships with well-armed men.'

King Sweyn's eyes were wide, but Sigvalde would not let him be heard, 'In return, I will then add just as many ships to the fleet and you know my warriors, it will not be a harmless force! Maybe I will contribute even more, but then the vessels will hardly be as large, and that will be fair, since you are the king, while I am only a fort chieftain.'

One hundred and twenty ships! So mighty a weight along the Norwegian coast would tilt the fjeld tops for the hooves of Skinfaxi! Svend

290

Silkenhair smiled cheekily, hesitantly lifting a hand, while King Haraldson took a slow drought of his mug, letting the silence draw out. Sigvalde did not push him but kept his carefree expression open as if they were talking about axe heads at a market and not expensive warships loaded with weapons and Vikings.

'Good. You shall have your sixty ships, I get the credit for Hakon's fall, too.'

The king's freckles glowed like snake eyes on his skin, 'And I choose the men myself. If the best hounds are not in the field, the wolves go hunting, but if you find even one useless housecarl among the men you receive, then I am ready to give you his weight in silver!'

His weight in silver? Hopefully Haraldson realised how much it would take to become a man revered by the Jomsvikings! The Bueson punched triumphantly into the air, but Arnulf shook his head, the worst had yet to come! The Stout sat upright on his bench, a half-gnawed leg in his stiffened hand, Torkel, on the other hand, seemed to have embers in his trousers, and Sigurd butted teeth with a long knife, although it could hardly find room in his mouth.

'That is a good answer and worthy of a king.'

Sigvalde's curls bobbed, satisfied, 'And I do not consider you a man who honours his words less than I. Therefore, I believe I will be ready to leave as soon as the funeral feast is over, for my ships are already fully equipped, and as your men seem so healthy, I see no reason why they should not be able to be ready for the voyage as soon as the food and weapons are carried on board.'

King Sweyn was struck dumb in front of the Jomschieftain, and a short rush of excited outbreaks swept along the benches, but Sigvalde boldly preserved his smile and raised his mug as if he were toasting the voyage. The fire in the men's eyes outshone the torches and hearth flames, and the glances swept between the faces like diving swallows. Arnulf held his breath, and King Sweyn hesitated. If the Dane lord had tired of his guests now, no one could honestly raise an eyebrow to it; like eagles he and Sigvalde had flown higher and higher over each other during the last day, and the winner risked getting his wings burned off. The air trembled from forced silence when the king stood up doggedly and looked over his hird, 'It will be as you want it, Sigvalde Earlson, though I probably should admit your haste is unexpected. However, you have the reputation of your cunning, and it is true that it can be difficult to crack the neck of the fjeldwolf, if he senses that the hunters are on his tail.'

Sweyn Haraldson's pallor was grey from bitterness, and the mug seemed to have doubled its weight in stone, as he raised it, 'Your visit is going to cost me more than I had expected, so enjoy the beer! It is not likely that soon hereafter a feast will be offered to Jomsborg again.'

Sigvalde, his arm friendly, clinked his mug with the king's, 'You will not be without feasts, my King. Great will we celebrate when you come to Jomsborg to collect your returning force and earl Hakon's head in a sack, and if you suffer deprivation now, then later you can travel north and throw a rope around Norway. That price is worth the loan of men.'

What more the two great men said to each other only they themselves heard, for now the cries could not be held back any longer, such important news had to be discussed promptly with the nearest table companions. Excited gestures, toppled mugs, food swept from tables and gathering men were besieged by companions from all sides, the desire for the voyage seemed great to Arnulf, and among the hirdmen talk quickly turned to who would be selected so when Svend Silkenhair proclaimed a toast to Sigvalde, there was no one near Arnulf who listened and drank with him. The relief wrestled with the excitement, now it was really certain that they would set out on the voyage, a storm without equal was about to rumble over Norway!

Bue the Stout could not sit still, he had to get up and slap his men on the back, stomp along the benches like an ox and bellow into the conversation. Svend's silken hair was tousled on the way, and Bue grabbed his son's empty mug and beckoned a long-limbed thrall girl to him to get it filled again. She obeyed smiling, and he grabbed her around the waist with a confident look and beat the other claw in Arnulf, so the sore shoulder twitched, 'Veulf!'

If he had to choke on his own pork, did that man not know normal cautiousness! Bue dragged him without the slightest annoyance off the bench with a sly face, after which he let go of the unfree, slapping his hand on her buttocks, 'Veulf! You have just as little sense to plan voyages as a pig has to brew beer, what do you think of Ysja here? There is not much of her, I must admit, but she is bold enough, and even a stick can be warmed if you set fire to it enough!'

Ysja smiled and Arnulf smiled with her, not knowing where was Bue going with his questions. A war party had just been initiated, who was in their right mind to think about women?

'I have no reason to contradict Ketil. He firmly believes that Sweyn Haraldson owns the prettiest girls who can be bought for silver. '

'Ha!'

Bue let go of the troubled shoulder, 'I thought probably she was your taste! And since you now have the habit of going to bed early, you can the warm her and the skins up nicely for me a bit. She knew herself where I lay yesterday.'

Arnulf looked at the Stout amazed. Did he mean what he said, or was he already senselessly drunk? Svend Silkenhair laughed loudly, 'Freyr's pride, Veulf, I really think the fat one is beginning to like you! And what about me? Me, your own flesh son, who languishes like a tethered buck, what have you got for me, you, you horny bull? Should I not also roll in skins instead of sitting here, fatigued by legion talk?'

Bue let out such a roar that Ysja, frightened, spilled mead and jumped back.

'You? There is no maiden to be found that you do not jump on as soon as I look the other way, jötnar curse me if I will actually also help you with it. Well, what will be of it? She is meant to be a gift, Twitwolf, if you are old enough for that kind of thing!'

With a start a wave of blood broke loose through his body, burning the sweat off the skin, old enough! Arnulf locked eyes with the Stout and angrily grabbed Ysja's wrist. Had he not proven himself to both Vagn and the king? How dare the Jomsman continue to fling insults! Bue's chest rumbled with delight, and he gave Ysja a push, so she tumbled into Arnulf, 'On my word if there are not nails on the Maidenskin! Just grab her! There is a law other than Jomsborg law, which is as important for a true Odin's warrior, and that is: fight when there is a fight, eat and drink, when there is pork and beer, and love when there are women! Away with you! That is an order.'

An order? Amused, Svend laughed loudly to himself. What order! Ysja willingly pulled Arnulf's sleeve, looking down under his belt where Odin's spear stood ready for combat. By Freyr, if he was going to journey among Jomsvikings, he was going to have to live as one. Without answering, he moved defiantly past the Stout and the Silkenhaired with Ysja in tow, he would show the burly nosey-snout who loved best! Freya herself would envy Ysja before the midnight moon was tired, so the other voyage men could sit here, licking their swords all night in longing for war, Fenrir swallow him raw, if there was anything to blame him for at dawn!

*****

The clouds were iron grey, axe head grey, blue-black just like domed helmets, glistening like chainmail, bulging like dark, beaten shield bosses and thunder rolled deep in the distance, wrapping itself around the Danish coast in a mighty ring, Thor followed his favourites, while the wind struck the sea spray hard like arrows, carving furrows in the naked skin. Setting sail in jötnar weather was not work for the weak-chested but with a contempt for danger they now faced the dark with defiance, all the straight masts dauntlessly conquering the canvases, creaking and croaking from top to keel.

As if all the sea's worst warriors had risen to crow, the longships stroked the foam from the waves, a spring tide of knife sharp bows, blood-hungry harm-bringing steeds, a fatal current, an indomitable disease, should thunder and woeful weather not follow so proud a gathering? Killing, killing and injury, chains of red-rimmed shields, chains of blood drops, chains of ominous predictions, who allowed himself to look at so mighty a fleet and still hope for life?

The Danes had not understood preparing for a voyage any less than the Jomsvikings. As soon as the men were selected, they left the feast to get ready in the best way they could, and the last day of the funeral feast passed with a hectic bustling. The ships were hurriedly checked for damage and weaknesses, blacksmiths worked red-hot iron, and baking and slaughter were not to delay the war voyage, if provisions were not ready for the voyage, then supplies would have to be found on the way.

Sigvalde and the king had been sitting with their closest allies at the high table, making plans, men with particular knowledge of earl Hakon and Norway had been summoned, and Torkel the Tall had regularly left his place to review the equipment and watch over the work outside. The progress went impressively quickly. Everyone knew their place, and although Arnulf had repeatedly offered, his help had not really been needed, on the contrary, but why worry about that, too?

Was he not here among hirdmen and Jomsvikings kicking full of life, as if three men were stuffed under his skin instead of one? The soreness disappeared, his feet could be set down with gravity and he was about to be strong, strong as never before! His warring blood finally seemed united: the eagle and the wolf with the legacy of the bear, perhaps maybe it was the drops from Vagn's chin gash that caused it to flow together. Fenrir lay on his back, his paws playing in the air, and Arnulf could see all the eyes, man that he was, a warrior about to go a-viking, and no one could take from him the gold band he carried unseen on his forehead!

Had Ysja not whimpered and clutched through the last two nights, wet with sweat from joy, eager and smiling, silent as a mute, but her body speaking volumes? Born to please were the unfree, and she had learned her skills well, if you took a thrall-girl with joy and kindness, you gave her life's flowers and more than that not one of the humblest could strive for!

The salty breaking waves licked the shields fixed along the shield rim, salty like tears, salty like blood as if the winter sea raged against the cliffs and rocks, and behind them sat the kingdom's master, sharp-eyed and high-born, living weapons with purpose and ingenuity, the flock of pride, of greatness, of deed! Who had enough fingers to count the ships and composure enough to hold out for so long? Did they see Sigvalde at the bow, at the front dragon in golden scales of armour, all the settlements trying to hide, pleading for mercy, hoping for the veil of rainfall, did they see his warriors clad in iron, the newly-sharpened spikes and blades, and did they see the black shield with the red yawning wolves? Serpents and stallions, bears and eagles, grisly creatures with gaping mouths, red-tongued, sharp-toothed, challengingly colourful, studded with bronze and silver, each ship craning its neck, every bow had eyes, fear and horror they induced, Helheim's fence was open, Ragnarök was near!

Arnulf did not dry the moisture off his face, despite showers regularly whipping over the sea. How could you worry about the water, when the body was carved in stone, and the heart was beating as if Norns had mistaken a child for an As and placed the heart of a god in him? So wildly burned the skin that it cooked under the battle-kyrtle, it steamed along his back, pulling at the scar, so his damaged eyelid quivered. He had been dizzy when the many ships sailed free of the fjord, sailing side-by-side for the length of a river, dizzy with excitement, every gust of wind put runes to the deed that was being embarked upon, his name should always be mentioned among the chosen, who left on the greatest voyage the Jomsvikings had ever made!

He looked back and shivered at the sight of the heads on the bows. Svend smiled from the opposite thwart but said nothing, and the Bueson's eyes glowed no less than his, even Vagn on the thwart behind seemed to be gripped by self-worth. Despite his wounds he wore chainmail again, and how he was suffering only Bjørn knew, no one who saw the dark warrior would find him weakened. The Bretlander had refused to let the Ågeson be alone for even a moment over the last few days, for although no one among the hird dared step forward, evil eyes followed his back, and Sigurd and Torkel had chosen to sleep with him in the side room despite all his angry objections. Aside from the issue caused by the king, there tended not to be hostility between men. Sweyn Haraldson's warriors were willing to let themselves be led by a man like

Sigvalde and the mutual respect was great, so the ships mingled indiscriminately between each other and old friendships were renewed, while new ones were made. The king himself said goodbye to each of his men and finally to Sigvalde, if not as a kinsman then honourably at least, and the Jomschieftain had not looked like a man who wanted to enter behind the royalseat's palisade again.

Arnulf returned Svend's smile. The Bueson had laughed at his pride and boldness, Cocky-wolf he had been called, but so too had most of the other Jomsvikings; Svend, himself included, had found it easy to laugh the last few days despite the seriousness and war plans, no one had spent all night alone at King Haraldson's, more women had come to the royalseat on the evening of the second day. What Frejdis would have thought was not good to think about, but did Trud not even send Stridbjørn to the thrall huts when she wanted to have peace? Embracing the girls on the hard beds improved breeding and secured stronger young, and when Bue had seen how happy Ysja was for Arnulf, he had generously found another skin-warmer with more fullness.

The smile was harder. That Ysja only had delighted because she had to, had to be good enough for an outlawed murderer. No woman, free or unfree, could yet take Frejdis' place. Fenrir had lent him his life; pleasure he had to obtain for himself.

'Just think, King Sweyn has a man running around in double chainmail! When I asked him why he bothered to lug around so much, he replied that it was because he could not abide the taste of onions.'

The Blood Fox grated its shield rim against Vagn's skeid and Little Ketil stood by the mast with his arms akimbo. His remark sparked laughter and Svend spat in the water, 'They have enough onions on the royal ships, but they will run dry for voyage-food. We plunder as soon as we arrive in Norway.'

'Yes, we do!'

Ketil's scarred face lit up with a grin, 'We will bang on earl Hakon's gate as soon as the first foot is put on the rocks, he should not fail to notice what guests he is receiving! Turn the sail.'

The Blood Fox changed direction so as not to clip its nose on the rear of Bue's ship and Arnulf watched the sprightly little warrior. Ysja slept with the hird now and Frejdis? Frejdis spoke, exasperated, with Trud over the wooden wool-combs while they mourned their common misfortune! He shook his head free of troublesome thoughts, 'Why onions?'

Svend laughed again, and Vagn leaned towards Arnulf with an expression that would frighten a child, 'Because, wolf whelp, then you know when you can save on care and wound-dressings. If you get hit in the stomach, you get onion soup to eat, and if your wound then smells of onions, it is because you will die, and there is no reason to spend more effort on you.'

He bared his teeth and sent Svend a sparkling glance, 'Double chainmail, what nonsense! If the arrow wants to go through, it will go through, unless one is made of wood. Ah, Ketil!'

He waved to *the Blood Fox*, 'You may well suggest the thin-skin eats a log before it gets going, then we can see if it helps!'

The crew laughed and Arnulf evaded attention by looking over at the nearest ship. Vagn the beast, he had already eaten wood, he had at least swallowed an anvil. Hard how they found amusement in blood and killings, had they not laughed themselves into seizures over Ottar's death? Maidenskin! Whelp! Colt! He would show them, by Fenrir he would! Did Serpenttooth not sing higher and more dangerously than ever before, and had he not found the spark in his sword and already learned more than Helge had ever shown him? All his powerless epithets they could burn in the first fire of the plunder, for now he would win respect for something other than being a skald and return home, if not as a Jomsviking, then at least a warrior!

*****

Norway came into sight at dusk on the evening of the second day. Sigvalde had chosen to begin his voyage in Vigen and intended to draw fire trails along the Norwegian coast, until earl Hakon looked up. Torkel the Tall knew the town of Tønsberg from a previous trip and thought that such rich dwellings would be a worthy landing site for the Jomsvikings. The vassal Øgmund the White also ruled over Tønsberg, and though he was young, he stood near Hakon. To harm him would hit earl Hakon hard, and the worse the Northmen were goaded, the more eager they would be to demand action from their earl and perhaps persuade him to stand against Sigvalde immediately rather than wait and rally men. Sigvalde gave permission for looting and prowling for women to anyone, for nothing and no one should be spared or shared, from the first night the skalds were to have ferocious deeds to make verses about!

Revisiting the twilight-wrapped fjelds tugged dew over his heart strings, and while the ships glided along the coast, Arnulf's mind was quiet and he pulled his cloak around him tightly on the thwart. The mighty mountains whispered confidentially over the water, they knew his secret and vowed to keep silent, and the evening chill embraced the returnee with wet kisses. Mountain dís and fjord wights murmured petitions for mercy and Gyrith turned in the bed with her arm around Little Ranvig while a smile adorned her sleep.

The last of the day's light dwindled, but the moon was revealingly clear, and when Torkel finally reached landfall, he gave orders that the sails were to be taken down and the oars laid out. The inhabitants of Tønsberg must certainly be in bed, but Sigvalde would not risk anything, so the fleet was rowed up the last bit as quietly and invisibly as possible. Arnulf pulled his oar regularly with his shipmates, looking over his shoulder. Slightly inclined, wooded stretches gave the fjeld feet fur and fields and pastures could be discerned behind a reasonable strand. The town of Tønsberg lay close to the water, and although it had to be near midnight, long rows of houses could be sensed in the moonlight. So many were there!

Arnulf completely forgot to row. Even if all the Haraldsfjord settlements were laid together, they would still not be able to cover half of the built area. There had to be several plank roads between the houses, which were arranged like cows in a barn, there was hardly room for pit houses and workshops, but maybe they were aligned in a row?

Svend nudged him with a displeased grunt and Arnulf grabbed the oar again. Stalls and canopies were erected on a large square in front of the houses, and several heavy ships were moored to a wide gangway. Lively trading had to take place here during the day, and on the strand, to one side, some tents stood that must be for housing the visiting traders, who did not sleep in the town itself.

Arnulf glanced at Svend. Wealth was here, good plundering, and after all the Jomsvikings had given him, a little silver in his belt pouch would not be bad! He looked over the men. All those warriors! The looting was not only for pleasure, it was a pure necessity! Few were the limbless in Jomsborg so if an arm or a leg was lost, it was about being rich so that if you survived, a farm could be purchased or a woman with inheritance betrothed.

Plundered goods. On Toke's raid Arnulf had only killed to defend the life of the Øystein's son and rescue Toste. Attacking was to be resisted, but sleeping men? And women! That struck below the ribs. He wanted to prove his worth against earl Hakon's men and who did not want to be on a healthy looting, but outright murder? Had he not killed enough? An armed man fell in battle, a sleeping one was miserably murdered. It should be possible to roar the enemy in Tønsberg aside without actually having to cut the way! But they could not believe his blood was soft, the sons of Odin. Blood companion to Vagn, praised by King Sweyn, would he hold back and chop wood rather than flesh? All the battles on the banner ground, if he was not warrior Viking now, he might as well leave the fleet immediately, throw Serpenttooth in the sea and walk over the fjelds to be a fisherman in Haraldsfjord! Wolfblood, Fenrir's raid, for the condemned everything was allowed, cursed to innocence, why should the rejected show goodness?

As an unexpected tidal wave swept skeids and longships up on the strand and shed breaking waves of armoured Vikings with drawn weapons. Tønsberg's dogs woke when Arnulf jumped ashore after Vagn and Svend and added his grip to those pulling the ship up on safe ground, but it was not ordinary summer peasants who carried out plunder at night, so even if the men in the town tumbled out of their beds with axes in hand, their fate was predetermined.

Despite weapons and chainmail, the Jomsviking force ran light-footed between the canopies and booths, and the obvious lack of defines showed how blindly the people of Tønsberg relied on their own courage and skill. A few moments passed, then screams and cries resounded among the houses, and the first roof was on fire. Arnulf stuck to Svend and Vagn and the deathly flow of warriors surrounded every building in a short time.

Tall and showy were the close houses, many with almost adjacent workshops and attics, and behind them were stables and small pit houses half-shrouded in darkness. Arnulf ran after the Bueson along a well-kept plank road that led directly towards the centre, and those most outstanding among the Jomsmen seemed to be allowed to choose prey before the others, in any case they all gave way for the Ågeson.

Men, women and children, thrall and old, all started to run out of the houses, panicking and searching for the forest in shifts or bare skin, but Helheim ruled the night! Toke would have let them save themselves, he would have let terror be enough and only attacked those who defended themselves or those who tried to recover their wealth but Sigvalde was heartless and Arnulf was not the son of Øystein. The infectious killing rage poisoned the will and incited with silver-hunger and striking-fever he beat away at the door of the house, Vagn chose the one with high-gables and elegant decor that stood out from among the others. The residents fled out a back door, taking refuge in the nearby storehouse, and from the attic they could better resist and Vagn yelled at Torkel the Tall that he should come and see if it was not Øgmund the White himself, who now stood trapped with his own cured meats. A spear was thrown through the half-open loft hatch, but Vagn stepped aside, laughing, 'Svend! Give me some fire, then you will get to hear how the hams here can brown, so it resonates all the way to Jomsborg, Svend! Svend? Disease beat him, Veulf where is Svend?'

Arnulf had left the door to help the Jomsvikings, who were shouting and beginning to pound the walls and pillars of the storehouse with axes and clubs, but Svend had disappeared in the turmoil. Torkel did also not seem to be nearby, so Vagn put his hands in front of his mouth to drown out screams and roars. Breathless, Arnulf leaned on Serpenttooth and saw with disgust a lame bitch being beaten down with a sax. A wild horse jumped past, slithering to its knees on the planks. Warriors fleeing flaming woodwork.

'Øgmund White! Come down, if you are a man, I want to talk to you, I have a message for earl Hakon.'

If Øgmund was among his people in the attic, the sight of Vagn did not apparently give him the desire to speak and the dark warrior laughed, so it could be heard despite a crashing roof. Just then Svend came out of the vassal's house with a screaming woman in tow. Her face was bloody, and her hand sat crookedly, so the Bueson had not been lenient, and a cry from the attic revealed who he had captured.

Arnulf looked indignantly from Svend to Vagn: were weapons not enough? With such superior strength did the heifers need to be crushed to lure out the bulls! Surrounded by warriors, the woman stood still, but she spat at Svend, snorting furiously.

'Who do we have there?'

Vagn brushed sparks off his sleeve and looked briefly at the captive.

'Øgmund's woman!'

Svend's grin shone as he twisted her arm and pushed her towards the storehouse, shouting at the door, 'Am I not right? Is this not your woman, Øgmund White? She says her name is Åse and it is all the same if you come down and defend her or not, I can amuse myself equally well, with or without onlookers!'

Arnulf clenched his teeth, so it tensed his temples. Leif Cleftnose had held the earl's daughter just like that ... before the vileness happened!

'Svend, your malicious buck!'

Vagn laughed lewdly and Arnulf wiped the sweat from his forehead. He should disappear now, he should get lost between the houses now and excuse himself with looting without admitting his weakness, Helge's misdeed, Jofrid's anguish, of course the Jomsmen would rape, but to witness it, that he did not need to do!

Still more houses caught fire along the plank road, Northmen were killed, probably more indoors than outdoors, and although the fighting continued, the plundering had already begun, the air was thick with smoke, anxiety and howls, so thick that it penetrated the skin, into the lungs, behind the eyes and let itself blend with discord and growing hatred. A shower of sparks fell on the plank road, burning holes in wool and leather. Muspelheim's folk rode over Bifrost, what honours could be harvested from killing unarmed weaklings and raping women?

'No!'

Åse screamed and writhed when a young white-haired man jumped from the attic and landed on his feet next to Vagn Ågeson. Enraged, his face convulsed and slashed, he lashed out against the Jomsviking, strong and tense from revenge. Vagn's answering blow seemed light, but the blade severed Øgmund's hand just above the wrist, and the lord of Tønsberg staggered back with a pained yell. Åse wailed terribly and Øgmund looked at her so crumbled and distraught that Arnulf froze on the spot. Then the vassal turned and fled, his arm bleeding profusely while Åse collapsed and cried like she wanted to die.

Toke. Gyrith. Arnulf stumbled to the wall of the house, his vision shimmering. He was a warrior, a warrior, Odin's blood, if his legs would not bear him now, he rushed over his own sword in that instant! Vagn and Svend pretended not to notice his girliness, for Vagn was about to wrestle a gold ring from the severed hand and Svend stared hungrily at Åse's buttocks.

'Now you become richer, Vagn Ågeson.'

Speckled with blood Little Ketil came, dragging a sack over his shoulder, closely followed by Bue and Sigurd, who certainly did not seem to have granted the Northmen keeping their own valuables.

'Let him run. Somebody should find Hakon, it would be shamelessly regretful if the earl did not hear anything about our landing.'

Vagn tried the ring and found it suited his little finger and Svend ripped open Åse's dress. Arnulf stared with his hand against the wall. He deserved to see Surtr's sword, did he not stand, peeking like a child through a knothole? Beautiful she was, golden skinned in the murderous burning glow, curvy like a snekke and large chested like Freya herself! Despite his own consternation, his manhood began to sense joy and Arnulf pressed himself up against the house's planks, breathless from self-loathing. Was it his own pride that rose? How could it? Should shame not have an end?

He wanted to get away and stepped forward, but Bue and Sigurd stood in the way, and Svend began to lustfully grope at his trousers. The death cries of Tønsberg were replaced by women's screams, but no conflict was harder than the one that raged in the chest! They were his companions! He had sailed with them, eaten with them, lived with them and trusted them, now contempt threatened to sweep that confidence away, although the worst deception was under the trousers!

'Biggest is first! Come on! Trousers down!'

Svend's eagerness swelled his desires freely from his trousers and Little Ketil was immediately up for the challenge. What he lacked in height, the Norns had made up in his manhood, for the shaft he revealed left nothing to complain about. Vagn's was dark-skinned, and Bue's thicker than most, but Sigurd seemed to be able to thrust to victory. Arnulf looked away, and Åse's cries grew silent while she looked up, careworn, wild-eyed like a caught lynx.

'What are you hesitating for, Veulf? Out with it! The contest is for everyone.'

Arnulf hid his dismay, staring back at Svend. By Trud's death would he stand here and squirm with his spear out for the eyes of everyone! They could force Åse, they were so many, but by Nidhogg's corpse-feathers not he! Gazes burned expectantly, smiles wide and the breathing was short.

'Ha, it wants out, see for yourself.'

Svend pointed cheerfully. His trousers strained from excitement, if the fire had not reddened his skin, Arnulf would have dropped dead from embarrassment! Bue was impatient, 'Let him be, Svend, you do not know how green-skinned he is? Only adult men can make a woman happy; whelps just play!'

Enraged, his betraying hands loosened his belt. Odin's spear jumped challengingly forward, as if it were endeavouring to bore a hole in the fat belly, and Little Ketil whistled, 'Whelps do you say? I will draw back from this contest, but let Veulf take her, it is the first time he is a-viking with us.'

'Yes, let Veulf take her. I think many owe him their lives for that skaldic verse he gave in the king's hall.'

Sigurd pulled up his trousers as an approvingly murmur spread, and Arnulf looked around, stunned. Impossible! He could not rape Øgmund's woman, what were they thinking!

302

'Thank you, but I can certainly wait…'

His smile did not falter, even though his heart was beating double, and the sweat cascade like a waterfall, 'I have already had a woman, over two nights, and it was not me who caught Åse White.'

'Never mind that, then you are warmed up, we will hold her, come on!'

Svend gestured, friendly, with his hand towards Åse and Ketil and Vagn threw her on her back with a hold on each arm. She fought, biting and kicking, but the Jomsmen were accustomed to scratching and were not daunted by a little resistance. They had obviously done this before and nailed her to the ground with a knee on each shoulder, and Åse sent Arnulf such a judgemental gaze that it should have turned all desire lame, but his manhood stood, stiff over her heaving breasts and swaying hips. He shook his head. They had better burn him up! Dishonour stood like a black wall behind the Jomsvikings; they would despise him, push him away, sail away with bawling laughter, defaming verses, Veulf, the whelp, who managed nothing, the beardless, who could not do what every thirteen year-old boy could offer and why? Because he would not rape a woman whose existence and honour were squandered, whose life was shattered and whose husband would probably bleed to death in the wilderness! She was expected to endure so many Vikings before dawn that she would probably not remember the first anyway! No power could save Åse White, but he himself would not throw away what little respect he so painstakingly had won from the Jomsvikings because of misguided mercy! How would she suffer by him taking her, he was not sharp-edged!

'Ah!'

Sigurd kicked Åse's legs apart, now it was about acting or fleeing like a dog! Brother murderer! Outlaw! Why behave like a man of honour, was his life not already forfeit? Arnulf peeled off his trousers with stiff hands as the warriors howled. What Åse shouted, foaming at the mouth, only the bloody corpses could hear, Svend and Sigurd forced her legs still while Arnulf threw himself over her, grinding in anger, in powerlessness, every thrust spawned nausea, spawned humiliation, spawned a rippling hunger, whelp, whelp, he was a man, a warrior, a Viking, a blood-brother, a hird's man, Veulf, Veulf, Veulf!

Åse's body twisted and flamed vigorously, she screamed and would have bitten again if Vagn had not grabbed her by the hair. Gasping, Arnulf saw his own saliva drool over the heavy breasts and his legs shook like straw in a storm when Svend finally pulled him up. Bue slapped him on the shoulder and Sigurd made ready to claim his right as Svend's silly laughing rattled worse than a whole nest full of crow chicks.

Arnulf pulled up his trousers with twitching fingers, deaf to the resounding pulse. Poison from the realm of Death etched icily on his hands, the fever raged, the belt was tightened too hard, to Helheim with it, to Helheim with all Danes and Northmen, to Helheim with all of Midgard! He stumped away without a word; they could believe what they wanted. Svend's laughter hung, the air was unbearably hot, and stank of blood, soot and tears. Helge turned his back, Toke put his arm around Jofrid, his mouth tight, and Frejdis wept so her wide-open eyes turned mud-black; he had failed them all as one.

He fell over each and every uneven plank he came across on the way, every dropped basket, every corpse, away, away, he had to get away; it didn't matter where to, mountains or sea could hide his shame! Tønsberg swayed past, house walls burst, liquid fire drifted into the lungs, he had done it again, of all misery, he had done it again! This time there was just no Toke Øysteinson to let loose and escape with, he had to die, only by leaving this life could the world be free of his endless misdeeds, Helheim had not torment enough in the Realm of Death for his misdeeds, he should be bound above Loki's head, so the poison alone hit him!

Dry sobs tore at his chest. Svend had killed everything, which was painstakingly struggled to its feet, it was Svend's fault, Svend's alone … damn if it was!

Arnulf stumbled out of the village, away from the houses, away from ships and tents, darkness called. Perhaps a human head did not sit on his neck at all, perhaps an evil spell was cast over him, maybe he was a child of the jötnar, had misdeeds and discontent not always followed him? Suppose Stridbjørn had been right all along, what if it was a black prophecy that he would be born in Egilssund to unleash unrest and annoyances on his family and village. Sigvalde's dragon stared after him, Vagn's skeid, *the Blood Fox*, the full range of pulled up sea stallions.

He had raped a woman! And what woman! Hakon's vassal's wife, a proud Norwegian family had been violated.

'Veulf!'

Out of breath, Svend overtook him at the water's edge, 'By Valhalla's shields, no matter how strong a force you are with, never go from it. We have just conquered a town! It is dark! Anyone could shoot you down or encircle you so far away from the ships.'

Arnulf groaned, hollow, turning to Svend. Fenrir was about to burst out of his skin, his teeth broke through, bristles stuck out of his neck, shoot him down?

'So let them shoot me down, what difference does it make, tell me that, what difference? Who would miss me anyway? Will not it just make Midgard more peaceful?'

Svend's excitement evaporated from sheer astonishment, 'Veulf! Have you horseflies in your ears? What do you mean? I would miss you, and you are not so ferocious that your death would be felt in Midgard.'

The wind tore at his hair, his long piss-yellow hair and Arnulf kicked a stone into the water, 'You? You! You miss nobody, do you? You were writhing with laughter over Ottar's death, you and Vagn and Ketil, and him you must have known better than me!'

Svend was serious and raised a cautionary hand, 'Turn off your fire! You judge too hastily; you believe only in the visible? I laughed, yes, I did, but that is how you cry in Jomsborg, do not you understand that? Otherwise, we have to sit and bawl like little girls, every time one of us does not return home. What are you so irascible about?'

'Irascible!'

Arnulf stamped, angry like a bull, around himself, the sand glowed through his shoes, 'I have committed rape, Svend Bueson that is what I am so irascible about! And now I am standing here, waiting for the Midgard Serpent to have mercy and swallow me raw, the water is deep enough!'

'You cannot mean that!'

The Silkenhaired lowered his arm, snorting, 'Åse White is laying her body down for a night's pleasure, but she does not need to die from it, we are at war, Tyr beat you, looting and desire are part of the payment for wounds and blood loss, man up! You did well. Be proud!'

Arnulf pressed his clenched fist against his forehead, 'Proud? Proud! I have assaulted a woman, I have cast shame and dishonour on the entire White lineage, my brother ... No, forget it, forget it! '

'Him you killed?'

'No!'

Painful fire swept through his body and his fists trembled in front of his chest. Arnulf shook his head violently, 'No, not him!'

The lungs were engulfed in iron, forced to obey, the tears dried up behind his heart, nothing could be revealed, nothing, Svend knew more than enough! Arnulf looked up with a forced calm. His voice quivered, hoarse and as thick as porridge, 'You cannot love, Svend, because you're constantly thinking of death! If you had ever loved, just once, you would never have been able to rape a woman, and you would never have forced me into doing it!'

'Forced you!'

Svend's jaw dropped, outraged, but Arnulf interrupted, 'My guilt was painful enough to carry already, I have had enough atonement for a lifetime.'

'No!'

Svend shook his head, emphatically, 'Think again, you skald-dreamer! What do you know about love? What maidens giggle about and call love is only an urge. A drive for pleasure, a bed-warmer, children and a thriving farm, but deep down, women are unreliable, and we know it well! How many men have not been pitted against each other by women, and how many are not miserably deceived? Men's friendships are faithful, men understand each other, risking their lives for each other, trusting each other.'

'Yes, like they trust a dog! And who told you all this nonsense? A woman? Do you think Øgmund jumped down and had his hand severed for fun? Was that clever? No, it was not, but what else could he do, he loves Åse, everybody can see that! Everybody except you maybe, who do not want other people to have what you yourself cannot have and therefore laugh at it!'

'He jumped not to be burned alive. Do you know what you are saying? It is not the White-lineage, you throw shame on, it is Jomsborg!'

'Svend!'

Arnulf had shouted, and the Bueson snarled and openly fought to keep his anger in check with a hand cramped around Snap's shaft. Arnulf heaved air into his lungs and gazed earnestly into the blue eyes, what did Silkenhair know of Frejdis' smile and sunny mind, what did he know about Jofrid's hatred and grief?

'I love a woman in my home village, love her so life has been grey for me! Now I have erred greatly against all Freya's sisters and daughters, and a worse disgrace does not exist!'

The Bueson opened his mouth, but Arnulf waved him silent, 'Because of rape my other brother lost his life and my own was nearly shattered, and now I have done what he did!'

Furious, he rubbed a runaway tear from his cheek, now he missed Brokkr's awl and strop, but Svend seemed to be trying to gather himself, wondering. He trotted a ring in the sand with lifted hands and then turned to face him again, 'Veulf! After the first killing, you curse yourself when the euphoria of victory turns cold, and after the first shield wall battle with sharp weapons, you terrify and become comrades with death. First raid, first sea-crossing, first rape, all are great experiences, violent experiences, but manhood is like oak bark; layer upon layer a boy grows into a warrior, changes him, and he becomes stronger if he does not wither and collapse.'

Arnulf ploughed his fingers through his hair, breathing all the way down to his stomach, 'Yes, it takes time to completely kill your own sense of justice! And it hurts! You talk about friendship. Who are you, Svend? Who are you underneath all your battle-kyrtles and chainmail, underneath all your scars?'

The Bueson's eyes flickered, now it was he running his fingers through his hair, 'You speak harshly. Was it not I who spared your life in the monastery and took you to Jomsborg? What would have happened to you without me? Have you yourself not exerted yourself on the banner ground?'

Arnulf blinked, regretting his words. One of Svend's eyelids quivered, he was shaken behind all his strength, shaken! Bue's son looked out over the sea, hard, his nostrils flaring, and Arnulf went a step forward, 'Forgive me!'

The last thing he wanted was to evoke Svend's disgust. Confidence could not be wrung out of someone, confidence could only be given, 'Forgive me!'

'Veulf!'

Svend sent him a long look and then reached out his hand, and Arnulf gripped it firmly. For a moment he could see, in the light of the flames, an unfamiliar light deep inside, behind the eyes, then he stared down, releasing his hand so as not to allow uninvited witnessing of his vulnerability, 'I have a friend, a good friend, who places women higher than anything else, and whatever objections you may have, he is a great Viking, who is neither afraid to kill nor to cry. He is a whole man, Svend.'

The Bueson became silent. The wind wrapped the coast and ships in a raw sea-breath, peeling away guilt and madness, so fatigue prodded his bones while Tønsberg burned, and the heat wrestled with the Norwegian night. Why all the talk, why all the anguish, why not just let the bark grow and thicken until nothing could harm the soft inner sap?

'Maybe I have something to learn, too, Veulf.'

Svend spoke low, ruminating over the back of one of his hands. The scars were light on the skin, and the index finger was crooked after a break.

'Maybe I should listen to you, like you listen to me.'

Arnulf bit his tongue, not answering, goose bumps on his skin and Svend turned his hand, close-minded, 'Can a man live without a shield?'

Arnulf nodded slowly, and Svend clenched hand and opened it again. He looked at it as if it were new, vulnerable, soft.

'I have taught you how to defend yourself ... Maybe you ...'

He wanted to say more but was fell silent. The screams from the town slipped into the fjelds and got lost in the dark. Seagull cries.

'Yes, I will, Svend Bueson. I do not take without giving anything back.'

Svend looked quickly at Arnulf. Then his smile started to grow so widely that his teeth shone, but instead of seizing the outstretched fist, Arnulf returned the smile and stroked his fingertips, as light as thistledown, over the palm to the Silkenhaired's amazement.

On silent wings, Huginn and Muninn flew through the night, Freya's hair lightly tickled her white neck while the hairs of Sleipnir's soft muzzle quivered. Only Heimdal heard Hrímfaxi's soft hoof beats and Frejdis' sweet breath whispered; her mouth close to his ear. He, who carries his heart in his hands, walks in a larger realm than the entrenched!

*****

The sun opened its eye early but obviously found the sight too ugly for the clouds pulled rapidly from the west and let the rain hiss in the smouldering remains of the fire in an attempt to flush the skeleton of Tønsberg clean of blood. Arnulf kept his back to the town, when the tents were taken down, what day would reveal ravens and wolves could observe, he himself was dull in all his limbs and had nothing to say to anyone. The warriors were otherwise boisterous enough, as if the newly acquired silver rattled against the chainmail, and bets were made on how many settlements Sigvalde would stop at before the evening.

Svend Bueson seemed contrary to his normal self, his mouth tame, but although he looked tired and like he had not slept, he helpfully counted the silver coins with Sigurd. He did not look Arnulf in the eye, and Arnulf had learned enough when sailing to know never to interrupt uninvited the close-sitting men, you could only be at peace and let your thoughts wander on your own thwart and if you did not participate in the talk, then staring or any other kind of inquiry was impolite.

The fleet set out, and when the wind was right, there was time to go over the evening's landing and tease good-naturedly. Arnulf wrapped himself in his cape, gazing into the distance, and the rain soon ceased, as if it wept only over Tønsberg. The men exchanged plunder and the shield rims grated against each other, while a lively crawling back and forth across the thwarts ensured that all everyone were satisfied with their share of the loot.

The next few settlements the fleet sailed past may have been warned, for they lay abandoned and Sigvalde sent only a single crew ashore to burn them down, anything of value was, needless to say, gone. What had Svend been restless about, he would not answer, and as the journey continued neither sword cut nor deed was required, he rolled himself into a sleeping skin between the thwarts and fell asleep.

To avoid wasting time Sigvalde let the ships spread out and did not send all to land whenever settlements appeared. A handful of ships at a time were allowed to go raiding and as Vagn still needed to rest a little, and none of the men on his skeid was poor except for Arnulf, the Jomschieftain thought it best that they stayed near his dragon. Sigvalde would rather not do without Vagn Ågeson should earl Hakon show up unexpectedly.

Arnulf was grateful to escape more unnecessary violence, and around midday he became tired of brooding over his own anger. What did it look like to sit and subdue yourself pale when the Norwegian earl would soon hear rumours that would force him to face Sigvalde like a raging bear? Just like Vagn could decide to sleep despite his pain, would he himself bury his loathing deep under a rock, it was not a given that he would escape alive from the coming battle, life should be lived proudly to the end! Was the skin on his arms not even a bit thicker than before, tougher than on the previous voyage, as rough as newly wrinkled oak bark? A few days yet, one for each finger, then nothing would get through, neither in nor out, and anyway the deep cries were so blurry that the wind over the sea could almost drown them out!

Svend seemed more composed after his nap. His gaze was warm and that Arnulf did not want to talk more about Åse White seemed to be a relief for him. Hungry, he took some sausage and bread from the food bag and Arnulf started asking questions. In the royalseat, he had trained persistently with Svend, and even if they could not exchange blows on the deck, there was still much more to learn, not least the uncomfortable idea of the confusion and tumult that must be enormous in so large a battle as they would likely find themselves in. The fight in the earl's courtyard had had untold costs and it was hard to sort out the arms and legs during the banner ground's great fights, so was it not likely to be much worse when more than two hundred ships met in open conflict? The Bueson laughed, his mouth full of bread, 'You are not going to fight them all together, Veulf, only those who are closest. Sigvalde leads the battle, and if just listen a little to what Vagn roars, there will not be much to worry about.'

Behind the assuredness of the words lurked a shadow of the nightly conversation: shared secrets, knowing wordless glances.

'And what if Vagn falls?'

Svend swallowed his mouthful and broke more off the bread, 'Then you are probably long dead, but if that does happen, then stick to Bue or Sigurd, Ketil will just run from you but I myself expect to stand for a moment. Find your peace, then you will know what to do.'

'Peace!'

Arnulf laughed tonelessly, grabbing a hunk of bread for himself, the experienced ones could probably get an overview, but peace, that was foolish talk, was Thor calm when he hunted the jötnar?

'Even when the sky and sea become one during the worst storm can the helmsman find peace in himself, for waves and wind do not have to go into his heart,' stated Svend, but Arnulf denied fierily, 'It is not peace, it is overview. Self-control. The outer breaks and the inner breaks, but the body can be forced with mastery, at least enough so the helm can be held.'

'Not necessarily.'

Svend softened a hard crust in his water mug, 'As soon as the fear is gone, peace takes its place.'

'Yes, but I'm not utterly fearless yet, Svend! I don't want to die.'

The Silkenhair tossed the crust overboard, 'No one wants to die! But you decide whether you will be overcome by fear. Look at Vagn, remember his single combat against Skarde, he won only because his peace is unshakable. He can be like a madman, shouting louder than most, but he knows all the time what he wants, he banished his fear long ago.'

Arnulf shook his head, it sounded too easy!

'Is it just about getting rid of your anxiety then?'

'No.'

Svend frowned and stared straight ahead, as the arms sank, 'How to explain it? Battle-peace is a condition. You see everything, react to everything, but you hover above it like an eagle, you are the fire's core and master, do you understand?'

His hands tensed, 'Everything happens quickly and slowly at the same time, it is as if speed can easily be increased. I feel my opponents and know so intensely where they are that I can almost close my eyes and like a plummeting buzzard feel which way they will move. They are

310

followed so closely that it seems possible to crawl into them and know their will, I become one with the enemy, therefore my attacks rarely miss when it really matters.'

It sounded fair and yet not. Words, great words, but pointless to use in front of hundreds of battle-ready Northmen. Arnulf squeezed his hunk of bread and did not let himself be persuaded, he had shared mind and blood with Sigvalde's stallion, but it still wasn't peace!

'Does Bue perhaps seem calm in a shield wall battle? He looks like Thor, who has just discovered that Mjolnir is stolen!'

Svend laughed, spluttering crumbs, 'You got me there! My father would probably agree with you, but that is simply because he is so thick-headed and well-larded that he is never in any real danger. Wait Veulf, just wait, but if something must be found, it must first be sought.'

He smiled without saying more, looking far out over the sea, munching; evidence of his own peace and Arnulf left him, turning on his thwart.

*****

In the late afternoon, Sigvalde gave the order to take the sails down, so the ships that had fallen far behind because of plundering, could catch up with the main fleet again, while he sent Sigurd onwards with some vessels to seek out a suitable place to overnight. After a moment, Bue and Vagn's skeid's came alongside the dragon and they climbed on board to hold council with Sigvalde and Torkel the Tall and Bjørn the Bretlander called Little Ketil over for a board game.

Arnulf was soon tired of keeping up with the game and stared, stiff-limbed, at the endless waves and cold steep mountainsides. He saw horsemen on land, riding like mad, but whether they could overtake Sigurd and his ships and warn the next settlement was doubtful, horses were not worth much along the fjeld coast. He followed a plank with his finger. Had Øgmund the White endured his walking through the wilderness? Did he find help or had everyone fled deeper into the country? Did he know what had happened to Åse? Of course he did!

Arnulf leaned against the shield rim. Jofrid. Had she given birth to Helge's rape child now? It weighed on his chest. Was the new-born child lying abandoned somewhere now, shivering, and calling to wild animals with his infant crying? He closed his eyes. Fenrir protect the child, even a rat could cause damage! Maybe people on the mountain pastures would hear it, perhaps their dogs, would the giant wolf bother to stand guard until someone with a heart arrived!

Svend interrupted his thoughts and began to talk about a lengthy tiresome quarrel Bue had once had at the Thing, and before his detailed account was finished, Sigvalde commanded the sails be set again, so the fleet could move on.

Sigurd had successfully found and emptied a larger settlement, and when the rest of the Jomsviking force arrived, newly slaughtered cattle and pigs had already been skilfully sizzled over a fire. Svend found blunt swords and went for Arnulf as soon as they had come ashore, Vagn did not help with either setting up the tents or mooring the ships. Bjørn attended to his wounds, and the Silkenhaired selected a steep slope for practicing sword work, and Arnulf had not defended himself long with a slipping foothold before the sweat was dripping from the ends of his hair. While the campsite grew up around the longhouses, and the dead were dragged out of the way and put into a secluded pile, Svend, hot-tempered, righted his stiff shield-wielding arm, 'If you do not follow my strokes more lively, I will split your shield all too easily, do you think it is made of stone?'

The Norwegian evening was bright, and it would be long before the meat was tender, so when Little Ketil shouted enthusiastically to Svend that he should stop the swordplay and come and see, Arnulf could have embraced him. The games on the slope had sweated through his clothes, but Svend believed he could take more, and grumbled loudly to Ketil, 'What is it that you have found that is so important? Veulf is hardly warmed up yet.'

'A knáttleikr ground! Haug and Kjartan just challenged Bue and Sigurd!'

Svend gave a yelp and flashed a grin, 'By Thor's death! That is not going to end quietly, come Veulf, I will not miss such grand a show, not even if I was given Draupnir!'

He crashed down on solid ground, and Arnulf followed breathlessly, throwing the training sword away. Knáttleikr! Not since the ice froze on Egilssund, and he and Rolf made a playing field on it and played against Tyrleif's sons, had he played knáttleikr. All fatigue was forgotten, and Little Ketil led the way through the village to a rocky field that seemed to have served as a domestic grazing pasture for the sizzling cattle.

Part of the legion had gathered here, around a playing field, marked by white straps in the earth, and in front of one goal stood the two challengers, swinging their bats while Bue and Sigurd were putting

312

their heads together at the opposite end. The ball was in the middle and Little Ketil, who with his small size was hardly an excellent knáttleikr player, proclaimed himself judge and grabbed the horn that hung from one of the goal posts. Svend pushed himself exorbitantly to the front row, and Arnulf saw no reason not to follow him. Vagn Ågeson did not have to push to get through, and Torkel the Tall gave Bue and Sigurd advice with grand gestures and eager eyes.

'Do you know Haug and Kjartan?'

Svend pointed unnecessarily and Arnulf shook his head.

'They are blood-brothers, Haug is from Bornholm like my family, and Kjartan came to Jomsborg last year, he the blond one with the braided beard.'

Arnulf nodded, looking at the heavily built Jomsviking, who was almost a head taller than his companion. Haug was stocky like a wild male boar and looked violent, there where he stood thrusting Gungnir into the goal with the ball bat, and although Bue had the weight of two, the bald Bornholmer appeared to be a worthy opponent for him.

'Who covers whom?'

Arnulf stretched his neck as Sigvalde came into sight and took up position on the fjord-facing side.

'I do not know, but it seems that Torkel has distributed the men.'

Torkel the Tall skidded off the field, and Bue stomped forward, patting his bat against Kjartan's while Sigurd slapped his bat into fist and waved to Haug. Then Ketil came forward, so he could accurately see if the ball flew over the targets or beside it, and immediately after the horn sounded for the first time. Sigurd and Haug switched playing field half and took five steps away from the ball while Bue and Kjartan went to stand in front of their own goal. Jeering shouts resounded against them and were thrown back by the nearby fjeld walls, and to Bue's annoyance those Bornholmers present thronged together and began shouting at Haug. Red-cheeked he rebuked his companions but then burst out laughing, and Ketil blew into the horn for the second time and elated, started the game.

Amidst vibrating roars Haug and Sigurd threw themselves against each other and the ball, and Sigurd was fastest and slid on his stomach into Haug's shoulder, so their heads banged together, but the ball was his! Bue struck out at it as Sigurd threw it, and the ball screamed over the fallen Jomsmen towards the blood-companion's goal where Kjartan met it with a practiced stroke and sent it back into the back of the Stout's brother. The laughter exploded and Svend screamed at Bue, while Haug caught the ball on his knees and biffed it towards the earl's sons' goal. It

313

went to the side and out over the back strap and Ketil blew the horn, while a hirdman collected the ball and ran back to put it in the centre of the playing field. Once again, the players stood ready, Haug with a bleeding nose, and again the match's start was sounded.

Now Arnulf shouted with them, and this time Sigurd did not throw himself but instead kicked the ball out of Haug's hand and struck it with the bat, so tufts of grass flew through the air. The ball whizzed towards the goal, but Kjartan was on guard again and he hammered it away to the opposite end of the playing field. Bue and Sigurd ran into Haug and tumbled to the ground, hunting for the ball, and Kjartan jumped to help his companion and locked Sigurd in a grappling hold. Bue rolled around with the ball in his fist and Haug on his back, but Sigurd could not free himself and the Bornholmers' loud roars for Haug were so rhythmic that a group of hirdmen began to roar at Bue from sheer spite.

Arnulf joined in, and Svend Silkenhair yelled to his father that he should rub Haug off against a stone. Like a mountain-jötunn, Bue got up on his legs with Haug as his rider, but he could not use the bat as the Bornholmer had a hold of it, and without it a goal could not be made. Bue jumped and writhed and ended up throwing himself down on his back, beating the air out of Haug's lungs. Ketil cried a warning, but although Haug gasped for breath like a fish on land, he managed to hit Bue's fingers with his own bat, so the ball rolled astray over the grass.

Meanwhile, Sigurd wrestled with Kjartan, so they both their heads were as red as smith's iron and Haug pulled himself free and crawled after the ball amid thunderous applause and whistling. Little Ketil scolded both Bue and Haug, but as they appeared to be roughly equally injured, he did not expel either of them from the playing field. The Stout shook his bruised hand, taking up the pursuit, and now Haug was chased like the hare before the dog, and not many goals came out if it.

Arnulf grinned at Svend and shouting encouragingly to Sigurd with raised arms, who with a great effort threw Kjartan on his back and was now struggling to be free of a leg grip. By chance he kicked Kjartan's elbow against a round stone and got loose, and now Haug was abandoned to the mercy of the earl's sons, for his companion was too slow to get up. The bald Bornholmer stopped and struck the bat in the ball and Bue could only blame himself for not moving out of the way and getting hit in the ribs. Sigurd leapt in vain, and the ball curved beautifully over the goal with such a roaring exhilaration that Little Ketil's subsequent horn blows were more for the eyes than the ears.

Arnulf laughed heartily, but Svend was mad, and the Bornholmers' tribute to Haug resulted in him pulling out Snap and making threatening thrusts against them. The ball was found and brought onto the playing field, and the four players, snorting like stallions, trotting around themselves, while Ketil shouted to the Jomsviking legion, asking if now it was time to expand the teams. The answer was unanimous, and Haug and Sigurd chose another two men each, who with wild gestures and roars went onto the field equipped with bats and fresh courage. Ketil gave Haug time to stuff wool in his bleeding nose, and Torkel quickly wound a linen strip around Bue's hand, so the game started again, and Haug felled Sigurd over the ball with a wild blow of his elbow to the throat.

The game was wild now, wild like the Plains of Ida, and the strength was not saved for earl Hakon! Bue had two men against him, and Sigurd rolled, coughing in the grass, but the other players on the team managed to escape until he could receive the ball with one knee on the ground. It flew safely to the target, but was caught at the last minute, and out of sheer fury Sigurd slammed his bat into a stone so it broke. That kind of self-imposed obstacle Ketil did not participate in, and while Sigurd staggered off the field to find himself a new bat with one hand pressed against his neck and Bue, foaming at the mouth, struggled to remove the leeches from himself, Kjartan took a tiny step towards the earl's sons goal and, grinning, sent the ball over the plank with a lazy strike, his companion held the last two men back with a deadly swinging bat.

Mockery and triumph gripped the Jomsborg flock, skirmishes occurred in the cluster of men, and Little Ketil called off the game, roaring for an armistice. Svend Silkenhair was nearly as red-faced as his father, and Torkel was close to brawling with Kjartan, so to avoid bloodshed Ketil started the match again despite his own displeasure. The players goaded each other, and fighting ceased, now the Jomsteam had to correct their disgrace, if they lost another goal to their opponents, they could just as well go to the half-raw roasts now.

With Berserker-like death-defiance, Sigurd and Haug crashed together and their companions after them, and the dispute over the ball seemed a pure wolf's fight to Arnulf, no trick was omitted, no grip was too vile, and Sigvalde's men could not seem to be violent enough. The torn-up grass on the knáttleikr field suffered far less than the tumbling men and the fight became less and less about the game that was played in Egilssund in wintertime. Like stampeding cattle blinded by the spring sun, the Jomsborg's heirs stripped the Norwegian soil naked and Utgard's Loki sat down with his back on the nearest mountain, nodding.

Kjartan was knocked unconscious by accident, Sigurd broke a tooth, and one of the new players had to limp off the field with a twisted foot, so replacements were needed.

Bue managed to get the ball over the goal, but after that the game was too hard for the bats to be used properly again, and Ketil sent Haug off the field for deliberately cutting the bat's edge into Sigurd's shoulder. The ball trickled over the back strap and was again brought back, but no goals came and after a good while, when Kjartan still had not woken up and another man had to be supported over the long side, Sigvalde commanded the match be stopped. He did not like to lose capable men on hostile ground and thought that earl Hakon would have laughed himself silly if he knew how eagerly the Jomsvikings were beating each other to the ground.

Disappointed but enlivened the warrior crowd dispelled, and mead and ointment were brought out for participating players. Bue the Stout toasted and cursed Haug and the entire flock of Bornholmers, and Sigurd rubbed his shoulder, saddened by the loss of his teeth, for he did not want to end up with as ugly a sight as his honourable brother! Vagn Ågeson had only praise for the game, and Little Ketil had finally awakened Kjartan, who was not hurt any worse than mead could flow manly into him.

The Bueson stated succinctly that the game had to be resumed as soon as earl Hakon's head was stuffed in King Sweyn's sack and Little Ketil had to pledge him that and drink a promise toast from Bue's mug. Even though the sweaty men had to be really sore, no complaints were heard from anyone; Kjartan was slightly unsteady on his feet, but he would not be cheated out of the spit-roasted pig.

Arnulf picked up a discarded bat, weighing it tentatively. It was not playfulness that was missing, but he could probably do without the pleasure of playing against the Jomsvikings. Evening breezes from the sea and mountains caused him to shiver in his sweat-wet clothes, and Svend noticed it and pulled his sax mercilessly out of its sheath again. The food was not ready and if a man became cold up north, it was not far to a sore throat and chest sickness, and Arnulf's clumsy shield wielding was still unsatisfactory and his footsteps as heavy as if a lazy troll fought!

Newly learned self-control met the familiar intoxicating wrath, and Arnulf stamped down towards the open grass plain with ill-concealed grumbles on the heels of Svend. Fenrir savage that Jomsson, but honour had to be defended!

*****

With alternating winds Sigvalde's force swept along the Norwegian coast, and the chieftain's mind did not become any milder as the days followed on from each another. The Jomsvikings went hard at the unfortunate villages that were spotted, and several war rumouring ships were captured and sank for Hræsvelgr's wings stroked the fleet quickly over the water. Yet more and more settlements were found abandoned, and despite his fearsome strength Sigvalde kept his force more together now, caution increased, and single lying farms were completely passed over in haste. Daring men were sent to lookout on the fjords and around the larger islands, and all on board were clad in chainmail and ready for battle. Hakon would certainly know which disease ravaged his flank, and the sight of the Danish force had to wake horror beyond the rottenness of Helheim. The brightly coloured ships and bow heads blazed against the grey and green sides of the fjelds and the red shield edges testified to an unbreakable unity, while the horrifying images let Norwegians know that every man on the thwarts was able to fight for himself!

Arnulf was careful with his combat training whenever an opportunity presented itself, and despite the rush, Sigvalde put his force ashore most days during the late afternoon, so weapons and muscles were not rusted solid from idleness.

On the skeid, the thoughts tumbled under the billowing sail. As the fickle wind blew, doubt and fire-blood pulled at his pounding heart, and death's presence fuelled the loss and deeply hidden fears. The folk of Egilssund seemed painfully near and Arnulf took his leave from them, his head bowed, one by one. Like shadows they stepped near to him, shadows, without speech, without gravity, but he knew them, by Fenrir, how he knew them, both spring and summer shrank to a dried apple! Trud's solid hands and Rolf's mulch smell could be sensed behind his closed eyes, and Frejdis cried until she was tired and worn out and finally accepted Arnulf's plea for forgiveness. She sadly caressed his hair, and even Stridbjørn was soft-spoken. Aslak and Halfred drank to him from the same bench as Asbjørn and Old Olav, and up along the fjeld ridges Helge rode his pitch-black stallion while he warded off the Valkyries.

Then they left him so as not to disturb the Jomsvikings' voyage, and for a time his body was empty like rusty chainmail. Adamant, Arnulf forced new life behind the iron rings and began to regard the country around him closely in an attempt to recall the landmarks, but even though he diligently compared Toke's sailing to Sigvalde's, the weather and vessels were too different for the stretch to be travelled at the same time

A churning stomach stone grew steadily greater, for he fought through every night, and again and again Haraldsfjord mirrored itself in the Norwegian coast, Toke should be warned but how? It had occurred to him easily enough in the royalseat, but now that he saw how futile the Northmen were at trying to forestall the fleet, the possibilities shrank into nothing, he could get hold of neither horse nor boat, and little would that benefit him.

Svend noticed the silence but did not ask. He surely thought Arnulf was wrestling with the doubt that gripped any inexperienced warrior before his first great fight. The laughter on the ships had sharp edges, the stories between the men became harsher and direct atrocities were, now and then, committed against the fjeld people who did not save themselves in time. Arnulf held himself free from participating in the deaths by fire and rape, but when Vagn went ashore, he had to go with him, and he could not stand farthest back all the time.

Ring by ring, the chainmail grew heavier on his heart, the shield covered both strokes and view, and even though the laws of Jomsborg commanded that no man flee from an enemy with the same strength and armour of his own, it did not command the killing of the weak and the fearful; Arnulf kept it steadfastly.

Svend Silkenhair's open gaze disappeared again behind glittering scales with blood shadows, and the fragile confidence that had escaped him that night in Tønsberg could not again be freed as long as the iron was tight around his chest.

Early on Arnulf began to limp due to an alleged blow to the knee, and his tardiness was subsequently not blamed for too much, though surprised only Bjørn the Bretlander that he could not see the injury. As Svend had said, the oak bark swelled up, the days of the voyage were unusual, and both guilt and shame could be hidden in the bark, but when Sigvalde, during an encampment at an abandoned harbour, asked Vagn to sail further as a lookout for slaughter animals, the courage was not yet as strong as that of the Jomscompanions for little did Arnulf care to sail away from the legion in a single skeid.

His concern was not shared by the dark warrior who in his quest for livestock began to roam between the islands, undaunted. Several rocks rose out of the water uselessly sheer, while others had grazing on the slopes, and one seemed to be inhabited and quite large, in any case both goats and cows were near the shore.

318

Vagn steered towards it and Arnulf stood up and searched the surroundings carefully. The sea struck from the north but stayed reassuredly in bays and coves, and he followed some low-flying geese and wanted to turn towards Svend to help with the impending landing when his breath suddenly froze to a block of ice between his ribs. There, like a seagull surrounded Æsir tower stood the white rock, the rock Toke had shown him! He could clearly see the back of it, there was no doubt! Out there, on the other side, the eider duck island had to be, he had sailed out there before, and near, amazingly near, lay Haraldsfjord's mouth, that he had not noticed any landmarks until now, had to be due solely to Sigvalde keeping his fleet behind the rocks and islets instead of sailing out in free water!

Arnulf heaved air and met Svend's questioning look. What the Bueson thought about his sudden agitation, was not to know, but Svend did not seem to falsehood, for he looked at the white rock with a surprised nod, then he poked those sitting in front and pointed, but the Jomsmen were not in the mood to admire unusual stones, the keel scraped against the bottom of the shore of the island, and everyone jumped ashore.

Weak-kneed Arnulf stepped onto the grass, now his promise bound, now the fate changed horses, now his northern friend needed help for his life! Silently he helped pull the skeid. Hodur's sight, he should have noticed where he was, much earlier, condemned as if the Norwegian coast could change him like a jötunn! But Sigvalde had set up camp, and Vagn was here, so unless other warriors were sent out, no one needed to enter Haraldsfjord at this moment and the settlements could not be seen from the sea.

The skeid creaked and sullenly bit ground and Arnulf stroked the hair uneasily from his eyes. What if Sigvalde from responsibility and sunken stomachs sent several boats out for flesh anyway, would it be Toke's fjord they sailed into? What if Little Ketil met Svend, boasting of killings, while Bue walked around proudly with the Øysteinson's silver chains around his neck when Vagn's men returned with the cattle!

Arnulf was pained! Could he steal the skeid and escape now while the cows were being captured? Impossible! He would never get it out alone, the sail was too heavy, and he could not fail and leave the Jomsvikings. But perhaps there were other vessels on the shore, perhaps a small boat? If the island hid a farm, then there was probably a rowing boat, just one, Fenrir's torment, even a trunk with oars could be used.

Vagn gave the sign to surround the grazing cows, who confidently lifted their heads, and his men spread out to identify them, but at that

319

moment a rough-haired man with a stick came into sight over the ridge. At the sight of the crew he stopped, astonished, bristling his yellow-grey eyebrows, but despite the warriors' tough exterior, he quickly regained his composure. Vagn was out for something other than killing and did not deign him much attention but told his men to drive the cows down to the ship before they were slaughtered, 'And if you find more animals, take them with you, we have enough space in front of the mast.'

Arnulf smacked his hand on the warm rear of a cow, clicking with his tongue. While the others were killing the cattle, he could take a detour around the island in search of bread and other food, and if there was a vessel anywhere, he would find it!

'Halt!'

The Northman stepped boldly forward, thrusting his stick in the ground, and Arnulf stopped at the order, mostly from wonder, for the last many farmers, he had met, had jumped to life.

'Who is in charge of your ship?'

Svend Silkenhair took a wide stance with his thumbs in his belt, watching him with a broad grin, 'That is Vagn Ågeson.'

The fjeld farmer seemed to know the name, the way his eyes opened, but undaunted he stood his ground while his eyes found Vagn, 'Then we have Jomsvikings in the country!'

He stared resolutely at the dark eyes, his mouth shrewdly drawn, 'I would probably think that you could find larger beef cattle than my cows and goats here, if that is what your intentions may be, so if you really want to be fed, you should listen to me!'

The hunt for livestock ceased and the Jomsmen proceeded to stare at the stout peasant, who was undoubtedly just trying to defend fur and property. Vagn put his hand on his sword hilt and leaned icily towards the Northman, 'If you can tell us something of Hakon earl's whereabouts, it is not impossible that your animals can be saved, but then you put your life in the truth of your words. What is your name?'

'Ulf.'

The man yielded to the earl's son and had to look away for a moment but then stood up for his cattle. 'Høj-Ulf after my island.'

Loathing surrounded him. No one threatened the island-dweller, so if he just kept his mouth shut and disappeared, he would be far luckier than many of his countrymen, but instead of fleeing, Høj-Ulf looked around, trade-desire in his eyes, his weight on his front leg, 'Earl Hakon put ashore here in Hjörungavádr late last night with a single ship. He is waiting for his men, and you can kill him now, if you will.'

320

Earl Hakon! Here! Arnulf looked back quickly as if the Norwegian force was on its way to topple the island's summit with lowered spears, but everything seemed peaceful. He stared at Ulf. Traitor! Did that wretch not even mind betraying his earl to the enemy without the slightest constraint? Why? Was it revenge or an ambush? Or was the man simply wrong in the head? Arnulf glanced at Svend, but none of the Jomsvikings reacted, and the sweat began to bead on Høð-Ulf's forehead. Had he equated his life with a herd of cattle and three goats? Vagn nodded slowly. 'In that case, you have redeemed your cows, but we are so unfamiliar with the area here, I think it is best that you come on board with us and show us the way to the earl.'

Høð-Ulf clutched his stick less cocky than before, shifting his weight to his back foot, 'I will certainly not fight my lord and my country men, so I will only go aboard your ship if you give me your word that I will be put ashore with peace as soon as you know the way.'

A predatory smile under dead eyes was the only promise Vagn gave him, but Høð-Ulf was content, now the choice was not given.

The livestock was left behind despite Svend's objections, the concerned Northman followed, and Arnulf stumbled over tussocks and rocks, while his thoughts struck falling stars in broad daylight. If Hakon was nearby, waiting for men, then the first ship he should do battle with would be *Twin Raven* and if the Northmen had gathered on the other side of Høð, then Toke had long been warned, and every infant, every thrall, every toothless lame throughout the North must already know of Sigvalde's war-voyage and be tightening sword belts, but Ulf glance had revealed such honest astonishment that they hardly knew how close their enemy was. If *Twin Raven* really was here, then he could almost shout to Toke from the top of Høð!

Arnulf clenched his fists, freezing from the sweat. Toke. Toke Øysteinson, the Northman who had prevented his suicide, defended him against Leif Cleftnose, given him the wolf-knife and fought with him, maybe he was just a few boats' length from the skeid! And maybe drowned on the other side of the western sea. Fenrir's fury! Wolf blood! The ravens tore his purpose into strips and his feet faltered as the skeid was pushed out, so Svend pulled him up over the shield rim, 'You should let Bjørn look at your knee, Veulf. Courage is one thing, stupidity is something else, and he could, at least, wrap a supportive bandage around it, if we must fight now, you need your legs with you.'

Arnulf looked at Svend, not understanding, but then hastened to nod. He had to stop revealing what was happening behind the eyes, no uninitiated should share in it.

'I'll do it myself when we reach the camp.'

Svend frowned but let it go for now the sail was being set and the ship could not set out fast enough. Grim Vagn took the helm, and the Bueson sat down across from Hød-Ulf with a teasing look as if he were about to haul confessions and breaches out of the Northman. Arnulf should have stolen away that night in Tønsberg. Ships had lay along the strand and he could have stolen a horse and got a head-start in the darkness, Norn sorcery and Odin's runes, why should everything be so difficult?

*****

The Jomsviking legion had clumped together on a smaller island, and Vagn had to squeeze his ship in between the others and moor it without a land grip. Even as he climbed onto the nearest deck, he shouted that Sigvalde and the earl's sons should be gathered and as Arnulf reached solid ground after Bjørn and Svend, Bue and Sigurd stood by the waterfront flanked by Sigvalde and Torkel, the war council had gathered.

Vagn commanded the Northman repeat his words to the Jomschieftain, and the stout fjeld peasant's voice trembled during the meeting with the many sharp glances. Sigvalde listened attentively and did not believe the man was lying about Hakon, but that the earl was hiding alone sounded unlikely. Neither Vagn nor the chieftain thought that Hød-Ulf had been sent out to lure the Jomsvikings in an ambush, but it was obvious that it was important to strike straight away, before every able-bodied man in Norway had gathered around their earl.

Arnulf had palpitations. It seemed unreal to have to meet the earl so suddenly. For many days, the game had been hunted, but now the bear's cave had been found and the hunting arrows were strangely heavy. All day he had sailed, the bonfires were lit, the food was ready to be prepared, but instead of settling down to talk, board games and weapon-play Sigvalde now gave the order that they were to prepare immediately for fierce battle.

His warriors received his words with victorious expressions and ominous glances, but no one shouted aloud, for the air was quiet between the islands, even the most tender gull cries could be heard from afar and earl Hakon could have people everywhere watching for the enemy. He lay

322

good here, in the middle of his kingdom, and no doubt several of his ships had managed to get further along the coast, all the people of the North had to be on the way!

Little Ketil slapped the palm of his hand in Svend's, the two Jomsvikings looked ready for a feast, and they took out their axes and mock-striked at each other, so the cut stroked over both the neck and the lower leg. Arnulf's fingers wound around Serpenttooth, seeking the bloody-minded strength of the sword. Now anger and mad rage had to be roused and so violently that life dared venture for deeds, but his heart galloped on a taut tether, and his courage did not want to strike a fire for friend-killing, as beautiful as Toke's smile spread over Haraldsfjord!

Most of the Jomsmen were equipped and armed, but once again the weapons and, buckles were checked, shield grips were shaken and bowstrings drawn and the ships' decks could well be cleared and goods placed under the planks, while bread was held under arms and teeth munched cold meats.

Arnulf helped, found his chest, pulled on a hood and a helmet and took out the shields. The sword and the knife slipped easily out of their sheaths, a belt kept the chainmail in place, and the perspiration ran from under his hair, the late afternoon sun was so warm.

Svend still toyed with Ketil and even found time to comb his golden hair to shining for his funeral, and Bue ordered his men ready, his largest broad axe over his shoulder. Just like before his single combat with Skarde, Vagn Ågeson went a little away by himself and knelt on one knee with his forehead on his shield's edge and his sword drawn over his thigh, and Arnulf saw many others do the same to ready their minds and make vows for weapons and protection, while Sigvalde took a gold ring off his arm and threw it into the sea to Odin.

All kinds of warriors breathed into the brotherhood of their red shield rims: the gloomy silence, the wild young love, the seriously experienced, the mighty and highly boasting, the cunning with sneaky low-held weapons, the broadest with the most heavy shields at the front, the fiery and menacing, the outwardly quiet, the exuberant, all taunting death, vengeful for companions and war-loving, all sons of Jomsborg or hirdmen of the Dane king. And between them Veulf the Outlaw, the brother-murderer from Egilssund; so worthy were the damned companions!

His stomach did not want to know food, but Arnulf forced pork down his throat, his body felt light, as light as an eider duck, downy and hollow all the way through. Maybe Hød-Ulf had not lied, perhaps the Norwegian earl was to be found truly alone with his closest housecarls, all

323

his men might have been sent on a recruitment voyage into the fjords and the longships would lie well-hidden and shelter, Hød appeared so abruptly. Hope was every man's right.

The newly erected tents were allowed to stand, and anything unnecessary was carried off the ships. Spears and arrows were laid ready, stones and shields, and strong rope was carefully secured so that the vessels could quickly be bound together if necessary. Hød-Ulf sat on a barrel, clutching his stick, and Sigvalde strode around, his red curls flaming down his chainmail. He should plait his hair, it fluttered so wildly, but Arnulf would like to see the man who would attempt to grab hold of the Jomschieftain's locks! Just as Bue rested a grand broad axe over his shoulder, although the leader of the force would hardly stand at the front of the skirmishes.

'Are you ready, Veulf?'

Svend's bared teeth were ready to bite under his twinkling gaze. He looked happy, his axe could not get to play soon enough, and his chainmail weighed less on him than swan feathers. The Northmen should be notified; they should, from pure pity, know how fast the Bueson could twist his arms, how easily he stepped, how deep Snap drank! Someone should tell them of Bue's strength, of Sigurd ingenuity, of Ketil's leg-looting and Vagn's merciless harvest, but maybe they already knew their enemy well enough from rumours and skaldic verses to want to fight as no fjord men had ever fought in Norwegian waters before.

'Yes, I'm ready.'

The voice sounded as hoarse as a cut blade but wild with defiance. He who hesitated fell first! Svend looked deep into his eyes, and Arnulf jerked again, betraying his own fickleness. Fenrir's honour, an earthy peasant lad he was not, his warrior-blood simmered, red as fire, dangerous steam whirled from it, soon bubbles would burst and woe to the wretched, splattering blows!

The Bueson stretched out his hands, and Arnulf took them with Thor's grip. The Jomsborgson was mad, mad from birth, his mind was like an unpredictable dog, but a better battle companion no one could wish for, the smile under the yellow hair promised lunacy and great hunting, Svend was ready for a game of knáttleikr with sharp weapons!

Armed for Ragnarök, the Jomsvikings rose on board. The thickest battle-kyrtles were worn, the heaviest chainmail, the strongest helmets, arms were laced well into leather, their weapons beat hard against each other, their round shields jarred, their spearheads flashed. The shields along the shield rim soaked themselves tough and supple with sea water, ready to intervene and wrestle damaging blades from the enemy and Sigvalde's banner waved over the dragon, as the oars were put out. Sitting as close as possible, the Vikings rowed forward and Vagn let his skeid come alongside the Jomschieftain's longship and commanded Høð-Ulf stand in the bow and show the way between the islands. The northern waters lay quiet, hesitant of its fate, and not a single drop of water was left untouched behind the fleet, every ripple was hit and the sea lapped bitterly against the banks and rocks as if the deep was sighing, preparing to mix blood with the fallen.

Arnulf pulled his oar with a look over his shoulder. Large and equal to each other the king's hird's ships slipped forward, Sweyn Haraldson's warriors, rocking death-snakes, and among them Sigvalde's diverse fleet: small, long, tall, blunt, light, he brought all vessels. Little Ketil's slender *Blood Fox* was like a red spear, Vagn's broader, shorter skeid was led with the same skill, as if it was his battle-axe, and just as scarred as the men at the oars, the sea horses snorted their curved bows forward.

The chainmail caught the battle-kyrtle with every stroke, and the weight made the oar seem easy. Just as little as the men resembled each other, just as many types of equipment and weapons they carried, some simple, some lavishly decorated, each had his favourite, only Arnulf used that which he had been able to borrow, but Serpenttooth was his own!

Høð-Ulf's posture was not proud in the bow of the skeid, and the longer the ships cleaved the fish kingdom, the more the Northman needed to change feet. Vagn kept a sharp eye on him, and near the dragon ship, he followed the trembling hand's direction. Sigvalde got up, his chin lifted, and Svend's warriors kept close to the curves of the next island. Arnulf craned his neck, stiffening his arms abruptly, for in the bay behind the island he saw it at once, as if hundreds of breeding giant seals were on the shore, but it was clearly not sea creatures that rested on the flat strand, it was ships!

The oar clashed with those to the sides, but the crew had now spotted the earl's hideout in Hjörungavádr and let the skeid drift while rumours spread like fire across the fleet. Høð-Ulf's treason had been right.

Hakon's longship was easy to identify, it was so red and big, and around it lay ships of all sizes, as numerous as fallen autumn foliage, more than under Sigvalde's command, much more! Every countryman must have rigged up, hastening to help the earl, proud snekkes lay as oath-brothers to fishing boats, cargo vessels, skeids, small humble boats, and even heavy broad knarrs were mixed in the teem.

Arnulf rested his oar over the sea, licking his lips. The Norwegian fleet flickered, doubling in size in the reflection of the water, and if Hakon had as many men as he had ships, the prospects were bleak!

'How miserable! Is that really all the goat breeder has to insult us with? It is reprehensible! By my life and blood, if Hakon is setting a simple cargo boat against me, I am sailing home again, I did not come here to pick lice out of mountain sheep.'

Vagn spat contemptuously into the water, but on land the enemy had now become aware of the Jomsvikings, and in an instant men swarmed to the strand, running, shouting, sounding horns; horses whinnied and the Northmen were taken completely by surprise and fell over soup pots and tent ropes.

Hakon Goat-Breeder? Then he was breeding horned sheep with blades and coins, the flock did not look harmless despite the confusion, and hot-tempered it bleated, a man could easily feel small, as if Vigridr billowed from life! Arnulf heaved air into his lungs. Behind him ship after ship came to Sigvalde's row and like low, roaring thunder clouds, they blocked the way to open sea; no one would be cheated out of the sight of the enemy; sniffing blood, the dogs necked onwards!

The laughter spread through the Danish force and Hød-Ulf seemed to think that he had kept his promise enough, because he suddenly jumped ashore and began to swim toward land like an otter with his head under water. Stones and half-hearted curses followed him, but despite the cold seeming to quickly ensnare his arms, slowing his strokes, Vagn grabbed a spear and threw it, and he threw it well, for Arnulf could no longer see neither man nor weapon.

He shaded his eyes, staring at the island's strand with a thumping heart. So many ships! Could he find a single leaf of the tree, a single straw in the field? It was difficult to distinguish, yet there was no doubt. There it was! There it was! Halfway up on the strand with its high, iron-sharp bow carved firmly into the sand, its two raven heads boldly raised, *Twin Raven*, Øystein Ravenslayer's proud vessel.

Arnulf had to grab the shield rim, his fingertips smarted. Toke! Toke was here! There on the island, among all the others, there he ran now, shouting, followed by Stentor and Leif Cleftnose and all the others from Haraldsfjord. The hatred boiled their anger rock-solid, no doubt they would use all their strength to try to crush the enemy, who, for to amuse the Dane king in a drinking-game, they now murdered the sons of the kingdom and raped its daughters!

Arnulf narrow his eyes, trying to look for Toke in the crowd, but the distance was too great, all the men appeared alike in the chainmail, and helmets hid faces and hair beyond recognition. He would do what Høð-Ulf did; throw himself into the sea and swim ashore, grasp his life friend around the neck, shake fists with Stentor, and even Leif Cleftnose could be tolerated in the moment!

A shoulder blow caused him to gasp and Svend laughed, 'It seems great, but my hands on Andrimner's platter if we are not the far more terrifying vision! Look around, Veulf. There is only one victor here and it is Sigvalde.'

Arnulf nodded, his gaze shifting. The appearance of the Jomsviking legion might paralyse the tight-hearted, so violent were the ships and shields, so heavily armed appeared the men, so clearly burned the colours against all the grey. He held Serpenttooth's hilt tightly. Foolish he was, as stupid as a child! He could not do anything to find Toke now, the battle had to stand, the fight had to first blow bays and fjelds from each other, then he could seek his friend, shield his life, command his freedom! Toke lived, *Twin Raven* had reached home safe and sound! Arnulf snorted. With the strength of two men he would fight, every blow would lead him further, he had made promises, and Vagn had a claim on his life, Svend his support, worthy were the companions who had given him a thwart on the voyage and were the king's rings not glowing on each hand? Even Toke would have to laugh if he saw him now!

'Yes, Svend. There is only one victor, and he is not standing alone!'

Svend's laughing drowned out the noise of the Northmen. 'Well said, Wolfblood. Show me now you can bite!'

Sigvalde's horn sounded in that moment. The tall Jomsviking had placed himself amidships, shouting orders with grand gestures. Strong as Tyr he stood, the scale-armour flashing in the sun, and his posture was prouder than the highest fjeld peaks.

'Come into one row, side by side. Bue and Sigurd! You take the outermost north flank, half of the ships to be between you and me. Bjørn! You take *the Black Snekke* and lie next to Vagn, and you both take the south flank, Vagn furthest out and the rest of the ships between us. Torkel! You lead *White Stallion* next to me! Get the bows ready and warm up the men. Hakon should be reluctant to believe it is his weak-kneed grandmothers who have come!'

The earl's sons shouted back, and with amazing skill the Jomsvikings began rowing the ships into place. The current was even in the water, and deeper than the anchor-rope's length did the warrior grave's bed reach, but the flowing sword serpent stretched from almost shore to shore and did not let itself drift in disarray with the Vikings' skilful oar strokes. Arnulf pulled the wolves shields free, and with a grinning from ear to ear, Little Ketil's laid his *Blood Fox* along Bjorn's inner side. Both Kjartan and Haug adorned his crew, Odin's delight, Sigvalde had such strong men in the south flank, and it should hold well!

Meanwhile the Northmen pushed out from the shore and after brief consideration grouped their ships after Sigvalde's battle orders. They were so many, the vessels lay in several rows, and Hakon's red wave-swine lay in the middle across from Sigvalde. Arnulf looked down into the water. Even naked a man could drown; it was so muscle-numbingly cold and with the weight of the weapons and the iron chainmail the sea would have no mercy! His body shuddered, remembering his last swim fight, and Arnulf again let his gaze sweep over the Norwegian force, seeking *Twin Raven*. To his great regret, the longship sailed towards the north flank, and where Toke sat, he was not able to see before it slipped behind the other vessels.

A massive blue ship with an iron-clad bow took up place in front of Vagn and Bjørn, and a tall fair-haired man with stern features under his helmet seemed to lead the crew. Over his chainmail he wore a red silk kyrtle, and his shield was adorned with a long-horned bull's head. At his ship's side, a snekke was the proud companion of the Northmen and Vagn Ågeson squinted narrowly, considering his opponents thoroughly but laughed aloud soon after, 'Look! There, on the snekke, next to the red warrior's ship. Beware, Svend, we have a dear kinsman against us, Øgmund White, upon my word, praise he must have, he would rather fight than be sick!'

Arnulf saw the handless vassal in the bow, and though his face was ravaged with fever and his posture was weak, his eyes blazed at Vagn's so dearly did the Northman want revenge! The Ågeson sent him a respectful nod, for even though he could taunt his enemies green from bile, when he felt like it; a worthy opponent would apparently be honoured.

Despite how easy it had been for the Jomsvikings, the Northmen were not able to align, and they had to endure many derogatory chants from the Danes. Not all ships were properly cleared, and from need much was thrown into the water, which later would be missed, without foothold there was no victory!

'Look there!'

Svend put a rigid hand on Arnulf's shoulder and pointed to a smaller ship near Hakon's proud red. A few handfuls of warriors, dressed in wolf skins, brandished weapons on the deck, and despite the cries their

328

wolf-like howling could clearly be heard. They wore neither battle-kyrtles nor chainmail, only hides behind the red-painted shields, and they moved wildly, while blood seemed to run from the bare arms.

'Ulfhednir!'

Svend shook his head, 'Keep away from those men, neither weapons nor runes can bite them. Dark power surrounds them, black magic powers, neither coins nor blade could match them. They are invulnerable, if you find one against you, flee! Only the best of us can keep such wild-blood men from life.'

Arnulf stared. It was hard to believe someone so fearless sounded worried.

'They don't even have helmets on!'

'Make no mistake! It is Helheim's force! They cut themselves before battle, go on a wild killing spree and that Hakon has placed them there is no coincidence.'

He looked at Arnulf tight-lipped, 'Veulf! In this conflict you are a wolf. Stay behind us and kill anyone who defies our shield wall, shadow our backs! If you stand at the front, you will swallow a sword before you manage to blink, and I will ...'

'War companions! Hirdmen! Precious sons of Jomsborg! Kinsmen and blood brothers, Einherjar and heirs to Valhalla!'

Vagn stood in the skeid's bow with axe and sword held high over his head. The long hair stroked his shoulders under the helmet's edge, and his eyes burned like coal. His mouth was wild, behind the chainmail black lava cooked, he was a warrior, a warrior in blood, in intention, in limb, a looter of life, the death realm's generous provider! The Jomsvikings turned their heads and were silent for as far as his voice could reach.

'Before my sword sees its sheath again, will the bay here be drained by corpses! Before I lower my axe, will the screams of Norwegian women have frozen the sea to ice all the way to Vigen! My courage can be measured with Odin's! My strength with Thor's! Who here will follow me into battle against earl Hakon and win a greater honour than Jomsborg could ever before boast of?'

A roar made the ships quake waves in the water, and the Vikings pulled out their weapons and shook their shields as Vagn swung his axe, so the skeid's figurehead almost left its life, 'I am so proud to stand before you that my chainmail is about to burst! In Asgard, the warriors beg Valkyries to gather better company, can you not hear Sigurd Fafnerslayers's and Starkad's cries? Will you toast with them with Heidrun's mead before the sun goes down? Together we will rip the heads from the Norwegian goats and use them as knáttleikr balls, who will help me comfort widows and daughters tonight, who will bathe in loot and gold, and who here will help hold earl Hakon until all our force has used him like a woman?'

A new roar rattled shields and weapons against each other, and Arnulf screamed with them, Vagn held the heart's pulse in a single grip.

'You are shining like Surtr's battle-folk! Hakon is already crying from the horror in his piss-wet pants, and he shall have more to weep over! Before the day fades, I will hang him up by the balls, and there he will be allowed to hang until he howls that he will kiss my ass!'

The laughter crashed, and the swords beat rumbles against the shield's surfaces. Vagn's will was an engulfing river, it took everything with it, breaths were drawn with one lung, weapons carried with one hand, Arnulf had faith, was faithful to the death! The Ågeson tossed his head, striking his axe against the earl's ship, 'So beleaguered is Hakon that he has rocked the cradles free for infants, set sail on them and staffed them with dogs! Woe to you who stands at the back, you will only get cold flesh to hit! Kill! Flense! Murder! Slay! Do we feel pain?'

'No!'

'Do we know fatigue?'

'No!'

'Do we know what fear is?'

'No!'

'Who wins the victory?'

'Us!'

'Who are we?'

'Sons of Jomsborg!'

Again, the dark warrior's cries were drowned out by enthusiastic roaring and rumbling, but he quietened them again. Frantically he grew, throwing his shadow completely over Sigvalde's dragon, froth sprayed, and the listeners became obsessed with a madness like a burning disease while the bear-earl's voice resounded all the way to Jötunheimr, 'Fight with me! Bleed with me! Win with me! If I falter, scorn me! If I flee, kill me! If I die, avenge me!'

Arnulf cried tears in his throat. With shame the last remaining fear and hesitation left his chest, Serpenttooth had to dance among its kinsmen, the shield-wolves howled, pulling at each other, woe to the Northmen, woe to earl Hakon, woe to all of Norway!

330

From Vagn to Bue, the Jomswarriors and hirdmen screamed and hollered with the earls' son's temper, ships blazed, and shields rumbled united in a single rhythm while the cries repeated Sigvalde's name.

Arnulf was a scale on the serpent, the fate ruled, Odin rode Sleipner over the soot-dark rolling clouds, and behind him beamed the late sun in the Valkyries' helmets. This was the day for honour and heroism, for bravery's deed and great revenge, Bifrost was open to Valhalla, and murder was the water bearing the fleet, zeal the blood that hammered the arms as rigid as man's spears and madness the breeze that drank sweat from the skin!

The Northmen also appeared to be whipped into action, their jaws howling from their limbs, and Sigvalde saw no reason to wait any longer. With a god-like roar he flung his spear towards earl Hakon and sacrificed the Norwegian fleet to the Æsir Lord, the oars were put into use, and the two forces approached each other, as inevitably as the increasing tide and the closer the Norwegian axes showed their newly-sharpened edges, the louder Arnulf shouted along to drown out the enemy's spouting! He saw everything from the thwart, everything. The countless country's defenders, many of whom had nothing more to place between blows and skin than layers of leather but whose hatred thickened the air, the spiky spears which roofed Hakon's fleet like a hedgehog's back, they squeezed their weapons, which for some were simply nail-tipped clubs, pointed sticks and firewood axes; the unpainted shields, and far behind the Norwegian force, a cow on a hillside shook flies from its neck with its muzzle in the grass. It was so peaceful! When the conflict was over and lineages had fallen, it would still stand there, only the night could disrupt its endless munching and patiently slouching tail.

Vagn commanded bows and slings be prepared, but before the arrows and stones were laid ready, a horn sounded from Hakon's red ship, and the next moment hissing swarms of arrows swirled in high arches over the water. Arnulf raised his shield, ducking behind it. Serpenttooth hissed so strongly that he had completely forgotten the initial skirmish, but Svend laughed when the Norwegian earl blundered, his attack reaching only the water between them and none of the Jomsvikings lifted anything to guard them other than snide laughter.

Embarrassed Arnulf lowered his arm, but soon after the danger was threatening enough and Vagn stretched his sword in the air to give the sign. The arrows were awaited with eerie tension, more cowardly weapons did not exist! Even the finest warriors had to pay with their lives to men who out of luck succeeded with their blind shots, and all toil and

331

ingenuity stood in vain against randomness, against a single toe long iron tip even Bue and Vagn could not do anything!

Both fleets tensed their bows and simultaneously released, and Arnulf curled, shuddering, into a ball of yarn behind the high raised wolf-shield when a hail of iron speckled the skeid like a full beard. It slammed against the shield, an arrow slipped by while another penetrated several hand-lengths through, and the edge was torn up by a tip that ended its fall with a dull clatter against his helmet. The hood mitigated the blow, Vagn shouted again, and Arnulf snapped the intruding arrow, daring a quick glance. The archers were scantily shielded by their companions, but the exposure was dangerous, and it was about getting the arrows in the air before Hakon's men loosened their strings. It sang and hissed, warnings barked, the Northmen had to stay in cover, and even before the bows were lowered, Vagn sent stones over the enemy. That rain was hardly so deadly, but men were beaten unconscious and bones crushed, Sigvalde would be satisfied, and the rowers strained themselves on.

Hakon's second volley flew close, it was difficult to achieve full shielding and the Vikings at the oars were not spared, although many turned with raised shields. The Northmen also shot burning arrows at their guests, but it was easy enough to extinguish incipient loose fires as long as close combat had not begun, and the cleared ships did not seem to be easily flammable. Svend jumped up, throwing his shield to Arnulf while he yelled for protection, for now he would row! Short of breath Arnulf returned Serpenttooth to its sheath and crawled to a free oar, while the soaked hair bristled the helmet from the scalp in sheer fear of arrows in the back, and only at the last minute did he manage to get both shields lifted before the ships were made to a drum-skin and chastened by the Northmen's anger.

'It is a dry rain falling from the fjelds, it does not give many crops!'

Svend's face shone with excitement as he helped a wounded rower aside and pulled the oar as if he alone would ram Hakon earl's fleet. Stones splintered the skeid, damaging the thin planks, and surprisingly powerful flint hammered the highest shield against his shoulder. Arnulf turned it a little to protect them both, and Svend managed some strokes between the forces' exchanges of shots, so swarms of arrows rattled against each other over the water, falling ill-timed and missing their target, and now Vagn shouted for heavier weapons, the buggers would get spears; flea bites alone would not fell them!

The Bueson looked back, sweat pouring into his eyes, and Arnulf suddenly remembered the two seas that broke the bow on Denmark's northern tip. Soon, very soon, the warring parties would run stakes through each other's lives, then the currents would break necks, and water and blood would mix with salt! Behind the shields, along the shield rim, short javelins were held ready, grips secured and weight proportioned, while archers scattered, sustaining their shooting, as long as there were still arrows to find on the deck. Death, death and darkness, was a fiery heart ever truly prepared to give up its life for another man's cause? Why were they here, the Danes and the Norwegians, when until recently they had shared a king in brotherhood?

Despite the danger, Sigvalde stood far ahead in the dragon, and on the outside of the north flank Bue the Stout's voice persistently poured splendid spite and curses on their opponents that Svend Silkenhair had to chuckle, shaking his head under the shields. The sweat dripped off Arnulf, and his mouth was as dry as cracked wood. Whoever hesitated, died first. Whoever lost overview, was killed. The enemy, their sight bound, was not dangerous. Blows would not necessarily kill. Agile shield wielding, light foot changes, do not look the enemy in the eye, never cross your legs. The first block was the sword's, the next the shield's and lastly his body dodged. It was so easy to remember it all on the banner ground's evenness, but now sense was failing, the limbs were heavy and stiff and soft, while fear sneaked around the body like a black wolverine hunting for sudden vulnerability. Fenrir! With Fenrir at his back he need not tremble, the wolf should have blood, saturated from Norwegian victims, and just with that thought the jötunn animal's ears pointed.

Vagn let the heavy weaponry go, and it was not weaklings who cast them, only the strongest arms let go of spears, and they made nice holes in Hakon's heap of men! Both on the red warrior's iron whale and on Øgmund the White's snekke people tumbled over the deck and shield rims and those ships lying behind drove forward from their need for revenge while the answer immediately rushed the other way, and if the arrows had caused reasonable damage, the spearheads stack much deeper. The sound was obscure, the sight tremble-inducing and the arms stiffened in spite, the nips of Helheim would not stop Svend's oar strokes! From the snekke, Øgmund slung weight into his shaft, Åse's redress, and how he knew that the bearer of the wolf-shield had been the first to defile only Freyr could answer, the spear caused Arnulf to tumble back over a thwart into the Bueson's shoulder, its point broken by the shield, deadeningly, releasing a sharp pain in his upper arm.

A short scream escaped his throat, so his jaws bit furiously together, the weight of the shaft pulled the point out of the flesh when the shield tipped, and by Odin's eye was it time to whine! Blood kisses were a warrior's ornament, Arnulf was up immediately with the Jomsman's support and his arm obeyed, it was no worse! Svend's gaze blazed watchfully, but Arnulf snorted, still wielding the shield in both hands, so the Bueson collected himself to follow his row-companions' oar-pulls and the next bunch of spears struck elsewhere.

The pierced shield was heavy, so Arnulf supported its edge by slanting it against the nearest thwart, to pull out the spear could cause life-threaten exposure. Despite the noise and the cries, the blood rushed in his ears, and through the wound his blood was poisoned with a bestial anger, fear gave way, the pain pulled together, now he knew why Ulfhednir cut themselves before battle! Fenrir's pulse pounded in his temples but Jomsborg's warrior-will kept madness in an ice-grip, he, who acted in anger during combat, drove the blade in his chest himself!

Vagn's men began to rise, rallying along the shield rim at the foreship, those in front with scale-laid shields, throwing hooks and free sword, and behind them the long spears and broad axes were held ready. Closely, the Northmen rowed forward, so close that the oars struck each other now and then when the current pulled awry and the iron whale and vassal's snekke seemed each lay their long side against the skeid's shield rim to squeeze the tallow of Vagn's crew. Bjørn the Bretlander gave the sign from *the Black Snekke* to attack the blue iron whale from the opposite side and Little Ketil yelled cheerfully from his *Blood Fox* while Haug and Kjartan clinked axes in their hunger for wounding. Although arrows and spears still flew scattered through the air, both fleets seemed to be making ready for close combat; threats, howls and weapon-roars thundered across the bay like never before, and Sigvalde shouted his last orders, foaming at the mouth. Immense was the strength of the gathered warriors! The water level rose up the fjelds with a crushing pressure, never had greater whales romped along the Norwegian coast, never had such sharp keels clefted the archipelago to strips!

The square on the deck was cramped and the thwarts were treacherous to fight over, much allowance for movement was not made, but the men apparently knew to keep together without clumping. Svend wanted to go to Vagn and let go of his oar. He snatched a stray shield and spear, nodding encouragingly to Arnulf, then in a few leaps he was among the warriors waiting at the bow and stood with one foot on each thwart to be part of the game over his companions' heads. Arnulf groaned. He was embroiled in a din and if the straps had not been fastened, the helmet would have washed into the neck from sweat. He threw away the broken shield, drew his sword, waiting on trembling knees behind the shield wall. The last armful of sea water retreated between the forces, while Bjørn howled to Bue's son that he was offering his neck to the enemy and should step down immediately, but Svend stood, and roars and screams put icicles on the ear-piercing noise of weapons, now, now, now! Now the fight against earl Hakon began in earnest!

The oars were pulled in, the drifting continued, and like two ravines, the forces crashed together, planks gave, shield edges burst, oars broke, ships glided in between each other, men stumbled, opponents were selected, splinters flew from the woodwork, dragon heads nipped and cries were replaced by hammering and crackling, as if a thousand smiths had come together at once, while shield rim sought shield rim in mutual encirclement!

The blue iron whale laid its side against the skeid, and in the shadow of their shields, the vessels combined their fate with rope-tethered hooks that were quickly lashed to the thwarts. Fiercely and furiously the battle was initiated and all the zeal and contempt Vagn had ignited, unleashed crushing blows. The Vikings were experienced; experienced and without thought for their own lives, every day they had trained and known each other, and no one placed themselves randomly, but the red warrior's folk set hard against hard, they appeared to be housecarls, hardened and feisty, the Ågeson would not have an easy harvest!

Øgmund White had less luck with his snekke, which was accidentally pushed aside by another Norwegian ship, and the skeid turned so Vagn's raised crew blocked the view of the fleets. Arnulf's gaze was on a lightning voyage, bursting and ready for the extreme, and he stared open-mouthed at the working chainmailed-shoulders in front of him, the undulating shield edges and the pumping elbows sticking points between the protection while broad axes swept over the shoulders of those in front. Wolf, he was a wolf and had to stay where he stood, and, he could not discern a single face, the conflict did not seem to be human, although the screams no longer testified to degrading soiling but to pain and the loss of life. Arnulf shuffled back and forth along the laid-down mast. Daft! The skeid had to be turned! War yelps and Valkyrie voyage and he could see nothing but the Jomsvikings legion-clothed backs, the weapons raised slightly, the pitching arms, but what happened, what happened over the shield rim, he knew it well from the banner ground. Wolf? Who could penetrate Vagn's shield wall, men died, the Gjallarhorn commanded, should he stand here, staring, just because Svend would

335

spare his inexperienced hirdman? Not a single ship was behind him, neither arrows nor stones threatened the vulnerable Jomsbacks and did Helge not stand at Asgard's wall, grinding his teeth in shame?

Arnulf stuck Serpenttooth in its sheath, threw away his shield and found a bow. Arrows still lay there, he pulled several from the woodwork and fasten them to his belt and if Svend could find foothold on the narrow thwarts, then Arnulf could too! He came up amidships, finally getting an overview, and for a moment his hands forgot their knowledge of the bow use. The two long fleet ranks were completely broken up, vessels were hopelessly jammed, intertwined and oar-less, subject to the current's whims, but there where the long sides were bound with rope, the fighting waved with a cruel ferocity and violence over the shield rim and the deck, men were toppled overboard to drown, horns and incomprehensible cries sounded, and rammed ships sank, while fires broke out in ropes and rolled sails. On the north flank, Bue and Sigurd held the ships together diligently as many rallied around them, but the Northmen's small vessels were easier and quicker to steer than the Danes' large longships. They still had arrows and Jomsvikings and hirdmen were surrounded by packs of barking fjeld dogs who tried to stick together and separate the selected crews.

Arnulf had to dodge a javelin and his forefoot nearly slipped on the smooth thwart. Sigvalde and Torkel the Tall had bound their ships together, and there was some order where the fleet still held the row, but Hakon's red ship lay just opposite, closely flanked by his most robust vessels and the Ulfhednirs' humble boat began to spew its insane howling brood around the earl.

Svend Silkenhair's laughter sounded shrill near Arnulf, and in front of his companions cleaving position were the faces of the enemy, and what faces! Contorted and revenge-driven with wide open mouths, the Northmen fought for kingdom and lineage, fiercely and devoted, spear slew shield, axe helmet, sword fire burned, and behind them stood the red warrior in all his implacable rigour, goading his countrymen on, the northern folk were paying dearly for Sigvalde's mead promise!

Resolutely, Arnulf nocked an arrow. It was mad to stand here, but no more than that Svend was also standing up in the crowd! The Bueson thrust with the spear, so the tip dripped, and he could reach far, the opponents found it difficult to defend from both above and below, and Arnulf took aim for the red warrior, it was an easy shot! His firing arm smarted but the leader of the force saw the threat, the shield managed to catch the arrow and in the next moment a handful of Norwegians were ready to shoot Arnulf and Svend down. The Silkenhaired stepped on the deck, and Arnulf became lonely on the thwarts and followed as the skeid leisurely pulled askew, revealing the struggle of the nearest vessels. Vagn's men were busy, and the arrows should not remain useless in his belt, and although the ground rocked, it was possible to pick Northmen off the other ships without hitting his own.

Arnulf shot. The arrows firmly reached their target, Helge had never considered his brother to be a bad archer. Deer, fox and hare, all animals near the village except the wolves knew his shots, should man then not also fear them? Dream-like killing from a distance! The screams did not make it out, no jolt went through the hand-curved blade, no blood-splattered guilt and honour on the arm; it seemed unreal when men fell, had he hit them at all, or had they dropped from wounds he didn't see? How effortless! Life gave up easier than lint from a stalk, why torment himself, who here deserved to survival anyway?

Arnulf had to step back to make room when fighting along the shield rim became difficult because of the fallen bodies. The formation opened up in glimpses and Arnulf saw, between his shot, the skirmish of those warriors in front. Blood. Guts. Severed arms. Crushed heads. Broken legs. He stared, glazed, and saw nothing, the earl's yard and the fight with Toke had only cost a scratch, child's knee, man's work was not worth admiring, now could Fenrir be expected, and last of all the day had to die!

Since those killed could not be dragged out of the way, many chose to step on the dead, although a treacherous foothold in the open flesh could result in a fateful tripping. On *the Black Snekke*, Bjørn shouted blood-cold to his men to hold together, and Ketil prevailed over *the Blood Fox's* fallen, making himself so low and bashful that the axe sneaked easily into a vulnerable, corpse-raised leg. Kjartan and Haug worked like a four-armed monster, beating rifts in the opposing ranks, but on the ships lying behind, the Norwegians were immediately ready to re-form their shield wall again, the Jomssons' efforts seemed to be in vain.

Arnulf felt his own growling, his lungs were halved, breathing so shallowly he had to gasp. Arrows, where were there more, odd that they hid in the emptiness, those he wrestled free from the planks were now damaged and rendered useless! Svend stood by Vagn under the skeid's head. All the combat training, the kinsmen had shared, obviously benefitted them: every step, every movement, every breath they knew of each other, the enemy was pushed without words, rider and horse, helmsman and ship, loving couples, nothing shared a deeper understanding than the two blood-companions' combined attack. Hakon's men shied away from the iron whale's shield rim, falling over their own dead, many of Vagn's Vikings went with them, and the fighting was pushed onto the red warrior's deck.

The battle called! Red mist rolled from the fjelds, and Arnulf threw away the bow, found a shield and pulled his sword. Violence was lord of the bay, warriors fell to Valhalla, skald verses dawned, men born and heroes burned to eternal fame! Both shield and sword hilt were wet, and his hair dripped. He tried to get over the ship's side, but too many still stood in the way on the enemy's deck, he could not squeeze through, and over the noise of weapons and shield-hammering urged the red warrior's sharp cry!

The Jomsvikings opened up unexpectedly, yielding as instructed, and a Boar's Snout of Norwegians penetrated over the shield rim, led by a scale-clad ox with a bloody sax. Vagn's companions fell on them from all sides, but the leader escaped, heading directly for Arnulf with rolling eyes and driving wounds. Those who hesitated! Arnulf narrowly escaped, and the sax burst behind him the thwart, Serpenttooth hissed along the cut blade with its next blow, slid along the arm and sought the armpit, but by Fenrir! The Northman had a knife in the other hand, where the shield had been before and Arnulf's back leg rammed the next thwart. The blade met Arnulf's nose, grating the helmet, then the Northman beat out with both arms, dropping his weapon, just as abruptly as he had come, he crashed and bumped his shoulder into Arnulf; dead, a broad axe silently planted in his back.

Arnulf staggered and fell, hurt his lower back on a thwart, lost the shield and rolled, groaning, with the sword in front of him. The blood ran down his throat, so he nearly choked, his head had to come up and his nostrils felt torn to the root, the way it flowed over his mouth. He snorted and stood up precariously on his legs. Out of the corner of his eye a misty shadow slid forward along the skeid's free aft shield rim and hooked firm, and Arnulf shook his head, leaning on Serpenttooth. His wound was aching. Øgmund! It was Øgmund the White's snekke, finally had the vassal gained mastery over his ship and rowed it into position, just as Ågeson's crew was divided over both skeid and iron whale.

Arnulf screamed a warning, fumbling for his shield. His cries were heard and the Jomsvikings called to Vagn that the force had to be held together. Although Øgmund's men were quick, Sigvalde's were quicker, and the intruders did not manage to set foot on the foreign vessels before the skeid was defended along the full length of the shield rim. Arnulf was pushed forward, no one was a wolf any longer, and Svend came rushing with a blow-marked spear in his hands. He stood behind Arnulf and the shield with a menacing grin, bloody as Sæhrímnir itself, and the planks shielded well his lower legs, but Nidhogg's rotten breath stood just opposite!

It felt like pushing against a hurricane on the shield when the enemy's spear came against it, and Serpenttooth forced the shaft aside without the slightest possibility of attack. If just one of the offensive spikes went to the side, Trud would lose her last son, and how to control the fight or break the enemy's rhythm, how to survive longer than a single gasp, so many spears pushed him backwards, tearing holes in the chainmail? The shield shrank, the chainmail seemed to become thinner, naked stood Arnulf against the blade wall, but Svend's support from behind instilled courage! The Bueson's spear ripped shield edges and pierced holes in bellies, the shaft beat knees aside, bared buttocks for shock and sneaked towards fatal wounds, but the battle came too close, and while Svend shortened the shaft, he lost the point and had to, without protection, resort to Snap beside Arnulf with a long knife in the other hand. Serpenttooth blocked blows and striked back, the shield held and Arnulf struck lightning against the nearest while he tried to keep his overview and perceptiveness. His face lowered, horse vision, movements in the corners of his eyes were the most dangerous! He got a broad axe behind him, which encountered kept the Northmen at bay, and in fear of death his arm followed the blocks and cuts, Svend had knocked into it, but the anxiety killed, in a moment he would be able to see his own rank from above when the Valkyries grabbed him by hair! Fenrir's rage and wolf-blood, he had come so far, he would live yet!

It stabbed against the helmet and rasped along the armour, and Svend swapped blows with a strong-limbed northern warrior, making him stumble forward over the edge of the shield rim where Serpenttooth met his neck, so Arnulf hissed his life in his grip. The slain's axe flew backwards, and Svend pulled another of Hakon's men in front of his companions' weapons, where he gave up breath, hit by his own earl.

It was so close now that the knives came into use, space was limited, shoulders rubbed against each other, and Arnulf hammered his sword hilt into the near foreheads. A blade tip slid paralysingly from wrist to elbow, so the leather-laces burst, and Serpenttooth trembled in stiff fingers, but by Helge's reputation if the sword should let go because of that, with a furious scream Arnulf jutted the shield's edge into his attacker's chin. Sneering, he stuck out his tongue against the teeth-chattering enemy, and when the Northman goaded, pressing forward, Snap separated him from anger with a bite to the neck.

Suddenly it darkened around the helmet, and an abrupt weakness took his legs out from under him. The axe continued to fall, striking his shoulder, and for the second time Arnulf reeled over backwards but had the sense to keep the shield over himself. He bumped his elbow in a mass of slimy intestines on the deck, sliding so his cheek rubbed against the fallen, while the shield covered the thwarts, and the skeid was seized by a whirlpool. The din of the battle drowned in masses of milling water, the sky was dark, and the sword lay across his chest as his hand sought the help of the nearest thwart. Blood and sweat, his stomach writhed, he paused only a moment, perhaps, then Arnulf gritted his teeth and fought to sit up, as giddy as a drunkard.

Svend was gone, and the entire aftship cleared, the fight was on Øgmund's snekke and a brief moment of peace allowed Arnulf time to get to his feet. It knocked horribly under the helm, and powerless he picked up Serpenttooth, but then strength flowed through him again, Odin had regretted his choice! His sword arm was bleeding, his body light and distant under the heavy armour, and his wounds painless; strange as if his pulse beat each and every feeling aside, maybe he was already dead?

On the Norwegian vessel, Hakon's folk fell in the water, and the bodies did not float for long, only the shields called to the sky riders where their bearers had gone down. Vagn had returned to the skeid's bow, holding an indomitable front, and on Bjørn's and Ketil's ships the amount of deaths was almost doubled. The wounded tried, wailing, to drag themselves out of danger, but no one thought it too tactless to stab them in the back, so many fought in vain. Scattered arrows and stones struck, cracking like at a feast and undamaged javelins were thrown in all directions by freestanding men: the air was dangerous, the water dangerous; life had no rights at Death's Thing, and even those who spoke best for themselves were sentenced penalties.

Arnulf smeared nose blood over his face. Shit! His nostrils felt quite loose, should he now run around as another Leif Cleftnose, scaring the life out of thrall-young?

On the snekke, Øgmund settled his score with Svend and his beleaguered companions gave them space. They stood in the aft, but *the White* could not do much more, he was so weakened, and it was not Northmen who weighed heavily on his ship. Arnulf yanked up the shield and climbed over the shieldwall to assist the Bueson but Snap had no time to wait. Svend swung the axe in the vassal's collarbone, and Åse lost man and honour without the slightest redress, the Jomsvikings did not know honour-prices. When Arnulf reached the Bueson, the snekke was almost cleared of vermin and Svend lighted up, laughing at the reunion. Pale cold ice sparkled from the sweaty gaze, the killer was ruthless, but he stared, over-excited, at Arnulf and bent abruptly above the fallen Øgmund. Everything he touched was soiled with blood, but he took a hold of it anyway, cutting a chunk off the nose of the vassal with the axe blade.

'Here! You look like you need a prettier muzzle! If it does not fit, I will gladly get you another.'

Svend handed the dripping nose over, bursting into a mad, wild laughter, threw it away again and slapped his red-smeared hand in Arnulf's shoulder, 'Veulf, you skrælling, I told you to stay behind me, I thought you were dead! Well fought!'

Arnulf grimaced, thrusting him away with a snort, but their fists met superficially and Svend fixed his helmet strap and sought his dropped shield. On the skeid, the battle against the iron whale was still unsettled, but unexpectedly the red warrior suddenly gave the word to retreat, and Arnulf saw the man, who from Hakon's red ship was diligently waving a banner and pointing the strict Northman down to the opposite flank. Ropes were cut, the hooks fell on the deck, and although the Jomsvikings were not inclined to let the enemy escape, the fjeld warriors set the oars hard in the water, abandoning the battle at the earl's command.

'What is happening?'

Arnulf squinted narrowly, trying to see over the battle ships' turmoils.

'It is my father. He is flaying the pelts from them on the north flank and the red force leader had to stand near the earl, as it was him who is going to turn the tide.'

Bue the Stout and Sigurd were surrounded by empty Norwegian boats, and the Jomsvikings seemed to have taken over the nearby ships. Svend set foot on the shield rim to jump back on the skeid but hesitated for a moment, coughing hollowly, and Arnulf lay his hand on the Silkenhaired's side, 'Are you wounded?'

The chainmail had holes in several places, and the battle-kyrtle could cover much. Svend spat, jumping onto his own deck, his footing not uncertain.

'Of course I am wounded, come on!'

Vagn shouted from the bow with a wave. Beside the skeid were both *the Black Snekke* and *Blood Fox,* being encircled by hot-headed peasants and the Ågeson roared to Bjørn that he should shake off the horseflies and bind the stem to Ketil's ship so they could form a cat snout. The iron whale was busy along the fleet, and in the middle of the bay the fighting was apparently equally between Sigvalde and earl Hakon. The ships lying between them lay sideways against each other in fierce combat and in many places, there was no room for oar strokes so throwing hooks were used extensively. If the mountain-jötnar did not come to the northern people's aid, it seemed that Norway would again be under the Danes' yoke, the Jomsmen's equipment was significantly better, and in the long run they should be able to endure most.

Arnulf followed Svend, who nudged Vagn with Snap over his shoulder.

'What is a cat snout?'

'Veulf, we are not on the banner ground! Gawp and ask afterwards.'

Svend pulled a spear out of a Jomsman, which had pinned him to the deck through his arm, and the Viking got up deathly pale at his help and asked for a strip of linen. Vagn shouted the men to the oars hoarsely before the next attack, and the crew divided themselves between thwarts and spears to keep the Northmen from life until the skeid was in place. The dark warrior stood like an oak, unswaying, invincible, if the sap was pouring from the grooves of the bark, he did not feel it, the fiery will bolstered the body's strength despite the blood loss!

Little Ketil threw the rope to one of Bjørn's men and their ship bows were attached to each other's heads while the skeid sought to grip *the Blood Fox's* aft. For a short while the three vessels lay like waddling geese, then the rowers forced *the Black Snekke's* and the skeid's free ends together so that the ships formed a solid triangle and Arnulf had to smile briefly from admiration. The Norwegians were so many, the Jomsvikings did not need to be able to move, they would be attacked, but now only one side of the ship lay clear for the enemy, and he who fired arrows against the cat's snout, risked hitting his own.

'Now, we hold position and kill and push the dead to the sea floor, so Hakon does not realise how greedily we eat here!'

Svend smiled harshly and would have said more but was silent for several of the enemy-filled ships seemed to have learned the rules of the game and were rowing briskly to catch up, and although it was difficult to control the vessels, as their will intended, more of them managed to lay diagonally into the Jomsvikings so as many ships as possible formed a bridge to the triangular shieldfort. Vagn's men formed rank along the shieldwall again, and Arnulf wolfed behind them and now large stuffed woolsacks were being set on fire on the Norwegian ships and thrown against the fighting warriors.

Arnulf leaped aside with a yell. The flames reached out for the planks, threatening to take hold of the life of the skeid, and he quickly stuck Serpenttooth back in its sheath, swapped his shield for a spear and impaled the nearest sack over the shield rim, before the planks caught fire. Several bags began to burn behind the ship-companions and Arnulf worked quickly with no thought of the fight, if the deck caught, the men would be trapped between flames and weapons, but when the enemy discovered how few results their efforts yielded, they soon ceased throwing.

Vagn's worn bear-roar scattered down-heartedness among his enemies, and the pumping blood flows made the deck slimy to stand on, the fjord folk fell and were shoved overboard in front of the Jomsvikings, but although the loss was odd, the Ågeson lost men. Arnulf held tightly to the spear and stood as part of the third row behind Svend. It was not easy to get to, but the shaft could be pried between those fighting from above and the tip find flesh with well-chosen jabs. The noise penetrated the bones: shock, blow, cut, crash, his arms quivered with the warmth of the blood.

The Bueson suddenly faltered back, sinking breathlessly down on a thwart with Snap supported against the planks, his gaze penetrating. The tip of a light hand-axe had taken hold in his shoulder blade, and Arnulf threw the spear down and grabbed the handle to wrestle it free. It was disgusting, and the first jolt did not release it, but Svend did not make a sound, only hugged Snap. The blood was soaked up by the thick battle-kyrtle and Svend, with an iron-will, wanted to get up again immediately, so Arnulf threw the axe away, pulling him up on his feet without a word. Toke would have screamed, Toke would be paled and lost his strength, but the Bueson sniffed fiercely, retrieving a dropped shield for new protection.

'Let me stand at the front! Just a moment.'

Svend wrested a smile loose, shaking his head, 'The goat maggots are losing their breath, if only Vagn can hold a little longer, then ... they are hitting him too hard.'

He frowned and raised his arm tentatively, ready to re-enter between his comrades and help Ågeson. The Northmen's shield wall was now surrounded by Jomsvikings and hirdmen who moved their ships into the siege and attacked from behind. New men could not come into the cat's snout as it was, and the enemy was obviously aware of Sigvalde's loss if Vagn fell so Svend pushed his way to his kinsman's side, and Arnulf tried mightily to help them with his spear. Again and again, the dark warrior roared his attacks towards the north flank over piles of corpses and his companions borrowed his courage and fought with their flank leader in blind faith. So many others could rule Jomsborg, Vagn was a warrior now; Arnulf understood the Bueson's words! As the Stout lit and held the north flank, Vagn was Sigvalde's south beacon, and as long as those two men stood fast, the Jomschieftain could concentrate on facing Hakon.

More ships came, and in a churning maelstrom the cat's snout was selected as the eye of the battle. The Northmen were pushed from both sides, Jomswarriors broke through, cleared the ship of men and joined Little Ketil and Bjørn, while the dead-filled vessels rocked laden with bodies and masterless, getting in the way of the living. The capable swordsmen gathered where the fighting was fiercest, and on both sides, they stumbled over the increasing number of fatalities.

Arnulf struck out until his arms trembled, weak from their wounds, but he kept going, and the men in front of him provided better protection against the enemy's spears than any shield. Then the smell of smoke reached him, and the cries from *Blood Fox* changed tone. The large longship was on fire, no one had managed to extinguish the fire in time, and now the flames were running along the deck, consuming thwarts and mast fish, the ship had to be vacated, and as a matter of urgency!

The Jomsvikings gathered on *the Black Snekke* and the skeid and *the Blood Fox* had to be cut free so the fire would not spread to the other vessels. Ketil wept, as he, as the last man, jumped from the ship and cut the ropes, he had been prepared for losing companions, but the ship had been his own. Vagn called every man over onto the skeid, as the binding with *the Black Snekke* had to be abandoned, the cat's nose split, and the Northmen tried to push the flaming longship into the side of Vagn's crew with their bows as they threw water over their own vessels. Spear and oars were used for protection, but it was not effective and it was Little Ketil himself who, held in Kjartan's iron fists, leaned forward, despite the fire, and cut a hole in the planks just under the water level.

Lopsided, *the Blood Fox* took in water and the Northmen abandoned their venture and any further attempts to put order on the battle failed. Arnulf was joined by Bjørn the Bretlander and Kjartan relieved Vagn of his efforts; now, for a while, there was enough manpower, and the hardest tried to breathe for a moment.

The Jomsvikings lay close to the Ågeson's ship, and fatigue began to reach the watchful eyes of the fjeld folk. Bjørn was drenched in blood, but given the way he moved, it was hardly his own, and Arnulf suspected the enemy did not want to cut an old man's body. A certain weakening gripped the formations and the Norwegian vessels pulled back a little, but

344

just as Arnulf started thinking about a drink of water, a violent shock went through the skeid. The iron whale had returned!

The sharpened bow had rammed the rudder in two, the shield rim was ruptured, but the planks held, and the red warrior shouted to Vagn from the stern while he shook his sword. Gone were the beginnings of exhaustion, a gust of wind seemed to go through the Jomsvikings, and the dark warrior took up the challenge with raised arms, 'Aslak! Aslak the Bald!'

His voice was now so torn, ripped, that he screamed like a raven, and a mighty helmetless, bald Jomsman who had stood near Bjørn the Bretlander on the black snekke, answered his call.

'Aslak! Would you like to shovel shit out of a pigsty?'

The bald giant laughed, beating his sword hilt on his chainmail rings, 'Well I would to, Vagn Ågeson, but do not be sure that you can eat more pork than I!'

'So come! Svend! Free the skeid and come along the iron whale's side, so the dead hogs do not get wet when they roll overboard.'

Vagn threw his shield away and grabbed a broad axe with both hands and with a few leaps he was in the blue ship's bow, and Aslak the Bald was no less agile, so they began their strikes simultaneously. Now the nearest skirmishes ceased, for wilder men had barely before caused the northern kingdom injury, and neither the Danes nor the fjord people would miss the sight of the heroes' last fight. Arnulf overheard Svend's call for setting the oars and went right up to the ship's side. Why was Vagn doing this? Was he mortally injured and wanted to die with honour, or was he just mad with pain and the lunacy of battle-bile?

The red warrior roused his men to go against the invaders, but the Jomsvikings cleaved forward along their thwarts with weighty blows and did not let anyone come near. Vagn swung so forcefully, starting the movement at the low heels so the axe split both wood and iron, while Aslak's sword swept housecarls down like swaying rye. They looked like Berserkers at work, but behind all the Ågeson's fury, his overview was clear; Svend knew his kinsman well! The longer the Jomswarriors fought, the clearer it was that fear was tearing through the enemy, and the red warrior raged to his carls if it was possible for two men to beat down the crew, who themselves had just broken the resistance of the Bue Veseteson himself! Svend looked, troubled, towards the north flank, but Arnulf did not care in the least about the Stout, only Odin could help the earlsons now!

Aslak was hit over the crown again and again, but his skull had to have been made of a shieldboss, like a jötunn he rushed forward and Vagn slashed his way to both sides without the slightest hesitation. He kept the distance even, so no short blade could reach him, and as long as his strikes kept their whirling rhythm, his opponents had to bite the planks from his strength.

The Jomsmen on the surrounding boats began to whoop and shout like at a knáttleikr match and the skeid turned towards the iron whale's shield rim but seemed to attack. As the weapons did not appear to bite the Bald's forehead, the ship's anvil behind the mast fish was loosened, and a powerful jötunn lifted it over his head and flung it towards the Ågeson's battle companion. Arnulf forgot to breathe as the iron lump flew through the air, and Vagn shouted a warning, but Aslak did not move in time and received the tip of the anvil in the crown of his head, falling sharply as the Northman boomed in triumph. At the same time, a man jumped towards Vagn with a club, hitting him in the helmet, and the Ågeson staggered towards him, thrusting with the axe, and so as not to fall onto the enemy's vessel, he jumped over the shield rim, where he landed, standing on the skeid's deck.

Arnulf took a step towards his blood-brother, the dark warrior needed help, and he could easily be mortally wounded, but Bjørn pushed him aside to come forward. The cheers were deafening, and while the iron whale's crew, hungry for revenge, chopped Aslak's corpse to sausage meat, Vagn sank down on a thwart, groaning, blood streaming down his face. He groped Kjartan's leg for support and the Bretlander pulled the helmet off him while Svend ordered the skeid come from the iron whale in a hurry. Both armies had apparently been beaten enough for now, and without further fighting, Norwegians and Danes rowed their vessels from one another to lie in a row and catch their breath.

Arnulf sat, breathless, and bowed his head, as the shield and sword slipped away from him. The chainmail was as heavy as soft rock, and the helmet slammed against the deck when the strap was loosened. He clasped the thwart, hearing only his own gasping breath, while his body began to shake from weakness and temporary relief and the wounds in his arms began to ache and compete with the nasal tear. It hurt, a snarling pain, but as long as the danger was still lurking, then the stabs and cuts would have to fend for themselves. The tumult continued behind the closed eyelids, and the thirst burned while the body screamed to be free of iron and leather, baked through as it was by the heat of the late sun. He raised his head slowly. Gazing out over the legion and the bay, searching for fjeld grass, the drowned warriors had lost their lives, but they dwelled in coolness! Everything seemed loathsome, unimaginably disgusting and loathsome; he was alive, but his chest was pierced, and the heart that loved Frejdis lost.

The cow was still munching on its slope, and the gulls screamed food to their young on a stone-wide rock in the middle of the bay, so little did the creature care about the fall of men.

'Are you badly hit?'

Little Ketil stood over him, his soaked sleeve pressed against a cheek tear, his eyes red from smoke and the loss of his ship. Arnulf shook his head, wiping his bleeding nose.

'Then help me with the others. Take the linen strips from the chest over there and wind them around the most bleeding wounds as hard as you can. It is not certain if Hakon will give us a long time to stem the blood loss, the battle can begin again at any moment.'

Arnulf nodded, accepting the outstretched hand, 'What about Vagn? Will he make it?'

Little Ketil laughed dully, pulling him up as he let go of his cheek, 'The man who can kill Vagn Ågeson is not yet born. He probably got a decent bump, but he is not known to be a milksop.'

His legs trembled defiantly, Arnulf stood up, stiffly, picked up Serpenttooth and studied the blunt-cut blade. A sax would have held up better with its wide, flat backside, but where sword-bitten men and weapons were, the battle would soon start again. Ketil stood with Kjartan bent over Haug, who had lost a hand and had an arrow through his shoulder, and although the Bornholmer did not cry when his companions pulled it out, he coughed up blood as if he were choking. Bjørn bound Vagn, and although Svend could also do with care, he pushed the dead Vikings overboard with a curly-bearded Jomsviking to prepare for renewed fighting. Severed limbs and spilled guts went the same way, and Arnulf had to sit down, dizzy and queasy like a frightened girl but then he bit his teeth and looked for the chest with the linen strips.

The most injured men were wrapped roughly unless they were dying, and water bags were pulled from under the loose deck planks. Haug endured, sitting with his back against the shield rim, trying to breathe without gulping blood and Kjartan sat with him and tried to stop the flow from his arm, while the Bueson cut cloth from a fallen man's kyrtle and stuffed it under his battle-kyrtle to soak his shoulder.

On the ships around the skeid, each crew was attending to their own, and the depopulated vessels sought each other to gather enough

347

manpower. The smell was sickly-sweet and the heat excruciating, so many men pulled off their clothes to keep it out, but when Arnulf had drunk and wanted to ease the weight of the body, Svend grabbed hold of his arm with a grim shake of the head, 'No, Veulf, do not remove your iron skin, you may sweat now, but the sun is low, and it is drawing in from the sea, remember, we are in Norway! It gets cold, and without armour you are too easy for weapons.'

He pointed to the west, where low ashen clouds rumbled against the blue sky and an insignificant puff of wind mumbled tantalisingly of a change of weather. Arnulf hid his disappointment, snorting his clogged nose free of blood. There were possibly no limits to what the Jomsvikings could endure, but he himself would soon boil unconscious in the battle-kyrtle if he did not get to cool off! He found a lost cloak, dipped it over the shield rim and wrung water over himself, but the salty sea sweat smarted so much on his nose that the body got no joy out of it.

The Norwegians had withdrawn to a good distance, and earl Hakon and his closest seemed to have left their people entirely for a while. The blue iron whale had disappeared, and *Twin Raven* remained so far away that it would be impossible for Toke to recognise him. On the north flank, Bue loomed on his ship alongside Sigurd, so both brothers were still alive, and Sigvalde and Torkel the Tall also seemed to be on their feet, despite that with his bold stand and red hair Ørvad Bullsax could well be confused with the Jomschieftain at this distance.

Vagn was standing again and putting his helmet on, and his expression did not reveal how deep the wounds were in his flesh. He spoke quietly with Haug, who between coughs could still find a twisted smile, and then called Bjørn and Svend over to the mast fish with a glance over the bay. Shouts and waves came from Sigvalde's dragon, while Arnulf headed for his blood companion, and the cry rang from ship to ship for the skeid to be rowed to the middle, Jomsborg's leader had words for Vagn Ågeson. The dark warrior commanded the oars be laid out, and the Vikings who still had strength, slowly pulled the heavy vessel forward alongside the many ships that were gradually being lined up again. Some of the oars had been lost and without a rudder, the remaining had to be used with care, but the Vikings knew their ship. Every time the skeid glided past a vessel, Vagn was greeted and he returned the cheers, and the fatigue relieved; such a strong vision inspired new courage in his companions.

Little Ketil and Kjartan also sought out midship, and despite exhaustion and disgust, pride touched Arnulf, so the armour could be worn, and he confidently dried blood on the back of his hand. Such strong fighters, such undaunted courage! It was possible Hakon still had many men with him, but against Jomsborg's force none could prevail, earl or not, Vagn would fulfil his promises even before the threatening clouds had fully gathered over the bay, and with him the other earl sons, King Sweyn could calmly lift his mug in Denmark.

Sigvalde waited at the shield rim and thanked Vagn for his efforts as the skeid came up alongside the dragon. The broad-shouldered, pale warrior seemed unharmed, but too many of his men sat injured on the thwarts, and bodies lay close to the nearest vessels. Shield rims and woodwork were marked by blows and the decks were slimy from blood, the fight must have been terrible here, the bodies of men lay on the decks like trees felled by winter storms.

'You held the south flank well, despite having Erik Hakonson in front of you, Bue could not stand against him, but I think it is about to be aligned over there.'

Sigvalde looked north, where the Stout shouted, pointing his vessel into place, although the current and increasing winds had a hold of the ships.

'Erik Hakonson? Is that the red-kyrtled man on the iron whale?'

Vagn dried drops of blood off his forehead and waved to Bue and Sigurd. Sigvalde nodded gloomily, stroking his fingers through his beard, 'Yes, it is, Vagn Ågeson, and though you deserved to have Torkel Lere swap places with Erik, let that be, because I want you to lie next to me when it starts again.'

A wildfire flickered over Vagn's face, and his gaze was sharp, 'Torkel Lere! Where is he? And what do you need me for here? If we lose the flank, then we are in real trouble.'

Despite the strife and wounds, Vagn still thought about his promise to kill Torkel Lere and embrace his daughter, Ingeborg! Arnulf looked at his companion, but the Bueson stared into the distance, despite standing near Sigvalde and he looked tired. The red-locked Jomschieftain raised his hand commandingly, 'Torkel has caused Bue and Sigurd severe anguish, and they even got him to give way, it was therefore that Erik left you for a while. But the battle has been tough here, look around! We have lost many people, and the Ulfhednirs' hunger for prey is insatiable; they spread much weakness throughout us, while they instil strength among their own, we are penetrated, Vagn! Hakon will undoubtedly set everything against me; you must beat his wolf-warriors and give your companions back strength.'

Sigvalde looked bitterly at the humble ship with the fur-clad warriors who were still yelling scattered howls and were not resting on the deck, and Vagn frowned with a bitter twitch of his lips, 'Who is to keep the flank?'

'I have already told Skargeir Torfinnson and Arngrim Rune to do it and they have kept flanks before.'

'Such a defeatist attitude does not suit you!'

Arnulf let his gaze glide between the two men. Was there a hidden challenge behind the words? Would Vagn take orders from the man his own grandfather had favoured over him? Bjørn the Bretlander laid a hand on his raised arm, 'If Strut-Harald's sons fall, Hakon will not rest until everyone is killed. Skargeir and Arngrim are good men, and Sigvalde rules over Jomsborg.'

The Ågeson snorted and spat on the floor, 'And well he does it! But you and Ketil must row back to the flank before the hog-earl rides his seahorse again, we cannot pull all the strongest weapon into the middle.'

'I will stay here, and if we can get Ketil behind the Ulfhednir they will get more surprises in the next collision than they probably think. Throw him over the shield wall, Vagn, he is not bigger!'

Bjørn smiled, but Little Ketil did not seem to be enjoying himself in the least, 'You would do better to throw Bue at their heads, Bjørn, then you will see how many ticks his fat belly can squash!'

Sigvalde's mouth pulled upwards, and Torkel the Tall joined them, his eyes warm, but Vagn scowled evilly, 'Thor's beard on a chopping block, we have bled just as much out on the flank as you and the men over there will be disappointed, but if you want it, I will stay. It is easier for me to reach Torkel Lere from the middle.'

Sigvalde's face was resolute, 'I do! Against the blood of Palnatoke, the earl will fall, Odin is with us.'

He held out his hand, and Vagn stepped forward and grabbed it without smiling, and then the leader of the legion nodded to the other men on the skeid, who swore continued allegiance to the Ågeson with a look. Jomsvikings and blood-companions, the red shield edges tied them together in brotherhood, and no man stood alone.

Arnulf sat down on the nearest thwart to rest, while there was time, and a many-freckled Jomsman with broken teeth pushed him from over the shield rim and handed him some linen strips, 'Here! You are bleeding. Tie it around your arm, there are enough wounds below the armour to drain life which cannot be reached.'

Arnulf nodded gratefully to him, the freckled one was not unknown from the banner ground and that he stood on Sigvalde's dragon was hardly accidental. Svend sank down on the thwart with him, and Vagn faltered unexpectedly at the shield rim, his eyes blinking, and had to support himself on Bjørn, but straight after pushed his foster-father away from him again. No one around him moved a muscle, so apparently no notice should be given that the dark warrior was showing signs of deterioration.

While Arnulf wrapped the tear tightly, a light, quivering buckhorn sounded, and there was excitement over on the Norwegian vessels. Behind them slid the red ship with earl Hakon, and after him came the iron whale and another longship. Svend sprang up immediately, and Arnulf arose to find his helmet. His heart started to trample like a tethered stallion, and a rush of anxiety clenched at his stomach. Not again! Not again! An overwhelming urge to flee seized his limbs, and the strap to the helmet twisted rebelliously, while the pain flowed in his arms, and his throbbing nose caused his vision to flicker. For a moment, he looked at Haug, who was badly wounded and had lost a hand, but whose sole task ahead was to stay alive, crouched behind a shield, while the others were fighting, and a cowardly envy reared in his mind. If Vagn did not shout courage back into him, Serpenttooth would drop limply from his hands as soon as the fjeld force came, but the Ågeson was injured, and certainly more than he cared to appear, and Sigvalde himself had expressed concerns.

Earl Hakon sailed alongside his people, shouting with conviction in his voice, and the Northmen got up, roaring certain replies. What it was, their commander had to tell could not be heard, as long as he his back was turned on the Danish force but Torkel the Tall took up the challenge and with surprising power began to warm the willingness of his comrades.

And Bue the Stout snorted like a bull from the north flank, so it went through chainmail and bones, while Skargeir Torfinnson and Arngrim Rune each in their own well-manned longship stroked in the opposite direction. Torkel, Vagn and Sigvalde roared fatigue and pain from the ships in turn, the dragon banner flickered under the threatening skies and cold winds whipped the sweat into the skin. Now it was again time for wild deeds and spear play, steadfast stood Jomsborg, the unwavering Danish hird, and together they were to smear shit and rottenness out of the northern people's intestines! Helheim's soot-black rooster crowed, Naglfar was breaking free and the ice jötnar were gripping clubs as Bifrost and the mountains trembled! Arnulf shouted and screamed fear in the face, he

351

could drown, and he would drown, but not without resistance, and if the body was afraid, the wolf-blood would have to flow alone! Anger and victory stood like shields in front of the fjeld earl, the last fight skid against the fleets like a great king; the final triumph, and burning from wounds and sweat his body suffered, what loss was it to let go?

The clamour of weapons resumed, sworn and revenge bound arms shook saxes and axes, raging in front of the helmsman as flaming hatred now ran glowingly down the blades, all had lost, all had a reason to seek blood-revenge now, even Tyr had to laugh at the battle, it was about to erupt so marvellously!

The Norwegian earl boldly let his red ship row in front of the legion, and although he came within reach of the skilled archers, he stood in the bow, head uncovered and hair flowing. Arnulf was silent and stared, his sword raised. Strong was the man who had set out against King Harald and cheated him of a tithe land, determined and brave, and that Hakon had been able to assemble such a large fleet so quickly, proved his people's faith and respect, Sigvalde could not have found a more worthy opponent elsewhere and to defeat him would be a tremendous achievement! Arnulf slowly lowered Serpenttooth. The earl was not standing alone under the dragon head, and the Joms' cries were dampened from disbelief and were replaced with wonder, for Hakon's companion was no warrior! The figure was small, the loose green robe was taken by the wind, and the hair was curled and waist long, it looked like ... it was a woman! A woman!

Dismayed Arnulf looked at Svend, who had completely forgotten Snap somewhere over by his helmet. Misfortune it was, an omen, ill-luck and black sorcery, no full-hearted man brought a woman with him into battle, she could not be an ordinary fjeld dweller, and the questions crept between the Vikings. Jomsborg, the men's fort, warriors who shunned women for the sake of the battle and the fellowship, should their first killing after the break in fighting be to fell a bosomed maiden, a daughter of Freya, a carrier of children? Was it Hakon's demeaning insult, or was she more than what she seemed to be, had Odin loaned the earl a Norn, a dís, or was she a seidhr, fostered in Niflheim?

Svend shook his head, and the green-clothed legion follower raised her arms, so the fingers bristled straight towards Sigvalde and began to chant stridently over the bay. Arnulf was ill at ease. Rune-knowledgeable she had to be, perhaps in cahoots with malevolent forces, why else lift the chin towards the most feared warrior legion that had come from Daneland, had she the right to stretch claws like a cat against Sigvalde Strut-Haraldson himself, protected only by skin and wool?

Vagn jeered, laughing insanely. Hakon was so pressured, he had picked up his old mother and brought her to the fight, now shirts would stand guard against what pinches and slaps had not managed to keep from life, but before the Ågeson had finished laughing, heavy hail beat down over the row of ships from the ashen clouds, and the arrow Kjartan shot at the seidhr, curved in its flight, crashing into the water. Arnulf was hit by a sharp hail in the lower lip, and it was followed by blazing pain in the wounds; the horse suddenly rode the man wrongly, Hakon's action was startled and incomprehensible!

Sigvalde boasted, laughing at his enemy, and the Jomsvikings around him again began to shout threateningly, but the beats on the shields sounded hollow and the din of the weapons fluttered over the waves like a winged gull. The Northmen took hold of the oars and shot water from the keels, and warriors stood as protection for their earl and the fate-boding woman. Arnulf turned his back on Hakon and tight-lipped laid out an oar to row in time with the others. Helge's brother was not afraid of a dress, it was cunning of the earl to put a milk-thrall in the bow, and he had near shaken the Danes' luck, but moaning in a foreign language and pointing fingers had never achieved victory against a superior force!

Hailstones drummed against chainmail and shields, unusually large whipping against the Danes and as he sat now, they did no harm to his back, but having to turn around and fight with their slap in the face would block his view! Did the woman reign over wind and weather, since it changed so astonishingly, had the day not been bright and warm until she came, and why was the wind now squealing against Sigvalde's fleet? The oar was heavy to handle and it was hard to stay on course without a rudder, but Vagn shouted cheerfully that hail in Bretland was so sharp it could cut up a lamb, and this did not bother hardened men and Bjørn agreed, shouting loudly. The men, who had taken off clothes earlier, now had to accept the ice-drops with bare skin, and the heat gave way to the cold like an extinguished flame.

The seidhr's chanting could be heard through the shouts and storms, it was strange, because even Bue's voice drowned in the din, and Arnulf snorted blood from his nose and pulled through grey water. Vagn Ågeson's broad shoulders were no longer an assurance of victory; the Ulfhednirs' howling pierced the ears with fiery needles, and a disturbing darkness lay over the Hjörungavádr. Sigvalde's Vikings were men, trained to meet ships and weapon blows but no one in the royalseat had promised to overcome sorcery-weather and runic power!

Arnulf heaved the oar in, drew Serpenttooth from its sheath and turned around. No man had to give way to an equal opponent, but the law of Jomsborg said nothing about sorcery and curses! Svend had risen with a javelin, and the Northmen seemed exuberant, as if they found themselves in the middle of a mead party and not a sea battle. Only scattered arrows bolted through the air, and the skeid was attached to the dragon, so no one could penetrate through to Sigvalde without having to go through Vagn's crew. Along the chieftain's ship's opposite shield rim was Torkel the Tall's white stallion, scratched and blood-soiled and around them the Jomsvikings and hirdmen held tight, if Sigvalde fell, Jomsborg fell and Hakon's line-up was strongest in the middle. High-sided vessels slid in front of the chieftain and were tied into a firm battlefield of a row of decks, and although it was tempting for those most outstanding among the warriors to go over the ships to the front, they remained by Sigvalde to hold position and avenge the men who now would give their lives voluntarily. On the south flack, Arngrim and Skargeir seemed to have the reigns in hand and Bue the Stout filled his place on the deck as never before with Sigurd by his side. He yelled to Svend, who waved back eagerly, and Vagn took stock of the entire legion and exchanged words with Ketil and the Jomsleader.

The Norwegian earl had again donned his helmet, so Arnulf could not see his face clearly, and his housecarls seemed fierce and aggressive, not least the stout broad man with the lush beard, who stood ... Leif! It was Leif! Leif Cleftnose! Arnulf's mouth fell open with an outburst. Of all the Northmen! And on that particular red ship! Leif Slinkyass, Leif Lousehaven, he shook his head and closed his mouth; that the Cleftnose stood near the earl should not be surprising. As hard as that Viking hit and shaped his words, he would naturally end up with the kingdom's great man in war. The ships were close enough now for the two nose bits to be discerned over the laughing, and the club was not blood-free, but Leif did not stand near his own settlement companions, Toke would have to stand against Bue alone.

It would not be long to the new clashes and the Ulfhednir warriors distributed in pairs over the front ships under their bow heads, blood dripping from their lips and knives between their teeth. Whether evil sorcery or dark forces protected them or not was not to know, but superior sword skill and certain death steamed from their wolf skins, and they reeked of the desire to kill.

The Jomsvikings took up arms and formed shieldwalls and Arnulf managed to get a glimpse of *Twin Raven* in front of Sigurd's snekke, before ships with standing men stole any vision. Possibly the two men up front looked like Toke and Stentor, but he was not sure, and Svend looked at him sharply over his shoulder, 'Hold the skeid, Veulf! Stay here, whatever happens, try not to stand at the front against Hakon housecarls and Ulfhednir.'

The wind began to drive the bound front back against Sigvalde's ship wall and the hail made the planks icy and treacherous to keep a foothold, and now Hakon's bows grated against those of the Danish force's, while sorcery-roused Northmen threw themselves against spears and swords in scorn of death.

The earl's dogs barked wildly, embittered claws rasped after throats and there, where Ulfhednir fought in front of their companions, Sigvalde's men had given way despite fierce defines. It was impossible to use a bow, and as the close combat was so far away, Arnulf could only clench his swords and spear without even choosing his weapon. Blinded by hail and wind many a Jomsviking's blow went awry, and while unproven Northmen with inferior weapons slew great scarred warriors, the seidhr's chanting screeched over the screams and the roars, and Sigvalde shouted that more than ordinary skill was required against sorcerers, so the men had to fight as best they could.

The fighting quickly moved over onto the bound front ships, and now Vagn rushed forward and with him went most of the skeid's crew. Arnulf hesitated, it was so wild, the shieldwalls burst; the overall battle broke up into smaller groups that held furiously together, contending with each other, while individual warriors ate into them from the back. Entire groups of men were simultaneously pushed overboard and they disappeared into the icy water, but when they now and then succeeded to pull an Ulfhednar over the shield rim, the chainmailless wolf held his head above water and was helped on board Hakon's nearest ship. Although they were not invulnerable, Arnulf did not see any wolf-warriors fall, and with terrible strength they heaped bodies around him.

Svend went with Vagn wherever he pressed forward, and Kjartan kept their backs free of enemies, while Little Ketil, round-shouldered, flew under the lower rims of the shields, like a low flying swallow, felling the fighters at their roots. Behind Northmen and Ulfhednir warriors, Arnulf caught sight of Leif Cleftnose and his swinging club again and again, and the big fjord man served his earl well, Hakon would owe him gold for his effort! Sigvalde stood rigid at the dragon's mast fish while Torkel the Tall returned to his own ship and with a loud cry flung encouragement and warnings over the confusion.

Restless, Arnulf wanted to move towards the shield rim; it was cowardly waiting on a nearly empty vessel, just because Svend wanted it that way, but Bjørn the Bretlander called him back. The old warrior obviously did not crave more scars and had remained on the skeid, despite still knowing how to fight back, and now the Jomsvikings had to reluctantly retreat over the front ships with large losses to follow, while the wind tore screams from behind and the hail nailed them to the water.

Under the sea a tremble ran from Jomsborg's faltering ramparts along the Norwegian coast and spread to the deck. The Vikings had stood so well before the rest, how was it possible for Hakon to have usurped the battle-luck with only the help of a woman? With inhuman strength the Ågeson tried to show himself as much as possible between his brothers, but he, too, was driven to climb over the shield rim to his own ship, and Svend limped, so he had to use a thwart to help him stand. Bjørn pulled Arnulf with him to the aftship where Haug, coughing, sat hidden behind a shield, and now the spear was selected and Serpenttooth was stuck in the sheath, for Svend stood so uncertainly that he had to have the support from behind. With great exertion, the shieldwall was reformed and the enemy kept from the deck, and a sharp skirmish over the shield rim at the foreship drowned out the seidhr's sinister curses for a moment. Arnulf broke free of Bjørn's grip while Svend limped behind his dark kinsman, wind and rain struck as pure pain, and the planks were so slippery from ice that the thwarts had to be used as anchors.

Again, Arnulf jabbed with the spear for his blood companion, the tip wedged through the smallest opening in front of it, tore the shaft free of dead flesh and he felt the pain of the hit burn in his fists. Svend's chainmail clad back was no longer straight, and with his shin over a thwart, a well-aimed blow could easily fell him. Had both flanks fallen then as all Hakon's force tried to trample over the foreships to shipwreck and invade Vagn's skeid all together? The bad weather increased and swelled to a howling hailstorm, the cold cut headwinds like sharpened knives, and the cry came that another sorceress could now be seen on Hakon's longship: Jomsborg was doomed! Arnulf screamed wordlessly to Svend and Vagn, screamed for life and resistance! They would not drop from the weather and goatherds, they were heroes, they were engaged in heroic deeds and if the Northmen could just be driven a few steps back to their own ships, the earl could be reached and victory be skinned from his fingers!

Out of the corner of his eye, he saw ships pull clear of Sigvalde's force and tack, large ships with many men. No! It did not make sense! Yes! Proud longships with stooped men at the oars rowed out of the bay, the fleeing hird was King Sweyn's, by Fenrir's fate and Loki's deceit, they fled like frightened rats! Such miserable weaklings had the Dane Lord in his bread that they gave way to pain and rain. Despicable! Treason! Sigvalde roared rooster-red from his dragon, waving his arms, but when the hirdmen simply turned their faces away without obeying, he wavered uncertainly back as if struck by weapons, and the weakening seemed to waft through the struggling Jomsmen like a gust of death from Helheim. Deprived of half the force, Vagn's and Bue's outpourings of strength would count as much as kicks from children and the Ågeson howled for Sigvalde to draw his sword and go forward among his men. Kjartan slipped in the hail and fell, and on the bound front ships, the Ulfhednir gathered behind the front row of men, ready to confront the dragon and the surrounding ships.

Along the rows of ships to both sides, it seemed that Hakon's legion had seized Jomsborg's life, from Skargeir to Sigurd the Danes were outnumbered and Arnulf's arms sank down as heavily as the sea. Frejdis! He would think of Frejdis when the nearest wolf-warrior wrenched his weapons free of his chest so as to forget him in the same breath! Forever doomed to fight Odin would put him on the Plains of Ida, and for eternity he would tap the blood from endless rows of opponents and drink himself into oblivion with Heidrun's mead. Suddenly Valhalla seemed far worse than any exile, if only disease would take him now so he could rest with Balder in dank shadows of Death's Realm instead!

The noise drew strangely back, the rhythmic cries sounded like they came from a remote valley: Hakon, Hakon, Hakon; they could have shouted something else, and Sigvalde's hoarse voice splintered hope and brave deeds like ice against the rocks. Escape! He waved his arms at Bue and Vagn, roaring that there was no reason to maintain the fight, they were not fleeing from men but from sorcery, and any man who gave up was excused, for the promise at the royalseat applied only to the earl of Norway, not sorcery and runic power! The ropes to the skeid and white stallion was severed, the dragon pushed back and the oars were placed in the water, and already a few fathoms out men and ships were blurred in the hailstorm, while a untamed triumphal roar blasted from the throats of Hakon's legion. Arnulf groaned. The celebrations crashed, weapons were temporarily eased back, and the moment should evidently be enjoyed to the full, the fjord people withdrew a step from the shield rim in wild enthusiasm.

'Sigvalde!'

Vagn's Fafnir's scream was torched. Arnulf stared after the dragon ship. Strut-Harald's son! On the run! Screwed like a kicked dog with its tail between its legs, Palnatoke's shame! Now the skaldic verses died, now the heroes sank, now lay skeids and fleet neck deep in lies! The dark warrior's Jomsvikings and Torkel's ship mates stood lame, but on the north flank, Bue the Stout fought so rampantly that the troubled water only badly managed to cover his slain before new fell after them.

'Sigvalde!'

Thickened by bile, as toxic as snake venom, the Ågeson hoarsely dragged his chieftain in front of the Thing. Arnulf had difficulty catching his breath. Bue was missing a hand from his left arm, and a man pressed forward and struck him in the face, so the blood gushed so forcefully that it could be seen all the way from the skeid.

'No!'

Svend uttered a terrible cry. Earl Hakon's red ship slid all the way to the bound front ships while the Northmen's hoots merged with Ulfhednirs' howls, the enemy was preparing to storm the skeid and was apparently just waiting for Hakon's orders to rhythmic throbbing and threatening air strikes. Bue the Stout cut his slayer across the middle and seemed to shout to his companions, as he stepped, shaking in death, up on the shield rim and jumped overboard, and Svend screamed as his body cramped together from madness. Arnulf threw away the spear and grabbed him by the shoulders. The Silkenhaired shook brutishly, shot stones under the skin and turned like a deranged bull that in the next blow would turn the fjelds to gravel! His eyes rolled, and his froth-soaked teeth were exposed.

'Sigvalde!'

Vagn ran over the thwarts from the bow with a spear in his hand, his face twisted. The helmet had fallen off his head, his long hair was dripping with blood and sweat, and his eyes threw coal-sparks over the wide-open mouth. His companions jumped to life, the Ågeson had eyes only for the dragon and let nothing stand in the way of his revenge. For Arnulf, it looked as if he intended to throw himself into the sea but, at the last moment, his free hand gripped the stern, and he leaned out into the storm, offering the last of his voice, 'Sigvalde! Turn or I will kill you! Only a wretch places his men under the mace and sails home to Denmark to cast himself into the arms of a woman! Bue was brave, but my spear will be your payment!'

The figure at the dragon's rudder was not bothered by the Ågeson's madness, and Vagn threw his weapon to Sigvalde so blood sprayed from his wounds. Life-taking, the spear hit the target between the shoulders, so the arms flung out to both sides, and Arnulf's grip on Svend's madness iced onto the chainmail's rings. Jomsborg's fall! When Palnatoke's heir killed the Jomsviking's leader, then, in truth, the entire fellowship of the fort died! For a moment, Hakon and the Norwegian force's presence paled against Vagn's deed. It was so incomprehensible, such boundless pain had to lie beneath such despairing hate! No one like the dark warrior had stood behind the Joms' lord, no one more faithful had laid his life before his chieftain, no one with greater assuredness assumed the risk and effort.

With an outburst that was not human, Svend tore himself free. He swung Snap and threw the shield to pull the sax out of his belt, and the next moment he crashed against the bow, made his way straight through his own ranks and jumped over the shield rim to avenge his father as bloodily as possible. Arnulf shouted for him in vain, but with appalling carelessness the Bueson crashed towards his own grave, forgetting everything he had so carefully impressed into his hirdman.

'That was not Sigvalde.'

Bjørn the Bretlander's mouth was pulled down in the seagull-white beard, and he shook his head in horror, clarifying, 'It was Ørvad Bullsax, Sigvalde is sitting at an oar.'

He strode towards Vagn, while the men on the skeid pursued Svend with a senseless fury and joined him in going berserk, with Kjartan and Little Ketil at the head. The last fight! Should Jomsborg meet its fate, the Vikings would willingly and with incomparable courage suffer death by the sword!

The Northmen on the bound ships departed and let the Ulfhednir meet Vagn's crew, while the buckhorn sounded, and Arnulf lost himself in the middle of the ship. Danes and Northmen melted together into a Frankish blade of clashing arms, sliding shields and dully glimmering helmets. Vagn croaked, beside himself, his arms over Bjørn's head in the aftship, while the dragon pulled out in the blurry weather with his confounded load. Sigvalde had been so still, he might now be frozen, therefore he had seized the oar, and now Torkel the Tall drew his *White Stallion* free from the fight and let it row out of the battle with Skidbladnir's haste. Sigurd seemed to believe he had fulfilled his pledge to stand shoulder-to-shoulder with his brother for his ship stroked after Torkel's and with them most of the others who were able to do so; only a few handfuls of crews who still had courage and determination rallied against Hakon, as fast as the oars could eat water to assist Vagn, and among them were Arngrim and Skargeir from the south flank.

Arnulf slowly pulled Serpenttooth out of its sheath for the last time in his life! As blood companion to Vagn, he owed his fraternity his arm. Deep down, from the feet, a corrosive heat began to rise through the legs, and without the slightest ripple it reached below the navel and spread ominously out through the body, as it consecrated the wolf-blood to Fenrir! Fear and concern fell from his shoulders like a rejected cape and an inner light penetrated the clouds' darkness from sight. The fatigue was gone, the pain evaporated, and the incalculable tangle of ships was as clear and simple as a game of the dogs after the hare. Even the hail lessened under the waning wind, and when Vagn ran past Arnulf, he followed, but before he could set foot on the shield rim to drown with honour in a sea of swords, a Northman jumped onto the skeid and wedged himself in between him and the planks with a beard fluttering roar.

Leif's eyes flashed with murderous joy, the club was wielded like a willow twig, and Serpenttooth glowed sharply in Arnulf's hand, seeking to slay Leif of its own accord with a dragon blow, as such an overwhelming craving for vengeance brought his body into such a position that Arnulf was nearly more surprised than the Cleftnose himself. He shouted challengingly and stared at the Northman in his broad chest. Now he would receive, now he would know what the price was for pushing his ship mate overboard in a storm; finally, finally his revenge time had come, a blow for him and a shock for Toke, Leif could lie there, life gulping out of his stomach, robbed of any joy over Hakon's victory. Surely the Damaged-Snout one thought he would find the same unproven farm boy as before, but he was mistaken, a fate twisting mistake! Impressive, the fjord man believed himself to be, but against the Jomsvikings he was like a hornless kid goat!

The club's swings were easy to avoid, and before it was lifted again, the sword had bitten a hole in the chainmail under his arm. Leif made a sound and aimed at the chest, and Arnulf escaped without any attempt to put the thin shield between them, but when he raised his arm and sucked in his stomach, something slimy got a hold of his back foot, which slid, slid in something that felt like uncooked sausages, intestines, a man's innards! Desperately his foot groped for resistance, his knee gave way, his weight slipped from under him, Thor's piss, a thwart should have been there! The crushing blow hit him under the shield arm, the battle-kyrtle received it, but the force was irresistible, shield and sword flew from his hands, the ship was sucked down, and his knees slammed against the shield rim as his body was hurled backward across the ship's side.

By Fenrir, no, not again, impossible! A glimpse of an uneasy smirk disappeared, then his back splashed into the waves, and all sound ceased, while the weight of the chainmail and battle-kyrtle dragged his body into the water with a staggering power. For a moment, every deed was paralysed by the icy water, and only the gaze watched; full of horror, he stared at the long drawn blood streaks and sinking men, some stiffened, others writhing in fright, but they all sank like shiny giant fish, pulled to the depths by the iron with strangled cries like slapped flies interrupted in urgent action, Ran's kingdom was silent! He was going to die! Being sucked down was terrible, the ships' seal bellies were lost in the fog, liquefied darkness, and Arnulf's fierce swimming strokes were of no use in the least. The panic threw its winding body around his stony, struck lungs, its teeth sinking, but his will shook him free with a heave, oversight was crucial, so as not to be blinded by fury! Down he went, upper body first, flowing quickly, the chainmail pulled, but it was not tight on his body; it had to come off, come off immediately before the pressure and suffocation took his consciousness.

The fingers were warm enough to loosen the helmet and belt, and Arnulf kicked his legs to turn his head vertical to the depths, if his crown struck the bottom now, it would break his neck! A fight for life! The sheath flew from him, Toke's silver knife flashed, lost over the helm in the semi-darkness, then the chainmail slid down over his chest as it should. For a moment, it hung around his head but rolled off after a wild twist, the battle-kyrtle followed sullenly, the cold cut his naked skin like a woodworker's plane, his shoulders and left hand were free, but then they both suddenly hung, stuck in the dressing on the sword arm, unwrenching and horrific as the last of the light faded and the pressure in his ears threatened to blow his head. No! Horror's madness! Clearly! He must continue to think clearly and not give in to the sickening anxiety, not give up, not faint so close to being free of the deadly iron skin. Ægir! Njord! If the bottom was reached, he could push his feet against it, but if the sea fell as the fjelds rose, he would die before! His lungs ached, the last of the air bubbled out of them, flashes of light flickered in his vision, the horror and cold were overpowering, it was impossible, impossible! Serpenttooth, where was the sword: his under arm could be cut off, what price was maiming in the face of drowning?

Arnulf forced his lower body down, grabbed the clinging chainmail sleeve between his knees and pulled the arm, using his other hand to help, so the rings pulled and peeled the skin around his wrist, and at last the iron-cloth released him. It was black, and even if the body was free, the trousers weighed him down, he would not get up without a fight. Stroke after stroke, his arms fractured cracks in the sea, but at the same time an invincible weakening barred his will, the light did not return, and the limbs began to jerk masterlessly, cramping in uncontrollable starts, air, he had to have air now, now! A sinking sword grazed a hole in his shoulder, shadows floated by, sinking shadows, where was the light, why it was not light, why could he not see the ships again, in what direction did the sky lay? Arnulf wriggled his hip desperately; if he, blind and deaf, had to bite his way, well, he would not drown, not end his life here! It pricked his skin, his limbs didn't obey, the rage was not enough, he could not, could not, his head reeled ... they would not ... legs ... Frejdis! Frejdis ... no ...

The air howled in his lungs but was immediately forced out with a rattling cough. Again, they heaved the storm in, in life-giving gasps, spluttering convulsively, while his knees pulled up under his stomach in the next fit of coughing, then the breath went clean through victorious and he could feel the grip in his hair.

'Now listen and give me that hand! Veulf, it is now, or I will let go again, do you think I can stand here until you have finished gulping?'

A slap in the face focused his eyes, and Arnulf tried with all his might to stretch an arm into the air, but he was weak, as weak as at death's door! Svend took hold and demanded the other too, and Arnulf obeyed dizzily, struggling with what little his body was capable of. The splintered planks tore into the bare skin and his body hung whale-heavy over the shield rim, then he slapped onto the deck and curled up, unimaginable that the Bueson found the strength for such a drag!

'Wake up, by Tyr's death, come to yourself!'

Svend struck again, pulling him over, and Arnulf blinked his eyes clear, while the pain from the club hit nearly took his breath away again. With his elbow pressed against his side, his dazed eyes slid around as his surroundings became clearer. Dying and dead remained on the abandoned skeid, whose deck, covered with bloody hail porridge and broken weapons and splintered shields, made any movement uncertain. Haug was still sitting behind his shield in the aft, and the fighting had not quite passed the front ships, the noise returned, tumbling and alive. Svend's gaze was deadly extinct as if a hope-ripping shadow had conquered and he was bloody, soaked from the inside out, only the golden hair shone like

Heimdallr's lures. He snorted like a bull again and stank of death, the fury was streaked with black from grief, 'Here! I saw you get beaten into the water. I could not save my father, but I have slain seven men for his life and refused to believe you would remain down there.'

Serpenttooth's hilt was pressed into Arnulf's hand and the Bueson frowned, 'You dropped it on the deck, can you stand? I must return to Vagn immediately, but you cannot fight without a helmet and chainmail, we can take one off one of those killed, come! Your ribs are not broken, if they were you would be bleeding from your mouth.'

Arnulf nodded but could not answer, his jaw trembled so badly. Svend helped him up, rough-handedly, onto his legs and picked up a shield for Serpenttooth. The battles last fights stood around and on the front ships, the Danes had either fled or lay wounded and cold on the rest of the drifting vessels in the bay, but both Arngrim and Skargeir's crews fought like berserkers to provide maximum support for Vagn's men. Arnulf breathed deeply, although it struck like lightning in his side. He grasped the weapon, his shield shivering from cold. The trousers were glued to his legs, but the hail clouds were driven further into the fjords and seidhrs or not the weather had been crucial to Hakon's side, shielding his kingdom and people.

Leif Cleftnose was not anywhere to be seen, Helheim take him, and life was on loan so could Vagn's defeat be less, somewhere in the swirling jumble on the bound ships the last Jomsleader hacked himself to undisputable reputation, and he lacked men.

Arnulf took some steps to get a grip of his body again, and although he froze like a newly sheared sheep in the late frost, his limbs obeyed again. It was odd to stand unchallenged so near to Odin's scythe! Like the cow on the slope, the gulls on the rock, had Bue's son just pulled him up for a new death? The icy darkness shuddered and released in his chest, replaced by the kills of the men of the legion.

Haug called hoarsely to Svend. He looked awful, his chest was dripping wet from coughing up blood and his wrist lay in a clotted cow dung, but he was not completely dead, although his voice was pale, 'Take mine. It is easier to take chainmail off a living man than a dead, just be careful with my shoulder.'

The Silkenhaired wanted to answer and limped over the mast fish but stiffened abruptly, for at that same moment a Norwegian warrior sprang onto the skeid at the bow, one helmetless warrior dressed in wolf skins!

The man's gaze was yellow, his piercing eyes merciless and they lurked from narrow crevices. A wolf's scalp was pulled over his crown, so the teeth rested on his forehead, and the Ulfhednar had cut both the face and up and down the bare arms, so the blood flowed through the battle-pelt cape and rolled in lines down the bare lower legs.

Wolf teeth were drilled through both earlobes and nose cartilage, and many more formed chains around his neck; he was in possession of so much ferocity that numerous animals must have given the man power, he had added many shadowy-lives to his own. Red was the shield, drenched with blood, and the sax was drenched by the recent killings.

Arnulf stared at the warrior. For a moment, his body screamed from suffering and powerlessness, then heat rolled defiantly through his bones, the Jomsmen were hit so hard and yet they fought on, he himself stood like a frolicsome spring colt! Yellow eyes. Stentor also had a yellow eye, yellow was terrifying, a sign of the proximity of the gods and knowledge of sorcery, but it did not make him fear! He held onto Serpenttooth easily, assuring himself, where the deck was free, 'We surround him, he is only one and not much better shielded than I.'

From the ships, Little Ketil's cry to the Bretlander resounded.

'Veulf, you are mad, you do not even have a battle-kyrtle, he will wound you with his eyes alone, find a spear and stand behind me! He is an Ulfhednar!'

Svend wavered and found only little support on his injured leg. He had to be exhausted from the blood loss and exertion and appalled at Bue's death, too. An arrow whizzed over his shoulder.

'Give me a spear, too, and fight down here! Maybe I have a single blow left in my arm.'

Haug coughed horridly from the speech, then bowed his head and sank down wearily on his side, looking like a man who could not hold as much as a spoon. The Ulfhednar came slowly closer over the thwarts, but only a broken spear could be seen and Svend composed himself, hissing, and took a stand, his axe and shield lowered, 'I will switch over and fight left-handed as soon as he reaches me, you stand diagonally behind my right side, making sure ...'

A sudden violent jolt shot through the Bueson and a sound of amazement escaped him. Then he crumbled, falling onto one knee, as his hands dropped what they held.

'Svend!'

Arnulf was with him in a jump and gripped his arms, horrified. Not Svend, not Svend! An arrow shaft stuck out from between the trembling hands and the Bueson forced his head up with an open-mouthed groan. He was hit in the stomach, the sweat poured from him, and the wolf warrior stopped, as if wanting to assess whether it was worthwhile to use weapons, or whether the enemy would die of his own accord, hit by a Norwegian arrow.

'Svend, by Fenrir, hold on! Sit down!'

Arnulf sat him down with his back against a thwart, Baldur's death, only now was the Wolf of Woe hit, and so much that his legs trembled beneath him! Svend heaved air with a stiffened face, 'Now Snap fails!'

He tried to smile but was suddenly serious, 'Flee! Swim ashore and save yourself.'

'No!'

Never! Had the Silkenhaired himself not just left his own companions to help the damned? Promises and bonds were what mattered now, now his own fate meant nothing! The bloody hand grabbed Arnulf in a painful cramp, 'You cannot ... stand against an Ulfhednar, flee!'

'No! I will not leave you!'

'Veulf!'

The Bueson breathed with forced calm, resting heavily against a thwart, and the buckhorn sounded again, as the clamour dwindled, 'You will have to ...'

'Svend!'

He should understand! Arnulf looked him straight in his eye, 'He is only a wolf, and I am not afraid of wolves, I have never been afraid of wolves!'

Vehemently, the Bueson mingled his mind with his through his eyes, then yielded his glittering scaly-hide to warm vulnerabilities, 'Odin stand with you.'

Arnulf shook his head, let go of his hand and pulled Svend's shield in front of him, 'Only Fenrir stands against wolves!'

He grabbed his own shield, stood up and took a few steps from Svend towards the Ulfhednar, whose face contorted in an expectant grin that revealed sharply filed teeth. A wolf. A beast. The wind hardened the bare skin, and the drops from the wet hair furrowed down his spine. Clothed in a pelt. The beast-man gave himself over fully to the horror, but for him who already had kinship with dark and wolves Hyrrokin's brood seemed neither invincible nor magic, the only sorcery that protected the Ulfhednar was that created by the enemy themselves!

Arnulf's gaze flamed in the Ulfhednar's, who held back his steps with a hint of surprise. Serpenttooth lost weight and floated in his hand, his heart slowed down, pulsing strength and heat through his body with a slow pounding beat, while everything around him froze and receded. A wolf. He had provoked and evaded Stridbjørn's bull, Sigvalde's white stallion had shared pulse with him, and now Arnulf felt the warmth from the animal, felt its will, knew its intention, and far from the forests of Egilssund came the howls of the pack of Danes, the grey-companions had trained their whelp well. Wolfblood! Helge was killed, Frejdis lost forever, Rolf dead, settlement and land wrested from hands and possibly after this Toke's friendship also, but he would not lose Svend! Svend should live, should learn to live, would rise again as soon as the wounds were healed, laugh his sparkling laughter, the Bueson was his!

Fenrir's dark, thick-flowing blood burned in his veins, his claws scraped against the sword hilt and his neck hairs stood behind the flattened ears, his throat rolled deep growls. He saw everything, he heard everything, and the injured nostrils opened up to catch any bashful scent of aim. The Ulfhednar stepped light-footed over the thwarts and slid forward on supple joints while the sax swept from side to side like a hunting tail. A devious smirk replaced his grin and Arnulf let his gaze slide down to his collar bone. Behind the wolf warrior stood the Norns, enveloped in black cloaks, flanked by the dís of fate with heavy jewellery of silver-dew and furthest back stood Helheim and the lord of the Æsir himself with his ravens, but what could a man in a wolf-pelt put up against Fenrir regardless of his hird?

The Ulfhednar set off, his sax raised but he broke the air slowly, deliberately, deeply calm, Arnulf had, long before he landed, stepped aside to let the attack float by and expose his opponent's vulnerability, the warrior probably had enough teeth, but not necessarily a bite! With surprising ingenuity the angry wolf twisted in his jump and pulled his claw heavily over the white chest, but the pain did not come and the Arnulf did not give the cut skin a thought, tense as a bowstring, he was focused on the sax's flight, and he pursued the animal behind the shield but without meeting anything other than wind. The skeid gave such little space and the planks were so greasy, the feet took hold with a bird's ease, and Arnulf weaved effortlessly away from the next blow. Wolf and snake, the sax was his master's companion; sliding, cutting, hissing like a gust from the grave, but Arnulf knew its path, the blade went after the neck, nipped the hilt and sweat hair off the pelt.

Again the wolf brandished iron towards flesh, the tip drove into the shoulder, so Serpenttooth gave in his grip, but it did not hurt, pain had no access to the fight; it could stand behind the planks and wail in the

366

water, Arnulf was raiding! The shield deflected the blows, the blade warded off strikes from his wrist, pushing from the elbow, his body twisting itself free at the forefront of the attacks, it would take more than a dog before Svend had something to fear!

Arnulf himself attacked, breaking the rhythm, jumping back and stopping his assault, rushed to the side from the sax, turning the wolf on his heel; Svend sat behind him, his will fighting with him. The Yawning Gap! Between the wolf's wheezing and Svend's quick panting, Arnulf attacked over the gap, the Ulfhednar followed every step, the sax forming whirlpools, struck shards off Serpenttooth and splintered the shield's rim. His hip was hit, the shock dull, and the injured muscles were sluggish like untanned ox hide. A gust of wind trembled around the body, and the warrior animal did not hesitate but now Arnulf got a blow under the beast's knees, and the wolf yielded backwards, slobbering from hatred.

Vermin attack Hati if the force should be allowed to perish like stores before the Fimbulwinter! His chest worked heavily, his shoulder was stiffer than before, the current flowed warm over his skin, perhaps the sax had drunk deeper than it had thirst for, in any case the weakening drew shivers, and he clenched his teeth. He was Svend's protection; defeat was not possible! That animal had not set foot on Midgard's backbone that could arouse his fear! The ribs whispered of Leif's strokes behind the shield surface, but the discomfort was knocked away during the next swarm of blockades, possibly the Jomsvikings suffered defeat, and possibly Sigvalde had lost his battle, but that did not warrant the Ulfhednar getting Svend!

The shields beat together, weight jarred weight, and the sax went over his shoulder towards his back but went awry thanks to Serpenttooth's answering blow. Feet ploughed furrows in the muck, Arnulf yelled sharply and escaped, but the wolf did not stumble, and the sax met his sword arm just above the elbow, heatedly and triumphant, and a snarling pain threatened to break through the palisade. Serpenttooth played angrily with its tongue, its neck wounded, pulling awry, but Helge had not given up his fight, even when his arm fell onto the deck! Arnulf turned aside and withdrew entirely behind the shield, catching the next blow softly, but the stab, the cut, the tear, it shook from his wrist to his shoulder, and the blade was heavy. The enemy was met but not injured, sorcery and spells, was the sword so blunt that it could no longer bite through simple wolf leather?

Even Jörmungandr would not slip by! The Ulfhednar staggered over an axe, cutting himself on the blade, but although Serpenttooth was quick, it won only a rift for his deed. The Wolf warrior pulled backwards with a resting grip and a death-sentencing glance at the Bueson and Arnulf had to stay where he was, bleeding; if he followed, the wolf would strike him and knock the life out of Svend. The beast waited, cowardly in the limpid silence, only the heaving of the lungs disturbed Hjörungavádr's peace, then Arnulf shouted sharply, wordlessly, about honour and action, threw spite with his eyes and shot Odin's spear from under the shield, and the Ulfhednar again followed his desire. Deep went the Wolfman's revenge for the disgrace into Arnulf's thighs, and before the failed leg found support, the Ulfhednar's wound-fire slid up under his armpit, cutting the muscle to bits as he lifted the sword.

Arnulf's shield edge caught the animal in the throat while a tidal wave of pain tore out a scream. Flames engulfed the open wounds, the will stumbled. Misfortune! Æsir laughter! No! Not a foot would he give, but the victory slipped away in the mire of shame over his boasting, the calm sank, his heart beat like a blacksmith, but the bellows was punctured and Arnulf had to rest the shield's edge against a thwart, weak in his limbs, awaiting the crouched, coughing wolf as it flickered and blinked from view. Svend! He had to protect Svend, had to continue the fight, had to force his arm to obey, a Jomsviking knew neither fatigue nor pain. With sweat and blood gushing from the body, the Serpent swelled, quivering his sluggish but magnificent tooth, the blade could not twist higher than the ribs and his leg shook uncontrollably. Mockery flowed from the yellow eye as the Ulfhednar, breathless, went for him, and the enemy hilt crushed Arnulf's fingers against the sword handle before the Northern Wolf failed in his footing again, crashing to deck on his knee.

Arnulf bent, dizzy and groaning, over the shield. He had to ... Svend! Serpenttooth's tip began its advance over the planks, only two fingers gripped like an infant, and the Wolfman got up and slid in front of the guard, the sax ready, while his yell was answered by the pack. Frejdis! A final blow for Frejdis, then he would die free from humiliation and failure, before the pain-frenzy swept over him, die and throw himself into Helge's embrace! With white-hot will, he turned sideways, calling on the conquered sword, and Serpenttooth tumbled astray behind his back, following the muscles that could still pull and hidden by the shield, the tip rushed from under the left elbow. Arnulf moved his defines up, and even though the shock was dull, it was deep enough!

The Ulfhednar, his leg bursting, grabbed the blade while the blood from his lungs poured out of his mouth. Arnulf let go of the hilt and tumbled back over a thwart, fumbling for Toke's knife, which was no longer on his hip. Gurgling, the wolf tried to reach him with the sax, but the cut could be kicked away and Hakon's beast crumpled, gulping. He flinched as if he were poisoned, blood snarling to foam and fixed his cursed yellow gaze at Arnulf, as the shadow wolves howled away from him, freed from their oath. He would not die, death was not one of his grey-fellows, but the wolf-pelt slid askew over his face, so the predators' teeth jutted into his eyes, Hyrrokkin's brood ate their brother!

Arnulf fought with the north wind in his ears. He was bleeding like a pig. Drenching like ice over fire. It didn't matter! Writhing, he forced his body up on the thwart and turned around towards Svend, who, pale, had pushed away the shield and followed him with his eyes, then it went black, and the planks hit his shoulder. Breath. The heartbeat. He could see again. He supported himself with his shield hand and sat up against the thwart. Water! A drink of water, then he could manage!

'Veulf!'

Svend reached out his arm out with a distorted smile. The uninjured hand met the Bueson's and his will rose again. No matter how badly he was hit, the arrow in Svend's stomach had to be removed before it killed him, but how? What had Helge said about arrows? It depended on the entry and barbs. Why was it so quiet? And was it darkening already? A hand was laid on the injured shoulder and Arnulf pulled together and looked up at Bjørn's bearded face.

'Sit quietly Veulf, you are bleeding badly.'

'But Svend ...'

'He is not bleeding dangerously, but you are about to pass out, be quiet.'

The Bretlander quickly loosened and lifted a deck-plank aside to retrieve a stock of linen strips stowed below and wound clips, how hasty he was! Arnulf let his gaze trail over the planks to the front ships. Everyone was dead! No, they just didn't fight anymore! The red ship was moving away and with it the Northmen and their vessels, Vagn's last flock remained, drizzle fell over the bay, the battle was over!

Earl Hakon had won!

Bjørn pulled the edges of the wound together and roughly wound the linen around the shoulder, and Arnulf bowed his head and, groaning, clenched his teeth while the skeid jumped a bend under him, ugh, it was nauseating! The pain stuck spearheads into him like the beaks of an endless flock of starlings, and the arm felt half-detached. No one could have so much pain! It had to cease, in a moment it would still, in a moment it would go by itself, it simply had to, he had to endure! The injured hand was quite cold. He looked up.

'Are you alive, Svend?'

Little Ketil squatted by the Bueson and pushed his hands away from his stomach for a better look. Svend did not seem to like the contact but did not resist, 'Hakon's feast food is tough to digest, but I live.'

'It is a nasty needle.'

Little Ketil's did not seem to want to touch the protruding arrow and Svend grimaced, 'It is not worth ... cooking onion soup for my sake.'

'No, I will certainly not peel onions for you.'

The little warrior pressed the Bueson's hard hand and stood up heavily, looking over Arnulf. Ketil usually moved so jauntily that his age was not something noticeable, but now he seemed worn. Arnulf shuddered. Bjørn's dressing supported the useless sword arm, and his solid hands were good. From the front the ships the surviving Jomsvikings came limping, supporting each other, injured and crestfallen, and Arngrim and Skargeir laid their ships on each side of the skeid. Vagn was still standing, stooping like a maimed bear, and Kjartan had to talk for him, the Ågeson had only hissing and crow squawks left. Hakon had had enough, had pulled his men back to allow the Danes bleed to death alone, too many Northmen had fallen, and now the earl set his guard in the bay, so the last of the Jomsvikings could not escape.

Another shiver pulled at his skin. Arnulf froze, that might be why he was trembling so much. Bjørn dressed his thighs thoroughly, and the thought of how deep the sax had struck, made his stomach turn. His hand he had to keep still, each time the sinews pulled the fingers, a knife cut them. A dream. A nightmare. Everything around him was going on at a distance, the sounds were woolly. Kjartan stumbled over to Haug and wounded men were carried over the shield rim and laid between the thwarts while dressings were found. With a gesture, Vagn called some men over to search for survivors among the fallen, and Bjørn sent him a worried look and worked quickly. Ketil threw a cloak to the Bretlander, who threw it around Arnulf's shoulders, and the warm wool instilled a bit of courage, the battle was over and he was not killed, after all!

Only silent comments were shared between the Jomsvikings, and those who still had some strength intact made every effort to stop the bleeding of the men, who seemed most likely to survive. The worst injured were prepared to die without reproach, and Vagn staggered over the thwarts and warriors to his kinsman and knelt down with a deep sigh. He said nothing, just took Svend's hands, bowed his head and squeezed them

370

against his chest, trembling all over. Then he grabbed the silken hair and pressed his forehead against the Bueson's and wordlessly they seemed to share a lifetime together, as Bjørn tried to wrap his arm. Arnulf winced. It hurt as though his elbow were in a fire! Bjørn's voice was gentle; he spoke to a frightened child, banishing evil creatures and predictions from the hearth, 'You will live, Veulf; if the fever does not take you, you will live and grow old like myself, be sure of it.'

He turned to the Ågeson, commanding harshly, 'Sit here! If you do not rest now, I myself will end up leading the surviving men, and I am tired.'

Vagn let go of Svend and sank to the floor, bleaker than ever. He was bone-white, his lips discoloured, his chainmail torn up in several places, and the sight of his many wounds caused Arnulf to be ashamed of his own whimpering. By Fenrir! The Jomsvikings around him were hit so they should be squirming in endless screams, but only few faces revealed complaints, the wailing in the bay was from Northmen!

Bjørn called to a blond curly-haired Viking and asked him to take care of the last stabs and lacerations, he himself would see to Vagn, and the curly-haired one replaced him willingly and wrapped the chest expertly, while the Bretlander unfastened the belt from the dark warrior to pull the chainmail off him. Ketil was waved over to help.

'You stood well, Veulf.'

The curly-haired one nodded appreciatively, and Vagn agreed with him, 'That fight I will remember, and so will the others who saw it. Do you know that Hakon noticed you?'

He whispered hoarsely but clearly enough, and Arnulf shook his head, 'Then he also knows from whom vengeance must be taken for the Ulfhednar's death!'

So many Jomsmen, and the victor was still able to pick him out as guilty for the loss of the Ulfhednar.

'The earl does not think like that, and I could see, you would win.'

Vagn's eyelids slid halfway.

'What do you mean?'

His gaze was hazy again, and Arnulf blinked, dizzy, the wolf warrior had killed him, but for his last strike!

'You were a wolf yourself, am I right? Do you not remember what I called you on the banner ground? Your blood did not betray you.'

The curly-haired one stuffed the end of the strip firmly around the chest and started on the hip. Arnulf wanted to answer, but Kjartan interrupted, sinking down heavily on a thwart. Forfeit, the big man stared in front of him, raising his words with a hollow voice, 'Haug will not survive. Maybe tonight, maybe tomorrow, but he cannot breathe properly, there is a hole in his lung, he is drowning.'

The broad hands took his face, but straight after he looked out over the bay with a hard gaze, where earl Hakon and his retinue were putting ashore on a flat strand. No one had answers to give, and Arnulf looked at the fallen Bornholmer. Little Ketil and Bjørn pulled the chainmail off Vagn and the Bretlander cautiously opened the wet battle-kyrtle, but Kjartan could rest no longer, 'What do we do now, Vagn Ågeson?'

'Find some water and let me and Ketil bind Vagn's wounds, Kjartan, otherwise you are going to ask your own reflection. Skargeir! Are you able to look at Svend Bueson?'

Bjørn was sharp-eyed and Haug's companion stood guiltily, while Skargeir left his ship to sit by the Bueson. Water! Arnulf would give gold for water! He was so tired! The drizzle soothed a little, and it was beginning to get dark, the night would be cold, cold and clammy. He closed his eyes. He did not want to see. Did not like the red. But the sounds did not leave his ears. Vagn's slow, controlled breathing, which sailed over Bjørn's healing hands like a snekke in deep swells, the Bretlander's subdued orders, the snap of the thin shaft, Svend's chainmail, which was laid on the deck, and his gasping, the squelch when the arrowhead was removed from the intestines, and the curly-haired one's sharp calls for more linen.

'Here!'

Arnulf felt a mug being pressed into his uninjured hand and drank without looking. The dizziness left him, the thoughts cleared and the worst of the thirst was satisfied for a moment.

'Thank you, Kjartan.'

Arnulf air sucked in. Lost. They had lost. Behind the agony the defeat smarted. The night saw the Jomsvikings left well enough alone, but as soon as dawn came, the Northmen would come after the survivors and what punishment they could find to befall Sigvalde's survivors, it was not worth thinking about. In addition to the killing of the Ulfhednar, earl Hakon would undoubtedly take him for a Jomsbrother, so maybe it was best to bleed to death on the skeid among companions rather than throwing shame on Jomsborg by acting like a weakling. The curly-haired Viking patted his shoulder and went immediately to give a hand to Skargeir.

'Sigvalde is a coward!'

372

'Sit still and lift your arm a little more, Sigvalde took responsibility for Jomsborg and he, who is responsible, is never miserable.'

Vagn spat, but Bjørn did not care and Arnulf glanced at them through narrow slits. Coward? Responsible? The Ågeson was too much warrior to lose in a battle. Perhaps that was why Palnatoke originally handed Jomsborg to Sigvalde and not to his grandson? Vagn would have fought until all were killed! The fort was now drained of men, at half strength but alive, and new would seek it, but the best of them all would never again step through the rampart's gate.

*****

While the gloom threw a mantle over fjelds and islands, and the rain ceased, the worst wounds were bound, and the men huddled on the three guarded ships. Like black shadows, the loose vessels drifted together in Hjörungavádr with subdued creaking, but now and then the moon got the seat of honour as the clouds drifted by one another, and the northern night was swaddled with summer. Arnulf crept up to Svend and asked him to lean on his shoulder, for as sore as he was, he was still able to move, and the Bueson looked troublingly weak. Vagn had stuck Snap in his belt when Svend was reluctant to be separated from the axe and he himself could not have it at his side. There was no food, and the water went quickly, and not everyone who had taken off a kyrtle earlier, could find new clothes, but Little Ketil gave Arnulf a large lamb's skin vest and helped him put Serpenttooth on his hip with a new sword belt. After a rest, the dark warrior called them together, where he sat, to counsel despite his weaknesses, and all who could manage it moved closer.

'We have two options.'

Vagn had righted himself and was pulled into his lacerated kyrtle again, 'We can stay here and let Hakon's thralls catch us tomorrow, which I am not so much in favour of, or we can go ashore and make all kinds of mischief for the Northmen that we can manage, and afterwards try to get to safety.'

Make mischief for the Northmen! Arnulf cast his eyes up on the moon. Get to safety? Who here was able to escape from the bay, not to mention stand upright with a sword? And how could the skeid possibly sail past the earl's guards without being accosted! Bjørn the Bretlander shook his head. His old face was deeply furrowed in the new night, furrowed by grief more than pain, 'We cannot fight, and you know it. But we certainly

373

cannot let Hakon pick us up like rabbits in a trap, and the ships have to stay here.'

'There are not many of us who can swim tonight.'

Little Ketil wound linen around his knee, 'But if we take the mast and yard, we can float with them inland, and then we can see how persistently Hakon minds his own vessels.'

An approving murmur went through the men in support of his statement and Vagn looked around. Haug and Svend had possibly enough strength to hang on to the mast if they got help, and Ketil's plan was not bad. As long as the ships lay where they lay, Hakon's watchmen would probably be satisfied for as tired as they were, they hardly had owl eyes.

'So let us put it into action immediately, now, while Hakon's men are scrambling to bind themselves and are not expecting anything other than that we remain here, groaning. How does it look on your ships, Arngrim and Skargeir?'

The two Jomsvikings declared their surviving companions ready to follow Vagn, and the strongest men got up at once to release the skeid's mast and yard and lift them into the water. Svend expressed no enthusiasm over the prospect of having to get into the water and Little Ketil came limping towards the thwart with a determined expression.

'Can you manage, Veulf? Then I will make sure to keep Svend afloat.'

Arnulf nodded fiercely. Yes, he could. His shield arm was in fair condition, and his left leg could still kick out, it looked much worse for the Bueson who could hardly hold himself up despite the shoulder-support.

'Do not look like me! Am I a worm? As long as I do not ... have to crawl on my stomach, I still have limbs enough to hold on.'

Svend was angry, angry at his own weakness.

'I am only helping you so Vagn does not strangle me if you drown. You and Bjørn; as long as you both breathe; he can endure anything.'

Little Ketil smiled and was forgiven, and the two long stems slipped in the water with the least possible noise. The bay was dark, but no darker than that sharp eyes could see what was happening, the water had to be crossed quietly, a splash and moan could reveal them all. Man after man was helped from the ship and found place along the floating wood, and Bjørn the Bretlander kept a lookout in the bow. Arnulf pulled off the lamb's skin vest so as not to drown in it. He carried it with him but was hardly able to limp or find support with his arm, and the icy saltwater smarted unbearably in his wounds, but the worst was the dizziness from the blood loss. Intoxicated, erratic, swirling mind. The wet vest was laid over the mast, the cold rolled the pain to a distance, and as soon as his shield arm got a hold of the roundness of the sail's wood, the eagerness of the action was aroused. Kjartan and Ketil lifted both Haug and Svend down from the shield rim, and Vagn was the last to leave the skeid after having bid farewell to the dying.

Softly, softly slid the conquered Jomsvikings over Hjörungavádr. With water up to their necks, every pair of eyes were vital, and the mast and yard had not been moved far before Arnulf realised how hopeless their actions were. Many were too badly injured to stay long in the water and a few fathoms out the first began to let go, to surrender and descend from their companions to drown in silence. The sea seemed to have taken the coldness from the hail, and Ketil had to keep a hold of Svend with all his might. Arnulf kicked as best he could, but even though the Vikings floated, their strength for forward movement was little, and when the top of the mast at last reached land, many were so exhausted that they had to be pulled up on the stony ground. Unkind rocks bristled, wide teeth in their mouths, but Arnulf was so exhausted, he almost did not feel the unevenness, and he crawled, dragging his affected leg over to a cattle-sized stone and sat panting with his back against it. The lamb's skin vest was soaked, never had iron been heavier, but wet wool was better shelter than naked skin, so he crept into it. His body shivered from cold and pain, and his fingers felt like they had been replaced by icicles, Thor give him strength if he were ever to leave his seat again! Around him, his shipmates slumped where they stood, battered and beaten after several days of storms at sea, and Svend tried, half senseless, to falter inland hanging between Ketil and Kjartan. Arnulf beckoned them to him. If they lay Bue's son on the ground, the life really would drain out of him.

'Put him up against me, then at least he will get a little warmth.'

He spread his legs so the Silkenhaired could rest up against his chest and avoid the cold of the stone, and the Jomsmen obeyed. Svend's head came to rest heavily against his shield shoulder and the weight increased the pressure on the wound and pushed his ribs, but the warmth was worth it.

'Where are we?'

The voice trembled.

'Inland, I suppose.'

Arnulf did not care where exactly but the Bueson sucked the warmth into him while his back went numb from the stone's ice. Was it now, they should steal a ship from Hakon? Vagn remained on his feet, and the strongest men sat down, silent and freezing, while Kjartan sneaked a

375

look along the round bank. Arnulf's eyes followed him, and the great Jomsman came quickly back with discouraging news, 'We are not inland, Vagn Ågeson.'

He threw his hands up, despairingly, 'This is that bird rock we saw in the middle of the bay. I believe we are now worse off than on the ships.'

Bird rock!

'You are wrong!'

The dark warrior lifted his clenched fist, but Kjartan shook his head, 'No.'

He turned his back to Vagn and sat with Haug, who lay crouching on the ground, bravely choking his coughing into his arm. Birds' rock! Impossible! How? The Northern earl had truly had seidhrs with him – even the islands moved for their will! Vagn wavered, and Bjørn Fosterfather stood up and grabbed his arm, 'Come. Sit. Now we rest, there is nothing else to be done.'

'No!'

The Ågeson stumbled unwillingly with him, and the Bretlander forced him to sit down next to Arnulf and Svend while the weary men around them moved closer together to better warm each other and endure.

'No!'

Vagn supported his head in his hands, groaning deeply, 'What have I led us out in! Why, Bjørn? Who is it that goes against us?'

Fiery, he looked up when the Bretlander put his arm around him, and his pain could be sensed and glimpsed as the pain flashed; pain that almost cut his body off from his mind.

'We walk the paths we must, rest now. You are hit hard, and I fear Hakon will not look mildly on you in the morning. '

'Hakon! Our death will become Sigvalde's shadow.'

Bjørn did not deny it, and Arnulf leaned his head against the stone, stiff, as if he were a corpse.

'And my promises! Them I will not be able to keep, on the contrary Torkel will come to adorn his farm with my head on a stick!'

The old man's answer was a breath intended only for the few, and though the words cut, the voice was gentle, 'Vagn, by Palnatoke's blood! You are a foot from breaching Jomsborg's laws, collect yourself! Spring the sax into your chest if you crave more dejection.'

The answer seemed to throw saltwater in the face of their heir, and Vagn became silent, tight-lipped. Arnulf stared blankly out over the water, promises! How could the Ågeson possible think of them now?

Proud words of killings and rape, now Torkel Lere himself would get to take his life as revenge for his craving after Ingeborg, but what did it all mean? They would die, die, and he did not even have the strength to fear! The mast bobbed onto the bank, as the yard was about to drift away, but no one cared to haul the trunks on to land. The silence was broken only by sighs and muffled movements, and the fire from Hakon's force glared in on the land. The earl's men had warmth. Mead. Food. Victory. Now and then, the sound of voices got louder over the bay, but otherwise the water was silent, brooding upon the slain and rocking the dying to eternal sleep. Jomsborg's sons. Dark Men. A shivering flock of downtrodden warriors, whose shimmering night-eyes reflected defeat, while they each prepared for their own death. Svend stirred uneasily, turning his head, 'Do you have water, Veulf?'

'No.'

Bue's son was warm, warmer than he should be; sweat had broken out on his icy forehead.

'It is possible to drink salt water. One ... of my kinsmen from Bornholm once went to sea without oars, and he ... survived by drinking salt water ... He ...'

'Arnulf.'

'Who? What do you mean?'

Was did it matter? Who here would lift their eyebrows for the sake of an outlaw?

'My name is Arnulf, not Veulf.'

The shadow of a former sparkling smile curled on his lips, and Svend fumbled with his hand for his. Arnulf took it and held firmly, and Vagn turned against him. Behind his back he made out Ketil's face.

'I am called Arnulf, and I killed my brother, Rolf. I did not mean to ... but it happened anyway.'

Behind the pain, the grass spread out softly. His mind untensed a little, released its hold, and Frejdis' downy-soft skin pressed relief on his wounds.

'I had to escape ... They had sentenced me an outlaw, I ...'

Vagn lifted his hand, soothingly, 'We know, you betrayed yourself long ago. Many men in Jomsborg share your story and are not looked down upon. Where are you from? Arnulf.'

They knew it! And said nothing. And Svend right from the beginning!

'Egilssund. My father's name is Stridbjørn.'

377

The Ågeson smiled, 'Then you have another brother, have not you? Helge Stridbjørnson's name was mentioned among the hird at the royalseat, and only for good.'

Arnulf looked into the black eyes without returning the smile. The burning pain in his thigh returned, gnawing a worm into the bone, 'Helge is dead.'

He could not muster up any more words, Gleipner's grip, why had he ever mentioned it?

'Were they good brothers?'

Arnulf nodded, tired, but his voice failed him, 'The best!'

He rested his head against the stone again, avoiding Vagn's stare. In the darkness, among the men, they stood, Stridbjørn's brothers, but his sword arm was destroyed. Never again would it wrestle in a Viking grasp with Helge, never again would he bump his fist with Rolf's, condemned! Vagn did not ask anything else, and both Bjørn and Ketil drew eyes to themselves. Wolves run in high grass, raiding on blunt claws, Svend's oppressed pain prevented him seeking refuge behind his eyelids. He suffered, the Bueson, suffered so his body was about to explode, as the fever rose. Arnulf drew his uninjured knees up to give Svend more support and continued to hold the clenched hand. Veulf, Arnulf, fate was the same regardless of the name.

'Tomorrow, I will find a boat, and then I will sail you home to Vesete on Bornholm. We will take Vagn with us. And Haug. Bjørn can take the helm. You just sit here and breathe, then it will be tomorrow again, and then I will lay you between the thwarts.'

A tremor went through the Silkenhaired, and the hand's grip became harder, 'Arnulf. I cannot ... Bue is dead!'

'I will tell your father's father about his death, you just need to gather your strength and get well, then I will sail you home to his farm, and rest myself there, too. We will get there quickly; the wind will turn south at dawn. I will stop at a fjord and get some freshly baked bread. And fresh milk.'

Svend sighed, quivering, and leaned his cheek against Arnulf, 'I can feel the shreds of the end of my life's thread.'

'It's just something you're seeing because you have a fever.'

'Hakon will kill us tomorrow. I will die well!'

Svend raised his head, 'Did you hear? I am tired now, but tomorrow I will die like a Jomsviking dies!'

'Sssh!'

Arnulf pulled his head back against his shoulder at the hair. 'You will not die; you are going to sail with me. Just sit here and rest, and I'll provide for you. Tomorrow I will be strong enough, just wait!'

Vagn rose, strained. Stumbling, curled up and pressing his hand against his side with a rock-crushing glance but he then straightened, looked up and took in the slain men. Like a helmsman looked at his shattered ship, a king's his burned land, he looked at his battle-brothers and then began to go to each in turn, exchanging words and gripping fists. The Ågeson said farewell and gave courage, gave promises of fidelity and honourable death, the conversations were soft, he knew each man, shared their minds and the only ones he did not lay hands on were Svend and Bjørn.

Arnulf closed his eyes, but the pain gave him no rest. The flesh was cut up, torn, split and a large black raven seemed to be hacking agony into one, while Nidhogg gnawed the other wound and sucked the blood, frozen as it was in his veins, he would not bleed to death! It hammered through his broken fingers, and the fatigue piled stones over his limbs, never again would he be able to get up, he could probably sleep from the cold but not the pain. The Bueson's breathing was strained, as if he was denying the torments, the exhaustion would eat even more mercilessly into his struggling body.

'Arnulf!'

Arnulf looked up into the dark warrior's face, and Vagn struggled to raise his voice so the men around could hear him, 'Arnulf Stridbjørnson, you fought like a Jomsviking today! You stood for Svend, and no one could have shielded him better, you slew an Ulfhednar! Tomorrow we will be killed one and all. It cannot be avoided, but will you die like one of us? Will you die a Jomsviking?'

A fire-hot roaring rinsed the blood wild and the eagle flapped its wings, so the south wind sang! The sky cleared itself of clouds and the fjelds blocked his flight upwards no more than the stones on the shore. Behind Vagn Ågeson stood Palnatoke, wide and mighty in the shadows of the mountains, and further south, where the nights were warm, Jomsborg spread its earthen rampart on the plain like an oath-ring of gold!

'Yes, I will, Vagn Ågeson!'

The voice was frayed and hoarse, the honour touched him so deeply. Vagn smiled broadly and turned to his men, 'Has anyone here an objection to Arnulf coming among us as a Jomsviking? After today, I see no reason for him to pass the tests.'

Only warm smiles and appreciative head shakes met Vagn who reached out both his hands to Arnulf, taking his unharmed hand in a kinsman's grasp, 'You know Jomsborg's laws and know the promises inherent in your answer! Therefore, your yes will be enough, as it is now, and we have all mingled blood today, but before that, you became my blood-brother, and that oath is binding! A name you have won, and you shall be known by it, Arnulf Wolfblood, be welcomed into the brotherhood and I wish your time with us, as short as it is, may bring you luck and honour.'

An approvingly murmur floated towards Arnulf, but only Bjørn, Ketil and Kjartan could stand on their feet to shake hands. Arnulf Wolfblood. For a moment, the walls of the hall rose up in the dark, the mead mugs clashed together, the long fire roared, and the laughter lifted the mood, then Sigvalde's longhouse and the ramparts of Jomsborg disappeared again, but they echoed in his chest, and the skaldic verses sounded. Svend smiled proudly and Vagn stood irresolute. Rather than silence, the Ågeson had probably wanted cries and feasting, which undoubtedly was custom when a new man joined Jomsborg but wound-heavy, he sank, feeble, his back against the stone and shoulder against Arnulf, 'Rest now, son of Stridbjørn, rest if you can, Odin will see to the celebrations of this! Even I have to sleep a little; I think Torkel Lere will request Hakon make something special out of my death, and I would like to be able to withstand as is expected of me.'

He closed his eyes, but Arnulf was too excited to think of life ending now, not as a Jomsviking! That word put chainmail between pain and desire, a chainmail of hope and unexpected force! Wolfblood!

'Earl Hakon does not need to prove his victory by tormenting our deaths.'

'Do not talk to Vagn about more now, my young Jomsman. He has carried a heavier burden today than most others.'

Bjørn was sharp but his eyes were warm and Arnulf was silent, silent in the still waters of joy, in the hope of spring, in the fragrance of buds, the day would dawn well again, and that more than once! Arnulf Wolfblood! He slowly let his eyes slide over his Jomsbrothers. As soon as he had risen, as soon as they all had ships-passage to the south, he would encircle his wolves' shields with red and hang one of them up on the most beautiful longhouse in Jomsborg, he would exchange blows with the Bueson on top of Jomsborg's ramparts and participate in banner ground fights without yielding! Sigvalde would lift his mug to him, Torkel the Tall would forget his scorn and Sigurd Buesbrother would send a man to

Egilssund with the good news. Indeed, King Sweyn might even ask the Thing to reverse its decision on the outlawry! It flickered before his eyes, as the pain jarred with the joy with cruel shocks. Veulf. Veulf. The ice was too thin! The shields were broken, Vagn was going to die, and Svend had already begun his journey on Slidr! No one, except the men on the bird rock, should hear about his appointment, Stridbjørn would forever condemn him, and Leif could, with glee, boast that the woman-shamer's brother had now drowned for the second time! Fenrir's rage! He touched his prey with his fingertips, only to lose the animal, and the fall was greater than the misfortune which had once hit him!

A ship was slowly rowed out of the darkness and set a course for the open sea behind the rock, a longship. Arnulf took a stand against his grief, regarding it with watchful resentment. The rowers did not seem to be in a hurry, had the warriors' escape been discovered? Mjölnir protected the fallen, after tonight Hakon's men could collect them, but not now, not as exhausted as they were! The ship seemed to want to slip by, soberly and without rocking its cargo unnecessarily and the two raven heads in the bow guarded its crew threateningly, their beaks dilated. The skin flinched, scalded, and Arnulf stared the night asunder, tense from heel to the roots of his hair. *Twin Raven!* Toke! Toke was out there! With a blink, he forced the eagle forward in the failing sight. The battle had been fought so near Haraldsfjord, the ship was apparently bearing its wounded back to the settlements immediately after parting with the earl that they should not be under the open sky, when women and care were waiting by the hearths. Toke would rather his men had a good night under their own roofs than himself be part of the honour and victory feasting that had to follow, and now Arnulf could see him, Arnulf could see him! He sat with Stentor under the raven heads, bareheaded, his gaze distant, towards the open, uninjured enough to lead his flock out of the bay, and the tears blurred in his eyes, so Arnulf had to wipe them away with the back of his hand. Toke! He lived! Freyr's favour! And Stentor lived, too! Both his chest and hand lifted, wanting to reach out for the ship but stiffened abruptly.

If he cried out now, Toke would put ashore on the rock immediately, he would burst into tears of joy and throw himself around Arnulf's neck, take him home, call Gyrith of the bed and ask Hildegun to find the ointment jars, but ...! Arnulf looked over the Jomsvikings. Earl Hakon would accuse Toke of treason if he helped the enemy after the injuries they had caused the North people. He would lead the Øystein's son to the Thing, pass judgement and accuse him of stealing the prisoners, disown him and give the seized chieftain seat to his valiant housecarl, Leif

Cleftnose, and what should Toke do with Svend, with Vagn, with Bjørn, Little Ketil, Kjartan and all the others? He himself could never leave them; definitely not as a Jomsviking! His heart ripped in two. For the sake of goodness, Toke would plunge himself and his descendants into misfortune, but Gyrith awaited him, Hildegun, Jofrid, Ranvig and the unborn child!

Tears streamed down his cheeks, and Svend turned his head, questioningly, but Arnulf did not see him, he saw only Toke, saw how *Twin Raven* curved from the rock, turning the aft to them, and saw the moon white keel-water cut the bay, as if it were his own chest! And silent. Made no sign. He did not lift Svend out of the way, to get up and have his arm damned, eternally damned, Toke and Gyrith should not be torn with him in his fall!

Arnulf bowed his head while pain and despair tormented his mind. Now he was drowning indeed, Jomsviking or not! Everything was lost, everything: life, desire, will, hope! The only thing that remained was a night full of cold, thirst and endless pain that would drain all courage. Finally, Fenrir had company on his wind-swept island, so generously did the jötunn-wolf reward his faithful blót-giving man at the end, with bitter suffering and miserable death. The Ravenbear help him for his mistake!

*****

One of earl Hakon's largest longships docked at the rock shortly after dawn, and even Vagn Ågeson was not in a position to resist when the Norwegians captured the Jomsvikings. Haug was still alive, but it was unnecessary to tie the Bornholmer, yet the housecarls threw ropes around him just as they threw ropes around everyone else, they were only allowed to support each other down to the ship before their hands were forced behind their back in loops and knots.

Arnulf did not make a sound, despite both his elbow and armpit being on fire, and Little Ketil loosened Svend's grip on his neck and let him gently slide down on a thwart before he himself took a seat and was bound. Vagn followed without a word, the pain was united, the fate and the defeat, all was said that had to be said. Heavy in the head and heavier in body, but with hazy air behind his eyes Arnulf let his shoulder lean supportively against Svend, who swaying, tried to remain seated with a pensive gaze. Feverish and glassy-eyed, the Silkenhaired endured, despite him whispering that Bue probably did not have to wait long for his coming at the end of the night. Arnulf had wanted to deny him and persuade him differently, but his strength was too little. Kjartan had fetched seawater in his helmet for those men who desired it. It was disgusting to drink, but the thirst was quenched for a moment. Bjørn had counted ten dead men, as the Norwegian ship approached, but when Vagn, stiff, had to fight to stand up, his palms against the stone, muttering about sword stabs, the Bretlander had shook his head.

The ship set out, and the men grasped the oars. In the bay, Hakon's men were plundering the drifting vessels for goods and weapons, the harvest was rich and joyous cries rang from the men every time a special, sumptuous blade was wrenched free from a dead man or a helmet with inlaid gold was dried clean. On land the loot was gathered around Hakon's banner pole in front of the camp ground, and the pile grew all the time, the victory was to be celebrated, and the earl praised and the cheering rose at the sight of the captured Jomsvikings, now awaited the pleasure of revenge for the injuries!

Arnulf stared down between his feet. The light was better than the darkness and the raw morning air pressed the night's torment away a little. When the ship reached land, when he and the others set foot on solid ground, he had to show no weakness, he must not express fear, he was now a Jomsviking, and he was about to die, so Vagn and Svend would recognise him, if he betrayed his promises, he would cast shame upon his companions. Jomsborg! He raised his head. Arnulf Wolfblood, the grey predator's scion, no death was so acrid that he would be unable to look it in the eye with a straight back! He stared hard at Hakon's banner, the Northmen on the banks and thralls by the fires, even if Leif Cleftnose himself were to cut him into strips, he would not murmur in the least!

A group of distinguishably clad men stood in conversation down by the water, and Arnulf recognised Erik Earlson in the red silk kyrtle. The large self-confident man with a gold ring on his forehead standing by his side could only be his father, Hakon, so alike in features was his son, but who the others were, none of the Jomsvikings seemed to know, only Vagn stiffened when a smooth-necked Northman in a blue cloak turned around and spotted him. The fjeldman jolted, then a wolverine-grin spread over his face, and Thor could not have looked more furious than the dark warrior whose lowered eyebrows leaned like bear claws over his eyes. Hakon's companion had to be Torkel Lere, and that he had heard about the Ågeson's promises were burned into his posture. Eagerly the vassal shared words with his earl, and what favour it was he asked for could only be guessed, but Hakon seemed to grant it to him, and the malicious laughter the vassal threw at the Ågeson announced revenge for more than just killing Northmen.

Leif Cleftnose was not to be found in the flock, and Hakon and his followers were silent as the longship ran its bow aground. Both the earl's and Erik's faces could now be seen clearly, and although there was scorn on the hard faces, neither of them radiated cruelty. The greying earl rested mightily in his condition and beautiful and empowering did his heir grace his side, and although their carls on the banks gathered to gloat about the captives, father and son remained standing with worthy expressions.

Thralls with ropes met Vagn's men on the strand, and despicable cries rained down over the Jomsvikings along with commands to leave the ship. The Ågeson stood up, as if he were a visiting king, and so strong was his spear's gaze that the condescending scolding words ceased, and faces turned away. One by one, the Jomscompanions followed after him, all proud and sharp-eyed and even Haug managed, out of sheer spite, to jump overboard without support. Svend stood up, surprisingly, as if there was nothing wrong with him, but behind his hot eyes Arnulf could see the dried softwood burning up in mighty flames. Incomprehensible how the Bueson managed to get his limbs to obey, he had been hit so violently. His life seemed to flame with a devouring fire. Die, he would die like a Jomsviking and if his heart ruptured, before Hakon decided how, the Stout would be pleased to welcome him by Asgard's wall!

Arnulf took courage from the Silkenhaired, shooing the pain away, the wounds would not determine how he drew his last breath! Brusquely the Jomsvikings were ordered to sit on the coarse sand in a long row, and Svend sat by Vagn, while Bjørn slid down on the Ågeson's other side and called for Arnulf. Arnulf would rather have sat with Svend, but the tightly-freckled man with the broken front teeth, who had stood on Sigvalde's ship, was to sit there; apparently he had chosen to die with Vagn rather than to save the life of his chieftain.

A solid thrall that the Northmen called Skofte, now tied all the Jomsvikings together by the feet with a long rope, and stood up to guard his catch, while the earl and his retinue went up to the tents and banner pole to divide the plunder, passing judgement on the Danes was not urgent. Several men were summoned, there were enough gifts to give, and many to be rewarded. Magnanimously, the earl gave away weapons and jewellery with praise, and now Leif Cleftnose also came hurrying, his clefted nose apparently had no trouble sniffing out gold, it was hard to watch, hard as a newly honoured Jomsviking! The rope twisted his sword arm, so it pounded under the bandages, but Arnulf refused to complain. If

384

Svend and the other seriously wounded could bear it, so could he! Silently the warriors sat, shoulder against shoulder, but Little Ketil quickly found it too sad, in any case, he leaned forward and grinned challenging at Vagn and Svend, 'I do not believe you have heard what Thorhal Buckbag has been doing this winter. You probably both remember that he was badly hit when Ejolf Icelander carried out his trails before the winter?'

Thorhal Buckbag! Little Ketil should be kicked and embraced! The mood changed abruptly, as if the men were sitting at a long table and not bound on the sandy shores and the Bueson grabbed the question like a knáttleikr ball. His voice cheerful, 'Ugly it is to come from Bretland to battle and not even hear all the news! What happened to him? When we set out, he lay writhing in Sigurd's longhouse.'

Ketil's laughter spread to more of the surrounding men, 'Thorhal, that bull, he probably felt that life was about to run from him, so he asked Sigvalde a favour. He so wanted to end his days with Godfred on Højbo, for he has five good and skilled daughters, who not least you, Svend, know very well.'

Svend laughed out loud, and glares came from the camp. Laughter was probably not what Hakon's carls expected from bleeding, defeated men. Disbelievingly, Arnulf blew a lock of hair away from his eyes. The Bueson could not laugh! Had the rest really done him such good? Where did this unexpected strength come from?

'Yes, I know them very well, especially the youngest! I believe Thorhal was cared for at Godfred's!'

'He was! It especially soothed his back when he embraced his daughters, and he was, of course, in pain. Before the winter feast began, three of them awaited children, Thorhal took a woman faster than Bue emptied a horn.'

Kjartan hooted, elated, 'Thorhal Buckbag! He made men turn pale and womenfolk blush; that he will be remembered for, though he was a fool with a longspear.'

Vagn had his say on spears of varying length and the Jomsvikings roared with laughter, red in the face, and Arnulf laughed with them. The last time he would laugh, laugh so the wounds leaked, laugh until the iron hit him and maybe even longer still!

'Did he recover? I do not recall having seen him since we returned from Bretland.'

The Silkenhaired waved in front of the men's heads.

'You have to say he died of overwork, but few die happier! He dreamed that the stomachs were bursting with sons and rose heavily from

385

his bed. Now Sigvalde will get thrice in return what he is about to lose, he said, and then he tumbled to the floor, grinning from ear to ear.'

Svend's laughter was light, Vagn's roaring and Bjørn's as deep as a full-fat ox humming. The earl's folk stared out angrily from the tents, but Ketil had more stories to tell, and Hakon's force did not get to eat in peace, when, after the first distribution of the goods, they sat down to do so. Arnulf did not hear much of their swaggering gloating over the victory, for the Jomsmen had decided to enjoy themselves and each word tripped over the heel of the last. Only when earl Hakon called Erik and Torkel Lere to him and, with a larger retinue, began to go down towards the captives at the strand, did Little Ketil keep his cheerfulness inside and the row of Jomsvikings became silent. Bjørn looked warmly at Arnulf, so the icy wind from the Death Realm swept their feet rigid, while the echo of laughter floated away over the bay, as free as thoughts.

Torkel Lere had a huge broad axe on his shoulder. The blue cloak he had let remain at the tents, so his arms could swing without hindrance, and he followed steadily in the earl's footsteps, staring at Vagn with scorn and triumph shining from his face. The vassal seemed satisfied by whatever torments he had in mind for Vagn, and Arnulf bit his tongue. Scary the way the axe drew eyes to it! It was beautiful, richly inlaid with silver and sparklingly sharp; surely it would cut well, and Torkel seemed to be a strong man. Leif Cleftnose was also among the retinue, and the lush beard was split wildly into two parts when he saw Arnulf among Vagn's men. If Torkel expressed the hatred for Jomsborg's strongest, then Leif expressed unmixed delight at his finding, and the vassal should apparently not be the only one to be granted a favour, because with persuasive gestures the Cleftnose pointed and spoke his case to the earl. Hakon fixed his eyes on Arnulf but then shook his head firmly. Whether he recognised the Ulfhednar slayer was unclear, but the prisoners' lives belonged to his whim, and however close Leif was to him, the Jomsvikings did not count as plunder, a reward to be distributed indiscriminately.

Arnulf looked at the Cleftnose as if Leif were a rotten sheep stomach and deigned him no further attention. He should not have the joy of being noticed, a miserable fjord fisherman that was what he was and what did a Jomsviking care for a slimy cod-eater? It was a curse to have to see death assisted by so disgusting a man and the humiliation smarted, but that stinking goat fart should not suspect his effect, Ran strangle him!

Arnulf snorted and tried to swallow, but his mouth was dry, and his body lacked moisture. The axe. So cool its shadow. If this should be so, then Torkel was likely to start in the middle of the row, rather that, than deedless await the blow and be present at his shipmates' deaths! Earl Hakon stopped in front of Vagn and his men began to smear the air with condescending shouts and demeaning questions, but not one of them received an answer, and the Ågeson's quiet gaze anchored deep in Hakon's. Torkel Lere shook each fist in turn and spat on his palms before the axe squealed some tentative gashes in front of him, and while the earl said not a word but weighed his opponents' bravery with his eyes and gave the sign to Torkel to begin his killing.

The nails pierced his skin and the sweat burst from the skin on his back. The outer men were the worst wounded and the last to leave ship, and the thrall, Skofte, loosened the first and led him away in front of the earl, whereupon he kicked the legs out from under the man and thrust him forward. The Jomsviking had bled much and offered no resistance, and it was not difficult for Torkel to find his target. The eyes he sent Ågeson were hideous, as if he was only warming up his sacrificial knife before the blót. Then the axe fell. It startled Arnulf when the head flew off and dumped to the ground, and the man had lost so much blood that his neck quickly ran dry. Bjørn's expression revealed nothing, and the row of men remained silent, but the fjeldmen's hoots and Leif's shouts stung, although Hakon raised his hand immediately after and stopped the noise. Arnulf clenched his teeth. Die as a Jomsviking! Die as a warrior! Would he be able to stand in front of the axe, would the terror not overwhelm him, beat screams for mercy from his throat and let him squirm at the earl's feet in an attempt to save his life? He had not been counted among Sigvalde's folk long!

The next man also lost his head quietly, and the thralls pulled the bodies out of the way, so the third man could advance. After him it was Haug and Arnulf was short of breath. Haug with the knáttleikr-ball in his hands, Haug with the Bornholmer-companions cries in his back, now the fathers on that rocky island would lose their sons, Bue was not the first, and Haug not the last.

The third man sank, freed from further torments, and Skofte the thrall cut Haug free and led him in front of the earl and Erik Hakonson. Hard trod the wild boar's hooves in the sand, hard and courageous. Torkel snorted, hesitantly, sizing up the heavy neck, whereby he leaned by the axe, facing his countrymen, 'Can it be seen now? I have been told that you can always tell if a man had beheaded three at once, but I do not think I can notice any change myself.'

The earl looked dryly at his vassal, 'You look just as flustered as you always have done, Torkel, continue now.'

387

Despite his pitiful condition, Haug was not easy to kick to the ground so Skofte borrowed a long-handled mallet to hit his legs with. No! Arnulf's clenched hands shook the rope. Thor beat Torkel and Helheim crack the earth, shame follow him, shame and deceit! The vassal spat and bent confidentially towards Haug, 'What do you really think about having to die, Jomsviking?'

The voice was mean but sincere in its curiosity, and Haug turned his head slowly towards him, blood pouring from his mouth. His kyrtle was drenched down to his trousers, drenched so it dripped, 'I like that I have to die. It will happen for me as it happened for my father. I die!'

His voice was dull, and his choice of words ended in gulps, but Torkel seemed to be satisfied with the answer, for he straightened up and quickly removed the head of the Bornholmer, so it rolled to Arngrim's feet. Blood gushed from the collapsed body, and Arnulf looked down, but Bjørn nudged him. His face had to be lifted, on a white neck, on the pounding thin-skinned, axe-promised neck, no man in the sand was allowed to express cowardice.

Haug's neck stump did not bleed dry before the body was pulled away to make room for Skargeir Torfinnson and the crack when the shinbone was fractured by Skofte's club made the Northern Lights flicker above Hjörungavádr. What man was that Norwegian earl that he found delight in so bloody a vision? Arnulf stared at Bjørn's command, but his eyes seemed to be turning in their hollows out of unwillingness; brave he appeared to be, brave he had decided to be, but the intention yielded to the disease of terror. He was anxious, scared like when Toke sailed from him, like when Leif's axe demanded his life, and when the chainmail pulled him under the water. True, he was not the feeblest of Jomsvikings – he had just fought for Svend's life and his own fate, and behind Serpenttooth's shiny blade, he was still just Stridbjørn's inept son from Egilssund, despised for his pointless straying and his headstrong mind!

Haug's glazed eyes stared right into the sun without blinking. The Bornholmer was no longer in pain trying to breath.

'And what do you feel, knowing that are about to die?'

Torkel lowered the axe to spare his sleeves from unnecessary stains and laughed, peering at the Ågeson. Skargeir sat erect on his knees and nodded to Vagn and Arngrim, before he took the time to answer, 'Everyone shall lose his life sooner or later, and I would be remembering Jomsborg's law badly if I whined from fear or was sorry to die.'

Such a proud man! Such worthy words! Arnulf tried unsuccessfully to moisten his lips. It was probably not enough to die fearlessly; the axe demanded words for reputation and honour, too! Harshly, he bit moisture into his mouth. What answer should be given to Torkel if the vassal continued to ask? What did he feel honestly about dying? Where were they, the words, those luminous words that would be remembered and repeated, words that men would later find strength in and respect; they had suddenly taken flight, golden sounds that otherwise were so easily captured and bent to his will.

Torkel shrugged and took a step back, taking a wide stance and swung the axe as hard as he could, and a quicker death Skargeir could not have wished for. The body fell, and it had enough blood that it both pumped and poured, and Hakon drew a step back so as not to soil his well-sewn shoes. Arnulf glanced down at the dwindling number of men in the row and then crept his eyes towards Leif. Would the Cleftnose even tell Toke about his death? Would he repeat his answer, his gaze, his fall? Well would he! Everything that could hurt Toke, he would gladly blurt out and more than once.

Arngrim Rune went willingly and knelt in his companions' blood, and Svend turned his face towards Arnulf. His glittering smile was edged with blood and most of the conifer tree was burned up, but his will seemed equally undaunted, free as that morning he had set Snap in Stefanus' neck. How could he? He must have black death in his stomach, being eaten all the way up to his heart, after such a life-draining night of woe he should be lying senseless on the ground. Arnulf's lips answered of their accord with a fiery smile. A little while yet, then he could run over the threshold to Valhalla, laughing, with his hand on the Bueson's shoulder; a little while yet, then Vagn would pound his axe in Odin's table and demand to know where his place was in the hall and Bue would spray mead over his beard, come tramping towards them, thump his Jomsmen on the back and shout to the Valkyries for more mugs! Fenrir could stay on his island until Ragnarök, Arnulf was now a Jomsviking and from now on obeyed only the One-Eyed's command! Odin! He looked up into the sky. The day was bright. The sun was out. Helge awaited him, bursting from impatience, he had waited all night, trudged from Bifrost to Valhalla and back again, shouted that his brother no longer stood near the jötunn-wolf but had won the respect of men and honour and proved his worth so Bragi could make songs about it! Therefore, Arnulf could smile to Svend and grasp his mind with his eyes, rope and body would rot to dirt from the axe's fall, but never had a man from Jomsborg lost courage and speech!

The Northmen were talking loudly together. Earl Hakon wanted for each Jomsviking to be asked like the first, for it could be amusing to know their thoughts and see if they really were as hard as rumour said, and although Erik Earleson did not think there was any reason to question the prisoners' courage as they now sat and had cheered themselves, he, too, was inflamed by this venture. Torkel Lere weighed his axe impatiently and then sent Arngrim an acidic look, 'What do you think about having to die?'

Arngrim sounded angry at Skargeir's death, and sharp-hatred sliced his voice, 'Fame, I have won, and only good will be spoken about me, so I would like to know death, but you will have to face disgrace and insults, as long as you live!'

He laughed tremendously and continued to laugh until the axe drove its wedge furiously through his neck, and Ketil was then cut free of the foot rope. A distance scream tore the clouds from the sky, a cry that began in Egilssund and hurried over the Dane Land to Jomsborg, to eventually roll between the mountains like thunder. Svend's smile withered away. It was bad to see a friend being thrown to the ground in front of him by thrall-fists, but the little warrior did not lose his glow for so little. Only two men, then the Bueson would stand for his turn, and Asgard lost itself behind Midgard's rim, Little Ketil was a good man, although his neck was among the thinnest. Torkel asked his question again, with the Northmen listening attentively. The Jomsvikings' courage seemed to baffle them, despite all the skaldic verses and stories. Ketil met the vassal's curiosity with his own and spoke unconcernedly, as if they were sitting at a table, 'I feel very good about having to die, but I will ask you to loosen my hands before you strike, for there is one thing we Jomsvikings have talked about many times, and we are finally able to find out for certain.'

He smiled subtly to Bjørn and Svend, and the earl gave a consenting sign to Skofte to cut the rope. The Northmen at the rear moved closer and Little Ketil drew his knife and held it up so everyone could see it, 'That, which we cannot agree on in Jomsborg, is whether you feel something after you are dead or not. Strike now Torkel Lere, and do not fumble with the axe. I will have a clean and quick cut, and if I feel anything after my throat is cut through, I will turn the knife blade upwards. The only thing that will annoy me then, is if Sigvalde and our brothers in the south do not get the message later.'

'They will get the message, you have my word on that, but give me your name, too, so they may know to whom the deed should be attributed.'

Earl Hakon just smiled, and Erik looked amazed at the little warrior whose boldness under the axe far surpassed the previous men's.

'Ketil Northmanslayer you can call me, for despite my size I felled more of your men yesterday than you and your heir felled Danes together!'

The Jomsviking turned the knife horizontally and Torkel gave a challenging nod and fixed his eyes on Vagn. Little Ketil! *The Blood Fox's* rider, the Separator of Feet from Legs, Svend's laughter companion, Arnulf wanted to throw himself on the vassal's legs, rip the weapon from him and plant it in his chest, throw him to the dogs, in the sea, down the mountains, no revenge was too ugly, for the killing he intended to do!

Torkel gripped the axe firmly and took aim, putting weight behind his swing, although it was not necessary. Ketil's head flew right over to the executed Jomswarriors and the arm fell with the body to the ground, without the knife turning either up or down. Flame-scorched sand! Hog-tied lungs! Arnulf wanted to tear off the ropes and with his wolf teeth bite the throat of the vassal to shreds. Did he not know what sort of men it was that he so stone-hearted killed? Did he not know how poorer he made Midgard by silencing such mighty heroes? Swans dying at the cackling of geese! Did madness know no limit? Earl Hakon had seen what a waste it was to splinter dignified lives; now that he himself had lost so many. Erik Earlson had to see that and talk sense to his father! So strongly had he fought against Vagn and enjoyed an equal opponent. A wise warlord would never let so useless a blood game continue!

Kjartan rose from the row and pulled himself free of Skofte's hands with contempt. The thrall followed him watchfully but apparently did not wish to risk anything, for the Jomsviking was big and did not seem in the least weakened, a kick could break the back of a larger man than Skofte. It was Torkel himself, who had to force the legs to kneel with the axe, but when Kjartan started to speak after the vassal had once again asked his question, it could only be poorly heard from him that the tendons were cut, 'I think just as my companions, who gave their lives here, did about having to die, but there is another thing that we Jomsvikings have talked about other than that Ketil named, and that is whether your eyes blink if you are struck in the middle of your face.

Some believe that the eyes blink by themselves, while others believe that it is something you are master of, so I would ask all here to watch carefully, and I will sit so my companions can see it.'

'You will get it as you want it, warrior. Hit the carl in the face, Torkel and hit him well!'

The earl nodded to his vassal, and Kjartan turned his back on him, pulling back a little, so Torkel had enough space to swing the axe without hitting anyone sitting. The Northmen moved out to the sides to look, while the vassal took stock of the angle, so the axe would take Kjartan right in his line of sight, and Vagn welcomed his companion's gaze and held it with deep respect and warmth. Then the great Jomsman fixed his eyes on the axe, and Arnulf saw no blinking when the weapon struck. The head was cut through the nose, the brain splattered before the blood, and Kjartan sat for a while before he collapsed as the Norwegians murmured, puzzled. Arnulf stared at the half-open mouth under the mush. The dead man had nice teeth and the vomit stiffened behind the lungs. So much horror could never be recovered from! The lust for life shrank, gloomy, as hard as coal and barren, and the pain cut with renewed strength. Trud's grief over her youngest was not in vain. Stridbjørn would, with disgust, tear the memory from his chest, and from now on no one in the village would dare to utter the disowned's name, only the forest wolves would know their loss from the stench of blood!

Torkel Lere went challengingly towards Vagn and let the axe drip over his head, his teeth bared, but the Ågeson's taunts to him were whispered so softly that no one else heard them, and the vassal's grip, white from tension, on the shaft started to vibrate while the lips pinched the mouth into a bloodless gash. For a moment, it looked as if Vagn would not have to wait for his turn, then Hakon's carl turned on his heel and strode off stiff-legged ready for his next murder.

Svend's side was exposed when the tightly freckled man with the broken front teeth stood up. Without letting himself feel the deaths of his companions, he went briskly over to the earl and, like Little Ketil, asked that his hand be freed. Arnulf had difficulty seeing him clearly as his heart began to beat now. It sloshed behind his ribs, as if whales were slapping their tails in the sea's roaring, in a moment it would be Svend and soon afterwards himself! His courage flickered treacherously, his will gasped from the splintered spear through his waist. He was fearless, he would be fearless, he had to be fearless when the axe drank!

The freckled one had his rope loosened, too.

'What are you up to? Is there more, you Jomsvikings shall have unravelled today?'

'No! But I have to piss and would like to relieve myself before I sit down to dinner in a better hall than yours.'

The earl looked at him with displeasure, but some of his housecarls began to laugh, and although Arnulf was careful not to look at Leif, he could not help but hear him.

'So, piss then, what difference will it make?'

Torkel Lere stamped his foot while Skofte cut the rope, and without haste the freckled one loosened his belt and let the stream strive for the earl's legs. Bjørn the Bretlander laughed softly, and a man further down the line shouted that the freckled one was free to gush a lake for him, too, so well had Norway's ruler regaled his guests! The current ebbed away, but his manhood hesitated between his fingers, and the Jomsman looked at Hakon, 'No, it does not make much of a difference, and many things were not as I had planned. My cock here had, in fact, anticipated being cared for in bed by your woman, earl Hakon, for so many good things are said about her, and she is known to be more generous than you!'

The freckled one shook his pecker dry and pulled up his pants, but Hakon was scarlet in the face and howled for Torkel to chop as a matter of urgency, for that man was so evil in his mind that there was no reason to keep him alive any longer. The axe grabbed the neck before more words could escape the Jomsviking, but as he was standing, the blade did not quite cut through, and it was some time before he finished jerking from the heavy wound, but Arnulf only had eyes for Svend. Skofte the thrall cut the Bueson free from the rope and pulled him up, and the Silkenhaired swayed but found familiar footing, while Torkel, annoyed, hacked the freckled one once more. Svend had bled from the laughter, so his trousers were wet all the way to his ankles, and only hatred and will held him upright now. The last soft wood branches burst, sparking together in a breath-taking sight, and the warmth radiated so hotly that the fever was clearly hidden.

Bue the Stout's son walked easily over to the earl and seemed to want to make a request, as the others had done, and Arnulf set his gaze on his straight back. The Ulfhednar fight had been useless, all the training on banner ground useless, Svend's upbringing with Vagn Ågeson useless, nothing could pull him free of the Norns' unbreakable threads, and even though the fjelds bowed and wept Baldur's tears over the bay, the earl had the look of a jötunn in his dry face.

'What do you think about having to die, Goldenhair?'

Torkel rested the axe over his shoulder, demandingly, but Svend spoke only to the earl, 'I have had my best time, and now such good men have been killed that I no longer have any desire to live.'

Fast and light was the voice, with a silver sheen his last words were sounded.

'As I am very careful with my hair, I do not want blood in it, therefore I ask you that one of your men hold it from my neck when Torkel

393

strikes. I will not be touched by thrall-hands, so it must be a man who does not stand under your vassal in rank, he cannot be particularly difficult to find an equal to, and he must pull the head to himself quickly, as soon as the blow falls, otherwise all my efforts will be in vain.'

Earl Hakon nodded, his eyes focused on the silken hair, but Torkel looked cross.

'That wish I would give you gladly, young Jomsman, such fair locks are a rare sight! Who here, of my hird, will hold the hair?'

A tall long-nosed Northman came out of the flock, and Svend nodded acceptingly and knelt for Torkel's axe. Arnulf had to lean against Bjørn, the pain shook his life so violently. Liquid fire surged through his lungs, now the vassal would slew Svend, now he would slaughter him like a ram, and nothing, nothing could stop the axe's fall! Vagn's wheezing breath promised eternal visitation on the Norwegian folk, and Bjørn sat tense, his sinews set in stone. Wailing arose from the ground, everything around Arnulf cried, screamed, cursed, now the prettiest gold ring of Jomsborg burst!

Svend leaned forward and the hirdman carefully pulled the silky hair from the neck, twisting his hands into it. He looked up at Torkel and nodded, his front foot ready to pull. The axe rose, blind and cold, Haug's blood was already clotted against the blade, but the freckled man's blood still dripped. If Vagn had hated Torkel Lere before, now his shadow raised like Jörmungandr of the Deep, and the vassal must have felt it, for he sent the dark warrior a gleeful grin, before, roaring, he swung his weapon towards Svend's outstretched neck.

Arnulf screamed, but the hirdman screamed louder for the Bueson pulled his head to himself with a violent jerk as the axe rushed, and the blade hit Hakon's carl at the elbow joints, severing his forearms.

A shock-storm went through the Northmen and the Jomsvikings battle-roared while the hapless henchman writhed on the ground in a frenzied torment. Spring jumped in the gasp, and Arnulf laughed from madness! Unscathed, Svend was unscathed, the weapon had bitten so misguidedly that another man's life was thrown away! Earl Hakon could lead his legion, rule his realm and kill prisoners, but in front of Bue's son, he came up shamefully short!

Svend jumped up in front of the enraged North Sea and with an infectious laugh, shook his head, then the bonded hands dangled around his shoulders, 'What kind of a lad is it who has his fingers in my hair? Such red jewellery have I never had before! What do you think of my ornament, Vagn, it is not manly?'

He stood so handsomely! Laughing, Bjørn nudged Arnulf with his elbow in the side just where Leif's club had hit, and Vagn hooted elated, 'The women around Jomsborg will now be envious! You should let that priceless treasure hang until it dries, even if they hinder the comb going through! Afterwards, you can nail them firmly under the beams in Bue's longhouse in memory of a man who kept what he promised to keep!'

Hakon's angry roar drowned out the Jomsmen, and he was so bad-tempered that his sword flew out of its sheath. Murder shone from the hird's eyes as they drew arms with the earl, and the fallen were carried away as Hakon aired his indignation, 'Grab that misfortune-bringer immediately and kill him! Kill them all, I will not listen to more! They are so hardened that we are being made a laughingstock.'

Arnulf struggled to regain his breath, and Torkel made to want to swing the axe into Svend, where he stood, but Erik Earlson walked coolly forward and grabbed the vassal by the arm as he lifted his other hand, composed, 'I would still like to know who the warriors are before they are killed, and not least this man, for he stood in front of me during the fight, and he stood well.'

He looked around commandingly and the cries ceased. Earl Hakon set fire to the water with his eyes, but then restrained himself, lowering the sword with a firm nod to his son. For a moment, they spoke without words, then Erik turned towards Svend and asked for all to hear, 'Who are you then, Goldenhair?'

All merriment left Svend, and he replied dignified without scorn and spite, 'Svend is my name. Bue the Stout was my father, and his father is Vesete, earl of Bornholm.'

The severed hands still held the hair but did not bleed anymore. Erik nodded appreciatively and asked on without animosity, 'How old are you, Svend Bueson?'

'Eighteen, if I am able to live another half year.'

The earl's son considered his opponent openly, and the silence around them was oppressive. Svend had helped clear Erik's ship, and he had helped Vagn eat into the store of men, but as the two faced each other, Arnulf felt almost a goodness between them and the tension was excruciating.

'You will probably survive that long and even longer! Will you accept peace, Svend Jomsman?'

Peace! Peace? After all the killings? They should be eaten raw, those Northmen, each and every one! By slimy serpents and maggots!

'It depends on who is offering it.'

The earth around the Bueson's feet darkened, and Arnulf saw weak twitches in his skin of his neck, where the hair was stroked apart. He had to hover directly over the pain, the fire burned now to the bone, who was holding him up? The One-Eyed himself?

'That is he, who has the power to do it! I am Erik Hakonson, and if I am allowed to decide, you will not lose your life.'

Earl Hakon cleared his throat brusquely and once more wills clashed. Then his expression softened and he let his discontent fly with a shrug, annoyed, 'I do not know what you are thinking since you want to free a man who has treated us so unusually badly, but if you absolutely want to hold your hand over him, I will not insist on his death.'

The red warrior turned to Svend, his eyebrows raised, but it was a little while before the Bueson replied, 'Well then, Erik Hakonson, I accept your peace. Maybe I, despite my current loathing for life ... yet have something to achieve ... I ...'

The knees gave way and he sank abruptly with a sigh, and the earl's son grabbed for his new weapon-companion came too late. Arnulf wanted to get up, but Bjørn held him back with a sharp outbreak, none of them could help, and Vagn's nostrils flared under the eagle eyes. Two hirdmen went forward and cut Svend's hands free, then carried him out of the way and laid him on a cloak, while a thrall was sent for water and that the Bueson so boldly had salvaged life lifted the mood of the Jomsvikings. Shoulder-nudges and appreciative nods were shared along the row of men. One hirdman worked the severed hands free of the hair without Svend seeming to sense it, and Hakon, dully, gave the order for Torkel to continue the executions.

The lightness was lost with the order, and the faces left Svend to turn towards Palnatoke's relative and the earl's vassal. Torkel Lere straightened up with overwhelming evil, and his face shone from so much abhorrence and disgust that it was only when Skofte went to loosen Vagn Ågeson that Arnulf really grasped the depth of his hatred. It was not easy to loosen the dark warrior from the foot rope, for it had wrapped around his legs in a peculiar manner, and it did not seem to fare very well for Skofte to have to crawl around Vagn's knees, as strong as the Jomsman was. Torkel tossed his head like a stallion, yelling exultantly, so it could be heard all the way up at the tent camp, 'Tell me, Vagn, you son of a skrælling, how does it feel in your chest knowing that you are about to die? I can understand that you are probably not afraid, but how does it feel that it is me wielding the axe?'

Vagn stamped his heel hard into the ground over Skofte's frayed sleeve so that the thrall had difficulty pulling his arm free, 'At dying, I have no complaint, it just pains me not to be able to fulfil my promises!'

He got up, banging his knee on the thrall's mouth so blood ran down Skofte's chin, and Erik Earlson still had his inquisitiveness intact, for he interrupted again with a wink, 'What is your name, Jomsviking, and what promises have you given, since you are so heavily committed to keeping them before you leave this life?'

Skofte whimpered, delayed his knife work, and dried his lips with his sleeve.

'I am Vagn, son of Åge Palnatokeson from Funen. I promised to kill your father's vassal and play with his daughter under the sleeping skins, no matter what he thinks of it, and dying before these duties are fulfilled did not occur to me at all, otherwise I would not have won such a great reputation!'

Before Erik Hakonson could formulate his response, Torkel Lere's face split into a cock-red roar, 'I know the ending for your reputation, and it will be dealt immediately!'

With mouth gaping and axe raised, he jumped up without thinking in the least of where the killing was taking place and Vagn made ready to meet his accelerating death with bear-flouncing jeers. Arnulf swallowed a thunderbolt, and the only man in Norway who apparently still believed in the Ågeson's life was Bjørn the Bretlander who snorted, kicking his foster son so violently in the knees that that warrior tumbled. Arnulf groaned, for the kick had caught his leg nastily in the foot rope and added pressure to his injured thigh, but Torkel's axe blow flew so powerfully wild that the vassal fell, banging his head on Vagn's knee. A collective gasp went through the crowd, and Vagn crept as agile as a cat over to the lost weapons as Skofte fled. Before Torkel had shaken away the mist from his vision and the hird could prevent anything, Vagn had cut himself free, seizing the axe in an upward spring. The blow was so deep that the vassal's entire chest was cleaved through and the Ågeson's revenge-cry drowned in the roars of the Jomsvikings, whereupon Vagn's name was shouted so the water in the bay trembled. Everyone in the coarse sand arose in triumph while Jomsborg's heir was surrounded by a circle of drawn sword tips, and the housecarls left no doubt of their intentions.

Arnulf stared at the earl and Erik, while Vagn's joyful cries split light through the din, 'Now I have fulfilled my first promise and feel considerably better than before, so I lack only the second!'

He pushed his abdomen forward in a sweaty grin, but Hakon looked baleful, and the Jomsvikings vigilantly kept their exultations inside to listen. Torkel was perhaps not closest to the earl, but the conquered should not have ventured to end his life! Angrily came the command to the hird to kill that instant, but once again Erik Earlson involved himself, demanding that this warrior also be freed and placed under his protection like Svend Bueson and for a moment no one breathed.

'Vagn is a good man and a great warrior. It seems to me a fruitful exchange, if we show him the honour of offering him Torkel Lere's place as your vassal, and if, in addition to taking care of Torkel's large farm, he would also look after his daughter, that trade will satisfy everyone.'

Earl Hakon folded his arms across his chest, looking at his heir, his face contorted as if he had sucked on a bitter plum. Vagn was a great warrior but also a bull who could not be shooed, and Norway's ruler was not stupid! Arnulf looked at the Ågeson. Erik spoke his case well, and a rapid sidelong glance was exchanged between the hird, but Vagn was stony-faced.

'There is great insight in your speech, Erik, so in this, too, you are allowed to advise as you will.'

The earl did not seem unhappy with his son and looked slowly around the circle, finally letting his eyes linger on Vagn, 'What do you think about the offer, Vagn Ågeson? Will you follow your young companion and accept peace and reputation as well as goods and possible heirs, or you will die as an outcast of Jomsborg? Leif Cleftnose told me you had spear you had left for Sigvalde.'

The housecarls lowered their swords a tad on the dark warrior's chest, and Vagn was not slow to answer. He spoke clearly despite the torn voice, as clearly as he was proud, 'I am not a horse that can be traded by great men at will, and I bestow spears on those who have earned it! Nothing is won in peace from you here unless it also applies to my brothers-in-arms, so either we are all freed as masters of our own lives, or we follow one another into death!'

Arnulf lost his breath. The sun stopped. Nidhogg's dripping teeth tickled the bare skin while the serpent, in confusion, sought to catch the scent of gluttony or disappointment. He looked at Hakon, like a drowning man in a remote boat.

'Easy. Your companions left their lives so valiantly, you and the rest of your men deserve to be free. We have defeated Sigvalde and broken the neck of his renowned legion, and here is ample evidence for the courage found in Jomsborg. Skofte! Cut them loose, and if anyone then wants to serve me instead of the man who fled Hjörungavádr like a hare, there is room in my hird!'

Arnulf saw the words freeze on the earl's mouth like frosty breath and the sounds around him flowed together into a throbbing roar. His breathing hissed like the beats of Hræsvelgr's wings while his thoughts stood still in stunned disbelief. Free? Was he free? Was he not going to die? Did Hakon's assurance really apply to all of them, or he had heard wrong? His eyes blinked in rhythm with his pulse. A hirdman of the Norwegian earl! How could Hakon let men kill one moment and then trust in their former oath-brothers in the next?

'Who are you, old man? What has driven you out on this voyage, you, who are bald and as white as a young seagull? It is indeed true, what I have heard said: every straw will stab at us Norwegians, when even warriors on the brink of the grave come to fight against us.'

Erik smiled at Bjørn and walked over himself to cut his hands free, while the surviving Jomsvikings greeted each other, elated, with wishes for long life and good health. Vagn sliced the foot rope with his knife, and earl Hakon nodded to the closest hirdmen to help loosen the rest of the prisoners.

'My name is Bjørn, and I am called the Bretlander and furthermore I am foster-father to Vagn Ågeson, so you can compare my colour to stronger animals than seagull chicks!'

Erik laughed loudly, offering him his sword hand, 'Are you the Bjørn the Bretlander that so brilliantly retrieved one of his men from the hall of King Sweyn?'

Arnulf felt a knife between his wrists and clenched his teeth as his wounded arm fell down by his side. Bjørn confirmed, pleased, and seemed to like the earl's son and Erik grasped fists with the old man before he cheerfully turned to Arnulf.

'Your name, I do not yet know, but that you slew an Ulfhednar is known by all! You defended your companion, so your reputation will grow from it, and such men can always find place among Norway's best warriors.'

Dumbfounded, Arnulf stared and stepped out of the cut foot rope, but before he could answer, Leif Cleftnose beat him to it, hate in his voice, 'I can tell you who the colt is! Arnulf Stridbjørnson is his name, and he is of good family, for one of his brothers raped Øystein Ravenslayer's daughter from Haraldsfjord, and he himself killed the other brother and is probably for the same reason an outlaw in Denmark.'

399

The tattling snot snout! If only his shield hand had control enough over Serpenttooth, the sword would slit both ears and maw, so they were worthy company for his nose! Arnulf grasped the hilt, but a brief look from Vagn made him hesitate. Amazed, Erik Earlson looked at Leif, but the Cleftnose was not finished, 'It is not honourable for you to give the wimp his freedom, and I have a quarrel with him, which I intend to end this instant! Give him to me, then I will have received plenty for my share of the loot and be only glad to! In addition to his limpness, he has less forethought between his ears than a spurless cockerel.'

What Hakon's son thought of the tirade Arnulf did not give time to hear, for his chest burned furiously at Leif, 'I am known as Arnulf Wolfblood, and I am a Jomsviking and blood-brother to Vagn Ågeson! You may decide for yourself, Erik Earlson, which of us best exhibits decent behaviour here, but I know about Leif; that he will go to any length to achieve his goals, and that his quests do not always serve him glory.'

Let Freya marry Thrymr before the Cleftnose should be allowed to draw the wolf-blood through the mud! Leif Cleftnose's eyes enlarged, trying in vain to fight any denial in Vagn's expression.

'Surtr's sword, you are so infuriating my cape is about to catch fire!'

Without anger, Erik walked between Arnulf and Leif, and Hakon stepped closer to interfere in the dispute. The earl looked to have more desire for beer and feasting than strife and quarrels, 'Leif Cleftnose! Hold your bold axe in its belt and listen to me now, enough blood has been spilled on Norwegian soil, and I do not give a man his freedom in one moment only to leave him to his enemy in the next. In my eyes, Arnulf Wolfblood proved his worth in the fight amply and that does not need further discussion.'

Hakon fell silent, as if he wanted to build the excitement, and when he spoke again, it was with a glance to the crowd and a raised voice, 'But you have made an outstanding effort, and I regret in the least that you stood on my ship. When Eye Einar fell in battle, I lost a faithful and esteemed vassal, but all those around me witnessed how bravely you fought and how you saved my life when I stumbled. Therefore, with great pleasure, I hereby give Romsdale, its hinterland and fjords into your hands and it is my belief that you will tend to Eye-Einar's duties as zealously as you watched my life yesterday!'

Excited shouts greeted the Norwegian earl and Leif closed his cod-mouth in a hurry and took the outstretched hand without a sound, but his muteness lasted no longer than a few farts for a roar broke through his beard, while his arms flapped the sun onto a wrong course. He laughed heartily, slammed his jaws together to again shake his Hakon, but laughed once more and yelled for mead, and in such abundance that he could swim in it.

All attention left Arnulf. Vagn turned to the others who had been released while the indignation over Leif's behaviour and undeserved luck surpassed any pain for a moment. The bearded-goat, the swaggering stinky bearded-goat! Serpenttooth screamed from its sheath, vassal of Romsdale! Over the hinterland! Fjords! Haraldsfjord! Arnulf wavered. Revenge, disease and deceit, Thor's anger, as soon as the wounds were healed, the dastardly swine-ass would pay! To reveal both brother-murder and rape to the holder of Norway's reigns and Toke! Toke was a dead man now, who was the chieftain of Haraldsfjord against the vassal of Romsdale? No matter how great the Son of Øystein had stood and excelled on *Twin Raven*, the earl would now listen most to Leif. Arnulf looked up into the fjelds. Behind the rocks lay the fjord, and he had once trod the path there with Stentor. Toke! The settlements had to be warned of Leif's new position, so no one should meet the brown-ended cleaved-spouted boaster unprepared, the Øystein's son could be granted one night to think before his worst enemy stood at the door.

The injured thigh felt more rotten and unsure than any fishing-net pile, and Arnulf drew Serpenttooth to seek support from the sword. Glowing stones were being pushed into the wounds, and an overwhelming faintness trespassed on his will. Hirdmen had surrounded Leif and were patting his back, like cows swatting flies, and both Hakon and Erik looked to be in favour of a mug of beer between the tents, but the Jomsvikings gathered around Vagn, and they were no less enthusiastic than the housecarls. Arnulf looked around, searching. Svend! Thor's death, he was so tired that the thoughts stumbled over each other. There he lay, the Bueson, lying as the Northmen had placed him, alone on the cloak with closed eyes. Vagn spoke hoarsely with the Jomsmen while he persistently ignored Bjørn's command to sit and surrender his mauled body to proper care, and Arnulf hobbled with Serpenttooth's help to Svend. What Leif intended to do, seemed suddenly distant and indifferent, as concern for Svend's state slammed into his mind, and when he reached the cloak and sank with a groan to his knees beside the Silkenhaired, all foreboding spread like flames in straw.

The Bueson's breathing came in gasps, strained, and his eyes seemed blind as he sensed Arnulf and turned his face towards him with a groping hand, 'Vagn?'

401

He had received water for his kyrtle was wet across his chest, but the drink had obviously not worked.

'No, it's me, Arnulf, I'm here. Here!'

Arnulf grabbed the seeking hand, and Svend smiled vaguely, but rolled convulsively, struggling to breathe. Blood seeped through the bandage around his stomach, and Arnulf was as cold as a corpse and frightened, powerlessly afraid! He should not lie like this, Bue's son, not so soon after having spoken up against Erik.

'Svend! Hold on! Breathe, lie still, I'm here and I won't let you go!'

He clutched the clenched hand and the Bueson lay once again, short of breath and wheezing through his half-separated lips.

'Arnulf!'

'Yes, Arnulf. Rest, lie still, then you'll get better, you're tired.'

'Yes ... tired!'

Svend twisted a smile from himself again, but his eyes stared past, and Arnulf suppressed the urge to seize the Silkenhaired's head and force him to look in the right direction, command him to man up, survive, live! He looked around frantically. Someone had to help! The Bueson was fatally wounded and had endured unimaginable feats, someone had to know what was to be done with an open stomach wound, but no one came forward, and Bjørn only had eyes for Vagn, who was sitting with his back against a pile of ship chests, and was about to remove his kyrtle. The words about onion soup, and to only care for the men who might be able to make it stabbed in his side like blades of ice. Svend squeezed his hand, 'I wanted to be a new brother for you ... A good brother.'

His eyes smarted, and their hands crushed as if one sought to push life into the other.

'You will be! You were already, otherwise I would not have defended you against the Ulfhednar.'

The Bueson grimaced, his face denying, 'It will not be like that ... and you know it, but ... take my place in Jomsborg ... take Snap, it is yours! The Ulfhednar ... scratched you. Can you feel his blood in your body now? If you dare, you can take his ... strength, Arnulf Wolfblood.'

Again, Svend huddled, and longer this time, but untensed a little again and found the strength to speak, 'Ask Vagn ... He will teach you ... aah!'

His body convulsed, and Arnulf let his hand go and, burning, stroked the yellow hair. Svend hit his fists in the sand with a snarling whine but then forced himself to lay still again, while he stubbornly tried to continue talking. Arnulf interrupted him, 'Svend! Use your strength on

402

yourself, then we can talk about this later. I will neither have Snap nor learn more from Vagn. I'll get Bjørn. He will know what you need.'

'No!'

The tense hand bored its fingers into his knees, 'There will be no later! Do not go! Tell ... Vagn ...'

Arnulf shook his head violently, 'But there will be a later, for I have promised to sail you home to Bornholm, to Vesete's farm and your ancestral lineage, remember that, and I will die as a Jomsviking, but I will not live to forsake life in battle! You have never had a choice, but I love a woman, and my blood shall end with me!'

The tears trickled over the quivering jaw, trickled, like from an icicle on the roasting spit. Svend was dying! Svend with the glittering laughter and the indomitable courage, he was dying, he was dying! Vagn knew it the moment the arrow struck, and the two kinsmen had said their parting taken on the deck.

Restrained sobbing mingled with Svend's feverish moaning and Arnulf leaned over the golden hair that had saved the failing life in vain, 'Live Svend! Live for my sake, for Vagn's and Vesete's sake! Get well on Bornholm, I'll find a woman for you, a woman who will teach you to love! I will not let you go, not even if all of Odin's legion will tear you away from me!'

'I cannot ... Do not fear death!'

'Yes, you can! You can!'

Arnulf stared into the not-seeing eyes and felt Svend's darkness. It whistled through the heart. He saw life and hope slide from the body, saw the defeat, heard the last song sound. Svend was suffering enough! The Bueson should not also bear his own despair.

'I will make a song about you, Svend Bueson, a great skaldic verse, and I will perform it in the greatest halls and for King Sweyn himself! All I will relate and raise in honour, everything, except your death!'

A wide smile spread the chapped lips that had to feel to dripping tears, 'Battle is hope, Arnulf, he ... who dies in battle, dies in ... hope!'

The Jomsson rolled his head against Arnulf's knees, struggling for breath again, fighting so much his shoulders shook. Arnulf bent over his convulsions and took the bewildered hand.

'My father ...'

Svend shook his head and was bleeding from the mouth, as if he had bitten himself.

'He's awaiting you together with Ketil and Haug and all the others.'

Helge! Rolf! With sudden strength, the Bueson came forward and rose up on his elbow with his eyes towards the sky, as if he were listening intently, 'Listen!'

He laughed, gasping, 'Can you not hear them? The sounds of hooves ... see! Chainmail ... spears ... they are red-haired, did you know that?'

Wildly he laughed, hollow and abrasive, straightened himself and waved exuberantly as if he could see what Arnulf could not. Then the strength betrayed him and Svend sank in violent spasms oblivious to Arnulf's cries. It jolted through his body, twitching the limbs, but the lungs heaved irregularly and did not grudge the struggling air. The gaze froze over the twisted drag of the mouth and Arnulf tried to raise Svend's upper body to help his breathing, but he was too heavy, heavy as frozen rock, and the injured sword arm was useless. The tears were silent, the mouth open, the life left the Bueson, left the Silkenhaired behind, betrayed him in the meanest way; the Valkyries took him, and it made little difference that Serpenttooth, distraught, split the air around the bed, Svend went limp, then like stone and gave up his groans. He was dead!

Still the heart of Arnulf hammered like a stallion's stamp, still the bellows drove burning air through his throat, but the silence under him were more weighty than the burial mound's silence and horror's black shadow paralysed sound and motion, as if all glow and joy should be entwined in sticky threads and be forgotten forever! The knuckles roasted bone-runes in his forehead while the lamb's wool vest was whipped off the naked flesh. Svend! Svend! Everything was lost, the stores empty, against the hunger stood not the slightest protection!

Arnulf collapsed into himself, while his breath burned the sinews of his forearm, and his hair hid the wretched remnants of charred hope. Here it ended! Here the last of his courage was killed! Now the fire extinguished, now his will sank forever, Baldur's voyage, the last word. The parting with a dream, the parting with Svend, the parting with Jomsborg. A wild urge to escape swept through his body, a headlong flight! He could not bear to see Svend's funeral, could not bear to hear the other warriors enumerate the fallen or talk about Sigvalde's failure and the hird's broken promises, he had to get away, and at once!

How the legs lifted his body upright did not matter, and that his shield arm felt Serpenttooth still could be used as support was its own business, stones filled his chest, black iron-heavy stone, why his feet were dragging him back to Vagn could be answered at another time, Arnulf was dead, cold, killed! Every step flamed to his waist, false hollow flames, each limped footstep had a sound, had a name: Discourage, Heart's Loss, Will Slayer, Hope's Plunderer, Life's Fall.

'He is dead!'

The steps paused uncertainly in front of Vagn and his mouth spoke by itself, 'Svend. He is dead.'

Serpenttooth's hilt was like ice, but his hand was colder, ready to drop, his body begged for rest and threatened to fail if he did not give in, but if he sat down next to Vagn, he would sit for eternity! He would roll up like an animal in hibernation, seek oblivion, lose his senses and never awake again. The Ågeson closed his eyes as his face convulsed, ploughing his fingers through his hair's hardened cakes of blood, but he did not seem about to get up, 'Of course, Svend is dead!'

He sat heavily, leaning against the ship chests with a mug of beer on his knee, white skinned, his words sluggish as if he could hardly muster to shape his tongue behind his discoloured lips. Bjørn had stuck his knife into a newly lit fire, and around them sat or lay the remaining Jomscompanions, resting with quiet talk and deep drags of the Norwegian beer. Vagn's wounds were scantily bound, but the soaked linen strips did not manage to cover the many injuries and Arnulf was still alive enough to become nauseated at the sight. Was Vagn going to die now, too? Fleetingly, another spear stabbed his chest but found no blood or pain there, only endless emptiness. The Ågeson looked up, exasperated, with a vague shake of his head, 'I am surely not dying, then I would have lain down, you know that Arnulf Wolfblood. Here!'

He reached up with the mug, and Arnulf supported the sword against his stomach and drank, so the beer sloshed down his throat, sucked in an insatiable gushing slug; thirst, it was thirst!

'Sit!'

Vagn took the empty mug and swept his hand over the coarse sand, but Arnulf remained standing, 'I have to leave you, Vagn. I cannot ... Not when Svend is dead! I have a friend on the other side of the mountain in Haraldsfjord, Toke is his name, Toke Øysteinson. There is a path there. All I need is a horse. A horse.'

He stared at the Ågeson as his thoughts stalled, 'I need a horse.'

'Arnulf!'

Vagn's mouth pulled, and he waved a deprecating hand, 'You cannot escape from your grief. You are wounded, you will die up there, and it is not good for man to be alone after a defeat. Sit down and drink with me until the darkness takes us, you may be standing now, but believe me! It will not be long until your strength will leave you, I know it, I have experienced it too many times before.'

'I am not escaping, and I did not kill one Ulfhednar to die on a fjeld path, I know the way, and yes, I'm tired, but not tired enough to drop off a horse! Toke should be warned against Leif Cleftnose, the new vassal will not treat him well.'

Vagn's gaze was penetrating, but the questions seemed to give way to respect, and his head bent sharply against his chest as a tremble curled in the clenched hand. Bjørn watched him silently, turning his knife in the fire, and the Ågeson looked up again with blurred eyes. The black eyes burned no longer over the laboured breathing, and never had Arnulf seen him so weak, his eyes were deep and vulnerable, it was Åge's son who sat here, not the warrior. Close flowed wordless thoughts from him, grief companions, blood-brothers, closer than that only the Bretlander could be to the Jomsman.

'Bjørn! Get Arnulf a horse, he means what he says, and by Tyr! The men, you give friendship to, Wolfblood, you are faithful to them until your last drop of blood.'

The eyelids slid halfway, and Arnulf shook damp hairs from his eyes, as the Bretlander left them without a word.

'Do not think more about me than you see. I have betrayed my own, so the shame has near eaten me up!'

'That was before you became a man, and I have not yet been mistaken in the blood-brothers I have chosen. Svend gave you Snap, did he not?'

Vagn fumbled the axe free from the belt that was lying on the discarded kyrtle and handed it to Arnulf, who took the precious weapon with dry bread in his throat. The Ågeson deserved the axe more than anyone else, not him, not when he had only known Svend such a short time.

'Would you rather keep it?'

'Because I was closer to him than you? No! What Svend gave me lives in my chest, I do not need his weapon.'

Snap fumbled its way down into the belt, the shaft still warm from the Bueson's battle grip and his shield hand gradually stopped moving over the sharp edge.

'It was all in vain, Vagn, the voyage, the battle and my stand against the Ulfhednar, we have lost everything. Everything.'

'No.'

Weary, Vagn shook his head, 'Nothing was in vain, battle is never useless! The honour triggered the voyage and the battle was magnificent but uneven, but least of all was your own fight in vain.'

'Svend is dead!'

'Svend received his mortal wound even before the Ulfhednar had reached you, but you did not notice. Other men had accepted his fate and left the ship to save their lives, so some might call your stand the work of a madman, I call it a deed of brotherhood. We all saw the fight, earl Hakon saw it, Odin saw it; you convinced the Northmen what Jomsborg stands for! You did not fail your companion, and you did not give up, though no one except I predicted your victory, you overcame the fear and found your inner warrior! Your fight was not in vain; on the contrary, it opened gates for you.'

Arnulf faltered, dazed, and closed his eyes for a moment. So many words! They slowly fell into place but still did not mean anything. Serpenttooth slipped in the sand. No one had proven himself more than Vagn himself!

'What gates? I found nothing, I fought so as not to lose.'

Vagn allowed himself to lighten and broke out into a smile as he carefully laid his sword arm better over his thigh and considered his wound, 'To be a warrior is many things. Courage, stamina, strength and the will to fight are just some of it, and every man in Jomsborg follows his own path, his own honour. We are very different, but the inner warrior is found in the eyes, the heart, and not only in those skilled in weapons. A fisherman may also be a warrior, a farmer, a mother, all who fight and refuse to give up, no matter how hard and hopeless fighting against it is: storms, hunger, disease, the warrior stands through it all, until life is taken from him.'

He looked up, 'You slew Hakon's wolf-warrior, and that will be known. Sigvalde will receive you with joy, but King Sweyn's housecarls will welcome you, too, and earl Hakon needs new men in his hird. Ride over the fjeld, Arnulf, rest and heal your wounds and then make your choice but remember that you first promised your sword to Jomsborg! Snap is the sign that you speak the truth, and whatever Sigvalde now thinks of me, he will not doubt your right to your reputation as a Jomsviking.'

Arnulf flickered his eyes restlessly over the bay and fjeld without being able to grasp the depth of his speech. Jomsborg? The royalseat? Hakon's hird? He was expelled, Vagn was delirious!

'I have killed my brother! I am an outlaw! Banished from my land!'

Vagn raised an eyebrow, 'The only reason that I myself was not dragged in front of the Thing as a young man for those killings I did was that no one dared, and the dead have not bothered me much since then. Anyone who has anything to complain about can speak to Serpenttooth about their issue.'

Arnulf was startled but then nodded. His legs shook under him, and his thigh could not endure much more agony! If only he could sit down, hide in the Ågeson's shadow, close his eyes, and refuse to ever see misery again.

'What will you do, Vagn? Sigvalde will hardly open the port for you again.'

Vagn could claim his inheritance to Jomsborg, could split the Viking's fidelity and probably take over rule after his stand against earl Hakon, but his place was in the shield wall, in the bow, not under the banner pole, he would be Jomsborg's misfortune, Jomsborg's bane.

The Ågeson seemed unconcerned, 'I have got a large farm in Vigen, you heard it yourself. A farm and a woman!'

He smiled again, surprisingly mild, and his chest lifted, 'Arnulf I have got the woman I long for, and as soon as tomorrow will I ask Bjørn to hold the oar and sail me to her. Come visit me in Vigen next summer and tell me about your companion, Toke, and I will teach you everything Svend did not have time to, but yesterday was my last fight and I will not draw my sword again.'

He looked clear in mind, and his hissing, muffled laughter smoothed Arnulf's astonishment and made the pain and fatigue retreated a little.

'You will not be a warrior anymore?'

'I will always be a warrior, but I will not fight anymore, look at me! My body cannot keep healing wounds, and I have pain that you will not even know in your worst nightmare. Now I have peace, and by next winter I will take Ingeborg with me to Funen to run my family's farm, become a father and beget sons, lots of sons. She will want me as soon as she sees who I am, and forget her father's hatred, and never has an enterprising man disappointed a warm-bosomed woman.'

He sighed, exhausted, and Arnulf was silent. His Jomscompanions around him were considerate, as if they were keeping their ears to themselves, but the men, Arnulf knew best, were killed or fled. The remaining would rest awhile, then say farewell to Vagn and sail south to Sigvalde, Bjørn would likely assist his foster son in Vigen and maybe later return to Bretland, and in Jomsborg the funeral feast would be longer and less cheerful than Strut-Harald earl's memorial feast in King Sweyn's hall.

'I will come to Vigen. Next summer.'

Vagn's eyes warmed, 'Never forget that we are blood-brothers. You saved my life with your skaldic verses at the royalseat, and I am also heir to half of Bretland and rule the law there, so if you are ever cornered, then come to me.'

Arnulf returned the smile, though black tears ran down inside his skin. Vagn Ågeson. He would be the last man standing in Ragnarök!

'Thank you, Vagn.'

Bjørn's return interrupted him, and amazingly enough the Bretlander led a red, strongly built horse with him by the hand. Cream-coloured was the mane, and it was well saddled, a healthy animal with kind eyes and Bjørn handed the reins to him with the utmost naturalness, as if he had just picked up a loaf of bread. The Ågeson did not seem surprised, and Arnulf accepted, as the horse tossed its head, 'Where did you find it? Is it on loan?'

'Earl Hakon gave it to me, or rather, he gives it to you along with the words that he can always use a man with a good sword and especially one with wolf-blood.'

'I cannot accept this! A horse! I killed one of his best men, and he gives me a horse!'

The Bretlander smiled, offering to help him into the saddle, 'Arnulf Wolfblood, do not look so startled! If the earl can replace his lost man with one who is just as brave, then a horse is not an unreasonable gift, and if you refuse his offer, he has just yet again proved his generosity and magnanimously and can only win honour from that. Put your knee here!'

Arnulf obeyed tamely, holding his injured hand close to his stomach as Bjørn pushed and helped the wounded legs over. The old man was strong, as strong as Starkad, and the loss of hair aside, he had kept his strength! Arnulf stuck Serpenttooth into its sheath as Snap balanced the weight of his belt. He looked down at Vagn Ågeson and Bjørn the Bretlander, looked down at the Jomsborg's keel, brutally broken by the ship but still confident in its sway, and the dark warrior swung his fist at him, 'Live well over winter, Arnulf. Then I can look forward to seeing you in better conditions and ensure that Ingeborg's beer is strong!'

Mutely, Arnulf nodded, taking the hand. There were no words and Bjørn gave his good leg a pat, 'Ride as best as you can, and make sure you stay in the saddle. If I hear that a dead man has been found in the fjeld, I will be mad!'

His furrowed smile was well-meant, and Arnulf pressed his hand with a nod, before he pulled the reins and turned the horse toward the fjeld. Such mighty men! Such proud warriors! The courage that was shown in Hjörungavádr should never be forgotten! The horse's eager trot made his wounded thigh slouch badly, and he looked back quickly. The battle that had been here would be remembered, every blow retold, every skirmish assessed, and the bravest heroic deeds would live on in songs and stories! Bjørn waved, and Arnulf tried to keep his leg calm with his hand. His chest hurt more than his wounds right now, but in a strange way his mind was elated. The battle between earl Hakon and Sigvalde would outlive him and anyone who had participated in it, and if Arnulf Wolfblood was ever mentioned by a long fire, it would give the whole campaign worth and purpose. Yes! It would! By Odin. The warriors' god.

*****

The fjeld was misty and cold but not so steep that the horse could not find its way, and as soon as it had fought its way up a little, narrow paths winding between rocks and stones came into view. Grass and small shrubs were sparse, where the raw mountain did not shoot through and though Arnulf was not unsure of the direction, as early as the first ascent he understood fully Vagn's warning, for his thigh began to hound him so unbearably with every step the horse took that he feared he would faint. Although he stopped the animal now and then, the pain shot just as ruthlessly into the wound as soon as he continued, and his knee dangled from the saddle under the torn asunder muscle without being controlled in the least.

Arnulf clenched his teeth and forced his thoughts from his leg, but his body was against him, as soon as one wound stopped burning, the other blazed, and the lack of sleep and food drained the last of the strength from his limbs. Damned! Had he not just stood unaided, talking with Vagn and Bjørn, how could the dullness gain control so violently, he should not go far! Sweat joined the fight, yet he froze like a dog in the dank air. It was as if the Jomsvikings had managed to throw a cloak of action around themselves and had been able to endure together, now he stood alone and had to bear the pain without the slightest encouragement, and the burden was heavier than expected.

The horse pushed on, trotting surely, and Stentor had identified and named some of the largest rocky peaks around the path, but how far exactly to Haraldsfjord was hard to figure out. He and the gothi had had other things to do than go straight the last time he was here, and long detours for sheep and cattle in the valleys had been necessary. Much had happened since, perhaps he remembered the direction wrongly and it was hard to find the way around as soon as the sea was out of sight.

Arnulf stopped the horse again and looked around. He froze! On the other side of the next ridge, bedrock sloped down to a waterfall, and from there he should be able to see the path that led over the next two ridges and down to Haraldsfjord; it was not far by ship as least. He nudged the horse to walk again, but this time he found it hard to endure the motion! The pain ate into his torn flesh, like poisonous, rough hands grabbing at the bones, crushing them, it hurt so much, a sickening hurt, a serpent had fastened itself to his shoulder, its teeth biting deep into his armpit, it felt as if his sword arm was hanging loose. Freyr! Toke! He would make it! Nine days had Odin hung impaled in Yggdrasil, nine days, so he could also ride over the fjeld and stay conscious for a while yet! Arnulf clenched the unharmed hand. Frejdis. He would think of Frejdis, of her hair, her breasts, her swaying hips, but instead of Freya's daughter, Rolf rose bloody chested, standing in the way of the inner eye, Rolf with his twisted mouth and reproachful expression. Arnulf looked down and shook his head. Delusions. Nightmares. Brother murderer's punishment, it was Jofrid's sorcery that brought forward the murdered!

The mist grew thicker or were his eyes blurred? Arnulf tried to wipe them clear, without success, and the pulse could now be felt in every scratch, felt as a mighty pounding drumbeat, a beat that never ceased but began again and again. It was so cold! His fingers were so stiff. Maybe he would lose them. Perhaps his limbs would drop off one at a time and, in the end, his head, like Ketil's and Haug's. A scream! He heard screams! No! It was only the echoes between his ears, the echo of the roars of many men, the echo of a discontinued life and if he were bleeding! Or was he? How could he be bleeding so much; he had bled so much during the night, but his skin was wet. It had to be sorcery, sorcery or Jötunheimr, the way his senses deceived him was not that natural. The light brown mane tickled his nose, reminding him of the cut through one nostril. The horsehair felt strange, harsh, only pigs had more prickly brushes, all other furs were soft, soft and warm, the mane seemed like grass. Grass in his nose. His nose? So, it was worse than good!

Arnulf straightened himself but, dizzy, had to grab the horse's mane while a plaintive wail reached him. The sounding cut him, rooted in his own chest, and the swaddled fear wrapped itself constrictingly around his heart. Clearly! He had to think clearly, the thoughts were slipping away

411

from him, his mind, his mind was rampant. He stared at the stony path between the rocky outcrops with open eyes but shook so violently from the cold that his fossilised fingers could hardly grab the mane any longer. Cold? No, it was fever, fever; the wound-fever had caught him!

His shield hand stroked sweat and loosened blood from his forehead, but even the fear did not instil new strength. Fever, so now it was important to hurry, hurry ... hurry ... the horse walked on. The path lay under the hooves. He just had to linger. Hold on. Remain seated. Why? Why should he remain seated, Vagn had forgot to answer that! What thoughts had driven him out on a leather-thin ice flake that the fever melted through in every moment? To warn Toke? To meet Toke's hatred and be rejected in the fjord? What had he fled from? And where to? How could the Øysteinson welcome him after the battle? The brother-murderer had killed Northmen, lots of Northmen, he had betrayed the Norwegian folk, his friend and fellow kinsmen and clashed swords with earl Hakon! The penalty for it was death, and if Toke himself did not wield the knife, there were probably others who would! Veulf, wounded, alone on the fjeld, dying. On his way to nothing. On the run from everything.

Arnulf crept, trembling over the horse's neck and twisted a lock of mane around his good hand as tightly as he could. Frejdis! She was lost. Helge killed. Everything was lost, why endure any longer? Why expose himself to the terrible suffering of being in the saddle, why not just slide down to a place with soft grass and remain there until ... until everything stopped. He had committed murder and had been outlawed for that; betrayal, killed warriors and rape hung like pendants from the same chain, and in Egilssund only shame remained, what was there to live for? Now it was getting dark, too! Already? The pain bit, so each step triggered groans, plaintive groans and his forehead hid against the horse's neck. Sleep. Forgetfulness. The stony grounds grew up against him. A warrior never gave up, no matter how strong the opposition was! A Jomsviking may not show ... show ... what was it now? Powerlessness? Abruptly his head rose itself with a jerk! Heels! Legs! There was a man at the animal's head, a man! The emptied heart thundered, but the will would not react. Arnulf tried to see clearly. Yes! A man was walking there, and now he turned his face and smiled.

Helge! It was Helge! Helge! Arnulf reached out his arm and tried to shout, but Helge did not take it, just shook his head and led the horse by the bridle, the horse whose front legs were now dripping with blood. Helge! In a silver shower of sparks. Arnulf wanted to smile, but his cheek rocked into the mane again, and the dread of his own incapacity defied the fever. Helge led the horse. His brother would lead him safely to Haraldsfjord; that was why he had come. Just like back in the sea. His struggle was over. Completely gone. Everything relaxed. Fell. His arm slid down. His body swayed in the breakers, the blood boiled, and the pain devoured any urge to scream. Arnulf stared several times through his own skull to determine what he was seeing, but Helge remained there, as real as the horse and the fjeld. His eyelids slipped shut. The mountains rose and fell as the hooves tramped, and his head dangled. Arnulf Wolfblood. A prouder Jomsviking had never set foot in Norway!

Not least he hit himself when the rocks welcomed him, and softly sank his head to rest against a stone, while the injured hand landed in a tuft of grass, the mountain's arms whispered about peace in the ear of the ice-cold sweating body. Peace. He had found peace. Like Vagn. The horse went on, Helge went on, but the mountains whispered the song of the dís ... No! Arnulf fought to come up onto his elbows. He screamed for the animal, but not a sound escaped his throat and his arm gave just as quickly as it had obeyed. No! No! The horse, without the horse he would die! Without the horse, he could not go on! Helge! He could not just go on ahead! He would not leave him here! Arnulf made an impossible attempt to come up onto his knees, but the mountains swam around him and the rocks danced, so sparks struck and darkness came. Helge! He had to go back, come back, and the stupid horse! His breathing's hissing rattle was everything the body would give, and Arnulf sailed. Sailed on the fever. Had to rest. Just a little. Just a moment. Helge returned again when he saw the saddle was empty.

The time dwindled. The wind tore at his mind. Brightly coloured tapestries struck the fjelds around him, herds of horses, foxes and birds swept past. Reindeer. Or was it a hedgehog? His skin lapped the cold of the mountain, but it soothed, and his heart continued to beat. His lungs drew. His heart and lungs, arms and legs were no more, only pulses and gasps and blurred stone that lay closest to his eyes, but soon after they disappeared into blackness, so his eyelids could be released from hanging open. Was this what it was to die? Was it so? It was nice! And sounds still remained. The fever took the pain, took the worry and the hunger but not the wind and the cries of the birds. The seagulls. Those who had called him out of Egilssund countless days ago. Led him away. Over the sea. Many seas. Ships. Proud dragons. He waited for the last ship now, for the last keel voyage, waited, and had time to wait, paralyzed in his own mind!

They flew away, the gulls, so it had to be evening or winter, but the cold was not stronger, and his body was already completely frozen to

413

death, it was just the head that lay here. Perhaps Torkel Lere had actually struck him in the neck with the axe? Torkel Lere? Well, he was dead, so it must have been someone else. Perhaps the men, whose horses he heard? Was it Helge who'd come back? Perhaps the Valkyries? But did they trample so heavily on stone ground? Should he open his eyes? No. Curiosity had been killed with his body; if they just took his head, then all would be fine.

Strong hands turned Arnulf over onto his back, and excited voices spoke together over him, but what they said could not be understood, and the sight went no further than differentiated hazy figures in the sky. The pain returned with a roar when his body was lifted, but the hands did not let him go, and wool pulled at his wounds. His neck bumped against a strange man's shoulder, and although his lungs gasped as if he were choking, he was not laid down again. Arnulf wanted to get down, wanted to ask the men for peace, wanted to beg and coerce, but his lips were solidified in day-old blood, and the arm around his waist was determined. To Helheim with Odin, the ride surely accelerated only the ship's arrival, the ship.

They took him between them, the strangers, a door to fiery heat was opened, and Arnulf sank down on a bed, the softest bed the Æsir had ever created! It was lined with down, lined with foal muzzles, with care and safety, and brushed lamb's wool slipped around his wounds, milder than a woman's hands. A king did not lay better! Freya no warmer! The smell of frying, sweat and boiling porridge mixed with the sound of children crying. Arnulf disappeared.

*****

The bottom of the ocean. He was laying on the seabed. Dark brooded over dark, the blackness was silent, and the current quiet, but the water burned. Turmoil. Pressure. It burned! Roasted! He had to get up, had to have the air! His chest was terribly heavy, chainmail lay over him, chainmail, red-hot from fire!

Arnulf screamed, struggling to be free of the melting iron, and the sickening stench of charring skin mixed with the storm of pain. Helheim was standing over him with Bjørn's glowing knife, hands held him as she cut, and he screamed, roared so his lungs slipped free of his chest. The seabed shot him from himself, he swam through blood, through vomit, through snot, ships' stems struck each other, heaps of severed heads hailed from the sky as shrill chanting wailed and Svend lamented from a horse of stone with his belly full of arrows.

Arnulf broke the water, clinging to Vagn's soot-dark hair but the Ågeson was gone. Odin rode against him, Fenrir howled, running on the water, and from the royalseat's stallion-trodden roof, Sweyn Haraldson yelled to Sigvalde that the hird blood in the beer brought the war voyage luck! Fear! Paralysing horror! Aslak swung the felling axe into Arnulf's wounds but then began to chop the hands off Bue the Stout and the Ulfhednar warriors made a circle around Frejdis, swearing revenge as they cut her skin into strips. She sat, singing, her hair flowing, and her face turned away and she did not see them coming.

Again, Helheim swept Arnulf with its knife, and he was crying, despite Vagn's echo roaring that he may not, he wept and sank to his knees for the Realm of Death's master, begging for his life. Renewed pain, Frejdis flew, Stridbjørn shook his head, Rolf stepped up to the Thing's stone his voice like thunder, and Helge's back disappeared into the fjeld, but Jofrid's sorcery swathed all the ice splinters. Stentor gathered the women, and Toste Skaldshield stood with him. Frejdis smiled on the other side of the midnight mountain but Arnulf could not reach her for ropes ensnared his severed limbs, but she smiled and blew the south wind towards him, and a lock of her long hair grazed his skin. Then Nidhogg twisted his body tightly around him, biting his teeth into his flesh, and Arnulf writhed, moaning in frenzied torment, feathers cut him, he could not tolerate the touch, could not breathe. Frejdis took his burning hand as Svend filed his golden hair with Snap and laughed that he could not feel pain. Frejdis. Frejdis. Arnulf moaned and could not lie still on the fire-stitched wounds, but she called him, stroking his forehead and she lay his injured hand against her heaving bosom.

Peace. She surrounded him with peace. A shield standing before the wild storms, muffling his screams. Offensive pain, scalded skin, Frejdis was the bird rock, and Arnulf bored his forehead into her lap, extinguished and anguished, a tormented brute.

*****

Voices. Faraway voices over the bed. Excitement. Concern. Joy. A hand on his neck. An edge against his hard lips. Water! Arnulf sucked greedily, parched from thirst, and most of it ran down the side, but he got some into himself, then his body shook abruptly, first coughing and then moaning in gasps. He hunched on his side but regretted it at once, his wounds chaffed so terribly, and soft hands pushed him back onto his back and held on. The voices came near. The thigh ... the armpit ... the hands held their grip, but Arnulf lay in the forge's embers and found peace like in a furious wasp nest! For the sake of freedom, he forced himself to stay quiet at the stings, and his captors released their hold again, while the voices asked eagerly. Words. Quantities of words. They beat his ears, thronged his mind, they wanted in, in, to be listened to and understood. One voice gave up and let the other talk, subdued and earnest, and Arnulf opened his eyes, his chest panting.

The glow of the fire cast a ring of light on the golden wealth of hair that flowed towards him, and a face came slowly through the mist and became clear, a face of radiant tenderness. Moist eyes, trembling smile, flawless teeth. Frejdis! Arnulf stiffened and blinked. Frejdis! Trickling longing rolled over his skin and loosened his heart at the root. Impossible! He was dreaming! Terrible fever hallucinations! He closed his eyes tightly and shook his head, but it was same sight again and he lost his self-belief. It had to be Freya herself, a Valkyrie in human form, a conjured dís of gold! Frejdis? He fumbled for her breathlessly, as tears sprang, and her clenched grip was so wild, crushing salvation, hope and joy shot through his arm and for a moment it pushed away the body's cry.

'Frejdis!'

The voice was unrecognisable, hoarse and worn from exertion. She nodded vigorously, stroking his hair with a quivering gentleness but grabbed so hungrily at the mane as if she would never let go again.

'Arnulf!'

Her eyes poured dew, which ran over, and she pressed his hand against her lips and leaned forward so that her breath could be felt, 'Arnulf!'

He shook his head, 'How...? ...Where?'

He looked around, but it went black, and the eyelids slid faithlessly together, only the clenched hand was left. Anxiety. Confusion. Heat! Thumping beats, cheers dogged by doubts, thoughts that would not move, would not be used explain the eyes' conquest, Frejdis was in Egilssund, Rolf was dead, how could she sit there? Where was he? Could hatred cry?

'Stay! Frejdis, stay!'

Moist warmth was pressed against his forehead.

'I'm not going anywhere, I'm sitting here! I'm with you constantly, don't be afraid.'

Frejdis! Birds soared on their wings, colours sang, only now did he know how hard his longing had worn on the agony rope. Arnulf could half see again, and the voice behind Frejdis spoke for more water, while there was time. She obeyed, raised his head again and put the mug to his lips, and Arnulf drank, drank life and courage back, so weakened that his throat's work exhausted him. The surroundings took a step forward, clear and colourful, his senses found him.

'You have nothing to fear, you are safe in Haraldsfjord. Your horse came bloody over the fjeld, and Toke and Stentor found you up there.'

Haraldsfjord!

'Toke?'

'Yes, me.'

Frejdis straightened up, and Toke stepped out of the shadows and leaned over the bed with a broad smile to borrow the unharmed hand. He looked tired and haggard, but his eyes were warm and the grasp wholehearted. Toke! A river of joy filled his chest, joy mixed with hard guilt.

'Toke! I ... I didn't mean, forgive me!'

The smile's dawn darkened, and Arnulf turned his head away, countryman killings, rape and failed warnings, he was not worthy to meet the Northman's eyes, but Toke shook his hand gently, 'Forgive you? Arnulf! Look at me! Why should I be angry, it is me who is desecrated with shame!'

Arnulf looked into Øysteinson's face, wanting to answer, but his voice failed. So many questions, so many winds! Now he lay, felled, with no strength to begin, and Toke shook head, his eyes gentle as if he heard the mind whispering the ballad of the will.

'Lie still, you are gravely wounded, and the fever has not quite let go. Although there is much to talk about, save it for later, it is enough that you know where you are, and that we are taking care of you. Rest now!'

'But Leif ...'

A heaving groan killed the words and Toke lay a finger against his lips, 'Sssh! I know all about Leif, he himself was here yesterday to tell us who is the new vassal in Romsdale but forget him now! It is obvious that you have fought with the Jomsvikings, so do not waste strength telling me that.'

'Yesterday?'

'Yes, yesterday. We found you three days ago, and the fever was about to kill you. Frejdis has fought and called for you for you listened to her voice and Stentor and I treated the worst of your wounds with glowing iron. I am sorry about the pain it caused you, but we burned the evil out and that helped greatly.'

417

He gave his hand a squeeze, passed it back to Frejdis and stood up. Her voice trembled as she grasped it. She still had tears to cry, 'I've been so scared! After my arrival in Haraldsfjord, Toke told me you were drowned somewhere west, and we cried together, Arnulf I was near death with grief!'

She wiped her nose on the back of her hand, 'Now you will live, and I will take care of your wounds, until you leap like a foal! Do you think you could eat a little? You are nothing but skin and bones and Hildegun has long had the soup warm.'

Arnulf nodded and closed his eyes. He wanted to think, answer, but the pain was so intense that they usurped too much attention. As long as she was seated. Was with him. His body would escape, would sleep and escape the senses, but his heart refused rest.

'Here!'

Toke handed Frejdis a bowl, a bowl full of vigour and the spoon hovered against Arnulf like a rope to life. It was difficult to eat, as exhausting as mountain climbing, but the soup was fatty and strong, and his stomach was happy to accept. No one said anything. Hildegun's smile slipped fleetingly past, behind Toke's back, and Gyrith and Jofrid's awake eyes flashed from the dusk, too. Jofrid Øysteindaughter. As big as a mountain. She had not given birth yet.

Arnulf gave up on the way to bottom of the bowl, but Frejdis was satisfied with his feat and pulled the skin up over his chest, 'Sleep now. Stentor has carved runes onto a wolf's tooth, it is around your neck, and Hildegun and Gyrith lay powerful herbs on your wounds.'

Arnulf fumbled at his chest and found a leather cord with a canine. Runes and herbs, could they win over what blades had destroyed? Would he be able to wield a sword again? Would he limp?

'Thank him for it. Why are you here, Frejdis? How ...'

His lungs lost their breath and Frejdis looked down while Toke, disapproving, touched her shoulder, 'Not now, he is too weak!'

Arnulf summoned sparks to his eyes, why not now, what did they know that could beat a man, who was already lying down? Stubbornly, he stared at Frejdis who shook her head towards Toke, so the hair fell over her shoulders, 'It is a weapon as powerful as hope!'

'Why, Frejdis?'

The soup had cleared his mind and the urge to rest slipped from him anyway, he ached so much. She looked up with a fixed gaze, 'Rolf sent me.'

418

Rolf! The dance of the fire stiffened, the shadows in Øystein's house, his heart, his blood, his mind, the only thing that moved was common sense, which fell. The lungs gasped and broke the curse, and the fear pressed in from all sides.

'Rolf?'

He could barely whisper, 'Rolf is dead!'

The stony ground burst deep, deep down, and the fjeld's roots split for the streams of boiling pitch.

'No! He lives! You didn't kill him, Arnulf! Toke told me you think you did, but Rolf is alive, though he was still very weak when I left him. '

'No!'

Arnulf curled up with his face pressed in both the healthy and the injured hand, 'No!'

Flesh jumped up, blood flowed, his body rolled as if it were untied cargo in a storm while the screams struggled to get out, 'I killed him! He died ... the knife!'

Sobbing grabbed his lungs, waves of tears and gasps, 'I killed him! I killed him!'

Arnulf cried like a child, uninhibited, flushing, groaning, and Frejdis drowned her hands in his hair with her mouth against his neck, 'No, he's not dead, he's not dead, and you are not an outlaw and never have been! You're a free man, Arnulf, you are free, not a murderer, you didn't kill your brother!'

Her crying slung onto his, her hair, her fingers, and Arnulf clung fast, as mast and ribs splintered. Rolf! Alive! Rolf was alive! The curse was broken! The ropes broke, the heart bled torrentially and the relief squealed like an April storm through the joints and mind, not dead, not a murderer, free, free to live, free to look people in the eye without guilt, free to ... to return home! He squirmed and stared at Frejdis, while a new horror abruptly tore the words down. Home! Home to Rolf, the man who had not died, the man who was betrothed to his beloved!

Frejdis grabbed his face between her hands and shook her head, black despair in her eyes, and Arnulf lay his forehead against hers, letting the current of wind and destiny flow. Swirling, whistling spindles of the Norns, round and round, darker and deeper, sweat, delirium, fever, pain, the fire went out, Frejdis slipped away from his grip, the fall went on, went on, dizzying nausea, salt, his hands searched but missed the grip and Arnulf knocked his head in Fenrir's meagre hip and remained lying.

*****

419

He awoke in darkness. Thirsty. Warm. Restless from difficult dreams, sweaty; hungry. Fever? No, it was a nightmare and not a fever that had turned the sleeping skins clammy. Arnulf laid the back of his hand across his forehead. His breathing allowed itself a lull, and behind it awaited the whole row, they would all meet him without resistance, the thought of Rolf, of Frejdis, Toke, vibrating and moonlit, even Sigvalde's sea battle did not match the events in Haraldsfjord! Rolf lived! And Frejdis did not hate him, his fears had been unfounded, nor was Toke angry. Arnulf breathed as deeply as his bruised ribs would allow, and for a little while a jingling pleasure held his body's ailments at bay, then it bit, in every place the skin was torn, bit so the moaning escaped him, and the bed beside him came alive.

She was naked, Frejdis, naked she had settled herself under the skins and her skin could be sensed in the glow of the wakeful embers. Such divine beauty! A remote desire stroked the crumpled spear on its head, such fair breasts, such an arched sway, such a waste to lie helpless when lust's goal was within reach. She slipped from the bed like a dís, returned with the mug without asking, and the thirst was deep, cracked to the bottom. Still without a word, she went around the dormant fire, pouring from the pot, carried with care, and Arnulf was silent so as not to release new tears. He lay in the grass behind the house in Egilssund, awaiting her in the night and with every spoonful of soup she led to his lips, she brought strength, hope, life. Frejdis! The longing seemed even stronger than before now that she sat there. Her light shone on everything, everything he had done, shouted, had had in mind, everything faded, but not Freya's daughter!

Behind her, the questions stood like watchmen in the black shadows, furry and prickly questions that contained unbearable answers, questions that would change the direction of the thread and break the spell. His thigh throbbed, it pulled over his chest, brewed in his injuries, cut in his armpit, nose, hip, ribs ... Frejdis put the bowl down and slid in under the skin, so his head could rest on her chest, and fingers interlaced the unharmed hand as if she was trying to bear some of his suffering. Her chest was chick-soft, downy, but it did not help his agony.

'It hurts so much!'

High flew the ball, and the bat seemed unbearably heavy. With a gust of wind, they sailed onto the pitch, the questions, ready to grab and throw back. Knáttleikr. Knáttleikr with heart and life.

420

'Such severe wounds require great bravery, and you are bearing it with the strength of two men, what happened, Arnulf? Your impetuous mind I recognise but not your courage!'

Her fingers slipped into the scar over the eye, searched the caves in his hair, and a sigh reached into the battered ribs.

'Much has happened, but you took my question.'

Arnulf squeezed her hand while a raven-flock of moans abruptly left his wounds, pulling his body. She waited, stroking his skin and drawing attention from his lacerations and only began to talk again when he lay heavily once more.

'You didn't kill Rolf, but he was so near death that no one thought to hope. I sat with him day and night, sat and heard his cries, and he yelled at you! He was angry. Miserable. The fever was terrible, and your parents were beside themselves with anxiety. Trud threw much of her jewellery into the marsh, and for three days Stridbjørn sat on Cattlehill, screaming to the Æsir to spare his son, cried, though he had no voice in the end. Halfred and Aslak had to drag him home and get him drunk before anyone could speak to him again.'

Arnulf sighed and bored his cheek deeper into her chest. The clouds drove through Stridbjørn's grey hair, hunting for the new moon, while the sludge ate the Gormsø-rings, amber beads and the dragon-buckle Helge brought home from Iceland.

'The wound fever raged for six days, and when it finally released, Rolf was so weak he couldn't speak. Trud set the thralls out to keep the calm around the house, so nothing should disturb his sleep, and the animals were moved. We sat with him, she and I, changed the dressing and gave him the lust for life, and Stridbjørn was gentle, like you've never seen him. Rolf wept, Arnulf, he was crying and found no solace in our words, suffering horribly from his wound, but the grief was worse. He felt cursed, abandoned by the gods and he could not forgive himself for what he had done. He feared for your anger with strangers and for being the cause of your death.'

Trembling, Arnulf smeared tears and snot on the downy skin while the stones rattled with remorse, 'I felt the same, Frejdis!'

'I know, Toke told me everything. Rolf loves you, Arnulf, and regretted what happened like no one before has regretted. Not that he had got my yes, but that he had been too cowardly to look you in the eye, and that he had humiliated you in the worst possible way. Every day he talked about your journey out there, and although Halfred said many times that no man had a sharper blade and was better to have at his side

421

in danger than Øystein Ravenslayer's son from Haraldsfjord, Rolf feared, so it frayed his health.'

Frejdis was silent in the darkness, and Arnulf hid his face in her ample bosom. Rolf, his beloved brother. Now his loss broke through, only now did he see how beautiful he was! Behind Helge's voyages and praised actions that man stepped forward, who Arnulf would support and live near to his death. Earth. Cattle. Children. Life. Laughter. A hand was outstretched, a solid worthy hand, forgiving and willing for renewed friendship. His own.

'A man from Gormsø sailed with *the Sea Swallow*, and we understood that the Bjarke he had met, had to be you. We guessed that you had fled to Norway, but no one dared sail to Haraldsfjord for certainty, not with all the killings Halfred and the crew had done and Stridbjørn's concern for blood vengeance weighed heavily upon him. When Rolf could finally stand on his feet again, he asked me to get you home. Men kill men, but Toke seemed proud enough to let a woman go in peace, and as the new chieftain of Haraldsfjord he should be able to vouch for my life. To win you back Rolf wagered the best he had.'

'Frejdis!'

Arnulf stared up at the eyes sparkling in the darkness, 'You risked your life for Rolf! The Northmen could have killed you! Leif Cleftnose is not a man of woman-honour, and he has wanted me dead several times, he rules in the outer-fjord village and meets strangers first!'

The golden hair swept around her face in denial, 'I didn't go for Rolf's sake, I did it for you! And for myself. Because ... because you took my life with you when you fled.'

'Frejdis!'

'Besides, I met only Gyrith and Hildegun and waited with them, *Twin Raven* reached home only two days before the order from earl Hakon came.'

The tears were new, but painful convulsions swept them aside and Frejdis welcomed his crushing grip and put her arm around him, unable to relieve him.

'I would have been betrothed to you after the voyage with Helge, I love you, Frejdis!'

The voice jumped between the whipped wave-ridges, had suffering no end? The swords stuck through the skin both ways!

'Not more than I love you! And you would have had my yes! Everything that happened is my fault, mine alone, don't you understand that? I should have defied my parents and Stridbjørn, defied my own urge for ensuring the lineage, if anyone carries guilt under the sun, it's me. '

'By Odin, no!'

Arnulf raised his head and shot his gaze in the blue glow, 'Three men stood against you and the worst was probably your mother's crying, you are not to blame, you had no choice, it was myself who squandered the opportunities I had, I was blinded by sailing with Helge. But I cannot kill Rolf again!'

His head sank, his neck was so slack.

'I cannot kill him again.'

Frejdis' excited, quivering voice was weak, 'No. But Rolf loves me, too, and I promised him my love to keep him in life, he will not renounce me, Arnulf, he can no more see me with you, than you can see me with him.'

She struggled not to burst under him, and Arnulf heard his own squeak.

'So, we have to live with you both, and share the nights between us.'

The fingers melted through his skin, holding his heart.

'For whose pleasure is that?'

Frejdis pulled away and sat up, wiping her face in the skin. For a moment, she pressed it hard against her forehead, then she straightened and looked at Arnulf, as she tried with all her might to collect herself, 'Forgive me, I have upset you much too dangerously, Toke will be furious! You are so sick that I can feel your pain all the way to my bones, you need to rest and sleep, not cry! Freya curse me if I lie here, drawing life from you instead of making you healthy.'

Arnulf put his hand over his forehead, closing his eyes. His heart stood open, nothing was hidden, as if glistening bronze serpents were winding themselves around each other: despair, longing, hate, joy, and he shook his head, 'You give me certainty. It is better than fear, so neither Toke nor Freya has anything to say to you. I will rest now. I'm tired. Tired.'

The screams piled in his chest like mountain pastures seeking sheep.

'Do not think, let it go, you need all the sleep you can get. I have broken my word to Toke about not telling you anything too early, don't reveal me by lying restless the rest of the night, lay the wolf to sleep!'

Frejdis lay close to him, and Arnulf nodded, wide awake and unbearably clear-sighted under his hand, sleep was a stranger, he stood alone in the bow in front of Frejdis and Rolf, in front of Leif Cleftnose and

Toke's future, Svend's death, Jomsborg's call and around the ship flowed blood and screams and killed men, how could he sleep, how would he ever be able to sleep again?

*****

At dawn, thralls began to move around, and when the smell of porridge drifted over the newly-lit fire, the women of the house and Toke found clothing. Ranvig woke with a yelp and was lifted up, and Jofrid complained about her weight and heartburn to Gyrith while Hildegun tiptoed to Arnulf's bed and bent over him. Frejdis slept deeply, and Arnulf smiled faintly at Toke's mother and took her hand. She did not seem any less tired and troubled than her son, but her hair had grown and her facial joy was sincere, 'It is good to see you awake, Arnulf Stridbjørnson, how did you rest during the night?'

'I have not slept since midnight but am happy to be here again. Thank you for taking care of me.'

'Of course we are taking care of you, and if you are in too much pain, take just a swig of strong beer. Øystein always had difficulty finding peace after a battle.'

Hildegun felt for the fever and nodded satisfied, 'It is progressing nicely, and now you must eat to put flesh on your bones again, you are not pretty to look at. Toke!'

She turned to her son without accepting other answer than a nod, 'Give Arnulf a reasonable meal and do not tire him unnecessarily, we will let Frejdis sleep.'

Toke had both a bowl and a smile when he sat on the edge of the bed, and Hildegun found tasks nearby so she could keep an eye on whether Arnulf got enough to eat. Gyrith wished him a good morning over Ranvig's bright locks but would not interfere in the peace of the food, but encouragingly agreed with Hildegun's relief that Arnulf was awake and nearly free of the fever. The bustle and chatter over the fire made Stridbjørn's longhouse soar into the light through the open door, and a longing for Egilssund flared up. Women, children's voices, family, the night's heavy visions evaporated, and talks around the fire played without chainmail. Arnulf swallowed the spoonfuls with a tightness in his chest, and that Jofrid sullenly kept her back turned did not destroy the good mood. However glorious Jomsborg was in Sigvalde's honour, it was a poor exchange compared to the wealth Toke ruled over.

'As soon as you are back on your feet, *Twin Raven* will set sail for Denmark. I promised Frejdis I would sail you home to Egilssund before the autumn storms set in.'

Toke smiled broadly over the bowl, unable to keep silent any longer.

Arnulf pushed the spoon away, 'It is a long time to autumn.'

'Not with those cuts, you gave yourself in the battle. You were more difficult to cobble together than a worn thrall-kyrtle, so it will probably be some time before you are worth sending on a sea-voyage again.'

Arnulf nodded, closing his eyes, 'Thank you, Toke. But I wonder if it also depends on how Leif Cleftnose positions himself? I wanted to warn you, by Odin, I did! As soon as the war voyage was planned, I swore to reach Haraldsfjord in time, but I had neither boat nor horse when I recognised the white rock, and we encountered earl Hakon that very same day.'

He was breathless for a moment, by Helheim, it was gruelling to form words! His gaze drifted up, 'I have killed Northmen, how many I do not know, and I did not even manage to stay awake so I could tell you about Leif's appointment.'

'Oh, Arnulf, do not distress yourself like that! I know you did your best, and it seems that your warning came too late anyway, and I have killed Danes, so it all evens out. You must sleep again now and become stronger, but ...'

His eyes flickered, as if something heavy lay on his mind, 'I have an apology to give you, no, more than that!'

Toke's gaze was urgent, 'It has weighed heavily that I sailed from you during the voyage! Ever since we found you in the fjeld, I wanted to explain and ask for forgiveness. I was horrified when I understood my own action, but we thought you had drowned, and the storm lasted for over a day. The only one who still had the courage to look for you was me. Even Stentor was opposed, it was so far to land when you were washed overboard.'

Arnulf sucked air, staring stared hard at Toke, 'I was not washed overboard! Leif pushed me!'

'What!'

Toke's face contorted in disbelief, then he shook his head and stood up with a start, running his hand through his hair, 'No!'

His fist hammered a nearby post, so the women by the fire froze. The Northman walked around himself, upset, 'It is not true! The miscreant! The dastardly rogue! Arnulf, by Freyr, if I have ever hated a man more!'

Arnulf pressed his hand against his armpit, 'Just as he has probably not told you that the day after the battle, he begged earl Hakon for my life? We sat, trapped on the strand, and Leif would waive his share of the war goods, if he could decide my fate, but then the earl gave him Romsdale and that caused him to forget about me.'

Toke sank down on the bed again with an agitated look, 'No, he has not told me that, but I have heard about the men Hakon had beheaded and the answers they gave Torkel Lere! They were fearless warriors – did you sit among them? One of them was supposed to be Palnatoke's kinsman, Bue the Stout's son and also the man who alone beat an Ulfhednar, after the battle was over.'

Arnulf nodded, trying to press the pain away from his armpit, 'I am that man Toke. The Ulfhednar was going to kill Svend Bueson, and I could not let him win that fight, but the wolves bite was to no avail. Svend ... he died shortly afterwards. He was my friend. It was he who took me westward and demanded a place for me on the ship, I ...'

The speech burned out, such overwhelming grief was in his breath, and behind the Norwegian, Hildegun broke into the conversation with authority, telling her son to spare his enfeebled guest, 'You two have a lot to explain, and there is nothing wrong with my own curiosity, but do you not see what all the talk is costing Arnulf? You would do better fetching strong beer until he can find a little peace from his agony.'

Toke bowed his head, but Arnulf waved his hand towards Hildegun, he was so tired, his chest had to be eased. Sleep was still an unreliable retinue, 'I would not say no to a drink, Hildegun, but grant us the peace to talk, I would like to be rid of what we have to say.'

He turned his gaze to Toke, 'I saw you on the night after the battle, Toke, I saw *Twin Raven* sail past the rocks in the bay that we sat upon, but I did not want to call down the earl's anger on you and the settlement by asking you to help the enemy. It was a terrible night!'

Toke shook his head, his eyes sharp, 'You saw me? Arnulf! You could have called out! We did not notice you, you could have called *Twin Raven* to the rock, the earl would never have known you were on board, by Freyr, why did you remain silent?'

'Sigvalde's warriors are my brothers now, I could not forsake them. I was accepted among them that night, I am a Jomsviking now, I am Arnulf Wolfblood.'

A mug was passed over Toke's shoulder, and Gyrith's dark eyes glittered behind him. The Northman grabbed the handle, but forgot to hand it further, 'Arnulf Wolfblood? Jomsviking?'

He looked from Arnulf to Gyrith, 'Did you hear that or am I losing my mind?'

Stentor's daughter laughed and Toke shook his head so the beer splashed over the edge of the mug and down the sleeve of his kyrtle, 'You owe me a skaldic verse now, Stridbjørnson, and I want to hear it from the beginning! Gyrith, get Stentor and wake Frejdis, for now I am going to get my Danish kinsman drunk and get the secrets out of him, by Thor's beard, look at those eyes!'

The Northman's grin blazed, and the mug was offered, 'He will live, by my honour, save your worrying Gyrith, no doubt he is suffering, but Arnulf will rise, neither sea nor weapons can subdue him, and once he has returned home, no prouder man than Stridbjørn from Egilssund will be found throughout the entire Danish kingdom!'

*****

Hildegun's strong beer was powerful, but however much Arnulf drank, the pain and nightmares continued. Excruciating agony shot through both his arm and his chest from his armpit, and in his thigh a fickle hird of sickening thumping remained, while his ribs reminded his lungs of Leif Cleftnose's strength with every breath. Arnulf bore holes in the bed straw. The wolftooth runes drove the fever away, but sleep had also departed the bed, except when horrific, drunken dreams of blood and screams held his body trapped, and the dead penetrated like shadows on his heaving chest. Frejdis had to hold his hands when Hildegun and Gyrith changed the dressings on the wounds, and as if that was not enough, then Toke and Stentor took hold to force his limbs to keep still. If the gothi could at least have consulted the Æsir about how long this misery was to persist, it would have been comforting, but like the ship now drifting without oars and direction, it was hard to show courage. His gaze was familiar now with every beam below the ceiling, each and every post, every sound in the house, the fight dragged on, and despite Hildegun's good meat, the fat disappeared completely from under his skin.

Sleep. Flight. Shelter. Exhausted, everything swam before his eyes; sleep was worth everything. Everything! Svend and Little Ketil gestured around the bed, so Arnulf feared he was going mad, if he could haggle, silver could buy rest, sorcery, just one full night of freedom! So giddy was

427

his head from sleep deprivation, it was unclear what was happening on either side of his skull. Frejdis sang quietly, stroking his hair and undamaged skin, but she did not manage to turn his mind from his body, the grief or the horror. If he could just have met his opponents one at a time! Only when she slipped down under the skin naked did he find relief from the burden of life.

The dark seemed to brood endlessly over the suffering, and no matter how beautiful Øystein's longhouse was, the light only fell onto the floor by the door. The sun. The giver of life. Fire's love and the delight of birds! It was so gloomy that his eyes forgot their proper use, they would be blind when they were finally freed, why even keep his face over the skins just for the sake of a flickering oil lamp? His skin yearned for wind, so much so it became loose on his bones, and Arnulf called on torrential rain and freezing winds, a midwinter storm and saltwater.

Frejdis believed that a sick day in bed was longer than ten healthy days outdoors and she did not count them, but she knew his longing and picked flowers from the fjelds, and they were fair, but they were not equal to the poppies that had kissed her body. She laughed about the incident, 'That day I twisted more than you do now, and if we don't pluck more this year, they will come back again after the winter.'

Arnulf pulled himself up with a smile, reaching for her, 'I won't let you go again, no matter what comes!'

Frejdis was grave and laid the flowers on the sleeping skin, 'My father and Stridbjørn made promises and Rolf lives on my faith. I'm afraid to face them when we return home, afraid if I can live with Rolf peacefully. His prosperity will ensure my parents' old age, and I am their only child.'

Arnulf let his hand fall, staring at the ceiling. Prosperity. Security. Rolf was a full storehouse built in strong oak!

'I have no inheritance, and the silver I took on the voyage has long been divided between the crew, for they believed me drowned, but even if I were rich, your father would hardly see me as a useful swap for Rolf. I have no reputation in Denmark, and I bitterly regretted my straying and mockery of Stridbjørn. I was stupid, Frejdis, so stupid. I have to live with that for eternity.'

'No, not stupid!'

Soft hands went through his hair, 'Free and kinsman with the wolves, and if they had not taught you, the Ulfhednar would have killed you! Your blood is wild, but that is why I did not stay in Egilssund, you will probably be unstable for your children, but I can take care of them myself – my skills with wool will see to that! Just promise to rally home, whole,

428

from your voyages with Toke Øysteinson, so I won't fear for our wealth, you will probably take Helge's place. Aslak has made the new ship seaworthy again.'

The hands sought and Arnulf took hold. Voyages with Toke?

'Where will it all end? Vagn Ågeson said Jomsborg; King Sweyn and earl Hakon would open their doors for me, but what I wish for most is so difficult to get! You overshadow even the Dane king, I wriggle so badly in your wool.'

Instead of smiling, Frejdis bowed her head, 'A strong arm with a quick sword, it's all they see. I want it all! Do you really want to settle for being counted among the blows, do you not aspire to more? They are only opening their hirds to you because so many were killed.'

'Frejdis!'

She took a flower stalk and twisted it between her fingers so it broke and Arnulf shook his head, 'Have I not just survived where others fell? Svend Bueson said that women have killed more warriors than any weapon, therefore men in Jomsborg live alone, they fear being disturbed in mind when they fight, but I cannot live like that! I can only live with you! Come with me, we'll build a farm, wherever you want it.'

'No.'

The hair fell over her eyes.

'You aren't thinking clearly. Who will help my parents when they grow old? The family goes as much back as it goes forward, and I can't let them down.'

'I am thinking clearly! And no one will be let down!'

Frejdis looked up. Her bright eyes sparkled. She was strong, as wilful as an Asynjur, proud as Egilssund's pride should be! Words, what use were words, only actions forced fate onto the right course! She wore the answer on her lips, the sleeping pelt lifted from the heat, and amber floated towards her skin, amber, which had caught the summer's last rays.

*****

Several conversations took place by the wall, and Frejdis whispered of her will and joy, as the downy skin promised games and pleasure as soon as strength had returned. When his face rested against her chest, the woe of the wounds was easier to endure, and Toke spent much time on the edge of the bed, too. He had to see to other weapon-sick companions, and concerns about their own future and Leif Cleftnose's new position burdened him greatly. He was no less plagued by nightmares of the battle than Arnulf, so he often came stealthily at night and, again and again, the battle was discussed in subdued tones, every blow, every death, possibly unworthy talk for a Jomsviking, but even Sigvalde's folk had the right to be disheartened by weakening and tortured by killing in secret.

'I fought for Gyrith and Ranvig, for my family and my village and my fjord, what did you fight for, Arnulf?'

Sharp but not accusatory, the question hung like a disease in the air, and the answer hovered long after like a stench above the bed, 'I fought because I was too cowardly to resist! For companionship's sake, for the sake of the thrill and so as not to be counted for nothing. What would have happened if I had refused? I thought I was an outlaw in Denmark.'

'Others have probably acted on less, but what would you have done if Vagn had sailed into Haraldsfjord? Blood companion or not, he would have found it difficult to spare the fjord for your sake, there were so many men with him.'

Silence followed the words, so Toke spoke further about the plundering, about Toste Skaldshield's bereaved family, about Leif, who now rowed with earl Hakon when he was not frequenting Romsdale, and about Jofrid who did not have the strength for much more. The funeral feast for Øystein he would have held immediately after his voyage west, but now those plans had to be forgotten for a while; at least, until things were certain. Arnulf struggled to sit up, but sat listening with his back leaning heavily against the leather-padded wall, a mug of beer in his hand, caring little for the prospect of the holmgang, which was to take place between Toke and Leif as soon as the Cleftnose returned to the fjord. Although Stentor and the women of the house never used it, Arnulf could not avoid hearing other men mention Toke's new nickname: he was called Maimed-arm because he could not lift his sword arm high enough; the trading man's axe throw seemed to have given him a permanent injury. It did not bode well for the holmgang's outcome, but the Northman's speed and resourcefulness was still intact, and Leif apparently took the single combat seriously and let time drag out so as not to be irritated by his own battle scratches at their meeting.

'I lost your wolf-knife in the battle when Leif knocked me overboard for the second time.'

Toke smiled regretfully, 'You got to make good use of it, not least when you defended my life at the earl's farm, and the possibility of loss is the curse of the best weapons. In return, you won a ring that many men will envy you for.'

Arnulf looked at the precious encircling golden serpent, nodding, 'Sweyn Haraldson in the royalseat has my hands, and Jomsborg my arms but my full fidelity Frejdis alone has.'

'Frejdis?'

Toke looked mild at her sleeping, 'She is beautiful, Arnulf, few women are better born, but Rolf is entitled to her, and if he is like you in any way, he will not give up that right, as long as he draws breath.'

Arnulf's sigh blew darkness over the embers, 'What shall I do? She is my life and I love my brother. Even now, when I know how it is to end, it makes me happy that I didn't kill him.'

Toke could not think of an answer, an answer that would neither be wrapped in lies nor dreams, and Arnulf rolled onto his side with a stifled groan, too tired to grapple with such difficult predictions, while the Northman got up to get a little sleep out of the night.

That Arnulf was under Toke's roof became quickly known, but no one had anything to say against it. Øystein's son was well liked and had led *Twin Raven* skilfully in Hjörungavádr, and Stentor had read nothing but good omens about the friendship, too. Gyrith was anxious for the future of her children. Hildegun shared her anxiety and said Leif Cleftnose may well pursue her son for life, but he would never dare touch the gothi's family, there was not much honour in driving pregnant or ageing women out of the fjord, and certainly with autumn approaching, so Toke was alone in his fear. After those words, she did not speak of fear again, but Toke's back was burned by her gaze, and the women's care for the master of the house almost outdid their care of Arnulf.

As long as the wounds healed only slowly, there was no talk of sailing to Denmark, and despite people in Egilssund no doubt being troubled by Frejdis' long absence, it did not occur to her to seek passage home alone. That Rolf's future wife shared a bed with his brother, only Jofrid dared to be disgusted over, but Hildegun beat her torrents to the ground, 'If it helps Arnulf get on his feet, then do not get involved, do you not see the light between them? It is the work of Freya and what comes out of it, only Frigg knows, but Frejdis did not come to Haraldsfjord from obedience alone, so they may well enjoy a little happiness in peace.'

Jofrid was silent after that but allowed herself to send snide glances and Gyrith seemed wistful about the impossible unity. Maybe the gothi-daughter grasped how deep the roots wove, Arnulf caught glimpses of himself in her penetrating gaze. Frejdis did not worry about Jofrid but tended to the wounds by day and Odin's spear at night and, together with Toke, supported him when Hildegun allowed the first tentative steps across the floor. His sword arm squirmed at the grip and his legs slid like cooked eel, while his thigh made severe objections to the effort, so it was not the proud walk of a great man, but Stentor had congratulations enough for the deed, 'Our Jomsviking can tread so heavily! Just wait, Arnulf, before the cold sets in, you will be able to drag my best horse to the ground, and while you might now feel you have reason to complain, I can see that your leg will carry you solidly again.'

The gothi stood leaning against the door frame with his arms folded, and Toke laughed exhilaratingly and led the fight against him, 'Yes, the Dane warrior is not made of dough and now we will go out, if it suits the handless friend of the Æsir by the door to jump out of the way in time!'

It was hard to participate in the fun, and as the sun rose, the hollow of his knee burst over the doorstep. His body was breathless, ashamed of its own uselessness and blinded by the light! Toke struggled with his weight to the wall of the house, and both the hand and the hair had to hide his eyes, as the tears flowed. The sun was so warm! Its power so mighty! Compared to that well of light even a king had to be counted as an insect and Arnulf drank life from its rays like a dry tree in the rain. He cried still, as Frejdis sat with him with a beer mug and dish of gannet, and village and fjord only became clear once his eyes remembered to praise the day's song.

*****

Frejdis helped Arnulf out into the sun several times a day after that, and peace was found by her soft arms and tickly hair. It was difficult to think of Rolf as her husband and Egilssund lay far from Haraldsfjord; Frejdis' intimate laughter overcame his body's ailments, and by the wall of the house the smile was easy to find. She remembered the blackberries and the dances on summer nights, and Arnulf leaned his neck heavily against the house, Gerdr had only been half as happy with Freyr as he was with Frejdis!

Toke cut a crutch, and Arnulf took great journeys around the house to build up his strength and steps; he even dragged the recalcitrant leg down to the water to sit on a rock and look out over the fjord. It was clear, mirroring the village and mountains, and *Twin Raven* adorned its surface, too, with its high-raised bow heads. Calmness was there, the water was like liquid silver, and the sighs no longer stack groaning thorns in his side. Arnulf moved the fingers of the healing hand gently and stared

432

out over the water. Svend Silkenhair smiled from the shadows of the rocks, but the screams' echo was not yet dead, only more thronged, as if pressed. Perhaps the shame of misdeeds never completely faded, maybe some men were chosen to carry the blame for such a stock of experience, maybe each one carried a deep secret in the chest of his mind, which was only reluctantly unlocked.

'It is a courageous journey you have embarked you on, Stridbjørnson, have you realised that the way back is uphill?'

Smiling, Toke sat beside him and shadowed his eyes with his hand, 'There is rest on the water today. You have grown, Arnulf, before you would have watched for the seagulls.'

Arnulf let his thumb slide over the crutch's planed timber, and Toke picked up a stone and rubbed it between his palms.

'You are quiet. Are you in pain?'

Pain? Was pain not a condition for Jomsborg's sons, was that not how the Bueson would have answered? Arnulf drilled a hole in the ground between his feet with his eyes, 'I raped a woman.'

He looked up at Toke, and the stone slid back from where it came.

'I raped a woman without wanting to, Sigvalde's warriors held her and taunted me, and if I had not done it, they would not have counted me a man. She was Øgmund White's and she did not like me.'

The fjord dragged his gaze again and Toke dried his hand over his knee, waiting to respond, anger probably had to gather first. Arnulf pressed his nails into his palms, now it hurt, but not in the flesh! Åse White apparently had neither father nor brother to invoke the law of vengeance and Øgmund was dead, perhaps the Norns had wrapped Helge's life-thread into his own?

'You have been a murderer. How does it feel to be a rapist? '

The words were edged.

'Only slightly better than having killed my brother.'

The sword hand gave at being clenched, and Toke remained seated with a pensive face, no hatred grew in his expression, 'Then you know well, what you should do another time. You do not win respect by doing what others expect, you earn respect when you stand up for yourself.'

He found his stone again and sent it plopping into the water, 'And I wonder if I did not help to avenge your misdeeds plentifully and thereby the right to release you of your agony? Your self-loathing earns you honour.'

433

'Why do you not hate me? I did everything wrong against you on the voyage.'

Toke shook his head with a hint of a smile, 'The will can break from pressure, I have no reason to hate. My respect you won long ago, and it was you who saved a mother and her daughter from Leif Cleftnose's heat, even if you received both laughter and scar from it. In my eyes Jomsvikings are predators, who live for killing and dying, but you have loved Frejdis always, have you not? You may have the wolf and the eagle in your name, but despite that you cannot live by the smell of blood alone, you need more than battles and voyages.'

Arnulf nodded and supported his elbow on his knee, 'Vagn Ågeson sailed to Vigen to live with Torkel Lere's daughter, Ingeborg. He will not fight again.'

'Then Vagn is, after all, a better man than I thought.'

Another stone was picked up and thrown into the sparkling sea.

'He is a dangerous man he is but also my blood-brother. Svend Silkenhair would have been my brother.'

Toke snorted and threw a new stone off after the ripples, 'Friendships are strongly linked around shared killing and danger, but less can bind just as hardened ties. You suffer by having brothers, but I have never had one, yet have always wanted one. I envy men, who win kinsmen with a single knife cut, but what blood binds, words bind no less.'

Arnulf straightened and let his discouragement go. Øysteinson with his great responsibility and full heart. Toke, who always found an answer and dared to let his will stand tall! More than life itself he owed the Northman, Freyr's chosen, Haraldsfjord's protector.

'Will you accept my brother-word, Toke? Despite it being presented with an injured hand, put forward by an incalculable mind?'

He forced his sword arm forward a little and Toke stiffened, his eyes blank. He stared at the bandaged hand and slowly lifted his eyes. That vulnerability, neither Svend nor Vagn possessed, trembled over his skin, and he took his hand, gently but firmly, nodding, 'Yes, Arnulf Stridbjørnson, yes, I will! And my grip does not count for less than the promises of great men! You were my brother already – from that moment you cut the rope in the thrall hut, and I have counted you as such ever since.'

The smile seared into Arnulf and Toke threw his head back abruptly and laughed, 'By Freyr, Wolfson, as long as you do not drag me into Jomsborg itself, then I will stand by you no matter what is thrown against your ship. Life should not be worn out from boredom, that oath you swore the day you were born, and Odin has not had any reason to yawn since in Hlidskjalf, Jörmungandr take you! Now, for my own protection's sake, I will have to make you another silver knife!'

*****

A messenger came during the afternoon from Leif, riding over the fjeld to set the day of the holmgang and Toke met him, standing tall, in front of the longhouse. The Cleftnose's challenge was simple, and Toke could not shake the vassal's conditions much: the loser was the man who first spilled blood on the ground, and he should thereafter, by the next spring at the latest, leave his village, while the winner would rule over Haraldsfjord. Gyrith erupted in loud crying at the words, and Hildegun's face greyed, but Toke agreed without batting an eye, and Arnulf let go of the crutch by his side and glared mockingly at Leif's man. Leave the fjord? Abandon land and farm? It was not enough for Leif to win over his opponent, he would send Øystein's son away, and it was surely only not to fall out with Stentor that he gave until spring!

Toke stood for a while at the door, watching the rider with a harsh gaze, while his fingers absently stroked the scar on his arm, Freyr was not here, Odin's favour had to follow the chosen one, and Arnulf shuddered in the breeze. Øystein, Sigtryg, ancestors grown in the fjeld, where could Toke make a new farm for his women and children, what other fjord would give its water to *Twin Raven's* keel? Without a word, the Northman strode off, and before Arnulf had got hold of the crutch, Hildegun went past him with chainmail and sword in her arms, heading for the forge, obviously only a master's hand should be allowed to repair and sharpen her son's weapon and protection.

That night the sound of heavy footsteps woke Arnulf, heavy hesitant steps. Tense from troubling dreams, he was awake immediately, but the danger was no greater than Jofrid going back and forth along the fireplace's embers, huge and big bellied with rocking life, the time had come. She had lit a single lamp but did not seem to use its light for much, her gaze was so distant, and Arnulf hid his watchful eyes. If others in the house were awake, they did not let on and Jofrid did not complain, she only paused, now and then, between steps and leaned against a post or against the wall as she breathed heavily.

Arnulf looked at the sleeping Frejdis. A birth. Perhaps Leif's messenger had triggered the pains, maybe fear had pushed the child into action, not a word was said about the challenge, since the rider had disappeared over the fjeld, but their minds had mulled gloomily and Gyrith had slumped over the loom. Jofrid rubbed her lower back. Soon he and Toke would be shooed out of the house so the women could be alone, but Jofrid did not seem to want to rush Helge's child out; her slow wandering around the embers continued at her own pace, and she did not seem to need help. Arnulf stared at the dark beams. He could not sleep, nightmares and anxiety waited in rest and his armpit ached. He closed his eyes. The child. Helge's child. The family stood to gain, but Jofrid was against its life. Restless, his gaze swept back through the semi-darkness, following Jofrid's fight. Did she feel the same as he had before the battle against earl Hakon? Was she scared? She was in pain, that way she leaned against the woodwork and drew breath, it must have been ugly to have to pass through an unchosen fight. It was Helge's misdeed! Arnulf ran his fingers through his hair. Helge. He could have at least survived, could have excused himself with drunkenness and tried to betroth himself to Jofrid to make good. Øystein and Stridbjørn could certainly share the feast beer easily, instead Jofrid had lost her father, and only a lame weakling stood as the child's defence. He squinted. Jofrid's fight, his own battle, they would stand equally well on their legs when the weapons should be drawn, rest was needed, but he could not find calm.

The steps divided the night. Like a country that was being meted out, Jofrid's movements were even more laboured at dawn, an endless wandering, increasingly impoverished, increasingly difficult footsteps, and she stopped now and again at the edge of her bed, seeking strength but not finding peace from her quest. Hildegun knew of her daughter's condition in the first grey daylight but did not disturb her, and as sleeping skins along the walls were lifted and clothes were found, chores and talk seemed more rushed and subdued than usual. Arnulf sat up against the wall with his hand at his armpit, his head was so heavy! He wanted to sleep all winter, sleep like a bear as soon as his body was free from pain and nightmares, Frejdis should bring thick skins to him, Helheim curse the Ulfhednar's bones!

Concerns about Leif Cleftnose's challenge seemed temporarily forgotten around the rekindled fire, Toke went to Stentor, so Freya could be called upon for assistance, and Frejdis spilled porridge over the yarn when she stumbled with the bowl. Breakfast was eaten on one side of the fire to give Jofrid space; it was charred, but Hildegun did not scold the thralls, and Arnulf was too tired to really be hungry. Toke returned on light legs, looking restless; he ate standing and Gyrith seemed to sense that Jofrid's biggest threat right now came from her brother, for she found a

436

smile and pulled him encouragingly by the sleeve, 'Torvald will break in his white-starred horse today, you should go and help him, do you remember how good a hand you gave with the brown, when it came down from the fjeld?'

'Torvald?'

'Yes, and Arnulf, you look like you could do with a little more sleep. Is it your armpit again? Should I get a drink of mead for you?'

'He has to go out!'

Jofrid had stopped in the middle of the floor and for the first time sent those wake a glance, 'Arnulf. He must go out. Now.'

It flamed red under her hair, Sif herself could not have ordered more fiercely, 'I said now!'

She staggered and fumbled to the nearest bed, and Hildegun got up quickly and went to her daughter with a sure nod to Toke, orders were given, from now on, the men had no place on the ship. Arnulf struggled to his feet and got a shoulder of support from Øysteinson while Frejdis, in a hurry, gathered up skins and wool and slipped past them. A thrall followed with a mead jug and mugs, and Jofrid's furious eyes stabbed holes in Arnulf's kyrtle, such wild hatred! His leg gave and had to be forced to obey, would she always only see him as Helge's brother and the goal of all revenge? Luck follow her anyway, Hildegun had to be encouraged to help her daughter as best as possible, but even Gyrith seemed so brusque at his presence that Arnulf limped off wordlessly with a solid grip on Toke's arm.

The lamb skins were laid along the wall of the house, and Toke sat with him and, despite the day's insignificant age, had a craving for mead and with a fleeting smile Frejdis slipped in through the door again to give Hildegun a hand. The morning was cool and the sky cloudless, and Arnulf pulled a skin around himself, and took the filled mug. The grass in the village was tired, the summer aged and the wool was starting to thicken on the sheep. Toke supported his mug on his knee, as if he had forgotten his sudden thirst and stared out over the fjord, his face a little lost, 'Do you know anything about childbirth?'

Childbirth? How livestock lambed, calved and foaled he understood, but women!

'Not in the least.'

'Gyrith gave birth to Ranvig in half a night, but Hodr from Tornevig's woman died when she gave the child last summer.'

He looked at Arnulf with big eyes, 'She screamed, so it could be heard far up in the fjelds, and afterwards she lay, burning with fever, Hodr was mad with grief. If my mother loses Jofrid, it will be more than she can bear, she has enough worries already, and Jofrid abhors the child! Maybe it will deprive her of the strength required, Freyr stand with us, I fear the day even more than I fear Leif Cleftnose's axe.'

'Jofrid is strong and hatred gives strength! She has good helpers around her, and Freya will listen to Stentor.'

Arnulf grimaced and took a sip of mead, his armpit was healing badly, but the amber liquid was easy enough to swallow. It did not work as well as earlier, perhaps his stomach had become accustomed to intoxication. Toke bowed his head and stroked his hair. Older, he had become older since the flight from Haraldsfjord and unwilling to share in more misfortune and fights. Arnulf shivered and placed the mug on the grass, 'Leif's axe is heavy, but you are fast, and the smith has sharpened Sigtryg's sword, so it resembles a lynx-claw. The blade does not need to go deep to cut its way to victory.'

Toke looked up anxiously, shaking his head, 'My arm is not yet healthy, I could feel it in Hjörungavádr, it lacks both strength and lifting. Leif's blows will be tough, and I have much to lose.'

His eyes shone sincerely, 'If I die, will you protect my women?'

Protect his women? With such a miserable body? Serpenttooth had no arm to blow.

'Odin is hardly lacking men in his hird after the battle, and what is all this talk of dying?'

The challenge applies only to blood on the ground, do you think Leif will risk his triumph over Romsdale for your sake? He is an ox, dodge and search for cuts, then he'll have lost before his second blow, but I will protect your women well; keep in mind, Frejdis is among them!'

Crestfallen, Toke drank deeply and struck out with his arm, 'The year will soon end. The settlements should be thinking of winter and supplies, and instead their strength has been spent on war. Men are still injured, families are mourning, and by a single unlucky sword blow, I may lose both home and companions! They trust me, the people in Haraldsfjord, we have had losses, but it went well for *Twin Raven's* crew in the battle, I am tired to death of battles and blood, and I am afraid! What will happen Gyrith and my children, my mother and my sister, if I am not here? Stentor himself has plenty to see to.'

Arnulf sought his shoulder with his hand, 'Sigtryg's sword will not betray the family, and Leif's good fortune makes him overconfident. There is a law among Jomsvikings which says that no man in the fort should show signs of worry or fear, no matter how hopeless his situation is, and maybe that's why Sigvalde's men are rarely broken on the battlefield.'

Toke must not lose his will, whether his words were true or not, he sat weighed down, he was a nut without a shell.

'It is possible, but I am not a Jomsviking.'

'No, but I am!'

Toke's features stiffened, then a sad smile broke through, and he grasped the hand on his shoulder, 'By Freyr, you are right! It is bad chainmail to bear defeat in advance, and he who does not sleep during the night, does not see clearly. Today Jofrid is giving birth and Frigg alone knows what will happen tomorrow. See! Stentor is coming now!'

He waved to the gothi, who was easily persuaded into sharing a drink and Stentor had sure omens from the women's intentions in the house, which eased the melancholy, and the talk turned. The sun took power above the fjelds, and Arnulf lingered between sips, lapping up hope. Gyrith's father had safety woven in his cloak, his presence relieved burdens and the yellow eye frightened evil away. He was a great man, and as soon as other men settled down in the grass, for the waiting time, their minds were lifted for a while. Everything other than what was going on inside was talked about, and when Toke looked like himself again, Arnulf came painstakingly to his feet and headed between the houses, so as not to neglect his hunt for health.

His knee was sluggish to bend, a burning knot was ignited in his thigh with the stretch, but the leg's support was better with each outing he made. Frejdis still bandaged his sword arm thoroughly to give the healing wounds support and his armpit some peace; it was still too soon to hoist the sails on *Twin Raven* but the longing grew! Arnulf stopped, breathless, gazing out over the fjord-mirror. Egilssund was so foremost in his mind that Rolf's call could be heard in his dreams. Stridbjørn's house, Trud's arms, Aslak's grin, Halfred's thundering voice; he closed his eyes, they were all there, but in Haraldsfjord Frejdis was his! True, he was no longer banished but he still had only refuge in Norway.

The red-haired smith greeted him from the forge, when Arnulf limped past, but back at the wall of the house, there was no news to hear, the birth was dragging out. Around midday, Frejdis came out with bread and cheese but had no more news other than Jofrid now sat more than she walked, and that it was hard that she suffered so. The men in the grass found something else to do, the words ran out, and the day put its chilly start to shame emphatically, so Toke slipped off his kyrtle and sat doggedly, in distant thoughts, while his fingers twisted around the belt-purse's shiny strings. Arnulf tried to find rest but was no less restless than Øysteinson, Jofrid's deep heaving of air could be sensed through the wall, as Helge's heir made demands. He went again, once around the house for each finger, and Skinfaxi diligently slid warmer colours over the fjord. It had to happen soon!

Toke went to the door and wanted to know if he was to be called in when the youngster had eventually learned to crawl, but Hildegun had no voice left for her son, and Gyrith's face was tight, 'If you do not find time to grapple with Torvald's horse, then give me time to grapple with your sister, she struggles such that each of your Vikings would long since have given up!'

'But will the child not come out? Should it be pulled? Why is she not giving birth?'

'Are you suffering so much pain from throwing yourself over a mead jug that you cannot grant Jofrid housecarls for her battle? Better you sit and talk loudly with Arnulf, so he does not hear what Helge is being called in here!'

What was Helge being called? The indignation raged, but the blame lay certain, so Arnulf was silent and sent Toke a look as Gyrith, snorting, turned at the door, leaving her husband to sit with his undone deeds. Hands clenched, and the sun stopped, a cow complained, but birthed the calf and the sheep squeezed out lambs, so the foxes hardly had time to get close, why had women learned to scare the life out of their males – were they afraid of not reaping praise enough afterwards? Foaming, Toke tore up the grass around him without trying to say anything sensible, and shortly after Stentor began to roam near the longhouse, keeping to himself, even the people of the next village were silent and took note.

The evening porridge had to be retrieved outside, for the thralls did not dare to come near Hildegun any longer. Shadows crept from thighs to toes, as Toke pulled his kyrtle over his head again and gave up trying to pretend that he had found any peace in his seat. Like a hungry wolf, he trotted back and forth and stopped half-exploded whenever a brash outburst snuck out the door, but Arnulf did not hear Jofrid, and Stentor's assurances slowly lost reliability. Maybe she lay there, unconscious from exertion, while Helge's child suffocated from lack of air! He straightened. Jofrid had now had pains since midnight – what had Freya to avenge? The scream struck like a knife in the stomach, driving through his wounds, so he writhed. Tearing asunder the dusk around the longhouse so bestially that voices broke into flaming squeals and Toke emitted a cry, running towards the door. Another cry followed, agonising and painfully tense, an omen of the woe of Vigridr, and then a third that was so full of defiance and force that shivers ran down Arnulf's spine.

Toke tore at the door, but it was bolted, and he stared aghast at Arnulf who, sweaty and clammy, came to his feet with his hand against the wall of the house, now it was happening, now! Life or death, he limped to Toke, but Stentor reached him first, and now came new cries, others' screams, thin and light but equally, furiously wild, and the tears pressed behind the eye's shield and drove the liquid through, while a consuming anxiety started to boil. The door was blocked! The door was locked to give Jofrid time to wield the dagger, time to kill, kill Helge's new-born baby! With breaking strength Arnulf pushed Toke aside and tugged on the handle and behind the planks an infant's screams defied fortune and fate so violently that it tore new life to itself. Numb, he pushed his shoulder into the door and screams became yelps, while Stentor's masterful hand forced him back, 'Arnulf, are you trying to beat yourself unconscious? Wait, you will tear your wounds!'

The gothi knocked authoritatively on the woodwork and, breathless, Arnulf leaned his weight against him, the pain took hold with eagle talons and the yelps came closer as if it were the new-born himself, who sought to make a hole in the longhouse. Then the door opened, and a thrall woman appeared, with the swaddled one crying in her hands, wanting to get past. Toke slinked around her and Stentor followed after, his forehead wrinkled, but Arnulf stood in the way with his hand against the door frame, staring at the swathed, writhing cloth. Helge's child. Helge himself!

'Where are you going with the child?'

The woman timidly avoided his eyes and spoke quietly, 'It is to be put out on the fjeld at once; that is Jofrid's decision.'

'That it must not, give it to me!'

The thrall quickly shook her head and held the bundle closer to her body, 'You cannot have it, such were the words, it is to be put out on the fjeld at once, Ram is to throw it in the Salmonfalls.'

Scorching sparks flew through the air, the Salmonfalls! Over his dead body! Arnulf let go of the frame and reached commandingly, 'Give me the child, or I will kill you! How dare you defy a free man's will!'

The thrall woman began to shake and blubber and made no resistance as he pulled the cloth aside to see. It was so slimy! Congealed in bloody cakes of fat, but he knew the will and the short dark look in the half-closed eyes made his heart jump. A boy! A strong and well-limbed boy! Svend Helgeson. A yelp, no, a roar, bade him to the fore in the shield

441

wall for his kin and Arnulf stood guardian of his kinsman and rocked the child over to his shield arm. Even if all Haraldsfjord's settlements were behind Jofrid, Little Svend would return to Egilssund before winter, his mother would give life and food, and Trud would be allowed to watch him grow, that oath he swore on Draupnir itself!

With victory in mind he stepped through the door and headed right towards the bed on the other side of the long fire where Gyrith and Hildegun seemed to be busy over Jofrid, who was still breathing heavily after her efforts. Water and blood stained the floor and Frejdis looked up from the suspended pot over the fire, her eyes anxious. Toke had sat down by his sister's head, and Stentor watched, withdrawn, as if he stood ready to fend off misdeeds and anger. Hildegun felt the shadow from behind and turned around with a bloody cloth in her hands, her expression sharp at the sight of Arnulf, sharp as never before. 'No, Arnulf, let the young one be and go out with it, you have before heard my opinion on this matter, and I would very reluctantly remind you that you are only a guest here. Give the thrall back its bundle.'

Her eyes sparkled in the light from the many hanging lamps, and the short hairs bristled with sweat. When Arnulf contented himself with stopping, she blocked the way quickly, but it was useless action, Helge's cry rang clear.

'You would do the same for Toke, and if we are going to talk about matters, then you are kinswoman to the child you are going to kill, he has the same standing as Ranvig! Step aside! I will not harm Jofrid!'

Rather Thor collapsed than he let go of Little Svend! Arnulf shot fiery wolf-blood in front of him, and Hildegun paled, 'If Helge had wanted a child, he would have acted differently and met Jofrid with gold instead of violence, so do not defend it for his sake, and a child of rape cannot be equated with Toke's offspring! Collect yourself and do not do any more damage than you can stand behind, Arnulf, for Toke's sake! You are not well, hand over the child, I am here to do the best for Jofrid.'

'It's a boy Hildegun, a son, your daughter's son, did you hear Jofrid? You birthed a son!'

Hildegun's words rammed hard, but behind Helge were the shadows of Stridbjørn and Trud and they wanted a part of their lineage. Toke rose abruptly, his face dark and Jofrid turned her face towards Arnulf. He had yelled the last bit loudly, but Jofrid's gaze strangled the next word. She was exhausted, weakened beyond recognition, but the pain in her expression did not come from the birth. Arnulf went around Hildegun, and the others fell silent, only the little one whimpered, craving the breast. Now the weaklings had to do combat, the struggle of the less abled. Gyrith pressed a cloth between Jofrid's bloody legs and pulled a fur for sleeping over her abdomen, then she stepped back as if she recognised the inevitable, she herself had birthed and carried a child.

'Jofrid ...'

'No!'

The screams had taken most of her voice and the words took the air from her body, but Arnulf stopped only when his knee encountered the side of the bed, so close that Little Svend's objections penetrated her skin.

'Jofrid, it is your child, yours! Helge is dead and will never come back, understand that and forget your hatred! The boy here will live, he is crying for you, he is freezing, your brother is his kinsman, your mother is a part of him, take him now, look!'

Arnulf pulled the blanket from Little Svend, and the boy kicked angrily at the cold and started to howl, but Jofrid looked past him, 'You will never understand the shame, Arnulf'

She gasped for air as if her lungs had no support from her belly anymore, 'Go! Your behaviour is unforgiveable, I do not want the fruit of humiliation and violence, do you not understand that?'

'I know everything there is to know about shame! And about violence.'

Arnulf used the worthless sword arm to help keep Little Svend against her, the muscles shaking at the grip, 'Look at him! Helge was a great man, and his son will not be any less! There is no man in Haraldsfjord, who does not want to be a foster father to the boy, it is yourself you are killing if Ram throws him in the Salmonfalls! Who will be betrothed to a child-murderer? I know what it is to have killed, by Freya, Jofrid!'

The wound under his arm opened, so it trickled down his kyrtle sleeve and the pain was nauseating. Little Svend slipped from his grip.

'If you do not go now, I will get Toke and Stentor to force you out!'

Jofrid's heavy breasts called to the boy, blushing from heat. Arnulf laid Little Svend on them, pulling the cloth from him. Jofrid wanted to push him down, but Arnulf grasped his sword hand around her wrist, although it caused everything to go black before his eyes, and held tightly, 'What do you want, Jofrid? I will give anything, anything, you just have to nurse the baby until I can take him home to Egilssund.'

He had to grab the woodwork, not much less breathless than Jofrid, 'I am not asking you to keep him, I am asking for his life! What is the price, Jofrid? If nothing else, let me pay a thrall-price for your son.'

His thigh trembled, and Arnulf took a wide stance, propped against the bed so as to lay Little Svend better towards a breast, and Jofrid wriggled loose, hitting out towards his injured armpit. It felt like the glowing tip of a point, and Arnulf writhed, groaning, over her, but Little Svend found the food source and latched on with overwhelming force. A sob escaped Hildegun's daughter, and her head shook while Toke's firm grip lay support on his shoulder and gently pulled Arnulf back a step. He staggered, but Jofrid had a hand on the little one now, and even though she was crying, she did not push Svend Helgeson away, 'I hate you, Arnulf! But fine! You will be allowed to pay, but I will not keep the child a day too long!'

Her eyes narrowed, as if she wanted to strike again, and Arnulf had to lean on Toke, his arm dangling, 'You can set the price yourself, and I give my word that I will take Svend with me as soon as possible.'

'I want Serpenttooth!'

The flickering flames stiffened; the words split him through the middle. Serpenttooth! Serpenttooth? Impossible! He stared in disbelief at Jofrid, who with a cat's gaze kept her arm around the suckling one; if he refused, it would cost a life!

'What do you want with a sword? You will get what it is worth in silver or take my skald-rings instead; they are more costly than any weapon, for they were given by a king! You know what Serpenttooth means to me.'

Surely it was Serpenttooth itself who had threatened her during the rape, now she was taking revenge and breaking Helge's neck, he had loved his blade so much.

'You get the boy and I get Serpenttooth, otherwise there is no deal!'

His legs gave way, and it began to drip from the fingers of his sword hand. Arnulf collapsed, hit by something so hard that his resistance broke. The hair danced down over his eyes, and his arm had to be kept close to his body so as not to fall off; she wanted to humiliate him, taunt him, wrestle the thing from him that meant the most to him, seize the last of Helge. A warrior without a sword. A Jomsviking without a weapon. Just as naked and defenceless as Helge's son did she want her opponent; dishonourable laughter, the exchange was even!

He looked up. Serpenttooth was no inheritance, the sword had been taken from Stridbjørn's table, no less stolen than the silver in the earl's farm, if anyone had a claim to it, it was Rolf as the second oldest. But Helge's intent lived in it! His grip, his will, his victories, it flowed in the

444

blade like the blood of silver, no other weapon would glide in his arm like Serpenttooth, would whisper and egg him on, defend and win! What use was wolf-blood without teeth?

Frejdis loosened Toke's hand from his shoulder and put her own arm around him. She had fetched the sword, sheathless, the blade glittered in the fire, and Arnulf grasped the hilt, as she helped him up without a word. Like the smell of burned frying, the silence thickened around him, and the glances behind it were serious, Stentor's chiselled features lurked from the loom and even Hildegun had no objections. Frejdis' heart pounded in her palm, beating a pulse in time with Arnulf's through his skin. Toke's women. Jomsborg's men. Arnulf heaved air in and went back to Jofrid's bed. Little Svend suckled, a little breathless, and smelled of womb and newness, and the fingers of his sword hand burned in the grip, his arm could hardly lift the weight. The final blow! The last farewell! Vagn's spear slammed into the wall behind Jofrid's bed, and Snap rang with the strength of an oath from its hook in the darkness. Serpenttooth cast a shadow over the boy, then the blade slid down over the outstretched hand, and Arnulf let go of the hilt without touching Jofrid's fingers. Tyr's hand. Odin's eye. Veulf's sword.

He turned to go but stumbled instead, and now the voices broke out around him: actions, orders, a thawing power of intent, of steps, of will, but his body stooped, stripped of all power, and even Frejdis' help burned hideously! His forehead sought the floor, could the defeated not sink where he fell, so deep a wound required no heroes, the tendons were blown, the light became dark!

Jofrid complained angrily, and Hildegun's commanding voice wove about Stentor's light talk, Toke's feet were uncertain on the floor, but in the end, they chose family, and the thralls were called in. Helge held out his hand, but Arnulf did not take it, and Frejdis' petitions to stop the bleeding were brushed aside, the wolf was wounded, and alone it would mourn the loss, he crawled along the row of beds, searching the darkness under the skins, his eyes were his own. Serpenttooth. Little Svend. Vigridr's burden. Arnulf bored his face into the pelt, painless from emptiness and trembling, so his bones wore each other down. It was done!

$$*****$$

When the sun was at its highest on the agreed date, Stentor carefully carried the folded holmgang skin out of the longhouse and laid it on the blót stone in sight of all. He was naked despite the stiff wind, but the cold did not make his white skin shrink, and the gothi's song over the square was carried out over the fjord, as if the people from other villages, who had not turned up, should be able to share in the event. With raised hands, those men, who had won or lost on the skin, were named and although it was not yet unfolded, Arnulf could sense the old blood stains on the bear skin that had not allowed themselves be cleaned away so they could bear witness to fate and pronouncements.

Ullr was invoked, Odin and Tyr, and both Toke's and Leif's swords were laid over the skin to take part in the pact. The gothi's voice rang invokingly; loudly he proclaimed the nature of the dispute and the terms, and the power of the blót stone secured foothold and equal bite of the weapons so that no malicious sorcery should have the power to dull any of the blades. The yellow eye shone through the wind-blown hair, Stentor was the guardian of justice, however much of a share he had in Toke's luck, for now the extent of his help was only to hold the shields for his daughter's husband, and Leif Cleftnose did not appear to fear his presence, for he stood stalwart in a cloak of blue. Arnulf straightened the crutch, silk and silver buckles, Leif was Leif, regardless of the men who now stood by his side, and although they could hunt Toke out of the fjord with force of arms and without the slightest exertion, the Cleftnose was wise enough not to break the law. First loss of blood on the skin, a cut he would risk for his right but no more, and the hird would prevent Toke from thinking otherwise, in case it was his blood that flowed first.

Stentor gave the opponents back their swords and lifted the stitched bearskins down onto flat ground. Respectfully, he began to spread it out, and memories could be seen in the eyes of those gathered, dangerous triumph glowed alongside bitterness and stale disgrace, but what the gothi himself remembered, he kept to himself. Four bears had given life, four steps long was the skin on each side, the hair rubbed off, lacerations stitched together, and Stentor slowly opened the little tiösnur-peg chest and one by one laid the manhood-shaped pegs next to the leather loops around the edges. Then he bent over them and carefully bonded the loops to the ground while chanting was mingled with words of law and his gaze remained between his legs, as the ritual commanded. The holmgang skin was to be kept in place with symbols of life's fertility and Arnulf shuddered, glancing around as Stentor completed his duties. Frejdis' rapid breathing blew on his neck, scared like a young bird that she was about to face danger so near, but the esteem and gratitude had won over the repugnance for violence, Toke's support should be clearly visible in front of Leif's power. Gyrith had left Ranvig with the thralls and stood closest to Toke, pale, her hair loose, but with flashing eyes, and on the belt hung a sheathless thin-bladed knife, as if she wanted to threaten the vassal and sow hesitation in his strikes. Hildegun stood beside Jofrid, who was sitting, tired, in the grass with Little Svend at her chest, and although she almost had not been able to stagger from the birthing bed, she had not wanted to let her brother fight alone. Toke's sister had been milder in recent days, Helgeson's warm skin had thawed her hard expression and anger, and the shadow that had hatched before birth no longer cooled the air around her. Serpenttooth had been tucked away and she had smiled at Arnulf as if she believed they had finally made amends, but the loss of the sword pained him more than all his wounds together, and that Little Svend had won life, did not alleviate the horror of the price. Empty hung the belt, the scabbard was barren, and the honour kept shamefully to itself; feet without shoes, beast without fur, more naked than the gothi was the unarmed warrior, and Arnulf had to harden his will so it would not fall, only Snap could still call fire into his blood. Frejdis had not once mentioned the weapon, only pressed closer to him at night and laid her hand over the wounded armpit to keep the stinging at bay, but she felt the loss and gave it space.

Stentor straightened up and walked around the holmgang skin once with hazel branches in his hands. Two steps from the pelt's corners, he stuck the hazel branches into the ground and then tied the sacred band around their base, the fighters had six steps each way at their disposal, if they set a foot outside the hazel branches they yielded ground, and if the set another foot out, it counted as flight. Arnulf laid the weakened sword hand on Snap. Svend's axe might bring Toke luck in the fight, it had hung near Vagn when Skarde was killed, and the square in front of the king's long table had not been much bigger.

The gothi stepped into the middle of the skin and let his gaze sweep around the circle while he slowly repeated Leif's challenge and instructed those present that no one should interfere. Intimate, acknowledging nods and murmurs met his words, and almost as many had come from the settlements as on the day Øystein's son had returned home with the message of the chieftain's death. Each combatant received three approved shields for the fight, after that they would have to settle for covering themselves with their weapons until the skin drank blood, and Toke remained motionless with his sword tip resting against the ground for as long as Stentor spoke. The helmet hid part of his face, but not his gloomy expression, and the damage to the chainmail from the earlier

447

battle had been thoroughly rectified. Thick gloves and bands of leather shielded hands and arms, vulnerable skin was protected, and a long knife hung ready in front of his abdomen in case his shield should fail. Stentor stepped off the skin and pulled on his trousers and kyrtle to hold the shields, and Gyrith stepped in front of Toke and shared her mind with him through her hands on his shoulders. It had rested heavily on him after Jofrid gave birth! Arnulf had shared his concern and gained insight into the gut-wrenching anxiety, this fight was not about plundered silver and enrichment, or the kingdom's protection or the gaining of honour, it was about his family, his children, his survival and his courage was bending from the weight of it all. Stentor had practised blows with him behind the blót stone, but every time he had seriously attacked his bad arm, Toke yielded and lost the fight.

Leif Cleftnose had no woman to receive luck from; in return he had men to promise a victory drink to, and the laughter rang loud around the Romsdaleman. New weapons, jewellery and clothing, a large farm and hird and familiarity with the earl, Leif was on a day out, only wanted to play, and the array of hard, armed men could easily cast doubt on Toke's blow. What law would Leif obey, if his blood fell first? The folk of Haraldsfjord held Toke in their hearts, but all had kinsmen to keep in mind and the Cleftnose's strength was obvious. He was heavily protected: the chainmail went to his knees, and the helmet was inlaid with silver, the Fjordviking had not come to lose this fight.

Arnulf hobbled forward, holding up Snap for the housecarls. Haug had not given up when the Ulfhednar had jumped on board the skeid and his shield arm had rested enough to cause injury, the wolf-blood snarled grimly at having to stand outside, but Leif's volatile, icy-cold gaze left no doubt about how little he regarded his Danish enemy. Today, this day the craving for revenge had to rest, now the desire to cleave more than the Norwegian's nose had to kept in check, but by Odin's eye! Leif should be allowed to whine from regret, squirm and howl for mercy, that mud-hog should be drowned, drowned in his own stinking froth and bile, and if Serpenttooth was not up for the fight, then the Bueson still had a grip on Snap!

Toke took the first shield and composedly entered the holmgang skin, his eyes fixed on the vassal, who, amidst jubilations and cheers, threw his cloak from him, and stomped forward with his sword raised, accompanied by the roars of his men. The gothi's daughter trembled at the noise, as if she were standing, exposed, in frosty weather, but no one's hand would she take comfort from; she would stand no less tall than Toke.

Leif also had a shield companion, and he stood so arrogantly near the skin, that his foot violated the sacred band; the vassal was not wanting for protection, and there were plenty of carls who wanted to make an impression and draw attention to themselves. Stentor raised his arm with the remaining shields resting against his thighs. At that moment he let it fall and announced the start of the combat, Leif jumped forward with a resounding roar and swung so violently after Toke that the shield split through the middle and the Northman stumbled out of the bear skin. He had to throw himself to the ground and roll away to avoid the next blow, and Leif and his men burst into such heartfelt laughter that Stentor managed to pass the second shield to the Øysteinson as he was getting to his feet.

'Are you retreating already? After the first blow? Toke! Man up! They did not talk about you so badly after Hjörungavádr that you have to flee from the reputation like a spring hare!'

Again the vassal's sword squealed through the air, direct and heavy, as if it were stone and not flesh that would be parted by its bite, and this time Toke evaded, unwaveringly, but with no time to reply, for Leif let his shield follow the blade and the boss hammered into his helmet while Sigtryg's sword rasped deafeningly over the chainmail. There would need to be more than a few paces of skins to skip from the fallen mountain, Toke went down on one knee, half-paralysed by the blow and had to swerve pitifully away from the axe again, whose blade-seeking blow made his sword arm sink.

Frejdis' fingers drilled holes through his sleeve, and Arnulf clenched her hand. Leif exposed himself, but Toke was too late to take advantage of it, and several times he did not notice his chances. Stubbornly, the Cleftnose knocked against the injured arm, as if he wanted to hammer the strength from it before his final blow, but Toke had recovered his footing and slipped away from him, leaving Arnulf more breathless than Frejdis. They moved so clumsily! Never would Svend have let such an opening go by, and had Leif pursued his first blow, he would already be the winner. They were holmgang men, by Thor, not blacksmiths! The gazes flickered. Toke seemed to catch his thoughts, for he roguishly grabbed a strike to immediately let it escape, so Leif tumbled past him, but when the Øysteinson's sword was ripe for a neck bite, the Cleftnose's shield companion intruded with a shield for his vassal, deflecting the blade tip.

Arnulf shouted furiously, and under the invading shield, Leif rammed his shield's rim into Toke's knees to kill his opponent's speed and gain time for his foothold. A yell revealed how well he had hit, but when the Cleftnose turned around, Toke met him hard enough to hold his stance. The swords clanged together, both sets of chainmail were met but the skins remained free of blood and the shield bosses clashed. The weapons sought under the shields, but the legs were well guarded and even Leif's ripped glove cost him no blood loss.

The shield companion reaped much repute from his brothers for his move, while Arnulf's cry hung alone over the meeting place, but now the Øysteinson's contorted face enflamed. He was still blinking from the blow to his helmet, but the fear seemed shot behind the hazels, quickly the shield sent Leif's blow askew, and in a few strikes the injured arm was allowed to rest. Fresh courage and kinsman's deeds, if he continued he was going to win and Arnulf rocked on his toes, as if his thigh had forgotten the Ulfhednar's sword.

Good advice and excited shouts resounded from the housecarls, and Leif was apparently tired of Toke parrying his blows, because with a shout he suddenly threw his shield away, seized the hilt with both hands and thrust the blade right through Toke's shield. Toke dodged the tip and ripped his opponent's chainmail at the side all the way up to the belt while the Cleftnose wrenched the shield from him and split it with a crushing blow into the bearskin so splinters flew. Despite the tear in the rings he avoided being wounded, but his move had been costly, for Sigtryg's sword tore laces and skin on the shieldarm's inner side and Leif only managed to press his forearm against the cracked chainmail at the last minute, so the blood flowed down on his kyrtle and not onto the skin under them. Again he was attacked, and again his shield companion intruded into the fight and pressed Toke's strike awry, and Stentor shouted angrily for calm among the challengers' men, so the holmgang should not be declared invalid.

The last shield came into use, and Toke tried violently to seize control of Leif's weapon, now the vassal had to fight one-handed so as not to spill blood, but his knee appeared to have been badly hit. The Cleftnose went directly for both sword arm and leg, and it was hard for Toke, his limbs weakened, to avoid the heavy blows. Time and again, he tried to reach under Leif's strikes, but his arm was clearly sluggish, and his quest to control the fight failed.

Arnulf clenched his teeth. Cold-blooded, the Øysteinson offered his neck to tempt the bull's attack, but as he leaned back to avoid a blow, his knee gave way under him, and if the shield edge had not caught Leif's elbow, the blow would have struck his chest instead of the tiösnur-peg that now lost its head. The Cleftnose kicked Toke's lowered shield to the ground and put his foot on it, squeezing his arm under the weight, while the sword hammered into the helmet, but Sigtryg's blade cut the vassal above the ankle, and Leif had to jump and land his foot, blood gushing, outside the holmgang skin, so it was grass not bearskin that sucked the moisture. Furious cries sounded from the hird, and Toke wavered on his feet, his wrist pressed against the helmet, heaving at a safe distance while Leif glanced down at his leg. For a moment, Arnulf feared that Toke would faint, but instead the Northman's eyes turned icily to his opponent as he lowered his hand, 'A foot on each side, what courage, will you yield or fight? You were less irresolute in Hjörungavádr, but maybe earl Hakon values most those men who value safety over daring deed! I have given you two wounds. Even if you understand how to keep your blood like a bitch keeps her shift, do I have to wait until the stream reaches the skin, or will you recognise your defeat?'

A pip escaped from Gyrith, the flames of anger took hold easily outside the fire of the law, Toke fanned it so carelessly.

'Whoever yields to whom must be up to each and every person here to judge, but with the way you creep on the bearskin, you ought to bleat less about dignified behaviour! You would like to rule over the fjord, but you dare not accept blows, if you are a man, step forward, otherwise I see no other way out than for Stentor to give me the victory and accuse you of cowardice.'

Was it the arm or the helmet blow that troubled Toke most, given he preferred to fight with words rather than with a blade? His eyes were rolling – did he see clearly or was the strength faltering under the chainmail, as the words intruded aimlessly? Leif's throw of his head triggered a roar from his hird and Toke yanked up his shield to rebuke the challenge. No one should call the chieftain of Haraldsfjord cowardly and the Cleftnose could not really be blamed for not wanting to bleed on the skin voluntarily. Looming, he stepped closer, his weight on his good leg, but both held back with their weapons, Leif did not seem to have reliable support any longer either. Tense Øystein Ravenslayer's son sought to find weaknesses in his opponent while he hobbled back and forth in front of Leif and the swords flashed in turn, probing without really searching for a bite. The pool of blood around the vassal's foot grew larger, and the bull did not like being lashed in one place, his chest rumbled under the furious gaze and Toke's hesitation caused the teeth to be bared.

The outcome was awaited so silently that Little Svend's burping at the breast could be heard, but then Gyrith's furious screams abruptly

451

broke through for two of Leif's housecarls had seized hold of her hair and were trying brutally to drag her down into the grass, as if they were about to assault her. It startled Toke, Arnulf reefed Snap out of his belt, and Stentor shouted orders, but Leif used his men's loyalty, threw a shield on the skin and stepped on it, while the sword took advantage of the inattentiveness. It sent Sigtryg's blade crushingly awry from the injured arm and whirled to hit Toke above the wrist, so the leather tore, and before the flying sword met the grass, Leif's weapon had opened the flesh over the injured knee. Little did it help Toke that his shield rim struck the Cleftnose's face, blood splattered from the wounds, his feet stumbled, and the skin was mottled by dark drops.

'No!'

Arnulf shouted with Snap raised against the hirdmen, Gyrith was released, and Leif raised his arms in the air, while the roar was greeted and lifted by the promise of the housecarls' triumph.

'No!'

The loss of favour, the betrayal of the Æsir, the axe handle thickened in the palm, Svend's blade quivered, calling on Helheim! Toke stared at his bleeding arm, faltered and sank to his knees with his mouth open; furious, disbelieving, his fingers fumbling over his leg, and such a violent cry escaped him that his palms pound the skin, while indignation sprang from his shoulders. Darkness swept the loss of the fjord over his lineage, Sigtryg and Øystein rose from the fjelds and Hildegun's short hair seemed to turn as grey as her skin, but the Cleftnose's hunger was not sated. It flowed from the nose and lips, yet he kicked his opponent down onto his back and planted a foot on Toke's throat, so the Northman had to fight for breath, rattling. The long knife was pulled out with a choked snarl, but so were the hird's weapons, and Arnulf froze on his way onto the skin while Frejdis grabbed his arm from behind; if he shoved Snap into the vassal now, the price would be too high!

'Stop! Lower all weapons! The next one to shed blood breaks the law and will be punished for it!'

Stentor had raised his arms, and the yellow eye burned so fiercely with the confidence of the Æsir's that not even the new vassal of Romsdale dared to defy the order, he only placed more weight onto the foot before he moved, so Toke had to roll onto his side, gasping. Arnulf heard his own wheezing through his teeth. The interrupted strike flamed in his hand through the axe handle, Loki should give up his place to Leif, if only that Northman would suffer from debilitating disease and shrunken manhood!

452

'Fine then, Stentor Gothi, but before you take your arms down, you would do well to use breath to tell people in Haraldsfjord who now reigns in the settlements! There is blood on the skin, and whether or not the man lying here, groaning, is the father of your daughter's child, it is still he who must vacate the fjord so as not to be a lawbreaker!'

Leif raised his chin, and Stentor looked at him, his voice as clear as ice, 'Right is right, Leif Vassal, and no matter what has happened, it was Toke Øysteinson who first spilled blood on the holmgang skin, and therefore it is he who has lost his case. The victor is chieftain over the fjord and before the livestock is put out to pasture next year, Toke must have sat a farm up elsewhere. On the other hand, Leif!'

His voice trembled with pent threats, 'On the other hand, it has been seen before that he who forces himself on a gothi's kinsmen and land, must later see himself abandoned by Odin when his need is greatest!'

The Cleftnose did not anger, and the craving for revenge did not seem to bite him, 'That is reasonable talk, Stentor, your daughter can do whatever comes to her, but if I or any of my men see Toke in the fjord after the first spring, we will kill him!'

Without waiting for an answer, Leif limped off the skin, and Arnulf stuck Snap in his belt, but Gyrith reached Toke first. Tears flowed down her cheeks, but instead of helping him up, she crouched with her face in her hands, as if she alone carried the blame for the defeat. The hird had acted dishonourably, but it was Toke himself, who had let himself be distracted, and the people of the fjord would hardly put up with violence against women in open fields, even if Leif were earl of Norway! Frejdis sank down over her as Toke struggled to his feet, his face frozen in a terrible expression. Threateningly, his steps stopped in front of the Cleftnose, who just swung his cloak around his shoulders, while a carl bound his ankle tightly, and the hatred almost did not allow his voice to penetrate, 'You won today but by Freyr, Leif, we have not seen the last of each other! Men of honour do not stand in your hird, and you gain little honour in victory by assaulting a woman!'

Toke swayed, his forehead sweat was bloody, but Leif looked so pleased that the words rebounded from the chainmail, only his men moved together, their stances asking for permission for revenge.

'Excellent carls I have in my retinue, and I will win every other day too, and you still have life and family and goods intact, so rejoice at my benevolence! Had you given me the chieftain's seat when I demanded it, you would not have run yourself out of the fjord, remember that! Other

453

men than I would have had your throat for your defiance, so be quiet and live, Toke. It is no shame to lose to a vassal, and I have never really wished you any harm, you put yourself in the way.'

Without waiting for an answer, he turned and waved his horse to him with his sleeve against his lip, and the crowd began muttering as it dissolved with stolen glances. As Toke stood now and with Leif in the village, no one had the desire to talk. Abandoned! So alone in bearing his misfortune! Even Stentor seemed confounded, forced to say those words, and the women were silent, paralysed with horror, while the grass at the meeting place was lightened from the pressure of feet. The crutch left marks on the skin, while Little Svend yelped when Jofrid got up and Arnulf put his hand on Toke's arm. The Northman was quivering as if he burned at the touch. The pent-up anger had turned his eyes stony, blind and dry.

'Leif forgot to mention that you still have a brother, come! Your arm looks ugly, and helmet-shock must be taken seriously. That gelded stud won only the holmgang, not the battle, but before I sit down with you, Hildegun should bind your wounds.'

'No, I should!'

Gyrith pushed Arnulf aside decisively and Toke's stiffening burst in her hands as she pulled the helmet off. With a hoarse yell, he drew her to him in an iron clad embrace, and Arnulf looked down. Frejdis' hand slid down along his arm and interlaced his fingers and Hildegun rushed back to the longhouse, as the last of the village folk left. The change of chieftains. The word of brothers did not fail, the misfortune demanded shoulders, shoulders held by will and Arnulf stubbornly rooted his feet in the bearskin under him. With his followers at his back, Leif Cleftnose rode up the pasture path without looking back, his cloak flapping around him like a flashy banner and the housecarls straight in the saddles, helmed like a sword pommel.

'I have failed you, Gyrith.'

Sorrow hung in his voice, broken despair and grief, and the Hjörungavádr night met Arnulf abruptly in the chest. Gyrith shook her hair in his face and led Toke over to the blót stone, 'My scream was Leif's victory, you would have hit him; no one in the fjord doubts that, they only fear the power from Romsdale.'

'Guesses alone.'

The chainmail tumbled down the stone, and Toke landed with a sigh as Gyrith wound a fold of her dress around his arm.

'I heard from earl Hakon's men that Thorbrand in Ulddale has land to trade, and Vifil Ramme's farm is for sale for he is going to sail to Iceland.

We will dispose of the cattle and build up there, the mares can stand on Stentor's land for now, the catch is good, the children will thrive and we can reach Hjalte Store's blót stone.'

He spoke as if he had a fever, and Gyrith laid her fingers over his lips, quietening him, 'Toke! We will get through this. Leif could have killed you, sit still, you head was badly hit.'

'Maybe we should go to Iceland? There is room for the livestock on *Twin Raven* and sheep farming is something you understand.'

The hand sought her hair again with a painful moan as his neck rubbed against the blót stone, 'Do you think they need another warrior in Jomsborg, Arnulf? Is that not where outlaws go?'

'You are not an outlaw!'

Stentor's words fell pithily, and the gothi knelt and looked his daughter's husband in the eye, 'In all of Midgard, there is only one fjord you are no longer welcome in and only then from the first spring. Now stop your mindless chatter, do something about the scratches and rest, and afterwards I will lend ear and insight to your plans, Arnulf is right. And the settlements of Haraldsfjord fear Leif, but if I can win them for you, maybe I can ask the earl to judge the dispute, so do not be overwhelmed. The holmgang was miserably won, and as your arm is injured, the fight was not equal, and you know that the villagers who retreated from Leif's shadow will return after sunset. But there was one, who drew his weapon for you and Gyrith.'

Toke accepted his outstretched hand with a long look, then nodded: 'You are right. Everything is dizzying. Excuse me.'

Tired, he looked up Arnulf, 'Thank you for the support, and especially for not striking anyway.'

Arnulf accepted with a nod. Did Leif believe he was off the hook? He would be cleverer, he who was first chosen by Snap would be felled when the axe found the right day.

Hildegun came with linen and a leather bag in her hands, and Jofrid stood wordlessly with Svend resting in her arms. Her face beamed with kindness and determination, and Toke seemed to find peace in her defiant smile; the band of loyalty and familiarity between them seemed to be bound with Gleipner's strength.

'Come.'

Frejdis tugged gently at Arnulf's sleeve, 'Toke has enough around him and he is dazed from Leif's blow, do you not see how he is sitting and still blinking from it?'

'He is my friend!'

'Yes, but you are burning with revenge, and he needs rest. Stentor help him in.'

Her hand pulled firmer.

'Leif should not get away with chasing him out of the fjord like a dog! There will soon be more to avenge than that wretch has life to pay with!'

The firewood was stacked in hard knotted logs of insults and vile misdeeds.

'True but come on. I think Stentor will hit him harder than all your weapons together, Odin lends him wisdom.'

Arnulf limped in time with Frejdis' swaying hips and her hand warmed one of his buttocks. The fingers pinched into the flesh, and a sigh swelled the promise of her bosom, 'Fates, Arnulf, they flow like brooks, stories are birthed but rarely die out; someone will carry them on forever, and even if your skald resounds with Toke's, he has no place in all of your verses.'

Skald? Stories? What words were worth scattering after a defeat?

'What do you mean? Toke lost, and it is my intention and duty to assist him, Leif is against us both.'

'I think the time has come to set sail for Egilssund.'

She stopped with open eyes and let go of her grip, 'You can go, Jofrid has given birth, Toke is not so gravely injured than he won't jump up again in a handful of days. You have to be reconciled with Rolf and your father, and if we wait any longer, storms will fall over the Norwegian coast, we are closer to winter up here. Since we must face the consequences, escape will not offer any peace, and your sleep deprivation does not strengthen your recovery, it is the cries of the dead in Hjörungavádr that nourishes nightmares, they echo through the fjord and fjeld, so it sucks the mind dry. You have to go home now, Arnulf, you have to go home, the time has come.'

*****

Twin Raven set out of Haraldsfjord under such a biting wind that Toke wrapped another blanket around Jofrid and Little Svend, even before the field of sea had clenched its teeth in the keel. The sail flapped and tore at the ropes, and Frejdis found Jofrid's warmth more enticing than the last glimpse of the fjord, she covered herself right up to her nose and armed her gaze with perseverance. The crew was sparse, and when the rain began a little later in the day, the tent canvas was set up and carefully

456

attached while Arnulf kept Toke company at the helm. Rough weather and wind tore away words, the weakened ached from wet and cold, and Gyrith's faint-hearted face haunted the fjelds like an incantation. Despite the unluckiness and the fear for the future, Toke had ordered the longship be made ready, for he wanted to stand by his word to sail the Danes home; Leif would not succeed in changing intentions and promises just because of a spot of blood spilled on a pelt.

The night-bed was clammy, and it did not become any milder on the following day's journey, but wrapped against skin Svend Helgeson suffered no fear, and food was fat and plentiful. Jofrid had become oddly glad for the boy, so amenable that she offered herself when Arnulf sought nourishment for the infant during the trip, and despite still walking slowly, her cheeks flushed at the little one so Gyrith had to smile behind her hand. Joy had otherwise abandoned the village and although many had spoken with Toke by the fire, only a few felt the urge to stand openly with him – if Leif could exile Øystein's son from the fjord, more could probably be forced to follow if they grumbled.

Hildegun and Gyrith had said goodbye warmly to Arnulf with a wish to meet again, but he was only really overwhelmed when Stentor, as a last act, gave him a chest in his hands, a chest containing the plundered silver and amber that the fjord people had shared among themselves after they thought him drowned in the storm. A few rings and beads were missing, but without requesting it, the Vikings had found it reasonable to give back what they themselves had not won, and a consensus that Jofrid was better off by having let her child live than by having Gram throw him in the Salmonfalls also prevailed.

'Frejdis said you did not find much rest last night. Do you fear seeing Egilssund again?'

Drizzle dripped from Toke's short beard, but he was well dressed and not unfriendly with the weather, his hand sure on the helm, and *Twin Raven* slid obedient to his will.

'Rest?'

Arnulf closed his eyes and rubbed his hand over his face, the lack of sleep kicking behind his forehead. If it had just been a single night, but they knew he lay awake most nights without moving so as not to disturb anyone. That rest that kept madness at bay, lay in nightmares alone.

'I am still in pain and hear screams every time I try to sleep, and if I dream, there are corpses everywhere. Åse White accuses me, and Rolf, too. He did not die that night, but that does not change the fact that I killed him, the nights have become my enemy, and yes, I'm worried about

457

the meeting. You couldn't say I rushed out of the sound as a great man, and you certainly didn't either!'

He looked up. Most of his ship companions were under the tent, and the women's talk could be heard through the hide, Jofrid and Frejdis were sharing words easily. Toke shook his head, 'Only men with hearts of wood sleep quietly after a battle, and if Rolf has forgiven you, you should forgive yourself, too. We fled, but I do not think Stridbjørn will lock me inside the thrall hut again, though it may be madness to set foot under his roof. That night my hatred was the size of my torment, but after everything that has happened, I will look upon him as my oath-brother's father and not think about the rest.'

He stared ahead, 'You chose Fenrir, and I stayed with Freyr, but I have since repeatedly thought about which god has stood closest to one of us. Death was great in Hjörungavádr, and before that I lost Toste Skaldshield and not least my father – it does something to the mind. I have difficulty seeing Toste in front of me on the Plain of Ida, he was never a great swordsman, and where do the women live in Valhalla?'

'Do you mean Gyrith?'

'Yes, and Ranvig and Hildegun and Jofrid. I was not so afraid to die before, but now! After the battle with earl Hakon, I cherish life, maybe that was why the holmgang was lost, Fenrir would probably have helped me better.'

'No.'

Arnulf shook his head, 'Fenrir is the rogue's protector, I realised that truth that night on the bird rock, so now I will put my faith in Odin, not the wolf.'

Toke smiled, 'Odin? The worthy warriors' god. Beautiful is his hall and mighty his hird, but I would languish! What happens when you die, Arnulf, do we know that, or are we only guessing?'

Arnulf stroked his fingers over a plank and blew moisture from his upper lip, 'Svend Bueson saw the Valkyries when he died.'

'Did he? Perhaps we see what we most wish for when the fire goes out.'

'Would you then rather live in the death realm of Helheim like Balder and Nanna?'

Harshness, cold and hunger; the air turned icy at the thought.

'To be with Gyrith, then yes, though it is a miserable fate to tempt. There are many death realms, Arnulf, some tolerable, some attractive and some terrible, but all divide families and friends when life ends.'

Toke moved uneasily, as if something was pressing him inside, 'There were many men in Hakon's legion, some of them came from the south. I talked half the night with one of them – he traded frequently in Hedeby and was a Christian.'

His gaze was sharp as if he were about to defend something dangerous, something inexcusable and Stentor's yellow eye seemed to suddenly glow through the clouds. Arnulf looked out over the water and bore his fingers into the plank, 'What did he have to say?'

'A strange story that has a hard time taking root as close as I stand to Haraldsfjord's gothi.'

His voice warmed, 'Imagine that death is not the beginning of endless battle, division or pure misery, imagine a life with your family gathered around you, both those who lived before and those to come, a life with kinsmen and companions, who just go on and on!'

Valhalla, Folkvang, Helheim, Hvergelmir, Trudvang, Niflheim, Gimli, Nastrond, Ran and Ægir. Maybe it did not matter if Leif Cleftnose lodged with Nidhogg.

'Has White Christ stolen Idun's apples?'

The smile broke through.

'He may have his own or something else, but summer has taught me that a long life is a rare treasure, and that every day should be highly valued. You have been with King Sweyn. Is it true that he is on good terms with all the gods?'

Arnulf shrugged, 'I saw nothing, but it is true that the Christians creep for their god. For me it is better to die standing than to live on my knees!'

'I would bend my knee to live with Gyrith. Kneeling does not need to be an expression of submission; it can be an expression of respect.'

'You do not mean that!'

Toke clenched his hand and stretched it out, 'A closed fist is strong, but in its heart lies emptiness. Battle without purpose is futile, and some things are greater than honour and pride, you know it yourself. Have you been sitting here without longing for Frejdis?'

Arnulf did not answer, and Toke looked searchingly along the grey-swaddled coast, 'Much has Freyr given; this year's hardships have been difficult. Right now everything is bursting in me, and I do not know in which direction the bow should be set, you have to go home, but where will my seat be? Everything sure has fallen, everything certain has failed, and my courage ... how can I know if luck will find me again?'

Arnulf locked eyes with him, 'Luck you find yourself! Let Leif enjoy his winter, he will not die happy, but it is best to get women and children out of the fjord in time.'

'Women and children.'

Toke nodded thoughtfully towards the tent and adjusted the helm. He was silent for a moment, and Arnulf stared out over the waves without seeing. A hand knotted around emptiness. Futile strength. White Christ's apples of life. A man was judged by his own actions, not by his God, and kneel? Never! They must laugh in Asgard so the walls cracked!

'It will be difficult for Jofrid when we have to turn, she is happy for Little Svend, happier than she will admit.'

A furrow split Toke's forehead, and his voice was muted. Happy? Her strike against Arnulf's armpit had been hurting for days!

'She felt otherwise after the birth.'

'Yes, but she did not know him then, do you not feel the warmth from her? Now she knows what you gave her that day, she is just too proud to say it aloud, and I have yet to hear of a mother who voluntarily gave up her child.'

He sighed, 'Why do you think she sails with us to her rapist's kinsmen? Not to hold them accountable or insist on revenge, her hatred boils no longer, a new era begins, she is not angry anymore, but she loves her son. And she cannot free herself of the shame of rape, it rests on her like a mist that lights up every time someone in the fjord looks at her, we talked about it, but she cannot dissolve it and believe something else.'

Arnulf straightened, defensive, 'She will not get Little Svend back by returning Serpenttooth to me!'

'Of course not, I just think ...'

Toke paused, shaking his head vigorously.

'Think what?'

'Forget it!'

Forget it? Fickle talk!

'You usually tell me what's on your mind.'

Toke looked away, rubbing his arm, 'Yes, but not now. Go in and get warm in the tent and tell Asfinn to come here, so he can take over the helm, I am tired, Arnulf. All the rocking is causing it to throb where Leif beat his sword into my helmet.'

It probably did not thump uglier than before, but Arnulf obeyed and only now felt the cold in his limbs. Frejdis was understandable, but Jofrid and Little Svend, Toke had to know what he was saying, he was a father; ugh, such irresoluteness! To want to kill and then fall in love with your victim, that required a woman! Arnulf snorted and struck the tent canvas aside. Frejdis! He stumbled against a thwart, shaking off the moisture, hunger and longing, lamb and skin, the body needed warmth and downy skin. Øystein Ravenslayer's son could think what he wanted, all alone.

*****

Dressed in waving grass, crops and heavy foliage in its hair Egilssund welcomed *Twin Raven* on its extensive strand. The settlement lay, as it always had done, but it looked smaller than before, and the houses leaned, weathered and earth-coloured; Stridbjørn's proud longhouse could not be compared to the royalseat and Jomsborg. The salt marshes, boats, the hill and the thrall huts, nothing had changed, and yet everything was different, it was incomprehensible that summer, with timeless indifference, had greened and matured, as if the entire voyage had just been a delusion. Toke's splendid red cloak weighed on Arnulf's shoulders, and the silver chains rubbed against each other on his neck. He handed the crutch to Frejdis, sucking air into his tense chest. Helge's brother could walk without support, he would not drag himself miserably from the ship and *Twin Raven* was not bringing defeat with it.

The first cry was from the seagulls. Their flight over the sail commanded the vessel forward, as if they wanted to honour the ravens by following, then the dogs barked, unleashing commotion in on the shore, steps froze, bursting into excited cries, burst into running, into orders; it was likely that nobody recognised *Twin Raven*, but who other than Frejdis could be expected with the sun so low and golden? It was cramped and painful to breathe, such deceitful knees, his heart's stallion beat so wildly, if he opened his mouth, its hooves would be heard over the water! Arnulf straightened himself with clammy hands, the village folk would see Frejdis and Toke but first and foremost Stridbjørn's son.

The people of the sound gathered on the strand. Aslak Shipbuilder and his journeymen were some of the first, Halfred's wide figure following, and Little Ivar; it glittered before his eyes, Old Olav and the sons of Tyrleif, Arnulf knew them all, what were they thinking at the sight, what greeting would they give? *Twin Raven* glided forward warrior-proud, the houses grew larger and the faces clearer, and he had to clench Frejdis' hand behind his back until she winced, in a little while he would have to live alone! New shouts, happy, dismayed; recognising and waving arms, Frejdis waved back, but Arnulf could not move his limbs, the eyes stared so

461

vehemently, driving moisture along Stridbjørn's longhouse. The grizzly bear had to hear the excitement, soon he would know who was coming. Would he run out of the hall or shut the door, and Rolf, what about Rolf? Was Frejdis right?

The sail was taken down and the oars placed in the water, the jetty promised the sea stallion rest and the desire to flee struck its claws in the unrest, which had remained on the strand since spring just waiting for its prey, shame, offence, mockery and misdeeds, Vagn Ågeson dwindled, King Sweyn and earl Hakon, only Stridbjørn's angry shouts and call for the thrall-whip were the welcome. The cloak demanded sweat, and Arnulf's tongue dried. Before defiance would have supported him, now he met revenge naked, and even if *Twin Raven* was a worthy vessel, Toke was banished from Haraldsfjord and his best men had remained in Norway.

The door of the longhouse opened, and Stridbjørn came proudly into sight. He did not hesitate long, for *Twin Raven* moved quickly, and behind him Trud followed, following in her blue dress with silver buckles. The blue dress! A sound caught in Arnulf's throat; she was not pushing him away!

The houses blocked the vision for the floating ship, and poorly did his gaze meet those gathered, as Toke rocked the shield rim to rest against the jetty, they all seemed to stand much too near, as if they found places right under his kyrtle. Arnulf looked past the faces to the forest, despite each of the bridge's planks calling with their own voice, particularly the split one, the one with the knothole, and the one Helge used to stumble over. The greetings fell silent, the silence pressed his stomach across the sound and the flickering glances – would the looks of fear or joy win? Frejdis' hand weakened. They were all here. Awaiting his first words, his first action and his challenge; silence was not known in the Woe Wolf's retinue, even the children were listening anxiously.

'Arnulf!'

The voice was hoarse. The assembled people gave way and Stridbjørn pressed forward, his chin lifted, 'Arnulf! You have returned!'

Egilssund's first man stopped abruptly. A stormy breath of fierce determination swept over the shield rim, wrapping itself around remorse and longing, then the cloth tore and bared skin, Strife's Bear. In his hands he held the bronze-gilded drinking horns, the tears trickled down his beard, his face furrowed by old sorrow, and Arnulf faltered, a mumble escaped his lips, as if the grizzly bear had encountered him with a spear in life. Helge's horn! Helge's homecoming! Had the name not sounded, he feared Stridbjørn was awake and dreaming. It resembled his father so little to show his mind!

The steps were slowly resumed and Aslak's journeymen took the ropes from Toke's crew. Stridbjørn stopped in front of the bridge planks again, as if he were tempting fate by stepping out over the water. His stance called over the sloshing beer; the offered horn was a plea, a plea for reconciliation, and behind him stood Trud, her mouth quivering. Heart-blown senses, Arnulf moved his feet from the deck and found his way over the bridge; his lameness and weakness and loathed face-disfiguring scars did not matter, Stridbjørn's glowing eyes alone drew him to him, so surely that Midgard faded around him.

'You have returned!'

Arnulf took the horn, unable to swallow. He had killed the Bear's second eldest son; he must feel anger. Smooth and hard was the bronze, shiny and cool was the beer, and the thirst whispered. Had the drink not floated in his throat, had he fallen, his heart pounded heavily, and the drops tickled down his chin, it was not a dream!

'I was called home.'

Who took the horn, he did not see, but Stridbjørn's chest and prickly beard rammed against him and the arms' embrace was crushing. Arnulf hid his face in the grey bear's hair, panting against the pain and clutching the kinsmanship to him with his shield arm, as if the grip would never be released again. So much evil! Such harsh words! Stridbjørn grasped him by the shoulders, pulling back with a sweeping glance. It was difficult to hide how much the sword arm burned from the grip.

'You are wounded! And were even wounded before this one.'

'I have learned to defend myself.'

'I know. Serpenttooth was gone.'

Stridbjørn loosened his captive, and Trud took over the welcome, gently, tenderly, and so touched that her words failed her, but the grizzly bear recovered his voice from the embrace, roaring victory and laughter, 'Have you seen it? My son has returned! He has been in combat but has come back here to stop the crying for Helge, I have sons again!'

Cheers and congratulations burst out around him, and Arnulf heard his name being mixed with the demand for a feast and mead and pork. A smile brewed on the corners of his mouth, but he had to let words sound before a hand could be given and his arm rose asking for quiet. Foolhardy to rely on his voice; he did not dare, and Toke and Jofrid were waved from the ship as Frejdis came on their heels.

463

Øystein's daughter could hardly support herself on her feet. She kept her face all the way down over her swaddled child, and Toke had to whisper to her, enticingly and persuasively, but the cloth stayed in her fingers before Little Svend found rest in his kinsman's hands. When Arnulf took him, Jofrid recoiled, trembling, and Toke's eyes turned black, as if he had sold his sister's life! Piles of swords, silk and gold rings, no trade seemed to outweigh Jofrid's loss, and Arnulf clenched his teeth before he raised the boy towards the hushed folk of the sound. She would have killed him! Did she deserve to keep what she once wanted murdered?

The infant became angry and he proved his strength with his screams, but then he fell silent in front of Stridbjørn's greybeard and the unknown attention and Toke put his arm around Jofrid to comfort and help her up. Arnulf handed the boy to Trud with trembling arms, and the words were given clearly, so everyone on the strand could hear them, 'This is Svend. He is Helge's son. Jofrid Øysteinsdaughter gave birth to him, and now he has returned to his ancestral village to grow up.'

It startled Trud, and her eyes opened in astonishment as she uttered a cry of pain, reaching out for the little one, as an excited murmur drowned out Jofrid's gasping tears.

'Helge's son?'

Dumbfounded, Stridbjørn stared at the boy, who was objecting to Trud's warm embrace.

'Yes. He was to be thrown in to the Salmonfalls, but I bought him with Serpenttooth.'

'Serpenttooth!'

The horror was evident, but the trade was acknowledged and Svend drew new tears from the eyes of his aging relative.

'Toke and Jofrid should be received with all the honours you have to give. Svend is young and Toke recovering from a holmgang, the journey has been tough for both of them, and Jofrid does not seem as eager to hand over her son as she was before.'

Stridbjørn nodded grimly, turning towards Toke, who vigilantly held his ground, a hand on his sister and the other on Sigtryg's sword. Whether or not he had fled as a thrall, Toke now stood in the village as a chieftain's son, and how much there was to tell and ask, the guests should not have to ferret out on the open strand. Stridbjørn towered over the Northman as the sound's leader, his gaze wrestling but briefly, then the grey bear softened and he offered his hand, 'As I see it now, I must admit to having wronged you, Toke Øysteinson, and blinded as I was by the loss of my son, you came to suffer an unreasonable punishment. You brought

464

Frejdis under your protection and brought Arnulf and Helge's son back, so you are welcome with all the respect a chieftain deserves, and my hope is that there will be no enmity between our families from now on.'

Toke smiled, accepting the hand firmly, 'My friendship with Arnulf has washed away the hatred and Helge's death cannot outweigh the loss of my father and twenty of his men, but I have not come to add grief on to grief. Be proud of your youngest son, Stridbjørn, and guard him well! A great story awaits, but you should know at once that both King Sweyn and earl Hakon think well of Arnulf, and he comes home a Jomsviking!'

Brokkr's forge, Toke could have waited for a moment! The fire could hear songs and chatter, new and more important than anything else was keeping Little Svend in his arms! Stridbjørn stood open-mouthed, letting go of the hand, and Toke's words drifted over the crowd like a fire loose in hay. Unbelievingly, the bear stared at Arnulf, as Trud's gasping breathing caused Svend to look up and stop; Thor's courage, it was different to stand tall in foreign countries, in Egilssund it had only ever led to spite and being cut down.

'Is that true?'

'Arnulf!'

The sea's surface closed over him, shutting out all noise and movement and his chest was torn open. The voice was strained, but it still sounded like Heimdal's horn, and Arnulf turned with a solidified cry in his throat: 'Rolf!'

A rush of anxiety swam through his stomach. There! He was really standing there, fully alive and hearty, despite the body resembling winter-hunger, and the skin as dull white as dried bones. Rolf! Only the eyes were the same as before, but they promised progress and recovery, they shone so strongly and the legs carried him. Arnulf heaved, a desire for words flowing from the depths, impetuous rivers of remorse and intention, but a stone lay across his neck and his feet refused, his lips could not even manage a smile. Rolf walked forward, uncertain on his feet. He smelled of fear, sadness and heavy thoughts and the raised hand was bony. To take it ... take the hand that before was dead ... his mind melted, Rolf must be able to look directly into the roar! Hope. The cry, that toppled the stone aside, sounded like it came from an animal, and Arnulf met the outstretched reconciliation, his eyes overflowing. The grasp was hard, hard from sharpened suffering.

'Rolf! Forgive me!'

'No!'

Rolf shook his head violently with a drawn face, 'Arnulf, it is me who is to blame! I have behaved inexcusably and can see that you have paid a terrible price for it.'

Strong was his arm despite his long confinement, strong to grapple with land and livestock.

'I killed you!'

'Only because I forced you to kill. If you humble a wolf, you get bitten, I knew that well, but I lost my composure. I stole and was too cowardly to stand by it. No one has regretted and suffered anguish as I do.'

Regret? Odin had seen greater regret than Rolf's!

'I stabbed my unarmed brother, it can't be atoned, and you were right to anger! That night I tried to kill myself, but Toke prevented it. I have hated myself ever since.'

How did you put brother-murder into words?

'Toke is my friend and should be rewarded for it but forget your hatred! Arnulf! We have not lost each other!'

A radiant smile dissolved the weight of the killing, and Arnulf met his open embrace with a trembling sigh. Twigs alone shielded the damaged chest, but Rolf seemed to know his own abilities and was not afraid to pull his weight and his face's goodwill was more than bearable as he again drew himself free, 'Jomsviking and Svend Helgeson's redeemer! Arnulf, you make me prouder than I ever was of Helge, we expected much from him as magnificent as he was. Are you here to stay?'

Again the bystanders came into the light, and the sound of chatter could be heard. Little Svend started howling so penetratingly that Trud nodded, smiling to Jofrid, who again pressed her boy to her, and relief and festivity gathered around Stridbjørn. Here to stay?

'Frigg knows the future.'

'Arnulf and Rolf! To see your hands together is probably worth slaughtering pigs for! Trud! Set the thralls to work and get the whelp-clothes out of the chest, and Halfred, help me take the table and the large beer barrel in, the sea air makes you thirsty, and there are more uncertain legs here than on the strand during calving. Toke and Jofrid, the seats of honour in my longhouse are yours. And Arnulf, if Toke's great words can keep to my questions, you should know that the *Sea Wolf* needs a man in the bow in spring. As hard as you stabbed Rolf, he named Helge's new ship after you anyway!' The *Sea Wolf*! A stern seat! Stridbjørn laughed at Arnulf's gaping face, 'Ran's cunning. If you get a thwart and Halfred in your tail, I can dare to hope that you will not run away again.'

With an abrupt shout, Frejdis cut off his speech and ran behind Arnulf, for now Hedin and Sigrun came into view, and the joy of seeing their daughter safe and sound triggered fierce hugs and mingled tears. The overwhelmingness struck, for the anxiety seemed to have been hard; Arnulf had been long about leaving Norway. Rolf smiled broadly and went to take part in the reunion, but when Frejdis saw him, laughing, and grabbed his hands, both light and chest were charred, and Arnulf had to look away. Ragnarök! On the same day he had opened his eyes to Frejdis after Hjörungavádr, the prediction was stated, but black liquid pitch spread through his body anyway, and the restless wolf-blood raged so the air seemed sparse. Escape! Either Rolf or himself would sacrifice himself, the sight was a burning branch in the face; away, he had to get away, vacate the strand and village, leave his kinsmen for the second time, Jomsborg! Arnulf looked towards the salt meadow. Where were the horses? Sigvalde would give him room, longings and pain were crushed by banner square fights, sword work and oak bark, Vagn had to teach him, and the Ulfhednar in his blood awakened!

'Arnulf! Stay!'

Toke blocked the path before his step found direction, 'Stop! She will not deceive you, you have to wait, give it time, there was no lie between you in Haraldsfjord. Look at me!'

Was everything revealed so easily? Did Toke already see the eagle's beating wings over the sound? Fimbulwinter! Arnulf looked into Toke's eyes, he stood in ice-flames, burning in the deadly cold and like the banks were full of folk, the danger of choking was imminent! The Øysteinson's smile was winning, but his grip on his shoulder was unbreakable, any attempt to fly would be thwarted.

'If you have any beer, Stridbjørn, then I and my men have a thirst and great stories, and do not hesitate to butcher the pig. Even when the ham is tender, there will be enough stories left and so that Arnulf is not accused of boasting, I will recount as if you had Suttungr's mead in the barrel.'

'Ha!'

Stridbjørn flung out his arm, 'Well said, Toke Øysteinson, I suspect that I am going to rejoice that Arnulf cut you lose that night and gave you your freedom back. He certainly believed you were too good a man to put to thrall work, and I have to admit he was right.'

The grizzly bear turned around and stomped towards the longhouse, and Toke's calmness forced Arnulf, but not harder than that Aslak's and Halfred's fists could be shaken on the way. Whether Frejdis still held Rolf's hand was not easy to see, and the Northman walked so eagerly towards the village, that Arnulf's thigh drew his attention. To Helheim then! Here he was, returned home as Helge's equal and luck was dragged through the dirt anyway, to Jotunheim with the sound and the longhouse, by Odin, now it was time to drink!

*****

The sea air was good. And the air was refreshing; his head howled. The beer's revenge ran right down his neck and his stomach rumbled. His feet had dug a hole in the sand, in case it became necessary. Arnulf righted himself on the stone and looked out at the sound and the sky through the cracks, it was not advisable to let too much light in. Luckily, the morning was grey. The morning? It had long been since midday!

He spat and tousled his hair. Frejdis and Rolf had been sitting cosily, talking and smiling, while the thunder in his chest rumbled and the beer flowed. Silent and gloomy, Arnulf had listened to Toke's long accounts, and only when he got up and talked about Jomsborg did the festive spirit find him. Svend Silkenhair had astounded; Vagn looked fiercely at the frightened peasants, the king spoke so his audience pressed themselves along the benches, and the intake of breaths from the horror of the beheadings flickered the flames. Arnulf had said much, many questions had been answered, and toasts delivered, but nothing had been able to relieve the pain of the intimacy between Rolf and Frejdis, and Toke followed him out, guardingly, whenever the beer had to trickle through.

Arnulf rubbed his forehead. The last to awaken. Rolf was out, he had surely sought Frejdis. Jofrid and Toke were nowhere to be found in the longhouse, they probably wanted to hear Rolf's intentions for the future. Saliva hit the mussels, his chosen targets. Home again. Home again and never had his blood been more restless! How could they, his village folk, how could they tend animals and churn butter, as if nothing had happened, how could they happily chat and fiddle with looms and hanging fishing nets. There, outside the sound, raged life; out there welled actions and proud promises across land-borders; the storm was trapped in his body, whipping seething foam through his limbs, and such vehement, great work could not simply be replaced by silence! Mighty stories by Stridbjørn's fire, courage and deeds to think of for a long time – was that all he had won? Admiration by the fire, admiration? All the uncontrollable craving, only Frejdis could tame the wolf and expel the pain, only Frejdis. Rolf was a double-edged sword that cut him through the middle! Arnulf squinted hard. If it had been anyone other than Rolf! He looked out again, looked at *Twin Raven* and the *Sea Wolf*. How long had he been sitting with his back to the village? Long enough to know the stone's crevices, but why turn and burn the sight, suppose Rolf stood, embracing Freya's gift, where was Toke to prevent an escape?

Arnulf threw pebbles at the mussels. At least he had reconciled with Aslak for borrowing the *Sea Swallow*; the shipbuilder had been angry, but his pride had returned unharmed, and Toke had promised him an evening voyage on *Twin Raven*. And Halfred was appeased, too, no, more, elated at the thought of next summer's voyage, Helge's heritage had been talked about around the table, and Stridbjørn had laid silver on the planks, silver for a new sword.

Steps approached behind him, and a mug was handed over his shoulder.

'Here. Drink up and get ready.'

Arnulf looked up at Toke, accepting the water. The Northman was serious, decisions hung in his posture and his lips were pinched together, as if he had exhausted his vocabulary over the beer. Arnulf drank deeply and kept the water down, and Toke gave a hand to help him up, 'Come.'

'Where are we going?'

'In. Much has happened while you have been sleeping, but you were probably also the one who drank the most.'

'I can walk by myself.'

Arnulf pulled his hand away and limped beside Toke. It had been easier with crutches, not least as the foothold slipped, but was too pitiful. Toke pulled his hand to his shoulder.

'You have probably also slept long.'

No one could blame a man for sleeping it off. The bloodshot eyes gave the answer, 'I have had difficult conversations.'

Difficult conversations? With whom? The plank road was a relief, and Toke directly him gently towards Stridbjørn's house while the misgivings pushed the crushing nausea from the path. It must have been about Jofrid, maybe she wanted to try to persuade Trud to get Little Svend back?

The longhouse was bright. All the oil lamps were lit and shortly after Arnulf walked over the threshold, he could see clearly. The traces of the feast had been cleared away, and with such brooding faces around the table, the beer barrels were unlikely to be reopened. He hesitated. Stridbjørn waited watchfully in his seat of honour, Trud sitting by him with an uneasy expression. Hedin and Sigrun had been summoned, and Frejdis,

469

seated between them, sent Arnulf a questioning look. Hedin and Sigrun? What had they to do with Toke's sister? Frejdis did not seem to know anything. Jofrid calmly rested her hands on the table, and Rolf looked as if he had been stabbed by the knife for a second time; sallow but clear, he asked Arnulf and Toke to sit as he wanted to start the meeting.

Tense, Arnulf straddled the bench, what was this about? Toke and Rolf exchanged glances, and Jofrid's calmness involved her in the conspiracy, perhaps she too knew what was going to happen?

'I asked for this meeting after speaking at length with Toke.' Rolf looked around, lingering briefly on Arnulf, and Hedin fidgeted impatiently, 'I think you know what this meeting is about. It is hard for me to sit here.'

He sighed and began, 'All summer I have been afraid of my own thoughts, and yesterday I saw that my worst fears were justified.'

Frejdis' large eyes looked over the table, impossible to escape, even if the meeting was hurting Rolf. She was anxious and Hedin was vigilant, his raw, worn fingers suspiciously stiff in his moustache.

'Frejdis and I are promised to each other, and without her care I would not have survived my wounds. I ...'

Rolf looked down for a moment but then continued resolutely, as uncertain glances passed between his table companions. Arnulf rubbed his palms on his trousers – had Toke revealed what he had seen in Haraldsfjord?

'Arnulf and Frejdis have long felt for one another, it is known, and I have had time for much thought.'

Here it was, the revelation, now everything newly won burst, was the reconciliation and reunion about to be declared invalid? Rolf did not find the words easily, 'They both returned, even if some in the village mumbled that we were unlikely to see them again if they found each other in foreign lands. And until yesterday, I had hoped. Helge had always ventured out, and we heard about King Sweyn and earl Hakon, but even if you sat by me, Frejdis, and gave me your mind, you did not give me your fidelity.'

Woe! Arnulf looked down with clenched fists, as if his ears were pounding, Hedin's humming was almost drowned out but not Trud's sigh. The drooping hair was little defence against Rolf's burning eyes.

'You came home worthy, Arnulf, but only one of us can live with Frejdis. If it is to be me, I would have to live with a woman who longs, and a brother who would tempt the dangers too boldly, and if it is you ...'

Arnulf stared aghast. Fenrir sank teeth into Rolf, so life gushed from him, Asgard freed of misdeed.

470

'Then there will only be one who has a wound to heal, even though it is the second time my chest has been hit.'

Tyr fell and crushed bones stuck out of the jötunn wolf's maw. Rolf's fists bored into the table's plank, and he was breathing heavily. Arnulf wanted to reach out to him, wanted to shout and pull the meat out of the wolf's mouth, but his body was rooted to the bench.

'What do you mean, Rolf? Frejdis is promised to you and I received both your and Stridbjørn's hand on it. Are you sitting here now, breaching that promise?'

Both Hedin's voice and face were sharp, but Rolf raised his fist, controlled, 'Wait until I am finished, Hedin, then I will listen.'

Frejdis combed her fringe with quivering fingers.

'Arnulf left in unfortunate circumstances but has returned with great honour, and he has more than amply proven his courage and ability. He is Helge's brother and will not be counted for less from now on. What I saw yesterday, Toke has honestly confirmed, but I have talked to more than him tonight.'

Jofrid bowed her head, and Rolf grew milder, but Hedin had grabbed the edge of the table and was only remaining in his seat because of Sigrun's hand on his arm.

'Helge acted badly towards Jofrid, so badly that she did not do well in Haraldsfjord after the abuse. The shame of a chieftain's daughter is greater than that of an ordinary woman. As the eldest brother, I will take Svend as my own son, but I would also take his mother into the bargain. Jofrid has given me her yes.'

Brash ice in a spring stream. The words struck, crushed and splintered, but they did not make sense, as long as disbelief remained. Given her yes? Frejdis stopped playing with her hair, bewildered, and Stridbjørn half rose out of his seat, but Hedin struck his fist on the table, so all other reactions were brushed aside, and so furiously did he lean towards Rolf that all amazement yielded. Jofrid! Jofrid and Rolf?

'You gave me and Frejdis your word, and you will stand by it! My daughter is not a gold ring that can be received or discarded after random whims, and you talk about disgrace and ordinary daughters! What about Frejdis' honour? Do you think she can be given to your little brother like a horse? Stridbjørn! Have you a part of this?'

Rolf stood up, breathless, but leaned no more forward. Give Frejdis away! Give up his longing?

'Arnulf will not be a bad man for Frejdis! His own sword he gave to save Helge's son and bring him home, so how much will he not sacrifice for his own? He has silver and the goodwill of great men, what more do you want, Hedin? Your daughter's unhappiness? Look at her! Ask her yourself if you dare to hear the answer.'

Coughing, he fell over the table, his hand against his chest, and Trud jumped up with a start to support him on the bench. Man for Frejdis? Rolf! He threw anguish in his own yard and not from remorse alone, even Helge would not have given so much! Arnulf froze and sweated at the same time, and Frejdis wept silently, her hand over her mouth. Did he give anything at all? Was he not just staring the truth in the face? Sigrun did not seem to know which of her kinsmen she should hold on to, and despite Toke looking like he wanted to say something, Hedin broke coarsely in, 'Arnulf gave a stolen sword, and though luck was with him, he is only a summer older than the last time he was here, and a mad dog does not come to his senses so quickly! Your brother is impulsive and has never taken responsibility for anything, on the contrary! Do you think I will voluntarily exchange the village's best man for a colt that has no idea in which direction it will turn tomorrow?'

Such great agitation could hardly be accommodated, his skin blushed, his insides tensed, 'Silver you say? It is plunder from killing, and even you yourself were stabbed! Arnulf stinks of war and violence, and the only reason he sits quietly on the bench right now is that he has not recovered from his recent scratches. Once the wolf has tasted blood, it will never tame.'

A hog could howl loudly with insults when its tail was pinched! Arnulf was indignant. For the first time Frejdis stood within reach, so that herring-splitter of a daughter-guardian was not going to stand in the way! He rose, his fingers on Snap, but Toke pulled him down, and Stridbjørn was the rare master over his anger, 'All this is new to me, Hedin, and I would have preferred to speak with Rolf alone first.'

He looked disapprovingly at Rolf, who was breathing normally again, and then he rested his heavy gaze on Toke and Jofrid before he continued, 'But maybe it is best this way. Jofrid Øysteinsdaughter is from a proud family that it is good to have ties with, no matter how much Toke has fallen out of favour with Romsdale`s vassal right now. Svend Helgeson and Frejdis win by it, and my sons will be linked as no brothers have been before. You will still have kinship with my family, Hedin, and I know you value that highly, and if the *Sea Wolf* sails out with *Twin Raven* next summer, heritage and land will not mean anything. Arnulf will know how to obtain what Frejdis needs.'

Arnulf met Rolf's glance, and even though the table stood between them, their minds melted together in a precious oath. Rolf's pain was excruciating to accept, but by Odin, he would laugh again, Jofrid would rise again and there would be no end to goodness.

'I expected more of you, Stridbjørn, than the breaking of words and the exchanging of earth for gold!'

Hedin's bitterness was raw, 'You have power, a longhouse and livestock, land and ships, while all that Sigrun and I get joy from is Frejdis. I want kinship but not at any price, and as Arnulf is wild, no other man would dare approach my daughter for fear of getting a knife in the stomach. He has never listened to you.'

The reigned-in resentment began to simmer dangerously and Arnulf, his teeth clenched, shoved his shoulder with all his might.

'Mind your mouth! As common sense fails you now, I will let your harsh words be, and the poverty you complain about will come to an end, and you know it! Do not pry me with pity, Frejdis' happiness will certainly ensure your old age.'

Stridbjørn made a face as if the agreements were already made, but Hedin found more to rumble about, 'Rolf will take care of his property, but Arnulf will die! Stridbjørn! Your son is a Jomsviking! He had made his vows to Jomsborg! Do you think Sigvalde will let him remain on his ancestral land until the strength of his youth leaves him? If Jomsborg calls, he will go, and if it does not call, he will ride out himself, you know his restlessness! And if he does not come home cold, he will come home mutilated and without his health and who should then take care of Frejdis' flock of children? Poverty and hunger, Stridbjørn, they are the last things you want for your sons' children!'

The blow found its target, for Stridbjørn grumbled and fell silent, and Hedin's questioning went around the table in search of answers. Arnulf rose slowly. If the man sitting across from him should turn contempt into respect, the blows should not arouse anger, 'I fully understand your concerns, Hedin, and they are well reasoned, after what you've seen. My summer you heard about yesterday, and I can testify that change not only requires time, it also requires events. I am not proud of my past behaviour, but the story that accompanied the beer was so long that you must realise that I have not returned home by luck alone. I am a Jomsviking, and what that will mean, I don't yet know, but I do know one thing and that is that my love for your daughter will never find its end. My life will be her shield, and my only desire her best, and to cast doubt on that promise is the same as casting a lie.'

Hedin was breathing heavily, and he stared for a moment at the wall behind Arnulf. Then he looked back, as if he were looking at mouldy porridge that he was being forced to eat, 'We will not get anywhere by quarrelling and I will concede that you might have changed a bit. But you also made promises to Jomsborg and not for fun, nobody forced you to make them. I am not blind; you are fond of Frejdis and have been long enough that I believe you, but what is it you want, Arnulf? Tell me, and if your answer is worthy then we can talk.'

He paused heavily, not demanding an answer, and Arnulf fell back on the bench with no attempt to defend himself. For a while no one said anything, only Jofrid moved to sit with Rolf and Frejdis sought shelter under Sigrun's arm. She had hope in her eyes, but fragile ice cradled it, and it would bear only those who stepped rightly.

'I think each of us needs to consider the situation, but I also know that I cannot stay here longer than tomorrow.'

Toke spoke softly, and sadness stalked him, 'I have my own battle in Norway, and winter will come to us before it will come to you at this time of year. My sadness about leaving Jofrid here is heavy, but my joy is great. Walk along the strand and change your mind, Hedin, then you will find out how to weigh up Arnulf as he deserves, give him time and watch him, then I will not be afraid for your choice.'

'Choice?'

Disarmed, Hedin shook his head, 'Small men have never had choice, Chieftainson, but your advice is wise.'

He stood with certainty and pulled Sigrun and Frejdis with him, 'Arnulf! You may think my words to you harsh, but the good of the family comes before everything else. I will give you two years and then I will talk to you again, and if your actions are better suited to my taste then than now, you may be allowed to ask Frejdis. Until then, I will hold with other men, who are pleased by my daughter, and you can trust my word. It is better given than Rolf's.'

'Two years!'

The horror hammered his self-control, two years! Impossible! With the outer part of his will shouting and jumping were kept in check, and his head nodded as if it wanted to express consent. Two years! By that time, the realms could be divided, children grown up, and hair turned grey! Frejdis raised her hand, groping, but Sigrun pushed her protectively against the door, as if her skin would be poisoned if it touched hot blood. Groaning, Arnulf supported his elbows on the table planks, and pressed his knuckles into his forehead. Two years. Hedin could demand anything! He could never be like Rolf, and Frejdis' father was not wrong in his claims, despite his hard objections. The door was opened, and the voices rose above the table, but the talk was incomprehensible and indifferent, Hedin's pronouncement was not to be changed, and no one, who had heard it, could say anything against his wisdom.

'Arnulf.'

Jofrid bent over him, stroking his clenched hands, 'Arnulf, you suffer, but I have seen enough of you and Frejdis to know that nothing can keep you apart. Look up now, because we are going to live together, and I would like to reconcile.'

Arnulf lowered the loosening hands. Jofrid beamed. Not for the love of Rolf but from the will to live and gather family around her; her goodness was new, exuberant and fully felt.

'I took Serpenttooth from you, and I know how hard that smarted. Svend is an infant, but there will come a day when someone will put the sword in his hand and teach him how to use it, and that will not be Rolf. Do you want to guard Serpenttooth and keep the blade sharp from use until then? Only when the sword begins to weigh on you will Svend be strong enough to bear it, and Helge would hardly care to see it hang rejected for so long.'

'Jofrid!'

Now the shield cracked in seriousness, seething blood drove through and his breathing stumbled. The answer got stuck in a nod towards Jofrid's smile; out, he had to get out, now his eyes were blurry! Staggering, Arnulf stood and looked at Stridbjørn and Trud. They were hardly unhappy that Hedin had taken hold of their unruly son, even though their faces were still shaken. The Grey Bear's faithful gruffness was on its way back in accustomed gestures, and love was clearly visible in Trud's features, a little too visible, he was no crawling infant!

Rolf left his seat and although Arnulf could no longer repress his tears, he held the river back, limping in front of him. Dying embers remained in Rolf's eyes, glowing and with impossible longing, and Arnulf took his cold hands and sank to his knees with his forehead pressed against the grip. If Toke could kneel to live with Gyrith, so could he! Rolf clasped him as if he were drowning, but at the same time, pulled him up and Arnulf turned his face away, stumbling on his legs, light, air; he was blind and strangled from the fire's smoke. He stumbled across the floor, past the loom and jars, out through the door, leaving the house and wicker fence, his feet knew the path and village; they had brought him safe from anger and punishment before and that Stridbjørn's youngest suddenly

475

needed loneliness did not raise any eyebrows, it only seemed a little odd that a lame Jomsviking was now making the journey.

*****

Arnulf stopped on top of the mound and stared out across the sound.

The water was rocking quietly, and a shoal of fish flashed at the water's surface.

He sat in the waving grass with his arms around his knees and let the weak breeze dry his cheeks. His skin was stiff from salt, and the fire was burning down to the sound of cattle grazing. The one-horned cow lifted its head, as if it was welcoming him back to the strand's seat of honour, and the gulls greeted him with rousing calls, but now he knew what they screamed. Arnulf closed his eyes. His pain was so great it did not hurt. His mind so full it was empty. His hair fluttered. His fears he gave to the wind. Everything disappeared except Frejdis' smile.

The sound of Toke coming up the hill, made him look up. The Northman smiled and sat down beside him, and Arnulf looked out over the water again. There was something safe in feeling the Øysteinson's shoulder against his. The sea spread so vastly. The sky vaulted so high. The summer had given two brothers, two brothers and one choice. He sighed and twisted a blade of grass around his finger. Frejdis, Jomsborg, King Sweyn and earl Hakon, the dispute in Haraldsfjord should probably also be counted; life could make a man tired, his heart could die, but his reputation he could not lose.

'What will happen now, Toke?'

Toke shook his head but did not seem worried. He smiled, as if he had a prediction to foresee, but then seemed to regret it, 'I do not know, Arnulf, I do not know.'

7 years later, spring 993

'Vagn's coming!' Frejdis' gaze burned. Breathless, she pushed the hair away from her face as indignation tugged at the corners of her mouth. 'The ship is in the sound. All five of them are there. I was able to count them from the shore meadow.' Her fingers twitched and she stomped as her chest puffed like a bellows; Arnulf quietly let the knife continue along the light-coloured wooden sword. But flames were coursing under his skin. Of course, Vagn would come!

Frejdis' keys rattled on her belt, and she wheezed heavily as Arnulf contented himself with feeling the blade with his thumb. It should not be too sharp. She turned as though being persecuted, cast a quick glance down at the sloping village and out across the sound but then turned towards Arnulf again to wrench an answer from him.

'I heard the shouts.' Arnulf let his hands fall and looked up. She was wild with rage. Her hair was tangled from haste and her pale green dress was damp from the heat under her arms.

'I hate that look, Arnulf! I hate the way you shut out everything else each time you disappear to become a Jomsviking again! Look at me!'

Always the same strife every spring, always the same pain. She leaned forwards, so her breasts weighed heavily on the neckline of her dress, and the tight belly slowed her down. Chains of amber and multicoloured glass beads dangled over him from the linked bronze brooches; her bosom had grown with the unborn child.

'Look at me and tell me if you're going to leave us this year too, so you can kill and ravage with your sword-minded friends? Vagn isn't even human! He's a corpse-raven and his black blood draws us all into misfortune, so why are you going a-viking with him?' She waved her hands: 'Haven't you bled enough for Jomsborg? Haven't you given so much that you should be allowed to put your children first now? Look at me and look at yourself! Haven't you long had your fill of plundered silver? We have so much in the chests we could live like earls for years.'

477

Should she now be the one to decide what meant the most to him! Arnulf's face grew sharp, but Frejdis took a step forward, stomach first: 'Should we call him Gunulf, if it's a boy? Or should I ask your father to choose a suitable name for the child?'

Gunulf? Arnulf stuck the knife hard in the sheath. Never had she understood the growth of pride and great deeds that Vagn brought with him. He held the wooden sword with his arm outstretched, assessing whether the blade was straight and flawless. The weight was comfortable, and the hilt was made to fit a six-year-old boy's hand. Torulf would be delighted with the sword over the summer.

'Vagn is my blood brother and Jomsborg's mightiest and strongest warrior, so don't talk badly of him. I always come home again, and you know that.'

Frejdis fumed, gesturing with her arm angrily. 'I know that Helge promised you the same thing before heading out on his last voyage, but maybe he came back? Do you think we need to shed more tears?'

Helge! The old grief was still raw enough for him to clench his teeth and discard the wooden sword. 'My brother is dead, but his son is alive. I take care of Little Svend like I take care of my own and Rolf's son!'

'You do, and you teach all three of them about violence and murder!' Frejdis bared her teeth as though she was going to bite: 'Rolf does better all the months you're away, for he tells the boys about breeding animals and crops and gives them the skills and ability to live safely and for a long time. He's always been your best brother. He only raises the axe when slaughtering.' Her eyes shone with tears, and she faltered from agitation and had to lean against the wall of the house behind Arnulf's stool. The baby weighed heavily in her abdomen, and she wiped her cheeks furiously with the back of her hand.

The sun suddenly became too hot over the longhouse, and Arnulf got up and looked out towards the sound. Shouts drew people away from their pursuits and their looms throughout the entire village, and a good many looked hesitantly down at the strand, while cheering children raced ahead. The ship on the shimmering sound was not big, but there were only five men to sail it, and no one doubted who was coming, for the shields erected along the shield rim were edged with red. The unbreakable rings of Jomsborg. Air penetrated his lungs. Soon they would be six.

'Frejdis.' Arnulf softened for the last time and pulled her to him. In a moment, promises and oaths would strap chainmail around his chest, blocking out all mollification, but before the wolf-blood awakened in earnest, she would have to listen.

478

'What is ours, Jomsborg can't threaten. My five blood brothers ensure you my life and my return. Together we form a shieldwall, impenetrable to any enemy; have I endured any significant wounds since Torulf was born? Give me your fear, so I can carry it away from here, for you should only think of me with joy, and I will sacrifice to Freja so this birth will be easier than the previous ones.' He embraced the reassuring warmth and the quivering fertility, the absorbing scent and the light hair, as his groin swelled. The downy skin. The swaying hips. The ember that Frejdis now lit should smoulder until the year grew old, and she knew he would not journey without it. His hands signed a blessing and slid over her dress, feeling and nipping; she would have to survive on that until the cold returned and her breasts enticed him once again.

'But your ring of blood brothers always stands in front, seeking out danger – and Vagn is the worst, for he yearns the most for Odin. You have more scars than all the men of the village put together, and you could easily receive a mortal wound in his company.' Frejdis clung to him, her forehead on his chest. 'I'm so afraid, Arnulf! I'm so fearful that I only sleep in the winter when you're home, and every time I hear a raven scream or a wolf howl, I think you're dead.' She looked up at him hungrily. 'Stay home, just this summer! Just until the baby is born, so you know whether it is a son. You have three children who love you, and Torulf may be the oldest, and braver than many, but he cries as much as Fenja and Thurid as soon as you are out of sight.'

Children and descendants; now the chainmail hardened with Jomsborg's call, and Arnulf lowered his eyebrows, wolfing down the torment. 'You know I can't stay home, for I will never let my Blood Ring and Jomsborg down, but that doesn't mean that I don't ...'

'Let us down? Which is most important? Chasing after glory and reputation in battle or protecting your offspring?'

'Frejdis!' Arnulf held her so tight that she winced. 'Be proud, for only the best and mightiest of all warriors are admitted to Jomsborg. Even kings tremble before Earl Sigvalde!'

'Yes, for so grim are the men in his grip that they refrain from living with women to avoid becoming soft and timid from being cared for. How can you do without me, Arnulf?' She wrestled herself free accusingly: 'You, who don't rape on your journeys out of faithfulness. Will you stay in Jomsborg for the winter the day Sigvalde demands it? Now that you have iron scales in front of your eyes!'

'Father!'

Not now! But Torulf came running around the longhouse with

479

Little Svend and Helge after him, and Arnulf retreated sweatily from Frejdis. The boys had sticks in their hands, as if their game had been interrupted.

'Father, Vagn has come! The Blood Ring is here!' Torulf stopped abruptly with a wavering look that immediately recognised the warrior wolf, and his lips trembled briefly before he managed to squeeze them tightly shut. His forehead furrowed. His fists tense. Hot-headed and long-haired like Arnulf himself. The Joms chainmail could not contain the strength of his heart beating beneath it.

'Torulf.' Arnulf looked down at his son, but then crouched to be at eye level with him, while Frejdis wiped her nose on her sleeve and sighed, as if Torulf's presence supported her accusation.

'Now you remember what I taught you during the winter! Listen to your Uncle Rolf in every aspect and be obedient. Listen and learn, but when you three brawl with each other and shoot bows and practise with weapons, then you listen only to me.'

Torulf nodded firmly, and Helge and Little Svend nodded with him. Not a day had passed without them following Arnulf like a shadow, and not a word had been wasted. Despite Little Svend being the oldest, Torulf preferred to make the decisions. His cousins stood behind him on fidgety feet.

'The sword is finished.' Arnulf nodded at the discarded weapon: 'Practise, just as I taught you. Never flee from a fight. And remember that you are the son of Arnulf Wolfblood.'

Torulf nodded again, fired up, while the others stood tall, proud to be of the same blood. Arnulf gave them a look only the men of Jomsborg could endure. 'Honour is the most important thing, for it binds men, and if a man doesn't value honour most, then no one can keep peace with each other. So, a word and a promise must never be broken, for where does an oath-breaker end after his death?'

It was Torulf who answered, his voice quivering slightly: 'He ends up on Náströnd in the hall that's woven by serpents dripping venom, and there he must suffer among scoundrels and murderers having been outcast by his own kind in life.'

Fresh tears swelled in Frejdis' eyes, but Torulf was puffed up with self-importance.

'It is Odin who selects from among the warriors, Torulf. He is present in battle, watching the fighting and then he chooses. Just as he once chose Uncle Helge and my best friend, Svend Silkenhair.'

How could new wounds be endured if the old ones did not attract attention every now and then? His hands wanted to comfort and encourage, but Torulf was not to become soft. Embraces and smiles belonged to winter.

'In ten years, all three of you will sit in the *Sea Wolf* with me when I set sail on my longship. If you strive and persist enough and can withstand my grasp by that time.' Arnulf pulled the silver chain with the little patterned spearhead over his head to put it around Torulf's neck. Then he got up, tussling with his roaring pride. It was the first winter the boys were truly old enough to understand and accept, and there was no joy in having to leave them so quickly. But Little Svend stood like a king at his father Helge's name, and so should the dead be honoured and remembered. So lived reputation.

Arnulf hesitated. The urge to hold Torulf and Frejdis and defy the call of Jomsborg bit deep, as deep as Fenris' teeth into Tyr's arm; but the loss of a hand had not enfeebled the god of war.

'There is no better woman than your mother, Torulf.' He looked at Frejdis, but had no more to say, for the parting only grew worse, and pain was a condition for the sons of Jomsborg. Frejdis understood that; sniffling hard, she started to walk, gathering her hair behind her back as she went. 'Are you welcoming Vagn and the others inside for a mug of beer? Should I have a pig set over the fire?'

So his blood brothers could sit on Stridbjørn's bench and be subjected to his family's silent reproaches?

'They don't drink where they're not welcome, and they haven't come too early this year.'

'I'll put some food in a bag; go and get the thralls to carry your chest and your shields down to the strand.' Her shoulders sank, but she would not allow herself to feel the sadness. Everything had long since been packed and the weapons sharpened with care. When Arnulf followed her around the house, he met only the blank faces of the people, who turned their backs on him. Stridbjørn's son had never been very well-liked in the village in Egilssund, nor had the fold ever grown accustomed to the Blood Ring.

A handful of children gathered, excitement etched all over their faces, but the women he could see between the houses seemed careworn, as though Frejdis had already been made a widow, and their ire scorched. As if the shadow of Jomsborg had not protected them all for years! As if his reputation did not keep all danger at bay, just as his silver bought enough food for the village when the weather turned bad.

481

He stopped, half-stumbling, and took in his surroundings. The farewell was to more than just his family. The round-shouldered houses lay dispersed down the slope to the water below Stridbjørn's strong longhouse, and the woven fences around the homes flanked the wooden planked road to the shore where Aslak Shipbuilder and his journeymen had enough space to swing their tools and work. Flora on the shore meadow had flowered early. And the cattle hill was freshly green. As was the frog marsh. Further afield, the shabby thrall huts wound their way to the forest, where the wolves, who had taught him not to fear, lived. As always, he saw all the new things he was about to leave, but as soon as the ship had rounded the first point, Egilssund would humbly recede to be replaced by thoughts of Jomsborg. Only half of his heart lay beating in Frejdis' hands. And a good chunk of it with the children, too, now that they were growing up. A man at odds with himself was never good. To love was to doubt, but Sigvalde's laws did not tolerate any weakness. The winters at home had to be paid for with courage.

He drew in a deep breath. Vagn's ship was not far from going aground, so Arnulf followed Frejdis resolutely into the longhouse, where she was already ordering the thralls about, 'Bread and cheese, Unn. And Groa, is the sleeping sack finished? Then fetch one of the smaller mead barrels, for that is to be brought, too. Are you sure you put needles and thread   in   the   chest?'

The darkness blinded him, but the fire in the hearth soon returned his eyesight. The loom stood right inside the door next to the baskets of wool and yarn, so everything could easily be carried out into the light, and cloaks and kyrtles hung from hooks as did dried herbs, hunting weapons and the splitting axe. On the suspended shelves were neat rows of jars and pots, and despite Rolf not fighting, several shields hung on the wall behind the narrow long table with the leather-covered bench. Stridbjørn's seat of honour was full of carved, wool-wrapped wooden animals, as if Fenja and Thurid had set them to pasture there. The dolls watched over them from the   armrest.

His stomach lurched, but time was not to be squandered, and Arnulf walked along the sleeping beds by the wall with Torulf on his heel. He had once shadowed Stridbjørn like his own son was now stealthily following him, but this was no time for memories. The belt was loosened and the tunic was pulled over his head and discarded randomly, and Frejdis stood ready with the magnificent work of winter. The new kyrtle had demanded great care, and she had kept him from wearing it before now. Poppy red and closely embroidered with yellow and green interlacing

482

patterns along the neatly woven edging. Her hands clenched the fabric as Torulf hurried past them, opening the chest in search of something. If only a blade would not cut through her labour. She had probably asked Jofrid to cast a protective seidhr on the kyrtle.

'The chainmail is at the bottom, under the cloak along with the wound clamps, and I've added four leg wraps if the sea is still cold. You can eat sheep legs tonight, and don't crush the ointment jar.' With eyes lowered, she handed him the kyrtle, and Arnulf quickly put it on. The heavy belt with the silver fastening hung over her arm. The new tunic fitted his body well, without restricting him, and the belt was drawn tight as Torulf hopefully held out his selection on his palms. The wolf-tooth chain with the heavy wolf head of gold from Hedeby; nobody owned a stronger piece of jewellery. Arnulf accepted it without a word, as Frejdis looked up. What was the power of Jomsborg compared to the daughter of Freya?

Torulf leapt onto the bed to lift the weapons down off the wall with the greatest of reverence. First Serpenttooth, Helge's serpent-entwined glory with its silver-thread embellished hilt. Then Snap, Svend Silkenhair's light silver-inlaid battle axe. Inherited weapons of heroic power. The long knife had to hang from the middle of the belt. Torulf was allowed to bear the silver-adorned helmet. The thralls carried the wolf shields; though they seemed frightened of the ferocious red predators, who chased each other with open-mouths on the black-painted linden wood within the blood-red border of the Jomsborg shield.

'Is it time?' Rolf appeared in the doorway, blocking out the sun, breathless more from movement than rushing, and Arnulf pointed to Serpenttooth and ploughed his fingers through his hair: 'Yes.'

Frejdis heard the sigh from the door; Rolf stroked his fair-haired beard and stepped towards Arnulf with darkness in his otherwise mild blue eyes. His wife, Jofrid, had Fenja and Thurid by the hand behind him. Helge and Little Svend appeared, too.

'Guard yourself vigilantly again this year, so I will not be slaughtering too much pork in preparation for next winter.' He took hold of Arnulf's shoulders in such a way that his might could be mistaken for a warrior's, but plough and cattle demanded strength, too.

'Tyr watches over me, but Odin decides, and he is known for his fickleness.' Arnulf clasped his arms, and Rolf nodded, despite the farewell smarting. 'Then I hope someday you find peace before the Valkyries come to reap you. The need for you at home is mounting, now Father is getting older and the little ones are growing. I have heard of other warriors who left Jomsborg to return home to peace with honour, and who were not dead.'

His grip should not slip into an embrace, for Vagn should not see any moisture in the corner of his eye, so Arnulf let go to better push Snap into his belt. 'You and Helge were always older. Neither of you had my wild mind, and you've always had to endure so much talk, especially when the Blood Ring comes calling.'

Rolf smiled resignedly and without being ashamed of the water welling in his eyes, and he reached out for Torulf, as though to give him the affection Arnulf had denied him. 'I will watch over Frejdis and the children, no matter what Odin thinks, and I will tell your next son so much about you that he will recognise his father easily upon your return.'

Your next son. The words stuck in his throat, but Jofrid pressed herself forward with the anxious little girls who barely remembered the last spring.

'You can at least smile at your daughters, given that it is us who must endure the grim solemnity of your departure. That way they will have something to think about when we cry tonight.' Without hesitating, she lifted Thurid up and forced his younger daughter into his arms, while Fenja was pushed against his thigh; the longhouse became hazy to his eyes. Vulnerability triumphed over toughness, and Arnulf squeezed Thurid to him so he could whisper into her fine hair, as he laid a hand on Fenja's shoulder. Jofrid's seidhr. She knew exactly how to plant the poison that Earl Sigvalde never quite got the better of, and the muscles around both his lips and abdomen began to tug as Thurid hooked the wolf-tooth chain around her finger. Frejdis shed fresh tears, and Torulf was having a hard time clenching his teeth tightly enough, but Stridbjørn's roar from the door blew the worst of the heat abruptly away from her cheeks, 'Garmr will probably growl again, for I hear my Eagle-Wolf is venturing out again to arm wrestle with his pack! Where are you? Oh, there! Come here so I can better glare at my progeny who has more fire and turmoil than responsibility and reason in his skull.' He gestured with his arm, as he leaned on the windowsill, still sharp, though more hunched and thinner in the beard than the previous year. 'How long will the mad hounds of Jomsborg steal from my grandchildren's father and Frejdis' affection? If you had courage, like we others have goodness, you would stay home!' The palm of his hand slammed against the doorframe. 'And your face will not grow more handsome from cavorting with that violent mob. Odin is not getting any more of my sons!'

Mad hounds? He stared testily at Arnulf's scarred nose and the deep axe furrow over both his eye and cheek. Only Stridbjørn dared bark like that when Vagn was nearby. Frejdis freed Thurid as Fenja was enclosed in Jofrid's hands and Rolf beckoned the boys to him.

'Surely you are neither unsatisfied with your wealth nor the shield my reputation lays over Egilssund?' Arnulf took a reluctant step towards the Grey Bear: 'You already have five grandchildren. Not including the unborn one, and if you give yet another son to the one-eyed All-Father, there would be ten new sons-in-law to fight for Frejdis the very next day. You'll never be alone.' He accepted the snort like a fist that was weathered from life but sharp with age.

'Stay here!' Stridbjørn growled in his throat as he shrugged and gesticulated with no expectation. 'Be glad Trud is no longer alive, for you would not have turned your back so easily on your mother's weeping.' He looked Arnulf sharply in his eye and lowered his voice, 'Remember, Loki did not bring about peace between the Æsir and the jötnar, Veulf. At first, he wanted the best for everyone and was jovial, helpful and clever, but he was untruthful and malevolent, too, and he ended up betraying those closest to him. And it is for that reason he is now being punished so the earth shakes with his torment. Do not forget Frejdis!'

No Jomsviking was to flee from battle, but he was allowed to seek out the sun when the darkness became too suffocating for him. Arnulf wedged past Stridbjørn for air. Loki? He ran his fingers through his hair again as he sniffed and regained his footing. What did Stridbjørn know about kinship to Loki?

He straightened the kyrtle. Petulant old man: Vagn was surely waiting on the strand now, and it did not serve anyone well to drag out the pain with begging and crying. He adjusted the wolf-chain that Thurid had tinkered with. Other lineages paid tribute to their departing sons with raised horns of mead and proud cries. Stridbjørn should adorn himself with his offspring's honour and bask in the glow of Jomsborg. They all should.

Across the sound, the seagulls screamed of fiery blood and outward journeys, and the wolf arched its neck, so the hairs bristled through the kyrtle. Wherever he went, they would follow, and when his shield found its place on the shield rim, Jofrid had to take Frejdis under her wing. But the summer was no longer than the days could be counted, and Fimbulwinter would begin one night. There was time enough.

Read more in JOMSVIKING, Book Two of *Arnulf – A Viking Saga*

Manufactured by Amazon.ca
Bolton, ON